PENGUIN BOOKS

The Lady in the Lake and Other Novels

'Chandler is an original stylist, creator of a character, Philip Marlowe, as immortal as Sherlock Holmes'   Anthony Burgess

'His books should be read and judged, not as escape literature, but as works of art'   W. H. Auden

'The Chandler-Marlowe prose is a highly-charged blend of laconic wit and imagistic poetry set to breakneck rhythms'
    Ross MacDonald

'The lively inventiveness of Chandler's language and his vigorous, crackling dialogue make Philip Marlowe as enduring a hero as Sherlock Holmes or James Bond, and more spellbinding than either'
    Sunday Times

'His best novels carry the crime story to levels of artistry that have rarely been matched'   Daily Mail

'Chandler gave birth to a different kind of detective . . . His incisive and illuminating prose reveals California in all its sun-bleached sordid reality'   The Times

About the Author

One of the great writers of detective fiction, Raymond Chandler was born in Chicago in 1888. When he was twelve his family emigrated to England, where he was educated at Dulwich College. After studying in France and Germany he returned to London in 1907, where he reluctantly joined the Civil Service. He left to take up writing and worked for a number of newspapers as a reporter, essayist, book-reviewer and writer of verse. In 1912 he sailed to America and eventually settled in California. After the First World War, during which he served in the Canadian Army, he went into business and became a top executive for an oil company. In 1924 he married Cissy Pascal. With the onset of the Depression in the early thirties he returned to writing, producing stories for pulp magazines such as *Black Mask*. By 1938 he had published sixteen stories and was working on his first novel, *The Big Sleep*, which was published in 1939. An instant success, it introduced, in the words of one critic, 'a new type of crime novel in which ingenuity of plot and detection combine with a distinctive and distinguished literary style'. Equally well-received were *Farewell, My Lovely* (1940), *The High Window* (1942), *The Lady in the Lake* (1943), *The Little Sister* (1949) and *The Long Good-Bye* (1953), all of which feature his famous detective Philip Marlowe. Many of his books have been adapted for the screen and he wrote screenplays for a number of films, including *Double Indemnity* and *Blue Dahlia*, both of which were nominated for an Oscar. He was elected President of the Mystery Writers of America. During his later years he suffered increasingly from depression and general ill health and he died in 1959 in California. Dilys Powell called his writing a 'peculiar mixture of harshness, sensuality, high polish and backstreet poetry' and Elizabeth Bowen described him as 'a craftsman so brilliant, he has an imagination so wholly original, that no consideration of modern American literature ought . . . to exclude him'.

RAYMOND CHANDLER

The Lady in the Lake and Other Novels

PENGUIN BOOKS
in association with Hamish Hamilton

PENGUIN BOOKS

Published by the Penguin Group
Penguin Books Ltd, 27 Wrights Lane, London w8 5tz, England
Penguin Putnam Inc., 375 Hudson Street, New York, New York 10014, USA
Penguin Books Australia Ltd, Ringwood, Victoria, Australia
Penguin Books Canada Ltd, 10 Alcorn Avenue, Toronto, Ontario, Canada m4v 3b2
Penguin Books India (P) Ltd, 11 Community Centre, Panchsheel Park, New Delhi – 110 017, India
Penguin Books (NZ) Ltd, Private Bag 102902, NSMC, Auckland, New Zealand
Penguin Books (South Africa) (Pty) Ltd, 5 Watkins Street, Denver Ext 4, Johannesburg 2094, South Africa

Penguin Books Ltd, Registered Offices: Harmondsworth, Middlesex, England

The High Window First published in Great Britain by Hamish Hamilton 1943
Published in Penguin Books 1951
Copyright 1943 by Raymond Chandler

The Lady in the Lake First published in Great Britain by Hamish Hamilton 1944
Published in Penguin Books 1952
Copyright 1944 by Raymond Chandler

The Little Sister First published in Great Britain by Hamish Hamilton 1949
Published in Penguin Books 1955
Copyright 1949 by Raymond Chandler

This omnibus edition published under the title *The Lady in the Lake and Other Novels*
in Penguin Classics 2001

1

Set in 9.5/12.5 pt PostScript Linotype Elektra
Typeset by Rowland Phototypesetting Ltd, Bury St Edmunds, Suffolk
Printed in England by Clays Ltd, St Ives plc

Contents

The High Window

1

The house was on Dresden Avenue in the Oak Knoll section of Pasadena, a big solid cool-looking house with burgundy brick walls, a terra-cotta tile roof, and a white stone trim. The front windows were leaded downstairs. Upstairs windows were of the cottage type and had a lot of rococo imitation stonework trimming around them.

From the front wall and its attendant flowering bushes a half-acre or so of fine green lawn drifted in a gentle slope down to the street, passing on the way an enormous deodar around which it flowed like a cool green tide around a rock. The sidewalk and the parkway were both very wide and in the parkway were three white acacias that were worth seeing. There was a heavy scent of summer on the morning and everything that grew was perfectly still in the breathless air they get over there on what they call a nice cool day.

All I knew about the people was that they were a Mrs Elizabeth Bright Murdock and family and that she wanted to hire a nice clean private detective who wouldn't drop cigar ashes on the floor and never carried more than one gun. And I knew she was the widow of an old coot with whiskers named Jasper Murdock who had made a lot of money helping out the community, and got his photograph in the Pasadena paper every year on his anniversary, with the years of his birth and death underneath, and the legend: *His Life Was His Service*.

I left my car on the street and walked over a few dozen stumble stones set into the green lawn, and rang the bell in the brick portico under a peaked roof. A low red brick wall ran along the front of the house the short distance from the door to the edge of the driveway. At the end of the walk, on a concrete block, there was a little painted Negro in white riding-breeches and a green jacket and a red cap. He was holding a whip, and there was an iron hitching ring in the block at his feet. He looked a little sad, as if he had been waiting there a long time and was getting discouraged. I went over and patted his head while I was waiting for somebody to come to the door.

After a while a middle-aged sourpuss in a maid's costume opened the front door about eight inches and gave me the beady eye.

'Philip Marlowe,' I said. 'Calling on Mrs Murdock. By appointment.'

The middle-aged sourpuss ground her teeth, snapped her eyes shut, snapped them open and said in one of those angular hardrock pioneer-type voices: 'Which one?'

'Huh?'

'Which Mrs Murdock?' she almost screamed at me.

'Mrs Elizabeth Bright Murdock,' I said. 'I didn't know there was more than one.'

'Well, there is,' she snapped. 'Got a card?'

She still had the door a scant eight inches open. She poked the end of her nose and a thin muscular hand into the opening. I got my wallet out and got one of the cards with just my name on it and put it in the hand. The hand and nose went in and the door slammed in my face.

I thought that maybe I ought to have gone to the back door. I went over and patted the little Negro on the head again.

'Brother,' I said, 'you and me both.'

Time passed, quite a lot of time. I stuck a cigarette in my mouth, but didn't light it. The Good Humour man went by in his little blue and white wagon, playing 'Turkey in the Straw' on his music box. A large black and gold butterfly fish-tailed in and landed on a hydrangea bush almost at my elbow, moved its wings slowly up and down a few times, then took off heavily and staggered away through the motionless hot scented air.

The front door came open again. The sourpuss said: 'This way.'

I went in. The room beyond was large and square and sunken and cool and had the restful atmosphere of a funeral chapel and something the same smell. Tapestry on the blank roughened stucco walls, iron grilles imitating balconies outside high side windows, heavy carved chairs with plush seats and tapestry backs and tarnished gilt tassels hanging down their sides. At the back a stained-glass window about the size of a tennis-court. Curtained french doors underneath it. An old musty, fusty, narrow-minded, clean and bitter room. It didn't look as if anybody ever sat in it or would ever want to. Marble-topped tables with crooked legs, gilt clocks, pieces of small statuary in two colours of marble. A lot of junk that would take a week to dust. A lot of money, and all wasted. Thirty years before, in the wealthy close-mouthed provincial town Pasadena then was, it must have seemed like quite a room.

We left it and went along a hallway and after a while the sourpuss opened a door and motioned me in.

'Mr Marlowe,' she said through the door in a nasty voice, and went away grinding her teeth.

2

It was a small room looking out on the back garden. It had an ugly red and brown carpet and was furnished as an office. It contained what you would expect to find in a small office. A thin, fragile-looking, blondish girl in shell glasses sat behind a desk with a typewriter on a pulled-out leaf at her left. She had her hands poised on the keys, but she didn't have any paper in the machine. She watched me come into the room with the stiff, half-silly expression of a self-conscious person posing for a snapshot. She had a clear, soft voice, asking me to sit down.

'I am Miss Davis, Mrs Murdock's secretary. She wanted me to ask you for a few references.'

'References?'

'Certainly. References. Does that surprise you?'

I put my hat on her desk and the unlighted cigarette on the brim of the hat. 'You mean she sent for me without knowing anything about me?'

Her lip trembled and she bit it. I didn't know whether she was scared or annoyed or just having trouble being cool and business-like. But she didn't look happy.

'She got your name from the manager of a branch of the California-Security Bank. But he doesn't know you personally,' she said.

'Get your pencil ready,' I said.

She held it up and showed me that it was freshly sharpened and ready to go.

I said: 'First off, one of the vice-presidents of that same bank. George S. Leake. He's in the main office. Then State Senator Huston Oglethorpe. He may be in Sacramento, or he may be at his office in the State Building in Los Angeles. Then Sidney Dreyfus, Jr, of Dreyfus, Turner & Swayne, attorneys in the Title-Insurance Building. Got that?'

She wrote fast and easily. She nodded without looking up. The light danced on her blonde hair.

'Oliver Fry of the Fry-Krantz Corporation, Oil Well Tools. They're over on East Ninth, in the industrial district. Then, if you would like a couple of cops, Bernard Ohls of the DA's staff, and Detective-Lieutenant Carl Randall of the Central Homicide Bureau. You think maybe that would be enough?'

'Don't laugh at me,' she said. 'I'm only doing what I'm told.'

'Better not call the last two, unless you know what the job is,' I said. 'I'm not laughing at you. Hot, isn't it?'

'It's not hot for Pasadena,' she said, and hoisted her phone book up on the desk and went to work.

While she was looking up the numbers and telephoning hither and yon I looked her over. She was pale with a sort of natural paleness and she looked healthy enough. Her coarse-grained coppery blonde hair was not ugly in itself, but it was drawn back so tightly over her narrow head that it almost lost the effect of being hair at all. Her eyebrows were thin and unusually straight and were darker than her hair, almost a chestnut colour. Her nostrils had the whitish look of an anaemic person. Her chin was too small, too sharp and looked unstable. She wore no make-up except orange-red on her mouth and not much of that. Her eyes behind the glasses were very large, cobalt blue with big irises and a vague expression. Both lids were tight so that the eyes had a slightly oriental look, or as if the skin of her face was naturally so tight that it stretched her eyes at the corners. The whole face had a sort of off-key neurotic charm that only needed some clever make-up to be striking.

She wore a one-piece linen dress with short sleeves and no ornament of any kind. Her bare arms had down on them, and a few freckles.

I didn't pay much attention to what she said over the telephone. Whatever was said to her she wrote down in shorthand, with deft easy strokes of the pencil. When she was through she hung the phone book back on a hook and stood up and smoothed the linen dress down over her thighs and said:

'If you will just wait a few moments –' and went towards the door.

Half-way there she turned back and pushed a top drawer of her desk shut at the side. She went out. The door closed. There was silence. Outside the window bees buzzed. Far off I heard the whine of a vacuum cleaner. I picked the unlighted cigarette off my hat, put it in my mouth and stood up. I went around the desk and pulled open the drawer she had come back to shut.

It wasn't any of my business. I was just curious. It wasn't any of my business that she had a small Colt automatic in the drawer. I shut it and sat down again.

She was gone about four minutes. She opened the door and stayed at it and said: 'Mrs Murdock will see you now.'

We went along some more hallway and she opened half of a double glass door and stood aside. I went in and the door was closed behind me.

It was so dark in there that at first I couldn't see anything but the outdoors light coming through thick bushes and screens. Then I saw that the room was a sort of sun porch that had been allowed to get completely overgrown outside. It was furnished with grass rugs and reed stuff. There was a reed chaise-longue over by the window. It had a curved back and enough cushions to stuff an elephant and there was a woman leaning back on it with a wine-glass in her hand. I could smell the thick scented alcoholic odour of the wine before I could see her properly. Then my eyes got used to the light and I could see her.

She had a lot of face and chin. She had pewter-coloured hair set in a ruthless permanent, a hard beak and large moist eyes with the sympathetic expression of wet stones. There was lace at her throat, but it was the kind of throat that would have looked better in a football sweater. She wore a greyish silk dress. Her thick arms were bare and mottled. There were jet buttons in her ears. There was a low glass-topped table beside her and a

7

bottle of port on the table. She sipped from the glass she was holding and looked at me over it and said nothing.

I stood there. She let me stand while she finished the port in her glass and put the glass down on the table and filled it again. Then she tapped her lips with a handkerchief. Then she spoke. Her voice had a hard baritone quality and sounded as if it didn't want any nonsense.

'Sit down, Mr Marlowe. Please do not light that cigarette. I'm asthmatic.'

I sat down in a reed rocker and tucked the still unlighted cigarette down behind the handkerchief in my outside pocket.

'I've never had any dealing with private detectives, Mr Marlowe. I don't know anything about them. Your references seem satisfactory. What are your charges?'

'To do what, Mrs Murdock?'

'It's a very confidential matter, naturally. Nothing to do with the police. If it had to do with the police, I should have called the police.'

'I charge twenty-five dollars a day, Mrs Murdock. And, of course, expenses.'

'It seems high. You must make a great deal of money.' She drank some more of her port. I don't like port in hot weather, but it's nice when they let you refuse it.

'No,' I said. 'It isn't. Of course, you can get detective work done at any price – just like legal work. Or dental work. I'm not an organization. I'm just one man and I work at just one case at a time. I take risks, sometimes quite big risks, and I don't work all the time. No, I don't think twenty-five dollars a day is too much.'

'I see. And what is the nature of the expenses?'

'Little things that come up here and there. You never know.'

'I should prefer to know,' she said acidly.

'You'll know,' I said. 'You'll get it all down in black and white. You'll have a chance to object, if you don't like it.'

'And how much retainer would you expect?'

'A hundred dollars would hold me,' I said.

'I should hope it would,' she said, and finished her port and poured the glass full again without even waiting to wipe her lips.

'From people in your position, Mrs Murdock, I don't necessarily have to have a retainer.'

'Mr Marlowe,' she said, 'I'm a strong-minded woman. But don't let me scare you. Because if you can be scared by me, you won't be much use to me.'

I nodded and let that one drift with the tide.

She laughed suddenly and then she belched. It was a nice light belch, nothing showy, and performed with easy unconcern. 'My asthma,' she said carelessly. 'I drink this wine as medicine. That's why I'm not offering you any.'

I swung a leg over my knee. I hoped that wouldn't hurt her asthma.

'Money,' she said, 'is not really important. A woman in my position is always overcharged and gets to expect it. I hope you will be worth your fee. Here is the situation. Something of considerable value has been stolen from me. I want it back, but I want more than that. I don't want anybody arrested. The thief happens to be a member of my family – by marriage.'

She turned the wine-glass with her thick fingers and smiled faintly in the dim light of the shadowed room. 'My daughter-in-law,' she said. 'A charming girl – tough as an oak board.'

She looked at me with a sudden gleam in her eyes.

'I have a damn fool of a son,' she said. 'But I'm very fond of him. About a year ago he made an idiotic marriage, without my consent. This was foolish of him because he is quite incapable of earning a living and he has no money except what I give him, and I am not generous with money. The lady he chose, or who chose him, was a night-club singer. Her name, appropriately enough, was Linda Conquest. They have lived here in this house. We didn't quarrel because I don't allow people to quarrel with me in my own house, but there has not been good feeling between us. I have paid their expenses, given each of them a car, made the lady a sufficient but not gaudy allowance for clothes and so on. No doubt she found the life rather dull. No doubt she found my son dull. I find him dull myself. At any rate, she moved out, very abruptly, a week or so ago, without leaving a forwarding address or saying good-bye.'

She coughed, fumbled for a handkerchief, and blew her nose.

'What was taken,' she went on, 'was a coin. A rare gold coin called a Brasher Doubloon. It was the pride of my husband's collection. I care nothing for such things, but he did. I have kept the collection intact since he died four years ago. It is upstairs, in a locked fireproof room, in a set of fireproof cases. It is insured, but I have not reported the loss yet. I don't want to, if I can help it. I'm quite sure Linda took it. The coin is said to be worth over ten thousand dollars. It's a mint specimen.'

'But pretty hard to sell,' I said.

'Perhaps. I don't know. I didn't miss the coin until yesterday. I should not have missed it then, as I never go near the collection, except that a man in Los Angeles named Morningstar, called up, said he was a dealer, and was the Murdock Brasher, as he called it, for sale? My son happened to take the call. He said he didn't believe it was for sale, it never had been, but that if Mr Morningstar would call some other time, he could probably talk to me. It was not convenient then, as I was resting. The man said he would do that. My son reported the conversation to Miss Davis, who reported it to me. I had her call the man back. I was faintly curious.'

She sipped some more port, flopped her handkerchief about and grunted.

'Why were you curious, Mrs Murdock?' I asked, just to be saying something.

'If the man was a dealer of any repute, he would know that the coin was not for sale. My husband, Jasper Murdock, provided in his will that no part of his collection might be sold, loaned or hypothecated during my lifetime. Nor removed from this house, except in case of damage to the house necessitating removal, and then only by action of the trustees. My husband' – she smiled grimly – 'seemed to feel that I ought to have taken more interest in his little pieces of metal while he was alive.'

It was a nice day outside, the sun shining, the flowers blooming, the birds singing. Cars went by on the street with a distant comfortable sound. In the dim room with the hard-faced woman and the winy smell everything seemed a little unreal. I tossed my foot up and down over my knee and waited.

'I spoke to Mr Morningstar. His full name is Elisha Morningstar and he has offices in the Belfont Buildings on Ninth Street in downtown Los Angeles. I told him the Murdock collection was not for sale, never had been, and, so far as I was concerned, never would be, and that I was surprised that he didn't know that. He hemmed and hawed and then asked me if he might examine the coin. I said certainly not. He thanked me rather dryly and hung up. He sounded like an old man. So I went upstairs to examine the coin myself, something I had not done in a year. It was gone from its place in one of the locked fireproof cases.'

I said nothing. She refilled her glass and played a tattoo with her thick fingers on the arm of the chaise-longue. 'What I thought then you can probably guess.'

I said: 'The part about Mr Morningstar, maybe. Somebody had offered the coin to him for sale and he had known or suspected where it came from. The coin must be very rare.'

'What they call a mint specimen is very rare indeed. Yes, I had the same idea.'

'How would it be stolen?' I asked.

'By anyone in this house, very easily. The keys are in my bag, and my bag lies around here and there. It would be a very simple matter to get hold of the keys long enough to unlock a door and a cabinet and then return the keys. Difficult for an outsider, but anybody in the house could have stolen it.'

'I see. How do you establish that your daughter-in-law took it, Mrs Murdock?'

'I don't – in a strictly evidential sense. But I'm quite sure of it. The servants are three women who have been here many, many years – long before I married Mr Murdock, which was only seven years ago. The gardener never comes in the house. I have no chauffeur, because either my son or my secretary drives me. My son didn't take it, first because he is not the kind of fool that steals from his mother, and second, if he had taken it, he could easily have prevented me from speaking to the coin dealer, Morningstar. Miss Davis – ridiculous. Just not the type at all. Too mousy. No, Mr Marlowe, Linda is the sort of lady who might do it just for spite, if nothing else. And you know what these night-club people are.'

'All sorts of people – like the rest of us,' I said. 'No signs of a burglar, I suppose? It would take a pretty smooth worker to lift just one valuable coin, so there wouldn't be. Maybe I had better look the room over, though.'

She pushed her jaw at me and muscles in her neck made hard

lumps. 'I have just told you, Mr Marlowe, that Mrs Leslie Murdock, my daughter-in-law, took the Brasher Doubloon.'

I stared at her and she stared back. Her eyes were as hard as the bricks in her front walk. I shrugged the stare off and said:

'Assuming that is so, Mrs Murdock, just what do you want done?'

'In the first place I want the coin back. In the second place I want an uncontested divorce for my son. And I don't intend to buy it. I dare say you know how these things are arranged.'

She finished the current instalment of port and laughed rudely.

'I may have heard,' I said. 'You say the lady left no forwarding address. Does that mean you have no idea at all where she went?'

'Exactly that.'

'A disappearance then. Your son might have some ideas he hasn't passed along to you. I'll have to see him.'

The big grey face hardened into even more rugged lines. 'My son knows nothing. He doesn't even know the doubloon has been stolen. I don't want him to know anything. When the time comes I'll handle him. Until then I want him left alone. He will do exactly what I want him to.'

'He hasn't always,' I said.

'His marriage,' she said nastily, 'was a momentary impulse. Afterwards he tried to act like a gentleman. I have no such scruples.'

'It takes three days to have that kind of momentary impulse in California, Mrs Murdock.'

'Young man, do you want this job or don't you?'

'I want it if I'm told the facts and allowed to handle the case as I see fit. I don't want it if you're going to make a lot of rules and regulations for me to trip over.'

She laughed harshly. 'This is a delicate family matter, Mr Marlowe. And it must be handled with delicacy.'

'If you hire me, you'll get all the delicacy I have. If I don't have enough delicacy, maybe you'd better not hire me. For instance, I take it you don't want your daughter-in-law framed. I'm not delicate enough for that.'

She turned the colour of a cold boiled beet and opened her mouth to yell. Then she thought better of it, lifted her port glass and tucked away some more of her medicine.

'You'll do,' she said dryly, 'I wish I had met you two years ago, before he married her.'

I didn't know exactly what this last meant, so I let it ride. She bent over sideways and fumbled with the key on a house telephone and growled into it when she was answered.

There were steps and the little copper-blonde came tripping into the room with her chin low, as if somebody might be going to take a swing at her.

'Make this man a cheque for two hundred and fifty dollars,' the old dragon snarled at her. 'And keep your mouth shut about it.'

The little girl flushed all the way to her neck. 'You know I never talk about your affairs, Mrs Murdock,' she bleated. 'You know I don't. I wouldn't dream of it, I –'

She turned with her head down and ran out of the room. As she closed the door I looked out at her. Her little lip was trembling but her eyes were mad.

'I'll need a photo of the lady and some information,' I said when the door was shut again.

'Look in the desk drawer.' Her rings flashed in the dimness as her thick grey finger pointed.

I went over and opened the single drawer of the reed desk and took out the photo that lay all alone in the bottom of the drawer, face up, looking at me with cool dark eyes. I sat down again with the photo and looked it over. Dark hair parted loosely in the middle and drawn back loosely over a solid piece of forehead. A wide cool go-to-hell mouth with very kissable lips. Nice nose, not too small, not too large. Good bone all over the face. The expression of the face lacked something. Once the something might have been called breeding, but these days I didn't know what to call it. The face looked too wise and too guarded for its age. Too many passes had been made at it and it had grown a little too smart in dodging them. And behind this expression of wiseness there was the look of simplicity of the little girl who still believes in Santa Claus.

I nodded over the photo and slipped it into my pocket, thinking I was getting too much out of it to get out of a mere photo, and in a very poor light at that.

The door opened and the little girl in the linen dress came in with a three-decker cheque book and a fountain-pen and made a desk of her arm for Mrs Murdock to sign. She straightened up with a strained smile and Mrs Murdock made a sharp gesture towards me and the little girl tore the cheque out and gave it to me. She hovered inside the door waiting. Nothing was said to her, so she went out softly again and closed the door.

I shook the cheque dry, folded it and sat holding it. 'What can you tell me about Linda?'

'Practically nothing. Before she married my son she shared an apartment with a girl named Lois Magic – charming names these people choose for themselves – who is an entertainer of some sort. They worked at a place called the Idle Valley Club, out Ventura Boulevard way. My son Leslie knows it far too well. I know nothing about Linda's family or origins. She said once she was born in Sioux Falls. I suppose she had parents. I was not interested enough to find out.'

Like hell she wasn't. I could see her digging with both hands, digging hard, and getting herself a double handful of gravel.

'You don't know Miss Magic's address?'

'No. I never did know.'

'Would your son be likely to know – or Miss Davis?'

'I'll ask my son when he comes in. I don't think so. You can ask Miss Davis. I'm sure she doesn't.'

'I see. You don't know of any other friends of Linda's?'

'No.'

'It's possible that your son is still in touch with her, Mrs Murdock – without telling you.'

She started to get purple again. I held my hand up and dragged a soothing smile over my face. 'After all he has been married to her a year,' I said. 'He must know something about her.'

'You leave my son out of this,' she snarled.

I shrugged and made a disappointed sound with my lips. 'Very well. She took her car, I suppose. The one you gave her?'

'A steel grey Mercury, 1940 model, a coupé. Miss Davis can give you the licence number, if you want that. I don't know whether she took it.'

'Would you know what money and clothes and jewels she had with her?'

'Not much money. She might have had a couple of hundred dollars, at most.' A fat sneer made deep lines around her nose and mouth. 'Unless, of course, she has found a new friend.'

'There's that,' I said. 'Jewellery?'

'An emerald and diamond ring of no very great value, a platinum Longines watch with rubies in the mounting, a very good cloudy amber necklace which I was foolish enough to give her myself. It has a diamond clasp with twenty-six small diamonds in the shape of a playing-card diamond. She had other things, of course. I never paid much attention to them. She dressed well but not strikingly. Thank God for a few small mercies.'

She refilled her glass and drank and did some more of her semi-social belching.

'That's all you can tell me, Mrs Murdock?'

'Isn't it enough?'

'Not nearly enough, but I'll have to be satisfied for the time being. If I find she did not steal the coin, that ends the investigation as far as I'm concerned. Correct?'

'We'll talk it over,' she said roughly. 'She stole it all right. And I don't intend to let her get away with it. Paste that in your hat, young man. And I hope you are even half as rough as you like to act, because these night-club girls are apt to have some very nasty friends.'

I was still holding the folded cheque by one corner down between my knees. I got my wallet out and put it away and stood up, reaching my hat off the floor.

'I like them nasty,' I said. 'The nasty ones have very simple minds. I'll report to you when there is anything to report, Mrs Murdock. I think I'll tackle this coin dealer first. He sounds like a lead.'

She let me get to the door before she growled at my back: 'You don't like me very well, do you?'

I turned to grin back at her with my hand on the knob. 'Does anybody?'

She threw her head back and opened her mouth wide and roared with laughter. In the middle of the laughter I opened the door and went out and shut the door on the rough mannish sound. I went back along the hall and knocked on the secretary's half-open door, then pushed it open and looked in.

She had her arms folded on her desk and her face down on the folded arms. She was sobbing. She screwed her head around and looked up at me with tear-stained eyes. I shut the door and went over beside her and put an arm around her thin shoulders.

'Cheer up,' I said. 'You ought to feel sorry for her. She thinks she's tough and she's breaking her back trying to live up to it.'

The little girl jumped erect, away from my arm. 'Don't touch me,' she said breathlessly. 'Please. I never let men touch me. And don't say such awful things about Mrs Murdock.'

Her face was all pink and wet with tears. Without her glasses her eyes were very lovely.

I stuck my long-waiting cigarette into my mouth and lit it.

'I – I didn't mean to be rude,' she snuffled. 'But she does humiliate me so. And I only want to do my best for her.' She snuffled some more and got a man's handkerchief out of her desk and shook it out and wiped her eyes with it. I saw on the hanging-down corner the initials L.M. embroidered in purple. I stared at it and blew cigarette smoke towards the corner of the room, away from her hair. 'Is there something you want?' she asked.

'I want the licence number of Mrs Leslie Murdock's car.'

'It's 2xIIII, a grey Mercury convertible, 1940 model.'

'She told me it was a coupé.'

'That's Mr Leslie's car. They're the same make and year and colour. Linda didn't take the car.'

'Oh. What do you know about a Miss Lois Magic?'

'I only saw her once. She used to share an apartment with Linda. She came here with a Mr – a Mr Vannier.'

'Who's he?'

She looked down at her desk. 'I – she just came with him. I don't know him.'

'Okay, what does Miss Lois Magic look like?'

'She's a tall, handsome blonde. Very – very appealing.'

'You mean sexy?'

'Well –' she blushed furiously, 'in a nice well-bred sort of way, if you know what I mean.'

'I know what you mean,' I said, 'but I never got anywhere with it.'

'I can believe that,' she said tartly.

'Know where Miss Magic lives?'

She shook her head, no. She folded the big handkerchief very carefully and put it in the drawer of her desk, the one where the gun was.

'You can swipe another one when that's dirty,' I said.

She leaned back in her chair and put her small neat hands on her desk and looked at me levelly.

'I wouldn't carry that tough-guy manner too far, if I were you, Mr Marlowe. Not with me, at any rate.'

'No?'

'No. And I can't answer any more questions without specific instructions. My position here is very confidential.'

'I'm not tough,' I said. 'Just virile.'

She picked up a pencil and made a mark on a pad. She smiled faintly up at me, all composure again.

'Perhaps I don't like virile men,' she said.

'You're a screwball,' I said, 'if ever I met one. Good-bye.'

I went out of her office, shut the door firmly, and walked back along the empty halls through the big silent sunken funereal living-room and out of the front door.

The sun danced on the warm lawn outside. I put my dark glasses on and went over and patted the little Negro on the head again.

'Brother, it's even worse than I expected,' I told him.

The stumble stones were hot through the soles of my shoes. I got into the car and started it and pulled away from the kerb.

A small sand-coloured coupé pulled away from the kerb behind me. I didn't think anything of it. The man driving it wore a dark porkpie type straw hat with a gay print band and dark glasses were over his eyes, as over mine.

I drove back towards the city. A dozen blocks later, at a traffic stop, the sand-coloured coupé was still behind me. I shrugged and just for the fun of it circled a few blocks. The coupé held its position. I swung into a street lined with immense pepper trees, dragged my car around in a fast U-turn and stopped against the kerbing.

The coupé came carefully around the corner. The blond head under the cocoa straw hat with the tropical print band didn't even turn my way.

The coupé sailed on and I drove back to the Arroyo Seco and on towards Hollywood. I looked carefully several times, but I didn't spot the coupé again.

3

I had an office in the Cahuenga Building, sixth floor, two small rooms at the back. One I left open for a patient client to sit in, if I had a patient client. There was a buzzer on the door which I could switch on and off from my private thinking parlour.

I looked into the reception-room. It was empty of everything but the smell of dust. I threw up another window, unlocked the communicating door and went into the room beyond. Three hard chairs and a swivel chair, flat desk with a glass top, five green filing-cases, three of them full of nothing, a calendar and a framed licence bond on the wall, a phone, a washbowl in a stained wood cupboard, a hat-rack, a carpet that was just something on the floor, and two open windows with net curtains that puckered in and out like the lips of a toothless old man sleeping.

The same stuff I had had last year, and the year before that. Not beautiful, not gay, but better than a tent on the beach.

I hung my hat and coat on the hat-rack, washed my face and hands in cold water, lit a cigarette and hoisted the phone book on to the desk. Elisha Morningstar was listed at 824 Belfont Building, 422 West Ninth Street. I wrote that down and the phone number that went with it and had my hand on the instrument when I remembered that I hadn't switched on the buzzer of the reception room. I reached over the side of the desk and clicked it on and caught it right in stride. Somebody had just opened the door of the outer office.

I turned my pad face down on the desk and went over to see who it was. It was a slim tall self-satisfied looking number in a tropical worsted suit of slate-blue, black and white shoes, a dull ivory-coloured shirt and a tie and display handkerchief the colour of jacaranda bloom. He was holding a long black cigarette-holder in a peeled black white pigskin glove and he was wrinkling his nose at the dead magazines on the library table and the chairs and the rusty floor covering and the general air of not much money being made.

As I opened the communicating door he made a quarter turn and stared at me out of a pair of rather dreamy pale eyes set close to a narrow nose. His skin was sun-flushed, his reddish hair was brushed back hard over a narrow skull, and the thin line of his moustache was much redder than his hair.

He looked me over without haste and without much pleasure. He blew some smoke delicately and spoke through it with a faint sneer.

'You're Marlowe?'

I nodded.

'I'm a little disappointed,' he said. 'I rather expected something with dirty fingernails.'

'Come inside,' I said, 'and you can be witty sitting down.'

I held the door for him and he strolled past me flicking cigarette-ash on the floor with the middle nail of his free hand. He sat down on the customer's side of the desk, took off the glove from his right hand and folded this with the other already off and laid them on the desk. He tapped the cigarette-end out of the long black holder, prodded the ash with a match until it stopped smoking, fitted another cigarette and lit it with a broad mahogany-coloured match. He leaned back in his chair with a smile of a bored aristocrat.

'All set?' I inquired. 'Pulse and respiration normal? You wouldn't like a cold towel on your head or anything?'

He didn't curl his lip because it had been curled when he came in. 'A private detective,' he said. 'I never met one. A shifty business, one gathers. Keyhole peeping, raking up scandal, that sort of thing.'

'You here on business,' I asked him, 'or just slumming?'

His smile was as faint as a fat lady at a fireman's ball.

'The name is Murdock. That probably means a little something to you.'

'You certainly made nice time over here,' I said, and started to fill a pipe.

He watched me fill the pipe. He said slowly: 'I understand my mother has employed you on a job of some sort. She has given you a cheque.'

I finished filling the pipe, put a match to it, got it drawing and leaned back to blow smoke over my right shoulder towards the open window. I didn't say anything.

He leaned forward a little more and said earnestly: 'I know being cagey is all part of your trade, but I am not guessing. A little worm told me, a simple garden worm, often trodden on, but still somehow surviving – like myself. I happened to be not far behind you. Does that help to clear things up?'

'Yeah,' I said. 'Supposing it made any difference to me.'

'You are hired to find my wife, I gather.'

I made a snorting sound and grinned at him over the pipe bowl.

'Marlowe,' he said, even more earnestly, 'I'll try hard, but I don't think I am going to like you.'

'I'm screaming,' I said. 'With rage and pain.'

'And if you will pardon a homely phrase, your tough guy act stinks.'

'Coming from you, that's bitter.'

He leaned back again and brooded at me with pale eyes. He fussed around in the chair, trying to get comfortable. A lot of people had tried to get comfortable in that chair. I ought to try it myself sometime. Maybe it was losing business for me.

'Why should my mother want Linda found?' he asked slowly. 'She hated her guts. I mean my mother hated Linda's guts. Linda was quite decent to my mother. What do you think of her?'

'Your mother?'

'Of course. You haven't met Linda, have you?'

'That secretary of your mother's has her job hanging by a frayed thread. She talks out of turn.'

He shook his head sharply. 'Mother won't know. Anyhow, Mother couldn't do without Merle. She has to have somebody to bully. She might yell at her or even slap her face, but she couldn't do without her. What did you think of her?'

'Kind of cute – in an old-world sort of way.'

He frowned. 'I mean Mother. Merle's just a simple little girl, I know.'

'Your powers of observation startle me,' I said.

He looked surprised. He almost forgot to fingernail the ash of his cigarette. But not quite. He was careful not to get any of it in the ashtray, however.

'About my mother,' he said patiently.

'A grand old war-horse,' I said. 'A heart of gold and the gold buried good and deep.'

'But why does she want Linda found? I can't understand it. Spending money on it, too. My mother hates to spend money. She thinks money is part of her skin. Why does she want Linda found?'

'Search me,' I said. 'Who said she did?'

'Why, you implied so. And Merle –'

'Merle's just romantic. She made it up. Hell, she blows her nose in a man's handkerchief. Probably one of yours.'

He blushed. 'That's silly. Look, Marlowe. Please, be reasonable and give me an idea what it's all about. I haven't much money, I'm afraid, but would a couple of hundred –'

'I ought to bop you,' I said. 'Besides, I'm not supposed to talk to you. Orders.'

'Why, for heaven's sake?'

'Don't ask me things I don't know. I can't tell you the answers. And don't ask me things I do know, because I won't tell you the answers. Where have you been all your life? If a man in my line of work is handed a job, does he go around answering questions about it to anyone that gets curious?'

'There must be a lot of electricity in the air,' he said nastily, 'for a man in your line of work to turn down two hundred dollars.'

There was nothing in that for me, either. I picked his broad mahogany match out of the tray and looked at it. It had thin yellow edges and there was white printing on it. ROSEMONT. H. RICHARDS '3 – the rest was burnt off. I doubled the match and squeezed the halves together and tossed it in the waste basket.

'I love my wife,' he said suddenly, and showed me the hard white edges of his teeth. 'A corny touch, but it's true.'

'The Lombardos are still doing all right.'

He kept his lips pulled back from his teeth and talked through them at me. 'She doesn't love me. I know of no particular reason why she should. Things have been strained between us. She was used to a fast-moving sort of life. With us, well, it has been pretty dull. We haven't quarrelled. Linda's the cool type. But she hasn't really had a lot of fun being married to me.'

'You're just too modest,' I said.

His eyes glinted, but he kept his smooth manner pretty well in place.

'Not good, Marlowe. Not even fresh. Look, you have the air of a decent sort of guy. I know my mother is not putting out two hundred and fifty bucks just to be breezy. Maybe it's not Linda. Maybe it's something else. Maybe –' he stopped and then said this very slowly, watching my eyes 'maybe it's Morny.'

'Maybe it is,' I said cheerfully.

He picked his gloves up and slapped the desk with them and put them down again. 'I'm in a spot there all right,' he said. 'But I didn't think she knew about it. Morny must have called her up. He promised not to.'

This was easy. I said: 'How much are you into him for?'

It wasn't so easy. He got suspicious again. 'If he called her up, he would have told her. And she would have told you,' he said thinly.

'Maybe it isn't Morny,' I said, beginning to want to drink very badly. 'Maybe the cook is with child by the iceman. But if it was Morny, how much?'

'Twelve thousand,' he said, looking down and flushing.

'Threats?'

He nodded.

'Tell him to go fly a kite,' I said. 'What kind of lad is he? Tough?'

He looked up again, his face being brave. 'I suppose he is. I suppose they all are. He used to be a screen heavy. Good-looking in a flashy way, a chaser. But don't get any ideas. Linda just worked there, like the waiters and the band. And if you are looking for her, you'll have a hard time finding her.'

I sneered at him politely.

'Why would I have a hard time finding her? She's not buried in the backyard, I hope.'

He stood up with a flash of anger in his pale eyes. Standing there leaning over the desk a little he whipped his right hand up in a neat enough gesture and brought out a small automatic, about .25 calibre, with a walnut grip. It looked like the brother of the one I had seen in the drawer of Merle's desk. The muzzle looked vicious enough pointing at me. I didn't move.

'If anybody tries to push Linda around, he'll have to push me around first,' he said tightly.

'That oughtn't to be too hard. Better get more gun – unless you're just thinking of bees.'

He put the little gun back in his inside-pocket. He gave me a straight hard look and picked his gloves up and started for the door.

'It's a waste of time talking to you,' he said. 'All you do is wisecrack.'

I said: 'Wait a minute,' and got up and went around the desk. 'It might be a good idea for you not to mention this interview to your mother, if only for the little girl's sake.'

He nodded. 'For the amount of information I got, it doesn't seem worth mentioning.'

'That straight goods about your owing Morny twelve grand?'

He looked down, then up, then down again. He said: 'Anybody who could get into Alex Morny for twelve grand would have to be a lot smarter than I am.'

I was quite close to him. I said: 'As a matter of fact, I don't even think you are worried about your wife. I think you know where she is. She didn't run away from you at all. She just ran away from your mother.'

He lifted his eyes and drew one glove on. He didn't say anything.

'Perhaps she'll get a job,' I said. 'And make enough money to support you.'

He looked down at the floor again, turned his body to the right a little and the gloved fist made a tight unrelaxed arc through the air upwards. I moved my jaw out of the way and caught his wrist and pushed it slowly back against his chest, leaning on it. He slid a foot back on the floor and began to breathe hard. It was a slender wrist. My fingers went around it and met.

We stood there looking into each other's eyes. He was breathing like a drunk, his mouth open and his lips pulled back. Small round spots of bright red flamed on his cheeks. He tried to jerk his wrist away, but I put so much weight on him that he had to take another short step back to brace himself. Our faces were now only inches apart.

'How come your old man didn't leave you some money?' I sneered. 'Or did you blow it all?'

He spoke between his teeth, still trying to jerk loose. 'If it's any of your rotten business and you mean Jasper Murdock, he wasn't my father. He didn't like me and he didn't leave me a cent. My father was a man named Horace Bright who lost his money in the crash and jumped out of his office window.'

'You milk easy,' I said, 'but you give pretty thin milk. I'm sorry for what I said about your wife supporting you. I just wanted to get your goat.'

I dropped his wrist and stepped back. He still breathed hard and heavily. His eyes on mine were very angry, but he kept his voice down.

'Well, you got it. If you're satisfied, I'll be on my way.'

'I was doing you a favour,' I said. 'A gun toter oughtn't to insult so easily. Better ditch it.'

'That's my business,' he said. 'I'm sorry I took a swing at you. It probably wouldn't have hurt much, if it had connected.'

'That's all right.'

He opened the door and went on out. His steps died along the corridor. Another screwball. I tapped my teeth with a knuckle in time to the sound of his steps as long as I could hear them. Then I went back to the desk, looked at my pad, and lifted the phone.

4

After the bell had rung three times at the other end of the line a light childish sort of girl's voice filtered itself through a hank of gum and said: 'Good morning. Mr Morningstar's office.'

'Is the old gentleman in?'

'Who is calling, please?'

'Marlowe.'

'Does he know you, Mr Marlowe?'

'Ask him if he wants to buy any early American gold coins.'

'Just a minute, please.'

There was a pause suitable to an elderly party in an inner office having his attention called to the fact that somebody on the telephone wanted to talk to him. Then the phone clicked and a man spoke. He had a dry voice. You might even call it parched.

'This is Mr Morningstar.'

'I'm told you called Mrs Murdock in Pasadena, Mr Morningstar. About a certain coin.'

'About a certain coin,' he repeated. 'Indeed. Well?'

'My understanding is that you wished to buy the coin in question from the Murdock collection.'

'Indeed? And who are you, sir?'

'Philip Marlowe. A private detective. I'm working for Mrs Murdock.'

'Indeed,' he said for the third time. He cleared his throat carefully. 'And what did you wish to talk to me about, Mr Marlowe?'

'About this coin.'

'But I was informed it was not for sale.'

'I still want to talk to you about it. In person.'

'Do you mean she has changed her mind about selling?'

'No.'

'Then I'm afraid I don't understand what you want, Mr Marlowe. What have we to talk about?' He sounded sly now.

I took the ace out of my sleeve and played it with a languid grace. 'The point is, Mr Morningstar, that at the time you called up you already knew the coin wasn't for sale.'

'Interesting,' he said slowly. 'How?'

'You're in the business, you couldn't help knowing. It's a matter of public record that the Murdock collection cannot be sold during Mrs Murdock's lifetime.'

'Ah,' he said. 'Ah.' There was a silence. Then, 'At three o'clock,' he said, not sharp, but quick. 'I shall be glad to see you here in my office. You probably know where it is. Will that suit you?'

'I'll be there,' I said.

I hung up and lit my pipe again and sat there looking at the wall. My face was stiff with thoughts, or with something that made my face stiff. I took Linda Murdock's photo out of my pocket, stared at it for a while, decided that the face was pretty commonplace after all, locked the photo away in my desk. I picked Murdock's second match out of my ashtray and looked it over. The lettering on this one read: TOP ROW W. D. WRIGHT '36.

I dropped it back in the tray, wondering what made this important. Maybe it was a clue.

I got Mrs Murdock's cheque out of my wallet, endorsed it, made out a deposit slip and a cheque for cash, got my bank-book out of the desk, and folded the lot under a rubber band and put them in my pocket.

Lois Magic was not listed in the phone book.

I got the classified section up on the desk and made a list of the half-dozen theatrical agencies that showed in the largest type and called them. They all had bright cheerful voices and wanted to ask a lot of questions, but they either didn't know or didn't care to tell anything about a Miss Lois Magic, said to be an entertainer.

I threw the list in the waste-basket and called Kenny Haste, a crime reporter on the *Chronicle*.

'What do you know about Alex Morny?' I asked him when we were through wisecracking at each other.

'Runs a plushy night-club and gambling joint in Idle Valley, about two miles off the highway back towards the hills. Used to be in pictures. Lousy actor. Seems to have plenty of protection. I never heard of him shooting anybody on the public square at high noon. Or at any other time for that matter. But I wouldn't like to bet on it.'

'Dangerous?'

'I'd say he might be, if necessary. All those boys have been to picture shows and know how night-club bosses are supposed to act. He has a bodyguard who is quite a character. His name's Eddie Prue, he's about six feet five inches tall and thin as an honest alibi. He has a frozen eye, the result of a war wound.'

'Is Morny dangerous to women?'

'Don't be Victorian, old top. Women don't call it danger.'

'Do you know a girl named Lois Magic, said to be an entertainer. A tall gaudy blonde, I hear.'

'No. Sounds as though I might like to.'

'Don't be cute. Do you know anybody named Vannier? None of these people are in the phone book.'

'Nope. But I could ask Gertie Arbogast, if you want to call back. He knows all the night-club aristocrats. And heels.'

'Thanks, Kenny. I'll do that. Half an hour?'

He said that would be fine, and we hung up. I locked the office and left.

At the end of the corridor, in the angle of the wall, a youngish blond man in a brown suit and a cocoa-coloured straw hat with a brown and yellow tropical print band was reading the evening paper with his back to the wall. As I passed him he yawned and tucked the paper under his arm and straightened up.

He got into the elevator with me. He could hardly keep his eyes open he was so tired. I went out on the street and walked a block to the bank to deposit my cheque and draw out a little folding money for expenses. From there I went to the Tigertail Lounge and sat in a shallow booth and drank a martini and ate a sandwich. The man in the brown suit posted himself at the end of the bar and drank coca-colas and looked bored and piled pennies in front of him, carefully smoothing the edges. He had his dark glasses on again. That made him invisible.

I dragged my sandwich out as long as I could and then strolled back to the telephone booth at the inner end of the bar. The man in the brown suit turned his head quickly and then covered the motion by lifting his glass. I dialled the *Chronicle* office again.

'Okay,' Kenny Haste said. 'Gertie Arbogast says Morny married your gaudy blonde not very long ago. Lois Magic. He doesn't know Vannier. He says Morny bought a place out beyond Bel-Air, a white house on Stillwood Crescent Drive, about five blocks north of Sunset. Gertie says Morny took it over from a busted flush named Arthur Blake Popham who got caught in a mail fraud rap. Popham's initials are still on the gates. And probably on the toilet paper, Gertie says. He was that kind of a guy. That's all we seem to know.'

'Nobody could ask more. Many thanks, Kenny.'

I hung up, stepped out of the booth, met the dark glasses above the brown suit under the cocoa straw hat and watched them turn quickly away.

I spun around and went back through a swing door into the kitchen and through that to the alley and along the alley a quarter block to the back of the parking lot where I had put my car.

No sand-coloured coupé succeeded in getting behind me as I drove off, in the general direction of Bel-Air.

5

Stillwood Crescent Drive curved leisurely north from Sunset Boulevard, well beyond the Bel-Air Country Club golf-course. The road was lined with walled and fenced estates. Some had high walls, some had low walls, some had ornamental iron fences, some were a bit old-fashioned and got along with tall hedges. The street had no sidewalk. Nobody walked in that neighbourhood, not even the postman.

The afternoon was hot, but not hot like Pasadena. There was a drowsy smell of flowers and sun, a swishing of lawn sprinklers gentle behind hedges and walls, the clear ratchety sound of lawn mowers moving delicately over serene and confident lawns.

I drove up the hill slowly, looking for monograms on gates. Arthur Blake Popham was the name. A. B. P. would be the initials. I found them almost at the top, gilt on a black shield, the gates folded back on a black composition driveway.

It was a glaring white house that had the air of being brand new, but the landscaping was well advanced. It was modest enough for the neighbourhood, not more than fourteen rooms and probably only one swimming pool. Its wall was low, made of brick with the concrete all oozed out between and set that way and painted over white. On top of the wall a low iron railing painted black. The name A. P. Morny was stencilled on the large silver-coloured postbox at the service entrance.

I parked my car on the street and walked up the black driveway to a side door of glittering white paint shot with patches of colour from the stained-glass canopy over it. I hammered on a large brass knocker. Back along the side of the house a chauffeur was washing off a Cadillac.

The door opened and a hard-eyed Filipino in a white coat curled his lip at me. I gave him a card.

'Mrs Morny,' I said.

He shut the door. Time passed, as it always does when I go calling. The swish of water on the Cadillac had a cool sound. The chauffeur was a little runt in breeches and leggings and a sweat-stained shirt. He looked like an overgrown jockey and he made the same kind of hissing noise as he worked on the car that a groom makes rubbing down a horse.

A red-throated humming-bird went into a scarlet bush beside the door, shook the long tubular blooms around a little, and zoomed off so fast he simply disappeared in the air.

The door opened, the Filipino poked my card at me. I didn't take it.

'What you want?'

It was a tight crackling voice, like someone tiptoeing across a lot of eggshells.

'Want to see Mrs Morny.'

'She's not at home.'

'Didn't you know that when I gave you the card?'

He opened his fingers and let the card flutter to the ground. He grinned, showing me a lot of cut-rate dental work.

'I know when she tell me.'

He shut the door in my face, not gently.

I picked the card up and walked along the side of the house to where the chauffeur was squirting water on the Cadillac sedan and rubbing the dirt off with a big sponge. He had red-rimmed eyes and a bang of corn-coloured hair. A cigarette hung exhausted at the corner of his lower lip.

He gave me the quick side glance of a man who is minding his own business with difficulty, I said:

'Where's the boss?'

The cigarette jiggled in his mouth. The water went on swishing gently on the paint.

'Ask at the house, Jack.'

'I done asked. They done shut the door in mah face.'

'You're breaking my heart, Jack.'

'How about Mrs Morny?'

'Same answer, Jack. I just work here. Selling something?'

I held my card so that he could read it. It was a business card this time. He put the sponge down on the running-board, and the hose on the cement. He stepped around the water to wipe his hands on a towel that hung at the side of the garage doors. He fished a match out of his pants, struck it and tilted his head back to light the dead butt that was stuck in his face.

His foxy little eyes flicked around this way and that and he moved behind the car, with a jerk of the head. I went over near him.

'How's the little old expense account?' he asked in a small careful voice.

'Fat with inactivity.'

'For five I could start thinking.'

'I wouldn't want to make it that tough for you.'

'For ten I could sing like four canaries and a steel guitar.'

'I don't like these plushy orchestrations,' I said.

He cocked his head sideways. 'Talk English, Jack.'

'I don't want you to lose your job, son. All I want to know is whether Mrs Morny is home. Does that rate more than a buck?'

'Don't worry about my job, Jack. I'm solid.'

'With Morny – or somebody else?'

'You want that for the same buck?'

'Two bucks.'

He eyed me over. 'You ain't working for him, are you?'

'Sure.'

'You're a liar.'

'Sure.'

'Gimme the two bucks,' he snapped.

I gave him two dollars.

'She's in the backyard with a friend,' he said. 'A nice friend. You got a friend that don't work and a husband that works, you're all set, see?' He leered.

'You'll be all set in an irrigation ditch one of these days.'

'Not me, Jack. I'm wise. I know how to play 'em. I monkeyed around these kind of people all my life.'

He rubbed the two dollar bills between his palms, blew on them, folded them longways and wideways and tucked them in the watch pocket of his breeches.

'That was just the soup,' he said. 'Now for five more –'

A rather large blond cocker spaniel tore around the Cadillac, skidded a little on the wet concrete, took off neatly, hit me in the stomach and thighs with all four paws, licked my face, dropped to the ground, ran around my legs, sat down between them, let his tongue out all the way and started to pant.

I stepped over him and braced myself against the side of the car and got my handkerchief out.

A male voice called: 'Here, Heathcliff. Here, Heathcliff.' Steps sounded on a hard walk.

'That's Heathcliff?' the chauffeur said sourly.

'Heathcliff?'

'Cripes, that's what they call the dog, Jack.'

'*Wuthering Heights?*' I asked.

'Now you're double-talking again,' he sneered. 'Look out – company.'

He picked up the sponge and the hose and went back to washing the car. I moved away from him. The cocker spaniel immediately moved between my legs again, almost tripping me.

'Here, Heathcliff,' the male voice called out louder, and a man came into view through the opening of a latticed tunnel covered with climbing roses.

Tall, dark, with a clear olive skin, brilliant black eyes, gleaming white teeth. Sideburns. A narrow black moustache. Sideburns too long, much too long. White shirt with embroidered initials on the pocket, white slacks, white shoes. A wrist-watch that curved half-way around a lean dark wrist, held on by a gold chain. A yellow scarf around a bronzed slender neck.

He saw the dog squatted between my legs and didn't like it. He snapped long fingers and snapped a clear hard voice:

'Here, Heathcliff. Come here at once!'

The dog breathed hard and didn't move, except to lean a little closer to my right leg.

'Who are you?' the man asked, staring me down.

I held out my card. Olive fingers took the card. The dog quietly backed out from between my legs, edged around the front of the car, and faded silently into the distance.

'Marlowe,' the man said. 'Marlowe, eh? What's this? A detective? What do you want?'

'Want to see Mrs Morny.'

He looked me up and down, brilliant black eyes sweeping slowly and the silky fringes of long eyelashes following them.

'Weren't you told she was not in?'

'Yeah, but I didn't believe it. Are you Mr Morny?'

'No.'

'That's Mr Vannier,' the chauffeur said behind my back, in the drawled, over-polite voice of deliberate insolence. 'Mr Vannier's a friend of the family. He comes here quite a lot.'

Vannier looked past my shoulder, his eyes furious. The chauffeur came around the car and spat the cigarette-stub out of his mouth with casual contempt.

'I told the shamus the boss wasn't here, Mr Vannier.'

'I see.'

'I told him Mrs Morny and you was here. Did I do wrong?'

Vannier said: 'You could have minded your own business.'

The chauffeur said: 'I wonder why the hell I didn't think of that.'

Vannier said: 'Get out before I break your dirty little neck for you.'

The chauffeur eyed him quietly and then went back into the gloom of the garage and started to whistle. Vannier moved his hot angry eyes over to me and snapped:

'You were told Mrs Morny was not in, but it didn't take. Is that it? In other words the information failed to satisfy you.'

'If we have to have other words,' I said, 'those might do.'

'I see. Could you bring yourself to say what point you wish to discuss with Mrs Morny?'

'I'd prefer to explain that to Mrs Morny herself.'

'The implication is that she doesn't care to see you.'

Behind the car the chauffeur said: 'Watch his right, Jack. It might have a knife in it.'

Vannier's olive skin turned the colour of dried seaweed. He turned on his heel and rapped at me in a stifled voice: 'Follow me.'

He went along the brick path under the tunnel of roses and through a white gate at the end. Beyond was a walled-in garden containing flower-beds crammed with showy annuals, a badminton court, a nice stretch of greensward, and a small tiled pool glittering angrily in the sun. Beside the pool there was a flagged space set with blue and white garden furniture, low tables with composition tops, reclining chairs with footrests and enormous cushions, and over all a blue and white umbrella as big as a small tent.

A long-limbed languorous type of showgirl blonde lay at her ease in one of the chairs, with her feet raised on a padded rest and a tall misted glass at her elbow, near a silver ice bucket and a Scotch bottle. She looked at us lazily as we came over the grass. From thirty feet away she looked like a lot of class. From ten feet away she looked like something made up to be seen from thirty feet away. Her mouth was too wide, her eyes were too blue, her make-up was too vivid, the thin arch of her eyebrows was almost fantastic in its curve and spread, and the mascara was so thick on her eyelashes that they looked like miniature iron railings.

She wore white duck slacks, blue and white open-toed sandals over bare feet and crimson lake toenails, a white silk blouse and a necklace of green stones that were not square-cut emeralds. Her hair was as artificial as a night-club lobby.

On the chair beside her there was a white straw garden hat with a brim the size of a spare tyre and a white satin chin-strap. On the brim of the hat lay a pair of green sun-glasses with lenses the size of doughnuts.

Vannier marched over to her and snapped out: 'You've got to can that nasty little red-eyed driver of yours, but quick. Otherwise I'm liable to break his neck any minute. I can't go near him without getting insulted.'

The blonde coughed lightly, flicked a handkerchief around without doing anything with it, and said:

'Sit down and rest your sex appeal. Who's your friend?'

Vannier looked for my card, found he was holding it in his hand and threw it on her lap. She picked it up languidly, ran her eyes over it, ran them over me, sighed and tapped her teeth with her fingernails.

'Big, isn't he? Too much for you to handle, I guess.'

Vannier looked at me nastily. 'All right, get it over with, whatever it is.'

'Do I talk to her?' I asked. 'Or do I talk to you and have you put it in English?'

The blonde laughed. A silvery ripple of laughter that held the unspoiled naturalness of a bubble dance. A small tongue played roguishly along her lips.

Vannier sat down and lit a gold-tipped cigarette and I stood there looking at them.

I said: 'I'm looking for a friend of yours, Mrs Morny. I understand that she shared an apartment with you about a year ago. Her name is Linda Conquest.'

Vannier flicked his eyes up, down, up, down. He turned his head and looked across the pool. The cocker spaniel named Heathcliff sat over there looking at us with the white of one eye.

Vannier snapped his fingers. 'Here, Heathcliff! Here, Heathcliff! Come here, sir!'

The blonde said: 'Shut up. The dog hates your guts. Give your vanity a rest, for heaven's sake.'

Vannier snapped: 'Don't talk like that to me.'

The blonde giggled and petted his face with her eyes.

I said: 'I'm looking for a girl named Linda Conquest, Mrs Morny.'

The blonde looked at me and said: 'So you said. I was just thinking. I don't think I've seen her in six months. She got married.'

'You haven't seen her in six months?'

'That's what I said, big boy. What do you want to know for?'

'Just a private inquiry I'm making.'

'About what?'

'About a confidential matter,' I said.

'Just think,' the blonde said brightly. 'He's making a private inquiry about a confidential matter. You hear that, Lou? Busting in on total strangers that don't want to see him is quite all right, though, isn't it, Lou? On account of he's making a private inquiry about a confidential matter.'

'Then you don't know where she is, Mrs Morny?'

'Didn't I say so?' Her voice rose a couple of notches.

'No. You said you didn't think you had seen her in six months. Not quite the same thing.'

'Who told you I shared an apartment with her?' the blonde snapped.

'I never reveal a source of information, Mrs Morny.'

'Sweetheart, you're fussy enough to be a dance director. I should tell you everything, you should tell me nothing.'

'The position is quite different,' I said. 'I'm a hired hand obeying instructions. The lady has no reason to hide out, has she?'

'Who's looking for her?'

'Her folks.'

'Guess again. She doesn't have any folks.'

'You must know her pretty well, if you know that,' I said.

'Maybe I did once. That don't prove I do now.'

'Okay,' I said. 'The answer is you know, but you won't tell.'

'The answer,' Vannier said suddenly, 'is that you're not wanted here and the sooner you get out the better we like it.'

I kept on looking at Mrs Morny. She winked at me and said to Vannier: 'Don't get so hostile, darling. You have a lot of charm, but you have small bones. You're not built for the rough work. That right, big boy?'

I said: 'I hadn't thought about it, Mrs Morny. Do you think Mr Morny could help me – or would?'

She shook her head. 'How would I know? You could try. If he don't like you, he has guys around that can bounce you.'

'I think you could tell me yourself, if you wanted to.'

'How are you going to make me want to?' Her eyes were inviting.

'With all these people around,' I said, 'how can I?'

'That's a thought,' she said, and sipped from her glass, watching me over it.

Vannier stood up very slowly. His face was white. He put his hand inside his shirt and said slowly, between his teeth: 'Get out, mug. While you can still walk.'

I looked at him in surprise. 'Where's your refinement?' I asked him. 'And don't tell me you wear a gun with your garden clothes.'

The blonde laughed, showing a fine strong set of teeth. Vannier thrust his hand under his left arm inside the shirt and set his lips. His black eyes were sharp and blank at the same time, like a snake's eyes.

'You heard me,' he said, almost softly. 'And don't write me off too quick. I'd plug you as soon as I'd strike a match. And fix it afterwards.'

I looked at the blonde. Her eyes were bright and her mouth looked sensual and eager, watching us.

I turned and walked away across the grass. About half-way across it I looked back at them. Vannier stood in exactly the same position, his hand inside his shirt. The blonde's eyes were still wide and her lips parted, but the shadow of the umbrella had dimmed her expression and at that distance it might have been either fear or pleased anticipation.

I went on over the grass, through the white gate and along the brick path under the rose arbour. I reached the end of it, turned, walked quietly back to the gate and took another look at them. I didn't know what there would be to see or what I cared about it when I saw it.

What I saw was Vannier practically sprawled on top of the blonde, kissing her.

I shook my head and went back along the walk.

The red-eyed chauffeur was still at work on the Cadillac. He had finished the wash job and was wiping off the glass and nickel with a large chamois. I went around and stood beside him.

'How you come out?' he asked me out of the side of his mouth.

'Badly. They tramped all over me,' I said.

He nodded and went on making the hissing noise of a groom rubbing down a horse.

'You better watch your step. The guy's heeled,' I said. 'Or pretends to be.'

The chauffeur laughed shortly. 'Under that suit? Nix.'

'Who is this guy Vannier? What does he do?'

The chauffeur straightened up, put the chamois over the sill of a window and wiped his hands on the towel that was now stuck in his waistband.

'Women, my guess would be,' he said.

'Isn't it a bit dangerous – playing with this particular woman?'

'I'd say it was,' he agreed. 'Different guys got different ideas of danger. It would scare me.'

'Where does he live?'

'Sherman Oaks. She goes over there. She'll go once too often.'

'Ever run across a girl named Linda Conquest? Tall, dark, handsome, used to be a singer with a band?'

'For two bucks, Jack, you expect a lot of service.'

'I could build it up to five.'

He shook his head. 'I don't know the party. Not by that name. All kinds of dames come here, mostly pretty flashy. I don't get introduced.' He grinned.

I got my wallet out and put three ones in his little damp paw. I added a business card.

'I like small close-built men,' I said. 'They never seem to be afraid of anything. Come and see me some time.'

'I might at that, Jack. Thanks. Linda Conquest, huh? I'll keep my ear-flaps off.'

'So long,' I said. 'The name?'

'They call me Shifty. I never knew why.'

'So long, Shifty.'

'So long. Gat under his arm – in them clothes? Not a chance.'

'I don't know,' I said. 'He made the motion. I'm not hired to gunfight with strangers.'

'Hell, that shirt he's wearing only got two buttons at the top. I noticed. Take him a week to pull a rod from under that.' But he sounded faintly worried.

'I guess he was just bluffing,' I agreed. 'If you hear mention of Linda Conquest, I'll be glad to talk business with you.'

'Okay, Jack.'

I went back along the black driveway. He stood there scratching his chin.

6

I drove along the block looking for a place to park so that I could run up to the office for a moment before going on downtown.

A chauffeur-driven Packard edged out from the kerb in front of a cigar store about thirty feet from the entrance to my building. I slid into the space, locked the car and stepped out. It was only then that I noticed the car in front of which I had parked was a familiar-looking sand-coloured coupé. It didn't have to be the same one. There were thousands of them. Nobody was in it. Nobody was near it that wore a cocoa straw hat with a brown and yellow band.

I went around to the street side and looked at the steering-post. No licence holder. I wrote the licence plate number down on the back of an envelope, just in case, and went on into my building. He wasn't in the lobby, or in the corridor upstairs.

I went into the office, looked on the floor for mail, didn't find any, bought myself a short drink out of the office bottle and left. I didn't have any time to spare to get downtown before three o'clock.

The sand-coloured coupé was still parked, still empty. I got into mine and started up and moved out into the traffic stream.

I was below Sunset on Vine before he picked me up. I kept on going, grinning, and wondering where he had hid. Perhaps in the car parked behind his own. I hadn't thought of that.

I drove south to Third and all the way downtown on Third. The sand-coloured coupé kept half a block behind me all the way. I moved over to Seventh and Grand, parked near Seventh and Olive, stopped to buy cigarettes I didn't need, and then walked east along Seventh without looking behind me. At Spring I went into the Hotel Metropole, strolled over to the big horseshoe cigar counter to light one of my cigarettes and then sat down in one of the old brown leather chairs in the lobby.

A blond man in a brown suit, dark glasses and the now familiar hat, came into the lobby and moved unobtrusively among the potted palms and the stucco arches to the cigar counter. He bought a package of cigarettes and broke it open standing there, using the time to lean his back against the counter and give the lobby the benefit of his eagle eye.

He picked up his change and went over and sat down with his back to a pillar. He tipped his hat down over his dark glasses and seemed to go to sleep with an unlighted cigarette between his lips.

I got up and wandered over and dropped into the chair beside him. I looked at him sideways. He didn't move. Seen at close quarters his face seemed young and pink and plump and the blond beard on his chin was very carelessly shaved. Behind the dark glasses his eyelashes flicked up and down rapidly. A hand on his knee tightened and pulled the cloth into wrinkles. There was a wart on his cheek just below the right eyelid.

I struck a match and held the flame to his cigarette. 'Light?'

'Oh – thanks,' he said, very surprised. He drew breath in until the cigarette tip glowed. I shook the match out, tossed it into the sand jar at my elbow and waited. He looked at me sideways several times before he spoke.

'Haven't I seen you somewhere before?'

'Over on Dresden Avenue in Pasadena. This morning.'

I could see his cheeks get pinker than they had been. He sighed.

'I must be lousy,' he said.

'Boy, you stink,' I agreed.

'Maybe it's the hat,' he said.

'The hat helps,' I said. 'But you don't really need it.'

'It's a pretty tough dollar in this town,' he said sadly. 'You can't do it on foot, you ruin yourself with taxi fares if you use taxis, and if you use your own car, it's always where you can't get to it fast enough. You have to stay too close.'

'But you don't have to climb in a guy's pocket,' I said. 'Did you want something with me or are you just practising?'

'I figured I'd find out if you were smart enough to be worth talking to.'

'I'm very smart,' I said. 'It would be a shame not to talk to me.'

He looked carefully around the back of his chair and on both sides of where we were sitting and then drew a small pigskin wallet out. He handed me a nice fresh card from it. It read: George Anson Phillips.

Confidential Investigations. 212, Seneger Building, 1924 North Wilcox Avenue, Hollywood. A Glenview telephone number. In the upper left-hand corner there was an open eye with an eyebrow arched in surprise and very long eyelashes.

'You can't do that,' I said, pointing to the eye. 'That's the Pinkerton's. You'll be stealing their business.'

'Oh, hell,' he said, 'what little I get wouldn't bother them.'

I snapped the card on my fingernail and bit down hard on my teeth and slipped the card into my pocket.

'You want one of mine – or have you completed your file on me?'

'Oh I know all about you,' he said. 'I was a deputy at Ventura the time you were working on the Gregson case.'

Gregson was a con man from Oklahoma City who was followed all over the United States for two years by one of his victims until he got so jittery that he shot up a service station attendant who mistook him for an acquaintance. It seemed a long time ago to me.

I said: 'Go on from there.'

'I remembered your name when I saw it on your registration this a.m. So when I lost you on the way into town I just looked you up. I was going to come in and talk, but it would have been a violation of confidence. This way I kind of can't help myself.'

Another screwball. That made three in one day, not counting Mrs Murdock, who might turn out to be a screwball, too.

I waited while he took his dark glasses off and polished them and put them on again and gave the neighbourhood the once over again. Then he said:

'I figured we could, maybe, make a deal. Pool our resources, as they say. I saw the guy go into your office, so I figured he had hired you.'

'You know who he was?'

'I'm working on him,' he said, and his voice sounded flat and discouraged. 'And where I am getting is no place at all.'

'What did he do to you?'

'Well, I'm working for his wife.'

'Divorce?'

He looked all around him carefully and said in a small voice: 'So she says. But I wonder.'

'They both want one,' I said. 'Each trying to get something on the other. Comical, isn't it?'

'My end I don't like so well. A guy is tailing me around some of the time. A very tall guy with a funny eye. I shake him but after a while I see him again. A very tall guy. Like a lamp-post.'

A very tall man with a funny eye. I smoked thoughtfully.

'Anything to do with you?' the blond man asked me a little anxiously.

I shook my head and threw my cigarette into the sand jar. 'Never saw him that I know of.' I looked at my strap watch. 'We better get together and talk this thing over properly, but I can't do it now. I have an appointment.'

'I'd like to,' he said. 'Very much.'

'Let's then. My office, my apartment, or your office, or where?'

He scratched his badly shaved chin with a well-chewed thumbnail.

'My apartment,' he said at last. 'It's not in the phone book. Give me that card a minute.'

He turned it over on his palm when I gave it to him and wrote slowly with a small metal pencil, moving his tongue along his lips. He was getting younger every minute. He didn't seem much more than twenty by now, but he had to be, because the Gregson case had been six years back.

He put his pencil away and handed me back the card. The address he had written on it was 204 Florence Apartments, 128 Court Street.

I looked at him curiously. 'Court Street on Bunker Hill?'

He nodded, flushing all over his blond skin. 'Not too good,' he said quickly. 'I haven't been in the chips lately. Do you mind?'

'No, why would I?'

I stood up and held a hand out. He shook it and dropped it and I pushed it down into my hip pocket and rubbed the palm against the handkerchief I had there. Looking at his face more closely I saw that there was a line of moisture across his upper lip and more of it along the side of his nose. It was not as hot as all that.

I started to move off and then I turned back to lean down close to his face and say: 'Almost anybody can pull my leg, but just to make sure, she's a tall blonde with careless eyes, huh?'

'I wouldn't call them careless,' he said.

I held my face together while I said: 'And just between the two of us this divorce stuff is a lot of hooey. It's something else entirely, isn't it?'

'Yes,' he said softly, 'and something I don't like more every minute I think about it. Here.'

He pulled something out of his pocket and dropped it into my hand. It was a flat key.

'No need for you to wait around in the hall, if I happen to be out. I have two of them. What time would you think you would come?'

'About four-thirty, the way it looks now. You sure you want to give me this key?'

'Why, we're in the same racket,' he said, looking up at me innocently, or as innocently as he could look through a pair of dark glasses.

At the edge of the lobby I looked back. He sat there peacefully, with the half-smoked cigarette dead between his lips and the gaudy brown and yellow band on his hat looking as quiet as a cigarette advertisement on the back page of the *Saturday Evening Post*.

We were in the same racket. So I wouldn't chisel him. Just like that. I could have the key to his apartment and go in and make myself at home. I could wear his slippers and drink his liquor and lift up his carpet and count the thousand-dollar bills under it. We were in the same racket.

7

The Belfont Building was eight stories of nothing in particular that had got itself pinched off between a large green and chromium cut-rate suit emporium and a three-storey and basement garage that made a noise like lion cages at feeding time. The small dark narrow lobby was as dirty as a chicken yard. The building directory had a lot of vacant space on it. Only one of the names meant anything to me and I knew that one already. Opposite the directory a large sign tilted against the fake marble wall said: *Space for Renting Suitable for Cigar Stand. Apply Room* 316.

There were two open-grille elevators but only one seemed to be running and that not busy. An old man sat inside it slack-jawed and watery-eyed on a piece of folded burlap on top of a wooden stool. He looked as if he had been sitting there since the Civil War and had come out of that badly.

I got in with him and said 'eight', and he wrestled the doors shut and cranked his buggy and we dragged upwards lurching. The old man breathed hard, as if he was carrying the elevator on his back.

I got out at my floor and started along the hallway and behind me the old man leaned out of the car and blew his nose with his fingers into a cartoon full of floor sweepings.

Elisha Morningstar's office was at the back, opposite the fire-door. Two rooms, both doors lettered in flaked black paint on pebbled glass. *Elisha Morningstar. Numismatist.* The one farther back said: *Entrance.*

I turned the knob and went into a small narrow room with two windows, a shabby little typewriter desk, closed, a number of wall cases of tarnished coins in tilted slots with yellowed typewritten labels under them, two brown filing-cases at the back against the wall, no curtains at the windows, and a dust-grey floor carpet so threadbare that you wouldn't notice the rips in it unless you tripped over one.

An inner wooden door was open at the back across from the filing-cases, behind the little typewriter desk. Through the door came the small sounds a man makes when he isn't doing anything at all. Then the dry voice of Elisha Morningstar called out:

'Come in, please. Come in.'

I went along and in. The inner office was just as small but had a lot more stuff in it. A green safe almost blocked off the front half. Beyond this a heavy old mahogany table against the entrance door held some dark books, some flabby old magazines, and a lot of dust. In the back wall a window was open a few inches, without effect on the musty smell. There was a hat-rack with a greasy black felt hat on it. There were three long-legged tables with glass tops and more coins under the glass tops. There was a heavy dark leather-topped desk midway of the room. It had the usual desk stuff on it, and in addition a pair of jeweller's scales under a glass dome and two large nickel-framed magnifying-glasses and a jeweller's eyepiece lying on a buff scratch pad, beside a cracked yellow silk handkerchief spotted with ink.

In the swivel chair at the desk sat an elderly party in a dark grey suit with high lapels and too many buttons down the front. He had some stringy white hair that grew long enough to tickle his ears. A pale grey bald patch loomed high up in the middle of it, like a rock above timberline. Fuzz grew out of his ears, far enough to catch a moth.

He had sharp black eyes which had a pouch under each eye, brownish purple in colour and traced with a network of wrinkles and veins. His cheeks were shiny and his short sharp nose looked as if it had hung over a lot of quick ones in its time. A Hoover collar which no decent laundry would have allowed on the premises nudged his Adam's apple and a black string tie poked a small hard knot out at the bottom of the collar, like a mouse getting ready to come out of a mousehole.

He said: 'My young lady had to go to the dentist. You are Mr Marlowe?' I nodded.

'Pray, be seated.' He waved a thin hand at the chair across the desk. I sat down. 'You have some identification, I presume?'

I showed it to him. While he read it I smelled him from across the desk. He had a sort of dry musty smell, like a fairly clean Chinaman.

He placed my card face down on top of his desk and folded his hands on it. His sharp black eyes didn't miss anything in my face.

'Well, Mr Marlowe, what can I do for you?'

'Tell me about the Brasher Doubloon.'

'Ah, yes,' he said. 'The Brasher Doubloon. An interesting coin.' He lifted his hands off the desk and made a steeple of the fingers, like an old-time family lawyer getting set for a little tangled grammar. 'In some ways the most interesting and valuable of all early American coins. As no doubt you know.'

'What I don't know about early American coins you could almost crowd into the Rose Bowl.'

'Is that so?' he said. 'Is that so? Do you want me to tell you?'

'What I'm here for, Mr Morningstar.'

'It is a gold coin, roughly equivalent to a twenty-dollar gold piece, and about the size of a half-dollar. Almost exactly. It was made for the State of New York in the year 1787. It was not minted. There were no mints until 1793, when the first mint was opened in Philadelphia. The Brasher Doubloon was coined probably by the pressure moulding process and its maker was a private goldsmith named Ephraim Brasher, or Brashear. Where the name survives it is usually spelled Brashear, but not on the coin. I don't know why.'

I got a cigarette into my mouth and lit it. I thought it might do something to the musty smell. 'What's the pressure moulding process?'

'The two halves of the mould were engraved in steel, in *intaglio*, of course. These halves were then mounted in lead. Gold blanks were pressed between them in a coin press. Then the edges were trimmed for weight and smoothed. The coin was not milled. There were no milling machines in 1787.'

'Kind of a slow process,' I said.

He nodded his peaked white head. 'Quite. And, since the surface-hardening of steel without distortion could not be accomplished at that time, the dies wore and had to be remade from time to time. With consequent slight variations in design which would be visible under strong magnification. In fact, it would be safe to say no two of the coins would be identical, judged by modern methods of microscopic examination. Am I clear?'

'Yeah,' I said. 'Up to a point. How many of these coins are there and what are they worth?'

He undid the steeple of fingers and put his hands back on the desk top and patted them gently up and down.

'I don't know how many there are. Nobody knows. A few hundred, a thousand, perhaps more. But of these very few indeed are uncirculated specimens in what is called mint condition. The value varies from a couple of thousand on up. I should say that at the present time, since the devaluation of the dollar, an uncirculated specimen, carefully handled by a reputable dealer, might easily bring ten thousand dollars, or even more. It would have to have a history, of course.'

I said: 'Ah,' and let smoke out of my lungs slowly and waved it away with the flat of my hand, away from the old party across the desk from me. He looked like a non smoker. 'And without a history and not so carefully handled – how much?'

He shrugged. 'There would be the implication that the coin was illegally acquired. Stolen, or obtained by fraud. Of course it might not

45

be so. Rare coins do turn up in odd places at odd times. In old strong boxes, in the secret drawers of desks in old New England houses. Not often, I grant you. But it happens. I know of a very valuable coin that fell out of the stuffing of a horsehair sofa which had been restored by an antique dealer. The sofa had been in the same room in the same house in Fall River, Massachusetts, for ninety years. Nobody knew how the coin got there. But generally speaking, the implication of theft would be strong. Particularly in this part of the country.'

He looked at the corner of the ceiling with an absent stare. I looked at him with a not so absent stare. He looked like a man who could be trusted with a secret – if it was his own secret.

He brought his eyes down to my level slowly and said: 'Five dollars, please.'

I said: 'Huh?'

'Five dollars, please.'

'What for?'

'Don't be absurd, Mr Marlowe. Everything I have told you is available in the public library. In Fosdyke's *Register*, in particular. You choose to come here and take up my time relating it to you. For this my charge is five dollars.'

'And suppose I don't pay it,' I said.

He leaned back and closed his eyes. A very faint smile twitched at the corners of his lips. 'You will pay it,' he said.

I paid it. I took the five out of my wallet and got up to lean over the desk and spread it out right in front of him, carefully. I stroked the bill with my fingertips, as if it was a kitten.

'Five dollars, Mr Morningstar,' I said.

He opened his eyes and looked at the bill. He smiled.

'And now,' I said, 'let's talk about the Brasher Doubloon that somebody tried to sell you.'

He opened his eyes a little wider. 'Oh, did somebody try to sell me a Brasher Doubloon? Now why would they do that?'

'They needed the money,' I said. 'And they didn't want too many questions asked. They knew or found out that you were in the business and that the building where you had your office was a shabby dump where anything could happen. They knew your office was at the end of a corridor and that you were an elderly man who would probably not make any false moves – out of regard for your health.'

'They seem to have known a great deal,' Elisha Morningstar said dryly.

'They knew what they had to know in order to transact their business. Just like you and me. And none of it was hard to find out.'

He stuck his little finger in his ear and worked it around and brought it out with a little dark wax on it. He wiped it off casually on his coat.

'And you assume all this from the mere fact that I called up Mrs Murdock and asked if her Brasher Doubloon was for sale?'

'Sure. She had the same idea herself. It's reasonable. Like I said over the phone to you, you would know that coin was not for sale. If you knew anything about the business at all. And I can see that you do.'

He bowed, about an inch. He didn't quite smile but he looked about as pleased as a man in a Hoover collar ever looks.

'You would be offered this coin for sale,' I said, 'in suspicious circumstances. You would want to buy it, if you could get it cheap and had the money to handle it. But you would want to know where it came from. And even if you were quite sure it was stolen, you could still buy it, if you could get it cheap enough.'

'Oh, I could, could I?' He looked amused, but not in a large way.

'Sure you could – if you are a reputable dealer. I'll assume you are. By buying the coin – cheap – you would be protecting the owner or his insurance carrier from complete loss. They'd be glad to pay you back your outlay. It's done all the time.'

'Then the Murdock Brasher has been stolen,' he said abruptly.

'Don't quote me,' I said. 'It's a secret.'

He almost picked his nose this time. He just caught himself. He picked a hair out of one nostril instead, with a quick jerk and a wince. He held it up and looked at it. Looking at me past it he said:

'And how much will your principal pay for the return of the coin?'

I leaned over the desk and gave him my shady leer. 'One grand. What did you pay?'

'I think you are a very smart young man,' he said. Then he screwed his face up and his chin wobbled and his chest began to bounce in and out and a sound came out of him like a convalescent rooster learning to crow again after a long illness.

He was laughing.

It stopped after a while. His face came all smooth again and his eyes, opened, black and sharp and shrewd.

'Eight hundred dollars,' he said. 'Eight hundred dollars for an uncirculated specimen of the Brasher Doubloon.' He chortled.

'Fine. Got it with you? That leaves you two hundred. Fair enough. A quick turnover, a reasonable profit and no trouble for anybody.'

'It is not in my office,' he said. 'Do you take me for a fool?' He reached an ancient silver watch out of his vest on a black fob. He screwed up his eyes to look at it. 'Let us say eleven in the morning,' he said. 'Come back with your money. The coin may or may not be here, but if I am satisfied with your behaviour, I will arrange matters.'

'That is satisfactory,' I said, and stood up. 'I have to get the money anyhow.'

'Have it in used bills,' he said almost dreamily. 'Used twenties will do. An occasional fifty will do no harm.'

I grinned and started for the door. Half-way there I turned around and went back to lean both hands on the desk and push my face over it.

'What did she look like?'

He looked blank.

'The girl that sold you the coin.'

He looked blanker.

'Okay,' I said. 'It wasn't a girl. She had help. It was a man. What did the man look like?'

He pursed his lips and made another steeple with his fingers. 'He was a middle-aged man, heavy set, about five feet seven inches tall and weighing around one hundred and seventy pounds. He said his name was Smith. He wore a blue suit, black shoes, a green tie and shirt, no hat. There was a brown bordered handkerchief in his outer pocket. His hair was dark brown sprinkled with grey. There was a bald patch about the size of a dollar on the crown of his head and a scar about two inches long running down the side of his jaw. On the left side, I think. Yes, on the left side.'

'Not bad,' I said. 'What about the hole in his right sock?'

'I omitted to take his shoes off.'

'Darn careless of you,' I said.

He didn't say anything. We just stared at each other, half curious, half hostile, like new neighbours. Then suddenly he went into his laugh again.

The five-dollar bill I had given him was still lying on his side of the desk. I flicked a hand across and took it.

'You won't want this now,' I said. 'Since we started talking in thousands.'

He stopped laughing very suddenly. Then he shrugged.

'At eleven a.m.,' he said. 'And no tricks, Mr Marlowe. Don't think I don't know how to protect myself.'

'I hope you do,' I said, 'because what you are handling is dynamite.'

I left him and tramped across the empty outer office and opened the door and let it shut, staying inside. There ought to be footsteps outside in the corridor, but his transom was closed and I hadn't made much noise coming on crepe rubber soles. I hoped he would remember that. I sneaked back across the threadbare carpet and edged in behind the door, between the door and the little closed typewriter desk. A kid trick, but once in a while it will work, especially after a lot of smart conversation, full of worldliness and sly wit. Like a sucker play in football. And if it didn't work this time, we would just be there sneering at each other again.

It worked. Nothing happened for a while except that a nose was blown. Then all by himself in there he went into his sick rooster laugh again. Then a throat was cleared. Then a swivel chair squeaked, and feet walked.

A dingy white head poked into the room, about two inches past the end of the door. It hung there suspended and I went into a state of suspended animation. Then the head was drawn back and four unclean fingernails came around the edge of the door and pulled. The door closed, clicked, was shut. I started breathing again and put my ear to the wooden panel.

The swivel chair squeaked once more. The threshing sound of a telephone being dialled. I lunged across to the instrument on the little typewriter desk and lifted it. At the other end of the line the bell had started to ring. It rang six times. Then a man's voice said: 'Yeah?'

'The Florence Apartments?'

'Yeah.'

'I'd like to speak to Mr Anson in Apartment two-o-four.'

'Hold the wire. I'll see if he's in.'

Mr Morningstar and I held the wire. Noise came over it, the blaring sound of a loud radio broadcasting a baseball game. It was not close to the telephone, but it was noisy enough.

Then I could hear the hollow sound of steps coming nearer and the harsh rattle of the telephone receiver being picked up and the voice said:

'Not in. Any message?'

'I'll call later,' Mr Morningstar said.

I hung up fast and did a rapid glide across the floor to the entrance door and opened it very silently, like snow falling, and let it close the same way, taking its weight at the last moment, so that the click of the catch would not have been heard three feet away.

I breathed hard and tight going down the hall, listening to myself. I pushed the elevator button. Then I got out the card which Mr George Anson Phillips had given me in the lobby of the Hotel Metropole. I didn't look at it in any real sense. I didn't have to look at it to recall that it referred to Apartment 204, Florence Apartments, 128 Court Street. I just stood there flicking it with a fingernail while the old elevator came heaving up in the shaft, straining like a gravel truck on a hairpin turn.

The time was three-fifty.

8

Bunker Hill is old town, lost town, shabby town, crook town. Once, very long ago, it was the choice residential district of the city, and there are still standing a few of the jigsaw Gothic mansions with wide porches and walls covered with round-end shingles and full corner bay windows with spindle turrets. They are all rooming houses now, their parquetry floors are scratched and worn through the once glossy finish and the wide sweeping staircases are dark with time and with cheap varnish laid on over generations of dirt. In the tall rooms hagged landladies bicker with shifty tenants. On the wide cool front porches, reaching their cracked shoes into the sun and staring at nothing, sit the old men with faces like lost battles.

In and around the old houses there are flyblown restaurants and Italian fruit-stands and cheap apartment houses and little candy stores where you can buy even nastier things than their candy. And there are ratty hotels where nobody except people named Smith and Jones sign the register and where the night clerk is half watchdog and half pander.

Out of the apartment houses come women who should be young but have faces like stale beer; men with pulled-down hats and quick eyes that look the street over behind the cupped hand that shields the match flame; worn intellectuals with cigarette coughs and no money in the bank; fly cops with granite faces and unwavering eyes; cokies and coke peddlers; people who look like nothing in particular and know it, and once in a while even men that actually go to work. But they come out early, when the wide cracked sidewalks are empty and still have dew on them.

I was earlier than four-thirty getting over there, but not much. I parked at the end of the street, where the funicular railway comes struggling up the yellow clay bank from Hill Street, and walked along Court Street to the Florence Apartments. It was dark brick in front, three stories, the lower windows at sidewalk level and masked by rusted screens and dingy net curtains. The entrance door had a glass panel and enough of the name left to be read. I opened it and went down three brass-bound steps into a hallway you could touch on both sides without stretching. Dim doors painted with numbers in dim paint. An alcove at the foot of the stairs with a pay telephone. A sign: *Manager Apt.* 106. At the back of the hallway a screen-door and in the alley beyond it four tall battered garbage pails in a line, with a dance of flies in the sunlit air above them.

I went up the stairs. The radio I had heard over the telephone was still blatting the baseball game. I read numbers and went up front. Apartment 204 was on the right side and the baseball game was right across the hall from it. I knocked, got no answer and knocked louder. Behind my back three Dodgers struck out against a welter of synthetic crowd noise. I knocked a third time and looked out of the front hall window while I felt in my pocket for the key George Anson Phillips had given me.

Across the street was an Italian funeral home, neat and quiet and reticent, white painted brick, flush with the sidewalk. Pietro Palermo Funeral Parlours. The thin green script of a neon sign lay across its façade, with a chaste air. A tall man in dark clothes came out of the front door and leaned against the white wall. He looked very handsome. He had dark skin and a handsome head of iron-grey hair brushed back from his forehead. He got out what looked at that distance to be a silver or platinum and black enamel cigarette case, opened it languidly with two long brown fingers and selected a gold-tipped cigarette. He put the case away and lit the cigarette with a pocket lighter that seemed to match the case. He put that away and folded his arms and stared at nothing with half-closed eyes. From the tip of his motionless cigarette a thin wisp of smoke rose straight up past his face, as thin and straight as the smoke of a dying campfire at dawn.

Another batter struck out or flew out behind my back in the recreated ball game. I turned from watching the tall Italian, put the key into the door of Apartment 204 and went in.

A square room with a brown carpet, very little furniture and that not inviting. The wall bed with the usual distorting mirror faced me as I opened the door and made me look like a two-time loser sneaking home from a reefer party. There was a birchwood easy-chair with some hard-looking upholstery beside it in the form of a davenport. A table before the window held a lamp with a shirred paper shade. There was a door on either side of the bed.

The door to the left led into a small kitchenette with a brown woodstone sink and a three-burner stove and an old electric icebox that clicked and began to throb in torment just as I pushed the door open. On the woodstone drainboard stood the remains of somebody's breakfast, mud at the bottom of a cup, a burnt crust of bread, crumbs on a board, a yellow slime of melted butter down the slope of a saucer, a smeared knife and a granite coffee-pot that smelled like sacks in a hot barn.

I went back around the wall bed and through the other door. It gave on a short hallway with an open space for clothes and a built-in dresser. On the dresser was a comb and a black brush with a few blond hairs in its black bristles. Also a can of talcum, a small flashlight with a cracked lens, a pad of writing-paper, a bank pen, a bottle of ink on a blotter, cigarettes and matches in a glass ashtray that contained half a dozen stubs.

In the drawers of the dresser were about what one suitcase would hold in the way of socks and underclothes and handkerchiefs. There was a dark grey suit on a hanger, not new but still good, and a pair of rather dusty black brogues on the floor under it.

I pushed the bathroom door. It opened about a foot and then stuck. My nose twitched and I could feel my lips stiffen and I smelled the harsh, sharp bitter smell from beyond the door. I leaned against it. It gave a little but came back, as though somebody was holding it against me. I poked my head through the opening.

The floor of the bathroom was too short for him, so his knees were poked up and hung outwards slackly and his head was pressed against the woodstone baseboard at the other end, not tilted up, but jammed tight. His brown suit was rumpled a little and his dark glasses stuck out of his breast-pocket at an unsafe angle. As if that mattered. His right hand was thrown across his stomach, his left hand lay on the floor, palm up, the fingers curled a little. There was a blood-caked bruise on the right side of his head, in the blond hair. His open mouth was full of shiny crimson blood.

The door was stopped by his leg. I pushed hard and edged around it and got in. I bent down to push two fingers into the side of his neck against the big artery. No artery throbbed there, or even whispered. Nothing at all. The skin was icy. It wouldn't have been icy. I just thought it was. I straightened up and leaned my back against the door and made hard fists in my pockets and smelled the cordite fumes. The baseball game was still going on, but through two closed doors it sounded remote.

I stood and looked down at him. Nothing in that, Marlowe, nothing at all. Nothing for you here, nothing. You didn't even know him. Get out, get out fast.

I pulled away from the door and pulled it open and went back through the hall into the living-room. A face in the mirror looked at me. A strained, leering face. I turned away from it quickly and took out the flat key George Anson Phillips had given me and rubbed it between my moist palms and laid it down beside the lamp.

I smeared the doorknob opening the door and the outside knob closing the door. The Dodgers were ahead seven to three, the first half of the eighth. A lady who sounded well on with her drinking was singing Frankie and Johnny, the roundhouse version, in a voice that even whisky had failed to improve. A deep man's voice growled to her to shut up and she kept on singing and there was a hard quick movement across the floor and a smack and a yelp and she stopped singing and the baseball game went right on.

I put the cigarette in my mouth and lit it and went back down the stairs and stood in the half dark of the hall angle looking at the little sign that read: *Manager, Apt.* 106.

I was a fool even to look at it. I looked at it for a long minute, biting the cigarette hard between my teeth.

I turned and walked down the hallway towards the back. A small enamelled plate on a door said: *Manager.* I knocked on the door.

9

A chair was pushed back, feet shuffled, the door opened.

'You the manager?'

'Yeah.' It was the same voice I had heard over the telephone. Talking to Elisha Morningstar.

He held an empty, smeared glass in his hand. It looked as if somebody had been keeping goldfish in it. He was a lanky man with carroty short hair growing down to a point on his forehead. He had a long narrow head packed with shabby cunning. Greenish eyes stared under orange eyebrows. His ears were large and might have flapped in a high wind. He had a long nose that would be into things. The whole face was a trained face, a face that would know how to keep a secret, a face that held the effortless composure of a corpse in the morgue.

He wore his vest open, no coat, a woven hair watchguard, and round blue sleeve garters with metal clasps.

I said: 'Mr Anson?'

'Two-o-four.'

'He's not in.'

'What should I do – lay an egg?'

'Neat,' I said. 'You have them all the time, or is this your birthday?'

'Beat it,' he said. 'Drift.' He started to close the door. He opened it again to say: 'Take the air. Scram. Push off.' Having made his meaning clear he started to close the door again.

I leaned against the door. He leaned against it on his side. That brought our faces close together. 'Five bucks,' I said.

It rocked him. He opened the door very suddenly and I had to take a quick step forward in order not to butt his chin with my head.

'Come in,' he said.

A living-room with a wall-bed, everything strictly to specifications, even to the shirred paper lampshade and the glass ashtray. This room was painted egg-yolk yellow. All it needed was a few fat black spiders painted on the yellow to be anybody's bilious attack.

'Sit down,' he said, shutting the door.

I sat down. We looked at each other with the clear innocent eyes of a couple of used-car salesmen.

'Beer?' he said.

'Thanks.'

He opened two cans, filled the smeared glass he had been holding, and reached for another like it. I said I would drink out of the can. He handed me the can.

'A dime,' he said.

I gave him a dime.

He dropped it into his vest and went on looking at me. He pulled a chair over and sat in it and spread his bony upjutting knees and let his empty hand droop between them.

'I ain't interested in your five bucks,' he said.

'That's fine,' I said. 'I wasn't really thinking of giving it to you.'

'A wisey,' he said. 'What gives? We run a nice respectable place here. No funny stuff gets pulled.'

'Quiet, too,' I said. 'Upstairs you could almost hear an eagle scream.'

His smile was wide, about three-quarters of an inch. 'I don't amuse easy,' he said.

'Just like Queen Victoria,' I said.

'I don't get it.'

'I don't expect miracles,' I said. The meaningless talk had a sort of cold bracing effect on me, making a mood with a hard, gritty edge.

I got my wallet out and selected a card from it. It wasn't my card. It read: *James B. Pollock, Reliance Indemnity Company, Field Agent.* I tried to remember what James B. Pollock looked like and where I had met him. I couldn't. I handed the carroty man the card.

He read it and scratched the end of his nose with one of the corners. 'Wrong john?' he asked, keeping his green eyes plastered to my face.

'Jewellery,' I said, and waved a hand.

He thought this over. While he thought it over I tried to make up my mind whether it worried him at all. It didn't seem to.

'We get one once in a while,' he conceded. 'You can't help it. He didn't look like it to me, though. Soft looking.'

'Maybe I got a bum steer,' I said. I described George Anson Phillips to him, George Anson Phillips alive, in his brown suit and his dark glasses and his cocoa straw hat with the brown and yellow print band. I wondered what had happened to the hat. It hadn't been up there. He must have got rid of it, thinking it was too conspicuous. His blond head was almost, but not quite, as bad.

'That sound like him?'

The carroty man took his time making up his mind. Finally he nodded yes, green eyes, watching me carefully, lean hard hand holding the card up to his mouth and running the card along his teeth like a stick along the palings of a picket fence.

'I didn't figure him for no crook,' he said. 'But, hell, they come all sizes and shapes. Only been here a month. If he looked like a wrong gee, wouldn't have been here at all.'

I did a good job of not laughing in his face. 'What say we frisk the apartment while he's out?'

He shook his head. 'Mr Palermo wouldn't like it.'

'Mr Palermo?'

'He's the owner. Across the street. Owns the funeral parlours. Owns this building and a lot of other buildings. Practically owns the district, if you know what I mean.' He gave me a twitch of the lip and a flutter of the right eyelid. 'Gets the vote out. Not a guy to crowd.'

'Well, while he's getting the vote out or playing with a stiff or whatever he's doing at the moment, let's go up and frisk the apartment.'

'Don't get me sore at you,' the carroty man said briefly.

'That would bother me like two per cent of nothing at all,' I said. 'Let's go up and frisk the apartment.' I threw my empty beer can at the waste basket and watched it bounce back and roll half-way across the room.

The carroty man stood up suddenly and spread his feet apart and dusted his hands together and took hold of his lower lip with his teeth.

'You said something about five,' he shrugged.

'That was hours ago,' I said. 'I thought better of it. Let's go up and frisk the apartment.'

'Say that just once more –' his right hand slid towards his hip.

'If you're thinking of pulling a gun, Mr Palermo wouldn't like it,' I said.

'To hell with Mr Palermo,' he snarled, in a voice suddenly furious, out of a face suddenly charged with dark blood.

'Mr Palermo will be glad to know that's how you feel about him,' I said.

'Look,' the carroty man said very slowly, dropping his hand to his side and leaning forward from the hips and pushing his face at me as hard as he could. 'Look. I was sitting here having myself a beer or two. Maybe three. Maybe nine. What the hell? I wasn't bothering anybody. It was a nice day. It looked like it might be a nice evening – then you come in.' He waved a hand violently.

'Let's go up and frisk the apartment,' I said.

He threw both fists forward in tight lumps. At the end of the motion he threw his hands wide open, straining the fingers as far as they would go. His nose twitched sharply.

'If it wasn't for the job,' he said.

I opened my mouth. 'Don't say it!' he yelled.

He put a hat on, but no coat, opened a drawer and took out a bunch of keys, walked past me to open the door and stood in it, jerking his chin at me. His face still looked a little wild.

We went out into the hall and along it and up the stairs. The ball game was over and dance music had taken its place. Very loud dance music. The carroty man selected one of his keys and put it in the lock of Apartment 204. Against the booming of the dance band behind us in the apartment across the way a woman's voice suddenly screamed hysterically.

The carroty man withdrew the key and bared his teeth at me. He walked across the narrow hallway and banged on the opposite door. He had to knock hard and long before any attention was paid. Then the door was jerked open and a sharp-faced blonde in scarlet slacks and a green pullover stared out with sultry eyes, one of which was puffed and the other had been socked several days ago. She also had a bruise on her throat and her hand held a tall cool glass of amber fluid.

'Pipe down, but soon,' the carroty man said. 'Too much racket. I don't aim to ask you again. Next time I call some law.'

The girl looked back over her shoulder and screamed against the noise of the radio: 'Hey, Del! The guy says to pipe down! You wanna sock him?'

A chair squeaked, the radio noise died abruptly and a thick, bitter-eyed dark man appeared behind the blonde, yanked her out of the way with one hand and pushed his face at us. He needed a shave. He was wearing trousers, street shoes and an undershirt.

He settled his feet in the doorway, whistled a little breath in through his nose and said:

'Buzz off. I just come in from lunch. I had a lousy lunch. I wouldn't want nobody to push muscle at me.' He was very drunk, but in a hard practised sort of way.

The carroty man said: 'You heard me, Mr Hench. Dim that radio and stop the rough-house in here. And make it sudden.'

The man addressed as Hench said: 'Listen, pickle-puss –' and heaved forward with his right foot in a hard stamp.

The carroty man's left foot didn't wait to be stamped on. The lean body moved back quickly and the thrown bunch of keys hit the floor behind, and clanked against the door of Apartment 204. The carroty man's right hand made a sweeping movement and came up with a woven leather blackjack.

Hench said: 'Yah!' and took two big handfuls of air in his two hairy hands, closed the hands into fists and swung hard at nothing.

The carroty man hit him on the top of his head and the girl screamed again and threw a glass of liquor in her boy friend's face. Whether because it was safe to do it now or because she made an honest mistake, I couldn't tell.

Hench turned blindly with his face dripping, stumbled and ran across the floor in a lurch that threatened to land him on his nose at every step. The bed was down and tumbled. Hench made the bed on one knee and plunged a hand under the pillow.

I said: 'Look out – gun.'

'I can fade that, too,' the carroty man said between his teeth and slid his right hand, empty now, under his open vest.

Hench was down on both knees. He came up on one and turned and there was a short black gun in his right hand and he was staring down at it, not holding it by the grip at all, holding it flat on his palm.

'Drop it!' the carroty man's voice said tightly and he went on into the room.

The blonde promptly jumped on his back and wound her long green arms around his neck, yelling lustily. The carroty man staggered and swore and waved his gun around.

'Get him, Del!' the blonde screamed. 'Get him good!'

Hench, one hand on the bed and one foot on the floor, both knees doubled, right hand holding the black gun flat on his palm, eyes staring down at it, pushed himself slowly to his feet and growled deep in his throat:

'This ain't my gun.'

I relieved the carroty man of the gun that was not doing him any good and stepped around him, leaving him to shake the blonde off his back as best he could. A door banged down the hallway and steps came along towards us.

I said: 'Drop it, Hench.'

He looked up at me, puzzled dark eyes suddenly sober.

'It ain't my gun,' he said and held it out flat. 'Mine's a Colt .32 – belly gun.'

I took the gun off his hand. He made no effort to stop me. He sat down on the bed, rubbed the top of his head slowly, and screwed his face up in difficult thought. 'Where the hell –' his voice trailed off and he shook his head and winced.

I sniffed the gun. It had been fired. I sprang the magazine out and counted the bullets through the small holes in the side. There were six. With one in the magazine, that made seven. The gun was a Colt .32, automatic, eight shot. It had been fired. If it had not been reloaded, one shot had been fired from it.

The carroty man had the blonde off his back now. He had thrown her into a chair and was wiping a scratch on his cheek. His green eyes were baleful.

'Better get some law,' I said. 'A shot has been fired from this gun and it's about time you found out there's a dead man in the apartment across the hall.'

Hench looked up at me stupidly and said in a quiet, reasonable voice: 'Brother, that simply ain't my gun.'

The blonde sobbed in a rather theatrical manner and showed me an open mouth twisted with misery and ham-acting. The carroty man went softly out of the door.

10

'Shot in the throat with a medium-calibre gun and a soft-nosed bullet,' Detective-Lieutenant Jesse Breeze said. 'A gun like this and bullets like is in here.' He danced the gun on his hand, the gun Hench had said was not his gun. 'Bullet ranged upwards and probably hit the back of the skull. Still inside his head. The man's dead about two hours. Hands and face cold, but body still warm. No rigor. Was sapped with something hard before being shot. Likely with a gun butt. All that mean anything to you boys and girls?'

The newspaper he was sitting on rustled. He took his hat off and mopped his face and the top of his almost bald head. A fringe of light-coloured hair around the crown was damp and dark with sweat. He put his hat back on, a flat-crowned panama, burned dark by the sun. Not this year's hat, and probably not last year's.

He was a big man, rather paunchy, wearing brown and white shoes and sloppy socks and white trousers with thin black stripes, an open-neck shirt showing some ginger-coloured hair at the top of his chest, and a rough sky-blue sports-coat not wider at the shoulders than a two-car garage. He would be about fifty years old and the only thing about him that very much suggested cop was the calm unwinking, unwavering stare of his prominent pale-blue eyes, a stare that had no thought of being rude, but that anybody but a cop would feel to be rude. Below his eyes across the top of his cheeks and the bridge of his nose there was a wide path of freckles, like a mine-field on a war map.

We were sitting in Hench's apartment and the door was shut. Hench had his shirt on and he was absently tying a tie with thick blunt fingers that trembled. The girl was lying on the bed. She had a green wrap-around thing twisted about her head, a purse by her side and a short squirrel coat across her feet. Her mouth was a little open and her face was drained and shocked.

Hench said thickly: 'If the idea is the guy was shot with the gun under the pillow, okay. Seems like he might have been. It ain't my gun and nothing you boys can think up is going to make me say it's my gun.'

'Assuming that to be so,' Breeze said, 'how come? Somebody swiped your gun and left this one. When, how, what kind of gun was yours?'

'We went out about three-thirty or so to get something to eat at the hashhouse around the corner,' Hench said. 'You can check that. We must have left the door unlocked. We were kind of hitting the bottle a little. I guess we were pretty noisy. We had the ball game going on the radio. I guess we shut it off when we went out. I'm not sure. You remember?' He looked at the girl lying white-faced and silent on the bed. 'You remember, sweet?'

The girl didn't look at him or answer him.

'She's pooped,' Hench said. 'I had a gun, a Colt .32, same calibre as that, but a belly gun. A revolver, not an automatic. There's a piece broken off the rubber grip. A Jew named Morris gave it to me three, four years

61

ago. We worked together in a bar. I don't have no permit, but I don't carry the gun neither.'

Breeze said: 'Hitting the hooch like you birds been and having a gun under the pillow sooner or later somebody was going to get shot. You ought to know that.'

'Hell, we didn't even know the guy,' Hench said. His tie was tied now, very badly. He was cold sober and very shaky. He stood up and picked a coat off the end of the bed and put it on and sat down again. I watched his fingers tremble lighting a cigarette. 'We don't know his name. We don't know anything about him. I see him maybe two, three times in the hall, but he don't even speak to me. It's the same guy, I guess. I ain't even sure of that.'

'It's the fellow that lived there,' Breeze said. 'Let me see now, this ball game is a studio re-broadcast, huh?'

'Goes on at three.' Hench said. 'Three to say four-thirty, or sometimes later. We went out about the last half the third. We was gone about an innings and a half, maybe two. Twenty minutes to half an hour. Not more.'

'I guess he was shot just before you went out,' Breeze said. 'The radio would kill the noise of the gun near enough. You must of left your door unlocked. Or even open.'

'Could be,' Hench said wearily. 'You remember, honey?'

Again the girl on the bed refused to answer him or even look at him.

Breeze said: 'You left your door open or unlocked. The killer heard you go out. He got into your apartment, wanting to ditch his gun, saw the bed down, walked across and slipped his gun under the pillow, and then imagine his surprise. He found another gun there waiting for him. So he took it along. Now if he meant to ditch his gun, why not do it where he did his killing? Why take the risk of going into another apartment to do it? Why the fancy pants?'

I was sitting in the corner of the davenport by the window. I put in my nickel's worth, saying: 'Suppose he had locked himself out of Phillips's apartment before he thought of ditching the gun? Suppose, coming out of the shock of his murder, he found himself in the hall still holding the murder gun. He would want to ditch it fast. Then if Hench's door was open and he had heard them go out along the hall –'

Breeze looked at me briefly and grunted: 'I'm not saying it isn't so. I'm just considering.' He turned his attention back to Hench. 'So now, if this turns out to be the gun that killed Anson, we got to try and trace *your* gun. While we do that we got to have you and the young lady handy. You understand that, of course?'

Hench said: 'You don't have any boys that can bounce me hard enough to make me tell it different.'

'We can always try,' Breeze said mildly. 'And we might just as well get started.'

He stood up, turned and swept the crumpled newspapers off the chair on to the floor. He went over to the door, then turned and stood looking at the girl on the bed. 'You all right, sister, or should I call for a matron?'

The girl on the bed didn't answer him.

Hench said: 'I need a drink. I need a drink bad.'

'Not while I'm watching you,' Breeze said, and went out of the door.

Hench moved across the room and put the neck of a bottle into his mouth and gurgled liquor. He lowered the bottle, looked at what was left in it and went over to the girl. He pushed her shoulder.

'Wake up and have a drink,' he growled at her.

The girl stared at the ceiling. She didn't answer him or show that she had heard him.

'Let her alone,' I said. 'Shock.'

Hench finished what was in the bottle, put the empty bottle down carefully and looked at the girl again, then turned his back on her and stood frowning at the floor. 'Jeeze, I wish I could remember better,' he said under his breath.

Breeze came back into the room with a young fresh-faced plain-clothes detective. 'This is Lieutenant Spangler,' he said. 'He'll take you down. Get going, huh?'

Hench went back to the bed and shook the girl's shoulder. 'Get on up, babe. We gotta take a ride.'

The girl turned her eyes without turning her head, and looked at him slowly. She lifted her shoulders off the bed and put a hand under her and swung her legs over the side and stood up, stamping her right foot, as if it was numb.

'Tough, kid – but you know how it is,' Hench said.

The girl put a hand to her mouth and bit the knuckle of her little finger, looking at him blankly. Then she swung the hand suddenly and hit him in the face as hard as she could. Then she half ran out of the door.

Hench didn't move a muscle for a long moment. There was a confused noise of men talking outside, a confused noise of cars down below in the street. Hench shrugged and cocked his heavy shoulders back and swept a slow look around the room, as if he didn't expect to see it again very soon, or at all. Then he went out past the young, fresh-faced detective.

The detective went out. The door closed. The confused noise outside was dimmed a little and Breeze and I sat looking at each other heavily.

11

After a while Breeze got tired of looking at me and dug a cigar out of his pocket. He slit the cellophane band with a knife and trimmed the end of the cigar and lit it carefully, turning it around in the flame, and holding the burning match away from it while he stared thoughtfully at nothing and drew on the cigar and made sure it was burning the way he wanted it to burn.

Then he shook the match out very slowly and reached over to lay it on the sill of the open window. Then he looked at me some more.

'You and me,' he said, 'are going to get along.'

'That's fine,' I said.

'You don't think so,' he said. 'But we are. But not because I took any sudden fancy to you. It's the way I work. Everything in the clear. Everything sensible. Everything quiet. Not like that dame. That's the kind of dame that spends her life looking for trouble and when she finds it, it's the fault of the first guy she can get her fingernails into.'

'He gave her a couple of shiners,' I said. 'That wouldn't make her love him too much.'

'I can see,' Breeze said, 'that you know a lot about dames.'

'Not knowing a lot about them has helped me in my business,' I said. 'I'm open-minded.'

He nodded and examined the end of his cigar. He took a piece of paper out of his pocket and read from it. 'Delmar B. Hench, 45, bartender, unemployed. Maybell Masters, 26, dancer. That's all I know about them. I've got a hunch there ain't a lot more to know.'

'You don't think he shot Anson?' I asked.

Breeze looked at me without pleasure. 'Brother, I just got here.' He took a card out of his pocket and read from that. 'James B. Pollock, Reliance Indemnity Company, Field Agent. What's the idea?'

'In a neighbourhood like this it's bad form to use your own name,' I said. 'Anson didn't either.'

'What's the matter with the neighbourhood?'

'Practically everything,' I said.

'What I would like to know,' Breeze said, 'is what you know about the dead guy?'

'I told you already.'

'Tell me again. People tell me so much stuff I get it all mixed up.'

'I know what it says on his card, that his name is George Anson Phillips, that he claimed to be a private detective. He was outside my office when I went to lunch. He followed me downtown, into the lobby of the Hotel Metropole. I led him there. I spoke to him and he admitted he had been following me and said it was because he wanted to find out if I was smart enough to do business with. That's a lot of baloney, of course. He probably hadn't quite made up his mind what to do and was waiting for something to decide him. He was on a job – he said – he had got leery of and he wanted to join up with somebody, perhaps somebody with a little more experience than he had, if he had any at all. He didn't act as if he had.'

Breeze said: 'And the only reason he picked on you is that six years ago you worked on a case in Ventura while he was a deputy up there.'

I said, 'That's my story.'

'But you don't have to get stuck with it,' Breeze said calmly. 'You can always give us a better one.'

'It's good enough,' I said. 'I mean it's good enough in the sense that it's bad enough to be true.'

He nodded his big slow head.

'What's your idea of all this?' he asked.

'Have you investigated Phillips's office address?'

He shook his head, no.

'My idea is you will find out he was hired because he was simple. He was hired to take this apartment here under a wrong name, and to do something that turned out to be not what he liked. He was scared. He wanted a friend, he wanted help. The fact that he picked me after so long a time and such little knowledge of me showed he didn't know many people in the detective business.'

Breeze got his handkerchief out and mopped his head and face again. 'But it don't begin to show why he had to follow you around like a lost pup instead of walking right up to your office door and in.'

'No,' I said, 'it doesn't.'

'Can you explain that?'

'No. Not really.'

'Well, how would you try to explain it?'

'I've already explained it in the only way I know how. He was undecided whether to speak to me or not. He was waiting for something to decide him. I decided by speaking to him.'

Breeze said: 'That is a very simple explanation. It is so simple it stinks.'

'You may be right,' I said.

'And as the result of this little hotel lobby conversation this guy, a total stranger to you, asks you to his apartment and hands you his key. Because he wants to talk to you.'

I said, 'Yes.'

'Why couldn't he talk to you then?'

'I had an appointment,' I said.

'Business?'

I nodded.

'I see. What you working on?'

I shook my head and didn't answer.

'This is murder,' Breeze said. 'You're going to have to tell me.'

I shook my head again. He flushed a little.

'Look,' he said tightly, 'you got to.'

'I'm sorry, Breeze,' I said. 'But so far as things have gone, I'm not convinced of that.'

'Of course you know I can throw you in the can as a material witness,' he said casually.

'On what grounds?'

'On the grounds that you are the one who found the body, that you gave a false name to the manager here, and that you don't give a satisfactory account of your relations with the dead guy.'

I said: 'Are you going to do it?'

He smiled bleakly. 'You got a lawyer?'

'I know several lawyers. I don't have a lawyer on a retainer basis.'

'How many of the commissioners do you know personally?'

'None. That is, I've spoken to three of them, but they might not remember me.'

'But you have good contacts in the mayor's office and so on?'

'Tell me about them,' I said. 'I'd like to know.'

'Look, buddy,' he said earnestly, 'you must got some friends somewhere. Surely.'

'I've got a good friend in the Sheriff's office, but I'd rather leave him out of it.'

He lifted his eyebrows. 'Why? Maybe you're going to need friends. A good word from a cop we know to be right might go a long way.'

'He's just a personal friend,' I said. 'I don't ride around on his back. If I get in trouble, it won't do him any good.'

'How about the homicide bureau?'

'There's Randall,' I said. 'If he's still working out of Central Homicide. I had a little time with him on a case once. But he doesn't like me too well.'

Breeze sighed and moved his feet on the floor, rustling the newspapers he had pushed down out of the chair.

'Is all this on the level – or are you just being smart? I mean about all the important guys you don't know?'

'It's on the level,' I said. 'But the way I am using it is smart.'

'It ain't smart to say so right out.'

'I think it is.'

He put a big freckled hand over the whole lower part of his face and squeezed. When he took the hand away there were round red marks on his cheeks from the pressure of thumb and fingers. I watched the marks fade.

'Why don't you go on home and let a man work?' he asked crossly.

I got up and nodded and went towards the door. Breeze said to my back: 'Gimme your home address.'

I gave it to him. He wrote it down. 'So long,' he said drearily; 'don't leave town. We'll want a statement – maybe tonight.'

I went out. There were two uniformed cops outside on the landing. The door across the way was open and a fingerprint man was still working inside. Downstairs I met two more cops in the hallway, one at each end of it. I didn't see the carroty manager. I went out the front door. There was an ambulance pulling away from the kerb. A knot of people hung around on both sides of the street, not as many as would accumulate in some neighbourhoods.

I pushed along the sidewalk. A man grabbed me by the arm and said: 'What's the damage, Jack?'

I shook his arm off without speaking or looking at his face and went on down the street to where my car was.

12

It was a quarter to seven when I let myself into the office and clicked the light on and picked a piece of paper off the floor. It was a notice from the Green Feather Messenger Service saying that a package was held awaiting my call and would be delivered upon request at any hour of the day or night. I put it on the desk, peeled my coat off, and opened the windows. I got a half-bottle of Old Taylor out of the deep drawer of the desk and drank a short drink, rolling it around on my tongue. Then I sat there holding the neck of the cool bottle and wondering how it would feel to be a homicide dick and find bodies lying around and not mind at all, not have to sneak out wiping doorknobs, not have to ponder how much I could tell without hurting a client and how little I could tell without too badly hurting myself. I decided I wouldn't like it.

I pulled the phone over and looked at the number on the slip and called it. They said my package could be sent right over. I said I would wait for it.

It was getting dark outside now. The rushing sound of the traffic had died a little and the air from the open window, not yet cool from the night, had that tired end-of-the-day smell of dust, automobile exhaust, sunlight rising from hot walls and sidewalks, the remote smell of food in a thousand restaurants, and perhaps, drifting down from the residential hills above Hollywood – if you had a nose like a hunting dog – a touch of that peculiar tomcat smell that eucalyptus trees give off in warm weather.

I sat there smoking. Ten minutes later the door was knocked on and I opened it to a boy in a uniform cap who took my signature and gave me a small square package, not more than two and a half inches wide, if that. I gave the boy a dime and listened to him whistling his way back to the elevators.

The label had my name and address printed on it in ink, in a quite fair imitation of typed letters, larger and thinner than pica. I cut the string that tied the label to the box and unwound the thin brown paper. Inside was a thin cheap cardboard box pasted over with brown paper and stamped *Made in Japan* with a rubber stamp. It would be the kind of box you would get in a Jap store to hold some small carved animal or a small piece of jade. The lid fitted down all the way and tightly. I pulled it off and saw tissue paper and cotton-wool.

Separating these I was looking at a gold coin about the size of a half-dollar, bright and shining as if it had just come from the mint.

The side facing me showed a spread eagle with a shield for a breast and the initials E. B. punched into the left wing. Around these was a circle of beading, between the beading and the smooth unmilled edge of the coin, the legend E PLURIBUS UNUM. At the bottom was the date 1787.

I turned the coin over on my palm. It was heavy and cold and my palm felt moist under it. The outer side showed a sun rising or setting behind a sharp peak of mountain, then a double circle of what looked like oak leaves, then more Latin, NOVA EBORACA COLUMBIA EXCELSIOR. At the bottom of this side, in smaller capitals, the name BRASHER.

I was looking at the Brasher Doubloon.

There was nothing else in the box or in the paper, nothing on the paper. The hand-written printing meant nothing to me. I didn't know anybody who used it.

I filled an empty tobacco-pouch half full, wrapped the coin up in tissue-paper, snapped a rubber band around it and tucked it into the tobacco in the pouch and put more in on top. I closed the zipper and put the pouch in my pocket. I locked the paper and string and box and label up in a filing cabinet, sat down again and dialled Elisha Morningstar's number on the phone. The bell rang eight times at the other end of the line. It was not answered. I hardly expected that. I hung up again, looked Elisha Morningstar up in the book and saw that he had no listing for a residence phone in Los Angeles or the outlying towns that were in the phone book.

I got a shoulder holster out of the desk and strapped it on and slipped a Colt .38 automatic into it, put on hat and coat, shut the windows again, put the whisky away, clicked the lights off and had the office door unlatched when the phone rang.

The ringing bell had a sinister sound, for no reason of itself, but because of the ears to which it rang. I stood there braced and tense, lips tightly drawn back in a half grin. Beyond the closed window the neon lights glowed. The dead air didn't move. Outside the corridor was still. The bell rang in darkness, steady and strong.

I went back and leaned on the desk and answered. There was a click and a droning on the wire and beyond that nothing. I depressed the connexion and stood there in the dark, leaning over, holding the phone with one hand and holding the flat riser on the pedestal down with the other. I didn't know what I was waiting for.

The phone rang again. I made a sound in my throat and put it to my ear again, not saying anything at all.

So we were there silent, both of us, miles apart maybe, each one holding a telephone and breathing and listening and hearing nothing, not even the breathing.

Then after what seemed a very long time there was the quiet remote whisper of a voice saying dimly, without any tone:

'Too bad for you, Marlowe.'

Then the click again and the droning on the wire and I hung up and went across the office and out.

13

I drove west on Sunset, fiddled around a few blocks without making up my mind whether anyone was trying to follow me, then parked near a drug-store and went into its phone booth. I dropped my nickel and asked the O-operator for a Pasadena number. She told me how much money to put in.

The voice which answered the phone was angular and cold. 'Mrs Murdock's residence.'

'Philip Marlowe here. Mrs Murdock, please.'

I was told to wait. A soft but very clear voice said: 'Mr Marlowe? Mrs Murdock is resting now. Can you tell me what it is?'

'You oughtn't to have told him.'

'That loopy guy whose handkerchief you cry into.'

'How dare you?'

'That's fine,' I said. 'Now let me talk to Mrs Murdock. I have to.'

'Very well. I'll try.' The soft clear voice went away and I waited a long wait. They would have to lift her up on the pillows and drag the port bottle out of her hard grey paw and feed her the telephone. A throat was cleared suddenly over the wire. It sounded like a freight train going through a tunnel.

'This is Mrs Murdock.'

'Could you identify the property we were talking about this morning, Mrs Murdock? I mean, could you pick it out from others just like it?'

'Well – are there others just like it?'

'There must be. Dozens, hundreds for all I know. Anyhow, dozens. Of course, I don't know where they are.'

She coughed. 'I don't really know much about it. I suppose I couldn't identify it then. But in the circumstances –'

'That's what I'm getting at, Mrs Murdock. The identification would seem to depend on tracing the history of the article back to you. At least to be convincing.'

'Yes. I suppose it would. Why? Do you know where it is?'

'Morningstar claims to have seen it. He says it was offered to him for sale – just as you suspected. He wouldn't buy. The seller was not a woman, he says. That doesn't mean a thing, because he gave me a detailed description of the party which was either made up or was a description of somebody he knew more than casually. So the seller may have been a woman.'

'I see. It's not important now.'

'Not important?'

'No. Have you anything else to report?'

'Another question to ask. Do you know a youngish blond fellow named George Anson Phillips? Rather heavy set, wearing a brown suit and a dark pork-pie hat with a gay band. Wearing that today. Claimed to be a private detective.'

'I do not. Why should I?'

'I don't know. He enters the picture somewhere. I think he was the one who tried to sell the article. Morningstar tried to call him up after I left. I snuck back into his office and overheard.'

'You what?'

'I snuck.'

'Please do not be witty, Mr Marlowe. Anything else?'

'Yes, I agreed to pay Morningstar one thousand dollars for the return of the – the article. He said he could get it for eight hundred. . . .'

'And where were you going to get the money, may I ask?'

'Well, I was just talking. This Morningstar is a downy bird. That's the kind of language he understands. And then again you might have wanted to pay it. I wouldn't want to persuade you. You could always go to the police. But if for any reason you didn't want to go to the police, it might be the only way you could get it back – buying it back.'

I would probably have gone on like that for a long time, not knowing just what I was trying to say, if she hadn't stopped me with a noise like a seal barking.

'This is all very unnecessary now, Mr Marlowe. I have decided to drop the matter. The coin has been returned to me.'

'Hold the wire a minute,' I said.

I put the phone down on the shelf and opened the booth door and stuck my head out, filling my chest with what they were using for air in the drug-store. Nobody was paying any attention to me. Up front the druggist, in a pale-blue smock, was chatting across the cigar counter. The counter boy was polishing glasses at the fountain. Two girls in slacks were playing the pinball machine. A tall, narrow party in a black shirt and a pale yellow scarf was fumbling magazines at the rack. He didn't look like a gunman.

I pulled the booth shut and picked up the phone and said: 'A rat was gnawing my foot. It's all right now. You got it back, you said. Just like that. How?'

'I hope you are not too disappointed,' she said in her uncompromising baritone. 'The circumstances are a little difficult. I may decide to explain and I may not. You may call at the house tomorrow morning. Since I do not wish to proceed with the investigation, you will keep the retainer as payment in full.'

'Let me get this straight,' I said. 'You actually got the coin back – not a promise of it, merely?'

'Certainly not. And I'm getting tired. So, if you –'

'One moment, Mrs Murdock. It isn't going to be as simple as all that. Things have happened.'

'In the morning you may tell me about them,' she said sharply, and hung up.

I pushed out of the booth and lit a cigarette with thick awkward fingers. I went back along the store. The druggist was alone now. He was sharpening a pencil with a small knife, very intent, frowning.

'That's a nice sharp pencil you have there,' I told him.

He looked up, surprised. The girls at the pinball machine looked at me, surprised. I went over and looked at myself in the mirror behind the counter. I looked surprised.

73

I sat down on one of the stools and said: 'A double Scotch, straight.'

The counter man looked surprised. 'Sorry, this isn't a bar, sir. You can buy a bottle at the liquor counter.'

'So it is,' I said. 'I mean, so it isn't. I've had a shock. I'm a little dazed. Give me a cup of coffee, weak, and a very thin ham sandwich on stale bread. No, I better not eat yet, either. Good-bye.'

I got down off the stool and walked to the door in a silence that was as loud as a ton of coal going down a chute. The man in the black shirt and yellow scarf was sneering at me over the *New Republic*.

'You ought to lay off the fluff and get your teeth into something solid, like a pulp magazine,' I told him, just to be friendly?

I went on out. Behind me somebody said: 'Hollywood's full of them.'

14

The wind had risen and had a dry taut feeling, tossing the tops of trees, and making the swung arc-light up the side street cast shadows like crawling lava. I turned the car and drove east again.

The hock shop was on Santa Monica, near Wilcox, a quiet old-fashioned little place, washed gently by the lapping waves of time. In the front window there was everything you could think of, from a set of trout flies in a thin wooden box to a portable organ, from a folding baby carriage to a portrait camera with a four-inch lens, from a mother-of-pearl lorgnette in a faded plush case to a single action Frontier Colt, .44 calibre, the model they still make for Western peace officers whose grandfathers taught them how to file the trigger and shoot by fanning the hammer back.

I went into the shop and a bell jangled over my head and somebody shuffled and blew his nose far at the back and steps came. An old Jew in a tall black skull-cap came along behind the counter, smiling at me over cut-out glasses.

I got my tobacco-pouch out, got the Brasher Doubloon out of that and laid it on the counter. The window in front was clear glass and I felt naked. No panelled cubicles with hand-carved spittoons and doors that locked themselves as you closed them.

The Jew took the coin and lifted it on his hand. 'Gold, is it? A gold hoarder you are, maybe,' he said, twinkling.

'Twenty-five dollars,' I said. 'The wife and the kiddies are hungry.'

'Oi, that is terrible. Gold, it feels, by the weight. Only gold and, maybe, platinum it could be.' He weighted it casually on a pair of small scales. 'Gold it is,' he said. 'So ten dollars you are wanting?'

'Twenty-five dollars.'

'For twenty-five dollars what would I do with it? Sell it, maybe? For fifteen dollars worth of gold is maybe in it. Okay. Fifteen dollars.'

'You got a good safe?'

'Mister, in this business are the best safes money can buy. Nothing to worry about here. It is fifteen dollars, is it?'

'Make out the ticket.'

He wrote it out partly with his pen and partly with his tongue. I gave my true name and address. Bristol Apartments, 1624 North Bristol Avenue, Hollywood.

'You are living in that district and you are borrowing fifteen dollars,' the Jew said sadly, and tore off my half of the ticket and counted out the money.

I walked down to the corner drug-store and bought an envelope and borrowed a pen and mailed the pawn-ticket to myself.

I was hungry and hollow inside. I went over to Vine to eat, and after that I drove downtown again. The wind was still rising and it was drier than ever. The steering-wheel had a gritty feeling under my fingers and the inside of my nostrils felt tight and drawn.

The lights were on here and there in the tall buildings. The green and chromium clothier's store on the corner of Ninth and Hill was a blaze of light. In the Belfont Building a few windows glowed here and there, but not many. The same old ploughhorse sat in the elevator on his piece of folded burlap, looking straight in front of him, blank-eyed, almost gathered to history.

I said: 'I don't suppose you know where I can get in touch with the building superintendent?'

75

He turned his head slowly and looked past my shoulder. 'I hear how in Noo York they got elevators that just whiz. Go thirty floors at a time. High speed. That's in Noo York.'

'The hell with New York,' I said. 'I like it here.'

'Must take a good man to run them fast babies.'

'Don't kid yourself, dad. All those cuties do is push buttons, say "Good morning, Mr Whoosis", and look at their beauty spots in the car mirror. Now you take a Model T job like this – it takes a man to run it. Satisfied?'

'I work twelve hours a day,' he said. 'And glad to get it.'

'Don't let the union hear you.'

'You know what the union can do?' I shook my head. He told me. Then he lowered his eyes until they almost looked at me. 'Didn't I see you before somewhere?'

'About the building super,' I said gently.

'Year ago he broke his glasses,' the old man said. 'I could of laughed. Almost did.'

'Yes. Where could I get in touch with him this time of the evening?'

He looked at me a little more directly.

'Oh, the building super? He's home, ain't he?'

'Sure. Probably. Or gone to the pictures. But where is home? What's his name?'

'You want something?'

'Yes.' I squeezed a fist in my pocket and tried to keep from yelling. 'I want the address of one of the tenants. The tenant I want the address of isn't in the phone book – at his home. I mean where he lives when he's not in his office. You know, home.' I took my hands out and made a shape in the air, writing the letters slowly, h-o-m-e.

The old man said: 'Which one?' It was so direct that it jarred me.

'Mr Morningstar.'

'He ain't home. Still in his office.'

'Are you sure?'

'Sure I'm sure. I don't notice people much. But he's old like me and I notice him. He ain't been down yet.'

I got into the car and said: 'Eight.'

He wrestled the doors shut and we ground our way up. He didn't look at me any more. When the car stopped and I got out he didn't speak or look at me again. He just sat there blank-eyed, hunched on the burlap and the wooden stool. As I turned the angle of the corridor he was still sitting there. And the vague expression was back on his face.

At the end of the corridor two doors were alight. They were the only two in sight that were. I stopped outside to light a cigarette and listen, but I didn't hear any sound of activity. I opened the door marked *Entrance* and stepped into the narrow office with the small closed typewriter desk. The wooden door was still ajar. I walked along to it and knocked on the wood and said: 'Mr Morningstar.'

No answer. Silence. Not even a sound of breathing. The hair moved on the back of my neck. I stepped around the door. The ceiling light glowed down on the glass cover of the jeweller's scales, on the old polished wood around the leather desk top, down the side of the desk, on a square-toed, elastic-sided black shoe, with a white cotton sock above it.

The shoe was at the wrong angle, pointing to the corner of the ceiling. The rest of the leg was behind the corner of the big safe. I seemed to be wading through mud as I went on into the room.

He lay crumpled on his back. Very lonely, very dead.

The safe door was wide open and keys hung in the lock of the inner compartment. A metal drawer was pulled out. It was empty now. There may have been money in it once.

Nothing else in the room seemed to be different.

The old man's pockets had been pulled out, but I didn't touch him except to bend over and put the back of my hand against his livid, violet-coloured face. It was like touching a frog's belly. Blood had oozed from the side of his forehead where he had been hit. But there was no powder smell on the air this time, and the violet colour of his skin showed that he had died of a heart stoppage, due to shock and fear, probably. That didn't make it any less murder.

I left the lights burning, wiped the doorknobs, and walked down the fire stairs to the sixth floor. I read the names on the doors going along, for no reason at all. *H. R. Teager, Dental Laboratories, L. Pridview, Public Accountant, Dalton and Rees Typewriting Service, Dr E. J. Blaskowitz*, and underneath the name in small letters: *Chiropractic Physician*.

The elevator came growling up and the old man didn't look at me. His face was as empty as my brain.

I called the Receiving Hospital from the corner, giving no name.

15

The chessmen, red and white bone, were lined up ready to go and had that sharp, competent and complicated look they always have at the beginning of a game. It was ten o'clock in the evening, I was home at the apartment, I had a pipe in my mouth, a drink at my elbow and nothing on my mind except two murders and the mystery of how Mrs Elizabeth Bright Murdock had got her Brasher Doubloon back while I still had it in my pocket.

I opened a little paper-bound book of tournament games published in Leipzig, picked out a dashing-looking Queen's Gambit, moved the white pawn to Queen's four, and the bell rang at the door.

I stepped around the table and picked the Colt .38 off the drop-leaf of the oak desk and went over to the door holding it down beside my right leg.

'Who is it?'

'Breeze.'

I went back to the desk to lay the gun down again before I opened the door. Breeze stood there looking just as big and sloppy as ever, but a little more tired. The young, fresh-faced dick named Spangler was with him.

They rode me back into the room without seeming to and Spangler shut the door. His bright young eyes flicked this way and that while Breeze let his older and harder ones stay on my face for a long moment, then he walked around me to the davenport.

'Look around,' he said out of the corner of his mouth.

Spangler left the door and crossed the room to the dinette, looked in there, recrossed and went into the hall. The bathroom door squeaked, his steps went farther along.

Breeze took his hat off and mopped his semi-bald dome. Doors opened and closed distantly. Closets. Spangler came back.

'Nobody here,' he said.

Breeze nodded and sat down, placing his panama beside him.

Spangler saw the gun lying on the desk. He said: 'Mind if I look?'

I said: 'Phooey on both of you.'

Spangler walked to the gun and held the muzzle to his nose, sniffing. He broke the magazine out, ejected the shell in the chamber, picked it up and pressed it into the magazine. He laid the magazine on the desk and held the gun so that light went into the open bottom of breech. Holding it that way he squinted down the barrel.

'A little dust,' he said. 'Not much.'

'What did you expect?' I said. 'Rubies?'

He ignored me, looking at Breeze and added: 'I'd say this gun has not been fired within twenty-four hours. I'm sure of it.'

Breeze nodded and chewed his lips and explored my face with his eyes. Spangler put the gun together neatly and laid it aside and went and sat down. He put a cigarette between his lips and lit it and blew smoke contentedly.

'We know damn well it wasn't a long .38 anyway,' he said. 'One of those things will shoot through a wall. No chance of the slug staying inside a man's head.'

'Just what are you guys talking about?' I asked.

Breeze said: 'The usual thing in our business. Murder. Have a chair. Relax. I thought I heard voices in here. Maybe it was the next apartment.'

'Maybe,' I said.

'You always have a gun lying around on your desk?'

'Except when it's under my pillow,' I said. 'Or under my arm. Or in the drawer of the desk. Or somewhere I can't just remember where I happened to put it. That help you any?'

'We didn't come here to get tough, Marlowe.'

'That's fine,' I said. 'So you prowl my apartment and handle my property without asking my permission. What do you do when you get tough – knock me down and kick me in the face?'

'Aw hell,' he said and grinned. I grinned back. We all grinned. Then Breeze said: 'Use your phone?'

I pointed to it. He dialled a number and talked to someone named Morrison, saying: 'Breeze at' – he looked down at the base of the phone and read the number off – 'any time now. Marlowe is the name that goes with it. Sure. Five or ten minutes is okay.'

He hung up and went to the davenport.

'I bet you can't guess why we're here.'

'I'm always expecting the brothers to drop in,' I said.

'Murder ain't funny, Marlowe.'

'Who said it was?'

'Don't you kind of act as if it was?'

'I wasn't aware of it.'

He looked at Spangler and shrugged. Then he looked at the floor. Then he lifted his eyes slowly, as if they were heavy, and looked at me again. I was sitting down by the chess table now.

'You play a lot of chess?' he asked, looking at the chessmen.

'Not a lot. Once in a while I fool around with a game here, thinking things out.'

'Don't it take two guys to play chess?'

'I play over tournament games that have been recorded and published. There's a whole literature about chess. Once in a while I work out problems. They're not chess, properly speaking. What are we talking about chess for? Drink?'

'Not right now,' Breeze said. 'I talked to Randall about you. He remembers you very well, in connexion with a case down at the beach.' He moved his feet on the carpet, as if they were very tired. His solid old face was lined and grey with fatigue. 'He said you wouldn't murder anybody. He says you are a nice guy, on the level.'

'That was friendly of him,' I said.

'He says you make good coffee and you get up kind of late in the mornings and are apt to run to a very bright line of chatter and that we should believe anything you say, provided we can check it by five independent witnesses.'

'To hell with him,' I said.

Breeze nodded exactly as though I had said just what he wanted me to say. He wasn't smiling and he wasn't tough, just a big solid man working at his job. Spangler had his head back on the chair and his eyes half closed and was watching the smoke from his cigarette.

'Randall says we should look out for you. He says you are not as smart as you think you are, but that you are a guy things happen to, and a guy like that could be a lot more trouble than a very smart guy. That's what he says, you understand. You look all right to me. I like everything in the clear. That's why I'm telling you.'

I said it was nice of him.

The phone rang. I looked at Breeze, but he didn't move, so I reached for it and answered it. It was a girl's voice. I thought it was vaguely familiar, but I couldn't place it.

'Is this Mr Philip Marlowe?'

'Yes.'

'Mr Marlowe, I'm in trouble, very great trouble. I want to see you very badly. When can I see you?'

I said: 'You mean tonight? Who am I talking to?'

'My name is Gladys Crane. I live at the Hotel Normandy on Rampart. When can you –'

'You mean you want me to come over there tonight?' I asked, thinking about the voice, trying to place it.

'I –' The phone clicked and the line was dead. I sat there holding it, frowning at it, looking across it at Breeze. His face was quietly empty of interest.

'Some girl says she's in trouble,' I said. 'Connexion broken.' I held the plunger down on the base of the phone waiting for it to ring again. The two cops were completely silent and motionless. Too silent, too motionless.

The bell rang again and I let the plunger up and said: 'You want to talk to Breeze, don't you?'

'Yeah.' It was a man's voice and it sounded a little surprised.

'Go on, be tricky,' I said, and got up from the chair and went out to the kitchen. I heard Breeze talking very briefly, then the sound of the phone being returned to the cradle.

I got a bottle of Four Roses out of the kitchen closet and three glasses. I got ice and ginger-ale from the ice-box and mixed three highballs and carried them in on a tray and sat the tray down on the cocktail table in front of the davenport where Breeze was sitting. I took two of the glasses, handed one to Spangler, and took the other to my chair.

Spangler held the glass uncertainly, pinching his lower lip between thumb and finger, looking at Breeze to see whether he would accept the drink.

Breeze looked at me very steadily. Then he sighed. Then he picked the glass up and tasted it and sighed again and shook his head sideways with a half smile; the way a man does when you give him a drink and he needs it very badly and it is just right and the first swallow is like a peek into a cleaner, sunnier, brighter world.

'I guess you catch on pretty fast, Mr Marlowe,' he said, and leaned back on the davenport completely relaxed. 'I guess now we can do some business together.'

'Not that way,' I said.

'Huh?' He bent his eyebrows together. Spangler leaned forward in his chair and looked bright and attentive.

'Having stray broads call me up and give me a song and dance so you can say they said they recognized my voice somewhere, sometime.'

'The girl's name is Gladys Crane,' Breeze said.

'So she told me. I never heard of her.'

'Okay,' Breeze said. 'Okay.' He showed me the flat of his freckled hand. 'We're not trying to pull anything that's not legitimate. We only hope you ain't, either.'

'Ain't either what?'

'Ain't either trying to pull anything not legitimate. Such as holding out on us.'

'Just why shouldn't I hold out on you, if I feel like it?' I asked. 'You're not paying my salary.'

'Look, don't get tough, Marlowe.'

'I'm not tough. I don't have any idea of being tough. I know enough about cops not to get tough with them. Go ahead and speak your piece and don't try to pull any more phonies like that telephone call.'

'We're on a murder case,' Breeze said. 'We have to try to run it the best we can. You found the body. You had talked to the guy. He had asked you to come to his apartment. He gave you his key. You said you didn't know what he wanted to see you about. We figured that maybe with time to think back you could have remembered.'

'In other words I was lying the first time,' I said.

Breeze smiled a tired smile. 'You been around enough to know that people always lie in murder cases.'

'The trouble with that is how are you going to know when I stop lying?'

'When what you say begins to make sense, we'll be satisfied.'

I looked at Spangler. He was leaning forward so far he was almost out of his chair. He looked as if he was going to jump. I couldn't think of any reason why he should jump, so I thought he must be excited. I looked back at Breeze. He was about as excited as a hole in the wall. He had one of his cellophane-wrapped cigars between his thick fingers and he was slitting the cellophane with a penknife. I watched him get the wrapping off and trim the cigar end with the blade and put the knife away, first wiping the blade carefully on his trousers. I watched him strike a wooden match and light the cigar carefully, turning it around in the flame, then, hold the match away from the cigar, still burning, and draw on the cigar till he decided it was properly lighted. Then he shook the match out and laid it down beside the crumpled cellophane on the glass top of the cocktail table. Then he leaned back and pulled up one leg of his trousers and smoked peacefully. Every motion had been exactly as it had been when he lit a cigar in Hench's apartment, and exactly as it always would be whenever he lit a cigar. He was that kind of man, and that made him dangerous. Not as dangerous as a brilliant man, but much more dangerous than a quick excitable one like Spangler.

'I never saw Phillips before today,' I said. 'I don't count that he said he saw me up in Ventura once, because I don't remember him. I met him just the way I told you. He tailed me around and I braced him. He wanted to talk to me, he gave me his key, I went to his apartment, used the key to let myself in when he didn't answer – as he had told me to do. He was dead. The police were called and through a set of events or incidents that had nothing to do with me, a gun was found under Hench's pillow. A gun that had been fired. I told you this and it's true.'

Breeze said: 'When you found him you went down to the apartment manager, guy named Passmore, and got him to go up with you without telling him anybody was dead. You gave Passmore a phony card and talked about jewellery.'

I nodded. 'With people like Passmore and apartment houses like that one, it pays to be a little on the cagey side. I was interested in Phillips. I thought Passmore might tell me something about him, if he didn't know he was dead, that he wouldn't be likely to tell me if he knew the cops were going to bounce in on him in a brief space of time. That's all there was to that.'

Breeze drank a little of his drink and smoked a little of his cigar and said: 'What I'd like to get in the clear is this. Everything you just told us might be strictly the truth, and yet you might not be telling us the truth. If you get what I mean.'

'Like what?' I asked, getting perfectly well what he meant.

He tapped on his knee and watched me with a quiet up from under look. Not hostile, not even suspicious. Just a quiet man doing his job.

'Like this. You're on a job. We don't know what it is. Phillips was playing at being a private dick. He was on a job. He trailed you around. How can we know, unless you tell us, that his job and your job don't tie in somewhere? And if they do, that's our business. Right?'

'That's one way to look at it,' I said. 'But it's not the only way, and it's not my way.'

'Don't forget this is a murder case, Marlowe.'

'I'm not. But don't you forget I've been around this town a long time, more than fifteen years. I've seen a lot of murder cases come and go. Some have been solved, some couldn't be solved, and some could have been solved that were not solved. And one or two or three of them have been solved wrong. Somebody was paid to take a rap, and the chances are it was known or strongly suspected. And winked at. But skip that. It happens, but not often. Consider a case like the Cassidy case. I guess you remember it, don't you?'

Breeze looked at his watch. 'I'm tired,' he said. 'Let's forget the Cassidy case. Let's stick to the Phillips case.'

I shook my head. 'I'm going to make a point, and it's an important point. Just look at the Cassidy case. Cassidy was a very rich man, a multi-millionaire. He had a grown-up son. One night the cops were called to his home and young Cassidy was on his back on the floor with blood all over his face and a bullet-hole in the side of his head. His secretary was lying on *his* back in an adjoining bathroom, with his head against the second bathroom door, leading to a hall, and a cigarette burned out between the fingers of his left hand, just a short burned-out stub that had scorched the skin between his fingers. A gun was lying by his right hand. He was shot in the head, not a contact wound. A lot of drinking had been done. Four hours had elapsed since the deaths and the family doctor had been there for three of them. Now, what did you do with the Cassidy case?'

Breeze sighed. 'Murder and suicide during a drinking spree. The secretary went haywire and shot young Cassidy. I read it in the papers or something. Is that what you want me to say?'

'You read it in the papers,' I said, 'but it wasn't so. What's more, you knew it wasn't so and the D.A. knew it wasn't so and the D.A.'s investigators were pulled off the case within a matter of hours. There was no inquest. But every crime reporter in town and every cop on every homicide detail knew it was Cassidy that did the shooting, that it was Cassidy that was crazy drunk, that it was the secretary who tried to handle him and couldn't and at last tried to get away from him, but wasn't quick enough. Cassidy's was a contact wound and the secretary's was not. The secretary was left-handed and he had a cigarette in his left hand when he was shot. Even if you are right-handed, you don't change a cigarette over to your other hand and shoot a man while casually holding the cigarette. They might do that on *Gang Busters*, but rich men's secretaries don't do it. And what were the family and the family doctor doing during the four hours they didn't call the cops? Fixing it so there would only be a superficial investigation. And why were no tests of the hands made for nitrates? Because you didn't want the truth. Cassidy was too big. But this was a murder case, too, wasn't it?'

'The guys were both dead,' Breeze said. 'What the hell difference did it make who shot who?'

'Did you ever stop to think,' I asked, 'that Cassidy's secretary might have had a mother or a sister or a sweetheart – or all three? That they had their pride and their faith and their love for a kid who was made out to be a drunken paranoiac because his boss's father had a hundred million dollars?'

Breeze lifted his glass slowly and finished his drink slowly and put it down slowly and turned the glass slowly on the glass top of the cocktail table. Spangler sat rigid, all shining eyes and lips parted in a sort of rigid half smile.

Breeze said: 'Make your point.'

I said: 'Until you guys own your own souls you don't own mine. Until you guys can be trusted every time and always, in all times and conditions, to seek the truth out and find it and let the chips fall where they may – until that time comes, I have a right to listen to my conscience, and protect my client the best way I can. Until I'm sure you won't do him more harm than you'll do the truth good. Or until I'm hauled before somebody that can make me talk.'

Breeze said: 'You sound to me just a little like a guy who is trying to hold his conscience down.'

'Hell,' I said. 'Let's have another drink. And then you can tell me about that girl you had me talk to on the phone.'

He grinned: 'That was a dame that lives next door to Phillips. She heard a guy talking to him at the door one evening. She works days as an usherette. So we thought maybe, she ought to hear your voice. Think nothing of it.'

'What kind of voice was it?'

'Kind of a mean voice. She said she didn't like it.'

'I guess that's what made you think of me,' I said.

I picked up the three glasses and went out to the kitchen with them.

16

When I got there I had forgotten which glass was which, so I rinsed them all out and dried them and was starting to make more drinks when Spangler strolled out and stood just behind my shoulder.

'It's all right,' I said. 'I'm not using any cyanide this evening.'

'Don't get too foxy with the old guy,' he said quietly to the back of my neck. 'He knows more angles than you think.'

'Nice of you,' I said.

'Say, I'd like to read up on that Cassidy case,' he said. 'Sounds interesting. Must have been before my time.'

'It was a long time ago,' I said. 'And it never happened. I was just kidding.' I put the glasses on the tray and carried them back into the living-room and set them around. I took mine over to my chair behind the chess table.

'Another phony,' I said. 'Your sidekick sneaks out to the kitchen and gives me advice behind your back about how careful I ought to keep on account of the angles you know that I don't think you know. He has just the right face for it. Friendly and open and an easy blusher.'

Spangler sat down on the edge of his chair and blushed. Breeze looked at him casually, without meaning.

'What did you find out about Phillips?' I asked.

'Yes,' Breeze said. 'Phillips. Well, George Anson Phillips is a kind of pathetic case. He thought he was a detective, but it looks as if he couldn't get anybody to agree with him. I talked to the sheriff at Ventura. He said George was a nice kid, maybe a little too nice to make a good cop, even if he had any brains. George did what they said and he would do it pretty well, provided they told him which foot to start on and how many steps to take which way and little things like that. But he didn't develop much, if you get what I mean. He was the sort of cop who would be likely to hang a pinch on a chicken thief, if he saw the guy steal the chicken and the guy fell down running away and hit his head on a post or something and knocked himself out. Otherwise it might get a little tough and George would have to go back to the office for instructions. Well, it wore the sheriff down after a while and he let George go.'

Breeze drank some more of his drink and scratched his chin with a thumbnail like the blade of a shovel.

'After that George worked in a general store at Simi for a man named Sutcliff. It was a credit business with little books for each customer and George would have trouble with the books. He would forget to write the stuff down or write it in the wrong book and some of the customers would straighten him out and some would let George forget. So Sutcliff thought

87

maybe George would do better at something else, and he came to Los Angeles. He had come into a little money, not much, but enough for him to get a licence and put up a bond and get himself a piece of an office. I was over there. What he had was desk room with another guy who claims he is selling Christmas cards. Name of Marsh. If George had a customer, the arrangement was Marsh would go for a walk. Marsh says he didn't know where George lived and George didn't have any customers. That is, no business came into the office that Marsh knows about. But George put an advertisement in the paper and he might have got a customer out of that. I guess he did, because about a week ago Marsh found a note on his desk that George would be out of town for a few days. That's the last he heard of him. So George went over to Court Street and took an apartment under the name of Anson and got bumped off. And that's all we know about George so far. Kind of a pathetic case.'

He looked at me with a level, uncurious gaze and raised his glass to his lips.

'What about this advertisement?'

Breeze put the glass down and dug a thin piece of paper out of his wallet and put it down on the cocktail table. I went over and picked it up and read it. It said:

> Why worry? Why be doubtful or confused? Why be gnawed by suspicion? Consult cool, careful, confidential, discreet investigator. George Anson Phillips. Glenview 9521.

I put it down on the glass again.

'It ain't any worse than lots of business personals,' Breeze said. 'It don't seem to be aimed at the carriage trade.'

Spangler said: 'The girl in the office wrote it for him. She said she could hardly keep from laughing, but George thought it was swell. The Hollywood Boulevard office of the *Chronicle*.'

'You checked that fast,' I said.

'We don't have any trouble getting information,' Breeze said. 'Except maybe from you.'

'What about Hench?'

'Nothing about Hench. Him and the girl were having a liquor party.

They would drink a little and sing a little and scrap a little and listen to the radio and go out to eat once in a while, when they thought of it. I guess it had been going on for days. Just as well we stopped it. The girl has two bad eyes. The next round Hench might have broken her neck. The world is full of bums like Hench – and his girl.'

'What about the gun Hench said wasn't his?'

'It's the right gun. We don't have the slug yet, but we have the shell. It was under George's body and it checks. We had a couple more fired and compared the ejector marks and the firing-pin dents.'

'You believe someone planted it under Hench's pillow?'

'Sure. Why would Hench shoot Phillips? He didn't know him.'

'How do you know that?'

'I know it,' Breeze said, spreading his hands. 'Look, there are things you know because you have them down in black and white. And there are things you know because they are reasonable and have to be so. You don't shoot somebody and then make a lot of racket calling attention to yourself, and all the time you have the gun under your pillow. The girl was with Hench all day. If Hench shot anybody, she would have some idea. She doesn't have any such idea. She would spill, if she had. What is Hench to her? A guy to play around with, no more. Look, forget Hench. The guy who did the shooting hears the loud radio and knows it will cover a shot. But all the same he saps Phillips and drags him into the bathroom and shuts the door before he shoots him. He's not drunk. He's minding his own business, and careful. He goes out, shuts the bathroom door, the radio stops. Hench and the girl go out to eat. Just happens that way.'

'How do you know the radio stopped?'

'I was told,' Breeze said calmly. 'Other people live in that dump. Take it the radio stopped and they went out. Not quiet. The killer steps out of the apartment and Hench's door is open. That must be because otherwise he wouldn't think anything about Hench's door.'

'People don't leave their doors open in apartment houses. Especially in districts like that.'

'Drunks do. Drunks are careless. Their minds don't focus well. And they only think of one thing at a time. The door was open – just a little maybe, but open. The killer went in and ditched his gun on the bed and found another gun there. He took that away, just to make it look worse for Hench.'

'You can check the gun,' I said.

'Hench's gun? We'll try to, but Hench says he doesn't know the number. If we find it, we might do something there. I doubt it. The gun we have we will try to check, but you know how those things are. You get just so far along and you think it is going to open up for you, and then the trail dies out cold. A dead end. Anything else you can think of that we might know that might be a help to you in your business?'

'I'm getting tired,' I said. 'My imagination isn't working very well.'

'You were doing fine a while back,' Breeze said. 'On the Cassidy case.'

I didn't say anything. I filled my pipe up again but it was too hot to light. I laid it on the edge of the table to cool off.

'It's God truth,' Breeze said slowly, 'that I don't know what to make of you. I can't see you deliberately covering up on any murder. And neither can I see you knowing as little about all this as you pretend to know.'

I didn't say anything, again.

Breeze leaned over to revolve his cigar butt in the tray until he had killed the fire. He finished his drink, put on his hat and stood up.

'How long you expect to stay dummied up?' he asked.

'I don't know.'

'Let me help you out. I give you till tomorrow noon, a little better than twelve hours. I won't get my post-mortem report before that anyway. I give you till then to talk things over with your party and decide to come clean.'

'And after that?'

'After that I see the Captain of Detectives and tell him a private eye named Philip Marlowe is withholding information which I need in a murder investigation, or I'm pretty sure he is. And what about it? I figure he'll pull you in fast enough to singe your breeches.'

I said: 'Oh-huh. Did you go through Phillips's desk?'

'Sure. A very neat young feller. Nothing in it at all, except a little kind of diary. Nothing in that either, except about how he went to the beach or took some girl to the pictures and she didn't warm up much. Or how he sat in the office and no business come in. One time he got a little sore about his laundry and wrote a whole page. Mostly it was just three or four lines. There was only one thing about. It was all done in a kind of printing.'

I said: 'Printing?'

'Yeah, printing in pen and ink. Not big block caps like people trying to disguise things. Just neat fast little printing as if the guy could write that way as fast and easy as any way.'

'He didn't write like that on the card he gave me,' I said.

Breeze thought about that for a moment. Then he nodded. 'True. Maybe it was this way. There wasn't any name in the diary either, in the front. Maybe the printing was just a little game he played with himself.'

'Like Pepys's shorthand,' I said.

'What was that?'

'A diary a man wrote in a private shorthand, a long time ago.'

Breeze looked at Spangler, who was standing up in front of his chair, tipping the last few drops of his glass.

'We better beat it,' Breeze said. 'This guy is warming up for another Cassidy case.'

Spangler put his glass down and they both went over to the door. Breeze shuffled a foot and looked at me sideways, with his hand on the doorknob.

'You know any tall blondes?'

'I'd have to think,' I said. 'I hope so. How tall?'

'Just tall. I don't know how tall that is. Except that it would be tall to a guy who is tall himself. A wop named Palermo owns that apartment house on Court Street. We went across to see him in his funeral parlours. He owns them too. He says he saw a tall blonde come out of the apartment house about three-thirty. The manager, Passmore, don't place anybody in the joint that he would call a tall blonde. The wop says she was a looker. I give some weight to what he says because he gave us a good description of you. He didn't see this tall blonde go in, just saw her come out. She was wearing slacks and a sports jacket and a wrap-around. But she had light blonde hair and plenty of it under the wrap-around.'

'Nothing comes to me,' I said. 'But I just remembered something else. I wrote the licence number of Phillips's car down on the back of an envelope. That will give you his former address, probably. I'll get it.'

They stood there while I went to get it out of my coat in the bedroom.

I handed the piece of envelope to Breeze and he read what was on it and tucked it into his billfold.

'So you just thought of this, huh?'

'That's right.'

'Well, well,' he said. 'Well, well.'

The two of them went along the hallway towards the elevator, shaking their heads.

I shut the door and went back to my almost untasted second drink. It was flat. I carried it to the kitchen and hardened it up from the bottle and stood there holding it and looking out of the window at the eucalyptus trees tossing their limber tops against the bluish dark sky. The wind seemed to have risen again. It thumped at the north window and there was a heavy slow pounding noise on the wall of the building, like a thick wire banging the stucco between insulators.

I tasted my drink and wished I hadn't wasted the fresh whisky on it. I poured it down the sink and got a fresh glass and drank some ice water.

Twelve hours to tie up a situation which I didn't even begin to understand. Either that or turn up a client and let the cops go to work on her and her whole family. Hire Marlowe and get your house full of law. Why worry? Why be doubtful and confused? Why be gnawed by suspicion? Consult cock-eyed, careless, clubfooted, dissipated investigator, Philip Marlowe, Glenview 7537. See me and you meet the best cops in town. Why despair? Why be lonely? Call Marlowe and watch the wagon come.

This didn't get me anywhere either. I went back to the living-room and put a match to the pipe that had cooled off now on the edge of the chess table. I drew the smoke in slowly, but it still tasted like the smell of hot rubber. I put it away and stood in the middle of the floor, pulling my lower lip out and letting it snap back against my teeth.

The telephone rang. I picked it up and growled into it.

'Marlowe?'

The voice was a harsh low whisper. It was a harsh low whisper I had heard before.

'All right,' I said. 'Talk it up whoever you are. Whose pocket have I got my hand in now?'

'Maybe you're a smart guy,' the harsh whisper said. 'Maybe you would like to do yourself some good.'

'How much good?'

'Say about five C's worth of good.'

'That's grand,' I said. 'Doing what?'

'Keeping your nose clean,' the voice said. 'Want to talk about it?'

'Where, when, and who to?'

'Idle Valley Club. Morny. Any time you get here.'

'Who are you?'

A dim chuckle came over the wire. 'Just ask at the gate for Eddie Prue.' The phone clicked dead. I hung it up.

It was near eleven-thirty when I backed my car out of the garage and drove towards Cahuenga Pass.

17

About twenty miles north of the pass a wide boulevard with flowering moss in the parkways turned towards the foothills. It ran for five blocks and died – without a house in its entire length. From its end a curving asphalt road dived into the hills. This was Idle Valley.

Around the shoulder of the first hill there was a low white building with a tiled roof beside the road. It had a roofed porch and a floodlighted sign on it read: *Idle Valley Patrol*. Open gates were folded back on the shoulders of the road, in the middle of which a square white sign standing on its point said STOP in letters sprinkled with reflector buttons. Another floodlight blistered the space of road in front of the sign.

I stopped. A uniformed man with a star and a strapped-on gun in a woven leather holster looked at my car, then at a board on a post.

He came over to the car. 'Good evening. I don't have your car. This is a private road. Visiting?'

'Going to the club.'

'Which one?'

'Idle Valley Club.'

'Eighty-seven seventy-seven. That's what we call it here. You mean Mr Morny's place?'

'Right.'

'You're not a member, I guess.'

'No.'

'I have to check you in. To somebody who is a member or to somebody who lives in the valley. All private property here, you know.'

'No gate crashers, huh?'

He smiled. 'No gate crashers.'

'The name is Philip Marlowe,' I said. 'Calling on Eddie Prue.'

'Prue?'

'He's Mr Morny's secretary. Or something.'

'Just a minute, please.'

He went to the door of the building, and spoke. Another uniformed man inside plugged in on a PBX. A car came up behind me and honked. The clack of the typewriter came from the open door of the patrol office. The man who had spoken to me looked at the honking car and waved it in. It slid around me and scooted off into the dark, a green long open convertible sedan with three dizzy-looking dames in the front seat, all cigarettes and arched eyebrows and go-to-hell expressions. The car flashed around a curve and was gone.

The uniformed man came back to me and put a hand on the car door. 'Okay, Mr Marlowe. Check with the officer at the club, please. A mile ahead on your right. There's a lighted parking lot and the number on the wall. Just the number. Eighty-seven seventy-seven. Check with the officer there, please.'

I said: 'Why would I do that?'

He was very calm, very polite, and very firm. 'We have to know exactly where you go. There's a great deal to protect in Idle Valley.'

'Suppose I don't check with him?'

'You kidding me?' His voice hardened.

'No. I just wanted to know.'

'A couple of cruisers would start looking for you.'

'How many are you in the patrol?'

'Sorry,' he said. 'About a mile ahead on the right, Mr Marlowe.'

I looked at the gun strapped to his hip, the special badge pinned to his shirt. 'And they call this a democracy,' I said.

He looked behind him and then spat on the ground and put a hand on the sill of the car door. 'Maybe you got company,' he said. 'I knew a fellow, belonged to the John Reed Club. Over in Boyle Heights, it was.'

'Tovarich,' I said.

'The trouble with revolutions,' he said, 'is that they get in the hands of the wrong people.'

'Check,' I said.

'On the other hand,' he said, 'could they be any wronger than the bunch of rich phonies that live around here?'

'Maybe you'll be living in here yourself some day,' I said.

He spat again. 'I wouldn't live in here if they paid me fifty thousand a year and let me sleep in chiffon pyjamas with a string of matched pink pearls around my neck.'

'I'd hate to make you the offer,' I said.

'You make me the offer any time,' he said. 'Day or night. Just make me the offer and see what it gets you.'

'Well, I'll run along now and check with the officer of the club,' I said.

'Tell him to go spit up his left trousers leg,' he said. 'Tell him I said so.'

'I'll do that,' I said.

A car came up behind and honked. I drove on. Half a block of dark limousine blew me off the road with its horn and went past me making a noise like dead leaves falling.

The wind was quiet out here and the valley moonlight was so sharp that the black shadows looked as if they had been cut with an engraving tool.

Around the curve the whole valley spread out before me. A thousand white houses built up and down the hills, ten thousand lighted windows and the stars hanging down over them politely, not getting too close, on account of the patrol.

The wall of the club building that faced the road was white and blank, with no entrance door, no windows on the lower floor. The number was small but bright in violet-coloured neon. 8777. Nothing else. To the side, under rows of hooded, downward-shining lights, were even rows of cars, set out in the white lined slots on the smooth black asphalt. Attendants in crisp clean uniforms moved in the lights.

The road went around to the back. A deep concrete porch there, with an overhanging canopy of glass and chromium, but very dim lights. I got out of the car and received a check with the licence number on it, carried it over to a small desk where a uniformed man sat and dumped it in front of him.

'Philip Marlowe,' I said. 'Visitor.'

'Thank you, Mr Marlowe.' He wrote the name and number down, handed me back my check and picked up a telephone.

A Negro, in a white linen double-breasted guards' uniform, gold epaulettes, a cap with a broad gold band, opened the door to me.

The lobby looked like a high-budget musical. A lot of light and glitter, a lot of scenery, a lot of clothes, a lot of sound, an all-star cast, and a plot with all the originality and drive of a split fingernail. Under the beautiful soft indirect lighting the wall seemed to go up for ever, and to be lost in soft lascivious stars that really twinkled. You could just manage to walk on the carpet without waders. At the back was a free-arched stairway with a chromium and white enamel gangway going up in wide shallow carpeted steps. At the entrance to the dining-room a chubby captain of waiters stood negligently with a two-inch satin stripe on his pants and a bunch of gold-plated menus under his arm. He had the sort of face that can turn from a polite simper to cold-blooded fury almost without moving a muscle.

The bar entrance was to the left. It was dusky and quiet and a bartender moved moth-like against the faint glitter of piled glassware. A tall handsome blonde, in a dress that looked like sea-water sifted over with gold dust, came out of the Ladies' Room touching up her lips and turned towards the arch, humming.

The sound of rhumba music came through the archway and she nodded her gold head in time to it, smiling. A short fat man with a red face and glittering eyes waited for her with a white wrap over his arm. He dug his thick fingers into her bare arm and leered up at her.

A check girl in peach-bloom Chinese pyjamas came over to take my hat and disapprove of my clothes. She had eyes like strange sins.

A cigarette girl came down the gangway. She wore an egret plume in her hair, enough clothes to hide behind a toothpick, one of her long beautiful naked legs was silver, and one was gold. She had the utterly disdainful expression of a dame who makes her dates by long distance.

I went into the bar and sank into a leather bar seat packed with down. Glasses tinkled gently, lights glowed softly, there were quiet voices whispering of love, or ten per cent, or whatever they whisper about in a place like that.

A tall, fine-looking man in a grey suit cut by an angel suddenly stood up from a small table by the wall and walked over to the bar and started to curse one of the barmen. He cursed him in a loud clear voice for a long minute, calling him about nine names that are not usually mentioned by tall, fine-looking men in well-cut grey suits. Everybody stopped talking and looked at him quietly. His voice cut through the muted rhumba music like a shovel through snow.

The barman stood perfectly still, looking at the man. The barman had curly hair and a clear warm skin and wide-set careful eyes. He didn't move or speak. The tall man stopped talking and stalked out of the bar. Everybody watched him out except the barman.

The barman moved slowly along the bar to the end where I sat and looking away from me, with nothing in his face but pallor. Then he turned to me and said:

'Yes, sir?'

'I want to talk to a fellow named Eddie Prue.'

'So?'

'He works here,' I said.

'Works here doing what?' His voice was perfectly level and as dry as dry sand.

'I understand he's the guy that walks behind the boss. If you know what I mean.'

'Oh, Eddie Prue.' He moved one lip slowly over the other and made small tight circles on the bar with his bar cloth. 'Your name?'

'Marlowe.'

'Marlowe. Drink while waiting?'

'A dry martini will do.'

'A martini. Dry, Veddy, veddy dry.'

'Okay.'

'Will you eat it with a spoon or a knife and fork?'

'Cut it in strips,' I said. 'I'll just nibble it.'

'On your way to school,' he said. 'Should I put the olive in a bag for you?'

'Sock me on the nose with it,' I said. 'If it will make you feel any better.'

'Thank you, sir,' he said. 'A dry martini.'

He took three steps away from me and then came back and leaned across the bar and said: 'I made a mistake in a drink. The gentleman was telling me about it.'

'I heard him.'

'He was telling me about it as gentlemen tell you about things like that. As big shot directors like to point out to you your little errors. And you heard him.'

'Yeah,' I said, wondering how long this was going to go on.

'He made himself heard – the gentleman did. So I come over here and practically insult you.'

'I got the idea,' I said.

He held up one of his fingers and looked at it thoughtfully.

'Just like that,' he said. 'A perfect stranger.'

'It's my big brown eyes,' I said. 'They have that gentle look.'

'Thanks, chum,' he said, and quietly went away.

I saw him talking into a phone at the end of the bar. Then I saw him working with a shaker. When he came back with the drink he was all right again.

18

I carried the drink over to a small table against the wall and sat down there and lit a cigarette. Five minutes went by. The music that was coming through the fret had changed in tempo without my noticing it. A girl was singing. She had a rich deep down around the ankles contralto that was pleasant to listen to. She was singing 'Dark Eyes' and the band behind her seemed to be falling asleep.

There was a heavy round of applause and some whistling when she ended.

A man at the next table said to his girl: 'They got Linda Conquest back with the band. I heard she got married to some rich guy in Pasadena, but it didn't take.'

The girl said: 'Nice voice. If you like female crooners.'

I started to get up but a shadow fell across my table and a man was standing there.

A great long gallows of a man with a ravaged face and a haggard frozen right eye that had a clotted iris and the steady look of blindness. He was so tall that he had to stoop to put his hand on the back of the chair across the table from me. He stood there sizing me up without saying anything and I sat there sipping the last of my drink and listening to the contralto voice singing another song. The customers seemed to like corny music in there. Perhaps they were all tired out trying to be ahead of the minute in the place where they worked.

'I'm Prue,' the man said in his harsh whisper.

'So I gathered. You want to talk to me, I want to talk to you, and I want to talk to the girl that just sang.'

'Let's go.'

There was a locked door at the back end of the bar. Prue unlocked it and held it for me and we went through that and up a flight of carpeted steps to the left. A long straight hallway with several closed doors. At the end of it a bright star cross-wired by the mesh of a screen. Prue knocked on a door near the screen and opened it and stood aside for me to pass him.

It was a cosy sort of office, not too large. There was a built-in upholstered corner seat by the french windows and a man in a white dinner-jacket was standing with his back to the room, looking out. He had grey hair. There was a large black and chromium safe, some filing-cases, a large globe in a stand, a small-built-in bar, and the usual broad heavy executive desk with the usual high-backed padded leather chair behind it.

I looked at the ornaments on the desk. Everything standard and all copper. A copper lamp, pen set and pencil tray, a glass and copper ashtray with a copper elephant on the rim, a copper letter opener, a copper thermos bottle on a copper tray, copper corners on the blotter holder. There was a spray of almost copper-coloured sweet peas in a copper vase.

It seemed like a lot of copper.

The man at the window turned around and showed me that he was going on fifty and had soft ash-grey hair and plenty of it, and a heavy handsome face with nothing unusual about it expect a short puckered scar in his left cheek that had almost the effect of a deep dimple. I remembered the dimple. I would have forgotten the man. I remembered that I had seen him in pictures a long time ago, at least ten years ago. I didn't remember the pictures or what they were about or what he did in them, but I remembered the dark heavy handsome face and the puckered scar. His hair had been dark then.

He walked over to his desk and sat down and picked up his letter opener and poked at the ball of his thumb with the point. He looked at me with no expression and said: 'You're Marlowe?'

I nodded.

'Sit down.' I sat down. Eddie Prue sat in a chair against the wall and tilted the front legs off the floor.

'I don't like peepers,' Morny said.

I shrugged.

'I don't like them for a lot of reasons,' he said. 'I don't like them in any way or at any time. I don't like them when they bother my friends. I don't like them when they bust in on my wife.'

I didn't say anything.

'I don't like them when they question my driver or when they get tough with my guests,' he said. I didn't say anything.

'In short,' he said. 'I just don't like them.'

'I'm beginning to get what you mean,' I said.

He flushed and his eyes glittered. 'On the other hand,' he said, 'just at the moment I might have a use for you. It might pay you to play ball with me. It might be a good idea. It might pay you to keep your nose clean.'

'How much might it pay me?' I asked.

'It might pay you in time and health.'

'I seem to have heard this record somewhere,' I said. 'I just can't put a name to it.'

He laid the letter-opener down and swung open a door in the desk and got a cut-glass decanter out. He poured liquid out of it in a glass and drank it and put the stopper back in the decanter and put the decanter back in the desk.

'In my business,' he said, 'tough boys come a dime a dozen. And would-be tough boys come a nickel a gross. Just mind your business and I'll mind my business and we won't have any trouble.' He lit a cigarette. His hand shook a little.

I looked across the room at the tall man sitting tilted against the wall, like a loafer in a country store. He just sat there without motion, his long arms hanging, his lined grey face full of nothing.

'Somebody said something about some money,' I said to Morny. 'What's that for? I know what the bawling out is for. That's you trying to make yourself think you can scare me.'

'Talk like that to me,' Morny said, 'and you are liable to be wearing lead buttons on your vest.'

'Just think,' I said. 'Poor old Marlowe with lead buttons on his vest.'

Eddie Prue made a dry sound in his throat that might have been a chuckle.

'And as for me minding my own business and not minding yours,' I said, 'it might be that my business and your business would get a little mixed up together. Through no fault of mine.'

'It better not,' Morny said. 'In what way?' He lifted his eyes quickly and dropped them again.

'Well, for instance, your hard boy here calling me up on the phone and trying to scare me to death. And later in the evening calling me up and talking about five C's and how it would do me some good to drive out here and talk to you. And, for instance, that same hard boy or somebody who looks just like him – which is a little unlikely – following around after a fellow in my business who happened to get shot this afternoon, on Court Street on Bunker Hill.'

Morny lifted his cigarette away from his lips and narrowed his eyes to look at the tip. Every motion, every gesture, right out of the catalogue.

'Who got shot?'

'A fellow named Phillips, a youngish blond kid. You wouldn't like him. He was a peeper.' I described Phillips to him.

'I never heard of him,' Morny said.

'And also, for instance, a tall blonde who didn't live there was seen coming out of the apartment house just after he was killed,' I said.

'What tall blonde?' His voice had changed a little. There was urgency in it.

'I don't know that. She was seen and the man who saw her could identify her, if he saw her again. Of course, she need not have anything to do with Phillips.'

'This man Phillips was a shamus?'

I nodded. 'I told you that twice.'

'Why was he killed, and how?'

'He was sapped and shot in his apartment. We don't know why he was killed. If we knew that, we would likely know who killed him. It seems to be that kind of a situation.'

'Who is "we"?'

'The police and myself. I found him dead. So I had to stick around.'

Prue let the front legs of his chair down on the carpet very quietly and looked at me. His good eye had a sleepy expression I didn't like.

Morny said: 'You told the cops what?'

I said: 'Very little. I gather from your opening remarks to me here that you know I am looking for Linda Conquest. Mrs Leslie Murdock. I've found her. She's singing here. I don't know why there should have been any secret about it. It seems to me that your wife or Mr Vannier might have told me. But they didn't.'

'What my wife would tell a peeper,' Morny said, 'you could put in a gnat's eye.'

'No doubt she had her reasons,' I said. 'However that's not very important now. In fact, it's not very important that I see Miss Conquest. Just the same I'd like to talk to her a little. If you don't mind.'

'Suppose I mind,' Morny said.

'I guess I would like to talk to her, anyway,' I said. I got a cigarette out of my pocket and rolled it around in my fingers and admired his thick and still-dark eyebrows. They had a fine shape, an elegant curve.

Prue chuckled. Morny looked at him and frowned and looked back at me, keeping the frown on his face.

'I asked you what you told the cops,' he said.

'I told them as little as I could. This man Phillips asked me to come and see him. He implied he was too deep in a job he didn't like, and needed help. When I got there he was dead. I told the police that. They didn't think it was quite the whole story. It probably isn't. I have until tomorrow noon to fill it out. So I'm trying to fill it out.'

'You wasted your time coming here,' Morny said.

'I got the idea that I was asked to come here.'

'You can go to hell back any time you want to,' Morny said. 'Or you can do a little job for me – for five hundred dollars. Either way you leave Eddie and me out of any conversations you might have with the police.'

'What's the nature of the job?'

'You were at my house this morning. You ought to have an idea.'

'I don't do divorce business,' I said.

His face turned white. 'I love my wife,' he said. 'We've only been married eight months. I don't want any divorce. She's a swell girl and she knows what time it is, as a rule. But I think she's playing with a wrong number at the moment.'

'Wrong in what way?'

'I don't know. That's what I want found out.'

'Let me get this straight,' I said. 'Are you hiring me on a job – or off a job I already have?'

Prue chuckled again against the wall.

Morny poured himself some more brandy and tossed it quickly down his throat. Colour came back into his face. He didn't answer me.

'And let me get another thing straight,' I said. 'You don't mind your wife playing around, but you don't want her playing with somebody called Vannier. Is that it?'

'I trust her heart,' he said slowly. 'But I don't trust her judgement. Put it that way.'

'And you want me to get something on this man Vannier?'

'I want to find out what he is up to.'

'Oh. Is he up to something?'

'I think he is. I don't know what.'

'You think he is – or you want to think he is?'

He stared at me levelly for a moment, then he pulled the middle drawer of his desk out, reached in and tossed a folded paper across to me. I picked it up and unfolded it. It was a carbon copy of a grey billhead. *Cal-Western Dental Supply Company*, and an address. The bill was for 30 *lb. Kerr's Crystobolite* $15.75, and 25 *lb. White's Albastone*, $7.75, plus tax. It was made out to *H. R. Teager, Will Call*, and stamped *Paid* with a rubber stamp. It was signed for in the corner: *L. G. Vannier*.

I put it down on the desk.

'That fell out of his pocket one night when he was here,' Morny said. 'About ten days ago. Eddie put one of his big feet on it and Vannier didn't notice he had dropped it.'

I looked at Prue, then at Morny, then at my thumb. 'Is this supposed to mean something to me?'

'I thought you were a smart detective. I figured you could find out.'

I looked at the paper again, folded it and put it in my pocket. 'I'm assuming you wouldn't give it to me unless it meant something,' I said.

Morny went to the black and chromium safe against the wall and opened it. He came back with five new bills spread out in his fingers like a poker hand. He smoothed them edge to edge, riffled them lightly, and tossed them on the desk in front of me.

'There's your five C's,' he said. 'Take Vannier out of my wife's life and there will be the same again for you. I don't care how you do it and I don't want to know anything about how you do it. Just do it.'

I poked at the crisp new bills with a hungry finger. Then I pushed them away. 'You can pay me when – and if – I deliver,' I said. 'I'll take my payment tonight in a short interview with Miss Conquest.'

Morny didn't touch the money. He lifted the square bottle and poured himself another drink. This time he poured one for me and pushed it across the desk.

'And as for this Phillips murder,' I said, 'Eddie here was following Phillips a little. You want to tell me why?'

'No.'

'The trouble with a case like this is that the information might come from somebody else. When a murder gets into the papers you never know what will come out. If it does, you'll blame me.'

He looked at me steadily and said: 'I don't think so. I was a bit rough when you came in, but you shape up pretty good. I'll take a chance.'

'Thanks,' I said. 'Would you mind telling me why you had Eddie call me up and give me the shakes?'

He looked down and tapped on the desk. 'Linda's an old friend of mine. Young Murdock was out here this afternoon to see her. He told her you were working for old lady Murdock. She told me. I didn't know what the job was. You say you don't take divorce business, so it couldn't be that the old lady hired you to fix anything like that up.' He raised his eyes on the last words and stared at me.

I stared back at him and waited.

'I guess I'm just a fellow who likes his friends,' he said. 'And doesn't want them bothered by dicks.'

'Murdock owes you some money, doesn't he?'

He frowned. 'I don't discuss things like that.'

He finished his drink, nodded and stood up. 'I'll send Linda up to talk to you. Pick your money up.'

He went to the door and out. Eddie Prue unwound his long body and stood up and gave me a dim grey smile that meant nothing and wandered off after Morny.

I lit another cigarette and looked at the dental supply company's bill again. Something squirmed at the back of my mind, dimly. I walked to the window and stood looking out across the valley. A car was winding up a hill towards a big house with a tower that was half glass brick with light behind it. The headlights of the car moved across it and turned in towards a garage. The lights went out and the valley seemed darker.

It was very quiet and quite cool now. The dance band seemed to be somewhere under my feet. It was muffled, and the tune was indistinguishable.

Linda Conquest came in through the open door behind me and shut it and stood looking at me with a cold light in her eyes.

19

She looked like her photo and not like it. She had the wide cool mouth, the short nose, the wide cool eyes, the dark hair parted in the middle and the broad white line between the parting. She was wearing a white coat over her dress, with the collar turned up. She had her hands in the pockets of the coat and a cigarette in her mouth.

She looked older, her eyes were harder, and her lips seemed to have forgotten to smile. They would smile when she was singing, in that staged artificial smile. But in repose they were thin and tight and angry.

She moved over to the desk and stood looking down, as if counting the copper ornaments. She saw the cut-glass decanter, took the stopper out, poured herself a drink and tossed it down with a quick flip of the wrist.

'You're a man named Marlowe?' she asked, looking at me. She put her hips against the end of the desk and crossed her ankles.

I said I was a man named Marlowe.

'By and large,' she said, 'I am quite sure I am not going to like you one damned little bit. So speak your piece and drift away.'

'What I like about this place is everything runs so true to type,' I said. 'The cop on the gate, the shine on the door, the cigarette and check girls, the fat greasy sensual Jew with the tall stately bored showgirl, the well-dressed, drunk and horribly rude director cursing the barman, the silent guy with the gun, the night-club owner with the soft grey hair and the B-picture mannerisms, and now you – the tall dark torcher with the negligent sneer, the husky voice, the hard-boiled vocabulary.'

She said: 'Is that so?' and fitted her cigarette between her lips and drew slowly on it. 'And what about the wise-cracking snooper with the last year's gags and the come-hither smile?'

'And what gives me the right to talk to you at all?' I said.

'I'll bite. What does?'

'She wants it back. Quickly. It has to be fast or there will be trouble.'

'I thought –' she started to say and stopped cold. I watched her remove the sudden trace of interest from her face by monkeying with her cigarette and bending her face over it. 'She wants what back, Mr Marlowe?'

'The Brasher Doubloon.'

She looked up at me and nodded, remembering – letting me see her remembering.

'Oh, the Brasher Doubloon.'

'I bet you completely forgot it,' I said.

'Well, no. I've seen it a number of times,' she said. 'She wants it back, you said. Do you mean she thinks I took it?'

'Yeah. Just that.'

'She's a dirty old liar,' Linda Conquest said.

'What you think doesn't make you a liar,' I said. 'It only sometimes makes you mistaken. Is she wrong?'

'Why would I take her silly old coin?'

'Well – it's worth a lot of money. She thinks you might need money. I gather she was not too generous.'

She laughed, a tight sneering little laugh. 'No,' she said. 'Mrs Elizabeth Bright Murdock would not rate as very generous.'

'Maybe you just took it for spite, kind of,' I said hopefully.

'Maybe I ought to slap your face.' She killed her cigarette in Morny's copper goldfish bowl, speared the crushed stub absently with the letter opener and dropped it into the waste-basket.

'Passing on from that to perhaps more important matters,' I said, 'will you give him a divorce?'

'For twenty-five grand,' she said, not looking at me. 'I should be glad to.'

'You're not in love with the guy, huh?'

'You're breaking my heart, Marlowe.'

'He's in love with you,' I said. 'After all, you did marry him.'

She looked at me lazily. 'Mister, don't think I didn't pay for that mistake.' She lit another cigarette. 'But a girl has to live. And it isn't always as easy as it looks. And so a girl can make a mistake, marry the wrong guy and the wrong family, looking for something that isn't there. Security, or whatever.'

'But not needing any love to do it,' I said.

'I don't want to be too cynical, Marlowe. But you'd be surprised how many girls marry to find a home, especially girls whose arm muscles are all tired out fighting off the kind of optimists that come into these gin and glitter joints.'

'You had a home and you gave it up.'

'It got to be too dear. That port-sodden old fake made the bargain too tough. How do you like her for a client?'

'I've had worse.'

She picked a shred of tobacco off her lips. 'You notice what she's doing to that girl?'

'Merle? I noticed she bullied her.'

'It isn't just that. She has her cutting out dolls. The girl had a shock of some kind and the old brute has used the effect of it to dominate the girl completely. In company she yells at her but in private she's apt to be stroking her hair and whispering in her ear. And the kid sort of shivers.'

'I didn't quite get all that,' I said.

'The kid's in love with Leslie, but she doesn't know it. Emotionally she's about ten years old. Something funny is going to happen in that family one of these days. I'm glad I won't be there.'

I said: 'You're a smart girl, Linda. And you're tough and you're wise. I suppose when you married him you thought you could get your hands on plenty.'

She curled her lip. 'I thought it would at least be a vacation. It wasn't even that. That's a smart, ruthless woman, Marlowe. Whatever she's got you doing, it's not what she says. She's up to something. Watch your step.'

'Would she kill a couple of men?'

She laughed.

'No kidding,' I said. 'A couple of men have been killed and one of them at least is connected with rare coins.'

'I don't get it,' she looked at me levelly. 'Murdered, you mean?'

I nodded.

'You tell Morny all that?'

'About one of them.'

'You tell the cops?'

'About one of them. The same one.'

She moved her eyes over my face. We stared at each other. She looked a little pale, or just tired. I thought she had grown a little paler than before.

'You're making that up,' she said between her teeth.

I grinned and nodded. She seemed to relax then.

'About the Brasher Doubloon?' I said. 'You didn't take it. Okay. About the divorce, what?'

'That's none of your affair.'

'I agree. Well, thanks for talking to me. Do you know a fellow named Vannier?'

'Yes.' Her face froze hard now. 'Not well. He's a friend of Lois.'

'A very good friend.'

'One of these days he's apt to turn out to be a small quiet funeral, too.'

'Hints,' I said, 'have sort of been thrown in that direction. There's something about the guy. Every time his name comes up the party freezes.'

She stared at me and said nothing. I thought that an idea was stirring at the back of her eyes, but if so it didn't come out. She said quietly:

'Morny will sure as hell kill him, if he doesn't lay off Lois.'

'Go on with you. Lois flops at the drop of a hat. Anybody can see that.'

'Perhaps Alex is the one person who can't see it.'

'Vannier hasn't anything to do with my job, anyway. He has no connexion with the Murdocks.'

She lifted a corner of her lip at me and said: 'No? Let me tell you something. No reason why I should. I'm just a great big open-hearted kid. Vannier knows Elizabeth Bright Murdock and well. He never came to the house but once while I was there, but he called on the phone plenty of times. I caught some of the calls. He always asked for Merle.'

'Well – that's funny,' I said. 'Merle, huh?'

She bent to crush out her cigarette and again she speared the stub and dropped it into the waste-basket.

'I'm very tired,' she said suddenly. 'Please go away.'

I stood there for a moment, looking at her and wondering. Then I said: 'Good night, and thanks. Good luck.'

I went out and left her standing there with her hands in the pockets of the white coat, her head bent and her eyes looking at the floor.

It was two o'clock when I got back to Hollywood and put the car away and went upstairs to my apartment. The wind was all gone but the air still had that dryness and lightness of the desert. The air in the apartment was dead and Breeze's cigar butt had made it a little worse than dead. I opened windows and flushed the place through while I undressed and stripped the pockets of my suit.

Out of them with other things came the dental supply company's bill. It still looked like a bill to one H. R. Teager for 30 lb. of crystobolite and 25 lb. of albastone.

I dragged the phone book up on the desk in the living-room and looked up Teager. Then the confused memory clicked into place. His address was 422 West Ninth Street. The address of the Belfont Building was 422 West Ninth Street.

H. R. Teager Dental Laboratories had been one of the names on doors on the sixth floor of the Belfont Building when I did my backstairs crawl away from the office of Elisha Morningstar.

But even the Pinkertons have to sleep, and Marlowe needed far, far more sleep than the Pinkertons. I went to bed.

20

It was just as hot in Pasadena as the day before and the big dark red brick house on Dresden Avenue looked just as cool and the little painted Negro waiting by the hitching block looked just as sad. The same butterfly landed on the same hydrangea bush – or it looked like the same one – the same heavy scent of summer lay on the morning, and the same middle-aged sourpuss with the frontier voice opened to my ring.

She led me along the same hallways to the same sunless sunroom. In it Mrs Elizabeth Bright Murdock sat in the same reed chaise-longue and as I came into the room she was pouring herself a slug from what looked like the same port bottle but was more probably a grandchild.

The maid shut the door, I sat down and put my hat on the floor, just like yesterday, and Mrs Murdock gave me the same hard level stare and said:

'Well?'

'Things are bad,' I said. 'The cops are after me.'

She looked as flustered as a side of beef. 'Indeed. I thought you were more competent than that.'

I brushed it off. 'When I left here yesterday morning a man followed me in a coupé. I don't know what he was doing here or how he got here. I suppose he followed me here, but I feel doubtful about that. I shook him off, but he turned up again in the hall outside my office. He followed me again, so I invited him to explain why and he said he knew who I was and he needed help and asked me to come to his apartment on Bunker Hill and talk to him. I went, after I had seen Mr Morningstar, and found the man shot to death on the floor of his bathroom.'

Mrs Murdock sipped a little port. Her hand might have shaken a little, but the light in the room was too dim for me to be sure. She cleared her throat.

'Go on.'

'His name is George Anson Phillips. A young, blond fellow, rather dumb. He claimed to be a private detective.'

'I never heard of him,' Mrs Murdock said coldly. 'I never saw him to my knowledge and I don't know anything about him. Did you think I employed him to follow you?'

'I didn't know what to think. He talked about pooling our resources and he gave me the impression that he was working for some member of your family. He didn't say so in so many words.'

'He wasn't. You can be quite definite on that.' The baritone voice was as steady as a rock.

'I don't think you know quite as much about your family as you think you do, Mrs Murdock.'

'I know you have been questioning my son – contrary to my orders,' she said coldly.

'I didn't question him. He questioned me. Or tried to.'

'We'll go into that later,' she said harshly. 'What about this man you found shot? You are involved with the police on account of him?'

'Naturally. They want to know why he followed me, what I was working on, why he spoke to me, why he asked me to come to his apartment and why I went. But that is only the half of it.'

She finished her port and poured herself another glass.

'How's your asthma?' I asked.

'Bad,' she said. 'Get on with your story.'

'I saw Morningstar. I told you about that over the phone. He pretended not to have the Brasher Doubloon, but admitted it had been offered to him and said he could get it. As I told you. Then you told me it had been returned to you, so that was that.'

I waited, thinking she would tell me some story about how the coin had been returned, but she just stared at me bleakly over the wineglass.

'So, as I had made a sort of arrangement with Mr Morningstar to pay him a thousand dollars for the coin –'

'You had no authority to do anything like that,' she barked.

I nodded, agreeing with her.

'Maybe I was kidding him a little,' I said. 'And I know I was kidding myself. Anyway, after what you told me over the phone I tried to get in touch with him to tell him the deal was off. He's not in the phone book except at his office. I went to his office. This was quite late. The elevator man said he was still in his office. He was lying on his back on the floor, dead. Killed by a blow on the head and shock, apparently. Old men die easily. The blow might not have been intended to kill him. I called the Receiving Hospital, but didn't give my name.'

'That was wise of you,' she said.

'Was it? It was considerate of me, but I don't think I'd call it wise. I want to be nice, Mrs Murdock. You understand that in your rough way, I hope. But two murders happened in the matter of hours and both the bodies were found by me. And both the victims were connected – in some manner – with your Brasher Doubloon.'

'I don't understand. This other, younger man also?'

'Yes. Didn't I tell you over the phone? I thought I did.' I wrinkled my brow, thinking back. I knew I had.

She said calmly: 'It's possible. I wasn't paying a great deal of attention to what you said. You see, the doubloon had already been returned. And you sounded a little drunk.'

'I wasn't drunk. I might have felt a little shock, but I wasn't drunk. You take all this very calmly.'

'What do you want me to do?'

I took a deep breath. 'I'm connected with one murder already, by having found the body and reported it. I may presently be connected with another, by having found the body and not reporting it. Which is much more serious for me. Even as far as it goes, I have until noon today to disclose the name of my client.'

'That,' she said, still much too calm for my taste, 'would be a breach of confidence. You are not going to do that, I'm sure.'

'I wish you'd leave that damn port alone and make some effort to understand the position,' I snapped at her.

She looked vaguely surprised and pushed her glass away – about four inches away.

'This fellow Phillips,' I said, 'had a licence as a private detective. How did I happen to find him dead? Because he followed me and I spoke to him and he asked me to come to his apartment. And when I got there he was dead. The police know all this. They may even believe it. But they don't believe the connexion between Phillips and me is quite that much of a coincidence. They think there is a deeper connexion between Phillips and me and they insist on knowing what I am doing, who I am working for. Is that clear?'

'You'll find a way out of all that,' she said. 'I expect it to cost me a little more money, of course.'

I felt myself getting pinched around the nose. My mouth felt dry. I needed air. I took another deep breath and another dive into the tub of blubber that was sitting across the room from me on the reed chaise-longue, looking as unperturbed as a bank president refusing a loan.

'I'm working for you,' I said, 'now, this week, today. Next week I'll be working for somebody else, I hope. And the week after that for still somebody else. In order to do that I have to be on reasonably good terms with the police. They don't have to love me, but they have to be fairly sure I am not cheating on them. Assume Phillips knew nothing about the Brasher Doubloon. Assume, even, that he knew about it, but that his death had nothing to do with it. I still have to tell the cops what I know about him. And they have to question anybody they want to question. Can't you understand that?'

'Doesn't the law give you the right to protect a client?' she snapped. 'If it doesn't, what is the use of anyone's hiring a detective?'

I got up and walked around my chair and sat down again. I leaned forward and took hold of my kneecaps and squeezed them until my knuckles glistened.

'The law, whatever it is, is a matter of give-and-take, Mrs Murdock. Like most other things. Even if I had the legal right to stay clammed-up – refuse to talk – and got away with it once, that would be the end of my business. I'd be a guy marked for trouble. One way or another they would get me. I value your business, Mrs Murdock, but not enough to cut my throat for you and bleed in your lap.'

She reached for her glass and emptied it.

'You seem to have made a nice mess of the whole thing,' she said. 'You didn't find my daughter-in-law and you didn't find my Brasher Doubloon. But you found a couple of dead men that I have nothing to do with and you have neatly arranged matters so that I must tell the police all my private and personal business in order to protect you from your own incompetence. That's what I see. If I am wrong, pray correct me.'

She poured some more wine and gulped it too fast and went into a paroxysm of coughing. Her shaking hand slid the glass on to the table, slopping the wine. She threw herself forward in her seat and got purple in the face.

I jumped up and went over and landed one on her beefy back that would have shaken the City Hall.

She let out a long strangled wail and drew her breath in rackingly and stopped coughing. I pressed one of the keys on her dictaphone-box and when somebody answered, metallic and loud, through the metal disk, I said: 'Bring Mrs Murdock a glass of water, quick!' and then let the key up again.

I sat down again and watched her pull herself together. When her breath was coming evenly and without effort, I said: 'You're not tough. You just think you're tough. You been living too long with people that are scared of you. Wait'll you meet up with some law. Those boys are professionals. You're just a spoiled amateur.'

The door opened and the maid came in with a pitcher of ice-water and a glass. She put them down on the table and went out.

I poured Mrs Murdock a glass of water and put it in her hand.

'Sip it, don't drink it. You won't like the taste of it, but it won't hurt you.'

She sipped, then drank half of the glass, then put the glass down and wiped her lips.

'To think,' she said raspingly, 'that out of all the snoopers for hire I could have employed, I had to pick out a man who would bully me in my own home.'

'That's not getting you anywhere, either,' I said. 'We don't have a lot of time. What's our story to the police going to be?'

'The police mean nothing to me. Absolutely nothing. And if you give them my name, I shall regard it as a thoroughly disgusting breach of faith.'

That put me back where we started.

'Murder changes everything, Mrs Murdock. You can't dummy up on a murder case. We'll have to tell them why you employed me and what to do. They won't publish it in the papers, you know. That is, they won't if they believe it. They certainly won't believe you hired me to investigate Elisha Morningstar just because he called up and wanted to buy the doubloon. They may not find out that you couldn't have sold the coin, if you wanted to, because they might not think of that angle. But they won't believe you hired a private detective just to investigate a possible purchaser. Why should you?'

'That's my business, isn't it?'

'No. You can't fob the cops off that way. You have to satisfy them that you are being frank and open and have nothing to hide. As long as they think you are hiding something they never let up. Give them a reasonable and plausible story and they go away cheerful. And the most reasonable and plausible story is always the truth. Any objection to telling it?'

'Every possible objection,' she said. 'But it doesn't seem to make much difference. Do you have to tell them that I suspected my daughter-in-law of stealing the coin and that I was wrong?'

'It would be better.'

'And that it has been returned and how?'

'It would be better.'

'That is going to humiliate me very much.'

I shrugged.

'You're a callous brute,' she said. 'You're a cold-blooded fish. I don't like you. I deeply regret ever having met you.'

'Mutual,' I said.

She reached a thick finger to a key and barked into the talking-box. 'Merle. Ask my son to come in here at once. And I think you may as well come in with him.'

She released the key, pressed her broad fingers together and let her hands drop heavily to her thighs. Her bleak eyes went up to the ceiling.

Her voice was quiet and sad, saying: 'My son took the coin, Mr Marlowe. My son. My own son.'

I didn't say anything. We sat there glaring at each other. In a couple of minutes they both came in and she barked at them to sit down.

21

Leslie Murdock was wearing a greenish slack suit and his hair looked damp, as if he had just been taking a shower. He sat hunched forward, looking at the white buck shoes on his feet, and turning a ring on his finger. He didn't have his long black cigarette-holder and he looked a little lonely without it. Even his moustache seemed to droop a little more than it had in my office.

Merle Davis looked just the same as the day before. Probably she always looked the same. Her copper blonde hair was dragged down just as tight, her shell-rimmed glasses looked just as large and empty, her eyes behind them just as vague. She was even wearing the same one-piece linen dress with short sleeves and no ornament of any kind, not even earrings.

I had the curious feeling of re-living something that had already happened.

Mrs Murdock sipped her port and said quietly:

'All right, son. Tell Mr Marlowe about the doubloon. I'm afraid he has to be told.'

Murdock looked up at me quietly and then dropped his eyes again. His mouth twitched. When he spoke his voice had the toneless quality, a flat tired sound, like a man making a confession after an exhausting battle with his conscience.

'As I told you yesterday in your office, I owe Morny a lot of money. Twelve thousand dollars. I denied it afterwards, but it's true. I do owe it. I didn't want Mother to know. He was pressing me pretty hard for payment. I suppose I knew I would have to tell her in the end, but I was weak enough to want to put it off. I took the doubloon, using her keys one afternoon when she was asleep and Merle was out. I gave it to Morny and he agreed to hold it as security because I explained to him that he couldn't get anything like twelve thousand dollars for it unless he could give its history and show that it was legitimately in his possession.'

He stopped talking and looked up at me to see how I was taking it. Mrs Murdock had her eyes on my face, practically puttied there. The little girl was looking at Murdock with her lips parted and an expression of suffering on her face.

Murdock went on. 'Morny gave me a receipt, in which he agreed to hold the coin as collateral and not to convert it without notice and demand. Something like that. I don't profess to know how legal it was. When this man Morningstar called up and asked about the coin I immediately became suspicious that Morny either was trying to sell it or that he was at least thinking of selling it and was trying to get a valuation on it from somebody who knew about rare coins. I was badly scared.'

He looked up and made a sort of face at me. Maybe it was the face of somebody being badly scared. Then he took his handkerchief out and wiped his forehead and sat holding it between his hands.

'When Merle told me Mother had employed a detective – Merle ought not to have told me, but Mother has promised not to scold her for it.' He looked at his mother. The old war-horse clamped her jaws and looked grim. The little girl had her eyes still on his face and didn't seem to be very worried about the scolding. He went on: 'Then I was sure she had missed the doubloon and had hired you on that account. I didn't really believe she had hired you to find Linda. I knew where Linda was all the time. I went to your office to see what I could find out. I didn't find out very much. I went to see Morny yesterday afternoon and told him about it. At first he laughed in my face, but when I told him that even my mother couldn't sell the coin without violating the terms of Jasper Murdock's will and that she would certainly set the police on him when I told her where the coin was, then he loosened up. He got up and went to the safe and got the coin out and handed it to me without a word. I gave him back his receipt and he tore it up. So I brought the coin home and told Mother about it.'

He stopped talking and wiped his face again. The little girl's eyes moved up and down with the motions of his hand.

In the silence that followed I said: 'Did Morny threaten you?'

He shook his head. 'He said he wanted his money and he needed it and I had better get busy and dig it up. But he wasn't threatening. He was very decent, really. In the circumstances.'

'Where was this?'

'At the Idle Valley Club, in his private office.'

'Was Eddie Prue there?'

The little girl tore her eyes away from his face and looked at me. Mrs Murdock said thickly: 'Who is Eddie Prue?'

'Morny's bodyguard,' I said. 'I didn't waste *all* my time yesterday, Mrs Murdock,' I looked at her son, waiting.

He said: 'No, I didn't see him. I know him by sight, of course. You would only have to see him once to remember him. But he wasn't around yesterday.'

I said: 'Is that all?'

He looked at his mother. She said harshly: 'Isn't it enough?'

'Maybe,' I said. 'Where is the coin now?'

'Where would you expect it to be?' she snapped.

I almost told her, just to see her jump. But I managed to hold it in. I said: 'That seems to take care of that, then.'

Mrs Murdock said heavily: 'Kiss your mother, son, and run along.'

He got up dutifully and went over and kissed her on the forehead. She patted his hand. He went out of the room with his head down and quietly shut the door. I said to Merle: 'I think you had better have him dictate that to you just the way he told it and make a copy of it and get him to sign it.'

She looked startled. The old woman snarled:

'She certainly won't do anything of the sort. Go back to your work, Merle. I wanted you to hear this. But if I ever again catch you violating my confidence, you know what will happen.'

The little girl stood up and smiled at her with shining eyes. 'Oh, yes, Mrs Murdock. I never will. Never. You can trust me.'

'I hope so,' the old dragon growled. 'Get out.'

Merle went out softly.

Two big tears formed themselves in Mrs Murdock's eyes and slowly made their way down the elephant hide of her cheeks, reached the corners of her fleshy nose and slid down her lip. She scrabbled around for her handkerchief, wiped them off and then wiped her eyes. She put the handkerchief away, reached for her wine and said placidly:

'I'm very fond of my son, Mr Marlowe. Very fond. This grieves me deeply. Do you think he will have to tell this story to the police?'

'I hope not,' I said. 'He'll have a hell of a time getting them to believe it.'

Her mouth snapped open and her teeth glinted at me in the dim light. She closed her lips and pressed them tight, scowling at me with her head lowered.

'Just what do you mean by that?' she snapped.

'Just what I said. The story doesn't ring true. It has a fabricated, over-simple sound. Did he make it up himself or did you think it up and teach it to him?'

'Mr Marlowe,' she said in a deadly voice, 'you are treading on very thin ice.'

I waved a hand. 'Aren't we all? All right, suppose it's true. Morny will deny it, and we'll be right back where we started. Morny will have to deny it, because otherwise it would tie him to a couple of murders.'

'Is there anything so unlikely about that being the exact situation?' she blared.

'Why should Morny, a man with backing, protection and some influence, tie himself to a couple of small murders in order to avoid tying himself to something trifling, like selling a pledge? It doesn't make sense to me.'

She stared, saying nothing. I grinned at her, because for the first time she was going to like something I said.

'I found your daughter-in-law, Mrs Murdock. It's a little strange to me that your son, who seems so well under your control, didn't tell you where she was.'

'I didn't ask him,' she said in a curiously quiet voice, for her.

'She's back where she started, singing with the band at the Idle Valley Club. I talked to her. She's a pretty hard sort of girl in a way. She doesn't like you very well. I don't find it impossible to think that she took the coin all right, partly from spite. And I find it slightly less impossible to believe that Leslie knew it or found it out and cooked up that yarn to protect her. He says he's very much in love with her.'

She smiled. It wasn't a beautiful smile, being on slightly the wrong kind of face. But it was a smile.

'Yes,' she said gently. 'Yes. Poor Leslie. He would do just that. And in that case' – she stopped and her smile widened until it was almost ecstatic – 'in that case my dear daughter-in-law may be involved in murder.'

I watched her enjoying the idea for a quarter of a minute. 'And you'd just love that,' I said.

She nodded, still smiling, getting the idea she liked before she got the rudeness in my voice. Then her face stiffened and her lips came together hard. Between them and her teeth she said:

'I don't like your tone. I don't like your tone at all.'

'I don't blame you,' I said. 'I don't like it myself. I don't like anything. I don't like this house or you or the air of repression in the joint, or the squeezed down face of the little girl or that twerp of a son you have, or this case or the truth I'm not told about it and the lies I am told about it and –'

She started yelling then, noise out of a splotched furious face, eyes tossing with fury, sharp with hate:

'Get out! Get out of this house at once! Don't delay one instant! Get out!'

I stood up and reached my hat off the carpet and said:

'I'll be glad to.'

I gave her a sort of tired leer and picked my way to the door and opened it and went out. I shut it quietly, holding the knob with a stiff hand and clicking the lock gently into place.

For no reason at all.

22

Steps gibbered along after me and my name was called and I kept on going until I was in the middle of the living-room. Then I stopped and turned and let her catch up with me, out of breath, her eyes trying to pop through her glasses and her shining copper-blonde hair catching funny little lights from the high windows.

'Mr Marlowe! Please! Please, don't go away. She wants you. She really does!'

'I'll be darned. You've got Sub-deb Bright on your mouth this morning. Looks all right, too.'

She grabbed my sleeve. 'Please!'

'The hell with her,' I said. 'Tell her to jump in the lake. Marlowe can get sore, too. Tell her to jump in two lakes, if one won't hold her. Not clever, but quick.'

I looked down at the hand on my sleeve and patted it. She drew it away swiftly and her eyes looked shocked.

'Please, Mr Marlowe. She's in trouble. She needs you.'

'I'm in trouble, too,' I growled. 'I'm up to my earflaps in trouble. What are you crying about?'

'Oh, I'm really fond of her. I know she's rough and blustery, but her heart is pure gold.'

'To hell with her heart, too,' I said. 'I don't expect to get intimate enough with her for that to make any difference. She's a fat-faced old liar. I've had enough of her. I think she's in trouble all right, but I'm not in the excavating business. I have to get told things.'

'Oh, I'm sure if you would only be patient –'

I put my arm around her shoulders, without thinking. She jumped about three feet and her eyes blazed with panic.

We stood there staring at each other, making breath noises, me with my mouth open as it too frequently is, she with her lips pressed tight and her little pale nostrils quivering. Her face was as pale as the unhandy make-up would let it be.

'Look,' I said slowly, 'did something happen to you when you were a little girl?'

She nodded, very quickly.

'A man scared you or something like that?'

She nodded again. She took her lower lip between her little white teeth.

'And you've been like this ever since?'

She just stood there, looking white.

'Look,' I said, 'I won't do anything to you that will scare you. Not ever.'

Her eyes melted with tears.

'If I touched you,' I said, 'it was just like touching a chair or a door. It didn't mean anything. Is that clear?'

'Yes.' She got a word out at last. Panic still twitched in the depths of her eyes, behind the tears. 'Yes.'

'That takes care of me,' I said. 'I'm all adjusted. Nothing to worry about in me any more. Now take Leslie. He has his mind on other things. You know he's all right – in the way we mean. Right?'

'Oh, yes,' she said. 'Yes, indeed.' Leslie was aces. With her. With me he was a handful of bird gravel.

'Now take the old wine barrel,' I said. 'She's rough and she's tough and she thinks she can eat walls and spit bricks, and she bawls you out, but she's fundamentally decent to you, isn't she?'

'Oh, she is, Mr Marlowe. I was trying to tell you –'

'Sure. Now why don't you get over it? Is he still around – this other one that hurt you?'

She put her hand to her mouth and gnawed the fleshy part at the base of the thumb, looking at me over it, as if it was a balcony.

'He's dead,' she said. 'He fell out of a – out of a – a window.'

I stopped her with my big right hand. 'Oh, that guy. I heard about him. Forget it, can't you?'

'No,' she said, shaking her head seriously behind the hand. 'I can't. I can't seem to forget it at all. Mrs Murdock is always telling me to forget it. She talks to me for the longest times telling me to forget it. But I just can't.'

'It would be a darn sight better,' I snarled, 'if she would keep her fat mouth shut about it for the longest times. She just keeps it alive.'

She looked surprised and rather hurt at that. 'Oh, that isn't all,' she said. 'I was his secretary. She was his wife. He was her first husband. Naturally she doesn't forget it either. How could she?'

I scratched my ear. That seemed sort of noncommittal. There was nothing much in her expression now except that I didn't really think she realized that I was there. I was a voice coming out of somewhere, but rather impersonal. Almost a voice in her own head.

Then I had one of my funny and often unreliable hunches. 'Look,' I said, 'is there someone you meet that has that effect on you? Some one person more than another?'

She looked all round the room. I looked with her. Nobody was under a chair or peeking at us through a door or a window.

'Why do I have to tell you?' she breathed.

'You don't. It's just how you feel about it.'

'Will you promise not to tell anybody – anybody in the whole world, not even Mrs Murdock?'

'Her last of all,' I said. 'I promise.'

She opened her mouth and put a funny little confiding smile on her face, and then it went wrong. Her throat froze up. She made a croaking noise. Her teeth actually rattled.

I wanted to give her a good hard squeeze but I was afraid to touch her. We stood. Nothing happened. We stood. I was about as much use as a humming-bird's spare egg would have been.

Then she turned and ran. I heard her steps going along the hall. I heard a door close.

I went after her along the hall and reached the door. She was sobbing behind it. I stood there and listened to the sobbing.

There was nothing I could do about it. I wondered if there was anything anybody could do about it.

I went back to the glass porch and knocked on the door and opened it and put my head in. Mrs Murdock sat just as I had left her. She didn't seem to have moved at all.

'Who's scaring the life out of that little girl?' I asked her.

'Get out of my house,' she said between her fat lips.

I didn't move. Then she laughed at me hoarsely.

'Do you regard yourself as a clever man, Mr Marlowe?'

'Well, I'm not dripping with it,' I said.

'Suppose you find out for yourself.'

'At your expense?'

She shrugged her heavy shoulders. 'Possibly. It depends. Who knows?'

'You haven't bought a thing,' I said. 'I'm still going to have to talk to the police.'

'I haven't bought anything,' she said, 'and I haven't paid for anything. Except the return of the coin. I'm satisfied to accept that for the money I have already given you. Now go away. You bore me. Unspeakably.'

I shut the door and went back. No sobbing behind the door. Very still, I went on.

I let myself out of the house. I stood there, listening to the sunshine burn the grass. A car started up in back and a grey Mercury came drifting along the drive at the side of the house. Mr Leslie Murdock was driving it. When he saw me he stopped.

He got out of the car and walked quickly over to me. He was nicely dressed; cream-coloured gabardine now, all fresh clothes, slacks, black and white shoes, with polished black toes, a sports coat of very small black and white check, black and white handkerchief, cream shirt, no tie. He had a pair of green sun-glasses on his nose.

He stood close to me and said in a low timid sort of voice: 'I guess you think I'm an awful heel.'

'On account of that story you told about the doubloon?'

'Yes.'

'That didn't affect my way of thinking about you in the least,' I said.

'Well —'

'Just what do you want me to say?'

He moved his smoothly tailored shoulders in a deprecatory shrug. His silly little reddish-brown moustache glittered in the sun.

'I suppose I like to be liked,' he said.

'I'm sorry, Murdock. I like your being that devoted to your wife. If that's what it is.'

'Oh. Didn't you think I was telling the truth? I mean, did you think I was saying all that just to protect her?'

'There was that possibility.'

'I see.' He put a cigarette into the long black holder, which he took from behind his display handkerchief. 'Well – I guess I can take it that you don't like me.' The dim movement of his eyes was visible behind the green lenses, fish moving in a deep pool.

'It's a silly subject,' I said. 'And damned unimportant. To both of us.'

He put a match to the cigarette and inhaled. 'I see,' he said quietly. 'Pardon me for being crude enough to bring it up.'

He turned on his heel and walked back to his car and got in. I watched him drive away before I moved. Then I went over and patted the little painted Negro boy on the head a couple of times before I left.

'Son,' I said to him, 'you're the only person around this house that's not nuts.'

23

The police loudspeaker-box on the wall grunted and a voice said: 'K.G.P.L. Testing.' A click and it went dead.

Detective-Lieutenant Jesse Breeze stretched his arms high in the air and yawned and said: 'Couple of hours late, ain't you?'

I said: 'Yes. But I left a message for you that I would be. I had to go to the dentist.'

'Sit down.'

He had a small littered desk across one corner of the room. He sat in the angle behind it, with a tall bare window to his left and a wall with a large calendar about eye height to his right. The days that had gone down to dust were crossed off carefully in soft black pencil, so that Breeze glancing at the calendar always knew exactly what day it was.

Spangler was sitting sideways at a smaller and much neater desk. It had a green blotter and an onyx pen set and a small brass calendar and an abalone shell full of ashes and matches and cigarette-stubs. Spangler was flipping a handful of bank pens at the felt back of a seat cushion on end against the wall, like a Mexican knife-thrower flipping knives at a target. He wasn't getting anywhere with it. The pens refused to stick.

The room had that remote, heartless, not quite dirty, not quite clean, not quite human smell that such rooms always have. Give a police department a brand new building and in three months all its rooms will smell like that. There must be something symbolic in it.

A New York police reporter wrote once that when you pass in beyond the green lights of the precinct station you pass clear out of this world into a place beyond the law.

I sat down. Breeze got a cellophone-wrapped cigar out of his pocket and the routine with it started. I watched it detail by detail, unvarying, precise. He drew in smoke, shook his match out, laid it gently in the black glass ashtray, and said: 'Hi, Spangler.'

Spangler turned his head and Breeze turned his head. They grinned at each other. Breeze poked the cigar at me.

'Watch him sweat,' he said.

Spangler had to move his feet to turn far enough around to watch me sweat. If I was sweating, I didn't know it.

'You boys are as cute as a couple of lost golf-balls,' I said. 'How in the world do you do it?'

'Skip the wisecracks,' Breeze said. 'Had a busy little morning?'

'Fair,' I said.

He was still grinning. Spangler was still grinning. Whatever it was Breeze was tasting he hated to swallow it.

Finally he cleared his throat, straightened his big freckled face out, turned his head enough so that he was not looking at me but could still see me and said in a vague empty sort of voice:

'Hench confessed.'

Spangler swung clear around to look at me. He leaned forward on the edge of his chair and his lips were parted in an ecstatic half-smile that was almost indecent.

I said: 'What did you use on him – a pickaxe?'

'Nope.'

They were both silent, staring at me.

'A wop,' Breeze said.

'A what?'

'Boy, are you glad?' Breeze said.

'You are going to tell me or are you just going to sit there looking fat and complacent and watch me being glad?'

'We like to watch a guy being glad,' Breeze said. 'We don't often get a chance.'

I put a cigarette in my mouth and jiggled it up and down.

'We used a wop on him,' Breeze said. 'A wop named Palermo.'

'Oh. You know something?'

'What?' Breeze asked.

'I just thought of what is the matter with policeman's dialogue.'

'What?'

'They think every line is a punch line.'

'And every pinch is a good pinch,' Breeze said calmly. 'You want to know – or you want to just wisecrack?'

'I want to know.'

'Was like this, then. Hench was drunk. I mean he was drunk deep inside, not just on the surface. Screwy drunk. He'd been living on it for weeks. He'd practically quit eating and sleeping. Just liquor. He'd got to the point where liquor wasn't making him drunk, it was keeping him sober. It was the last hold he had on the real world. When a guy gets like that and you take his liquor away and don't give him anything to hold him down, he's a lost cuckoo.'

I didn't say anything. Spangler still had the same erotic leer on his young face. Breeze tapped the side of his cigar and no ash fell off and he put it back in his mouth and went on.

'He's a psycho case, but we don't want any psycho case made out of our pinch. We make that clear. We want a guy that don't have any psycho record.'

'I thought you were sure Hench was innocent.'

Breeze nodded vaguely. 'That was last night. Or maybe I was kidding a little. Anyway in the night, bang, Hench is bugs. So they drag him over to the hospital ward and shoot him full of hop. The jail doc. does. That's between you and me. No hop in the record. Get the idea?'

'All too clearly,' I said.

'Yeah.' He looked vaguely suspicious of the remark, but he was too full of his subject to waste time on it. 'Well, this a.m. he is fine. Hop still working, the guy is pale but peaceful. We go see him. How you doing, kid? Anything you need? Any little thing at all? Be glad to get it for you. They treating you nice in here? You know the line.'

'I do,' I said. 'I know the line.'

Spangler licked his lips in a nasty way.

'So after a while he opens his trap just enough to say "Palermo". Palermo is the name of the wop across the street that owns the funeral home and the apartment house and stuff. You remember? Yeah, you remember. On account of he said something about a tall blonde. All hooey. Them wops got tall blondes on the brain. In sets of twelve. But this Palermo is important. I asked around. He gets the vote out up there. He's a guy that can't be pushed around. Well, I don't aim to push him around. I say to Hench, "You mean Palermo's a friend of yours?" He says, "Get Palermo." So we come back here to the hutch and phone Palermo and Palermo says he will be right down. Okay. He is here very soon. We talk like this: Hench wants to see you, Mr Palermo. I wouldn't know why. He's a poor guy, Palermo says. A nice guy. I think he's okay. He wanta see me, that'sa fine. I see him. I see him alone. Without any coppers. I say, Okay, Mr Palermo, and we go over to the hospital ward and Palermo talks to Hench and nobody listens. After a while Palermo comes out and he says, Okay, copper. He make the confess. I pay the lawyer, maybe. I like the poor guy. Just like that. He goes away.'

I didn't say anything. There was a pause. The loudspeaker on the wall put out a bulletin and Breeze cocked his head and listened to ten or twelve words and then ignored it.

'So we go in with a steno and Hench gives us the dope. Phillips made a pass at Hench's girl. That was day before yesterday, out in the hall. Hench was in the room and he saw it, but Phillips got into his apartment and shut the door before Hench could get out. But Hench was sore. He socked the girl in the eye. But that didn't satisfy him. He got to brooding, the way a drunk will brood. He says to himself, that guy can't make a pass at my girl. I'm the boy that will give him something to remember me by. So he keeps an eye open for Phillips. Yesterday afternoon he sees Phillips go into his apartment. He tells the girl to go for a walk. She don't want to go for a walk, so Hench socks her in the other eye. She goes for a walk. Hench knocks on Phillips's door and Phillips opens it. Hench is a little surprised at that, but I told him Phillips was expecting you. Anyway, the door opens and Hench goes in and tells Phillips how he feels and what he is going to do and Phillips is scared and pulls a gun. Hench hits him with a sap. Phillips falls down and Hench ain't satisfied. You hit a guy with a sap and he falls down and what have you? No satisfaction, no revenge. Hench picks the gun off the floor and he is very drunk there being dissatisfied and Phillips grabs for his ankle. Hench doesn't know why he did what he did then. He's all fuzzy in the head. He drags Phillips into the bathroom and gives him the business with his own gun. You like it?'

'I love it,' I said. 'But what is the satisfaction in it for Hench?'

'Well, you know how a drunk is. Anyway, he gives him the business. Well it ain't Hench's gun, you see, but he can't make a suicide out of it. There wouldn't be any satisfaction for him in that. So Hench takes the gun away and puts it under his pillow and takes his own gun out and ditches it. He won't tell us where. Probably passes it to some tough guy in the neighbourhood. Then he finds the girl and they eat.'

'That was a lovely touch,' I said. 'Putting the gun under his pillow. I'd never in the world have thought of that.'

Breeze leaned back in his chair and looked at the ceiling. Spangler, the big part of the entertainment over, swung around in his chair and picked up a couple of bank pens and threw one at the cushion.

'Look at it this way,' Breeze said. 'What was the effect of that stunt? Look how Hench did it. He was drunk, but he was smart. He found that gun and showed it before Phillips was found dead. First we get the idea that a gun is under Hench's pillow that killed a guy – been fired anyway – and then we get the stiff. We believed Hench's story. It seemed reasonable. Why would we think any man would be such a sap as to do what Hench did? It doesn't make any sense. See we believed somebody put the gun under Hench's pillow and took Hench's gun away and ditched it. And suppose Hench ditched the death gun instead of his own, would he have been any better off? Things being what they were we would be bound to suspect him. And that way he wouldn't have started our minds thinking any particular way about him. The way he did he got us thinking he was a harmless drunk that went out and left his door open and somebody ditched a gun on him.'

He waited, with his mouth a little open and the cigar in front of it, held up by a hard freckled hand, and his pale blue eyes full of dim satisfaction.

'Well,' I said, 'if he was going to confess anyway, it wouldn't have made very much difference. Will he cop a plea?'

'Sure. I think so. I figure Palermo could get him off with manslaughter. Naturally, I'm not sure.'

'Why would Palermo want to get him off with anything?'

'He kind of likes Hench. And Palermo is a guy we can't push around.'

I said: 'I see.' I stood up. Spangler looked at me sideways along glistening eyes. 'What about the girl?'

'Won't say a word. She's smart. We can't do anything to her. Nice neat little job all around. You wouldn't kick, would you? Whatever your business is, it's still your business. Get me?'

'And the girl is a tall blonde,' I said. 'Not of the freshest, but still a tall blonde. Although only one. Maybe Palermo doesn't mind.'

'Hell, I never thought of that,' Breeze said. He thought about it and shook it off. 'Nothing in that, Marlowe. Not enough class.'

'Cleaned up and sober, you never can tell,' I said. 'Class is a thing that has a way of dissolving rapidly in alcohol. That all you want with me?'

'Guess so.' He slanted the cigar up and aimed it at my eye. 'Not that I wouldn't like to hear your story. But I don't figure I have an absolute right to insist on it the way things are.'

'That white of you, Breeze,' I said. 'And you, too, Spangler. A lot of the good things in life to both of you.'

They watched me go out, both with their mouths a little open.

I rode down to the big marble lobby and went and got my car out of the official parking lot.

24

Mr Pietro Palermo was sitting in a room which, except for a mahogany roll-top desk, a sacred triptych in gilt frames and a large ebony and ivory crucifixion, looked exactly like a Victorian parlour. It contained a horseshoe sofa and chairs with carved mahogany frames and antimacassars of fine lace. There was an ormolu clock on the grey-green marble mantel, a grandfather clock ticking lazily in the corner, and some wax flowers under a glass dome on an oval table with a marble top and curved elegant legs. The carpet was thick and full of gentle sprays of flowers. There was even a cabinet for bric-à-brac and there was plenty of bric-à-brac in it, little cups of fine china, little figurines in glass and porcelain, odds and ends of ivory and dark rosewood, painted saucers, an early American set of swan salt-cellars, stuff like that.

Long lace curtains hung across the windows, but the room faced south and there was plenty of light. Across the street I could see the windows of the apartment where Geroge Anson Phillips had been killed. The street between was sunny and silent.

The tall Italian with the dark skin and the handsome head of iron grey hair read my card and said:

'I got business in twelve minutes. What you want, Meester Marlowe?'

'I'm the man that found the dead man across the street yesterday. He was a friend of mine.'

His cold black eyes looked me over silently. 'That'sa not what you tell Luke.'

'Luke?'

'He manage the joint for me.'

'I don't talk much to strangers, Mr Palermo.'

'That'sa good. You talk to me, huh?'

'You're a man of standing, an important man. I can talk to you. You saw me yesterday. You described me to the police very accurately, they said.'

'Si. I see much,' he said without emotion.

'You saw a tall blonde woman come out of there yesterday.'

He studied me. 'Not yesterday. Wasa two three days ago. I tell the coppers yesterday.' He snapped his long dark fingers. 'The coppers, bah!'

'Did you see any strangers yesterday, Mr Palermo?'

'Is back way in and out,' he said. 'Is stair from second floor also.' He looked at his wrist-watch.

'Nothing there then,' I said. 'This morning you saw Hench.'

He lifted his eyes and ran them lazily over my face.

'The coppers tell you that, huh?'

'They told me you got Hench to confess. They said he was a friend of yours. How good a friend they didn't know, of course.'

'Hench make the confess, huh?' He smiled, a sudden brilliant smile.

'Only Hench didn't do the killing.' I said.

'No?'

'No.'

'That'sa interesting. Go on, Meester Marlowe.'

'The confession is a lot of baloney. You got him to make it for some reason of your own.'

He stood up and went to the door and called out: 'Tony.'

He sat down again. A short, tough-looking wop came into the room, looked at me and sat down against the wall in a straight chair.

'Tony, thees man a Meester Marlowe. Look, take the card.'

Tony came to get the card and sat down with it. 'You look at thees man very good, Tony. Not forget him, huh?'

Tony said: 'Leave it to me, Mr Palermo.'

Palermo said: 'Was a friend to you, huh? A good friend, huh?'

'Yes.'

'That'sa bad. Yeah. That'sa bad. I tell you something. A man's friend is a man's friend. So I tell you. But you don't tell anybody else. Not the damn coppers, huh?'

'No.'

'That'sa promise, Meester Marlowe. That'sa something not to forget. You not forget?'

'I won't forget.'

'Tony, he not forget you. Get the idea?'

'I gave you my word. What you tell me is between us here.'

'That'sa fine. Okay. I come of large family. Many sisters and brothers. One brother very bad. Almost so bad as Tony.'

Tony grinned.

'Okay, thees brother live very quiet. Across the street. Gotta move. Okay, the coppers fill the joint up. Not so good. Ask too many questions. Not good for business, not good for thees bad brother. You get the idea?'

'Yes,' I said. 'I get the idea.'

'Okay, thees Hench no good, but poor guy, drunk, no job. Pay no rent, but I got lotsa money. So I say, Look, Hench, you make the confess. You sick man. Two three weeks sick. You go into court. I have a lawyer for you. You say to hell with the confess. I was drunk. The damn coppers are stuck. The judge he turn you loose and you come back to me and I take care of you. Okay? So Hench say okay, make the confess. That's all.'

I said: 'And after two or three weeks the bad brother is a long way from here and the trail is cold and the cops will likely just write the Phillips killing off as unsolved. Is that it?'

'Si.' He smiled again. A brilliant warm smile, like the kiss of death.

'That takes care of Hench, Mr Palermo,' I said. 'But it doesn't help me much about my friend.'

He shook his head and looked at his watch again. I stood up. Tony stood up. He wasn't going to do anything, but it's better to be standing up. You move faster.

'The trouble with you birds,' I said, 'is you make mystery of nothing. You have to give the password before you bite a piece of bread. If I went down to headquarters and told the boys anything you have told me, they would laugh in my face. And I would be laughing with them.'

'Tony don't laugh much,' Palermo said.

'The earth is full of people who don't laugh much, Mr Palermo,' I said. 'You ought to know. You put a lot of them where they are.'

'Is my business,' he said, shrugging enormously.

'I'll keep my promise,' I said. 'But in case you should get to doubting that, don't try to make any business for yourself out of me. Because in my part of town I'm a pretty good man and if the business got made out of Tony instead, it would be strictly on the house. No profit.'

Palermo laughed. 'That'sa good,' he said. 'Tony. One funeral – on the house. Okay.'

He stood up and held his hand out, a fine strong warm hand.

25

In the lobby of the Belfont Building, in the single elevator that had light in it, on the piece of folded burlap, the same watery-eyed relic sat motionless, giving his imitation of the forgotten man. I got in with him and said: 'Six.'

The elevator lurched into motion and pounded its way upstairs. It stopped at six, I got out, and the old man leaned out of the car to spit and said in a dull voice:

'What's cookin'?'

I turned around all in one piece, like a dummy on a revolving platform. I stared at him.

He said: 'You got a grey suit on today.'

'So I have,' I said. 'Yes.'

'Looks nice,' he said. 'I like the blue you was wearing yesterday, too.'

'Go on,' I said. 'Give out.'

'You rode up to eight,' he said. 'Twice. Second time was late. You got back on at six. Shortly after that the boys in blue came bustlin' in.'

'Any of them up there now?'

He shook his head. His face was like a vacant lot. 'I ain't told them anything,' he said. 'Too late to mention it now. They'd eat my ass off.'

I said: 'Why?'

'Why I ain't told them? The hell with them. You talked to me civil. Damn few people do that. Hell, I know you didn't have nothing to do with that killing.'

'I played you wrong,' I said. 'Very wrong.' I got a card out and gave it to him. He fished a pair of metal-framed glasses out of his pocket, perched them on his nose and held the card a foot away from them. He read it slowly, moving his lips, looked at me over the glasses, handed me back the card.

'Better keep it,' he said. 'Case I get careless and drop it. Mighty interestin' life yours, I guess.'

'Yes and no. What was the name?'

'Grandy. Just call me Pop. Who killed him?'

'I don't know. Did you notice anybody going up there or coming down – anybody that seemed out of place in this building, or strange to you?'

'I don't notice much,' he said. 'I just happened to notice you.'

'A tall blonde, for instance, or a tall slender man with sideburns, about thirty-five years old.'

'Nope.'

'Everybody going up or down about then would ride in your car.'

He nodded his worn head. 'Less they used the fire stairs. They come out in the alley, bar-lock door. Party would have to come in this way, but there's stairs back of the elevator to the second floor. From there they can get to the fire stairs. Nothing to it.'

I nodded. 'Mr Grandy, could you use a five-dollar bill – not as a bribe in any sense, but as a token of esteem from a sincere friend?'

'Son, I could use a five-dollar bill so rough Abe Lincoln's whiskers would be all lathered up with sweat.'

I gave him one. I looked at it before I passed it over. It was Lincoln on the five, all right.

He tucked it small and put it away deep in his pocket. 'That's right nice of you,' he said. 'I hope to hell you don't think I was fishin'.'

I shook my head and went along the corridor, reading the names again. *Dr E. J. Blaskowitz, Chiropractic Physician. Dalton and Rees Typewriting Service. L. Pridview, Public Accountant.* Four blank doors. *Moss Mailing Company.* Two more blank doors. *H. R. Teager, Dental Laboratories.* In the same relative position as the Morningstar office two floors above, but the rooms were cut up differently. Teager had only one door and there was more wall space in between his door and the next one.

The knob didn't turn. I knocked. There was no answer. I knocked harder, with the same result. I went back to the elevator. It was still at the sixth floor. Pop Grandy watched me come as if he had never seen me before.

'Know anything about H. R. Teager?' I asked him.

He thought. 'Heavy-set, oldish, sloppy clothes, dirty finger-nails, like mine. Come to think I didn't see him in today.'

'Do you think the super would let me into his office to look around?'

'Pretty nosey, the super is. I wouldn't recommend it.'

He turned his head very slowly and looked up the side of the car. Over his head on a big metal ring a key was hanging. A pass-key. Pop Grandy turned his head back to normal position, stood up off his stool and said: 'Right now I gotta go to the can.'

He went. When the door had closed behind him I took the key off the cage wall and went back along to the office of H. R. Teager, unlocked it and went in.

Inside was a small windowless ante-room on the furnishings of which a great deal of expense had been spared. Two chairs, a smoking-stand from a cut-rate drug-store, a standing lamp from the basement of some borax emporium, a flat stained wood table with some old picture magazines on it. The door closed behind me on the door-closer and the place went dark except for what little light came through the pebbled glass panel. I pulled the chain switch of the lamp and went over to the inner door in a wall that cut across the room. It was marked: *H. R. Teager. Private*. It was not locked.

Inside it there was a square office with two uncurtained east windows and very dusty sills. There was a swivel-chair and two straight chairs, both plain hard stained wood, and there was a squarish flat-topped desk. There was nothing on the top of it except an old blotter and a cheap pen set and a round glass ashtray with cigar ash in it. The drawers of the desk contained some dusty paper linings, a few wire clips, rubber bands, worndown pencils, pens, rusty pen points, used blotters, four uncancelled two-cent stamps, and some printed letterheads, envelopes and bill forms.

The wire paper-basket was full of junk. I almost wasted ten minutes going through it rather carefully. At the end of that time I knew what I was pretty sure of already: that H. R. Teager carried on a small business as a dental technician doing laboratory work for a number of dentists in unprosperous sections of the city, the kind of dentists who have shabby offices on second floor walk-ups over stores, who lack both the skill and the equipment to do their own laboratory work, and who like to send it out to men like themselves, rather than to the big efficient hard-boiled laboratories who wouldn't give them any credit.

I did find one thing. Teager's home address at 1354B Toberman Street on the receipted part of a gas bill.

I straightened up, dumped the stuff back into the basket and went over to the wooden door marked *Laboratory*. It had a new Yale lock on it and the pass-key didn't fit it. That was that. I switched off the lamp in the outer office and left.

The elevator was downstairs again. I rang for it and when it came up I sidled in around Pop Grandy, hiding the key, and hung it up over his head. The ring tinkled against the cage. He grinned.

'He's gone,' I said. 'Must have left last night. Must have been carrying a lot of stuff. His desk is cleaned out.'

Pop Grandy nodded. 'Carried two suitcases. I wouldn't notice that, though. Most always does carry a suitcase. I figure he picks up and delivers his work.'

'Work such as what?' I asked as the car growled down. Just to be saying something.

'Such as makin' teeth that don't fit,' Pop Grandy said. 'For poor old bastards like me.'

'You wouldn't notice,' I said, as the doors struggled open on the lobby. 'You wouldn't notice the colour of a humming-bird's eye at fifty feet. Not much you wouldn't.'

He grinned. 'What's he done?'

'I'm going over to his house and find out,' I said. 'I think most likely he's taken a cruise to nowhere.'

'I'd shift places with him,' Pop Grandy said. 'Even if he only got to Frisco and got pinched there, I'd shift places with him.'

26

Toberman Street. A wide dusty street, off Pico. No. 1354B was an upstairs flat, south, in a yellow and white frame building. The entrance door was on the porch, beside another marked 1352B. The entrances to the downstairs flats were at right angles, facing each other across the width of the porch. I kept on ringing the bell, even after I was sure that nobody would answer it. In a neighbourhood like that there is always an expert window-peeker.

Sure enough the door of 1354A was pulled open and a small bright-eyed woman looked out at me. Her dark hair had been washed and waved and was an intricate mass of bobby pins.

'You want Mrs Teager?' she shrilled.

'Mr or Mrs.'

'They gone away last night on their vacation. They loaded up and gone away late. They had me stop the milk and the paper. They didn't have much time. Kind of sudden, it was.'

'Thanks. What kind of car do they drive?'

The heart-rending dialogue of some love serial came out of the room behind her and hit me in the face like a wet dish-towel.

The bright-eyed woman said: 'You a friend of theirs?' In her voice, suspicion was as thick as the ham in her radio.

'Never mind,' I said in a tough voice. 'All we want is our money. Lots of ways to find out what car they were driving.'

The woman cocked her head, listening. 'That's Beula May,' she told me with a sad smile. 'She won't go to the dance with Doctor Myers. I was scared she wouldn't.'

'Aw hell,' I said, and went back to my car and drove on home to Hollywood.

The office was empty. I unlocked my inner room and threw the windows up and sat down.

Another day drawing to its end, the air dull and tired, the heavy growl of homing traffic on the boulevard, and Marlowe in his office nibbling a drink and sorting the day's mail. Four advertisements; two bills; a handsome coloured postcard from a hotel in Santa Rosa where I had stayed for four days last year, working on a case; a long, badly typed letter from a man named Peabody in Sausalito, the general and slightly cloudy drift of which was that a sample of the handwriting of a suspected person would, when exposed to the searching Peabody examination, reveal the inner emotional characteristics of the individual, classified according to both the Freudian and Jung systems.

There was a stamped addressed envelope inside. As I tore the stamp off and threw the letter and envelope away I had a vision of a pathetic old rooster in long hair, black felt hat and black bow tie, rocking on a rickety porch in front of a lettered window, with the smell of ham hocks and cabbage coming out of the door at his elbow.

I sighed, retrieved the envelope, wrote its name and address on a fresh one, folded a dollar bill into a sheet of paper and wrote on it: 'This is positively the last contribution.' I signed my name, sealed the envelope, stuck a stamp on it and poured another drink.

I filled and lit my pipe and sat there smoking. Nobody came in, nobody called, nothing happened, nobody cared whether I died or went to El Paso.

Little by little the roar of the traffic quieted down. The sky lost its glare. Over in the west it would be red. An early neon light showed a block away, diagonally over roofs. The ventilator churned dully in the wall of the coffee shop down in the alley. A truck filled and backed and growled its way out on to the boulevard.

Finally the telephone rang. I answered it and the voice said: 'Mr Marlowe? This is Mr Shaw. At the Bristol.'

'Yes, Mr Shaw. How are you?'

'I'm very well, thanks, Mr Marlowe. I hope you are the same. There's a young lady here asking to be let into your apartment. I don't know why.'

'Me neither, Mr Shaw. I didn't order anything like that. Does she give a name?'

'Oh yes. Quite. Her name is Davis. Miss Merle Davis. She is – what shall I say ? – quite verging on the hysterical.'

'Let her in,' I said, rapidly. 'I'll be there in ten minutes. She's the secretary of a client. It's a business matter entirely.'

'Quite. Oh yes. Shall I – er – remain with her?'

'Whatever you think,' I said and hung up.

Passing the open door of the wash cabinet I saw a stiff excited face in the glass.

27

As I turned the key in my door and opened it Shaw was already standing up from the davenport. He was a tall man with glasses and a high-domed bald head that made his ears look as if they had slipped down on his head. He had the fixed smile of polite idiocy on his face.

The girl sat in my easy-chair behind the chess table. She wasn't doing anything, just sitting there.

'Ah, there you are, Mr Marlowe,' Shaw chirped. 'Yes. Quite. Miss Davis and I have been having such an interesting little conversation. I was telling her I originally came from England. She hasn't – er – told me where she came from.' He was half-way to the door saying this.

'Very kind of you, Mr Shaw,' I said.

'Not at all,' he chirped. 'Not at all. I'll just run along now. My dinner, possibly –'

'It's very nice of you,' I said. 'I appreciate it.'

He nodded and was gone. The unnatural brightness of his smile seemed to linger in the air after the door closed like the smile of a Cheshire cat.

I said: 'Hello, there.'

She said: 'Hello.' Her voice was quite calm, quite serious. She was wearing a brownish linen coat and skirt, a broad-brimmed low-crowned straw hat with a brown velvet band that exactly matched the colour of her shoes and the leather trimming on the edges of her linen envelope bag. The hat was tilted rather daringly, for her. She was not wearing her glasses.

Except for her face she would have looked all right. In the first place her eyes were quite mad. There was white showing all around the iris and they had a sort of fixed look. When they moved the movement was so stiff that you could almost hear something creak. Her mouth was in a tight line at the corners, but the middle part of her upper lip kept lifting off her teeth, upwards and outwards as if fine threads attached to the edge of the lip were pulling it. It would go up so far that it didn't seem possible, and then the entire lower part of her face would go into a spasm and when the spasm was over her mouth would be tight shut, and then the process would slowly start all over again. In addition to this there was something wrong with her neck, so that very slowly her head was drawn around to the left about forty-five degrees. It would stop there, her neck would twitch, and her head would slide back the way it had come.

The combination of these two movements, taken with the immobility of her body, the tight-clasped hands in her lap, and the fixed stare of her eyes, was enough to start anybody's nerves backfiring.

There was a can of tobacco on the desk, between which and her chair was the chess table with the chessmen in their box. I got the pipe out of my pocket and went over to fill it at the can of tobacco. That put me just on the other side of the chess table from her. Her bag was lying on the edge of the table, in front of her and a little to one side. She jumped a little when I went over there, but after that she was just like before. She even made an effort to smile.

I filled the pipe and struck a paper match and lit it and stood there holding the match after I had blown it out.

'You're not wearing your glasses,' I said.

She spoke. Her voice was quiet, composed. 'Oh, I only wear them around the house and for reading. They're in my bag.'

'You're in the house now,' I said. 'You ought to be wearing them.'

I reached casually for the bag. She didn't move. She didn't watch my hands. Her eyes were on my face. I turned my body a little as I opened the bag. I fished the glass case out and slid it across the table.

'Put them on,' I said.

'Oh, yes, I'll put them on,' she said. 'But I'll have to take my hat off, I think . . .'

'Yes, take your hat off,' I said.

She took her hat off and held it on her knees. Then she remembered about the glasses and forgot about the hat. The hat fell on the floor while she reached for the glasses. She put them on. That helped her appearance a lot, I thought.

While she was doing this I got the gun out of her bag and slid it into my hip pocket. I didn't think she saw me. It looked like the same Colt .25 automatic with the walnut grip that I had seen in the top right-hand drawer of her desk the day before.

I went back to the davenport and sat down and said: 'Well, here we are. What do we do now? Are you hungry?'

'I've been over to Mr Vannier's house,' she said.

'Oh.'

'He lives in Sherman Oaks. At the end of Escamillo Drive. At the very end.'

'Quite, probably,' I said without meaning, and tried to blow a smoke ring, but didn't make it. A nerve in my cheek was trying to twang like a wire. I didn't like it.

'Yes,' she said in her composed voice, with her upper lip still doing the hoist and flop movement and her chin still swinging around at anchor and back again. 'It's very quiet there. Mr Vannier has been living there three years now. Before that he lived in the Hollywood hills, on Diamond Street. Another man lived with him there, but they didn't get along very well, Mr Vannier said.'

'I feel as if I could understand that, too,' I said. 'How long have you known Mr Vannier?'

'I've known him eight years. I haven't known him very well. I have had to take him a – a parcel now and then. He liked to have me bring it myself.'

I tried again with a smoke ring. Nope.

'Of course,' she said, 'I never liked him very well. I was afraid he would – I was afraid he –'

'But he didn't,' I said.

For the first time her face got a human natural expression – surprise.

'No,' she said. 'He didn't. That is, he didn't really. But he had his pyjamas on.'

'Taking it easy,' I said. 'Lying around all afternoon with his pyjamas on. Well, some guys have all the luck, don't they?'

'Well you have to know something,' she said seriously. 'Something that makes people pay you money. Mrs Murdock has been wonderful to me, hasn't she?'

'She certainly has,' I said. 'How much were you taking him today?'

'Only five hundred dollars. Mrs Murdock said that was all she could spare, and she couldn't really spare that. She said it would have to stop. It couldn't go on. Mr Vannier would always promise to stop, but he never did.'

'It's a way they have,' I said.

'So there was only one thing to do. I've known that for years, really. It was all my fault and Mrs Murdock has been so wonderful to me. It couldn't make me any worse than I was already, could it?'

I put my hand up and rubbed my cheek hard, to quiet the nerve. She forgot that I hadn't answered her and went on again.

'So I did it,' she said. 'He was there in his pyjamas, with a glass beside him. He was leering at me. He didn't even get up to let me in. But there was a key in the front door. Somebody had left a key there. It was – it was –' her voice jammed in her throat.

'It was a key in the front door,' I said. 'So you were able to get in.'

'Yes.' She nodded and almost smiled again. 'There wasn't anything to it, really. I don't even remember hearing the noise. But there must have been a noise, of course. Quite a loud noise.'

'I suppose so,' I said.

'I went over quite close to him, so I couldn't miss,' she said.

'And what did Mr Vannier do?'

'He didn't do anything at all. He just leered, sort of. Well, that's all there is to it. I didn't like to go back to Mrs Murdock and make any more trouble for her. And for Leslie.' Her voice hushed on the name, and hung suspended, and a little shiver rippled over her body. 'So I came here,' she said. 'And when you didn't answer the bell, I found the office and asked the manager to let me in and wait for you. I knew you would know what to do.'

'And what did you touch in the house while you were there?' I asked. 'Can you remember at all? I mean, besides the front door. Did you just go in at the door and come out without touching anything in the house?'

She thought and her face stopped moving. 'Oh, I remember one thing,' she said. 'I put the light out. Before I left. It was a lamp. One of these lamps that shine upwards, with big bulbs. I put that out.'

I nodded and smiled at her. Marlowe, one smile, cheerful.

'What time was this – how long ago?'

'Oh, just before I came over here. I drove. I had Mrs Murdock's car. The one you asked about yesterday. I forgot to tell you that she didn't take it when she went away. Or did I? No, I remember now I did tell you.'

'Let's see,' I said. 'Half an hour to drive here, anyway. You've been here close to an hour. That would be about five-thirty when you left Mr Vannier's house. And you put the light off.'

'That's right.' She nodded again, quite brightly. Pleased at remembering. 'I put the light out.'

'Would you care for a drink?' I asked her.

'Oh, no.' She shook her head quite vigorously. 'I never drink anything at all.'

'Would you mind if I had one?'

'Certainly not. Why should I?'

I stood up, gave her a studying look. Her lip was still going up and her head was still going round, but I thought not so far. It was like a rhythm which is dying down.

It was difficult to know how far to go with this. It might be that the more she talked, the better. Nobody knows very much about the time of absorption of a shock.

I said: 'Where is your home?'

'Why – I live with Mrs Murdock. In Pasadena.'

'I mean, your real home. Where your folks are.'

'My parents live in Wichita,' she said. 'But I don't go there – ever. I write once in a while, but I haven't seen them for years.'

'What does your father do?'

'He has a dog and cat hospital. He's a veterinarian. I hope they won't have to know. They didn't about the other time. Mrs Murdock kept it from everybody.'

'Maybe they won't have to know,' I said. 'I'll get my drink.'

I went out round the back of her chair to the kitchen and poured it and I made it a drink that was a drink. I put it down in a lump and took the little gun off my hip and saw that the safety was on. I smelled the muzzle, broke out the magazine. There was a cartridge in the chamber, but it was one of those guns that won't fire when the magazine is out. I held it so that I could look into the breech. The cartridge in there was the wrong size and was crooked against the breech block. It looked like a .32. The cartridges in the magazine were the right size, .25's. I fitted the gun together again and went back to the living-room.

I hadn't heard a sound. She had just slid forward in a pile in front of the chair, on top of her nice hat. She was as cold as a mackerel.

I spread her out a little and took her glasses off and made sure she hadn't swallowed her tongue. I wedged my folded handkerchief into the corner of her mouth so that she wouldn't bite her tongue when she came out of it. I went to the phone and called Carl Moss.

'Phil Marlowe, Doc. Any more patients or are you through?'

'All through,' he said. 'Leaving. Trouble?'

'I'm home,' I said. 'Four-o-eight Bristol Apartments, if you don't remember. I've got a girl here who has pulled a faint. I'm not afraid of the faint, I'm afraid she may be nuts when she comes out of it.'

'Don't give her any liquor,' he said. 'I'm on my way.'

I hung up and knelt down beside her. I began to rub her temples. She opened her eyes. The lips started to lift. I pulled the handkerchief out of her mouth. She looked up at me and said: 'I've been over to Mr Vannier's house. He lives in Sherman Oaks. I –'

'Do you mind if I lift you up and put you on the davenport? You know me – Marlowe, the big boob that goes around asking all the wrong questions.'

'Hello,' she said.

I lifted her. She went stiff on me, but she didn't say anything. I put her on the davenport and tucked her skirt down over her legs and put a pillow under her head and picked her hat up. It was as flat as a flounder. I did what I could to straighten it out and laid it aside on the desk.

She watched me sideways, doing this.

'Did you call the police?' she asked softly.

'Not yet,' I said. 'I've been too busy.'

She looked surprised. I wasn't quite sure, but I thought she looked a little hurt, too.

I opened up her bag and turned my back to her to slip the gun back into it. While I was doing that I took a look at what else was in the bag. The usual oddments, a couple of handkerchiefs, lipstick, a silver and red enamel compact with powder in it, a couple of tissues, a purse with some hard money and a few dollar bills, no cigarettes, no matches, no tickets for the theatre.

I pulled open the zipper pocket at the back. That held her driver's licence and a flat packet of bills, ten fifties. I riffled them. None of them brand new. Tucked into the rubber band that held them was a folded paper. I took it out and opened it and read it. It was neatly typewritten, dated that day. It was a common receipt form and it would, when signed, acknowledge the receipt of $500. 'Payment on Account.'

It didn't seem as if it would ever be signed now. I slipped money and receipt into my pocket. I closed the bag and looked over at the davenport.

She was looking at the ceiling and doing that with her face again. I went into my bedroom and got a blanket to throw over her.

Then I went into the kitchen for another drink.

28

Dr Carl Moss was a big burly Jew with a Hitler moustache, pop eyes and the calmness of a glacier. He put his hat and bag on a chair and went over and stood looking down at the girl on the davenport inscrutably.

'I'm Dr Moss,' he said. 'How are you?'

She said: 'Aren't you the police?'

He bent down and felt her pulse and then stood there watching her breathing. 'Where does it hurt, Miss –'

'Davis,' I said. 'Miss Merle Davis.'

'Miss Davis.'

'Nothing hurts me,' she said, staring up at him. 'I – I don't even know why I'm lying here like this. I thought you were the police. You see, I killed a man.'

'Well, that's a normal human impulse,' he said. 'I've killed dozens.' He didn't smile.

She lifted her lip and moved her head round for him.

'You know you don't have to do that,' he said, quite gently. 'You feel a twitch of the nerves here and there and you proceed to build it up and dramatize it. You can control it, if you want to.'

'Can I?' she whispered.

'If you want to,' he said. 'You don't have to. It doesn't make any difference to me either way. Nothing pains at all, eh?'

'No.' She shook her head.

He patted her shoulder and walked out to the kitchen. I went after him. He leaned his hips against the sink and gave me a cool stare. 'What's the story?'

'She's the secretary of a client. A Mrs Murdock in Pasadena. The client is rather a brute. About eight years ago a man made a hard press at Merle. How hard I don't know. Then – I don't mean immediately – but around that time he fell out of a window or jumped. Since then she can't have a man touch her – not in the most casual way, I mean.'

'Uh-huh.' His pop eyes continued to read my face. 'Does she think he jumped out of the window on her account?'

'I don't know. Mrs Murdock is the man's widow. She married again and her second husband is dead too. Merle has stayed with her. The old woman treats her like a rough parent treats a naughty child.'

'I see. Regressive.'

'What's that?'

'Emotional shock, and the subconscious attempt to escape back to childhood. If Mrs Murdock scolds her a good deal but not too much, that would increase the tendency. Identification of childhood subordination with childhood protection.'

'Do we have to go into that stuff?' I growled.

He grinned at me calmly. 'Look, pal. The girl's obviously a neurotic. It's partly induced and partly deliberate. I mean to say that she really enjoys a lot of it. Even if she doesn't realize that she enjoys it. However, that's not of immediate importance. What's this about killing a man?'

'A man named Vannier who lives in Sherman Oaks. There seems to be some blackmail angle. Merle had to take him his money, from time to time. She was afraid of him. I've seen the guy. A nasty type. She went over there this afternoon and she says she shot him.'

'Why?'

'She says she didn't like the way he leered at her.'

'Shot him with what?'

'She had a gun in her bag. Don't ask me why. I don't know. But if she shot him, it wasn't with that. The gun's got a wrong cartridge in the breech. It can't be fired as it is. Also it hasn't been fired.'

'This is too deep for me,' he said. 'I'm just a doctor. What did you want me to do with her?'

'Also,' I said, ignoring the question, 'she said the lamp was turned on and it was about five-thirty of a nice summery afternoon. And the guy was wearing his sleeping-suit and there was a key in the lock of the front door. And he didn't get up to let her in. He just sort of sat there sort of leering.'

He nodded and said: 'Oh.' He pushed a cigarette between his heavy lips and lit it. 'If you expect me to tell you whether she really thinks she shot him, I can't do it. From your description I gather that the man is shot. That's so?'

'Brother, I haven't been there. But that much seems pretty clear.'

'If she thinks she shot him and isn't just acting – and, God, how these types do act! – that indicates it was not a new idea to her. You say she carried a gun. So perhaps it wasn't. She may have a guilt complex. Wants to be punished, wants to expiate some real or imaginary crime. Again I ask what do you want me to do with her? She's not sick, she's not loony.'

'She's not going back to Pasadena.'

'Oh.' He looked at me curiously. 'Any family?'

'In Wichita. Father's a vet. I'll call him, but she'll have to stay here tonight.'

'I don't know about that. Does she trust you enough to spend the night in your apartment?'

'She came here of her own free will, and not socially. So I guess she does.'

He shrugged and fingered the sidewall of his coarse black moustache. 'Well, I'll give her some nembutal and we'll put her to bed. And you can walk the floor wrestling with your conscience.'

'I have to go out,' I said. 'I have to go over there and see what has happened. And she can't stay here alone. And no man, not even a doctor, is going to put her to bed. Get a nurse. I'll sleep somewhere else.'

'Phil Marlowe,' he said. 'The shop-soiled Galahad. Okay. I'll stick around until the nurse comes.'

He went back into the living-room and telephoned the Nurses' Registry. Then he telephoned his wife. While he was telephoning, Merle sat up on the davenport and clasped her hands primly in her lap.

'I don't see why the lamp was on,' she said. 'It wasn't dark in the house at all. Not that dark.'

I said: 'What's your dad's first name?'

'Dr Wilbur Davis. Why?'

'Wouldn't you like something to eat?'

At the telephone Carl Moss said to me: 'Tomorrow will do for that. This is probably just a lull.' He finished his call, hung up, went to his bag and came back with a couple of yellow capsules in his hand on a fragment of cotton. He got a glass of water, handed her the capsules and said: 'Swallow.'

'I'm not sick, am I?' she said, looking up at him.

'Swallow, my child, swallow.'

She took them and put them in her mouth and took the glass of water and drank.

I put my hat on and left.

On the way down in the elevator I remembered that there hadn't been any keys in her bag, so I stopped at the lobby floor and went out through the lobby to the Bristol Avenue side. The car was not hard to find. It was parked crookedly about two feet from the kerb. It was a grey Mercury convertible and its licence number was 2XIIII. I remembered that this was the number of Linda Murdock's car.

A leather keyholder hung in the lock. I got into the car, started the engine, saw that there was plenty of gas, and drove it away. It was a nice eager little car. Over Cahuenga Pass it had the wings of a bird.

29

Escamillo Drive made three jogs in four blocks, for no reason that I could see. It was very narrow, averaged about five houses to a block and was overhung by a section of shaggy brown foothill on which nothing lived at this season except sage and manzanita. In its fifth and last block, Escamillo Drive did a neat little curve to the left, hit the base of the hill hard, and died without a whimper. In this last block were three houses, two on the opposite entering corners, one at the dead end. This was Vannier's. My spotlight showed the key still in the door.

It was a narrow English type bungalow with a high roof, leaded front windows, a garage to the side, and a trailer parked beside the garage. The early moon lay quietly on its small lawn. A large oak tree grew almost on the front porch. There was no light in the house now, none visible from the front at least.

From the lay of the land a light in the living-room in the daytime did not seem utterly improbable. It would be a dark house except in the morning. As a love-nest the place had its points, but as a residence for a blackmailer I didn't give it very high marks. Sudden death can come to you anywhere, but Vannier had made it too easy.

I turned into his driveway, backed to get myself pointed out of the dead end, and then drove down to the corner and parked there. I walked back in the street because there was no sidewalk. The front door was made of iron-bound oak planks, bevelled where they joined. There was a thumb latch instead of a knob. The head of the flat key projected from the lock. I rang the bell, and it rang with that remote-sound of a bell ringing at night in an empty house. I walked round the oak tree and poked the light of my pencil flash between the leaves of the garage door. There was a car in there. I went back round the house and looked at a small flowerless yard, walled in by a low wall of fieldstone. Three more oak trees, a table and a couple of all-metal chairs under one of them. A rubbish burner at the back. I shone my light into the trailer before I went back to the front. There didn't seem to be anybody in the trailer. Its door was locked.

I opened the front door, leaving the key in the lock. I wasn't going to work any dipsy-doodle in this place. Whatever was, was. I just wanted to make sure. I felt round on the wall inside the door for a light switch, found one and tilted it up. Pale flame bulbs in pairs in wall brackets went on all around the room, showing me the big lamp Merle had spoken of, as well as other things. I went over to switch the lamp on, then back to switch the wall light off. The lamp had a big bulb inverted in a porcelain glass bowl. You could get three different intensities of light. I clicked the button switch around until I had all there was.

The room ran from front to back, with a door at the back and an arch up front to the right. Inside that was a small dining-room. Curtains were half-drawn across the arch, heavy pale green brocade curtains, far from new. The fireplace was in the middle of the left wall, bookshelves opposite and on both sides of it, not built in. Two davenports angled across the corners of the room and there was one gold chair, one pink chair, one brown chair, one brown and gold jacquard chair with footstool.

Yellow pyjama legs were on the footstool, bare ankles, feet in dark green morocco leather slippers. My eyes ran up from the feet, slowly, carefully. A dark green figured silk robe, tied with a tasselled belt. Open above the belt showing a monogram on the pocket of the pyjamas. A handkerchief neat in the pocket, two stiff points of white linen. A yellow neck, the face turned sideways, pointed at a mirror on the wall. I walked round and looked in the mirror. The face leered all right.

The left arm and hand lay between a knee and the side of the chair, the right arm hung outside the chair, the ends of the fingers touching the rug. Touching also the butt of a small revolver, about .32 calibre, a belly gun, with practically no barrel. The right side of the face was against the back of the chair, but the right shoulder was dark brown with blood and there was some on the right sleeve. Also on the chair. A lot of it on the chair.

I didn't think his head had taken that position naturally. Some sensitive soul had not liked the right side of it.

I lifted my foot and gently pushed the footstool sideways a few inches.

The heels of the slippers moved reluctantly over the jacquard surface, not with it. The man was as stiff as a board. So I reached down and touched his ankle. Ice was never half as cold.

On a table at his right elbow was half of a dead drink, an ashtray full of butts and ash. Three of the butts had lipstick on them. Bright Chinese-red lipstick. What a blonde would use.

There was another ashtray beside another chair. Matches in it and a lot of ash, but no stubs.

On the air of the room a rather heavy perfume struggled with the smell of death, and lost. Although defeated, it was still there.

I poked through the rest of the house, putting lights on and off. Two bedrooms, one furnished in light wood, one in red maple. The light one seemed to be a spare. A nice bathroom with tan and mulberry tiling and a stall shower with a glass door. The kitchen was small. There were a lot of bottles on the sink. Lots of bottles, lots of glass, lots of fingerprints, lots of evidence. Or not, as the case might be.

I went back to the living-room and stood in the middle of the floor breathing with my mouth as far as possible and wondering what the score would be when I turned this one in. Turn this one in and report that I was the fellow who had found Morningstar and run away. The score would be low, very low. Marlowe, three murders. Marlowe practically kneedeep in dead men. And no reasonable, logical, friendly account of himself whatsoever. But that wasn't the worst of it. The minute I opened up I would cease to be a free agent. I would be through with doing whatever it was I was doing and with finding out whatever it was I was finding out.

Carl Moss might be willing to protect Merle with the mantle of Aesculapius, up to a point. Or he might think it would do her more good in the long run to get it all off her chest, whatever it was.

I wandered back to the jacquard chair and set my teeth and grabbed enough of his hair to pull the head away from the chair back. The bullet had gone in at the temple. The set-up could be for suicide. But people like Louis Vannier do not commit suicide. A blackmailer, even a scared blackmailer, has a sense of power, and loves it.

I let the head go back where it wanted to go and leaned down to scrub my hand on the nap of the rug. Leaning down I saw the corner of a picture frame under the lower shelf of the table at Vannier's elbow. I went round and reached for it with a handkerchief.

The glass was cracked across. It had fallen off the wall. I could see the small nail. I could make a guess how it had happened. Somebody standing at Vannier's right, even leaning over him, somebody he knew and had no fear of, had suddenly pulled a gun and shot him in the right temple. And then, startled by the blood or the recoil of the shot, the killer had jumped back against the wall and knocked the picture down. It had landed on a corner and jumped under the table. And the killer had been too careful to touch it, or too scared.

I looked at it. It was a small picture, not interesting at all. A guy in doublet and hose, with lace at his sleeve ends, and one of those round puffy velvet hats with a feather, leaning far out of a window and apparently calling out to somebody downstairs. Downstairs not being in the picture. It was a colour reproduction of something that had never been needed in the first place.

I looked round the room. There were other pictures, a couple of rather nice water-colours, some engravings – very old-fashioned this year, engravings, or are they? Half a dozen in all. Well, perhaps the guy liked the picture, so what? A man leaning out of a high window. A long time ago.

I looked at Vannier. He wouldn't help me at all. A man leaning out of a high window, a long time ago.

The touch of the idea at first was so light that I almost missed it and passed on. A touch of a feather, hardly that. The touch of a snowflake. A high window, a man leaning out – a long time ago.

It snapped in place. It was so hot it sizzled. Out of a high window a long time ago – eight years ago – a man leaning – too far – a man falling – to his death. A man named Horace Bright.

'Mr Vannier,' I said with a little touch of admiration, 'you played that rather neatly.'

I turned the picture over. On the back dates and amounts of money were written. Dates over almost eight years, amounts mostly of $500, a few $750's, two for $1,000. There was a running total in small figures. It was $11,100. Mr Vannier had not received the latest payment. He had been dead when it arrived. It was not a lot of money, spread over eight years. Mr Vannier's customer had bargained hard.

The cardboard back was fastened into the frame with steel gramophone needles. Two of them had fallen out. I worked the cardboard loose and tore it a little getting it loose. There was a white envelope between the back and the picture. Sealed, blank. I tore it open. It contained two square photographs and a negative. The photos were just the same. They showed a man leaning far out of a window with his mouth open yelling. His hands were on the brick edges of the window-frame. There was a woman's face behind his shoulder.

He was a thinnish dark-haired man. His face was not very clear, nor the face of the woman behind him. He was leaning out of a window and yelling or calling out.

There I was holding the photograph and looking at it. And so far as I could see, it didn't mean a thing. I knew it had to. I just didn't know why. But I kept on looking at it. And in a little while something was wrong. It was a very small thing, but it was vital. The position of the man's hands, lined against the corner of the wall where it was cut out to make the window-frame. The hands were not holding anything, they were not touching anything. It was the inside of his wrists that lined against the angle of the bricks. The hands were in air.

The man was not leaning. He was falling.

I put the stuff back in the envelope and folded the cardboard back and stuffed that into my pocket also. I hid frame, glass and picture in the linen closet under towels.

All this had taken too long. A car stopped outside the house. Feet came up the walk.

I dodged behind the curtains in the archway.

30

The front door opened and then quietly closed.

There was a silence, hanging in the air like a man's breath in frosty air, and then a thick scream, ending in a wail of despair.

Then a man's voice, tight with fury, saying: 'Not bad, not good. Try again.'

The woman's voice said: 'My God, it's Louis! He's dead!'

The man's voice said: 'I may be wrong; but I still think it stinks.'

'My God! He's dead, Alex. Do something – for God's sake – *do* something!'

'Yeah,' the hard, tight voice of Alex Morny said. 'I ought to. I ought to make you look just like him. With blood and everything. I ought to make you just as dead, just as cold, just as rotten. No, I don't have to do that. You're that already. Just as rotten. Eight months married and cheating on me with a piece of merchandise like that. My God! What did I ever think of to put in with a chippy like you?'

He was almost yelling at the end of it.

The woman made another wailing noise.

'Quit stalling,' Morny said bitterly. 'What do you think I brought you over here for? You're not kidding anybody. You've been watched for weeks. You were here last night. I've been here already today. I've seen what there is to see. Your lipstick on cigarettes, your glass that you drank out of. I can see you now, sitting on the arm of his chair, rubbing his greasy hair, and then feeding him a slug while he was still purring. Why?'

'Oh, Alex – darling – don't say such awful things.'

'Early Lillian Gish,' Morny said. 'Very early Lillian Gish. Skip the agony, Toots. I have to know how to handle this. What the hell you think I'm here for? I don't give one little flash in hell about you any more. Not any more, Toots, not any more, my precious darling angel blonde mankiller. But I do care about myself and my reputation and my business. For instance, did you wipe the gun off?'

Silence. Then the sound of a blow. The woman wailed. She was hurt, terribly hurt. Hurt in the depths of her soul. She made it rather good.

'Look, angel,' Morny snarled. 'Don't feed me the ham. I've been in pictures. I'm a connoisseur of ham. Skip it. You're going to tell me how this was done if I have to drag you around the room by your hair. Now – did you wipe off the gun?'

Suddenly she laughed. An unnatural laugh, but clear and with a nice tinkle to it. Then she stopped laughing, just as suddenly.

Her voice said: 'Yes.'

'And the glass you were using?'

'Yes.' Very quiet now, very cool.

'And you put his prints on the gun?'

'Yes.'

He thought in the silence. 'Probably won't fool them,' he said. 'It's almost impossible to get a dead man's prints on a gun in a convincing way. However. What else did you wipe off.'

'N-nothing. Oh, Alex. Please don't be so brutal.'

'Stop it. *Stop it!* Show me how you did it, how you were standing, how you held the gun.'

She didn't move.

'Never mind about the prints,' Morny said. 'I'll put better ones on. Much better ones.'

She moved slowly across the opening of the curtains and I saw her. She was wearing pale-green gabardine slacks, a fawn-coloured leisure jacket with stitching on it, a scarlet turban with a gold snake in it. Her face was smeared with tears.

'Pick it up,' Morny yelled at her. 'Show me!'

She bent beside the chair and came up with the gun in her hand and her teeth bared. She pointed the gun across the opening in the curtains, towards the space of room where the door was.

Morny didn't move, didn't make a sound.

The blonde's hand began to shake and the gun did a queer up and down dance in the air. Her mouth trembled and her arm fell.

'I can't do it,' she breathed. 'I ought to shoot you but I can't.'

The hand opened and the gun thudded to the floor.

Morny went swiftly past the break in the curtains, pushed her out of the way and with his foot pushed the gun back to about where it had been.

'You couldn't do it,' he said thickly. 'You couldn't do it. Now watch.'

He whipped a handkerchief out and bent to pick the gun up again. He pressed something and the gate fell open. He reached his right hand into his pocket and rolled a cartridge in his fingers, moving his fingertips on the metal, pushed the cartridge into a cylinder. He repeated the performance four times more, snapped the gate shut, then opened it and spun it a little to set it in a certain spot. He placed the gun down on the floor, withdrew his hand and handkerchief and straightened up.

'You couldn't shoot me,' he sneered, 'because there was nothing in the gun but one empty cartridge. Now it's loaded again. The cylinders are in the right place. One shot has been fired. And your fingerprints are on the gun.'

The blonde was very still, looking at him with haggard eyes.

'I forgot to tell you,' he said softly, '*I* wiped the gun off. I thought it would be so much nicer to be *sure* your prints were on it. I was pretty sure they were – but I felt as if I would like to be *quite* sure. Get it?'

The girl said quietly: 'You're going to turn me in?'

His back was towards me. Dark clothes. Felt hat pulled low. So I couldn't see his face. But I could just about see the leer with which he said:

'Yes, angel, I am going to turn you in.'

'I see,' she said, and looked at him levelly. There was a sudden grave dignity in her over-emphasized chorus-girl's face.

'I'm going to turn you in, angel,' he said slowly, spacing his words as if he enjoyed the act. 'Some people are going to be sorry for me and some people are going to laugh at me. But it's not going to do my business any harm. Not a bit of harm. That's one nice thing about a business like mine. A little notoriety won't hurt it at all.'

'So I'm just publicity value to you, now,' she said. 'Apart, of course, from the danger that you might have been suspected yourself.'

'Just so,' he said. 'Just so.'

'How about my motive?' she asked, still calm, still level-eyed and so gravely contemptuous that he didn't get the expression at all.

'I don't know,' he said. 'I don't care. You were up to something with him. Eddie tailed you downtown to a street on Bunker Hill where you met a blond guy in a brown suit. You gave him something. Eddie dropped you and tailed the guy to an apartment house near there. He tried to tail him some more, but he had a hunch the guy spotted him, and he had to drop it. I don't know what it was all about. I know one thing, though. In that apartment house a young guy named Phillips was shot yesterday. Would you know anything about that, my sweet?'

The blonde said: 'I wouldn't know anything about it. I don't know anybody named Phillips and strangely enough I didn't just run up and shoot anybody out of sheer girlish fun.'

'But you shot Vannier, my dear,' Morny said almost gently.

'Oh, yes,' she drawled. 'Of course. We were wondering what my motive was. You get it figured out yet?'

'You can work that out with the johns,' he snapped. 'Call it a lover's quarrel. Call it anything you like.'

'Perhaps,' she said, 'when he was drunk he looked just a little like you. Perhaps that was the motive.'

He said: 'Ah,' and sucked his breath in.

'Better-looking,' she said. 'Younger, with less belly. But with the same god-damned self-satisfied smirk.'

'Ah,' Morny said, and he was suffering.

'Would that do?' she asked him softly.

He stepped forward and swung a fist. It caught her on the side of the face and she went down and sat on the floor, a long leg straight out in front of her, one hand to her jaw, her very blue eyes looking up at him.

'Maybe you oughtn't to have done that,' she said. 'Maybe I won't go through with it, now.'

'You'll go through with it, all right. You won't have any choice. You'll get off easy enough. Christ, I know that. With your looks. But you'll go through with it, angel. Your fingerprints are on that gun.'

She got to her feet slowly, still with the hand to her jaw.

Then she smiled. 'I knew he was dead,' she said. 'That is my key in the door. I'm quite willing to go downtown and say I shot him. But don't lay your smooth white paw on me again – if you want my story. Yes. I'm quite willing to go to the cops. I'll feel a lot safer with them than I feel with you.'

Morny turned and I saw the hard white leer of his face and the scar dimple in his cheek twitching. He walked past the opening in the curtain. The front door opened again. The blonde stood still a moment, looked back over her shoulder at the corpse, shuddered slightly, and passed out of my line of vision.

The door closed. Steps on the walk. Then car doors opening and closing. The motor throbbed, and the car went away.

31

After a long time I moved out from my hiding-place and stood looking around the living-room again. I went over and picked the gun up and wiped it off very carefully and put it down again. I picked the three rouge-stained cigarette-stubs out of the tray on the table and carried them into the bathroom and flushed them down the toilet. Then I looked around for the second glass with her fingerprints on it. There wasn't any second glass. The one that was half full of a dead drink I took to the kitchen and rinsed out and wiped on a dish-towel.

Then the nasty part. I kneeled on the rug by his chair and picked up the gun and reached for the trailing bone-stiff hand. The prints would not be good, but they would be prints and they would not be Lois Morny's. The gun had a checked rubber grip, with a piece broken off on the left side below the screw. No prints on that. An index print on the right side of the barrel, two fingers on the trigger guard, a thumb print on the flat piece on the left side, behind the chambers. Good enough.

I took one more look around the living-room.

I put the lamp down to a lower light. It still glared too much on the dead yellow face. I opened the front door, pulled the key out and wiped it off and pushed it back into the lock. I shut the door and wiped the thumb-latch off and went my way down the block to the Mercury.

I drove back to Hollywood and locked the car up and started along the sidewalk past the other parked cars to the entrance of the Bristol.

A harsh whisper spoke to me out of darkness, out of a car. It spoke my name. Eddie Prue's long blank face hung somewhere up near the roof of a small Packard, behind its wheel. He was alone in it. I leaned on the door of the car and looked in at him.

'How you making out, shamus?'

I tossed a match down and blew smoke at his face. I said: 'Who dropped that dental supply company's bill you gave me last night? Vannier, or somebody else?'

159

'Vannier.'

'What was I supposed, to do with it – guess the life history of a man named Teager?'

'I don't go for dumb guys,' Eddie Prue said.

I said: 'Why would he have it in his pocket to drop ? And if he did drop it, why wouldn't you just hand it back to him? In other words, seeing that I'm a dumb guy, explain to me why a bill for dental supplies should get anybody all excited and start trying to hire private detectives. Especially gents like Alex Morny, who don't like private detectives.'

'Morny's a good head,' Eddie Prue said coldly.

'He's the fellow for whom they coined the phrase, "as ignorant as an actor".'

'Skip that. Don't you know what they use that dental stuff for?'

'Yeah. I found out. They use albastone for making moulds of teeth and cavities. It's very hard, very fine grain and retains any amount of fine detail. The other stuff, crystobolite, is used to cook out the wax in an invested wax model. It's used because it stands a great deal of heat without distortion. Tell me you don't know what I'm talking about.'

'I guess you know how they make gold inlays,' Eddie Prue said. 'I guess you do, huh?'

'I spent two of my hours learning today. I'm an expert. What does it get me?'

He was silent for a little while, and then he said: 'You ever read the paper?'

'Once in a while.'

'It couldn't be you read where an old guy named Morningstar was bumped off in the Belfont Building on Ninth Street, just two floors above where this H. R. Teager had his office. It couldn't be you read that, could it?'

I didn't answer him. He looked at me for a moment longer, then he put his hand forward to the dash and pushed the starter-button. The motor of his car caught and he started to ease in the clutch.

'Nobody could be as dumb as you act,' he said softly. 'Nobody ain't. Good night to you.'

The car moved away from the kerb and drifted down the hill towards Franklin. I was grinning into the distance as it disappeared.

I went up to the apartment and unlocked the door and pushed it open a few inches and then knocked gently. There was movement in the room. The door was pulled open by a strong-looking girl with a black stripe on the cap of her white nurse's uniform.

'I'm Marlowe. I live here.'

'Come in, Mr Marlowe. Dr Moss told me.'

I shut the door quietly and we spoke in low voices. 'How is she?' I asked.

'She's asleep. She was already drowsy when I got here. I'm Miss Lymington. I don't know very much about her except that her temperature is normal and her pulse still rather fast, but going down. A mental disturbance, I gather.'

'She found a man murdered,' I said. 'It shot her full of holes. Is she hard enough asleep so that I could go in and get a few things to take to the hotel?'

'Oh, yes. If you're quiet. She probably won't wake. If she does, it won't matter.'

I went over and put some money on the desk. 'There's coffee and bacon and eggs and bread and tomato juice and oranges and liquor here,' I said. 'Anything else you'll have to phone for.'

'I've already investigated your supplies,' she said, smiling.

'We have all we need until after breakfast tomorrow. Is she going to stay here?'

'That's up to Dr Moss. I think she'll be going home as soon as she is fit for it. Home being quite a long way off, in Wichita.'

'I'm only a nurse,' she said. 'But I don't think there is anything the matter with her that a good night's sleep won't cure.'

'A good night's sleep and a change of company,' I said, but that didn't mean anything to Miss Lymington.

I went along the hallway and peeked into the bedroom. They had put a pair of my pyjamas on her. She lay almost on her back with one arm outside the bedclothes. The sleeve of the pyjama coat was turned up six inches or more. The small hand below the end of the sleeve was in a tight fist. Her face looked drawn and white and quite peaceful. I poked about in the closet and got a suitcase and put some junk in it. As I started back out I looked at Merle again. Her eyes opened and looked straight up at the ceiling. Then they moved just enough to see me and a faint little smile tugged at the corners of her lips.

'Hello.' It was a weak spent little voice, a voice that knew its owner was in bed and had a nurse and everything.

'Hello.'

I went around near her and stood looking down, with my polished smile on my clear-cut features.

'I'm all right,' she whispered. 'I'm fine. Aren't I?'

'Sure.'

'Is this your bed I'm in?'

'That's all right. It won't bite you.'

'I'm not afraid,' she said. A hand came sliding towards me and lay palm up, waiting to be held. I held it. 'I'm not afraid of you. No woman would ever be afraid of you, would she?'

'Coming from you,' I said, 'I guess that's meant to be a compliment.'

Her eyes smiled, then got grave again. 'I lied to you,' she said softly. 'I – I didn't shoot anybody.'

'I know. I was over there. Forget it. Don't think about it.'

'People are always telling you to forget unpleasant things. But you never do. It's so kind of silly to tell you to, I mean.'

'Okay,' I said, pretending to be hurt. 'I'm silly. How about making some more sleep?'

She turned her head until she was looking into my eyes. I sat on the edge of the bed, holding her hand.

'Will the police come here?' she asked.

'No. And try not to be disappointed.'

She frowned. 'You must think I'm an awful fool.'

'Well – maybe.'

A couple of tears formed in her eyes and slid out at the corners and rolled gently down her cheeks.

'Does Mrs Murdock know where I am?'

'Not yet. I'm going over to tell her.'

'Will you have to tell her – everything?'

'Yeah, why not?'

She turned the head away from me. 'She'll understand,' her voice said softly. 'She knows the awful thing I did eight years ago. The frightful terrible thing.'

'Sure,' I said. 'That's why she's been paying Vannier money all this time.'

'Oh, dear,' she said, and brought her other hand out from under the bedclothes and pulled away the other I was holding so that she could squeeze them tightly together. 'I wish you hadn't had to know that. I wish you hadn't. Nobody ever knew but Mrs Murdock. My parents never knew. I wish you hadn't.'

The nurse came in at the door and looked at me severely.

'I don't think she ought to be talking like this, Mr Marlowe. I think you should leave now.'

'Look, Miss Lymington, I've known this little girl two days, You've only known her two hours. This is doing her a lot of good.'

'It might bring on another – er – spasm,' she said, severely avoiding my eyes.

'Well, if she has to have it, isn't it better for her to have it now, while you're here, and get it over with? Go on out to the kitchen and buy yourself a drink.'

'I never drink on duty,' she said coldly. 'Besides, somebody might smell my breath.'

'You're working for me now. All my employees are required to get liquored up from time to time. Besides, if you had a good dinner and were to eat a couple of the Chasers in the kitchen cabinet, nobody would smell your breath.'

She gave me a quick grin and went back out of the room. Merle had been listening to this as if it was a frivolous interruption to a very serious play. Rather annoyed.

'I want to tell you all about it,' she said breathlessly. 'I –'

I reached over and put a paw over her two locked hands. 'Skip it. I know. Marlowe knows everything – except how to make a decent living. It doesn't amount to beans. Now you're going back to sleep and tomorrow I'm going to take you on the way back to Wichita – to visit your parents. At Mrs Murdock's expense.'

'Why, that's wonderful of her,' she cried, her eyes opening wide and shining. 'But she's always been wonderful to me.'

I got up off the bed. 'She's a wonderful woman,' I said, grinning down at her. 'Wonderful. I'm going over there now and we're going to have a perfectly lovely talk over the teacups. And if you don't go to sleep right now, I won't let you confess to any more murders.'

'You're horrid,' she said. 'I don't like you.' She turned her head away and put her arms back under the bedclothes and shut her eyes.

I went towards the door. At the door I swung round and looked back quickly. She had one eye open, watching me. I gave her a leer and it snapped shut in a hurry.

I went back to the living-room, gave Miss Lymington what was left of my leer, and went out with my suitcase.

I drove over to Santa Monica Boulevard. The hock-shop was still open. The old Jew in the tall black skull-cap seemed surprised that I was able to redeem my pledge so soon. I told him that was the way it was in Hollywood.

He got the envelope out of the safe and tore it open and took my money and pawnticket and slipped the shining gold coin out on his palm.

'So valuable this is I am hating to give it back to you,' he said. 'The workmanship, you understand, the workmanship is beautiful.'

'And the gold in it must be worth all of twenty dollars,' I said.

He shrugged and smiled and I put the coin in my pocket and said good night to him.

32

The moonlight lay like a white sheet on the front lawn except under the deodar where there was the thick darkness of black velvet. Lights in two lower windows were lit and in one upstairs room visible from the front. I walked across the stumble stones and rang the bell.

I didn't look at the little painted Negro by the hitching-block. I didn't pat his head tonight. The joke seemed to have worn thin.

A white-haired, red-faced woman I hadn't seen before opened the door and I said: 'I'm Philip Marlowe. I'd like to see Mrs Murdock. Mrs Elizabeth Murdock.'

She looked doubtful. 'I think she's gone to bed,' she said. 'I don't think you can see her.'

'It's only nine o'clock.'

'Mrs Murdock goes to bed early.' She started to close the door.

She was a nice old thing and I hated to give the door the heavy shoulder. I just leaned against it.

'It's about Miss Davis,' I said. 'It's important. Could you tell her that?'

'I'll see.'

I stepped back and let her shut the door.

A mocking-bird sang in a dark tree nearby. A car tore down the street much too fast and skidded round the next corner. The thin shreds of a girl's laughter came back along the dark street as if the car had spilled them out in its rush.

The door opened after a while and the woman said: 'You can come in.'

I followed her across the big empty entrance room. A single dim light burned in one lamp, hardly reaching to the opposite wall. The place was too still, and the air needed freshening. We went along the hall to the end and up a flight of stairs with a carved handrail and newel post. Another hall at the top, a door open towards the back.

I was shown in at the open door and the door was closed behind me. It was a big sitting-room with a lot of chintz, a blue and silver wallpaper, a couch, a blue carpet and french windows open on a balcony. There was an awning over the balcony.

Mrs Murdock was sitting in a padded wing chair with a card-table in front of her. She was wearing a quilted robe and her hair looked a little fluffed out. She was playing solitaire. She had the pack in her left hand and she put a card down and moved another one before she looked up at me.

Then she said: 'Well?'

I went over by the card-table and looked down at the game. It was Canfield.

'Merle's at my apartment,' I said. 'She threw an ing-bing.'

Without looking up she said: 'And just what is an ing-bing, Mr Marlowe?'

She moved another card, then two more quickly.

'A case of the vapours, they used to call it,' I said. 'Ever catch yourself cheating at that game?'

'It's no fun if you cheat,' she said gruffly. 'And very little if you don't. What's this about Merle? She has never stayed out like this before. I was getting worried about her.'

I pulled a slipper chair over and sat down across the table from her. It put me too low down. I got up and got a better chair and sat in that.

'No need to worry about her,' I said. 'I got a doctor and a nurse. She's asleep. She was over to see Vannier.'

She laid the pack of cards down and folded her big grey hands on the edge of the table and looked at me stolidly.

'Mr Marlowe,' she said, 'you and I had better have something out. I made a mistake calling you in the first place. That was my dislike of being played for a sucker, as you would say, by a hard-boiled little animal like Linda. But it would have been much better, if I had not raised the point at all. The loss of the doubloon would have been much easier to bear than you are. Even if I had never got it back.'

'But you did get it back,' I said.

She nodded. Her eyes stayed on my face. 'Yes. I got it back. You heard how.'

'I didn't believe it.'

'Neither did I,' she said calmly. 'My fool of a son was simply taking the blame for Linda. An attitude I find childish.'

'You have a sort of knack,' I said, 'of getting yourselves surrounded with people who take such attitudes.'

She picked her cards up again and reached down to put a black ten on a red jack, both cards that were already in the layout. Then she reached sideways to a small heavy table on which was her port. She drank some, put the glass down and gave me a hard, level stare.

'I have a feeling that you are going to be insolent, Mr Marlowe.'

I shook my head. 'Not insolent. Just frank. I haven't done so badly for you, Mrs Murdock. You did get the doubloon back. I kept the police away from you – so far. I didn't do anything on the divorce, but I found

Linda – your son knew where she was all the time – and I don't think you'll have any trouble with her. She knows she made a mistake marrying Leslie. However, if you don't think you got value –'

She made a humph noise and played another card. She got the ace of diamonds up to the top line. 'The ace of clubs is buried, darn it. I'm not going to get it out in time.'

'Kind of slide it out,' I said, 'when you're not looking.'

'Hadn't you better,' she said very quietly, 'get on with telling me about Merle? And don't gloat too much, if you have found out a few family secrets, Mr Marlowe.'

'I'm not gloating about anything. You sent Merle to Vannier's place this afternoon, with five hundred dollars.'

'And if I did?' She poured some of her port and sipped, eyeing me steadily over the glass.

'When did he ask for it?'

'Yesterday. I couldn't get it out of the bank until today. What happened?'

'Vannier's been blackmailing you for about eight years, hasn't he? On account of something that happened on 26 April 1933?'

A sort of panic twitched in the depths of her eyes, but very far back, very dim, and somehow as though it had been there for a long time and had just peeped out at me for a second.

'Merle told me a few things,' I said. 'Your son told me how his father died. I looked up the records and the papers today. Accidental death. There had been an accident in the street under his office and a lot of people were craning out of windows. He just craned out too far. There was some talk of suicide because he was broke and had fifty thousand life insurance for his family. But the coroner was nice and slid past that.'

'Well?' she said. It was a cold hard voice, neither a croak nor a gasp. A cold, hard, utterly composed voice.

'Merle was Horace Bright's secretary. A queer little girl in a way, over-timid, not sophisticated, a little-girl mentality, likes to dramatize herself, very old-fashioned ideas about men, all that sort of thing. I figure he got high one time and made a pass at her and scared her out of her socks.'

'Yes?' Another cold hard monosyllable prodding me like a gun-barrel.

'She brooded and got a little murderous inside. She got a chance and passed right back at him. While he was leaning out of a window. Anything in it?'

'Speak plainly, Mr Marlowe. I can stand plain talk.'

'Good grief, how plain do you want it? She pushed her employer out of a window. Murdered him, in two words. And got away with it. With your help.'

She looked down at the left hand clenched over her cards. She nodded. Her chin moved a short inch, down, up.

'Did Vannier have any evidence?' I asked. 'Or did he just happen to see what happened and put the bite on you and you paid him a little now and then to avoid scandal – and because you were really very fond of Merle?'

She played another card before she answered me. Steady as a rock.

'He talked about a photograph,' she said. 'But I never believed it. He couldn't have taken one. And if he had taken one, he would have shown it to me – sooner or later.'

I said: 'No, I don't think so. It would have been a very fluky shot, even if he happened to have the camera in his hand, on account of the doings down below in the street. But I can see he might not have dared to show it. You're a pretty hard woman, in some ways. He might have been afraid you would have him taken care of. I mean that's how it might look to him, a crook. How much have you paid him?'

'That's none –' she started to say, then stopped and shrugged her big shoulders. A powerful woman, strong, rugged, ruthless, and able to take it. She thought. 'Eleven thousand one hundred dollars, not counting the five hundred I sent him this afternoon.'

'Ah. It was pretty darn nice of you, Mrs Murdock. Considering everything.'

She moved a hand vaguely, made another shrug. 'It was my husband's fault,' she said. 'He was drunk, vile. I don't think he really hurt her, but, as you say, he frightened her out of her wits. I – I can't blame her too much. She has blamed herself enough all these years.'

'She had to take the money to Vannier in person?'

'That was her idea of penance. A strange penance.'

I nodded. 'I guess that would be in character. Later you married Jasper

Murdock and you kept Merle with you and took care of her. Anybody else know?'

'Nobody. Only Vannier. Surely he wouldn't tell anybody.'

'No. I hardly think so. Well, it's all over now. Vannier is through.'

She lifted her eyes slowly and gave me a long level gaze. Her grey head was a rock on top of a hill. She put the cards down at last and clasped her hands tightly on the edge of the table. The knuckles glistened.

I said: 'Merle came to my apartment when I was out. She asked the manager to let her in. He phoned me and I said yes. I got over there quickly. She told me she had shot Vannier.'

Her breath was a faint swift whisper in the stillness of the room.

'She had a gun in her bag, God knows why. Some idea of protecting herself against men, I suppose. But somebody – Leslie, I should guess – had fixed it to be harmless by jamming a wrong size cartridge in the breech. She told me she had killed Vannier and fainted. I got a doctor friend of mine. I went over to Vannier's house. There was a key in the door. He was dead in a chair, long dead, cold, stiff. Dead long before Merle went there. She didn't shoot him. Her telling me that was just drama. The doctor explained it after a fashion, but I won't bore you with it. I guess you understand all right.'

She said: 'Yes. I think I understand. And now?'

'She's in bed, in my apartment. There's a nurse there. I phoned Merle's father long-distance. He wants her to come home. That all right with you?'

She just stared.

'He doesn't know anything,' I said quickly. 'Not this or the other time. I'm sure of that. He just wants her to come home. I thought I'd take her. It seems to be my responsibility now. I'll need that last five hundred that Vannier didn't get – for expenses.'

'And how much more?' she asked brutally.

'Don't say that. You know better.'

'Who killed Vannier?'

'Looks like he committed suicide. A gun at his right hand. Temple contact wound. Morny and his wife were there while I was. I hid. Morny's trying to pin it on his wife. She was playing games with Vannier. So she probably thinks he did it, or had it done. But it shapes up like suicide.

The cops will be there by now. I don't know what they will make of it. We just have to sit tight and wait it out.'

'Men like Vannier,' she said grimly, 'don't commit suicide.'

'That's like saying girls like Merle don't push people out of windows. It doesn't mean anything.'

We stared at each other, with that inner hostility that had been there from the first. After a moment I pushed my chair back and went over to the french windows. I opened the screen and stepped out on to the porch. The night was all around, soft and quiet. The white moonlight was cold and clear, like the justice we dream of but don't find.

The trees down below cast heavy shadows under the moon. In the middle of the garden there was a sort of garden within a garden. I caught the glint of an ornamental pool. A lawn swing beside it. Somebody was lying in the lawn swing and a cigarette-tip glowed as I looked down.

I went back into the room. Mrs Murdock was playing solitaire again. I went over to the table and looked down.

'You got the ace of clubs out,' I said.

'I cheated,' she said without looking up.

'There was one thing I wanted to ask you,' I said. 'This doubloon business is still cloudy, on account of a couple of murders which don't seem to make sense now that you have the coin back. What I wondered was if there was anything about the Murdock Brasher that might identify it to an expert – to a man like old Morningstar.'

She thought, sitting still, not looking up. 'Yes. There might be. The coinmaker's initials, E.B., are on the left wing of the eagle. Usually, I'm told, they are on the right wing. That's the only thing I can think of.'

I said: 'I think that might be enough. You did actually get the coin back, didn't you? I mean that wasn't just something said to stop my ferreting around?'

She looked up swiftly and then down. 'It's in the strong room at this moment. If you can find my son, he will show it to you.'

'Well, I'll say good night. Please have Merle's clothes packed and sent to my apartment in the morning.'

Her head snapped up again and her eyes glared. 'You're pretty high-handed about all this, young man.'

'Have them packed,' I said. 'And send them. You don't need Merle any more – now that Vannier is dead.'

Our eyes locked hard and held locked for a long moment. A queer stiff smile moved the corners of her lips. Then her head went down and her right hand took the top card off the pack held in her left hand and turned it and her eyes looked at it and she added it to the pile of unplayed cards below the layout, and then turned the next card, quietly, calmly, in a hand as steady as a stone pier in a light breeze.

I went across the room and out, closed the door softly, went along the hall, down the stairs, along the lower hall past the sun-room and Merle's little office, and out into the cheerless, stuffy, unused living-room that made me feel like an embalmed corpse just to be in it.

The french doors at the back opened and Leslie Murdock stepped in and stopped, staring at me.

33

His slack suit was rumpled and also his hair. His little reddish moustache looked just as ineffectual as ever. The shadows under his eyes were almost pits.

He was carrying his long black cigarette-holder, empty, and tapping it against the heel of his left hand as he stood, not liking me, not wanting to meet me, not wanting to talk to me.

'Good evening,' he said stiffly. 'Leaving?'

'Not quite yet. I want to talk to you.'

'I don't think we have anything to talk about. And I'm tired of talking.'

'Oh, yes we have. A man named Vannier.'

'Vannier? I hardly know the man. I've seen him around. What I know I don't like.'

'You know him a little better than that,' I said.

He came forward into the room and sat down in one of the I-dare-you-to-sit-in-me chairs and leaned forward to cup his chin in his right hand and look at the floor.

'All right,' he said wearily. 'Get on with it. I have a feeling you are going to be very brilliant. Remorseless flow of logic and intuition and all that rot. Just like a detective in a book.'

'Sure. Taking the evidence piece by piece, putting it all together in a neat pattern, sneaking in an odd bit I had on my hip here and there, analysing the motives and characters and making them out to be quite different from what anybody – or I myself – and finally making a sort of world-weary pounce on the least promising suspect.'

He lifted his eyes and almost smiled. 'Who thereupon turns as pale as paper, froths at the mouth, and pulls a gun out of his right ear.'

I sat down near him and got a cigarette out. 'That's right. We ought to play it together some time. You got a gun?'

'Not with me. I have one. You know that.'

'Have it with you last night when you called on Vannier?'

He shrugged and bared his teeth. 'Oh. Did I call on Vannier last night?'

'I think so. Deduction. You smoke Benson & Hedges Virginia ciga-rettes. They leave a firm ash that keeps its shape. An ashtray at his house had enough of those little grey rolls to account for at least two cigarettes. But no stubs in the tray. Because you smoke them in a holder and a stub from a holder looks different. So you removed the stubs. Like it?'

'No.' His voice was quiet. He looked down at the floor again.

'That's an example of deduction. A bad one. For there might not have been any stubs, but if there had been and they had been removed, it might have been because they had lipstick on them. Of a certain shade that would at least indicate the colouring of the smoker. And your wife has a quaint habit of throwing her stubs into the waste-basket.'

'Leave Linda out of this,' he said coldly.

'Your mother still thinks Linda took the doubloon and that your story about taking it to give to Alex Morny was just a cover-up to protect her.'

'I said leave Linda out of it.' The tapping of the black holder against his teeth had a sharp quick sound, like a telegraph key.

'I'm willing to,' I said. 'But I didn't believe your story for a different reason. This.' I took the doubloon out and held it on my hand under his eyes.

He stared at it tightly. His mouth set.

'This morning when you were telling your story this was hocked on Santa Monica Boulevard for safe keeping. It was sent to me by a would-be detective named George Phillips. A simple sort of fellow who allowed himself to get into a bad spot through poor judgement and over-eagerness for a job. A thickset blond fellow in a brown suit, wearing dark glasses and a rather gay hat. Driving a sand-coloured Pontiac, almost new. You might have seen him hanging about in the hall outside my office yesterday morning. He had been following me around and before that he might have been following you around.'

He looked genuinely surprised. 'Why would he do that?'

I lit my cigarette and dropped the match in a jade ashtray that looked as if it had never been used as an ashtray.

'I said he might have. I'm not sure he did. He might have just been watching this house. He picked me up here and I don't think he followed me here.' I still had the coin on my hand. I looked down at it, turned it over by tossing it, looked at the initials E.B. stamped into the left wing, and put it away. 'He might have been watching the house because he had been hired to peddle a rare coin to an old coin dealer named Morningstar. And the old coin dealer somehow suspected where the coin came from, and told Phillips, or hinted to him, and that the coin was stolen. Incidentally, he was wrong about that. If your Brasher Doubloon is really at this moment upstairs, then the coin Phillips was hired to peddle was not a stolen coin. It was a counterfeit.'

His shoulders gave a quick little jerk, as if he was cold. Otherwise he didn't move or change position.

'I'm afraid it's getting to be one of those long stories after all,' I said, rather gently. 'I'm sorry. I'd better organize it a little better. It's not a pretty story, because it has two murders in it, maybe three. A man named Vannier and a man named Teager had an idea. Teager is a dental technician in the Belfont Buildings, old Morningstar's building. The idea was to counterfeit a rare and valuable gold coin, not too rare to be marketable, but rare enough to be worth a lot of money. The method they thought of was about what a dental technician uses to make a gold inlay. Requiring the same materials, the same apparatus, the same skill. That is, to reproduce a model exactly, in gold, by making a matrix in a hard white fine cement called albastone, then making a replica of the model in that matrix in moulding-wax, complete in the finest detail, then investing the wax, as they call it, in another kind of cement called crystobolite, which has the property of standing great heat without distortion. A small opening is left from the wax to outside by attaching a steel pin which is withdrawn when the cement sets. Then the crystobolite casting is cooked over a flame until the wax boils out through this small opening, leaving a hollow mould of the original model. This is clamped against a crucible on a centrifuge and molten gold is shot into it by centrifugal force from the crucible. Then the crystobolite, still hot, is held under cold water and it disintegrates, leaving the gold core with a gold pin attached representing the small opening. This is trimmed off, the casting is cleaned in acid and polished and you have, in this case, a brand new Brasher Doubloon, made of solid gold and exactly the same as the original. You get the idea?'

He nodded and moved a hand wearily across his head.

'The amount of skill this would take,' I went on, 'would be just what a dental technician would have. The process would be of no use for a current coinage, if we had a gold coinage, because the material and labour would cost more than the coin would be worth. But for a gold coin that was valuable through being rare, it would fit fine. So that's what they did. But they had to have a model. That's where you came in. You took the doubloon all right, but not to give to Morny. You took it to give to Vannier. Right?'

He stared at the floor and didn't speak.

'Loosen up,' I said. 'In the circumstances it's nothing very awful. I suppose he promised you money, because you needed it to pay off gambling debts and your mother is close. But he had a stronger hold over you than that.'

He looked up quickly then, his face very white, a kind of horror in his eyes.

'How did you know that?' he almost whispered.

'I found out. Some I was told, some I researched, some I guessed. I'll get to that later. Now Vannier and his pal have made a doubloon and they want to try it out. They wanted to know their merchandize would stand up under inspection by a man supposed to know rare coins. So Vannier had the idea of hiring a sucker and getting him to try to sell the counterfeit to old Morningstar, cheap enough so the old guy would think it was stolen. They picked George Phillips for their sucker, through a silly ad. he was running in the paper for business. I think Lois Morny was Vannier's contact with Phillips, at first, anyway. I don't think she was in the racket. She was seen to give Phillips a small package. This package may have contained the doubloon Phillips was to try to sell. But when he showed it to old Morningstar he ran into a snag. The old man knew his coin collections and his rare coins. He probably thought the coin was genuine enough – it would take a lot of testing to show it wasn't – but the way the maker's initials were stamped on the coin was unusual and suggested to him that the coin might be the Murdock Brasher. He called up here and tried to find out. That made your mother suspicious and the coin was found to be missing and she suspected Linda, whom she hates, and hired me to get it back and put the squeeze on Linda for a divorce, without alimony.'

'I don't want a divorce,' Murdock said hotly. 'I never had any such idea. She had no right –' he stopped and made a despairing gesture and a kind of sobbing sound.

'Okay, I know that. Well, old Morningstar threw a scare into Phillips, who wasn't crooked, just dumb. He managed to get Phillips's phone number out of him. I heard the old man call that number, eavesdropping in his office after he thought I had left. I had just offered to buy the doubloon back for a thousand dollars and Morningstar had taken up the offer, thinking he could get the coin from Phillips, make himself some money and everything lovely. Meantime Phillips was watching this house, perhaps to see if any cops were coming and going. He saw me, saw my car, got my name off the registration and it just happened he knew who I was.

'He followed me around trying to make up his mind to ask me for help until I braced him in a downtown hotel and he mumbled about knowing me from a case in Ventura when he was a deputy up there, and about being in a spot he didn't like and about being followed around by a tall guy with a funny eye. That was Eddie Prue, Morny's side-winder. Morny knew his wife was playing games with Vannier and had her shadowed. Prue saw her make contact with Phillips near where he lived on Court Street, Bunker Hill, and then followed Phillips until he thought Phillips had spotted him, which he had. And Prue, or somebody working for Morny, may have seen me go to Phillips's apartment on Court Street. Because he tried to scare me over the phone and later asked me to come and see Morny.'

I got rid of my cigarette-stub in the jade ashtray, looked at the bleak, unhappy face of the man sitting opposite me, and ploughed on. It was heavy going, and the sound of my voice was beginning to sicken me.

'Now we come back to you. When Merle told you your mother had hired a dick, that threw a scare into *you*. You figured she had missed the doubloon and you came steaming up to my office and tried to pump me. Very debonair, very sarcastic at first, very solicitous for your wife, but very worried. I don't know what you think you found out, but you got in touch with Vannier. You now had to get the coin back to your mother in a hurry, with some kind of story. You met Vannier somewhere and he gave you a doubloon. Chances are it's another counterfeit. He would be likely to hang on to the real one. Now Vannier sees his racket in danger of blowing up before it gets started. Morningstar has called your mother and I have been hired. Morningstar has spotted something. Vannier goes down to Phillips's apartment, sneaks in the back way and has it out with Phillips, trying to find out where he stands.

'Phillips doesn't tell him he has already sent the counterfeit doubloon to me, addressing it in a kind of printing afterwards found in a diary in his office. I infer that from the fact Vannier didn't try to get it back from me. I don't know what Phillips told Vannier, of course, but the chances are he told him the job was crooked, that he knew where the coin came from, and that he was going to the police or to Mrs Murdock. And Vannier pulled a gun, knocked him on the head and shot him. He searched him and the apartment and didn't find the doubloon. So he went to Morningstar. Morningstar didn't have the counterfeit doubloon either, but Vannier probably thought he had. He cracked the old man's skull with a gunbutt and went through the safe, perhaps found some money, perhaps found nothing, at any rate left the appearance of a stick-up behind him. Then Mr Vannier breezed on home, still rather annoyed because he hadn't found the doubloon, but with the satisfaction of a good afternoon's work under his vest. A couple of nice neat murders. That left you.'

34

Murdock flicked a strained look at me, then his eyes went to the black cigarette-holder he still had clenched in his hand. He tucked it in his shirt pocket, stood up suddenly, ground the heels of his hands together and sat down again. He got a handkerchief out and mopped his face.

'Why me?' he asked in a thick strained voice.

'You knew too much. Perhaps you knew about Phillips, perhaps not. Depends how deep you were in it. But you knew about Morningstar. The scheme had gone wrong and Morningstar had been murdered. Vannier couldn't just sit back and hope you wouldn't hear about that. He had to shut your mouth, very, very tight. But he didn't have to kill you to do it. In fact, killing you would be a bad move. It would break his hold on your mother. She's a cold, ruthless, grasping woman, but hurting you would make a wildcat of her. She wouldn't care what happened.'

Murdock lifted his eyes. He tried to make them blank with astonishment. He only made them dull and shocked.

'My mother – what – ?'

'Don't kid me any more than you have to,' I said. 'I'm tired to death of being kidded by the Murdock family. Merle came to my apartment this evening. She's there now. She had been over to Vannier's house to bring him some money. Blackmail money. Money that had been paid to him off and on for eight years. I know why.'

He didn't move. His hands were rigid with strain on his knees. His eyes had almost disappeared into the back of his head. They were doomed eyes.

'Merle found Vannier dead. She came to me and said she had killed him. Let's not go into why she thinks she ought to confess to other people's murders. I went over there and he had been dead since last night. He was as stiff as a wax dummy. There was a gun lying on the floor by his right hand. It was a gun I had heard described, a gun that belonged to a man named Hench, in an apartment across the hall from Phillips's apartment. Somebody ditched the gun that killed Phillips and took Hench's gun. Hench and his girl were drunk and left their apartment open. It's not proved that it was Hench's gun, but it will be. If it is Hench's gun, and Vannier committed suicide, it ties Vannier to the death of Phillips. Lois Morny also ties him to Phillips, in another way. If Vannier didn't commit suicide – and I don't believe he did – it might still tie him to Phillips. Or it might tie somebody else to Phillips, somebody who also killed Vannier. There are reasons why I don't like that idea.'

Murdock's head came up. He said: 'No?' in a suddenly clear voice. There was a new expression on his face, something bright and shining and at the same time just a little silly. The expression of a weak man being proud.

I said: 'I think you killed Vannier.'

He didn't move and the bright shining expression stayed on his face.

'You went over there last night. He sent for you. He told you he was in a jam and that if the law caught up with him, he would see that you were in the jam with him. Didn't he say something like that?'

'Yes,' Murdock said quietly. 'Something exactly like that. He was drunk and a bit high and he seemed to have a sense of power. He gloated, almost. He said if they got him in the gas chamber I would be sitting right beside him. But that wasn't all he said.'

'No. He didn't want to sit in the gas chamber and he didn't at the time see any very good reason why he should, if you kept your mouth good and tight. So he played his trump card. His first hold on you, what made you take the doubloon and give it to him, even if he did promise you money as well, was something about Merle and your father. I know about it. Your mother told me what little I hadn't put together already. That was his first hold and it was pretty strong. Because it would let you justify yourself. But last night he wanted something still stronger. So he told you the truth and said he had proof.'

He shivered, but the light clear proud look managed to stay on his face.

'I pulled a gun on him,' he said, almost in a happy voice. 'After all, she is my mother.'

'Nobody can take that away from you.'

He stood up, very straight, very tall. 'I went over to the chair he sat in and reached down and put the gun against his face. He had a gun in the pocket of his robe. He tried to get it, but he didn't get it in time. I took it away from him. I put my gun back in my pocket. I put the muzzle of the other gun against the side of his head and told him I would kill him, if he didn't produce his proof and give it to me. He began to sweat and babble that he was just kidding me. I clicked back the hammer on the gun to scare him some more.'

He stopped and held a hand out in front of him. The hand shook but as he stared down at it it got steady. He dropped it to his side and looked me in the eye.

'The gun must have been filed or had a very light action. It went off. I jumped back against the wall and knocked a picture down. I jumped from surprise that the gun went off, but it kept the blood off me. I wiped the gun off and put his fingers around it and then put it down on the floor close to his hand. He was dead at once. He hardly bled except the first spurt. It was an accident.'

'Why spoil it?' I half-sneered. 'Why not make it a nice clean honest murder?'

'That's what happened. I can't prove it, of course. But I think I might have killed him anyway. What about the police?'

I stood up and shrugged my shoulders. I felt tired, spent, drawn out and sapped. My throat was sore from yapping and my brain ached from trying to keep my thoughts orderly.

'I don't know about the police,' I said. 'They and I are not very good friends, on account of they think I am holding out on them. And God knows they are right. They may get to you. If you weren't seen, if you didn't leave any fingerprints around, and even if you did, if they don't have any other reason to suspect you and get your fingerprints to check, then they may never think of you. If they find out about the doubloon and that it was the Murdock Brasher, I don't know where you stand. It all depends on how well you stand up to them.'

'Except for mother's sake,' he said, 'I don't very much care. I've always been a flop.'

'And on the other hand,' I said, ignoring the feeble talk, 'if the gun really has a very light action and you get a good lawyer and tell an honest story and so on, no jury will convict you. Juries don't like blackmailers.'

'That's too bad,' he said. 'Because I am not in a position to use that defence. I don't know anything about blackmail. Vannier showed me where I could make some money, and I needed it badly.'

I said: 'Uh-huh. If they get you where you need the blackmail dope, you'll use it all right. Your old lady will make you. If it's her neck or yours, she'll spill.'

'It's horrible,' he said. 'Horrible to say that.'

'You were lucky about that gun. All the people we know have been playing with it, wiping prints off and putting them on. I even put a set on myself just to be fashionable. It's tricky when the hand is stiff. But I had to do it. Morny was over there having his wife put hers on. He thinks she killed Vannier, so she probably thinks he did.'

He just stared at me. I chewed my lip. It felt as stiff as a piece of glass.

'Well, I guess I'll just be running along now,' I said.

'You mean you are going to let me get away with it?' His voice was getting a little supercilious again.

'I'm not going to turn you in, if that's what you mean. Beyond that I guarantee nothing. If I'm involved in it, I'll have to face up to the situation. There's no question of morality involved. I'm not a cop nor a common informer nor an officer of the court. You say it was an accident. Okay, it was an accident. I wasn't a witness. I haven't any proof either way. I've been working for your mother and whatever right to my silence that gives her, she can have. I don't like her, I don't like you. I don't like this house. I didn't particularly like your wife. But I like Merle. She's kind of silly and morbid, but she's kind of sweet, too. And I know what has been done to her in this damn family for the past eight years. And I know she didn't push anybody out of any window. Does that explain matters?'

He gobbled, but nothing came that was coherent.

'I'm taking Merle home,' I said. 'I asked your mother to send her clothes to my apartment in the morning. In case she kind of forgets, being busy with her solitaire game, would you see that that is done?'

He nodded dumbly. Then he said in a queer small voice: 'You are going – just like that? I haven't – I haven't even thanked you. A man I hardly know, taking risks for me – I don't know what to say.'

'I'm going the way I always go,' I said. 'With an airy smile and a quick flip of the wrist. And with a deep and heartfelt hope that I won't be seeing you in the fishbowl. Good night.'

I turned my back on him and went to the door and out. I shut the door with a quiet, firm click of the lock. A nice, smooth exit, in spite of all the nastiness. For the last time I went over and patted the little painted Negro on the head and then walked across the long lawn by the moon-drenched shrubs and the deodar tree to the street and my car.

I drove back to Hollywood, bought a pint of good liquor, checked in at the Plaza, and sat on the side of the bed staring at my feet and lapping the whisky out of the bottle.

Just like any common bedroom drunk.

When I had enough of it to make my brain fuzzy enough to stop thinking, I undressed and got into bed, and after a while, but not soon enough, I went to sleep.

35

It was three o'clock in the afternoon and there were five pieces of luggage inside the apartment door, side by side on the carpet. There was my yellow cowhide, well scraped on both sides from being pushed around in the boots of cars. There were two nice pieces of airplane luggage, both marked L.M. There was an old black imitation walrus thing marked M.D. and there was one of these little leatherette overnight cases which you can buy in drugstores for a dollar forty-nine.

Dr Carl Moss had just gone out of the door cursing me because he had kept his afternoon class of hypochondriacs waiting. The sweetish smell of his Fatima poisoned the air for me. I was turning over in what was left of my mind what he had said when I asked him how long it would take Merle to get well.

'It depends what you mean by well. She'll always be high on nerves and low on animal emotion. She'll always breathe thin air and smell snow. She'd have made a perfect nun. The religious dream, with its narrowness, its stylized emotions and its grim purity, would have been a perfect release for her. As it is, she will probably turn out to be one of these acid-faced virgins that sit behind little desks in public libraries and stamp dates in books.'

'She's not that bad,' I had said, but he had just grinned at me with his wise Jew face and gone out of the door. 'And besides, how do you know they are virgins?' I added to the closed door, but that didn't get me any farther.

I lit a cigarette and wandered over to the window and after a while she came through the doorway from the bedroom part of the apartment and stood there looking at me with her eyes dark-ringed and a pale composed little face without any make-up except on the lips.

'Put some rouge on your cheeks,' I told her. 'You look like the snow maiden after a hard night with the fishing fleet.'

She went back and put some rouge on her cheeks. When she came back again she looked at the luggage and said softly: 'Leslie lent me two of his suitcases.'

I said: 'Yeah,' and looked her over. She looked very nice. She had a pair of long-waisted, rust-coloured slacks on, and Bata shoes and a brown and white print shirt and an orange scarf. She didn't have her glasses on. Her large clear cobalt eyes had a slightly dopey look, but not more than you would expect. Her hair was dragged down tight, but I couldn't do anything much about that.

'I've been a terrible nuisance,' she said. 'I'm terribly sorry.'

'Nonsense. I talked to your father and mother both. They're tickled to death. They've only seen you twice in over eight years and they feel as if they had almost lost you.'

'I'll love seeing them for a while,' she said, looking down at the carpet.

'It's very kind of Mrs Murdock to let me go. She's never been able to spare me for long.' She moved her legs as if she wondered what to do with them in slacks, although they were her slacks and she must have had to face the problem before. She finally put her knees close together and clasped her hands on top of them.

'Any little talking we might have to do,' I said, 'or anything you might want to say to me, let's get it over with now. Because I'm not driving half-way across the United States with a nervous breakdown in the seat beside me.'

She bit a knuckle and sneaked a couple of quick looks at me around the side of the knuckle. 'Last night' – she said, and stopped and coloured.

'Let's use a little of the old acid,' I said. 'Last night you told me you killed Vannier and then you told me you didn't. I know you didn't. That's settled.'

She dropped the knuckles, looked at me levelly, quiet, composed and the hands on her knees now not straining at all.

'Vannier was dead a long time before you got there. You went there to give him some money for Mrs Murdock.'

'No – for me,' she said. 'Although, of course, it was Mrs Murdock's money. I owe her more than I'll ever be able to repay. Of course, she doesn't give me much salary, but that would hardly –'

I said roughly: 'Her not giving you much salary is a characteristic touch and your owing her more than you can ever repay is more truth than poetry. It would take the Yankee outfield with two bats each to give her what she has coming from you. However, that's unimportant now. Vannier committed suicide because he had got caught out in a crooked job. That's flat and final. The way you behaved was more or less an act. You got a severe nervous shock seeing his leering dead face in a mirror and that shock merged into another one a long time ago and you just dramatized it in your screwy little way.'

She looked at me shyly and nodded her copper-blonde head, as if in agreement.

'And you didn't push Horace Bright out of any window,' I said.

Her face jumped then and turned startlingly pale. 'I – I –' her hand went to her mouth and stayed there and her shocked eyes looked at me over it.

'I wouldn't be doing this,' I said, 'if Dr Moss hadn't said it would be all right and we might as well hand it to you now. I think, maybe, you think you killed Horace Bright. You had a motive and an opportunity and just for a second I think you might have had the impulse to take advantage of the opportunity. But it wouldn't be in your nature. At the last minute you would hold back. But at that last minute probably something snapped and you pulled a faint. He did actually fall, of course, but you were not the one that pushed him.'

I held it a moment and watched the hand drop down again to join the other one and the two of them twine together and pull hard on each other.

'You were made to think you had pushed him,' I said. 'It was done with care, deliberation and the sort of quiet ruthlessness you only find in a certain kind of woman dealing with another woman. You wouldn't think of jealousy to look at Mrs Murdock now – but if that was a motive, she had it. She had a better one – fifty thousand dollars' life insurance – all that was left from a ruined fortune. She had the strange wild possessive love for her son such women have. She's cold, bitter, unscrupulous, and she used you without mercy or pity, as insurance, in case Vannier ever blew his top. You were just a scapegoat to her. If you want to come out of this pallid sub-emotional life you have been living, you have got to realize and believe what I am telling you. I know it's tough.'

'It's utterly impossible,' she said quietly, looking at the bridge of my nose. 'Mrs Murdock has been wonderful to me always. It's true I never remembered very well – but you shouldn't say such awful things about people.'

I got out the white envelope that had been in the back of Vannier's picture. Two prints in it and a negative. I stood in front of her and put a print on her lap.

'Okay, look at it. Vannier took it from across the street.'

She looked at it. 'Why, that's Mr Bright,' she said. 'It's not a very good picture, is it? And that's Mrs Murdock – Mrs Bright she was then – right behind him. Mr Bright looks mad.' She looked up at me with a sort of mild curiosity.

'If he looks mad there,' I said, 'you ought to have seen him a few seconds later, when he bounced.'

'When he what?'

'Look,' I said, and there was a kind of desperation in my voice now, 'that is a snapshot of Mrs Elizabeth Bright Murdock giving her first husband the heave out of his office window. He's falling. Look at the position of his hands. He's screaming with fear. She is behind him and her face is hard with rage – or something. Don't you get it at all? This is what Vannier has had for proof all these years. The Murdocks never saw it, never really believed it existed. But it did. I found it last night, by a fluke of the same sort that was involved in the taking of the picture. Which is a fair sort of justice. Do you begin to understand?'

She looked at the photo again and laid it aside. 'Mrs Murdock has always been lovely to me,' she said.

'She made you the goat,' I said, in the quietly strained voice of a stage manager at a bad rehearsal. 'She's a smart, tough, patient woman. She knows her complexes. She'll even spend a dollar to keep a dollar, which is what few of her type will do. I hand it to her. I'd like to hand it to her with an elephant gun, but my polite breeding restrains me.'

'Well,' she said, 'that's that.' And I could see she had heard one word in three and hadn't believed what she had heard. 'You must never show this to Mrs Murdock. It would upset her terribly.'

I got up and took the photo out of her hand and tore it into small pieces and dropped them in the waste-basket.

'Maybe you'll be sorry I did that,' I told her, not telling her I had another and the negative. 'Maybe some night – three months – three years from now – you will wake up in the night and realize I have been telling you the truth. And, maybe, then you will wish you could look at that photograph again. And, maybe, I am wrong about this, too. Maybe you would be very disappointed to find out you hadn't really killed anybody. That's fine. Either way it's fine. Now we are going downstairs and get in my car and we are going to drive to Wichita to visit your parents. And I don't think you are going back to Mrs Murdock, but it may well be that I am wrong about that, too. But we are not going to talk about this any more. Not any more.'

'I haven't any money,' she said.

'You have five hundred dollars that Mrs Murdock sent you. I have it in my pocket.'

'That's really awfully kind of her,' she said.

'Oh hell and fireflies,' I said and went out to the kitchen and gobbled a quick drink, before we started. It didn't do me any good. It just made me want to climb up the wall and gnaw my way across the ceiling.

36

I was gone ten days. Merle's parents were vague, kind, patient people, living in an old frame house in a quiet shady street. They cried when I told them as much of the story as I thought they should know. They said they were glad to have her back and they would take good care of her and they blamed themselves a lot, and I let them do it.

When I left, Merle was wearing a bungalow apron and rolling pie-crust. She came to the door wiping her hands on the apron and kissed me on the mouth and began to cry and ran back into the house, leaving the doorway empty until her mother came into the space with a broad homely smile on her face to watch me drive away.

I had a funny feeling as I saw the house disappear, as though I had written a poem and it was very good and I had lost it and would never remember it again.

I called Lieutenant Breeze when I got back and went down to ask him how the Phillips case was coming. They had cracked it very neatly, with the right mixture of brains and luck you always have to have. The Mornys never went to the police after all, but somebody called and told about a shot in Vannier's house and hung up quickly. The fingerprint man didn't like the prints on the gun too well, so they checked Vannier's hand for powder nitrates. When they found them they decided it was suicide after all. Then a dick named Lackey working out of Central Homicide thought to work on the gun a little and he found that a description of it had been distributed, and a gun like it was wanted in connexion with the Phillips killing. Hench identified it, but better than that they found a half-print of his thumb on the side of the trigger, which, not ordinarily being pulled back, had not been wiped off completely.

With that much in hand and a better set of Vannier's prints than I could make, they went over Phillips's apartment again and also over Hench's. They found Vannier's left hand on Hench's bed and one of his fingers on the underside of the toilet flush lever in Phillip's place. Then they got to work in the neighbourhood with photographs of Vannier, and proved he had been along the alley twice and on a side street at least three times. Curiously, nobody in the apartment house had seen him, or would admit it.

All they lacked now was a motive. Teager obligingly gave them that by getting himself pinched in Salt Lake City trying to peddle a Brasher Doubloon to a coin dealer who thought it was genuine but stolen. He had a dozen of them at his hotel, and one of them turned out to be genuine. He told them the whole story and showed a minute mark that he had used to identify the genuine coin. He didn't know where Vannier got it and they never found out because there was enough in the papers to make the owner come forward, if it had been stolen. And the owner never did. And the police didn't care any more about Vannier once they were convinced he had done murder. They left it at suicide, although they had a few doubts.

They let Teager go after a while, because they didn't think he had any idea of murder being done and all they had on him was attempted fraud. He had bought the gold legally and counterfeiting an obsolete New York State coin didn't come under the federal counterfeiting laws. Utah refused to bother with him.

They never believed Hench's confession. Breeze said he just used it for a squeeze on me, in case I was holding out. He knew I couldn't keep quiet if I had proof that Hench was innocent. It didn't do Hench any good, either. They put him in the line-up and pinned five liquor-store hold-ups on him and a wop named Gaetano Prisco, in one of which a man was shot dead. I never heard whether Prisco was a relative of Palermo's, but they never caught him, anyway.

'Like it?' Breeze asked me, when he had told me all this, or all that had then happened.

'Two points not clear,' I said. 'Why did Teager run away and why did Phillips live on Court Street under a phony name?'

'Teager ran away because the elevator man told him old Morningstar had been murdered and he smelled a hook-up. Phillips was using the name of Anson because the finance company was after his car and he was practically broke and getting desperate. That explains why a nice young boob like him could get roped in to something that must have looked shady from the start.'

I nodded and agreed that could be so.

Breeze walked to his door with me. He put a hard hand on my shoulder and squeezed.

'Remember that Cassidy case you were howling about to Spangler and me that night in your apartment?'

'Yes.'

'You told Spangler there wasn't any Cassidy case. There was – under another name. I worked on it.'

He took his hand off my shoulder and opened the door for me and grinned straight into my eyes.

'On account of the Cassidy case,' he said, 'and the way it made me feel, I sometimes give a guy a break he could perhaps not really deserve. A little something paid back out of the dirty millions to a working stiff – like me – or like you. Be good.'

It was night. I went home and put my old house clothes on and set the chessmen out and mixed a drink and played over another Capablanca. It went fifty-nine moves. Beautiful, cold, remorseless chess, almost creepy in its silent implacability.

When it was done I listened at the open window for a while and smelled the night. Then I carried my glass out to the kitchen and rinsed it and filled it with ice water and stood at the sink sipping it and looking at my face in the mirror.

'You and Capablanca,' I said.

The Lady in the Lake

1

The Treloar Building was, and is, on Olive Street, near Sixth, on the west side. The sidewalk in front of it had been built of black and white rubber blocks. They were taking them up now to give to the government, and a hatless pale man with a face like a building superintendent was watching the work and looking as if it was breaking his heart

I went past him through an arcade of speciality shops into a vast black and gold lobby. The Gillerlain Company was on the seventh floor, in front, behind swinging double plate-glass doors bound in platinum. Their reception-room had Chinese rugs, dull silver walls, angular but elaborate furniture, sharp shiny bits of abstract sculpture on pedestals and a tall display in a triangular showcase in the corner. On tiers and steps and islands and promontories of shining mirror-glass it seemed to contain every fancy bottle and box that has ever been designed. There were creams and powders and soaps and toilet waters for every season and every occasion. There were perfumes in tall thin bottles that looked as if a breath would blow them over and perfumes in little pastel phials tied with ducky satin bows, like little girls at a dancing class. The cream of the crop seemed to be something very small and simple in a squat amber bottle. It was in the middle at eye height, had a lot of space to itself and was labelled *Gillerlain Regal, The Champagne of Perfumes*. It was definitely the stuff to get. One drop of that in the hollow of your throat and the matched pink pearls started falling on you like summer rain.

A neat little blonde sat off in a far corner at a small PBX, behind a railing and well out of harm's way. At a flat desk in line with the doors was a tall, lean, dark-haired lovely whose name, according to the titled embossed plaque on her desk, was Miss Adrienne Fromsett.

She wore a steel-grey business suit and under the jacket a dark blue shirt and a man's tie of lighter shade. The edges of the folded handkerchief in the breast pocket looked sharp enough to slice bread. She wore a linked bracelet and no other jewellery. Her dark hair was parted and fell in loose but not unstudied waves. She had a smooth ivory skin and rather severe eyebrows and large dark eyes that looked as if they might warm up at the right time and in the right place.

I put my plain card, the one without the tommy gun in the corner, on her desk and asked to see Mr Derace Kingsley.

She looked at the card and said: 'Have you an appointment?'

'No appointment.'

'It is very difficult to see Mr Kingsley without an appointment.'

That wasn't anything I could argue about.

'What is the nature of your business, Mr Marlowe?'

'Personal.'

'I see. Does Mr Kingsley know you, Mr Marlowe?'

'I don't think so. He may have heard my name. You might say I'm from Lieutenant M'Gee.'

'And does Mr Kingsley know Lieutenant M'Gee?'

She put my card beside a pile of freshly typed letterheads. She leaned back and put one arm on the desk and tapped lightly with a small gold pencil.

I grinned at her. The little blonde at the PBX cocked a shell-like ear and smiled a small fluffy smile. She looked playful and eager, but not quite sure of herself, like a new kitten in a house where they don't care much about kittens.

'I'm hoping he does,' I said. 'But maybe the best way to find out is to ask him.'

She initialled three letters rapidly, to keep from throwing her pen set at me. She spoke again without looking up.

'Mr Kingsley is in conference. I'll send your card in when I have an opportunity.'

I thanked her and went and sat in a chromium and leather chair that was a lot more comfortable than it looked. Time passed and silence descended on the scene. Nobody came in or went out. Miss Fromsett's elegant hand moved over her papers and the muted peep of the kitten at the PBX was audible at moments, and the little click of the plugs going in and out.

I lit a cigarette and dragged a smoking stand beside the chair. The minutes went by on tiptoe, with their fingers to their lips. I looked the place over. You can't tell anything about an outfit like that. They might be making millions, and they might have the sheriff in the back room, with his chair tilted against the safe.

Half an hour and three or four cigarettes later a door opened behind Miss Fromsett's desk and two men came out backwards, laughing. A third man held the door for them and helped them laugh. They all shook hands heartily and the two men went across the office and out. The third man dropped the grin off his face and looked as if he had never grinned in his life. He was a tall bird in a grey suit and he didn't want any nonsense.

'Any calls?' he asked in a sharp bossy voice.

Miss Fromsett said softly: 'A Mr Marlowe to see you. From Lieutenant M'Gee. His business is personal.'

'Never heard of him,' the tall man barked. He took my card, didn't even glance at me, and went back into his office. His door closed on the pneumatic closer and made a sound like 'phooey'. Miss Fromsett gave me a sweet sad smile and I gave it back to her in the form of an obscene leer. I ate another cigarette and more time staggered by. I was getting to be very fond of the Gillerlain Company.

Ten minutes later the same door opened again and the big shot came out with his hat on and sneered that he was going to get a hair-cut. He started off across the Chinese rug in a swinging athletic stride, made about half the distance to the door and then did a sharp cutback and came over to where I was sitting.

'You want to see me?' he barked.

He was about six feet two and not much of it soft. His eyes were stone grey with flecks of cold light in them. He filled a large size in smooth grey flannel with a narrow chalk stripe, and filled it elegantly. His manner said he was very tough to get along with.

I stood up. 'If you're Mr Derace Kingsley.'

'Who the hell did you think I was?'

I let him have that trick and gave him my other card, the one with the business on it. He clamped it in his paw and scowled down at it.

'Who's M'Gee?' he snapped.

'He's just a fellow I know.'

'I'm fascinated,' he said, glancing back at Miss Fromsett. She liked it. She liked it very much. 'Anything else you would care to let drop about him?'

'Well, they call him Violets M'Gee,' I said. 'On account of he chews little throat pastilles that smell of violets. He's a big man with soft silvery hair and a cute little mouth made to kiss babies with. When last seen he was wearing a neat blue suit, wide-toed brown shoes, grey homburg hat, and he was smoking opium in a short briar pipe.'

'I don't like your manner,' Kingsley said in a voice you could have cracked a brazil nut on.

'That's all right,' I said. 'I'm not selling it.'

He reared back as if I had hung a week-old mackerel under his nose. After a moment he turned his back on me and said over his shoulder:

'I'll give you exactly three minutes. God knows why.'

He burned the carpet back past Miss Fromsett's desk to his door, yanked it open and let it swing to in my face. Miss Fromsett liked that too, but I thought there was a little sly laughter behind her eyes now.

2

The private office was everything a private office should be. It was long and dim and quiet and air-conditioned and its windows were shut and its grey venetian blinds half-closed to keep out the July glare. Grey drapes matched the grey carpeting. There was a large black and silver safe in the corner and a low row of low filing cases that exactly matched it. On the wall there was a huge tinted photograph of an elderly party with a chiselled beak and whiskers and a wing collar. The Adam's apple that edged through his wing collar looked harder than most people's chins.

The plate underneath the photograph read: *Mr Matthew Gillerlain, 1860–1934.*

Derace Kingsley marched briskly behind about eight hundred dollars' worth of executive desk and planted his backside in a tall leather chair. He reached himself a panatela out of a copper and mahogany box and trimmed it and lit it with a fat copper desk lighter. He took his time about it. It didn't matter about my time. When he had finished this, he leaned back and blew a little smoke and said:

'I'm a business man. I don't fool around. You're a licensed detective, your card says. Show me something to prove it.'

I got my wallet out and handed him things to prove it. He looked at them and threw them back across the desk. The celluloid holder with the photostat of my licence in it fell to the floor. He didn't bother to apologize.

'I don't know M'Gee,' he said. 'I know Sheriff Petersen. I asked for the name of a reliable man to do a job. I suppose you are the man.'

'M'Gee is in the Hollywood sub-station of the sheriff's office,' I said. 'You can check on that.'

'Not necessary. I guess you might do, but don't get flip with me. And remember when I hire a man he's my man. He does exactly what I tell him and he keeps his mouth shut. Or he goes out fast. Is that clear? I hope I'm not too tough for you.'

'Why not leave that an open question?' I said.

He frowned. He said sharply: 'What do you charge?'

'Twenty-five a day and expenses. Eight cents a mile for my car.'

'Absurd,' he said. 'Far too much. Fifteen a day flat. That's plenty. I'll pay the mileage, within reason, the way things are now. But no joy-riding.'

I blew a little grey cloud of cigarette smoke and fanned it with my hand. I said nothing. He seemed a little surprised that I said nothing.

He leaned over the desk and pointed with his cigar. 'I haven't hired you yet,' he said, 'but if I do, the job is absolutely confidential. No talking it over with your cop friends. Is that understood?'

'Just what do you want done, Mr Kingsley?'

'What do you care? You do all kinds of detective work, don't you?'

'Not all kinds. Only the fairly honest kinds.'

He stared at me level-eyed, his jaw tight. His grey eyes had an opaque look.

'For one thing I don't do divorce business,' I said. 'And I get a hundred down as a retainer – from strangers.'

'Well, well,' he said, in a voice suddenly soft. 'Well, well.'

'And as for your being too tough for me,' I said, 'most of the clients start out either by weeping down my shirt or bawling me out to show who's boss. But usually they end up very reasonable – if they're still alive.'

'Well, well,' he said again, in the same soft voice, and went on staring at me. 'Do you lose very many of them?' he asked.

'Not if they treat me right,' I said.

'Have a cigar,' he said.

I took a cigar and put it in my pocket.

'I want you to find my wife,' he said. 'She's been missing for a month.'

'Okay,' I said. 'I'll find your wife.'

He patted his desk with both hands. He stared at me solidly. 'I think you will at that,' he said. Then he grinned. 'I haven't been called down like that in four years,' he said.

I didn't say anything.

'Damn it all,' he said, 'I liked it. I liked it fine.' He ran a hand through his thick dark hair. 'She's been gone a whole month,' he said. 'From a cabin we have in the mountains. Near Puma Point. Do you know Puma Point?'

I said I knew Puma Point.

'Our place is three miles from the village,' he said, 'partly over a private road. It's on a private lake. Little Fawn Lake. There's a dam three of us put up to improve the property. I own the tract with two other men. It's quite large, but undeveloped and won't be developed now for some time, of course. My friends have cabins, I have a cabin and a man named Bill Chess lives with his wife in another cabin rent-free and looks after the place. He's a disabled veteran with a pension. That's all there is up there. My wife went up the middle of May, came down twice for week-ends, was due down the 12th of June for a party and never showed up. I haven't seen her since.'

'What have you done about it?' I asked.

'Nothing. Not a thing. I haven't even been up there.' He waited, wanting me to ask why.

I said: 'Why?'

He pushed his chair back to get a locked drawer open. He took out a folded paper and passed it over. I unfolded it and saw it was a postal telegraph form. The wire had been filed at El Paso on June 14th, at 9.19 a.m. It was addressed to Derace Kingsley, 965 Carson Drive, Beverly Hills, and read:

AM CROSSING TO GET MEXICAN DIVORCE STOP WILL MARRY
CHRIS STOP GOOD LUCK AND GOODBYE CRYSTAL

I put this down on my side of the desk and he was handing me a large and very clear snapshot on glazed paper which showed a man and a woman sitting on the sand under a beach umbrella. The man wore trunks and the woman what looked like a very daring sharkskin bathing suit. She was a slim blonde, young and shapely and smiling. The man was a hefty dark handsome lad with fine shoulders and legs, sleek dark hair and white teeth. Six feet of a standard type of home-wrecker. Arms to hold you close and all his brains in his face. He was holding a pair of dark glasses in his hand and smiling at the camera with a practised and easy smile.

'That's Crystal,' Kingsley said, 'and that's Chris Lavery. She can have him and he can have her and to hell with them both.'

I put the photo down on the telegram. 'All right, what's the catch?' I asked him.

'There's no telephone up there,' he said, 'and there was nothing important about the affair she was coming down for. So I got the wire before I gave much thought to it. The wire surprised me only mildly. Crystal and I have been washed up for years. She lives her life and I live mine. She has her own money and plenty of it. About twenty thousand a year from a family holding corporation that owns valuable oil leases in Texas. She plays around and I knew Lavery was one of her playmates. I might have been a little surprised that she would actually marry him, because the man is nothing but a professional chaser. But the picture looked all right so far, you understand?'

'And then?'

'Nothing for two weeks. Then the Prescott Hotel in San Bernardino got in touch with me and said a Packard Clipper registered to Crystal Grace Kingsley at my address was unclaimed in their garage and what about it. I told them to keep it and I sent them a cheque. There was nothing much in that either. I figured she was still out of the state and that if they had gone in a car at all, they had gone in Lavery's car. The day before yesterday, however, I met Lavery in front of the Athletic Club down on the corner here. He said he didn't know where Crystal was.'

Kingsley gave me a quick look and reached a bottle and two tinted glasses up on the desk. He poured a couple of drinks and pushed one over. He held his against the light and said slowly:

'Lavery said he hadn't gone away with her, hadn't seen her in two months, hadn't had any communication with her of any kind.'

I said, 'You believed him?'

He nodded, frowning, and drank his drink and pushed the glass to one side. I tasted mine. It was Scotch. Not very good Scotch.

'If I believed him –' Kingsley said, 'and I was probably wrong to do it – it wasn't because he's a fellow you have to believe. Far from it. It's because he's a no-good son of a bitch who thinks it is smart to lay his friends' wives and brag about it. I feel he would have been tickled pink to stick it into me and break it off that he had got my wife to run away with him and leave me flat. I know these tomcats and I know this one too well. He rode a route for us for a while and he was in trouble all the time. He couldn't keep his hands off the office help. And apart from all that there was this wire from El Paso and I told him about it, and why would he think it worth while to lie about it?'

'She might have tossed him out on his can,' I said. 'That would have hurt him in his deep place – his Casanova complex.'

Kingsley brightened up a little, but not very much. He shook his head. 'I still more than half-way believe him,' he said. 'You'll have to prove me wrong. That's part of why I wanted you. But there's another and very worrying angle. I have a good job here, but a job is all it is. I can't stand scandal. I'd be out of here in a hurry if my wife got mixed up with the police.'

'Police?'

'Among her other activities,' Kingsley said grimly, 'my wife occasionally finds time to lift things in department stores. I think it's just a sort of delusion of grandeur she gets when she has been hitting the bottle too hard, but it happens, and we have had some pretty nasty scenes in managers' offices. So far I've been able to keep them from filing charges, but if something like that happened in a strange city where nobody knew her' – he lifted his hands and let them fall with a smack on the desk – 'well, it might be a prison matter, mightn't it?'

'Has she ever been finger-printed?'

'She has never been arrested,' he said.

'That's not what I mean. Sometimes in large department stores they make it a condition of dropping shoplifting charges that you give them your prints. It scares the amateurs and builds up a file of kleptomaniacs in their protective association. When the prints come in a certain number of times they call time on you.'

'Nothing like that has happened to my knowledge,' he said.

'Well, I think we might almost throw the shoplifting angle out of this for the time being,' I said. 'If she got arrested, she would get searched. Even if the cops let her use a Jane Doe name on the police blotter, they would be likely to get in touch with you. Also she would start yelling for help when she found herself in a jam.' I tapped the blue-and-white telegraph form. 'And this is a month old. If what you are thinking about happened around that time, the case would have been settled by now. If it was a first offence, she would get off with a scolding and a suspended sentence.'

He poured himself another drink to help him with his worrying. 'You're making me feel better,' he said.

'There are too many other things that could have happened,' I said. 'That she did go away with Lavery and they split up. That she went away with some other man and the wire is a gag. That she went away alone or with a woman. That she drank herself over the edge and is holed up in some private sanatorium taking a cure. That she got into some jam we have no idea of. That she met with foul play.'

'Good God, don't say that,' Kingsley exclaimed.

'Why not? You've got to consider it. I get a very vague idea of Mrs Kingsley – that she is young, pretty, reckless, and wild. That she drinks and does dangerous things when she drinks. That she is a sucker for the men and might take up with a stranger who might turn out to be a crook. Does that fit?'

He nodded. 'Every word of it.'

'How much money would she have with her?'

'She liked to carry enough. She has her own bank and her own bank account. She could have any amount of money.'

'Any children?'

'No children.'

'Do you have the management of her affairs?'

He shook his head. 'She hasn't any – excepting depositing cheques and drawing out money and spending it. She never invests a nickel. And her money certainly never does me any good, if that's what you are thinking.' He paused and then said: 'Don't think I haven't tried. I'm human and it's not fun to watch twenty thousand a year go down the drain and nothing to show for it but hangovers and boy friends of the class of Chris Lavery.'

'How are you with her bank? Could you get a detail of the cheques she has drawn for the past couple of months?'

'They wouldn't tell me. I tried to get some information of the sort once, when I had an idea she was being blackmailed. All I got was ice.'

'We can get it,' I said, 'and we may have to. It will mean going to the Missing Persons Bureau. You wouldn't like that?'

'If I had liked that, I wouldn't have called you,' he said.

I nodded, gathered my exhibits together and put them away in my pockets. 'There are more angles to this than I can even see now,' I said, 'but I'll start by talking to Lavery and then taking a run up to Little Fawn Lake and asking questions there. I'll need Lavery's address and a note to your man in charge at the mountain place.'

He got a letterhead out of his desk and wrote and passed it over. I read: 'Dear Bill: This will introduce Mr Philip Marlowe who wishes to look over the property. Please show him my cabin and assist him in every way. Yrs Derace Kingsley.'

I folded this up and put it in the envelope he had addressed while I was reading it. 'How about the other cabins up there?' I asked.

'Nobody up this year so far. One man's in government service in

Washington and the other is at Fort Leavenworth. Their wives are with them.'

'Now Lavery's address,' I said.

He looked at a point well above the top of my head. 'In Bay City. I could find the house but I forget the address. Miss Fromsett can give it to you, I think. She needn't know why you want it. She probably will. And you want a hundred dollars, you said.'

'That's all right,' I said. 'That's just something I said when you were tramping on me.'

He grinned. I stood up and hesitated by the desk looking at him. After a moment I said: 'You're not holding anything back, are you – anything important?'

He looked at his thumb. 'No. I'm not holding anything back. I'm worried and I want to know where she is. I'm damn worried. If you get anything at all, call me any time, day or night.'

I said I would do that, and we shook hands and I went back down the long cool office and out to where Miss Fromsett sat elegantly at her desk.

'Mr Kingsley thinks you can give me Chris Lavery's address,' I told her and watched her face.

She reached very slowly for a brown leather address book and turned the leaves. Her voice was tight and cold when she spoke.

'The address we have is 623 Altair Street, in Bay City. Telephone Bay City 12523. Mr Lavery has not been with us for more than a year. He may have moved.'

I thanked her and went on to the door. From there I glanced back at her. She was sitting very still, with her hands clasped on her desk, staring into space. A couple of red spots burned in her cheeks. Her eyes were remote and bitter.

I got the impression that Mr Chris Lavery was not a pleasant thought to her.

3

Altair Street lay on the edge of the V forming the inner end of a deep canyon. To the north was the cool blue sweep of the bay out to the point about Malibu. To the south the beach town of Bay City was spread out on a bluff above the coast highway.

It was a short street, not more than three or four blocks, and ended in a tall iron fence enclosing a large estate. Beyond the gilded spikes of the fence I could see trees and shrubs and a glimpse of lawn and part of a curving driveway, but the house was out of sight. On the inland side of Altair Street the houses were well kept and fairly large, but the few scattered bungalows on the edge of the canyon were nothing much. In the short half-block ended by the iron fence were only two houses, on opposite sides of the street and almost directly across from each other. The smaller was number 623.

I drove past it, turned the car in the paved half-circle at the end of the street and came back to park in front of the lot next to Lavery's place. His house was built downwards, one of those clinging vine effects, with the front door a little below street level, the patio on the roof, the bedrooms in the basement, and a garage like the corner pocket on a pool table. A crimson bougainvillea was rustling against the front wall and the flat stones of the front walk were edged with Korean moss. The door was narrow, grilled and topped by a lancet arch. Below the grille there was an iron knocker. I hammered on it.

Nothing happened. I pushed the bell at the side of the door and heard it ring inside not very far off and waited and nothing happened. I worked on the knocker again. Still nothing. I went back up the walk and along to the garage and lifted the door far enough to see that a car with white side-walled tyres was inside. I went back to the front door.

A neat black Cadillac coupé came out of the garage across the way, backed, turned and came along past Lavery's house, slowed, and a thin man in dark glasses looked at me sharply, as if I hadn't any business to be there. I gave him my steely glare and he went on his way.

I went down Lavery's walk again and did some more hammering on his knocker. This time I got results. The judas window opened and I was looking at a handsome bright-eyed number through the bars of the grille.

'You make a hell of a lot of noise,' a voice said.

'Mr Lavery?'

He said he was Mr Lavery and what about it. I poked a card through the grille. A large brown hand took the card. The bright brown eyes came back and the voice said: 'So sorry. Not needing any detectives today, please.'

'I'm working for Derace Kingsley.'

'The hell with both of you,' he said, and banged the judas window.

I leaned on the bell beside the door and got a cigarette out with my free hand and had just struck the match on the woodwork beside the door when it was yanked open and a big guy in bathing trunks, beach sandals and a white terrycloth bathrobe started to come out at me.

I took my thumb off the bell and grinned at him. 'What's the matter?' I asked him. 'Scared?'

'Ring that bell again,' he said, 'and I'll throw you clear across the street.'

'Don't be childish,' I told him. 'You know perfectly well I'm going to talk to you and you're going to talk to me.'

I got the blue-and-white telegram out of my pocket and held it in front of his bright brown eyes. He read it morosely, chewed his lips and growled:

'Oh for Chrissake, come on in then.'

He held the door wide and I went in past him, into a dim pleasant room with an apricot Chinese rug that looked expensive, deep-sided chairs, a number of white drum lamps, a big Capehart in the corner, a long and very wide davenport in pale tan mohair shot with dark brown, and a fireplace with a copper screen and an overmantel in white wood. A fire was laid behind the screen and partly masked by a large spray of manzanita bloom. The bloom was turning yellow in places but was still pretty. There was a bottle of Vat 69 and glasses on a tray and a copper icebucket on a low round burl walnut table with a glass top. The room went clear to the back of the house and ended in a flat arch through which showed three narrow windows and the top few feet of the white iron railing of the staircase going down.

Lavery swung the door shut and sat on the davenport. He grabbed a cigarette out of a hammered silver box and lit it and looked at me irritably. I sat down opposite him and looked him over. He had everything in the way of good looks the snapshot had indicated. He had a terrific torso and magnificent thighs. His eyes were chestnut brown and the whites of them slightly grey-white. His hair was rather long and curled a little over his temples. His brown skin showed no signs of dissipation. He was a nice piece of beef, but to me that was all he was. I could understand that women would think he was something to yell for.

'Why not tell us where she is?' I said. 'We'll find out eventually anyway, and if you tell us now we won't be bothering you.'

'It would take more than a private dick to bother me,' he said.

'No, it wouldn't. A private dick can bother anybody. He's persistent and used to snubs. He's paid for his time and he would just as soon use it to bother you as any other way.'

'Look,' he said, leaning forward and pointing his cigarette at me. 'I know what that wire says, but it's the bunk. I didn't go to El Paso with Crystal Kingsley. I haven't seen her in a long time – long before the date of that wire. I haven't had any contact with her. I told Kingsley that.'

'He didn't have to believe you.'

'Why would I lie to him?' He looked surprised.

'Why wouldn't you?'

'Look,' he said earnestly, 'it might seem so to you, but you don't know her. Kingsley has no strings on her. If he doesn't like the way she behaves he has a remedy. These proprietary husbands make me sick.'

'If you didn't go to El Paso with her,' I said, 'why did she send this telegram?'

'I haven't the faintest idea.'

'You can do better than that,' I said. I pointed to the spray of manzanita in the fireplace. 'You pick that up at Little Fawn Lake?'

'The hills around here are full of manzanita,' he said contemptuously.

'It doesn't bloom like that down here.'

He laughed. 'I was up there the third week in May. If you have to know. I suppose you can find out. That's the last time I saw her.'

'You didn't have any idea of marrying her?'

He blew smoke and said through it: 'I've thought of it, yes. She has money. Money is always useful. But it would be too tough a way to make it.'

I nodded, but didn't say anything. He looked at the manzanita spray in the fireplace and leaned back to blow smoke in the air and show me the strong brown line of his throat. After a moment, when I still didn't say anything, he began to get restless. He glanced down at the card I had given him and said:

'So you hire yourself out to dig up dirt? Doing well it?'

'Nothing to brag about. A dollar here, a dollar there.'

'And all of them pretty slimy,' he said.

'Look, Mr Lavery, we don't have to get into a fight. Kingsley thinks you know where his wife is, but won't tell him. Either out of meanness or motives of delicacy.'

'Which way would he like it?' the handsome brown-faced man sneered.

'He doesn't care, as long as he gets the information. He doesn't care a great deal what you and she do together or where you go or whether she divorces him or not. He just wants to feel sure that everything is all right and that she isn't in trouble of any kind.'

Lavery looked interested. 'Trouble? What kind of trouble?' He licked the word around on his brown lips, tasting it.

'Maybe you won't know the kind of trouble he is thinking of.'

'Tell me,' he pleaded sarcastically. 'I'd just love to hear about some kind of trouble I didn't know about.'

'You're doing fine,' I told him. 'No time to talk business, but always time for a wisecrack. If you think we might try to get a hook into you because you crossed a state line with her, forget it.'

'Go climb up your thumb, wise guy. You'd have to prove I paid the freight, or it wouldn't mean anything.'

'This wire has to mean something,' I said stubbornly. It seemed to me that I had said it before, several times.

'It's probably just a gag. She's full of little tricks like that. All of them silly, and some of them vicious.'

'I don't see any point in this one.'

He flicked cigarette ash carelessly at the glass-top table. He gave me a quick up from under look and immediately looked away.

'I stood her up,' he said slowly. 'It might be her idea of a way to get back at me. I was supposed to run up there one week-end. I didn't go. I was – sick of her.'

I said: 'Uh-huh,' and gave him a long steady stare. 'I don't like that so well. I'd like it better if you did go to El Paso with her and had a fight and split up. Could you tell it that way?'

He flushed solidly behind the sunburn.

'God damn it,' he said, 'I told you I didn't go anywhere with her. Not anywhere. Can't you remember that?'

'I'll remember it when I believe it.'

He leaned over to snub out his cigarette. He stood up with an easy movement, not hurried at all, pulled the belt of his robe tight, and moved out to the end of the davenport.

'All right,' he said in a clear tight voice. 'Out you go. Take the air. I've had enough of your third-degree tripe. You're wasting my time and your own – if it's worth anything.'

I stood up and grinned at him. 'Not a lot, but for what it's worth I'm being paid for it. It couldn't be, for instance, that you ran into a little unpleasantness in some departmental store – say at the stocking or jewellery counter.'

He looked at me very carefully, drawing his eyebrows down at the corners and making his mouth small.

'I don't get it,' he said, but there was thought behind his voice.

'That's all I wanted to know,' I said. 'And thanks for listening. By the way, what line of business are you in – since you left Kingsley?'

'What the hell business is it of yours?'

'None. But of course I can always find out,' I said, and moved a little way towards the door, not very far.

'At the moment I'm not doing anything,' he said coldly. 'I expect a commission in the Navy almost any day.'

'You ought to do well at that,' I said.

'Yeah. So long, snooper. And don't bother to come back. I won't be at home.'

I went over to the door and pulled it open. It stuck on the lower sill, from the beach moisture. When I had it open, I looked back at him. He was standing there narrow-eyed, full of muted thunder.

'I may have to come back,' I said. 'But it won't be just to swop gags. It will be because I find something out that needs talking over.'

'So you still think I'm lying,' he said savagely.

'I think you have something on your mind. I've looked at too many faces not to know. It may not be any of my business. If it is, you're likely to have to throw me out again.'

'A pleasure,' he said. 'And next time bring somebody to drive you home. In case you land on your fanny and knock your brains out.'

Then without any rhyme or reason that I could see, he spat on the rug in front of his feet.

It jarred me. It was like watching the veneer peel off and leave a tough kid in an alley. Or like hearing an apparently refined woman start expressing herself in four-letter words.

'So long, beautiful hunk,' I said, and left him standing there. I closed the door, had to jerk it to get it shut, and went up the path to the street. I stood on the sidewalk looking at the house across the way.

4

It was a wide shallow house with rose stucco walls faded out to a pleasant pastel shade and trimmed with dull green at the window frames. The roof was of green tiles, round rough ones. There was a deeply inset front door framed in a mosaic of multi-coloured pieces of tiling and a small flower garden in front, behind a low stucco wall topped by an iron railing which the beach moisture had begun to corrode. Outside the wall to the left was the three-car garage, with a door opening inside the yard and a concrete path going from there to a side door of the house.

Set into the gate post was a bronze tablet which read: 'Albert S. Admore, M.D.'

While I was standing there staring across the street, the black Cadillac

I had already seen came purring around the corner and then down the block. It slowed and started to sweep outwards to get turning space to go into the garage, decided my car was in the way of that, and went on to the end of the road and turned in the widened-out space in front of the ornamental iron railing. It came back slowly and went into the empty third of the garage across the way.

The thin man in sun-glasses went along the sidewalk to the house, carrying a double-handled doctor's bag. Half-way along he slowed down to stare across at me. I went along towards my car. At the house he used a key and as he opened the door he looked across at me again.

I got into the Chrysler and sat there smoking and trying to make up my mind whether it was worth while hiring somebody to pull a tail on Lavery. I decided it wasn't, not the way things looked so far.

Curtains moved at a lower window close to the side door Dr Almore had gone in at. A thin hand held them aside and I caught the glint of light on glasses. They were held aside for quite some time, before they fell together again.

I looked along the street at Lavery's house. From this angle I could see that his service porch gave on a flight of painted wooden steps to a sloping concrete walk and a flight of concrete steps ending in the paved alley below.

I looked across at Dr Almore's house again, wondering idly if he knew Lavery and how well. He probably knew him, since theirs were the only two houses in the block. But being a doctor, he wouldn't tell me anything about him. As I looked, the curtains which had been lifted apart were now completely drawn aside.

The middle segment of the triple window they had masked had no screen. Behind it, Dr Almore stood staring across my way, with a sharp frown on his thin face. I shook cigarette ash out of the window and he turned abruptly and sat down at a desk. His double-handled bag was on the desk in front of him. He sat rigidly, drumming on the desk beside the bag. His hand reached for the telephone, touched it and came away again. He lit a cigarette and shook the match violently, then strode to the window and stared out at me some more.

This was interesting, if at all, only because he was a doctor. Doctors, as a rule, are the least curious of men. While they are still internes they hear enough secrets to last them a lifetime. Dr Almore seemed interested in me. More than interested, bothered.

I reached down to turn the ignition key, then Lavery's front door opened and I took my hand away and leaned back again. Lavery came briskly up the walk of his house, shot a glance down the street and turned to go into his garage. He was dressed as I had seen him. He had a rough towel and a steamer rug over his arm. I heard the garage door lift up, then the car door open and shut, then the grind and cough of the starting car. It backed up the steep incline to the street, white steamy exhaust pouring from its rear end. It was a cute little blue convertible, with the top folded down and Lavery's sleek dark head just rising above it. He was now wearing a natty pair of sun-goggles with very wide white sidebows. The convertible swooped off down the block and danced around the corner.

There was nothing in that for me. Mr Christopher Lavery was bound for the edge of the broad Pacific, to lie in the sun and let the girls see what they didn't necessarily have to go on missing.

I gave my attention back to Dr Almore. He was on the telephone now, not talking, holding it to his ear, smoking and waiting. Then he leaned forward as you do when the voice comes back, listened, hung up and wrote something on a pad in front of him. Then a heavy book with yellow sides appeared on his desk and he opened it just about in the middle. While he was doing this he gave one quick look out of the window, straight at the Chrysler.

He found his place in the book, leaned down over it and quick puffs of smoke appeared in the air over the pages. He wrote something else, put the book away, and grabbed for the telephone again. He dialled, waited, began to speak quickly, pushing his head down and making gestures in the air with his cigarette.

He finished his call and hung up. He leaned back and sat there brooding, staring down at his desk, but not forgetting to look out of the window every half-minute. He was waiting, and I waited with him, for no reason at all. Doctors make many phone calls, talk to many people. Doctors look out of their front windows, doctors frown, doctors show nervousness, doctors have things on their mind and show the strain. Doctors are just people, born to sorrow, fighting the long grim fight like the rest of us.

But there was something about the way this one behaved that intrigued me. I looked at my watch, decided it was time to get something to eat, lit another cigarette and didn't move.

It took about five minutes. Then a green sedan whisked around the corner and bore down the block. It coasted to a stop in front of Dr Almore's house and its tall buggy-whip aerial quivered. A big man with dusty blond hair got out and went up to Dr Almore's front door. He rang the bell and leaned down to strike a match on the step. His head came around and he stared across the street exactly at where I was sitting.

The door opened and he went into the house. An invisible hand gathered the curtains at Dr Almore's study window and blanked the room. I sat there, and stared at the sun-darkened lining of the curtains. More time trickled by.

The front door opened again and the big man loafed casually down the steps and through the gate. He snapped his cigarette end off into the distance and rumpled his hair. He shrugged once, pinched the end of his chin, and walked diagonally across the street. His steps in the quiet were leisurely and distinct. Dr Almore's curtains moved apart again behind him. Dr Almore stood in his window and watched.

A large freckled hand appeared on the sill of the car door at my elbow. A large face, deeply lined, hung above it. The man had eyes of metallic blue. He looked at me solidly and spoke in a deep harsh voice.

'Waiting for somebody?' he asked.

'I don't know,' I said. 'Am I?'

'I'll ask the questions.'

'Well, I'll be damned,' I said. 'So that's the answer to the pantomime.'

'What pantomime?' He gave me a hard level unfriendly stare from his very blue eyes.

I pointed across the street with my cigarette. 'Nervous Nellie and the telephone. Calling the cops, after first getting my name from the Auto Club, probably, then looking it up in the city directory. What goes on?'

'Let me see your driver's licence.'

I gave him back his stare. 'You fellows ever flash a buzzer – or is acting tough all the identification you need?'

'If I have to get tough, fellow, you'll know it.'

I leaned down and turned my ignition key and pressed the starter. The motor caught and idled down.

'Cut that motor,' he said savagely, and put his foot on the running-board.

I cut the motor again and leaned back and looked at him.

'God damn it,' he said, 'do you want me to drag you out of there and bounce you on the pavement?'

I got my wallet out and handed it to him. He drew the celluloid pocket out and looked at my driver's licence, then turned the pocket over and looked at the photostat of my other licence on the back. He rammed it contemptuously back into the wallet and handed me the wallet. I put it away. His hand dipped and came up with a blue-and-gold police badge.

'Degarmo, detective-lieutenant,' he said in his heavy brutal voice.

'Pleased to meet you, lieutenant.'

'Skip it. Now tell why you're down here casing Almore's place.'

'I'm not casing Almore's place, as you put it, lieutenant. I never heard of Dr Almore and I don't know of any reason why I should want to case his house.'

He turned his head to spit. I was meeting the spitting boys today.

'What's your grift then? We don't like peepers down here. We don't have one in town.'

'Is that so?'

'Yeah, that's so. So come on, talk it up. Unless you want to ride down to the clubhouse and sweat it out under the bright lights.'

I didn't answer him.

'Her folks hire you?' he asked suddenly.

I shook my head.

'The last boy that tried it ended up on the road gang, sweetheart.'

'I bet it's good,' I said, 'if only I could guess. Tried what?'

'Tried to put the bite on him,' he said thinly.

'Too bad I don't know how,' I said. 'He looks like an easy man to bite.'

'That line of talk don't buy you anything,' he said.

'All right,' I said. 'Let's put it this way. I don't know Dr Almore, never heard of him, and I'm not interested in him. I'm down here visiting a friend and looking at the view. If I'm doing anything else, it doesn't happen to be any of your business. If you don't like that, the best thing to do is to take it down to headquarters and see the day captain.'

He moved a foot heavily on the running-board and looked doubtful. 'Straight goods?' he asked slowly.

'Straight goods.'

'Aw hell, the guy's screwy,' he said suddenly and looked back over his shoulder at the house. 'He ought to see a doctor.' He laughed, without any amusement in the laugh. He took his foot off my running-board and rumpled his wiry hair.

'Go on – beat it,' he said. 'Stay off our reservation, and you won't make any enemies.'

I pressed the starter again. When the motor was idling gently I said: 'How's Al Norgaard these days?'

He stared at me. 'You knew Al?'

'Yeah. He and I worked on a case down here a couple of years ago – when Wax was chief of police.'

'Al's in the military police. Wish I was,' he said bitterly. He started to walk away and then swung sharply on his heel. 'Go on, beat it before I change my mind,' he snapped.

He walked heavily across the street and through Dr Almore's front gate again.

I let the clutch in and drove away. On the way back to the city, I listened to my thoughts. They moved fitfully in and out, like Dr Almore's thin nervous hands pulling at the edges of his curtains.

Back in Los Angeles I ate lunch and went up to my office in the Cahuenga Building to see what mail there was. I called Kingsley from there.

'I saw Lavery,' I told him. 'He told me just enough dirt to sound frank. I tried to needle him a little, but nothing came of it. I still like the idea that they quarrelled and split up and that he hopes to fix it up with her yet.'

'Then he must know where she is,' Kingsley said.

'He might, but it doesn't follow. By the way, a rather curious thing happened to me on Lavery's street. There are only two houses. The other belongs to a Dr Almore.' I told him briefly about the rather curious thing.

He was silent for a moment at the end and then he said: 'Is this Dr Albert Almore?'

'Yes.'

'He was Crystal's doctor for a time. He came to the house several times when she was – well, when she had been overdrinking. I thought him a little too quick with a hypodermic needle. His wife – let me see, there was something about his wife. Oh yes, she committed suicide.'

I said, 'When?'

'I don't remember. Quite a long time now. I never knew them socially. What are you going to do now?'

I told him I was going up to Puma Lake, although it was a little late in the day to start.

He said I would have plenty of time and that they had an hour more of daylight in the mountains.

I said that was fine and we hung up.

5

San Bernardino baked and shimmered in the afternoon heat. The air was hot enough to blister my tongue. I drove through it gasping, stopped long enough to buy a pint of liquor in case I fainted before I got to the mountains, and started up the long grade to Crestline. In fifteen miles the road climbed five thousand feet, but even then it was far from cool. Thirty miles of mountain driving brought me to the tall pines and a place called Bubbling Springs. It had a clapboard store and a gas pump, but it felt like paradise. From there on it was cool all the way.

The Puma Lake dam had an armed sentry at each end and one in the middle. The first one I came to had me close all the windows of the car before crossing over the dam. About a hundred yards from the dam a rope with cork floats barred the pleasure boats from coming any closer. Beyond these details the war did not seem to have done anything much to Puma Lake.

Canoes paddled about on the blue water and rowing-boats with out-board motors put-putted and speedboats showing off like fresh kids made wide swathes of foam and turned on a dime and girls in them shrieked and dragged their hands in the water. Jounced around in the wake of the speedboats people who had paid two dollars for a fishing licence were trying to get a dime of it back in tired-tasting fish.

The road skimmed along a high granite outcrop and dropped to meadows of coarse grass in which grew what was left of the wild irises and white and purple lupin and bugle flowers and columbine and pennyroyal and desert paint brush. Tall yellow pines probed at the clear blue sky. The road dropped again to lake level and the landscape began to be full of girls in gaudy slacks and snoods and peasant handkerchiefs and rat rolls and fat-soled sandals and fat white thighs. People on bicycles wobbled cautiously over the highway and now and then an anxious-looking bird thumped past on a power-scooter.

A mile from the village the highway was joined by another lesser road which curved back into the mountains. A rough wooden sign under the highway sign said: *Little Fawn Lake* 1¾ *miles*. I took it. Scattered cabins were perched along the slopes for the first mile and then nothing. Presently another very narrow road debouched from this one and another rough wood sign said: *Little Fawn Lake. Private Road. No Trespassing.*

I turned the Chrysler into this and crawled carefully around huge bare granite rocks and past a little waterfall and through a maze of black oak-trees and ironwood and manzanita and silence. A blue-jay squawked on a branch and a squirrel scolded at me and beat one paw angrily on the pine cone it was holding. A scarlet-topped woodpecker stopped probing in the bark long enough to look at me with one beady eye and then dodge behind the tree trunk to look at me with the other one. I came to a five-barred gate and another sign.

Beyond the gate the road wound for a couple of hundred yards through trees and then suddenly below me was a small oval lake deep in trees and rocks and wild grass, like a drop of dew caught in a curled leaf. At the near end of it was a rough concrete dam with a rope hand-rail across the top and an old millwheel at the side. Near that stood a small cabin of native pine with the bark on it.

Across the lake the long way by the road and the short way by the top of the dam a large redwood cabin overhung the water and farther along, each well separated from the others, were two other cabins. All three were shut up and quiet, with drawn curtains. The big one had orange-yellow venetian blinds and a twelve-paned window facing on the lake.

At the far end of the lake from the dam was what looked like a small pier and band pavilion. A warped wooden sign on it was painted in large white letters: *Camp Kilkare*. I couldn't see any sense in that in these surroundings, so I got out of the car and started down towards the nearest cabin. Somewhere behind it an axe thudded.

I pounded on the cabin door. The axe stopped. A man's voice yelled from somewhere. I sat down on a rock and lit a cigarette. Steps came around the corner of the cabin, uneven steps. A man with a harsh face and a swarthy skin came into view carrying a double-bitted axe.

He was heavily built and not very tall and he limped as he walked, giving his right leg a little kick out with each step and swinging the foot in a shallow arc. He had a dark unshaven chin and steady blue eyes and grizzled hair that curled over his ears and needed cutting badly. He wore blue denim pants and a blue shirt open on a brown muscular neck. A cigarette hung from the corner of his mouth. He spoke in a tight tough city voice.

'Yeah?'

'Mr Bill Chess?'

'That's me.'

I stood up and got Kingsley's note of introduction out of my pocket and handed to him. He squinted at the note, then clumped into the cabin and came back with glasses perched on his nose. He read the note carefully and then again. He put it in his shirt pocket, buttoned the flap of the pocket and put his hand out.

'Pleased to meet you, Mr Marlowe.'

We shook hands. He had a hand like a wood rasp.

'You want to see Kingsley's cabin, huh? Glad to show you. He ain't selling for Chrissake?' He eyed me steadily and jerked a thumb across the lake.

'He might,' I said. 'Everything's for sale in California.'

'Ain't that the truth? That's his – the redwood job. Lined with knotty pine, composition roof, stone foundations and porches, full bath and shower, venetian blinds all around, big fireplace, oil-stove in the big bedroom – and brother, you need it in the spring and autumn – Pilgrim combination gas and wood range, everything first class. Cost about eight thousand and that's money for a mountain cabin. And private reservoir in the hills for water.'

'How about electric light and telephone?' I asked, just to be friendly.

'Electric light, sure. No phone. You couldn't get one now. If you could, it would cost plenty to string the lines out here.'

He looked at me with steady blue eyes and I looked at him. In spite of his weathered appearance he looked like a drinker. He had the thickened and glossy skin, the too noticeable veins, the bright glitter in the eyes.

I said: 'Anybody living there now?'

'Nope. Mrs Kingsley was here a few weeks back. She went down the hill. Back any day, I guess. Didn't he say?'

I looked surprised. 'Why? Does she go with the cabin?'

He scowled and then put his head back and burst out laughing. The roar of his laughter was like a tractor backfiring. It blasted the woodland silence to shreds.

'Jesus, if that ain't a kick in the pants!' he gasped. 'Does she go with the –' He put out another bellow and then his mouth shut tight as a trap.

'Yeah, it's a swell cabin,' he said, eyeing me carefully.

'The beds comfortable?' I asked.

He leaned forward and smiled. 'Maybe you'd like a face full of knuckles,' he said.

I stared at him with my mouth open. 'That one went by me too fast,' I said. 'I never laid an eye on it.'

'How would I know if the beds are comfortable?' he snarled, bending down a little so that he could reach me with a hard right, if it worked out that way.

'I don't know why you wouldn't know,' I said. 'I won't press the point. I can find out for myself.'

'Yah,' he said bitterly, 'think I can't smell a dick when I meet one? I played hit and run with them in every state in the Union. Nuts to you, pal. And nuts to Kingsley. So he hires himself a dick to come up here and see am I wearing his pyjamas, huh? Listen, Jack, I might have a stiff leg and all, but the women I could get –'

I put a hand out, hoping he wouldn't pull it off and throw it in the lake.

'You're slipping your clutch,' I told him. 'I didn't come up here to inquire into your love life. I never saw Mrs Kingsley. I never saw Mr Kingsley until this morning. What the hell's the matter with you?'

He dropped his eyes and rubbed the back of his hand viciously across his mouth, as if he wanted to hurt himself. Then he held the hand in front of his eyes and squeezed it into a hard fist and opened it again and stared at the fingers. They were shaking a little.

'Sorry, Mr Marlowe,' he said slowly. 'I was out on the roof last night and I've got a hangover like seven Swedes. I've been up here alone for a month and it's got me talking to myself. A thing happened to me.'

'Anything a drink would help?'

His eyes focused sharply on me and glinted. 'You got one?'

I pulled the pint of rye out of my pocket and held it so that he could see the green label over the cap.

'I don't deserve it,' he said. 'God damn it, I don't. Wait till I get a couple of glasses or would you come into the cabin?'

'I like it out here. I'm enjoying the view.'

He swung his stiff leg and went into his cabin and came back carrying a couple of small cheese glasses. He sat down on the rock beside me, smelling of dried perspiration.

I tore the metal cap off the bottle and poured him a stiff drink and a light one for myself. We touched glasses and drank. He rolled the liquor on his tongue and a bleak smile put a little sunshine into his face.

'Man, that's from the right bottle,' he said. 'I wonder what made me sound off like that. I guess a guy gets the blues up here all alone. No company, no real friends, no wife.' He paused and added with a sideways look. 'Especially no wife.'

I kept my eyes on the blue water of the tiny lake. Under an overhanging rock a fish surfaced in a lance of light and a circle of widening ripples. A light breeze moved the tops of the pines with a noise like a gentle surf.

'She left me,' he said slowly. 'She left me a month ago. Friday the 12th of June. A day I'll remember.'

I stiffened, but not too much to pour more whisky into his empty glass. Friday the 12th of June was the day Mrs Crystal Kingsley was supposed to have come into town for a party.

'But you don't want to hear about that,' he said. And in his faded blue eyes was the deep yearning to talk about it, as plain as anything could possibly be.

'It's none of my business,' I said. 'But if it would make you feel any better –'

He nodded sharply. 'Two guys will meet on a park bench,' he said, 'and start talking about God. Did you ever notice that? Guys that wouldn't talk about God to their best friend.'

'I know that,' I said.

He drank and looked across the lake. 'She was one swell kid,' he said softly. 'A little sharp in the tongue sometimes, but one swell kid. It was love at first sight with me and Muriel. I met her in a joint in Riverside, a year and three months ago. Not the kind of joint where a guy would expect to meet a girl like Muriel, but that's how it happened. We got married. I loved her. I knew I was well off. And I was too much of a skunk to play ball with her.'

I moved a little to show him I was still there, but I didn't say anything for fear of breaking the spell. I sat with my drink untouched in my hand. I like to drink, but not when people are using me for a diary.

He went on sadly: 'But you know how it is with marriage – any marriage. After a while a guy like me, a common no-good guy like me, he wants to feel a leg. Some other leg. Maybe it's lousy, but that's the way it is.'

He looked at me and I said I had heard the idea expressed.

He tossed his second drink off. I passed him the bottle. A blue-jay went up a pine-tree hopping from branch to branch without moving his wings or even pausing to balance.

'Yeah,' Bill Chess said. 'All these hillbillies are half-crazy and I'm getting that way too. Here I am sitting pretty, no rent to pay, a good pension cheque every month, half my bonus money in war bonds, I'm married to as neat a little blonde as ever you clapped an eye on and all the time I'm nuts and I don't know it. I go for *that*.' He pointed hard at the redwood cabin across the lake. It was turning the colour of ox blood in the late afternoon light. 'Right in the front yard,' he said, 'right under the windows, and a showy little tart that means no more to me than a blade of grass. Jesus, what a sap a guy can be.'

He drank his third drink and steadied the bottle on a rock. He fished a cigarette out of his shirt, fired a match on his thumb-nail and puffed rapidly. I breathed with my mouth open, as silent as a burglar behind a curtain.

'Hell,' he said at last, 'you'd think if I had to jump off the dock I'd go a little ways from home and pick me a change in types at least. But little roundheels over there ain't even that. She's a blonde like Muriel, same size and weight, same type, almost the same colour eyes. But, brother, how different from then on in. Pretty, sure, but no prettier to anybody and not half so pretty to me. Well, I'm over there burning trash that morning and minding my own business, as much as I ever mind it. And she comes to the back door of the cabin in peekaboo pyjamas so thin you can see the pink of her nipples against the cloth. And she says in her lazy, no-good voice: "Have a drink, Bill. Don't work so hard on such a beautiful morning." And me, I like a drink too well and I go to the kitchen door and take it. And then I take another and then I take another and then I'm in the house. And the closer I get to her the more bedroom her eyes are.'

He paused and swept me with a hard level look.

'You asked me if the beds over there were comfortable and I got sore. You didn't mean a thing. I was just too full of remembering. Yeah – the bed I was in was comfortable.'

He stopped talking and I let his words hang in the air. They fell slowly and after them was silence. He leaned to pick the bottle off the rock and stare at it. He seemed to fight with it in his mind. The whisky won the fight, as it always does. He took a long savage drink out of the bottle and then screwed the cap on tightly, as if that meant something. He picked up a stone and flicked it into the water.

'I came back across the dam,' he said slowly, in a voice already thick with alcohol. 'I'm as smooth as a new piston head. I'm getting away with something. Us boys can be so wrong about those little things, can't we? I'm not getting away with anything at all. Not anything at all. I listen to Muriel telling me and she don't even raise her voice. But she tells me things about myself I didn't even imagine. Oh yeah, I'm getting away with it lovely.'

'So she left you,' I said, when he fell silent.

'That night. I wasn't even here. I felt too mean to stay even half-sober. I hopped into my Ford and went over to the north side of the lake and holed up with a couple of no-goods like myself and got good and stinking. Not that it did me any good. Along about 4 a.m. I got back home and Muriel had gone, packed up and gone, nothing left but a note on the bureau and some cold cream on the pillow.'

He pulled a dog-eared piece of paper out of a shabby old wallet and passed it over. It was written in pencil on blue-lined paper from a note-book. It read:

'I'm sorry, Bill, but I'd rather be dead than live with you any longer. Muriel.'

I handed it back. 'What about over there?' I asked, pointing across the lake with a glance.

Bill Chess picked up a flat stone and tried to skip it across the water, but it refused to skip.

'Nothing over there,' he said. 'She packed up and went down the same night. I didn't see her again. I don't want to see her again. I haven't heard a word from Muriel in the whole month, not a single word. I don't have any idea at all where she's at. With some other guy, maybe. I hope he treats her better than I did.'

He stood up and took keys out of his pocket and shook them. 'So if you want to go across and look at Kingsley's cabin, there isn't a thing to stop you. And thanks for listening to the soap opera. And thanks for the liquor. Here.' He picked the bottle up and handed me what was left of the pint.

6

We went down the slope to the bank of the lake and the narrow top of the dam. Bill Chess swung his stiff leg in front of me, holding on to the rope hand-rail set in iron stanchions. At one point water washed over the concrete in a lazy swirl.

'I'll let some out through the wheel in the morning,' he said over his shoulder. 'That's all the darn thing is good for. Some movie outfit put it up three years ago. They made a picture up here. That little pier down at the other end is some more of their work. Most of what they built is torn down and hauled away, but Kingsley had them leave the pier and the millwheel. Kind of gives the place a touch of colour.'

I followed him up a flight of heavy wooden steps to the porch of the Kingsley cabin. He unlocked the door and we went into hushed warmth. The closed-up room was almost hot. The light filtering through the slatted blinds made narrow bars across the floor. The living-room was long and cheerful and had Indian rugs, padded mountain furniture with metal-strapped joints, chintz curtains, a plain hardwood floor, plenty of lamps and a little built-in bar with round stools in one corner. The room was neat and clean and had no look of having been left at short notice.

We went into the bedrooms. Two of them had twin beds and one a large double bed with a cream-coloured spread having a design in plum-coloured wool stitched over it. This was the master bedroom, Bill Chess said. On a dresser of varnished wood there were toilet articles and accessories in jade-green enamel and stainless steel, and an assortment of cosmetic oddments. A couple of cold cream jars had the wavy gold brand of the Gillerlain Company on them. One whole side of the room consisted of closets with sliding doors. I slid one open and peeked inside. It seemed to be full of women's clothes of the sort they wear at resorts. Bill Chess watched me sourly while I pawed them over. I slid the door shut and pulled open a deep shoe drawer underneath. It contained at least half a dozen pairs of new-looking shoes. I heaved the drawer shut and straightened up.

Bill Chess was planted squarely in front of me, with his chin pushed out and his hard hands in knots on his hips.

'So what did you want to look at the lady's clothes for?' he asked in an angry voice.

'Reasons,' I said. 'For instance, Mrs Kingsley didn't go home when she left here. Her husband hasn't seen her since. He does not know where she is.'

He dropped his fists and twisted them slowly at his sides. 'Dick it is,' he snarled. 'The first guess is always right. I had myself about talked out of it. Boy, did I open up to you. Nellie with her hair in her lap. Boy, am I a smart little egg!'

'I can respect a confidence as well as the next fellow,' I said, and walked around him into the kitchen.

There was a big green-and-white combination range, a sink of lacquered yellow pine, an automatic water-heater in the service porch, and opening off the other side of the kitchen a cheerful breakfast-room with many windows and an expansive plastic breakfast set. The shelves were gay with coloured dishes and glasses and a set of pewter serving-dishes.

Everything was in apple-pie order. There were no dirty cups or plates on the drain-board, no smeared glasses or empty liquor bottles hanging around. There were no ants and no flies. Whatever loose living Mrs Derace Kingsley indulged in she managed without leaving the usual Greenwich Village slop behind her.

I went back to the living-room and out on the front porch again and waited for Bill Chess to lock up. When he had done that and turned to me with his scowl well in place I said:

'I didn't ask you to take your heart out and squeeze it for me, but I didn't try to stop you either. Kingsley doesn't have to know his wife made a pass at you, unless there's a lot more behind all this than I can see now.'

'The hell with you,' he said, and the scowl stayed right where it was.

'All right, the hell with me. Would there be any chance your wife and Kingsley's wife went away together?'

'I don't get it,' he said.

'After you went to drown your troubles they could have had a fight and made up and cried down each other's necks. Then Mrs Kingsley might have taken your wife down the hill. She had to have something to ride in, didn't she?'

It sounded silly, but he took it seriously enough.

'Nope. Muriel didn't cry down anybody's neck. They left the weeps out of Muriel. And if she did want to cry on a shoulder, she wouldn't have picked little roundheels. And as for transportation, she has a Ford of her own. She couldn't drive mine easily on account of the way the controls are switched over for my stiff leg.'

'It was just a passing thought,' I said.

'If any more like it pass you, let them go right on,' he said.

'For a guy that takes his long wavy hair down in front of complete strangers, you're pretty damn touchy,' I said.

He took a step towards me. 'Want to make something of it?'

'Look, pal,' I said. 'I'm working hard to think you are a fundamentally good egg. Help me out a little, can't you?'

He breathed hard for a moment and then dropped his hands and spread them helplessly.

'Boy, can I brighten up anybody's afternoon,' he sighed. 'Want to walk back around the lake?'

'Sure, if your leg will stand it.'

'Stood it plenty of times before.'

We started off side by side, as friendly as puppies again. It would probably last all of fifty yards. The roadway, barely wide enough to pass a car, hung above the level of the lake and dodged between high rocks. About half-way to the far end another smaller cabin was built on a rock foundation. The third was well beyond the end of the lake, on a patch of almost level ground. Both were closed up and had that long-empty look.

Bill Chess said after a minute or two: 'That straight, good little roundheels lammed off?'

'So it seems.'

'You are a real dick or just a shamus?'

'Just a shamus.'

'She go with some guy?'

'I should think it likely.'

'Sure she did. It's a cinch. Kingsley ought to be able to guess that. She had plenty of friends.'

'Up here?'

He didn't answer me.

'Was one of them named Lavery?'

'I wouldn't know,' he said.

'There's no secret about this one,' I said. 'She sent a wire from El Paso saying she and Lavery were going to Mexico.' I dug the wire out of my pocket and held it out. He fumbled his glasses loose from his shirt and stopped to read it. He handed the paper back and put his glasses away again and stared out over the blue water.

'That's a little confidence for you to hold against some of what you gave me,' I said.

'Lavery was up here once,' he said slowly.

'He admits he saw her a couple of months ago, probably up here. He claims he hasn't seen her since. We don't know whether to believe him. There's no reason why we should and no reason why we shouldn't.'

'She isn't with him now, then?'

'He says not.'

'I wouldn't think she would fuss with little details like getting married,' he said soberly. 'A Florida honeymoon would be more in her line.'

'But you can't give me any positive information? You didn't see her go or hear anything that sounded authentic?'

'Nope,' he said. 'And if I did, I doubt if I would tell. I'm dirty, but not that kind of dirty.'

'Well, thanks for trying,' I said.

'I don't owe you any favours,' he said. 'The hell with you and every other God-damn snooper.'

'Here we go again,' I said.

We had come to the end of the lake now. I left him standing there and walked out on the little pier. I leaned on the wooden railing at the end of it and saw that what had looked like a band pavilion was nothing but two pieces of propped-up wall meeting at a flat angle towards the dam. About two feet deep of overhanging roof was stuck on the wall, like a coping. Bill Chess came up behind me and leaned on the railing at my side.

'Not that I don't thank you for the liquor,' he said.

'Yeah. Any fish in the lake?'

'Some smart old bastards of trout. No fresh stock. I don't go for fish much myself. I don't bother with them. Sorry I got tough again.'

I grinned and leaned on the railing and stared down into the deep, still water. It was green when you looked down into it. There was a swirl of movement down there and a swift greenish form moved in the water.

'There's Granpa,' Bill Chess said. 'Look at the size of that old bastard. He ought to be ashamed of himself getting so fat.'

Down below the water there was what looked like an underwater flooring. I couldn't see the sense of that. I asked him.

'Used to be a boat landing before the dam was raised. That lifted the water level so far the old landing was six feet under.'

A flat-bottomed boat dangled on a frayed rope tied to a post of the pier. It lay in the water almost without motion, but not quite. The air was peaceful and calm and sunny and held a quiet you don't get in cities. I could have stayed there for hours doing nothing but forgetting all about Derace Kingsley and his wife and her boy friends.

There was a hard movement at my side and Bill Chess said, 'Look there!' in a voice that growled like mountain thunder.

His hard fingers dug into the flesh of my arm until I started to get mad. He was bending far out over the railing, staring down like a loon, his face as white as the weather tan would let it get. I looked down with him into the water at the edge of the submerged staging.

Languidly at the edge of this green and sunken shelf of wood something waved out from the darkness, hesitated, waved back again out of sight under the flooring.

The something had looked far too much like a human arm.

Bill Chess straightened his body rigidly. He turned without a sound and clumped back along the pier. He bent to a loose pile of stones and heaved. His panting breath reached me. He got a big one free and lifted it breast high and started back out on the pier with it. It must have weighed a hundred pounds. His neck muscles stood out like ropes under canvas under his taut brown skin. His teeth were clamped tight and his breath hissed between them.

He reached the end of the pier and steadied himself and lifted the rock high. He held it a moment poised, his eyes staring down now, measuring. His mouth made a vague, distressful sound and his body lurched forward hard against the quivering rail and the heavy stone smashed down into the water.

The splash it made went over both of us. The rock fell straight and true and struck on the edge of the submerged planking, almost exactly where we had seen the thing wave in and out.

For a moment the water was a confused boiling, then the ripples widened off into the distance, coming smaller and smaller with a trace of froth at the middle, and there was a dim sound as of wood breaking under water, a sound that seemed to come to us a long time after it should have been audible. An ancient rotted plank popped suddenly through the surface, stuck out a full foot of its jagged end, and fell back with a flat slap and floated off.

The depths cleared again. Something moved in them that was not a board. It rose slowly, with an infinitely careless languor, a long dark twisted something that rolled lazily in the water as it rose. It broke surface casually, lightly, without haste. I saw wool, sodden and black, a leather jerkin blacker than ink, a pair of slacks. I saw shoes and something that bulged nastily between the shoes and the cuffs of the slacks. I saw a wave of dark blonde hair straighten out in the water and hold still for a brief instant as if with a calculated effect, and then swirl into a tangle again.

The thing rolled over once more and an arm flapped up barely above the skin of the water and the arm ended in a bloated hand that was the hand of a freak. Then the face came. A swollen pulpy grey white mass without features, without eyes, without mouth. A blotch of grey dough, a nightmare with human hair on it.

A heavy necklace of green stones showed on what had been a neck, half-embedded, large rough green stones with something that glittered joining them together.

Bill Chess held the hand-rail and his knuckles were polished bones.

'Muriel!' his voice said croakingly. 'Sweet Christ, it's Muriel!'

His voice seemed to come to me from a long way off, over a hill, through a thick silent growth of trees.

7

Behind the window of the board shack one end of a counter was piled with dusty folders. The glass upper half of the door was lettered in flaked black paint. *Chief of Police. Fire Chief. Town Constable. Chamber of Commerce.* In the lower corners a USO card and a Red Cross emblem were fastened to the glass.

I went in. There was a pot-bellied stove in the corner and a roll-top desk in the other corner behind the counter. There was a large blue print map of the district on the wall and beside that a board with four hooks on it, one of which supported a frayed and much-mended mackinaw. On the counter beside the dusty folders lay the usual sprung pen, exhausted blotter and smeared bottle of gummy ink. The end wall beside the desk was covered with telephone numbers written in hard-bitten figures that would last as long as the wood and looked as if they had been written by a child.

A man sat at the desk in a wooden armchair whose legs were anchored to flat boards, fore and aft, like skis. A spittoon big enough to coil a hose in was leaning against the man's right leg. He had a sweat-stained Stetson on the back of his head and his large hairless hands were clasped comfortably over his stomach, above the waistband of a pair of khaki pants that had been scrubbed thin years ago. His shirt matched the pants except that it was even more faded. It was buttoned tight to the man's thick neck and undecorated by a tie. His hair was mousy-brown except at the temples, where it was the colour of old snow. He sat more on his left hip than his right, because there was a hip holster down inside his right hip pocket, and a half-foot of forty-five gun reared up and bored into his solid back. The star on his left breast had a bent point.

He had large ears and friendly eyes and his jaws munched slowly and he looked as dangerous as a squirrel and much less nervous. I liked everything about him. I leaned on the counter and looked at him and he looked at me and nodded and loosed half a pint of tobacco juice down his right leg into the spittoon. It made a nasty sound of something falling into water.

I lit a cigarette and looked round for an ash-tray.

'Try the floor, son,' the large friendly man said.

'Are you Sheriff Patton?'

'Constable and deputy-sheriff. What law we got to have around here I'm it. Come election anyways. There's a couple of good boys running against me this time and I might get whupped. Job pays eighty a month, cabin, firewood and electricity. That ain't hay in these little old mountains.'

'Nobody's going to whip you,' I said. 'You're going to get a lot of publicity.'

'That so?' he asked indifferently and ruined the spittoon again.

'That is, if your jurisdiction extends over to Little Fawn Lake.'

'Kingsley's place. Sure. Something bothering over there, son?'

'There's a dead woman in the lake.'

That shook him to the core. He unclasped his hands and scratched one ear. He got to his feet by grasping the arms of his chair and deftly kicking it back from under him. Standing up he was a big man and hard. The fat was just cheerfulness.

'Anybody I know?' he inquired uneasily.

'Muriel Chess. I guess you know her. Bill Chess's wife.'

'Yep, I know Bill Chess.' His voice hardened a little.

'Looks like suicide. She left a note which sounded as if she was just going away. But it could be a suicide note just as well. She's not nice to look at. Been in the water a long time, about a month judging by the circumstances.'

He scratched his other ear. 'What circumstances would that be?' His eyes were searching my face now, slowly and calmly, but searching. He didn't seem in any hurry to blow his whistle.

'They had a fight a month ago. Bill went over to the north shore of the lake and was gone some hours. When he got home she was gone. He never saw her again.'

'I see. Who are you, son?'

'My name is Marlowe. I'm up from L.A. to look at the property. I had a note from Kingsley to Bill Chess. He took me around the lake and we went out on that little pier the movie people built. We were leaning on the rail and looking down into the water and something that looked like an arm waved out under the submerged flooring, the old boat landing. Bill dropped a heavy rock in and the body popped up.'

Patton looked at me without moving a muscle.

'Look, sheriff, hadn't we better run over there? The man's half-crazy with shock and he's there all alone.'

'How much liquor has he got?'

'Very little when I left. I had a pint, but we drank most of it talking.'

He moved over to the roll-top desk and unlocked a drawer. He brought up three or four bottles and held them against the light.

'This baby's near full,' he said, patting one of them. 'Mount Vernon. That ought to hold him. County don't allow me no money for emergency liquor, so I just have to seize a little here and there. Don't use it myself. Never could understand folks letting theirselves get gummed up with it.'

He put the bottle on his left hip and locked the desk up and lifted the flap in the counter. He fixed a card against the inside of the glass door panel. I looked at the card as we went out. It read: *Back in Twenty Minutes – Maybe*.

'I'll run down and get Doc Hollis,' he said. 'Be right back and pick you up. That your car?'

'Yes.'

'You can follow along then, as I come back by.'

He got into a car which had a siren on it, two red spotlights, two fog-lights, a red and white fire plate, a new airraid horn on top, three axes, two heavy coils of rope and a fire-extinguisher in the back seat, extra petrol and oil and water-cans in a frame on the running-board, an extra spare tyre roped to the one on the rack, the stuffing coming out of the upholstery in dingy wads, and half an inch of dust over what was left of the paint.

Behind the right-hand lower corner of the windshield there was a white card printed in block capitals. It read:

VOTERS, ATTENTION! KEEP JIM PATTON CONSTABLE. HE IS TOO
OLD TO GO TO WORK

He turned the car and went off down the street in a swirl of white dust.

8

He stopped in front of a white frame building across the road from the stage depot. He went into the white building and presently came out with a man who got into the back seat with the axes and the rope. The official car came back up the street and I fell in behind it. We sifted along the main stem through the slacks and shorts and French sailor jerseys and knotted bandannas and knobby knees and scarlet lips. Beyond the village we went up a dusty hill and stopped at a cabin. Patton touched the siren gently and a man in faded blue overalls opened the cabin door.

'Get in, Andy. Business.'

The man in blue overalls nodded morosely and ducked back into the cabin. He came back out wearing an oyster-grey lion-hunter's hat and got in under the wheel of Patton's car while Patton slid over. He was about thirty, dark, lithe, and had the slightly dirty and slightly underfed look of the native.

We drove out to Little Fawn Lake with me eating enough dust to make a batch of mud pies. At the five-barred gate Patton got out and let us through and we went on down to the lake. Patton got out again and went to the edge of the water and looked along towards the little pier. Bill Chess was sitting naked on the floor of the pier, with his head in his hands. There was something stretched out on the wet planks beside him.

'We can ride a ways more,' Patton said.

The two cars went on to the end of the lake and all four of us trooped down to the pier behind Bill Chess's back. The doctor stopped to cough rackingly into a handkerchief and then look thoughtfully at the handkerchief. He was an angular bug-eyed man with a sad sick face.

The thing that had been a woman lay face down on the boards with a rope under the arms. Bill Chess's clothes lay to one side. His stiff leg, flat and scarred at the knee, was stretched out in front of him, the other leg bent up and his forehead resting against it. He didn't move or look up as we came down behind him.

Patton took the pint bottle of Mount Vernon off his hip and unscrewed the top and handed it.

'Drink hearty, Bill.'

There was a horrible, sickening smell in the air. Bill Chess didn't seem to notice it, nor Patton nor the doctor. The man called Andy got a dusty brown blanket out of the car and threw it over the body. Then without a word he went and vomited under a pine-tree.

Bill Chess drank a long drink and sat holding the bottle against his bare bent knee. He began to talk in a stiff wooden voice, not looking at anybody, not talking to anybody in particular. He told about the quarrel and what happened after it, but not why it had happened. He didn't mention Mrs Kingsley even in the most casual way. He said that after I left him he had got a rope and stripped and gone down into the water and got the thing out. He had dragged it ashore and then got it up on his back and carried it out on the pier. He didn't know why. He had gone back into the water again then. He didn't have to tell us why.

Patton put a cut of tobacco into his mouth and chewed on it silently, his calm eyes full of nothing. Then he shut his teeth tight and leaned down to pull the blanket off the body. He turned the body over carefully, as if it might come to pieces. The late afternoon sun winked on the necklace of large green stones that were partly embedded in the swollen neck. They were roughly carved and lustreless, like soapstone or false jade. A gilt chain with an eagle clasp set with small brilliants joined the ends. Patton straightened his broad back and blew his nose on a tan handkerchief.

'What you say, Doc?'

'About what?' the bug-eyed man snarled.

'Cause and time of death.'

'Don't be a damn fool, Jim Patton.'

'Can't tell nothing, huh?'

'By looking at that? Good God!'

Patton sighed. 'Looks drowned all right,' he admitted. 'But you can't always tell. There's been cases where a victim would be knifed or poisoned or something, and they would soak him in the water to make things look different.'

'You get many like that up here?' the doctor inquired nastily.

'Only honest to God murder I ever had up here,' Patton said, watching Bill Chess out of the corner of his eye, 'was old Dad Meacham over on the north shore. He had a shack in Sheedy Canyon, did a little panning in summer on an old placer claim he had back in the valley near Belltop. Folks didn't see him around for a while in late fall, then come a heavy snow and his roof caved in to one side. So we was over there trying to prop her up a bit, figuring Dad had gone down the hill for the winter without telling anybody, the way them old prospectors do things. Well by gum, old Dad never went down the hill at all. There he was in bed with most of a kindling axe in the back of his head. We never did find out who done it. Somebody figured he had a little bag of gold hid away from the summer's panning.'

He looked thoughtfully at Andy. The man in the lion-hunter's hat was feeling a tooth in his mouth. He said:

''Course we know who done it. Guy Pope done it. Only Guy was dead nine days of pneumonia before we found Dad Meacham.'

'Eleven days,' Patton said.

'Nine,' the man in the lion-hunter's hat said.

'Was all of six years ago, Andy. Have it your own way, son. How you figure Guy Pope done it?'

'We found about three ounces of small nuggets in Guy's cabin along with some dust. Never was anything bigger'n sand on Guy's claim. Dad had nuggets all of a pennyweight, plenty of times.'

'Well, that's the way it goes,' Patton said, and smiled at me in a vague manner. 'Fellow always forgets something, don't he? No matter how careful he is.'

'Cop stuff,' Bill Chess said disgustedly and put his pants on and sat down again to put on his shoes and shirt. When he had them on he stood up and reached down for the bottle and took a good drink and laid the bottle carefully on the planks. He thrust his hairy wrists out towards Patton.

'That's the way you guys feel about it, put the cuffs on and get it over,' he said in a savage voice.

Patton ignored him and went over to the railing and looked down. 'Funny place for a body to be,' he said. 'No current here to mention, but what there is would be towards the dam.'

Bill Chess lowered his wrists and said quietly: 'She did it herself, you darn fool. Muriel was a fine swimmer. She dived down in and swum under the boards there and just breathed water in. Had to. No other way.'

'I wouldn't quite say that, Bill,' Patton answered him mildly. His eyes were as blank as new plates.

Andy shook his head. Patton looked at him with a sly grin. 'Crabbin' again, Andy?'

'Was nine days, I tell you. I just counted back,' the man in the lion-hunter's hat said morosely.

The doctor threw his arms up and walked away, with one hand to his head. He coughed into his handkerchief again, and again looked into the handkerchief with passionate attention.

Patton winked at me and spat over the railing. 'Let's get on to this one, Andy.'

'You ever try to drag a body six feet under water?'

'Nope, can't say I ever did, Andy. Any reason it couldn't be done with a rope?'

Andy shrugged. 'If a rope was used, it will show on the corpse. If you got to give yourself away like that, why bother to cover up at all?'

'Question of time,' Patton said. 'Fellow has his arrangements to make.'

Bill Chess snarled at them and reached down for the whisky. Looking at their solemn mountain faces I couldn't tell what they were really thinking.

Patton said absently: 'Something was said about a note.'

Bill Chess rummaged in his wallet and drew the folded piece of ruled paper loose. Patton took it and read it slowly.

'Don't seem to have any date,' he observed.

Bill Chess shook his head sombrely. 'No. She left a month ago. June 12th.'

'Left you once before, didn't she?'

'Yeah.' Bill Chess stared at him fixedly. 'I got drunk and stayed with a chippy. Just before the first snow last December. She was gone a week and came back all prettied up. Said she just had to get away for a while and had been staying with a girl she used to work with in L.A.'

'What was the name of this party?' Patton asked.

'Never told me and I never asked her. What Muriel did was all silk with me.'

'Sure. Note left that time. Bill?' Patton asked smoothly.

'No.'

'This note here looks middling old,' Patton said, holding it up.

'I carried it a month,' Bill Chess growled. 'Who told you she left me before?'

'I forget,' Patton said. 'You know how it is in a place like this. Not much folks don't notice. Except maybe in summer time where there's a lot of strangers about.'

Nobody said anything for a while and then Patton said absently: 'June 12th you say she left? Or you thought she left? Did you say the folks across the lake were up here then?'

Bill Chess looked at me and his face darkened again. 'Ask this snoopy guy – if he didn't already spill his guts to you.'

Patton didn't look at me at all. He looked at the line of mountains far beyond the lake. He said gently: 'Mr Marlowe here didn't tell me anything at all, Bill, except how the body come up out of the water and who it was. And that Muriel went away, as you thought, and left a note you showed him. I don't guess there's anything wrong in that, is there?'

There was another silence and Bill Chess stared down at the blanket-covered corpse a few feet away from him. He clenched his hands and a thick tear ran down his cheek.

'Mrs Kingsley was here,' he said. 'She went down the hill that same day. Nobody was in the other cabins. Perrys and Farquhars ain't been up at all this year.'

Patton nodded and was silent. A kind of charged emptiness hung in the air, as if something that had not been said was plain to all of them and didn't need saying.

Then Bill Chess said wildly: 'Take me in, you sons of bitches! Sure I did it! I drowned her. She was my girl and I loved her. I'm a heel, always was a heel, always will be a heel, but just the same I loved her. Maybe you guys wouldn't understand that. Just don't bother to try. Take me in, damn you!'

Nobody said anything at all.

Bill Chess looked down at his hard brown fist. He swung it up viciously and hit himself in the face with all his strength.

'You rotten son of a bitch,' he breathed in a harsh whisper.

His nose began to bleed slowly. He stood and the blood ran down his lip, down the side of his mouth, to the point of his chin. A drop fell sluggishly to his shirt.

Patton said quietly: 'Got to take you down the hill for questioning, Bill. You know that. We ain't accusing you of anything, but the folks down there have got to talk to you.'

Bill Chess said heavily: 'Can I change my clothes?'

'Sure. You go with him, Andy. And see what you can find to kind of wrap up what he got here.'

They went off along the path at the edge of the lake. The doctor cleared his throat and looked out over the water and sighed.

'You'll want to send the corpse down in my ambulance, Jim, won't you?'

Patton shook his head. 'Nope. This is a poor county, Doc. I figure the lady can ride cheaper than what you get for that ambulance.'

The doctor walked away from him angrily, saying over his shoulder: 'Let me know if you want me to pay for the funeral.'

'That ain't no way to talk,' Patton sighed.

9

The Indian Head Hotel was a brown building on a corner across from the new dance hall. I parked in front of it and used its rest-room to wash my face and hands and comb the pine needles out of my hair, before I went into the dining-drinking parlour that adjoined the lobby. The whole place was full to overflowing with males in leisure jackets and liquor breaths and females in high-pitched laughs, ox-blood finger-nails and dirty knuckles. The manager of the joint, a low budget tough guy in shirt sleeves and a mangled cigar, was prowling the room with watchful eyes.

At the cash desk a pale-haired man was fighting to get the war news on a small radio that was as full of static as the mashed potatoes were full of water. In the deep back corner of the room, a hillbilly orchestra of five pieces, dressed in ill-fitting white jackets and purple shirts, was trying to make itself heard above the brawl at the bar and smiling glassily into the fog of cigarette smoke and the blur of alcoholic voices. At Puma Point summer, that lovely season, was in full swing.

I gobbled what they called the regular dinner, drank a brandy to sit on its chest and hold it down, and went out on to the main street. It was still broad daylight but some of the neon signs had been turned on, and the evening reeled with the cheerful din of motor horns, children screaming, bowls rattling, skeeballs clunking, .22s snapping merrily in shooting-galleries, juke boxes playing like crazy, and behind all this out on the lake the hard barking roar of the speedboats going nowhere at all and acting as though they were racing with death.

In my Chrysler a thin, serious-looking, brown-haired girl in dark slacks was sitting smoking a cigarette and talking to a dude ranch cowboy who sat on my running-board. I walked around the car and got into it. The cowboy strolled away hitching his jeans up. The girl didn't move.

'I'm Birdie Keppel,' she said cheerfully. 'I'm the beautician here daytimes and evenings I work on the *Puma Point Banner*. Excuse me sitting in your car.'

'That's all right,' I said. 'You want to just sit or you want me to drive you somewhere?'

'You can drive down the road a piece where it's quieter, Mr Marlowe. If you're obliging enough to talk to me.'

'Pretty good grapevine you've got up here,' I said and started the car.

I drove down past the post office to a corner where a blue-and-white arrow marked *Telephone* pointed down a narrow road towards the lake. I turned down that, drove down past the telephone office, which was a log cabin with a tiny railed lawn in front of it, passed another small cabin and pulled up in front of a huge oak-tree that flung its branches all the way across the road and a good fifty feet beyond it.

'This do, Miss Keppel?'

'Mrs. But just call me Birdie. Everybody does. This is fine. Pleased to meet you, Mr Marlowe. I see you come from Hollywood, that sinful city.'

She put a firm brown hand out and I shook it. Clamping bobbie pins into fat blondes had given her a grip like a pair of iceman's tongs.

'I was talking to Doc Hollis,' she said, 'about poor Muriel Chess. I thought you could give me some details. I understand you found the body.'

'Bill Chess found it really. I was just with him. You talk to Jim Patton?'

'Not yet. He went down the hill. Anyway, I don't think Jim would tell me much.'

'He's up for re-election,' I said. 'And you're a newspaper woman.'

'Jim's no politician, Mr Marlowe, and I could hardly call myself a newspaper woman. This little paper we get out up here is a pretty amateurish proposition.'

'Well, what do you want to know?' I offered her a cigarette and lit it for her.

'You might just tell me the story.'

'I came up here with a letter from Derace Kingsley to look at his property. Bill Chess showed me around, got talking to me, told me his wife had moved out on him and showed me the note she left. I had a bottle along and he punished it. He was feeling pretty blue. The liquor loosened him up, but he was lonely and aching to talk anyway. That's how it happened. I didn't know him. Coming back around the end of the lake we went out on the pier and Bill spotted an arm waving out from under the planking down in the water. It turned out to belong to what was left of Muriel Chess. I guess that's all.'

'I understand from Doc Hollis she had been in the water a long time. Pretty badly decomposed and all that.'

'Yes. Probably the whole month he thought she had been gone. There's no reason to think otherwise. The note's a suicide note.'

'Any doubt about that, Mr Marlowe?'

I looked at her sideways. Thoughtful dark eyes looked out at me under fluffed-out brown hair. The dusk had begun to fall now, very slowly. It was no more than a slight change in the quality of the light.

'I guess the police always have doubts in these cases,' I said.

'How about you?'

'My opinion doesn't go for anything.'

'But for what it's worth?'

'I only met Bill Chess this afternoon,' I said. 'He struck me as a quick-tempered lad and from his own account he's no saint. But he seems to have been in love with his wife. And I can't see him hanging around there for a month knowing she was rotting down in the water under that pier. Coming out of his cabin in the sunlight and looking along that soft blue water and seeing in his mind what was under it and what was happening to it. And knowing he put it there.'

'No more can I,' Birdie Keppel said softly. 'No more could anybody. And yet we know in our minds that such things have happened and will happen again. Are you in the real-estate business, Mr Marlowe?'

'No.'

'What line of business are you in, if I may ask?'

'I'd rather not say.'

'That's almost as good as saying,' she said. 'Besides, Doc Hollis heard you tell Jim Patton your full name. And we have an L.A. city directory in our office. I haven't mentioned it to anyone.'

'That's nice of you,' I said.

'And what's more, I won't,' she said. 'If you don't want me to.'

'What does it cost me?'

'Nothing,' she said. 'Nothing at all. I don't claim to be a very good newspaper woman. And we wouldn't print anything that would embarrass Jim Patton. Jim's the salt of the earth. But it does open up, doesn't it?'

'Don't draw any wrong conclusions,' I said. 'I had no interest in Bill Chess whatever.'

'No interest in Muriel Chess?'

'Why should I have any interest in Muriel Chess?'

She snuffed her cigarette out carefully into the ash-tray under the dashboard. 'Have it your own way,' she said. 'But here's a little item you might like to think about, if you don't know it already. There was a Los Angeles copper named De Soto up here about six weeks back, a big roughneck with damn poor manners. We didn't like him and we didn't open up to him much. I mean the three of us in the *Banner* office didn't. He had a photograph with him and he was looking for a woman called Mildred Haviland, he said. On police business. It was an ordinary photograph, an enlarged snapshot, not a police photo. He said he had information the woman was staying up here. The photo looked a good deal like Muriel Chess. The hair seemed to be reddish and in a very different style than she has worn it here, and the eyebrows were all plucked to narrow arches, and that changes a woman a good deal. But it did look a good deal like Bill Chess's wife.'

I drummed on the door of the car and after a moment I said, 'What did you tell him?'

'We didn't tell him anything. First off, we couldn't be sure. Second, we didn't like his manner. Third, even if we had been sure and had liked his manner, we likely would not have sicked him on to her. Why would we? Everybody's done something to be sorry for. Take me. I was married once – to a professor of classical languages at Redlands University.' She laughed lightly.

'You might have got yourself a story,' I said.

'Sure. But up here we're just people.'

'Did this man De Soto see Jim Patton?'

'Sure, he must have. Jim didn't mention it.'

'Did he show you his badge?'

She thought and then shook her head. 'I don't recall that he did. We just took him for granted, from what he said. He certainly acted like a tough city cop.'

'To me that's a little against his being one. Did anybody tell Muriel about this guy?'

She hesitated, looking quietly out through the windshield for a long moment before she turned her head and nodded.

'I did. Wasn't any of my damn business, was it?'

'What did she say?'

'She didn't say anything. She gave a funny little embarrassed laugh, as if I had been making a bad joke. Then she walked away. But I did get the impression that there was a queer look in her eyes, just for an instant. You still not interested in Muriel Chess, Mr Marlowe?'

'Why should I be? I never heard of her until I came up here this afternoon. Honest. And I never heard of anybody named Mildred Haviland either. Drive you back to town?'

'Oh no, thanks. I'll walk. It's only a few steps. Much obliged to you. I kind of hope Bill doesn't get into a jam. Especially a nasty jam like this.'

She got out of the car and hung on one foot, then tossed her head and laughed. 'They say I'm a pretty good beauty operator,' she said. 'I hope I am. As an interviewer I'm terrible. Good night.'

I said good night and she walked off into the evening. I sat there watching her until she reached the main street and turned out of sight. Then I got out of the Chrysler and went over towards the telephone company's little rustic building.

10

A tame doe deer with a leather dog collar on wandered across the road in front of me. I patted her rough hairy neck and went into the telephone office. A small girl in slacks sat at a small desk working on the books. She got me the rate to Beverly Hills and the change for the coin box. The booth was outside, against the front wall of the building.

'I hope you like it up here,' she said. 'It's very quiet, very restful.'

I shut myself into the booth. For ninety cents I could talk to Derace Kingsley for five minutes. He was at home and the call came through quickly but the connexion was full of mountain static.

'Find anything up there?' he asked me in a three-highball voice. He sounded tough and confident again.

'I've found too much,' I said. 'And not at all what we want. Are you alone?'

'What does that matter?'

'It doesn't matter to me. But I know what I'm going to say. You don't.'

'Well, get on with it, whatever it is,' he said.

'I had a long talk with Bill Chess. He was lonely. His wife had left him – a month ago. They had a fight and he went out and got drunk and when he came back she was gone. She left a note saying she would rather be dead than live with him any more.'

'I guess Bill drinks too much,' Kingsley's voice said from very far off.

'When he got back, both the women had gone. He has no idea where Mrs Kingsley went. Lavery was up here in May, but not since. Lavery admitted that much himself. Lavery could, of course, have come up again while Bill was out getting drunk, but there wouldn't be a lot of point to that and there would be two cars to drive down the hill. And I thought that possibly Mrs K. and Muriel Chess might have gone away together, only Muriel also had a car of her own. But that idea, little as it was worth, has been thrown out by another development. Muriel Chess didn't go away at all. She went down into your little private lake. She came back up today. I was there.'

'Good God!' Kingsley sounded properly horrified. 'You mean she drowned herself?'

'Perhaps. The note she left could be a suicide note. It would read as well that way as the other. The body was stuck down under that old submerged landing below the pier. Bill was the one who spotted an arm moving down there while we were standing on the pier looking down into the water. He got her out. They've arrested him. The poor guy's pretty badly broken up.'

'Good God!' Kingsley said again. 'I should think he would be. Does it look as if he –' He paused as the operator came in on the line and demanded another forty-five cents. I put in two quarters and the line cleared.

'Look as if he what?'

Suddenly very clear, Kingsley's voice said: 'Look as if he murdered her?'

I said: 'Very much. Jim Patton, the constable up here, doesn't like the note not being dated. It seems she left him once before over some woman. Patton sort of suspects Bill might have saved up an old note. Anyhow they've taken Bill down to San Bernardino for questioning and they've taken the body down to be post-mortemed.'

'And what do you think?' he asked slowly.

'Well, Bill found the body himself. He didn't have to take me around by that pier. She might have stayed down in the water very much longer, or for ever. The note could be old because Bill had carried it in his wallet and handled it from time to time, brooding over it. It could just as easily be undated this time as another time. I'd say notes like that are undated more often than not. The people who write them are apt to be in a hurry and not concerned with dates.'

'The body must be pretty far gone. What can they find out now?'

'I don't know how well equipped they are. They can find out if she died by drowning, I guess. And whether there are any marks of violence that wouldn't be erased by water and decomposition. They could tell if she had been shot or stabbed. If the hyoid bone in the throat was broken, they could assume she was throttled. The main thing for us is that I'll have to tell why I came up here. I'll have to testify at an inquest.'

'That's bad,' Kingsley growled. 'Very bad. What do you plan to do now?'

'On my way home I'll stop at the Prescott Hotel and see if I can pick up anything there. Were your wife and Muriel Chess friendly?'

'I guess so. Crystal's easy enough to get along with most of the time. I hardly knew Muriel Chess.'

'Did you ever know anybody named Mildred Haviland?'

'What?'

I repeated the name.

'No,' he said. 'Is there any reason why I should?'

'Every question I ask you ask another right back,' I said. 'No, there isn't any reason why you should know Mildred Haviland. Especially if you hardly knew Muriel Chess. I'll call you in the morning.'

'Do that,' he said, and hesitated. 'I'm sorry you had to walk into such a mess,' he added, and then hesitated again and said good night and hung up.

The bell rang again immediately and the long-distance operator told me sharply I had put in five cents too much money. I said the sort of thing I would be likely to put into an opening like that. She didn't like it.

I stepped out of the booth and gathered some air into my lungs. The tame doe with the leather collar was standing in the gap in the fence at the end of the walk. I tried to push her out of the way, but she just leaned against me and wouldn't push. So I stepped over the fence and went back to the Chrysler and drove back to the village.

There was a hanging light in Patton's headquarters but the shack was empty and his 'Back in Twenty Minutes' sign was still against the inside of the glass part of the door. I kept on going down to the boat-landing and beyond to the edge of a deserted swimming-beach. A few put-puts and speedboats were still fooling around on the silky water. Across the lake tiny yellow lights began to show in toy cabins perched on miniature slopes. A single bright star glowed low in the north-east above the ridge of the mountains. A robin sat on the spike top of a hundred-foot pine and waited for it to be dark enough for him to sing his good-night song.

In a little while it was dark enough and he sang and went away into the invisible depths of sky. I snapped my cigarette into the motionless water a few feet away and climbed back into the car and started back in the direction of Little Fawn Lake.

11

The gate across the private road was padlocked. I put the Chrysler between two pine-trees and climbed the gate and pussy-footed along the side of the road until the glimmer of the little lake bloomed suddenly at my feet. Bill Chess's cabin was dark. The three cabins on the other side were abrupt shadows against the pale granite outcrop. Water gleamed white where it trickled across the top of the dam, and fell almost sound-lessly along the sloping outer face to the brook below. I listened, and heard no other sound at all.

The front door of the Chess cabin was locked. I padded along to the back and found a brute of a padlock hanging at that. I went along the walls feeling window screens. They were all fastened. One window higher up was screenless, a small double cottage window half-way down the north wall. This was locked too. I stood still and did some more listening. There was no breeze and the trees were as quiet as their shadows.

I tried a knife blade between the two halves of the small window. No soap. The catch refused to budge. I leaned against the wall and thought and then suddenly I picked up a large stone and smacked it against the place where the two frames met in the middle. The catch pulled out of dry wood with a tearing noise. The window swung back into darkness. I heaved up on the sill and wangled a cramped leg over and edged through the opening. I rolled and let myself down into the room. I turned, grunting a little from the exertion at that altitude, and listened again.

A blazing flash beam hit me square in the eyes.

A very calm voice said: 'I'd rest right there, son. You must be all tuckered out.'

The flash pinned me against the wall like a squashed fly. Then a light switch clicked and a table lamp glowed. The flash went out. Jim Patton was sitting in an old brown Morris chair beside the table. A fringed brown scarf hung over the end of the table and touched his thick knee. He wore the same clothes he had worn that afternoon, with the addition of a leather jerkin which must have been new once, say about the time of Grover Cleveland's first term. His hands were empty except for the flash. His eyes were empty. His jaws moved in gentle rhythm.

'What's on your mind, son – besides breaking and entering?'

I poked a chair out and straddled it and leaned my arms on the back and looked around the cabin.

'I had an idea,' I said. 'It looked pretty good for a while, but I guess I can learn to forget it.'

The cabin was larger than it had seemed from outside. The part I was in was the living-room. It contained a few articles of modest furniture, a rag rug on the pineboard floor, a round table against the end wall and two chairs set against it. Through an open door the corner of a big black cookstove showed.

Patton nodded and his eyes studied me without rancour. 'I heard a car coming,' he said. 'I knew it had to be coming here. You walk right nice though. I didn't hear you walk worth a darn. I've been a mite curious about you, son.'

I said nothing.

'I hope you don't mind me callin' you "son",' he said. 'I hadn't ought to be so familiar, but I got myself into the habit and I can't seem to shake it Anybody that don't have a long white beard and arthritis is "son" to me.'

I said he could call me anything that came to mind. I wasn't sensitive.

He grinned. 'There's a mess of detectives in the L.A. phone book,' he said. 'But only one of them is called Marlowe.'

'What made you look?'

'I guess you might call it lowdown curiosity. Added to which Bill Chess told me you was some sort of dick. You didn't bother to tell me yourself.'

'I'd have got around to it,' I said. 'I'm sorry it bothered you.'

'It didn't bother me none. I don't bother at all easy. You got any identification with you?'

I got my wallet out and showed him this and that.

'Well, you got a good build on you for the work,' he said, satisfied. 'And your face don't tell a lot of stories. I guess you was aiming to search the cabin.'

'Yeah.'

'I already pawed around considerable myself. Just got back and come straight here. That is, I stopped by my shack a minute and then come. I don't figure I could let you search the place, though.' He scratched his ear. 'That is, dum if I know whether I could or not. You telling who hired you?'

'Derace Kingsley. To trace his wife. She skipped out on him a month ago. She started from here. So I started from here. She's supposed to have gone away with a man. The man denies it. I thought maybe something up here might give me a lead.'

'And did anything?'

'No. She's traced pretty definitely as far as San Bernardino and then El Paso. There the trail ends. But I've only just started.'

Patton stood up and unlocked the cabin door. The spicy smell of the pines surged in. He spat outdoors and sat down again and rumpled the mousy brown hair under his Stetson. His head with the hat off had the indecent look of heads that are seldom without hats.

'You didn't have no interest in Bill Chess at all?'

'None whatever.'

'I guess you fellows do a lot of divorce business,' he said. 'Kind of smelly work, to my notion.'

I let that ride.

'Kingsley wouldn't have asked help from the police to find his wife, would he?'

'Hardly,' I said. 'He knows her too well.'

'None of what you've been saying don't hardly explain your wanting to search Bill's cabin,' he said judiciously.

'I'm just a great guy to poke around.'

'Hell,' he said, 'you can do better than that.'

'Say I am interested in Bill Chess then. But only because he's in trouble and rather a pathetic case – in spite of being a good deal of a heel. If he murdered his wife, there's something here to point that way. If he didn't, there's something to point that way too.'

He held his head sideways, like a watchful bird. 'As for instance what kind of thing?'

'Clothes, personal jewellery, toilet articles, whatever a woman takes with her when she goes away, not intending to come back.'

He leaned back slowly. 'But she didn't go away, son.'

'Then the stuff should be still here. But if it was still here, Bill would have noticed she hadn't taken it. He would know she hadn't gone away.'

'By gum, I don't like it either way,' he said.

'But if he murdered her,' I said, 'then he would have to get rid of the things she ought to have taken with her, if she had gone away.'

'And how do you figure he would do that, son?' The yellow lamplight made bronze of one side of his face.

'I understand she had a Ford car of her own. Except for that I'd expect him to burn what he could burn and bury what he could not burn out in the woods. Sinking it in the lake might be dangerous. But he couldn't burn or bury her car. Could he drive it?'

Patton looked surprised. 'Sure. He can't bend his right leg at the knee, so he couldn't use the foot-brake very handy. But he could get by with the hand-brake. All that's different on Bill's own Ford is the brake pedal is set over on the left side of the post, close to the clutch, so he can shove them both down with one foot.'

I shook ash from my cigarette into a small blue jar that had once contained a pound of orange honey, according to the small gilt label on it.

'Getting rid of the car would be his big problem,' I said. 'Wherever he took it he would have to get back, and he would rather not be seen coming back. And if he simply abandoned it on a street, say, down in San Bernardino, it would be found and identified very quickly. He wouldn't want that either. The best stunt would be to unload it on a hot car dealer, but he probably doesn't know one. So the chances are he hid it in the woods within walking distance of here. And walking distance for him would not be very far.'

'For a fellow that claims not to be interested, you're doing some pretty close figuring on all this,' Patton said dryly. 'So now you've got the car hid out in the woods. What then?'

'He has to consider the possibility of its being found. The woods are lonely, but rangers and woodcutters get around in them from time to time. If the car is found, it would be better for Muriel's stuff to be found in it. That would give him a couple of outs – neither one very brilliant but both at least possible. One, that she was murdered by some unknown party who fixed things to implicate Bill when and if the murder was discovered. Two, that Muriel did actually commit suicide, but fixed things so that he would be blamed. A revenge suicide.'

Patton thought all this over with calm and care. He went to the door to unload again. He sat down and rumpled his hair again. He looked at me with solid scepticism.

'The first one's possible like you say,' he admitted. 'But only just, and I don't have anybody in mind for the job. There's that little matter of the note to be got over.'

I shook my head. 'Say Bill already had the note from another time. Say she went away, as he thought, without leaving a note. After a month had gone by without any word from her he might be just worried and uncertain enough to show the note, feeling it might be some protection to him in case anything had happened to her. He didn't say any of this, but he could have had it in his mind.'

Patton shook his head. He didn't like it. Neither did I. He said slowly: 'As to your other notion, it's just plain crazy. Killing yourself and fixing things so as somebody else would get accused of murdering you don't fit in with my simple ideas of human nature at all.'

'Then your ideas of human nature are too simple,' I said. 'Because it has been done, and when it has been done, it has nearly always been done by a woman.'

'Nope,' he said, 'I'm a man fifty-seven years old and I've seen a lot of crazy people, but I don't go for that worth a peanut shell. What I like is that she did plan to go away and did write the note, but he caught her before she got clear and saw red and finished her off. Then he would have to do all them things we been talking about.'

'I never met her,' I said. 'So I wouldn't have any idea what she would be likely to do. Bill said he met her in a place in Riverside something over a year ago. She may have had a long and complicated history before that. What kind of girl was she?'

'A mighty cute little blonde when she fixed herself up. She kind of let herself go with Bill. A quiet girl, with a face that kept its secrets. Bill says she had a temper, but I never seen any of it. I seen plenty of nasty temper in him.'

'And did you think she looked like the photo of somebody called Mildred Haviland?'

His jaws stopped munching and his mouth became almost primly tight. Very slowly he started chewing again.

'By gum,' he said, 'I'll be mighty careful to look under the bed before I crawl in tonight. To make sure you ain't there. Where did you get that information?'

'A nice little girl called Birdie Keppel told me. She was interviewing me in the course of her spare-time newspaper job. She happened to mention that an L.A. cop named De Soto was showing the photo around.'

Patton smacked his thick knee and hunched his shoulders forward.

'I done wrong there,' he said soberly. 'I made one of my mistakes. This big bruiser showed his picture to darn near everybody in town before he showed it to me. That made me kind of sore. It looked some like Muriel, but not enough to be sure by any manner of means. I asked him what she was wanted for. He said it was police business. I said I was in that way of business myself, in an ignorant countrified kind of way. He said his instructions were to locate the lady and that was all he knew. Maybe he did wrong to take me up short like that. So I guess I done wrong to tell him I didn't know anybody that looked like his little picture.'

The big calm man smiled vaguely at the corner of the ceiling, then brought his eyes down and looked at me steadily.

'I'll thank you to respect this confidence, Mr Marlowe. You done right nicely in your figuring too. You ever happen to go over to Coon Lake?'

'Never heard of it.'

'Back about a mile,' he said, pointing over his shoulder with a thumb, 'there's a little narrow wood road turns over west. You can just drive in and miss the trees. It climbs about five hundred feet in another mile and comes out by Coon Lake. Pretty little place. Folks go up there to picnic once in a while, but not often. It's hard on tyres. There's two three small shallow lakes full of reeds. There's snow up there even now in the shady places. There's a bunch of old hand-hewn log cabins that's been falling down ever since I recall, and there's a big broken-down frame building that Montclair University used to use for a summer camp maybe years back. They ain't used it in a very long time. This building sits back from the lakes in heavy timber. Round at the back of it there's a wash-house with an old rusty boiler and along of that there's a big woodshed with a sliding door hung on rollers. It was built for a garage, but they kept their wood in it and they locked it up out of season. Wood's one of the few things people will steal up here, but folks who might steal it off a pile wouldn't break a lock to get it. I guess you know what I found in that woodshed.'

'I thought you went down to San Bernardino.'

'Changed my mind. Didn't seem right to let Bill ride down there with his wife's body in the back of the car. So I sent it down in Doc's ambulance and I sent Andy down with Bill. I figured I kind of ought to look around a little more before I put things up to the sheriff and the coroner.'

'Muriel's car was in the woodshed?'

'Yep. And two unlocked suit-cases in the car. Packed with clothes and packed kind of hasty, I thought. Women's clothes. The point is, son, no stranger would have known about that place.'

I agreed with him. He put his hand into the slanting side pocket of his jerkin and brought out a small twist of tissue paper. He opened it up on his palm and held the hand out flat.

'Take a look at this.'

I went over and looked. What lay on the tissue was a thin gold chain with a tiny lock hardly larger than a link of the chain. The gold had been snipped through, leaving the lock intact. The chain seemed to be about seven inches long. There was white powder sticking to both chain and paper.

'Where would you guess I found that?' Patton asked.

I picked the chain up and tried to fit the cut ends together. They didn't fit. I made no comment on that, but moistened a finger and touched the powder and tasted it.

'In a can or box of confectioner's sugar,' I said. 'The chain is an anklet. Some women never take them off, like wedding-rings. Whoever took this one off didn't have the key.'

'What do you make of it?'

'Nothing much,' I said. 'There wouldn't be any point in Bill cutting it off Muriel's ankle and leaving that green necklace on her neck. There wouldn't be any point in Muriel cutting it off herself – assuming she had lost the key – and hiding it to be found. A search thorough enough to find it wouldn't be made unless her body was found first. If Bill cut it off, he would have thrown it into the lake. But if Muriel wanted to keep it and yet hide it from Bill, there's some sense in the place where it was hidden.'

Patton looked puzzled this time. 'Why is that?'

'Because it's a woman's hiding-place. Confectioner's sugar is used to make cake icing. A man would never look there. Pretty clever of you to find it, sheriff.'

He grinned a little sheepishly. 'Hell, I knocked the box over and some of the sugar spilled,' he said. 'Without that I don't guess I ever would have found it.' He rolled the paper up again and slipped it back into his pocket. He stood up with an air of finality.

'You staying up here or going back to town, Mr Marlowe?'

'Back to town. Until you want me for the inquest. I suppose you will.'

'That's up to the coroner, of course. If you'll kind of shut that window you bust in, I'll put this lamp out and lock up.'

I did what he said and he snapped his flash on and put out the lamp. We went out and he felt the cabin door to make sure the lock had caught. He closed the screen softly and stood looking across the moonlit lake.

'I don't figure Bill meant to kill her,' he said sadly. 'He could choke a girl to death without meaning to at all. He has mighty strong hands. Once done, he has to use what brains God gave him to cover up what he done. I feel real bad about it, but that don't alter the facts and the probabilities. It's simple and natural and the simple and natural things usually turn out to be right.'

I said: 'I should think he would have run away. I don't see how he could stand it to stay here.'

Patton spat into the black velvet shadow of a manzanita bush. He said slowly: 'He had a government pension and he would have to run away from that too. And most men can stand what they've got to stand, when it steps up and looks them straight in the eye. Like they're doing all over the world right now. Well, good night to you. I'm going to walk down to that little pier again and stand there awhile in the moonlight and feel bad. A night like this, and we got to think about murders.'

He moved quietly off into the shadows and became one of them himself. I stood there until he was out of sight and then went back to the locked gate and climbed over it. I got into the car and drove back down the road looking for a place to hide.

12

Three hundred yards from the gate a narrow track, sifted over with brown oak leaves from last autumn, curved around a granite boulder and disappeared. I followed it around and bumped along the stones of the outcrop for fifty or sixty feet, then swung the car around a tree and set it pointing back the way it had come. I cut the lights and switched off the motor and sat there waiting.

Half an hour passed. Without tobacco it seemed a long time. Then far off I heard a car motor start up and grow louder and the white beam of headlights passed below me on the road. The sound faded into the distance and a faint dry tang of dust hung in the air for a while after it was gone.

I got out of my car and walked back to the gate and to the Chess cabin. A hard push opened the sprung window this time. I climbed in again and let myself down to the floor and poked the flash I had brought across the room to the table lamp. I switched the lamp on and listened a moment, heard nothing and went out to the kitchen. I switched on a hanging bulb over the sink.

The wood-box beside the stove was neatly piled with split wood. There were no dirty dishes in the sink, no foul-smelling pots on the stove. Bill Chess, lonely or not, kept his house in good order. A door opened from the kitchen into the bedroom, and from that a very narrow door led into a tiny bathroom which had evidently been built on to the cabin fairly recently. The clean celotex lining showed that. The bathroom told me nothing.

The bedroom contained a double bed, a pinewood dresser with a round mirror on the wall above it, a bureau, two straight chairs and a tin waste-basket. There were two oval rag rugs on the floor, one on each side of the bed. On the walls Bill Chess had tacked up a set of war maps from the *National Geographic*. There was a silly-looking red-and-white flounce on the dressing-table.

I poked around in the drawers. An imitation leather trinket-box with an assortment of gaudy costume jewellery had not been taken away. There was the usual stuff women use on their faces and finger-nails and eyebrows, and it seemed to me that there was too much of it. But that was just guessing. The bureau contained both man's and woman's clothes, not a great deal of either. Bill Chess had a very noisy check shirt with starched matching collar, among other things. Underneath a sheet of blue tissue paper in one corner I found something I didn't like. A seemingly brand-new peach-coloured silk slip trimmed with lace. Silk slips were not being left behind that year, not by any woman in her senses.

This looked bad for Bill Chess. I wondered what Patton had thought of it.

I went back to the kitchen and prowled the open shelves above and beside the sink. They were thick with cans and jars of household staples. The confectioner's sugar was in a square brown box with a torn corner. Patton had made an attempt to clean up what was spilled. Near the sugar were salt, borax, baking-soda, cornstarch, brown sugar and so on. Something might be hidden in any of them.

Something that had been clipped from a chain anklet whose cut ends did not fit together.

I shut my eyes and poked a finger out at random and it came to rest on the baking-soda. I got a newspaper from the back of the wood-box and spread it out and dumped the soda out of the box. I stirred it around with a spoon. There seemed to be an indecent lot of baking-soda, but that was all there was. I funnelled it back into the box and tried the borax. Nothing but borax. Third time lucky. I tried the cornstarch. It made too much fine dust, and there was nothing but cornstarch.

The sound of distant steps froze me to the ankles. I reached up and yanked the light out and dodged back into the living-room and reached for the lamp switch. Much too late to be of any use, of course. The steps sounded again, soft and cautious. The hackles rose on my neck.

I waited in the dark, with the flash in my left hand. A deadly long two minutes crept by. I spent some of the time breathing, but not all.

It wouldn't be Patton. He would walk up to the door and open it and tell me off. The careful quiet steps seemed to move this way and that, a movement, a long pause, another movement, another long pause. I sneaked across to the door and twisted the knob silently. I yanked the door wide and stabbed out with the flash.

It made golden lamps of a pair of eyes. There was a leaping movement and a quick thudding of hoofs back among the trees. It was only an inquisitive deer.

I closed the door again and followed my flashlight beam back into the kitchen. The small round glow rested squarely on the box of confectioner's sugar.

I put the light on again, lifted the box down and emptied it on the newspaper.

Patton hadn't gone deep enough. Having found one thing by accident he had assumed that was all there was. He hadn't seemed to notice that there ought to be something else.

Another twist of white tissue showed in the fine white powdered sugar. I shook it clean and unwound it. It contained a tiny gold heart, no larger than a woman's little finger-nail.

I spooned the sugar back into the box and put the box back on the shelf and crumpled the piece of newspaper into the stove. I went back to the living-room and turned the table lamp on. Under that brighter light the tiny engraving on the back of the little gold heart could just be read without a magnifying-glass.

It was in script. It read: 'Al to Mildred. June 28th, 1938. With all my love.'

Al to Mildred. Al somebody to Mildred Haviland. Mildred Haviland was Muriel Chess. Muriel Chess was dead – two weeks after a cop named De Soto had been looking for her.

I stood there, holding it, wondering what it had to do with me. Wondering, and not having the faintest glimmer of an idea.

I wrapped it up again and left the cabin and drove back to the village.

Patton was in his office telephoning when I got around there. The door was locked. I had to wait while he talked. After a while he hung up and came to unlock the door.

I walked in past him and put the twist of tissue paper on his counter and opened it up.

'You didn't go deep enough into the powdered sugar,' I said.

He looked at the little gold heart, looked at me, went around behind the counter and got a cheap magnifying-glass off his desk. He studied the back of the heart. He put the glass down and frowned at me.

'Might have known if you wanted to search that cabin, you was going to do it,' he said gruffly. 'I ain't going to have trouble with you, am I, son?'

'You ought to have noticed that the cut ends of the chain didn't fit,' I told him.

He looked at me sadly. 'Son, I don't have your eyes.' He pushed the little heart around with his square blunt finger. He stared at me and said nothing.

I said: 'If you were thinking that anklet meant something Bill could have been jealous about, so was I – provided he ever saw it. But strictly on the cuff I'm willing to bet he never did see it and that he never heard of Mildred Haviland.'

Patton said slowly: 'Looks like maybe I owe this De Soto party an apology, don't it?'

'If you ever see him,' I said.

He gave me another long empty stare and I gave it right back to him. 'Don't tell me, son,' he said. 'Let me guess all for myself that you got a brand-new idea about it.'

'Yeah. Bill didn't murder his wife.'

'No. She was murdered by somebody out of her past. Somebody who had lost track of her and then found it again and found her married to another man and didn't like it. Somebody who knew the country up here – as hundreds of people do who don't live here – and knew a good place to hide the car and the clothes. Somebody who hated and could dissimulate. Who persuaded her to go away with him and when everything was ready and the note was written, took her around the throat and gave her what he thought was coming to her and put her in the lake and went his way. Like it?'

'Well,' he said judiciously, 'it does make things kind of complicated, don't you think? But there ain't anything impossible about it. Not one bit impossible.'

'When you get tired of it, let me know. I'll have something else,' I said.

'I'll just be doggone sure you will,' he said, and for the first time since I had met him he laughed.

I said good night again and went out, leaving him there moving his mind around with the ponderous energy of a homesteader digging up a stump.

13

At somewhere around eleven I got down to the bottom of the grade and parked in one of the diagonal slots at the side of the Prescott Hotel in San Bernardino. I pulled an overnight bag out of the boot and had taken three steps with it when a bellhop in braided pants and a white shirt and black bow-tie yanked it out of my hand.

The clerk on duty was an egg-headed man with no interest in me or in anything else. He wore parts of a white linen suit and he yawned as he handed me the desk pen and looked off into the distance as if remembering his childhood.

The hop and I rode a four by four elevator to the second floor and walked a couple of blocks around corners. As we walked it got hotter and hotter. The hop unlocked a door into a boy's-size room with one window on an air-shaft. The air-conditioner inlet up in the corner of the ceiling was about the size of a woman's handkerchief. The bit of ribbon tied to it fluttered weakly, just to show that something was moving.

The hop was tall and thin and yellow and not young and as cool as a slice of chicken in aspic. He moved his gum around in his face, put my bag on a chair, looked up at the grating and then stood looking at me. He had eyes the colour of a drink of water.

'Maybe I ought to have asked for one of the dollar rooms,' I said. 'This one seems a mite close-fitting.'

'I reckon you're lucky to get one at all. This town's fair bulgin' at the seams.'

'Bring us up some ginger ale and glasses and ice,' I said.

'Us?'

'That is, if you happen to be a drinking man.'

'I reckon I might take a chance this late.'

He went out. I took off my coat, tie, shirt and undershirt and walked around in the warm draught from the open door. The draught smelled of hot iron. I went into the bathroom sideways – it was that kind of bathroom – and doused myself with tepid cold water. I was breathing a little more freely when the tall languid hop returned with a tray. He shut the door and I brought out a bottle of rye. He mixed a couple of drinks and we made the usual insincere smiles over them and drank. The perspiration started from the back of my neck down my spine and was half-way to my socks before I put the glass down. But I felt better all the same. I sat on the bed and looked at the hop.

'How long can you stay?'

'Doing what?'

'Remembering.'

'I ain't a damn bit of use at it,' he said.

'I have money to spend,' I said, 'in my own peculiar way.' I got my wallet unstuck from the lower part of my back and spread tired-looking dollar bills along the bed.

'I beg yore pardon,' the hop said. 'I reckon you might be a dick.'

'Don't be silly,' I said. 'You never saw a dick playing solitaire with his own money. You might call me investigator.'

'I'm interested,' he said. 'The likker makes my mind work.'

I gave him a dollar bill. 'Try that on your mind. And can I call you Big Tex from Houston?'

'Amarillo,' he said. 'Not that it matters. And how do you like my Texas drawl? It makes me sick, but I find people go for it.'

'Stay with it,' I said. 'It never lost anybody a dollar yet.'

He grinned and tucked the folded dollar neatly into the watch pocket of his pants.

'What were you doing on Friday, June 12th?' I asked him. 'Late afternoon or evening. It was a Friday.'

He sipped his drink and thought, shaking the ice around gently and drinking past his gum. 'I was right here, six to twelve shift,' he said.

'A woman, slim, pretty blonde, checked in here and stayed until time for the night train to El Paso. I think she must have taken that because she was in El Paso Sunday morning. She came here driving a Packard Clipper registered to Crystal Grace Kingsley, 965 Carson Drive, Beverly Hills. She may have registered as that, or under some other name, and she may not have registered at all. Her car is still in the hotel garage. I'd like to talk to the boys that checked her in and out. That wins another dollar – just thinking about it.'

I separated another dollar from my exhibit and it went into his pocket with a sound like caterpillars fighting.

'Can do,' he said calmly.

He put his glass down and left the room, closing the door. I finished my drink and made another. I went into the bathroom and used some more warm water on my torso. While I was doing this the telephone on the wall tinkled and I wedged myself into the minute space between the bathroom door and the bed to answer it.

The Texas voice said: 'That was Sonny. He was inducted last week. Another boy we call Les checked her out. He's here.'

'Okay. Shoot him up, will you?'

I was playing with my second drink and thinking about the third when a knock came and I opened the door to a small, green-eyed rat with a tight, girlish mouth.

He came in almost dancing and stood looking at me with a faint sneer. 'Drink?'

'Sure,' he said coldly. He poured himself a large one, and added a whisper of ginger ale, put the mixture down in one long swallow, tucked a cigarette between his smooth little lips and snapped a match alight while it was coming up from his pocket. He blew smoke and went on staring at me. The corner of his eye caught the money on the bed, without looking directly at it. Over the pocket of his shirt, instead of a number, the word *Captain* was stitched.

'You Les?' I asked him.

'No.' He paused. 'We don't like dicks here,' he added. 'We don't have one of our own and we don't care to bother with dicks that are working for other people.'

'Thanks,' I said. 'That will be all.'

'Huh?' The small mouth twisted unpleasantly.

'Beat it,' I said.

'I thought you wanted to see me,' he sneered.

'You're the bell captain?'

'Check.'

'I wanted to buy you a drink. I wanted to give you a buck. Here.' I held it out to him. 'Thanks for coming up.'

He took the dollar and pocketed it, without a word of thanks. He hung there, smoke trailing from his nose, his eyes tight and mean.

'What I say here goes,' he said.

'It goes as far as you can push it,' I said. 'And that couldn't be very far. You had your drink and you had your graft. Now you can scram out.'

He turned with a swift tight shrug and slipped out of the room noiselessly.

Four minutes passed, then another knock, very light. The tall boy came in grinning. I walked away from him and sat on the bed again.

'You didn't take to Les, I reckon?'

'Not a great deal. Is he satisfied?'

'I reckon so. You know what captains are. They have to have their cut. Maybe you better call me Les, Mr Marlowe.'

'So you checked her out.'

'No, that was all a stall. She never checked in at the desk. But I remember the Packard. She gave me a dollar to put it away for her and to look after her stuff until train time. She ate dinner here. A dollar gets you remembered in this town. And there's been talk about the car bein' left so long.'

'What was she like to look at?'

'She wore a black and white outfit, mostly white, and a panama hat with a black and white band. She was a neat blonde lady like you said. Later on she took a hack to the station. I put her bags into it for her. They had initials on them but I'm sorry I can't remember the initials.'

'I'm glad you can't,' I said. 'It would be too good. Have a drink. How old would she be?'

He rinsed the other glass and mixed a civilized drink for himself.

'It's mighty hard to tell a woman's age these days,' he said. 'I reckon she was about thirty, or a little more or a little less.'

I dug in my coat for the snapshot of Crystal and Lavery on the beach and handed it to him.

He looked at it steadily and held it away from his eyes, then close.

'You won't have to swear to it in court,' I said.

He nodded. 'I wouldn't want to. These small blondes are so much of a pattern that a change of clothes or light or make-up makes them all alike or all different.' He hesitated, staring at the snapshot.

'What's worrying you?' I asked.

'I'm thinking about the gent in this snap. He enter into it at all?'

'Go on with that,' I said.

'I think this fellow spoke to her in the lobby, and had dinner with her. A tall good-lookin' jasper, built like a fast light-heavy. He went in the hack with her too.'

'Quite sure about that?'

He looked at the money on the bed.

'Okay, how much does it cost?' I asked wearily.

He stiffened, laid the snapshot down and drew the two folded bills from his pocket and tossed them on the bed.

'I thank you for the drink,' he said, 'and to hell with you.' He started for the door.

'Oh, sit down and don't be so touchy,' I growled.

He sat down and looked at me stiff-eyed.

'And don't be so damn southern,' I said. 'I've been knee-deep in hotel hops for a lot of years. If I've met one who wouldn't pull a gag, that's fine. But you can't expect me to expect to meet one that wouldn't pull a gag.'

He grinned slowly and nodded quickly. He picked the snapshot up again and looked at me over it.

'This gent takes a solid photo,' he said. 'Much more so than the lady. But there was another little item that made me remember him. I got the impression the lady didn't quite like him walking up to her so openly in the lobby.'

I thought that over and decided it didn't mean anything much. He might have been late or have missed some earlier appointment. I said:

'There's a reason for that. Did you notice what jewellery the lady was wearing? Rings, ear-pendants, anything that looked conspicuous or valuable?'

He hadn't noticed, he said.

'Was her hair long or short, straight or waved or curly, natural blonde or bleached?'

He laughed. 'Hell, you can't tell that last point, Mr Marlowe. Even when it's natural they want it lighter. As to the rest, my recollection is it was rather long, like they're wearing it now and turned in a little at the bottom and rather straight. But I could be wrong.' He looked at the snapshot again. 'She has it bound back here. You can't tell a thing.'

'That's right,' I said. 'And the only reason I asked you was to make sure that you didn't over-observe. The guy that sees too much detail is just as unreliable a witness as the guy that doesn't see any. He's nearly always making half of it up. You check just about right, considering the circumstances. Thanks very much.'

I gave him back his two dollars and a five to keep them company. He thanked me, finished his drink and left softly. I finished mine and washed off again and decided I would rather drive home than sleep in that hole. I put my shirt and coat on again and went downstairs with my bag.

The red-headed rat of a captain was the only hop in the lobby. I carried my bag over to the desk and he didn't move to take it off my hands. The egg-headed clerk separated me from two dollars without even looking at me.

'Two bucks to spend the night in this manhole,' I said, 'when for free I could have a nice airy ashcan.'

The clerk yawned, got a delayed reaction and said brightly: 'It gets quite cool here about three in the morning. From then on until eight, or even nine, it's quite pleasant.'

I wiped the back of my neck and staggered out to the car. Even the seat of the car was hot at midnight.

I got home about two-forty-five and Hollywood was an ice-box. Even Pasadena had felt cool.

14

I dreamed I was far down in the depths of icy green water with a corpse under my arm. The corpse had long blonde hair that kept floating around in front of my face. An enormous fish with bulging eyes and a bloated body and scales shining with putrescence swam around leering like an elderly roué. Just as I was about to burst from lack of the air, the corpse came alive under my arm and got away from me and then I was fighting with the fish and the corpse was rolling over and over in the water, spinning its long hair.

I woke up with a mouth full of sheet and both hands hooked on the head-frame of the bed and pulling hard. The muscles ached when I let go and lowered them. I got up and walked the room and lit a cigarette, feeling the carpet with bare toes. When I had finished the cigarette, I went back to bed.

It was nine o'clock when I woke up again. The sun was on my face. The room was hot. I showered and shaved and partly dressed and made the morning toast and eggs and coffee in the dinette. While I was finishing up there was a knock at the apartment door.

I went to open it with my mouth full of toast. It was a lean serious-looking man in a severe grey suit.

'Floyd Greer, lieutenant, Central Detective Bureau,' he said and walked into the room.

He put out a dry hand and I shook it. He sat down on the edge of a chair, the way they do, and turned his hat in his hands and looked at me with the quiet stare they have.

'We got a call from San Bernardino about that business up at Puma Lake. Drowned woman. Seems you were on hand when the body was discovered.'

I nodded and said, 'Have some coffee?'

'No, thanks. I had breakfast two hours ago.'

I got my coffee and sat down across the room from him.

'They asked us to look you up,' he said. 'Give them a line on you.'

'Sure.'

'So we did that. Seems like you have a clean bill of health so far as we are concerned. Kind of coincidence a man in your line would be around when the body was found.'

'I'm like that,' I said. 'Lucky.'

'So I just thought I'd drop around and say howdy.'

'That's fine. Glad to know you, lieutenant.'

'Kind of a coincidence,' he said again, nodding. 'You up there on business, so to speak?'

'If I was,' I said, 'my business had nothing to do with the girl who was drowned, so far as I know.'

'But you couldn't be sure?'

'Until you've finished with a case, you can't ever be quite sure what its ramifications are, can you?'

'That's right.' He circled his hat brim through his fingers again, like a bashful cowboy. There was nothing bashful about his eyes. 'I'd like to feel sure that if these ramifications you speak of happened to take in this drowned woman's affairs, you would put us wise.'

'I hope you can rely on that,' I said.

He bulged his lower lip with his tongue. 'We'd like a little more than a hope. At the present time you don't care to say?'

'At the present time I don't know anything that Patton doesn't know.'

'Who's he?'

'The constable up at Puma Point.'

The lean serious man smiled tolerantly. He cracked a knuckle and after a pause said: 'The San Berdoo D.A. will likely want to talk to you – before the inquest. But that won't be very soon. Right now they're trying to get a set of prints. We lent them a technical man.'

'That will be tough. The body's pretty far gone.'

'It's done all the time,' he said. 'They worked out the system back in New York where they're all the time pulling in floaters. They cut patches of skin off the fingers and harden them in a tanning solution and make stamps. It works well enough as a rule.'

'You think this woman had a record of some kind?'

'Why, we always take prints of a corpse,' he said. 'You ought to know that.'

I said: 'I didn't know the lady. If you thought I did and that was why I was up there, there's nothing in it.'

'But you wouldn't care to say just why you *were* up there,' he persisted.

'So you think I'm lying to you,' I said.

He spun his hat on a bony forefinger. 'You got me wrong, Mr Marlowe. We don't think anything at all. What we do is investigate and find out. This stuff is just routine. You ought to know that. You been around long enough.' He stood up and put his hat on. 'You might let me know if you have to leave town. I'd be obliged.'

I said I would and went to the door with him. He went out with a duck of his head and a sad half-smile. I watched him drift languidly down the hall and punch the elevator button.

I went back out to the dinette to see if there was any more coffee. There was about two-thirds of a cup. I added cream and sugar and carried my cup over to the telephone. I dialled Police Headquarters downtown and asked for the Detective Bureau and then for Lieutenant Floyd Greer.

The voice said: 'Lieutenant Greer is not in the office. Anybody else do?'

'De Soto in?'

'Who?'

I repeated the name.

'What's his rank and department?'

'Plain clothes something or other.'

'Hold the line.'

I waited. The burring male voice came back after a while and said: 'What's the gag? We don't have a De Soto on the roster. Who's this talking?'

I hung up, finished my coffee and dialled the number of Derace Kingsley's office. The smooth and cool Miss Fromsett said he had just come in and put me through without a murmur.

'Well,' he said, loud and forceful at the beginning of a fresh day, 'what did you find out at the hotel?'

'She was there all right. And Lavery met her there. The hop who gave me the dope brought Lavery into it himself, without any prompting from me. He had dinner with her and went with her in a cab to the railroad station.'

'Well, I ought to have known he was lying,' Kingsley said slowly. 'I got the impression he was surprised when I told him about the telegram from El Paso. I was just letting my impressions get too sharp. Anything else?'

'Not there. I had a cop calling on me this morning, giving me the usual looking over and warning not to leave town without letting him know. Trying to find out why I went to Puma Point. I didn't tell him as he wasn't even aware of Jim Patton's existence, it's evident that Patton didn't tell anybody.'

'Jim would do his best to be decent about it,' Kingsley said. 'Why were you asking me last night about some name – Mildred something or other?'

I told him, making it brief. I told him about Muriel Chess's car and clothes being found and where.

'That looks bad for Bill,' he said. 'I know Coon Lake myself, but it would never have occurred to me to use that old woodshed – or even that there was an old woodshed. It not only looks bad, it looks premeditated.'

'I disagree with that. Assuming he knew the country well enough it wouldn't take him any time to search his mind for a likely hiding-place. He was very restricted as to distance.'

'Maybe. What do you plan to do now?' he asked.

'Go up against Lavery again, of course.'

He agreed that that was the thing to do. He added: 'This other, tragic as it is, is really no business of ours, is it?'

'Not unless your wife knew something about it.'

His voice sounded sharply, saying: 'Look here, Marlowe, I think I can understand your detective instinct to tie everything that happens into one compact knot, but don't let it run away with you. Life isn't like that at all – not life as I have known it. Better leave the affairs of the Chess family to the police and keep your brains working on the Kingsley family.'

'Okay,' I said.

'I don't mean to be domineering,' he said.

I laughed heartily, said good-bye, and hung up. I finished dressing and went down to the basement for the Chrysler. I started for Bay City again.

15

I drove past the intersection of Altair Street to where the cross street continued to the edge of the canyon and ended in a semicircular parking place with a sidewalk and a white wooden guard fence around it. I sat there in the car a little while, thinking, looking out to sea and admiring the blue-grey fall of the foothills towards the ocean. I was trying to make up my mind whether to try handling Lavery with a feather or go on using the back of my hand and the edge of my tongue. I decided I could lose nothing by the soft approach. If that didn't produce for me – and I didn't think it would – nature could take its course and we could bust up the furniture.

The paved alley that ran along half-way down the hill below the houses on the outer edge was empty. Below that, on the next hillside street, a couple of kids were throwing a boomerang up the slope and chasing it with the usual amount of elbowing and mutual insult. Farther down still a house was enclosed in trees and a red brick wall. There was a glimpse of washing on the line in the backyard and two pigeons strutted along the slope of the roof bobbing their heads. A blue and tan bus trundled along the street in front of the brick house and stopped and a very old man got off with slow care and settled himself firmly on the ground and tapped with a heavy cane before he started to crawl back up the slope.

The air was clearer than yesterday. The morning was full of peace. I left the car where it was and walked along Altair Street to No. 623.

The venetian blinds were down across the front windows and the place had a sleepy look. I stepped down over the Korean moss and punched the bell and saw that the door was not quite shut. It had dropped in its frame, as most of our doors do, and the spring bolt hung a little on the lower edge of the lock plate. I remembered that it had wanted to stick the day before, when I was leaving.

I gave the door a little push and it moved inward with a light click. The room beyond was dim, but there was some light from west windows. Nobody answered my ring. I didn't ring again. I pushed the door a little wider and stepped inside.

The room had a hushed warm smell, the smell of late morning in a house not yet opened up. The bottle of Vat 69 on the round table by the davenport was almost empty and another full bottle waited beside it. The copper ice-bucket had a little water in the bottom. Two glasses had been used, and half a siphon of carbonated water.

I fixed the door about as I had found it and stood there and listened. If Lavery was away I thought I would take a chance and frisk the joint. I didn't have anything much on him, but it was probably enough to keep him from calling the cops.

In the silence time passed. It passed in the dry whirr of the electric clock on the mantel, in the far-off toot of an auto horn on Aster Drive, in the hornet drone of a plane over the foothills across the canyon, in the sudden lurch and growl of the electric refrigerator in the kitchen.

I went farther into the room and stood peering around and listening and hearing nothing except those fixed sounds belonging to the house, and having nothing to do with the humans in it. I started along the rug towards the archway at the back.

A hand in a glove appeared on the slope of the white metal railing, at the edge of the archway, where the stairs went down. It appeared and stopped.

It moved and a woman's hat showed, then her head. The woman came quietly up the stairs. She came all the way up, turned through the arch and still didn't seem to see me. She was a slender woman of uncertain age, with untidy brown hair, a scarlet mess of a mouth, too much rouge on her cheekbones, shadowed eyes. She wore a blue tweed suit that looked like the dickens with a purple hat that was doing its best to hang on to the side of her head.

She saw me and didn't stop or change expression in the slightest degree. She came slowly on into the room, holding her right hand away from her body. Her left hand wore the brown glove I had seen on the railing. The right-hand glove that matched it was wrapped around the butt of a small automatic.

She stopped then and her body arched back and a quick distressful sound came out of her mouth. Then she giggled, a high nervous giggle. She pointed the gun at me, and came steadily on.

I kept on looking at the gun and not screaming.

The woman came close. When she was close enough to be confidential she pointed the gun at my stomach and said:

'All I wanted was my rent. The place seems well taken care of. Nothing broken. He has always been a good tidy careful tenant. I just didn't want him to get too far behind in the rent.'

A fellow with a kind of strained and unhappy voice said politely: 'How far behind is he?'

'Three months,' she said. 'Two hundred and forty dollars. Eighty dollars is very reasonable for a place as well furnished as this. I've had a little trouble collecting before, but it always came out very well. He promised me a cheque this morning. Over the telephone. I mean he promised to give it to me this morning.'

'Over the telephone,' I said. 'This morning.'

I shuffled around a bit in an inconspicuous sort of way. The idea was to get close enough to make a side swipe at the gun, knock it outwards and then jump in fast before she could bring it back in line. I've never had a lot of luck with the technique, but you have to try it once in a while. This looked like the time to try it.

I made about six inches, but not nearly enough for a first down. I said: 'And you're the owner?' I didn't look at the gun directly. I had a faint, a very faint hope that she didn't know she was pointing it at me.

'Why, certainly. I'm Mrs Fallbrook. Who did you think I was?'

'Well, I thought you might be the owner,' I said. 'You talking about the rent and all. But I didn't know your name.' Another eight inches. Nice smooth work. It would be a shame to have it wasted.

'And who are you, if I may inquire?'

'I just came about the car payment,' I said. 'The door was open just a teeny weensy bit and I kind of shoved in. I don't know why.'

I made a face like a man from the finance company coming about the car payment. Kind of tough, but ready to break into a sunny smile.

'You mean Mr Lavery is behind in his car payments?' she asked, looking worried.

'A little. Not a great deal,' I said soothingly.

I was all set now. I had the reach and I ought to have the speed. All it needed was a clean sharp sweep inside the gun and outward. I started to take my left foot out of the rug.

'You know,' she said, 'it's funny about this gun. I found it on the stairs. Nasty oily things, aren't they? And the stair carpet is a very nice grey chenille. Quite expensive.'

And she handed me the gun.

My hand went out for it, as stiff as an eggshell, almost as brittle. I took the gun. She sniffed with distaste at the glove which had been wrapped around the butt. She went on talking in exactly the same tone of cockeyed reasonableness. My knees cracked, relaxing.

'Well, of course, it's much easier for you,' she said. 'About the car, I mean. You can just take it away, if you have to. But taking a house with nice furniture in it isn't so easy. It takes time and money to evict a tenant. There is apt to be bitterness and things get damaged, sometimes on purpose. The rug on this floor cost over two hundred dollars, second-hand. It's only a jute rug, but it has a lovely colouring, don't you think? You'd never know it was only jute, second-hand. But that's silly too because they're always second-hand after you've used them. And I walked over here too, to save my tyres for the government. I could have taken a bus part way, but the darn things never come along except going in the wrong direction.'

I hardly heard what she said. It was like surf breaking beyond a point, out of sight. The gun had my interest.

I broke the magazine out. It was empty. I turned the gun and looked into the breech. That was empty too. I sniffed the muzzle. It reeked.

I dropped the gun into my pocket. A six-shot .25-calibre automatic. Emptied out. Shot empty, and not too long ago. But not in the last half-hour either.

'Has it been fired?' Mrs Fallbrook inquired pleasantly. 'I certainly hope not.'

'Any reason why it should have been fired?' I asked her. The voice was steady, but the brain was still bouncing.

'Well, it was lying on the stairs,' she said. 'After all, people do fire them.'

'How true that is,' I said. 'But Mr Lavery probably had a hole in his pocket. He isn't home, is he?'

'Oh no.' She shook her head and looked disappointed. 'And I don't think it's very nice of him. He promised me the cheque and I walked over –'

'When was it you phoned him?' I asked.

'Why, yesterday evening.' She frowned, not liking so many questions.

'He must have been called away,' I said.

She stared at a spot between my big brown eyes.

'Look, Mrs Fallbrook,' I said. 'Let's not kid around any more, Mrs Fallbrook. Not that I don't love it. And not that I like to say this. But you didn't shoot him, did you – on account of he owed you three months' rent?'

She sat down very slowly on the edge of a chair and worked the tip of her tongue along the scarlet slash of her mouth.

'Why, what a perfectly horrid suggestion,' she said angrily. 'I don't think you are nice at all. Didn't you say the gun had not been fired?'

'All guns have been fired sometime. All guns have been loaded some-time. This one is not loaded now.'

'Well, then –' she made an impatient gesture and sniffed at her oily glove.

'Okay, my idea was wrong. Just a gag anyway. Mr Lavery was out and you went through the house. Being the owner, you have a key. Is that correct?'

'I didn't mean to be interfering,' she said, biting a finger. 'Perhaps I ought not to have done it. But I have a right to see how things are kept.'

'Well, you looked. And you're sure he's not here?'

'I didn't look under the beds or in the icebox,' she said coldly. 'I called out from the top of the stairs when he didn't answer my ring. Then I went down to the lower hall and called out again. I even peeped into the bedroom.' She lowered her eyes as if bashfully and twisted a hand on her knee.

'Well, that's that,' I said.

She nodded brightly. 'Yes, that's that. And what did you say your name was?'

'Vance,' I said. 'Philo Vance.'

'And what company are you employed with, Mr Vance?'

'I'm out of work right now,' I said. 'Until the police commissioner gets in a jam again.'

She looked startled. 'But you said you came about a car payment.'

'That's just part-time work,' I said. 'A fill-in job.'

She rose to her feet and looked at me steadily. Her voice was cold saying: 'Then in that case I think you had better leave now.'

I said: 'I thought I might take a look around first, if you don't mind. There might be something you missed.'

'I don't think that is necessary,' she said. 'This is my house. I'll thank you to leave now, Mr Vance.'

I said: 'And if I don't leave, you'll get somebody who will. Take a chair again, Mrs Fallbrook. I'll just glance through. This gun, you know, is kind of queer.'

'But I told you I found it lying on the stairs,' she said angrily. 'I don't know anything else about it. I don't know anything about guns at all. I – I never shot one in my life.' She opened a large blue bag and pulled a handkerchief out of it and sniffled.

'That's your story,' I said. 'I don't have to get stuck with it.'

She put her left hand to me with a pathetic gesture, like the erring wife in *East Lynne*.

'Oh, I shouldn't have done!' she cried. 'It was horrid of me. I know it was. Mr Lavery will be furious.'

'What you shouldn't have done,' I said, 'was let me find out the gun was empty. Up to then you were holding everything in the deck.'

She stamped her foot. That was all the scene lacked. That made it perfect.

'Why, you perfectly loathsome man,' she squawked. 'Don't you dare touch me! Don't you take a single step towards me! I won't stay in this house another minute with you. How *dare* you be so insulting –'

She caught her voice and snapped it in mid-air like a rubber band. Then she put her head down, purple hat and all, and ran for the door. As she passed me she put a hand out as if to stiff-arm me, but she wasn't near enough and I didn't move. She jerked the door wide and charged out through it and up the walk to the street. The door came slowly shut and I heard her rapid steps above the sound of its closing.

I ran a finger-nail along my teeth and punched the point of my jaw with a knuckle, listening. I didn't hear anything anywhere to listen to. A six-shot automatic, fired empty.

'Something,' I said out loud, 'is all wrong with this scene.'

The house seemed now to be abnormally still. I went along the apricot rug and through the archway to the head of the stairs. I stood there for another moment and listened again.

I shrugged and went quietly down the stairs.

16

The lower hall had a door at each end and two in the middle side by side. One of these was a linen closet and the other was locked. I went along to the end and looked in at a spare bedroom with drawn blinds and no sign of being used. I went back to the other end of the hall and stepped into a second bedroom with a wide bed, a café-au-lait rug, angular furniture in light wood, a box mirror over the dressing-table and a long fluorescent lamp over the mirror. In the corner a crystal greyhound stood on a mirror-top table and beside him a crystal box with cigarettes in it.

Face powder was spilled around on the dressing-table. There was a smear of dark lipstick on a towel hanging over the waste basket. On the bed were pillows side by side, with depressions in them that could have been made by heads. A woman's handkerchief peeped from under one pillow. A pair of sheer black pyjamas lay across the foot of the bed. A rather too emphatic trace of chypre hung in the air.

I wondered what Mrs Fallbrook had thought of all this.

I turned around and looked at myself in the long mirror of a closet door. The door was painted white and had a crystal knob. I turned the knob in my handkerchief and looked inside. The cedar-lined closet was fairly full of man's clothes. There was a nice friendly smell of tweed. The closet was not entirely full of man's clothes.

There was also a woman's black and white tailored suit, mostly white, black and white shoes under it, a panama with a black and white rolled band on a shelf above it. There were other woman's clothes, but I didn't examine them.

I shut the closet door and went out of the bedroom, holding my handkerchief ready for more doorknobs.

The door next the linen closet, the locked door, had to be the bathroom. I shook it, but it went on being locked. I bent down and saw there was a short, slit-shaped opening in the middle of the knob. I knew then that the door was fastened by pushing a button in the middle of the knob inside, and that the slit-like opening was for a metal key without wards that would spring the lock open in case somebody fainted in the bathroom, or the kids locked themselves in and got sassy.

The key for this ought to be kept on the top shelf of the linen closet but it wasn't. I tried my knife blade, but that was too thin. I went back to the bedroom and got a flat nail-file off the dresser. That worked. I opened the bathroom door.

A man's sand-coloured pyjamas were tossed over a painted hamper. A pair of heelless green slippers lay on the floor. There was a safety-razor on the edge of the wash-bowl and a tube of cream with the cap off. The bathroom window was shut, and there was a pungent smell in the air that was not quite like any other smell.

Three empty shells lay bright and coppery on the nile-green tiles of the bathroom floor, and there was a nice clean hole in the frosted pane of the window. To the left and a little above the window were two scarred places in the plaster where the white showed behind the paint and where something, such as a bullet, had gone in.

The shower curtain was green and white oiled silk and it hung on shiny chromium rings and it was drawn across the shower opening. I slid it aside, the rings making a thin scraping noise, which for some reason sounded indecently loud.

I felt my neck creak a little as I bent down. He was there all right – there wasn't anywhere else for him to be. He was huddled in the corner under the two shining faucets, and water dripped slowly on his chest from the chromium showerhead.

His knees were drawn up but slack. The two holes in his naked chest were dark blue and both of them were close enough to his heart to have killed him. The blood seemed to have been washed away.

His eyes had a curiously bright and expectant look, as if he smelled the morning coffee and would be coming right out.

Nice efficient work. You have just finished shaving and stripped for the shower and you are leaning in against the shower curtain and adjusting the temperature of the water. The door opens behind you and somebody comes in. The somebody appears to have been a woman. She has a gun. You look at the gun and she shoots it.

She misses with three shots. It seems impossible, at such short range, but there it is. Maybe it happens all the time. I've been around so little.

You haven't anywhere to go. You could lunge at her and take a chance, if you were that kind of fellow, and if you were braced for it. But leaning in over the shower faucets, holding the curtains closed, you are off balance. Also you are apt to be somewhat petrified with panic, if you are at all like other people.

That is where you go. You go into it as far as you can, but a shower stall is a small place and the tiled wall stops you. You are backed up against the last wall there is now. You are all out of space, and you are all out of living. And then there are two more shots, possibly three, and you slide down the wall, and your eyes are not even frightened any more now. They are just the empty eyes of the dead.

She reaches in and turns the shower off. She sets the lock of the bathroom door. On her way out of the house she throws the empty gun on the stair carpet. She should worry. It is probably your gun.

Is that right? It had better be right.

I bent and pulled at his arm. Ice couldn't have been any colder or any stiffer. I went out of the bathroom, leaving it unlocked. No need to lock it now. It only makes work for the cops.

I went into the bedroom and pulled the handkerchief out from under the pillow. It was a minute piece of linen rag with a scalloped edge embroidered in red. Two small initials were stitched in the corner, in red. A.F.

'Adrienne Fromsett,' I said. I laughed. It was a rather ghoulish laugh.

I shook the handkerchief to get some of the chypre out of it and folded it up in a tissue and put it in a pocket. I went back upstairs to the living-room and poked around in the desk against the wall. The desk contained no interesting letters, phone numbers or provocative match-folders. Or if it did, I didn't find them.

I looked at the phone. It was on a small table against the wall beside the fireplace. It had a long cord so that Mr Lavery could be lying on his back on the davenport, a cigarette between his smooth brown lips, a tall cool one at the table at his side, and plenty of time for a nice long cosy conversation with a lady friend. An easy, languid, flirtatious, kidding, not too subtle and not too blunt conversation, of the sort he would be apt to enjoy.

All that wasted too. I went away from the telephone to the door and set the lock so I could come in again and shut the door tight, pulling it hard over the sill until the lock clicked. I went up the walk and stood in the sunlight looking across the street at Dr Almore's house.

Nobody yelled or ran out of the door. Nobody blew a police whistle. Everything was quiet and sunny and calm. No cause for excitement whatever. It's only Marlowe, finding another body. He does it rather well by now. Murder-a-day Marlowe, they call him. They have the meat wagon following him around to follow up on the business he finds.

A nice enough fellow, in an ingenious sort of way.

I walked back to the intersection and got into my car and started it and backed it and drove away from there.

17

The bellhop at the Athletic Club was back in three minutes with a nod for me to come with him. We rode up to the fourth floor and went around a corner and he showed me a half-open door.

'Around to the left, sir. As quietly as you can. A few of the members are sleeping.'

I went into the club library. It contained books behind glass doors and magazines on a long central table and a lighted portrait of the club's founder. But its real business seemed to be sleeping. Outward-jutting bookcases cut the room into a number of small alcoves and in the alcoves were high-backed leather chairs of an incredible size and softness. In a number of the chairs old boys were snoozing peacefully, their faces violet with high blood pressure, thin racking snores coming out of their pinched noses.

I climbed over a few feet and stole around to the left. Derace Kingsley was in the very last alcove in the far end of the room. He had two chairs arranged side by side, facing into the corner. His big dark head just showed over the top of one of them. I slipped into the empty one and gave him a quick nod.

'Keep your voice down,' he said. 'This room is for after-luncheon naps. Now what is it? When I employed you it was to save me trouble, not to add trouble to what I already had. You made me break an important engagement.'

'I know,' I said, and put my face close to his. He smelled of highballs, in a nice way. 'She shot him.'

His eyebrows jumped and his face got that stony look. His teeth clamped tight. He breathed softly and twisted a large hand on his kneecap.

'Go on,' he said, in a voice the size of a marble.

I looked back over the top of my chair. The nearest old geezer was sound asleep and blowing the dusty fuzz in his nostrils back and forth as he breathed.

'No answer at Lavery's place,' I said. 'Door slightly open. But I noticed yesterday it sticks on the sill. Pushed it open. Room dark, two glasses with drinks having been in them. House very still. In a moment a slim dark woman calling herself Mrs Fallbrook, landlady, came up the stairs with her glove wrapped around a gun. Said she had found it on the stairs. Said she came to collect her three months' back rent. Used her key to get in. Inference is she took the chance to snoop around and look the house over. Took the gun from her and found it had been fired recently, but didn't tell her so. She said Lavery was not home. Got rid of her by making her mad and she departed in high dudgeon. She may call the police, but it's much more likely she will just go out and hunt butterflies and forget the whole thing – except the rent.'

I paused. Kingsley's head was turned towards me and his jaw muscles bulged with the way his teeth were clamped. His eyes looked sick.

'I went downstairs. Signs of a woman having spent the night. Pyjamas, face powder, perfume, and so on. Bathroom locked, but got it open. Three empty shells on the floor, two shots in the wall, one in the window. Lavery in the shower stall, naked and dead.'

'My God!' Kingsley whispered. 'Do you mean to say he had a woman with him last night and she shot him this morning in the bathroom?'

'Just what did you think I was trying to say?' I asked.

'Keep your voice down,' he groaned. 'It's a shock, naturally. Why in the bathroom?'

'Keep your own voice down,' I said. 'Why not in the bathroom? Could you think of a place where a man would be more completely off guard?'

He said: 'You don't know that a woman shot him. I mean, you're not sure, are you?'

'No,' I said. 'That's true. It might have been somebody who used a small gun and emptied it carelessly to look like a woman's work. The bathroom is downhill, facing outwards on space and I don't think shots down there would be easily heard by anyone not in the house. The woman who spent the night might have left – or there need not have been any woman at all. The appearances could have been faked. You might have shot him.'

'What would I want to shoot him for?' he almost bleated, squeezing both kneecaps hard. 'I'm a civilized man.'

That didn't seem to be worth an argument either. I said: 'Does your wife own a gun?'

He turned a drawn miserable face to me and said hollowly: 'Good God, man, you can't really think that!'

'Well, does she?'

He got the words out in small gritty pieces. 'Yes – she does. A small automatic.'

'You buy it locally?'

'I – I didn't buy it at all. I took it away from a drunk at a party in San Francisco a couple of years ago. He was waving it around, with an idea that that was very funny. I never gave it back to him.' He pinched his jaw hard until his knuckles whitened. 'He probably doesn't even remember how or when he lost it. He was that kind of a drunk.'

'This is working out almost too neatly,' I said. 'Could you recognize this gun?'

He thought hard, pushing his jaw out and half-closing his eyes. I looked back over the chairs again. One of the elderly snoozers had waked himself up with a snort that almost blew him out of his chair. He coughed, scratched his nose with a thin dried-up hand, and fumbled a gold watch out of his vest. He peered at it bleakly, put it away, and went to sleep again.

I reached in my pocket and put the gun in Kingsley's hand. He stared down at it miserably.

'I don't know,' he said slowly. 'It's like it, but I can't tell.'

'There's a serial number on the side,' I said.

'Nobody remembers the serial numbers of guns.'

'I was hoping you wouldn't,' I said. 'It would have worried me very much.'

His hand closed around the gun and he put it down beside him in the chair.

'The dirty rat,' he said softly. 'I suppose he ditched her.'

'I don't get it,' I said. 'The motive was inadequate for you, on account of you're a civilized man. But it was adequate for her.'

'It's not the same motive,' he snapped. 'And women are more impetuous than men.'

'Like cats are more impetuous than dogs.'

'How?'

'Some women are more impetuous than some men. That's all that means. We'll have to have a better motive, if you want your wife to have done it.'

He turned his head enough to give me a level stare in which there was no amusement. White crescents were bitten into the corners of his mouth.

'This doesn't seem to me a very good spot for the light touch,' he said. 'We can't let the police have this gun. Crystal had a permit and the gun was registered. So they will know the number, even if I don't. We can't let them have it.'

'But Mrs Fallbrook knows I had the gun.'

He shook his head stubbornly. 'We'll have to chance that. Yes, I know you're taking a risk. I intend to make it worth your while. If the set-up were possible for suicide, I'd say put the gun back. But the way you tell it, it isn't.'

'No. He'd have to have missed himself with the first three shots. But I can't cover up a murder, even for a ten-dollar bonus. The gun will have to go back.'

'I was thinking of more money than that,' he said quietly. 'I was thinking of five hundred dollars.'

'Just what did you expect to buy with it?'

He leaned close to me. His eyes were serious and bleak, but not hard. 'Is there anything in Lavery's place, apart from the gun, that might indicate Crystal has been there lately?'

'A black and white dress and a hat like the bellhop in Bernardino described on her. There may be a dozen things I don't know about. There almost certainly will be fingerprints. You say she was never printed, but that doesn't mean they won't get her prints to check. Her bedroom at home will be full of them. So will the cabin at Little Fawn Lake. And her car.'

'We ought to get the car –' he started to say. I stopped him.

'No use. Too many other places. What kind of perfume does she use?'

He looked blank for an instant. 'Oh – Gillerlain Regal, the Champagne of Perfumes,' he said woodenly. 'A Chanel number once in a while.'

'What's this stuff of yours like?'

'A kind of chypre. Sandalwood chypre.'

'The bedroom reeks with it,' I said. 'It smelled like cheap stuff to me. But I'm no judge.'

'Cheap?' he said, stung to the quick. 'My God, cheap? We get thirty dollars an ounce for it.'

'Well, this stuff smelled more like three dollars a gallon.'

He put his hands down hard on his knees and shook his head.

'I'm talking about money,' he said. 'Five hundred dollars. A cheque for it right now.'

I let the remark fall to the ground, eddying like a soiled feather. One of the old boys behind us stumbled to his feet and groped his way wearily out of the room.

Kingsley said gravely: 'I hired you to protect me from scandal, and, of course, to protect my wife, if she needed it. Through no fault of yours the chance to avoid scandal is pretty well shot. It's a question of my wife's neck now. I don't believe she shot Lavery. I have no reason for that belief. None at all. I just feel the conviction. She may even have been there last night, this gun may even be her gun. It doesn't prove she killed him. She would be as careless with the gun as with anything else. Anybody could have got hold of it.'

'The cops down there won't work very hard to believe that,' I said. 'If the one I met is a fair specimen, they'll just pick the first head they see and start swinging with their blackjacks. And hers will certainly be the first head they see when they look the situation over.'

He ground the heels of his hands together. His misery had a theatrical flavour, as real misery so often has.

'I'll go along with you up to a point,' I said. 'The set-up down there is almost too good, at first sight. She leaves clothes there she has been seen wearing and which can probably be traced. She leaves the gun on the stairs. It's hard to think she would be as dumb as that.'

'You give me a little heart,' Kingsley said wearily.

'But none of that means anything,' I said. 'Because we are looking at it from the angle of calculation, and people who commit crimes of passion or hatred just commit them and walk out. Everything I have heard indicates that she is a reckless, foolish woman. There's no sign of planning in any of the scene down there. There's every sign of a complete lack of planning. But even if there wasn't a thing down there to point to your wife, the cops would tie her up to Lavery. They will investigate his background, his friends, his women. Her name is bound to crop up somewhere along the line, and when it does, the fact that she has been out of sight for a month will make them sit up and rub their horny palms with glee. And of course they'll trace the gun, and if it's her gun –'

His hand dived for the gun in the chair beside him.

'Nope,' I said. 'They'll have to have the gun. Marlowe may be a very smart guy and very fond of you personally, but he can't risk the suppression of such vital evidence as the gun that killed a man. Whatever I do has to be on the basis that your wife is an obvious suspect, but that the obviousness can be wrong.'

He groaned and put his big hand out with the gun in it. I took it and put it away. Then I took it out again and said: 'Lend me your handkerchief. I don't want to use mine. I might be searched.'

He handed me a stiff white handkerchief and I wiped the gun off carefully all over and dropped it into my pocket. I handed him back the handkerchief.

'My prints are all right,' I said. 'But I don't want yours on it. Here's the only thing I can do. Go back down there and replace the gun and call the law. Ride it out with them and let the chips fall where they have to. The story will have to come out. What I was doing down there and why. At the worst they'll find her and prove she killed him. At the best they'll find her a lot quicker than I can and let me use my energies proving that she didn't kill him, which means, in effect, proving that someone else did. Are you game for that?'

He nodded slowly. He said: 'Yes – and the five hundred stands. For showing Crystal didn't kill him.'

'I don't expect to earn it,' I said. 'You may as well understand that now. How well did Miss Fromsett know Lavery? Out of office hours?'

His face tightened up like a charleyhorse. His fists went into hard lumps on his thighs. He said nothing.

'She looked kind of queer when I asked her for his address yesterday morning,' I said.

He let a breath out slowly.

'Like a bad taste in the mouth,' I said. 'Like a romance that fouled out. Am I too blunt?'

His nostrils quivered a little and his breath made noise in them for a moment. Then he relaxed and said quietly:

'She – she knew him rather well – at one time. She's a girl who would do about what she pleased in that way. Lavery was, I guess, a fascinating bird – to women.'

'I'll have to talk to her,' I said.

'Why?' he asked shortly. Red patches showed in his cheeks.

'Never mind why. It's my business to ask all sorts of questions of all sorts of people.'

'Talk to her then,' he said tightly. 'As a matter of fact she knew the Almores. She knew Almore's wife, the one who killed herself. Lavery knew her too. Could that have any possible connexion with this business?'

'I don't know. You're in love with her, aren't you?'

'I'd marry her tomorrow if I could,' he said stiffly.

I nodded and stood up. I looked back along the room. It was almost empty now. At the far end a couple of elderly relics were still blowing bubbles. The rest of the soft-chair boys had staggered back to whatever it was they did when they were conscious.

'There's just one thing,' I said, looking down at Kingsley. 'Cops get very hostile when there is a delay in calling them after a murder. There's been delay this time and there will be more. I'd like to go down there as if it was the first visit today. I think I can make it that way, if I leave the Fallbrook woman out.'

'Fallbrook?' He hardly knew what I was talking about. 'Who the hell – oh yes, I remember.'

'Well, don't remember. I'm almost certain they'll never hear a peep from her. She's not the kind to have anything to do with the police of her own free will.'

'I understand,' he said.

'Be sure you handle it right then. Questions will be asked you *before* you are told Lavery is dead, before I'm allowed to get in touch with you – so far as they know. Don't fall into any traps. If you do, I won't be able to find anything out. I'll be in the clink.'

'You could call me from the house down there – before you call the police,' he said reasonably.

'I know. But the fact that I don't will be in my favour. And they'll check the phone calls one of the first things they do. And if I call you from anywhere else, I might just as well admit that I came up here to see you.'

'I understand,' he said again. 'You can trust me to handle it.'

We shook hands and I left him standing there.

18

The Athletic Club was on a corner across the street and half a block down from the Treloar Building. I crossed and walked north to the entrance. They had finished laying rose-coloured concrete where the rubber sidewalk had been. It was fenced around, leaving a narrow gangway in and out of the building. The space was clotted with office help going in from lunch.

The Gillerlain Company's reception-room looked even emptier than the day before. The same fluffy little blonde was tucked in behind the PBX in the corner. She gave me a quick smile and I gave her the gunman's salute, a stiff forefinger pointing at her, the three lower fingers tucked back under it, and the thumb wiggling up and down like a western gun-fighter fanning his hammer. She laughed heartily, without making a sound. This was more fun than she had had in a week.

I pointed to Miss Fromsett's empty desk and the little blonde nodded and pushed a plug in and spoke. A door opened and Miss Fromsett swayed elegantly out to her desk and sat down and gave me her cool expectant eyes.

'Yes, Mr Marlowe? Mr Kingsley is not in, I'm afraid.'

'I just came from him. Where do we talk?'

'Talk?'

'I have something to show you.'

'Oh, yes?' She looked me over thoughtfully. A lot of guys had probably tried to show her things, including etchings. At another time I wouldn't have been above taking a flutter at it myself.

'Business,' I said. 'Mr Kingsley's business.'

She stood up and opened the gate in the railing. 'We may as well go into his office then.'

We went in. She held the door for me. As I passed her I sniffed. Sandalwood. I said:

'Gillerlain Regal, the Champagne of Perfumes?'

She smiled faintly, holding the door. 'On my salary?'

'I didn't say anything about your salary. You don't look like a girl who has to buy her own perfume.'

'Yes, that's what it is,' she said. 'And if you want to know, I detest wearing perfume in the office. He makes me.'

We went down the long dim office and she took a chair at the end of the desk. I sat where I had sat the day before. We looked at each other. She was wearing tan today, with a ruffled jabot at her throat. She looked a little warmer, but still no prairie fire.

I offered her one of Kingsley's cigarettes. She took it, took a light from his lighter, and leaned back.

'We needn't waste time being cagey,' I said. 'You know by now who I am and what I am doing. If you didn't know yesterday morning, it's only because he loves to play big shot.'

She looked down at the hand that lay on her knee, then lifted her eyes and smiled almost shyly.

'He's a great guy,' she said. 'In spite of the heavy executive act he likes to put on. He's the only guy that gets fooled by it after all. And if you only knew what he has stood from that little tramp –' She waved her cigarette. 'Well, perhaps I'd better leave that out. What was it you wanted to see me about?'

'Kingsley said you knew the Almores.'

'I knew Mrs Almore. That is, I met her a couple of times.'

'Where?'

'At a friend's house. Why?'

'At Lavery's house?'

'You're not going to be insolent, are you, Mr Marlowe?'

'I don't know what your definition of that would be. I'm going to talk business as if it was business, not international diplomacy.'

'Very well.' She nodded slightly. 'At Chris Lavery's house, yes. I used to go there – once in a while. He had cocktail parties.'

'Then Lavery knew the Almores – or Mrs Almore.'

She flushed very slightly. 'Yes. Quite well.'

'And a lot of other women – quite well, too. I don't doubt that. Did Mrs Kingsley know her too?'

'Yes, better than I did. They called each other by their first names. Mrs Almore is dead, you know. She committed suicide, about a year and a half ago.'

'Any doubt about that?'

She raised her eyebrows, but the expression looked artificial to me, as if it just went with the question I asked, as a matter of form.

She said: 'Have you any particular reason for asking that question in that particular way? I mean, has it anything to do with – with what you are doing?'

'I didn't think so. I still don't know that it has. But yesterday Dr Almore called a cop just because I looked at his house. After he had found out from my car licence who I was. The cop got pretty tough with me, just for being there. He didn't know what I was doing and I didn't tell him I had been calling on Lavery. But Dr Almore must have known that. He had seen me in front of Lavery's house. Now why would he think it necessary to call a cop? And why would the cop think it smart to say that the last fellow who tried to put the bite on Almore ended up on the road gang? And why would the cop ask me if her folks – meaning Mrs Almore's folks, I suppose – had hired me? If you can answer any of those questions, I might know whether it's any of my business.'

She thought about it for a moment, giving me one quick glance while she was thinking, and then looking away again.

'I only met Mrs Almore twice,' she said slowly. 'But I think I can answer your questions – all of them. The last time I met her was at Lavery's place, as I said, and there were quite a lot of people there. There was a lot of drinking and loud talk. The women were not with their husbands and the men were not with their wives, if any. There was a man there named Brownwell who was very tight. He's in the Navy now,

I heard. He was ribbing Mrs Almore about her husband's practice. The idea seemed to be that he was one of those doctors who run around all night with a case of loaded hypodermic needles, keeping the local fast set from having pink elephants for breakfast. Florence Almore said she didn't care how her husband got his money as long as he got plenty of it and she had the spending of it. She was tight too, and not a very nice person sober, I should imagine. One of these slinky glittering females who laugh too much and sprawl all over their chairs, showing a great deal of leg. A very light blonde with high odour and indecently large baby-blue eyes. Well, Brownwell told her not to worry, it would always be a good racket. In and out of the patient's house in fifteen minutes and anywhere from ten to fifty bucks a trip. But one thing bothered him, he said, however a doctor could get hold of so much dope without underworld contacts. He asked Mrs Almore if they had many nice gangsters to dinner at their house. She threw a glass of liquor in his face.'

I grinned, but Miss Fromsett didn't. She crushed her cigarette out in Kingsley's big copper and glass tray and looked at me soberly.

'Fair enough,' I said. 'Who wouldn't, unless he had a large hard fist to throw?'

'Yes. A few weeks later, Florence Almore was found dead in the garage late at night. The door of the garage was shut and the car motor was running.' She stopped and moistened her lips slightly. 'It was Chris Lavery who found her. Coming home at God knows what o'clock in the morning. She was lying on the concrete floor in pyjamas, with her head under a blanket which was also over the exhaust pipe of the car. Dr Almore was out. There was nothing about the affair in the papers, except that she had died suddenly. It was well hushed up.'

She lifted her clasped hands a little and then let them fall slowly into her lap again. I said:

'Was something wrong with it, then?'

'People thought so, but they always do. Some time later I heard what purported to be the lowdown. I met this man Brownwell on Vine Street and he asked me to have a drink with him. I didn't like him, but I had half an hour to kill. We sat at the back of Levy's bar and he asked me if I remembered the babe who threw the drink in his face. I said I did. The conversation then went something very like this. I remember it very well.

'Brownwell said: "Our pal Chris Lavery is sitting pretty, if he ever runs out of girl friends he can touch for dough."

'I said: "I don't think I understand."

'He said: "Hell, maybe you don't want to. The night the Almore woman died she was over to Lou Condy's place losing her shirt at roulette. She got into a tantrum and said the wheels were crooked and made a scene. Condy practically had to drag her into his office. He got hold of Dr Almore through the Physicians' Exchange and after a while the doc came over. He shot her with one of his busy little needles. Then he went away, leaving Condy to get her home. It seems he had a very urgent case. So Condy took her home and the doc's office nurse showed up, having been called by the doc, and Condy carried her upstairs and the nurse put her to bed. Condy went back to his chips. So she had to be carried to bed and yet the same night she got up and walked down to the family garage and finished herself off with monoxide. What do you think of that?" Brownwell was asking me.

'I said: "I don't know anything about it. How do you?"

'He said: "I know a reporter on the rag they call a newspaper down there. There was no inquest and no autopsy. If any tests were made, nothing was told about them. They don't have a regular coroner down there. The undertakers take turns at being acting coroner, a week at a time. They're pretty well subservient to the political gang naturally. It's easy to fix a thing like that in a small town, if anybody with any pull wants it fixed. And Condy had plenty at that time. He didn't want the publicity of an investigation and neither did the doctor."'

Miss Fromsett stopped talking and waited for me to say something. When I didn't, she went on: 'I suppose you know what all this means to Brownwell?'

'Sure. Almore finished her off and then he and Condy between them bought a fix. It has been done in cleaner little cities than Bay City ever tried to be. But that isn't all the story, is it?'

'No. It seems Mrs Almore's parents hired a private detective. He was a man who ran a night watchman service down there and he was actually the second man on the scene that night, after Chris. Brownwell said he must have had something in the way of information, but he never got a chance to use it. They arrested him for drunk driving and he got a jail sentence.'

I said: 'Is that all?'

She nodded. 'And if you think I remember it too well, it's part of my job to remember conversations.'

'What I was thinking was that it doesn't have to add up to very much. I don't see where it has to touch Lavery, even if he was the one who found her. Your gossipy friend Brownwell seems to think what happened gave somebody a chance to blackmail the doctor. But there would have to be some evidence, especially when you're trying to put the bite on a man who has already cleared himself with the law.'

Miss Fromsett said: 'I think so too. And I'd like to think blackmail was one of the nasty little tricks Chris Lavery didn't quite run to. I think that's all I can tell you, Mr Marlowe. And I ought to be outside.'

She started to get up. I said: 'It's not quite all. I have something to show you.'

I got the little perfumed rag that had been under Lavery's pillow out of my pocket and leaned over to drop it on the desk in front of her.

19

She looked at the handkerchief, looked at me, picked up a pencil and pushed the little piece of linen around with the eraser end.

'What's on it?' she asked. 'Flyspray?'

'Some kind of sandalwood, I thought.'

'A cheap synthetic. Repulsive is a mild word for it. And why did you want me to look at this handkerchief, Mr Marlowe?' She leaned back again and stared at me with level cool eyes.

'I found it in Chris Lavery's house, under the pillow on his bed. It has initials on it.'

She unfolded the handkerchief without touching it by using the rubber tip of the pencil. Her face got a little grim and taut.

'It has two letters embroidered on it,' she said in a cold angry voice. 'They happen to be the same letters as my initials. Is that what you mean?'

'Right,' I said. 'He probably knows half a dozen women with the same initials.'

'So you're going to be nasty after all,' she said quietly.

'Is it your handkerchief – or isn't it?'

She hesitated. She reached out to the desk and very quietly got herself another cigarette and lit it with a match. She shook the match slowly, watching the small flame creep along the wood.

'Yes, it's mine,' she said, 'I must have dropped it there. It's a long time ago. And I assure you I didn't put it under a pillow on his bed. Is that what you wanted to know?'

I didn't say anything, and she added: 'He must have lent it to some woman who – who would like this kind of perfume.'

'I get a mental picture of the woman,' I said. 'And she doesn't quite go with Lavery.'

Her upper lip curled a little. It was a long upper lip. I like long upper lips.

'I think,' she said, 'you ought to do a little more work on your mental picture of Chris Lavery. Any touch of refinement you may have noticed is purely coincidental.'

'That's not a nice thing to say about a dead man,' I said.

For a moment she just sat there and looked at me as if I hadn't said anything and she was waiting for me to say something. Then a slow shudder started at her throat and passed over her whole body. Her hands clenched and the cigarette bent into a crook. She looked down at it and threw it into the ash-tray with a quick jerk of her arm.

'He was shot in his shower,' I said. 'And it looks as if it was done by some woman who spent the night there. He had just been shaving. The woman left a gun on the stairs and this handkerchief on the bed.'

She moved very slightly in her chair. Her eyes were perfectly empty now. Her face was as cold as a carving.

'And did you expect me to be able to give you information about that?' she asked me bitterly.

'Look, Miss Fromsett, I'd like to be smooth and distant and subtle about all this too. I'd like to play this sort of game just once the way somebody like you would like it to be played. But nobody will let me – not the clients, nor the cops, nor the people I play against. However hard I try to be nice I always end up with my nose in the dirt and my thumb feeling for somebody's eye.'

She nodded as if she had only just barely heard me. 'When was he shot?' she asked, and then shuddered slightly again.

'This morning, I suppose. Not long after he got up. I said he had just shaved and was going to take a shower.'

'That,' she said, 'would probably have been quite late. I've been here since eight-thirty.'

'I didn't think you shot him.'

'Awfully kind of you,' she said. 'But it is my handkerchief, isn't it? Although not my perfume. But I don't suppose policemen are very sensitive to quality in perfume – or in anything else.'

'No – and that goes for private detectives too,' I said. 'Are you enjoying this a lot?'

'God,' she said, and put the back of her hand hard against her mouth.

'He was shot at five or six times,' I said. 'And missed all but twice. He was cornered in the shower-stall. It was a pretty grim scene, I should think. There was a lot of hate on one side of it. Or a pretty cold-blooded mind.'

'He was quite easy to hate,' she said emptily. 'And poisonously easy to love. Women – even decent women – make such ghastly mistakes about men.'

'All you're telling me is that you once thought you loved him, but not any more, and that you didn't shoot him.'

'Yes.' Her voice was light and dry now, like the perfume she didn't like to wear at the office. 'I'm sure you'll respect the confidence.' She laughed shortly and bitterly. 'Dead,' she said. 'The poor, egotistical, cheap, nasty, handsome, treacherous guy. Dead and cold and done with. No, Mr Marlowe, I didn't shoot him.'

I waited, letting her work it out of her. After a moment she said quietly: 'Does Mr Kingsley know?'

I nodded.

'And the police, of course.'

'Not yet. At least not from me. I found him. The house door wasn't quite shut. I went in. I found him.'

She picked the pencil up and poked at the handkerchief again. 'Does Mr Kingsley know about this scented rag?'

'Nobody knows about that, except you and me, and whoever put it there.'

'Nice of you,' she said dryly. 'And nice of you to think what you thought.'

'You have a certain quality of aloofness and dignity that I like,' I said. 'But don't run it into the ground. What would you expect me to think? Do I pull the hankie out from under the pillow and sniff it and hold it out and say, "Well, well, Miss Adrienne Fromsett's initials and all. Miss Fromsett must have known Lavery, perhaps very intimately. Let's say, just for the book, as intimately as my nasty little mind can conceive. And that would be pretty damn intimately. But this is cheap synthetic sandalwood and Miss Fromsett wouldn't use cheap scent. And this was under Lavery's pillow and Miss Fromsett just never keeps her hankies under a man's pillow. Therefore this has absolutely nothing to do with Miss Fromsett. It's just an optical delusion.'

'Oh, shut up,' she said.

I grinned.

'What kind of girl do you think I am?' she snapped.

'I came in too late to tell you.'

She flushed, but delicately and all over her face this time. Then, 'Have you any idea who did it?'

'Ideas, but that's all they are. I'm afraid the police are going to find it simple. Some of Mrs Kingsley's clothes are hanging in Lavery's closet. And when they know the whole story – including what happened at Little Fawn Lake yesterday – I'm afraid they'll just reach for the handcuffs. They have to find her first. But that won't be so hard for them.'

'Crystal Kingsley,' she said emptily. 'So he couldn't be spared even that.'

I said: 'It doesn't have to be. It could be an entirely different motivation, something we know nothing about. It could have been somebody like Dr Almore.'

She looked up quickly, then shook her head. 'It could be,' I insisted.

'We don't know anything against it. He was pretty nervous yesterday, for a man who has nothing to be afraid of. But, of course, it isn't only the guilty who are afraid.'

I stood up and tapped on the edge of the desk looking down at her. She had a lovely neck. She pointed to the handkerchief.

'What about that?' she asked dully.

'If it was mine, I'd wash that cheap scent out of it.'

'It has to mean something, doesn't it? It might mean a lot.'

I laughed. 'I don't think it means anything at all. Women are always leaving their handkerchiefs around. A fellow like Lavery would collect them and keep them in a drawer with a sandalwood sachet. Somebody would find the stock and take one out to use. Or he would lend them, enjoying the reactions to the other girl's initials. I'd say he was that kind of a heel. Good-bye, Miss Fromsett, and thanks for talking to me.'

I started to go, then I stopped and asked her: 'Did you hear the name of the reporter down there who gave Brownwell all his information?'

She shook her head.

'Or the name of Mrs Almore's parents?'

'Not that either. But I could probably find that out for you. I'd be glad to try.'

'How?'

'Those things are usually printed in death notices, aren't they? There is pretty sure to have been a death notice in the Los Angeles papers.'

'That would be very nice of you,' I said. I ran a finger along the edge of the desk and looked at her sideways. Pale ivory skin, dark and lovely eyes, hair as light as hair can be and eyes as dark as night can be.

I walked back down the room and out. The little blonde at the PBX looked at me expectantly, her small red lips parted, waiting for more fun.

I didn't have any more. I went out.

20

No police cars stood in front of Lavery's house, nobody hung around on the sidewalk and when I pushed the front door open there was no smell of cigar or cigarette smoke inside. The sun had gone away from the windows and a fly buzzed softly over one of the liquor glasses. I went down to the end and hung over the railing that led downstairs. Nothing moved in Mr Lavery's house. Nothing made sound except very faintly down below in the bathroom the quiet trickle of water dripping on a dead man's shoulder.

I went to the telephone and looked up the number of the police department in the directory. I dialled and while I was waiting for an answer, I took the little automatic out of my pocket and laid it on the table beside the telephone.

When the male voice said: 'Bay City police – Smoot talking,' I said: 'There's been a shooting at 623 Altair Street. Man named Lavery lives there. He's dead.'

'Six-two-three Altair. Who are you?'

'The name is Marlowe.'

'You there in the house?'

'Right.'

'Don't touch anything at all.'

I hung up, sat down on the davenport and waited.

Not very long. A siren whined far off, growing louder with great surges of sound. Tyres screamed at a corner, and the siren wail died to a metallic growl, then the silence, and the tyres screamed again in front of the house. The Bay City police conserving rubber. Steps hit the sidewalk and I went over to the front door and opened it.

Two uniformed cops barged into the room. They were the usual large size and they had the usual weathered faces and suspicious eyes. One of them had a carnation tucked under his cap, behind his right ear. The other one was older, a little grey and grim. They stood and looked at me warily, then the older one said briefly:

'All right, where is it?'

'Downstairs in the bathroom, behind the shower curtain.'

'You stay here with him, Eddie.'

He went rapidly along the room and disappeared. The other one looked at me steadily and said out of the corner of his mouth:

'Don't make any false moves, buddy.'

I sat down on the davenport again. The cop ranged the room with his eyes. There were sounds below stairs, feet walking. The cop with me suddenly spotted the gun lying on the telephone table. He charged at it violently, like a downfield blocker.

'This the death gun?' he almost shouted.

'I should imagine so. It's been fired.'

'Ha!' He leaned over the gun, baring his teeth at me, and put his hand to his holster. His finger tickled the flap off the stud and he grasped the butt of the black revolver.

'You should what?' he barked.

'I should imagine so.'

'That's very good,' he sneered. 'That's very good indeed.'

'It's not that good,' I said.

He reeled back a little. His eyes were being careful of me. 'What you shoot him for?' he growled.

'I've wondered and wondered.'

'Oh, a wisenheimer.'

'Let's just sit down and wait for the homicide boys,' I said. 'I'm reserving my defence.'

'Don't give me none of that,' he said.

'I'm not giving you any of anything. If I had shot him, I wouldn't be here. I wouldn't have called up. You wouldn't have found the gun. Don't work so hard on the case. You won't be on it more than ten minutes.'

His eyes looked hurt. He took his cap off and the carnation dropped to the floor. He bent and picked it up and twirled it between his fingers, then dropped it behind the fire screen.

'Better not do that,' I told him. 'They might think it's a clue and waste a lot of time on it.'

'Aw hell.' He bent over the screen and retrieved the carnation and put it in his pocket. 'You know all the answers, don't you, buddy?'

The other cop came back up the stairs, looking grave. He stood in the middle of the floor and looked at his wristwatch and made a note in a notebook and then looked out of the front windows, holding the venetian blinds to one side to do it.

The one who had stayed with me said: 'Can I look now?'

'Let it lie, Eddie. Nothing in it for us. You call the coroner?'

'I thought Homicide would do that.'

'Yeah, that's right. Captain Webber will be on it and he likes to do everything himself.' He looked at me and said: 'You're a man named Marlowe?'

I said I was a man named Marlowe.

'He's a wise guy, knows all the answers,' Eddie said.

The older one looked at me absently, looked at Eddie absently, spotted the gun lying on the telephone table and looked at that not at all absently.

'Yeah, that's the death gun,' Eddie said. 'I ain't touched it.'

The other nodded. 'The boys are not so fast today. What's your line, mister? Friend of his?' He made a thumb towards the floor.

'Saw him yesterday for the first time. I'm a private operative from L.A.'

'Oh.' He looked at me very sharply. The other cop looked at me with deep suspicion.

'Cripes, that means everything will be all balled up,' he said.

That was the first sensible remark he had made. I grinned at him affectionately.

The older cop looked out of the front window again. 'That's the Almore place across the street, Eddie,' he said.

Eddie went and looked with him. 'Sure is,' he said. 'You can read the plate. Say, this guy downstairs might be the guy –'

'Shut up,' the other one said and dropped the venetian blind. They both turned around and stared at me woodenly.

A car came down the block and stopped and a door slammed and more steps came down the walk. The older of the prowl-car boys opened the door to two men in plain clothes, one of whom I already knew.

21

The one who came first was a small man for a cop, middle-aged, thin-faced, with a permanently tired expression. His nose was sharp and bent a little to one side, as if somebody had given it the elbow one time when it was into something. His blue pork-pie hat was set very square on his head and chalk-white hair showed under it. He wore a dull brown suit and his hands were in the side pockets of the jacket, with the thumbs outside the seam.

The man behind him was Degarmo, the big cop with the dusty blond hair and the metallic blue eyes and the savage, lined face who had not liked my being in front of Dr Almore's house.

The two uniformed men looked at the small man and touched their caps.

'The body's in the basement, Captain Webber. Been shot twice after a couple of misses, looks like. Dead quite some time. This party's name is Marlowe. He's a private eye from Los Angeles. I didn't question him beyond that.'

'Quite right,' Webber said sharply. He had a suspicious voice. He passed a suspicious eye over my face and nodded briefly. 'I'm Captain Webber,' he said. 'This is Lieutenant Degarmo. We'll look at the body first.'

He went along the room. Degarmo looked at me as if he had never seen me before and followed him. They went downstairs, the older of the two prowl men with them. The cop called Eddie and I stared each other down for a while.

I said: 'This is right across the street from Dr Almore's place, isn't it?'

All the expression went out of his face. There hadn't been much to go. 'Yeah. So what?'

'So nothing,' I said.

He was silent. The voices came up from below, blurred and indistinct. The cop cocked his ear and said in a more friendly tone: 'You remember that one?'

'A little.'

He laughed. 'They killed that one pretty,' he said. 'They wrapped it up and hid it in back of the shelf. The top shelf in the bathroom closet. The one you can't reach without standing on a chair.'

'So they did,' I said. 'I wonder why.'

The cop looked at me sternly. 'There was good reasons, pal. Don't think there wasn't. You know this Lavery well?'

'Not well.'

'On to him for something?'

'Working on him a little,' I said. 'You knew him?'

The cop called Eddie shook his head. 'Nope, I just remembered it was a guy from this house found Almore's wife in the garage that night.'

'Lavery may not have been here then,' I said.

'How long's he been here?'

'I don't know,' I said.

'Would be about a year and a half,' the cop said, musingly. 'The L.A. papers give it any play?'

'Paragraph on the Home Counties page,' I said, just to be moving my mouth.

He scratched his ear and listened. Steps were coming back up the stairs. The cop's face went blank and he moved away from me and straightened up.

Captain Webber hurried over to the telephone and dialled the number and spoke, then held the phone away from his ear and looked back over his shoulder.

'Who's deputy coroner this week, Al?'

'Ed Garland,' the big lieutenant said woodenly.

'Call Ed Garland,' Webber said into the phone. 'Have him come over right away. And tell the flash squad to step on it.'

He put the phone down and barked sharply: 'Who handled this gun?'

I said: 'I did.'

He came over and teetered on his heels in front of me and pushed his small sharp chin up at me. He held the gun delicately on a handkerchief in his hand.

'Don't you know enough not to handle a weapon found at the scene of a crime?'

'Certainly,' I said. 'But when I handled it I didn't know there had been a crime. I didn't know the gun had been fired. It was lying on the stairs and I thought it had been dropped.'

'A likely story,' Webber said bitterly. 'You get a lot of that sort of thing in your business?'

'A lot of what sort of thing?'

He kept his hard stare on me and didn't answer.

I said: 'How would it be for me to tell you my story as it happened?'

He bridled at me like a cockerel. 'Suppose you answer my questions exactly as I choose to put them.'

I didn't say anything to that. Webber swivelled sharply and said to the two uniformed men: 'You boys can get back to your car and check in with the despatcher.'

They saluted and went out, closing the door softly until it stuck, then getting as mad at it as anybody else. Webber listened until their car went away. Then he put the bleak and callous eye on me once more.

'Let me see your identification.'

I handed him my wallet and he rooted in it. Degarmo sat in a chair and crossed his legs and stared up blankly at the ceiling. He got a match out of his pocket and chewed the end of it. Webber gave me back my wallet. I put it away.

'People in your line make a lot of trouble,' he said.

'Not necessarily,' I said.

He raised his voice. It had been sharp enough before. 'I said they make a lot of trouble, and a lot of trouble is what I meant. But get this straight. You're not going to make any in Bay City.'

I didn't answer him. He jabbed a forefinger at me.

'You're from the big town,' he said. 'You think you're tough and you think you're wise. Don't worry. We can handle you. We're a small place, but we're very compact. We don't have any political tug-of-war down here. We work on the straight line and we work fast. Don't worry about us, mister.'

'I'm not worrying,' I said. 'I don't have anything to worry about. I'm just trying to make a nice clean dollar.'

'And don't give me any of the flip talk,' Webber said. 'I don't like it.'

Degarmo brought his eyes down from the ceiling and curled a fore-finger to stare at the nail. He spoke in a heavy bored voice.

'Look, chief, the fellow downstairs is called Lavery. He's dead. I knew him a little. He was a chaser.'

'What of it?' Webber snapped, not looking away from me.

'The whole set-up indicates a dame,' Degarmo said. 'You know what these private eyes work at. Divorce stuff. Suppose we'd let him tie into it, instead of just trying to scare him dumb.'

'If I'm scaring him,' Webber said, 'I'd like to know it. I don't see any signs of it.'

He walked over to the front window and yanked the venetian blind up. Light poured into the room almost dazzlingly, after the long dimness. He came back bouncing on his heels and poked a thin hard finger at me and said:

'Talk.'

I said, 'I'm working for a Los Angeles businessman who can't take a lot of loud publicity. That's why he hired me. A month ago his wife ran off and later a telegram came which indicated she had gone with Lavery. But my client met Lavery in town a couple of days ago and he denied it. The client believed him enough to get worried. It seems the lady is pretty reckless. She might have taken up with some bad company and got into a jam. I came down to see Lavery and he denied to me that he had gone with her. I half believed him but later I got reasonable proof that he had been with her in a San Bernardino hotel the night she was believed to have left the mountain cabin where she had been staying. With that in my pocket I came down to tackle Lavery again. No answer to the bell, the door was slightly open. I came inside, looked around, found the gun and searched the house. I found him. Just the way he is now.'

'You had no right to search the house,' Webber said coldly.

'Of course not,' I agreed. 'But I wouldn't be likely to pass up the chance either.'

'The name of this man you're working for?'

'Kingsley.' I gave him the Beverly Hills address. 'He manages a cosmetic company in the Treloar Building on Olive. The Gillerlain Company.'

Webber looked at Degarmo. Degarmo wrote lazily on an envelope. Webber looked back at me and said: 'What else?'

'I went up to this mountain cabin where the lady had been staying. It's at a place called Little Fawn Lake, near Puma Point, forty-six miles into the mountains from San Bernardino.'

I looked at Degarmo. He was writing slowly. His hand stopped a moment and seemed to hang in the air stiffly, then it dropped to the envelope and wrote again. I went on:

'About a month ago the wife of the caretaker at Kingsley's place up there had a fight with him and left, as everybody thought. Yesterday she was found drowned in the lake.'

Webber almost closed his eyes and rocked on his heels. Almost softly he asked: 'Why are you telling me this? Are you implying a connexion?'

'There's a connexion in time. Lavery had been up there. I don't know of any other connexion, but I thought I'd better mention it.'

Degarmo was sitting very still, looking at the floor in front of him. His face was tight and he looked even more savage than usual. Webber said:

'This woman that was drowned? Suicide?'

'Suicide or murder. She left a good-bye note. But her husband has been arrested on suspicion. The name is Chess. Bill and Muriel Chess, his wife.'

'I don't want any part of that,' Webber said sharply. 'Let's confine ourselves to what went on here.'

'Nothing went on here,' I said, looking at Degarmo. 'I've been down here twice. The first time I talked to Lavery and didn't get anywhere. The second time I didn't talk to him and didn't get anywhere.'

Webber said slowly: 'I'm going to ask you a question and I want an honest answer. You won't want to give it, but now will be as good a time as later. You know I'll get it eventually. The question is this. You have looked through the house and I imagine pretty thoroughly. Have you seen anything that suggests to you that this Kingsley woman has been here?'

'That's not a fair question,' I said. 'It calls for a conclusion of the witness.'

'I want an answer to it,' he said grimly. 'This isn't a court of law.'

'The answer is yes,' I said. 'There are women's clothes hanging in a closet downstairs that have been described to me as being worn by Mrs Kingsley at San Bernardino the night she met Lavery there. The description was not exact though. A black and white suit, mostly white, and a panama hat with a rolled black and white band.'

Degarmo snapped a finger against the envelope he was holding. 'You must be a great guy for a client to have working for him,' he said. 'That puts the woman right in this house where a murder has been committed and she is the woman he's supposed to have gone away with. I don't think we'll have to look far for the killer, chief.'

Webber was staring at me fixedly, with little or no expression on his face but a kind of tight watchfulness. He nodded absently to what Degarmo had said.

I said: 'I'm assuming you fellows are not a pack of damn fools. The clothes are tailored and easy to trace. I've saved you an hour by telling you, perhaps even no more than a phone call.'

'Anything else?' Webber asked quietly.

Before I could answer, a car stopped outside the house, and then another. Webber skipped over to open the door. Three men came in, a short, curly-haired man and a large ox-like man, both carrying heavy black leather cases. Behind them a tall thin man in a dark-grey suit and black tie. He had very bright eyes and a poker face.

Webber pointed a finger at the curly-haired man and said: 'Downstairs in the bathroom, Busoni. I want a lot of prints from all over the house, particularly any that seem to be made by a woman. It will be a long job.'

'I do all the work,' Busoni grunted. He and the ox-like man went along the room and down the stairs.

'We have a corpse for you, Garland,' Webber said to the third man. 'Let's go down and look at him. You've ordered the wagon?'

The bright-eyed man nodded briefly and he and Webber went downstairs after the other two.

Degarmo put the envelope and pencil away. He stared at me woodenly.

I said: 'Am I supposed to talk about our conversation yesterday – or is that a private transaction?'

'Talk about it all you like,' he said. 'It's our job to protect the citizen.'

'You talk about it,' I said. 'I'd like to know more about the Almore case.'

He flushed slowly and his eyes got mean. 'You said you didn't know Almore.'

'I didn't yesterday, or know anything about him. Since then I've learned that Lavery knew Mrs Almore, that she committed suicide, that Lavery found her dead, and that Lavery has at least been suspected of blackmailing him – or of being in a position to blackmail him. Also both your prowl-car boys seemed interested in the fact that Almore's house was across the street from here. And one of them remarked that the case had been killed pretty, or words to that effect.'

Degarmo said in a slow deadly tone: 'I'll have the badge off the son of a bitch. All they do is flap their mouths. God damn empty-headed bastards.'

'Then there's nothing in it,' I said.

He looked at his cigarette. 'Nothing in what?'

'Nothing in the idea that Almore murdered his wife, and had enough pull to get it fixed.'

Degarmo came to his feet and walked over to lean down at me. 'Say that again,' he said softly.

I said it again.

He hit me across the face with his open hand. It jerked my head around hard. My face felt hot and large.

'Say it again,' he said softly.

I said it again. His hand swept and knocked my head to one side again.

'Say it again.'

'Nope. Third time lucky. You might miss.' I put a hand up and rubbed my cheek.

He stood leaning down, his lips drawn back over his teeth, a hard animal glare in his very blue eyes.

'Any time you talk like that to a cop,' he said, 'you know what you got coming. Try it on again and it won't be the flat of a hand I'll use on you.'

I bit hard on my lips and rubbed my cheek.

'Poke your big nose into our business and you'll wake up in an alley with the cats looking at you,' he said.

I didn't say anything. He went and sat down again, breathing hard. I stopped rubbing my face and held my hand out and worked the fingers slowly, to get the hard clench out of them.

'I'll remember that,' I said. 'Both ways.'

22

It was early evening when I got back to Hollywood and up to the office. The building had emptied out and the corridors were silent. Doors were open and the cleaning women were inside with their vacuum cleaners and their dry mops and dusters.

I unlocked the door to mine and picked up an envelope that lay in front of the mail slot and dropped it on the desk without looking at it. I ran the windows up and leaned out, looking at the early neon lights glowing, smelling the warm, foody air that drifted up from the alley ventilator of the coffee shop next door.

I peeled off my coat and tie and sat down at the desk and got the office bottle out of the deep drawer and bought myself a drink. It didn't do any good. I had another, with the same result.

By now Webber would have seen Kingsley. There would be a general alarm out for his wife, already, or very soon. The thing looked cut and dried to them. A nasty affair between two rather nasty people, too much loving, too much drinking, too much proximity ending in a savage hatred and a murderous impulse and death.

I thought this was all a little too simple.

I reached for the envelope and tore it open. It had no stamp. It read: 'Mr Marlowe: Florence Almore's parents are a Mr and Mrs Eustace Grayson, at present residing at the Rossmore Arms, 640 South Oxford Avenue. I checked this by calling the listed phone number. Yrs ADRIENNE FROMSETT.'

An elegant handwriting, like the elegant hand that wrote it. I pushed it to one side and had another drink. I began to feel a little less savage. I pushed things around on the desk. My hands felt thick and hot and awkward. I ran a finger across the corner of the desk and looked at the streak made by the wiping off of the dust. I looked at the dust on my finger and wiped that off. I looked at my watch. I looked at the wall. I looked at nothing.

I put the liquor bottle away and went over to the wash-bowl to rinse the glass out. When I had done that I washed my hands and bathed my face in cold water and looked at it. The flush was gone from the left cheek, but it looked a little swollen. Not very much, but enough to make me tighten up again. I brushed my hair and looked at the grey in it. There was getting to be plenty of grey in it. The face under the hair had a sick look. I didn't like the face at all.

I went back to the desk and read Miss Fromsett's note again. I smoothed it out on the glass and sniffed it and smoothed it out some more and folded it and put it in my coat pocket.

I sat very still and listened to the evening grow quiet outside the open windows. And very slowly I grew quiet with it.

23

The Rossmore Arms was a gloomy pile of dark red brick built around a huge forecourt. It had a plush-lined lobby containing silence, tubbed plants, a bored canary in a cage as big as a dog-house, a smell of old carpet dust and the cloying fragrance of gardenias long ago.

The Graysons were on the fifth floor in front, in the north wing. They were sitting together in a room which seemed to be deliberately twenty years out of date. It had fat overstuffed furniture and brass doorknobs, shaped like eggs, a huge wall mirror in a gilt frame, a marble-topped table in the window and dark red plush side drapes by the windows. It smelled of tobacco smoke and behind that the air was telling me they had had lamb chops and broccoli for dinner.

Grayson's wife was a plump woman who might once have had big baby-blue eyes. They were faded out now and dimmed by glasses and slightly protuberant. She had kinky white hair. She sat darning socks with her thick ankles crossed, her feet just reaching the floor, and a big wicker sewing basket in her lap.

Grayson was a long, stooped, yellow-faced man with high shoulders, bristly eyebrows and almost no chin. The upper part of his face meant business. The lower part was just saying good-bye. He wore bifocals and he had been gnawing fretfully at the evening paper. I had looked him up in the city directory. He was a C.P.A. and looked it every inch. He even had ink on his fingers and there were four pencils in the pocket of his open vest.

He read my card carefully for the seventh time and looked me up and down and said slowly:

'What is it you want to see us about, Mr Marlowe?'

'I'm interested in a man named Lavery. He lives across the street from Dr Almore. Your daughter was the wife of Dr Almore. Lavery is the man who found your daughter the night she – died.'

They both pointed like bird dogs when I deliberately hesitated on the last word. Grayson looked at his wife and she shook her head.

'We don't care to talk about that,' Grayson said promptly. 'It is much too painful to us.'

I waited a moment and looked gloomy with them. Then I said: 'I don't blame you. I don't want to make you. I'd like to get in touch with the man you hired to look into it, though.'

They looked at each other again. Mrs Grayson didn't shake her head this time.

Grayson asked: 'Why?'

'I'd better tell you a little of my story.' I told them what I had been hired to do, not mentioning Kingsley by name. I told them the incident with Degarmo outside Almore's house the day before. They pointed again on that.

Grayson said sharply: 'Am I to understand that you were unknown to Dr Almore, had not approached him in any way, and that he nevertheless called a police officer because you were outside his house?'

I said: 'That's right. Had been outside for at least an hour though. That is, my car had.'

'That's very queer,' Grayson said.

'I'd say that was one very nervous man,' I said. 'And Degarmo asked me if her folks – meaning your daughter's folks – had hired me. Looks as if he didn't feel safe yet, wouldn't you say?'

'Safe about what?' He didn't look at me saying this. He re-lit his pipe, slowly, then tamped the tobacco down with the end of a big metal pencil and lit it again.

I shrugged and didn't answer. He looked at me quickly and looked away. Mrs Grayson didn't look at me, but her nostrils quivered.

'How did he know who you were?' Grayson asked suddenly.

'Made a note of the car licence, called the Auto Club, looked up the name in the directory. At least that's what I'd have done and I saw him through his window making some of the motions.'

'So he has the police working for him,' Grayson said.

'Not necessarily. If they made a mistake that time, they wouldn't want it found out now.'

'Mistake!' He laughed almost shrilly.

'Okay,' I said. 'The subject is painful but a little fresh air won't hurt it. You've always thought he murdered her, haven't you? That's why you hired this dick – detective.'

Mrs Grayson looked up with quick eyes and ducked her head down and rolled up another pair of mended socks.

Grayson said nothing.

I said: 'Was there any evidence, or was it just that you didn't like him?'

'There was evidence,' Grayson said bitterly, and with a sudden clearness of voice, as if he had decided to talk about it after all. 'There must have been. We were told there was. But we never got it. The police took care of that.'

'I heard they had this fellow arrested and sent up for drunk driving.'

'You heard right.'

'But he never told you what he had to go on?'

'No.'

'I don't like that,' I said. 'That sounds a little as if this fellow hadn't made up his mind whether to use his information for your benefit or keep it and put a squeeze on the doctor.'

Grayson looked at his wife again. She said quietly: 'Mr Talley didn't impress me that way. He was a quiet unassuming little man. But you can't always judge, I know.'

I said: 'So Talley was his name. That was one of the things I hoped you would tell me.'

'And what were the others?' Grayson asked.

'How can I find Talley – and what it was that laid the groundwork of suspicion in your minds. It must have been there, or you wouldn't have hired Talley without a better showing from him that *he* had grounds.'

Grayson smiled very thinly and primly. He reached for his little chin and rubbed it with one long yellow finger.

Mrs Grayson said: 'Dope.'

'She means that literally,' Grayson said at once, as if the single word had been a green light. 'Almore was, and no doubt is, a dope doctor. Our daughter made that clear to us. In his hearing too. He didn't like it.'

'Just what do you mean by a dope doctor, Mr Grayson?'

'I mean a doctor whose practice is largely with people who are living on the raw edge of nervous collapse, from drink and dissipation. People who have to be given sedatives and narcotics all the time. The stage comes when an ethical physician refuses to treat them any more, outside a sanatorium. But not the Dr Almores. *They* will keep on as long as the money comes in, as long as the patient remains alive and reasonably sane, even if he or she becomes a hopeless addict in the process. A lucrative practice,' he said primly, 'and I imagine a dangerous one to the doctor.'

'No doubt of that,' I said. 'But there's a lot of money in it. Do you know a man named Condy?'

'No. We know who he was. Florence suspected he was a source of Almore's narcotic supply.'

I said: 'Could be. He probably wouldn't want to write himself too many prescriptions. Did you know Lavery?'

'We never saw him. We knew who he was.'

'Ever occur to you that Lavery might have been blackmailing Almore?'

It was a new idea to him. He ran his hand over the top of his head and brought it down over his face and dropped it to his bony knee. He shook his head.

'No. Why should it?'

'He was first to the body,' I said. 'Whatever looked wrong to Talley must have been equally visible to Lavery.'

'Is Lavery that kind of man?'

'I don't know. He has no visible means of support, no job. He gets around a lot, especially with women.'

'It's an idea,' Grayson said. 'And those things can be handled very discreetly.' He smiled wryly. 'I have come across traces of them in my work. Unsecured loans, long outstanding. Investments on the face of them worthless made by men who would not be likely to make worthless investments. Bad debts that should obviously be charged off and have not been, for fear of inviting scrutiny from the income-tax people. Oh yes, those things can easily be arranged.'

I looked at Mrs Grayson. Her hands had never stopped working. She had a dozen pairs of darned socks finished. Grayson's long bony feet would be hard on socks.

'What's happened to Talley? Was he framed?'

'I don't think there's any doubt about it. His wife was very bitter. She said he had been given a doped drink in a bar and he had been drinking with a policeman. She said a police car was waiting across the street for him to start driving and that he was picked up at once. Also that he was given only the most perfunctory examination at the jail.'

'That doesn't mean too much. That's what he told her after he was arrested. He'd tell her something like that automatically.'

'Well, I hate to think the police are not honest,' Grayson said. 'But these things are done, and everybody knows it.'

I said: 'If they made an honest mistake about your daughter's death, they would hate to have Talley show them up. It might mean several lost jobs. If they thought what he was really after was blackmail, they wouldn't be too fussy about how they took care of him. Where is Talley now? What it all boils down to is that if there was any solid clue, he either had it or was on the track of it and knew what he was looking for.'

Grayson said: 'We don't know where he is. He got six months, but that expired long ago.'

'How about his wife?'

He looked at his own wife. She said briefly: '1618½ Westmore Street, Bay City. Eustace and I sent her a little money. She was badly off.'

I made a note of the address and leaned back in my chair and said:

'Somebody shot Lavery this morning in his bathroom.'

Mrs Grayson's pudgy hands became still on the edges of the basket. Grayson sat with his mouth open, holding his pipe in front of it. He made a noise of clearing his throat softly, as if in the presence of the dead. Nothing ever moved slower than his old black pipe going back between his teeth.

'Of course it would be too much to expect,' he said and let it hang in the air and blew a little pale smoke at it, and then added, 'that Dr Almore had any connexion with that.'

'I'd like to think he had,' I said. 'He certainly lives at a handy distance. The police think my client's wife shot him. They have a good case too, when they find her. But if Almore had anything to do with it, it must surely arise out of your daughter's death. That's why I'm trying to find out something about that.'

Grayson said: 'A man who has done one murder wouldn't have more than twenty-five per cent of the hesitation in doing another.' He spoke as if he had given the matter considerable study.

I said: 'Yeah, maybe. What was supposed to be the motive for the first one?'

'Florence was wild,' he said sadly. 'A wild and difficult girl. She was wasteful and extravagant, always picking up new and rather doubtful friends, talking too much and too loudly, and generally acting the fool. A wife like that can be very dangerous to a man like Albert S. Almore. But I don't believe that was the prime motive, was it, Lettie?'

He looked at his wife, but she didn't look at him. She jabbed a darning-needle into a round ball of wool and said nothing.

Grayson sighed and went on: 'We had reason to believe he was carrying on with his office nurse and that Florence had threatened him with a public scandal. He couldn't have anything like that, could he? One kind of scandal might too easily lead to another.'

I said: 'How did he do the murder?'

'With morphine, of course. He always had it, he always used it. He was an expert in the use of it. Then when she was in a deep coma he would have placed her in the garage and started the car motor. There was no autopsy, you know. But if there had been, it was known that she had been given a hypodermic injection that night.'

I nodded and he leaned back satisfied and ran his hand over his head and down his face and let it fall slowly to his bony knee. He seemed to have given a lot of study to this angle too.

I looked at them. A couple of elderly people sitting there quietly, poisoning their minds with hate, a year and a half after it had happened. They would like it if Almore had shot Lavery. They would love it. It would warm them clear down to their ankles.

After a pause I said: 'You're believing a lot of this because you want to. It's always possible that she committed suicide, and that the cover-up was partly to protect Condy's gambling club and partly to prevent Almore having to be questioned at a public hearing.'

'Rubbish,' Grayson said sharply. 'He murdered her all right. She was in bed, asleep.'

'You don't know that. She might have been taking dope herself. She might have established a tolerance for it. The effect wouldn't last long in that case. She might have got up in the middle of the night and looked at herself in the glass and seen devils pointing at her. These things happen.'

'I think you have taken up enough of our time,' Grayson said.

I stood up. I thanked them both and made a yard towards the door and said: 'You didn't do anything more about it after Talley was arrested?'

'Saw an assistant district attorney named Leach,' Grayson grunted. 'Got exactly nowhere. He saw nothing to justify his office in interfering. Wasn't even interested in the narcotic angle. But Condy's place was closed up about a month later. That might have come out of it somehow.'

'That was probably the Bay City cops throwing a little smoke. You'd find Condy somewhere else, if you knew where to look. With all his original equipment intact.'

I started for the door again and Grayson hoisted himself out of his chair and dragged across the room after me. There was a flush on his yellow face.

'I didn't mean to be rude,' he said. 'I guess Lettie and I oughtn't to brood about this business the way we do.'

'I think you've both been very patient,' I said. 'Was there anybody else involved in all this that we haven't mentioned by name?'

He shook his head, then looked back at his wife. Her hands were motionless holding the current sock on the darning-egg. Her head was tilted a little to one side. Her attitude was of listening, but not to us.

I said: 'The way I got the story, Dr Almore's office nurse put Mrs Almore to bed that night. Would that be the one he was supposed to be playing around with?'

Mrs Grayson said sharply: 'Wait a minute. We never saw the girl. But she had a pretty name. Just give me a minute.'

We gave her a minute. 'Mildred something,' she said, and snapped her teeth.

I took a deep breath. 'Would it be Mildred Haviland, Mrs Grayson?'

She smiled brightly and nodded. 'Of course, Mildred Haviland. Don't you remember, Eustace?'

He didn't remember. He looked at us like a horse that has got into the wrong stable. He opened the door and said: 'What does it matter?'

'And you said Talley was a small man,' I bored on. 'He wouldn't for instance be a big loud bruiser with an overbearing manner?'

'Oh no,' Mrs Grayson said. 'Mr Talley is a man of not more than medium height, middle-aged, with brownish hair and a very quiet voice. He had a sort of worried expression. I mean, he looked as if he always had it.'

'Looks as if he needed it,' I said.

Grayson put his bony hand out and I shook it. It felt like shaking hands with a towel-rack.

'If you get him,' he said and clamped his mouth hard on his pipe stem, 'call back with a bill. If you get Almore, I mean, of course.'

I said I knew he meant Almore, but that there wouldn't be any bill.

I went back along the silent hallway. The self-operating elevator was carpeted in red plush. It had an elderly perfume in it, like three widows drinking tea.

24

The house on Westmore Street was a small frame bungalow behind a larger house. There was no number visible on the smaller house, but the one in front showed a stencilled 1618 beside the door, with a dim light behind the stencil. A narrow concrete path led along under windows to the house at the back. It had a tiny porch with a single chair on it. I stepped up on the porch and rang the bell.

It buzzed not very far off. The front door was open behind the screen but there was no light. From the darkness a querulous voice said:

'What is it?'

I spoke into the darkness. 'Mr Talley in?'

The voice became flat and without tone. 'Who wants him?'

'A friend.'

The woman sitting inside in the darkness made a vague sound in her throat which might have been amusement. Or she might just have been clearing her throat.

'All right,' she said. 'How much is this one?'

'It's not a bill, Mrs Talley. I suppose you are Mrs Talley?'

'Oh, go away and let me alone,' the voice said. 'Mr Talley isn't here. He hasn't been here. He won't be here.'

I put my nose against the screen and tried to peer into the room. I could see the vague outlines of its furniture. From where the voice came from also showed the shape of a couch. A woman was lying on it. She seemed to be lying on her back and looking up at the ceiling. She was quite motionless.

'I'm sick,' the voice said. 'I've had enough trouble. Go away and leave me be.'

I said: 'I've just come from talking to the Graysons.'

There was a little silence, but no movement, then a sigh. 'I never heard of them.'

I leaned against the frame of the screen door and looked back along the narrow walk to the street. There was a car across the way with parking lights burning. There were other cars along the block.

I said: 'Yes, you have, Mrs Talley. I'm working for them. They're still in there pitching. How about you? Don't you want something back?'

The voice said: 'I want to be let alone.'

'I want information,' I said. 'I'm going to get it. Quietly, if I can. Loud, if it can't be quiet.'

The voice said: 'Another copper, eh?'

'You know I'm not a copper, Mrs Talley. The Graysons wouldn't talk to a copper. Call them up and ask them.'

'I never heard of them,' the voice said. 'I don't have a phone, if I knew them. Go away, copper. I'm sick. I've been sick for a month.'

'My name is Marlowe,' I said. 'Philip Marlowe. I'm a private eye in Los Angeles. I've been talking to the Graysons. I've got something, but I want to talk to your husband.'

The woman on the couch let out a dim laugh which barely reached across the room. 'You've got something,' she said. 'That sounds familiar. My God it does! You've got something. George Talley had something too – once.'

'He can have it again,' I said, 'if he plays his cards right.'

'If that's what it takes,' she said, 'you can scratch him off right now.'

I leaned against the door-frame and scratched my chin instead. Somebody back on the street had clicked a flashlight on. I didn't know why. It went off again. It seemed to be near my car.

The pale blur of face on the couch moved and disappeared. Hair took its place. The woman had turned her face to the wall.

'I'm tired,' she said, her voice now muffled by talking at the wall. 'I'm so damn tired. Beat it, mister. Be nice and go away.'

'Would a little money help any?'

'Can't you smell the cigar smoke?'

I sniffed. I didn't smell any cigar smoke. I said, 'No.'

'They've been here. They were here two hours. God, I'm tired of it all. Go away.'

'Look, Mrs Talley –'

She rolled on the couch and the blur of her face showed again. I could almost see her eyes, not quite.

'Look yourself,' she said. 'I don't know you. I don't want to know you. I have nothing to tell you. I wouldn't tell it, if I had. I live here, mister, if you call it living. Anyway, it's the nearest I can get to living. I want a little peace and quiet. Now you get out and leave me alone.'

'Let me in the house,' I said. 'We can talk this over. I think I can show you –'

She rolled suddenly on the couch again and feet struck the floor. A tight anger came into her voice.

'If you don't get out,' she said, 'I'm going to start yelling my head off. Right now. Now!'

'Okay!' I said quickly. 'I'll stick my card in the door. So you won't forget my name. You might change your mind.'

I got the card out and wedged it into the crack of the screen door. I said: 'Well, good night, Mrs Talley.'

No answer. Her eyes were looking across the room at me, faintly luminous in the dark. I went down off the porch and back along the narrow walk to the street.

Across the way a motor purled gently in the car with the parking lights on. Motors purl gently in thousands of cars on thousands of streets, everywhere.

I got into the Chrysler and started it up.

25

Westmore was a north and south street on the wrong side of town. I drove north. At the next corner I bumped over disused interurban tracks and on into a block of junk yards. Behind wooden fences the decomposing carcasses of old automobiles lay in grotesque designs, like a modern battlefield. Piles of rusted parts looked lumpy under the moon. Roof-high piles, with alleys between them.

Headlights glowed in my rear view mirror. They got larger. I stepped on the gas and reached keys out of my pocket and unlocked the glove compartment. I took a .38 out and laid it on the car seat close to my leg.

Beyond the junk yards there was a brickfield. The tall chimney of the kiln was smokeless, far off over waste land. Piles of dark bricks, a low wooden building with a sign on it, emptiness, no one moving, no light.

The car behind me gained. The low whine of a lightly touched siren growled through the night. The sound loafed over the fringes of a neglected golf course to the east, across the brickyard to the west. I speeded up a bit more, but it wasn't any use. The car behind me came up fast and a huge red spotlight suddenly glared all over the road.

The car came up level and started to cut in. I stood the Chrysler on its nose, swung out behind the police car, and made a U turn with half an inch to spare. I gunned the motor the other way. Behind me sounded the rough clashing of gears, the howl of an infuriated motor, and the red spotlight swept for what seemed miles over the brickyard.

It wasn't any use. They were behind me and coming fast again. I didn't have any idea of getting away. I wanted to get back where there were houses and people to come out and watch and perhaps to remember.

I didn't make it. The police car heaved up alongside again and a hard voice yelled:

'Pull over, or we'll blast a hole in you!'

I pulled over to the kerb and set the brake. I put the gun back in the glove compartment and snapped it shut. The police car jumped on its springs just in front of my left front fender. A fat man slammed out of it roaring.

'Don't you know a police siren when you hear one? Get out of that car!'

I got out of the car and stood beside it in the moonlight. The fat man had a gun in his hand.

'Gimme your licence!' he barked in a voice as hard as the blade of a shovel.

I took it out and held it out. The other cop in the car slid out from under the wheel and came around beside me and took what I was holding out. He put a flash on it and read.

'Name of Marlowe,' he said. 'Hell, the guy's a shamus. Just think of that, Cooney.'

Cooney said: 'Is that all? Guess I won't need this.' He tucked the gun back in his holster and buttoned the leader flap down over it. 'Guess I can handle this with my little flippers,' he said. 'Guess I can at that.'

The other one said: 'Doing fifty-five. Been drinking, I wouldn't wonder.'

'Smell the bastard's breath,' Cooney said.

The other one leaned forward with a polite leer. 'Could I smell the breath, shamus?'

I let him smell the breath.

'Well,' he said judiciously, 'he ain't staggering. I got to admit that.'

''S a cold night for summer. Buy the boy a drink, Officer Dobbs.'

'Now that's a sweet idea,' Dobbs said. He went to the car and got a half-pint bottle out of it. He held it up. It was a third full. 'No really solid drinking here,' he said. He held the bottle out. 'With our compliments, pal.'

'Suppose I don't want a drink,' I said.

'Don't say that,' Cooney whined. 'We might get the idea you wanted feet-prints on your stomach.'

I took the bottle and unscrewed the cap and sniffed. The liquor in the bottle smelled like whisky. Just whisky.

'You can't work the same gag all the time,' I said.

Cooney said: 'Time is eight twenty-seven. Write it down, Officer Dobbs.'

Dobbs went to the car and leaned in to make a note on his report. I held the bottle up and said to Cooney: 'You insist that I drink this?'

'Naw. You could have me jump on your belly instead.'

I tilted the bottle, locked my throat, and filled my mouth with whisky. Cooney lunged forward and sank a fist in my stomach. I sprayed the whisky and bent over choking. I dropped the bottle.

I bent to get it and saw Cooney's fat knee rising at my face. I stepped to one side and straightened and slammed him on the nose with everything I had. His left hand went to his face and his voice howled and his right hand jumped to his gun holster. Dobbs ran at me from the side and his arm swung low. The blackjack hit me behind the left knee, the leg went dead and I sat down hard on the ground, gritting my teeth and spitting whisky.

Cooney took his hand away from his face full of blood.

'Jesus,' he cracked in a thick horrible voice. 'This is blood, my blood.' He let out a wild roar and swung his foot at my face.

I rolled far enough to catch it on my shoulder. It was bad enough taking it there.

Dobbs pushed between us and said: 'We got enough, Charlie. Better not get it all gummed up.'

Cooney stepped backwards three shuffling steps and sat down on the running-board of the police car and held his face. He groped for a handkerchief and used it gently on his nose.

'Just gimme a minute,' he said through the handkerchief. 'Just a minute, pal. Just one little minute.'

Dobbs said, 'Pipe down. We got enough. That's the way it's going to be.' He swung the blackjack slowly beside his leg. Cooney got up off the running-board and staggered forward. Dobbs put a hand against his chest and pushed him gently. Cooney tried to knock the hand out of his way.

'I gotta see blood,' he croaked. 'I gotta see more blood.'

Dobbs said sharply, 'Nothing doing. Pipe down. We got all we wanted.'

Cooney turned and moved heavily away to the other side of the police car. He leaned against it, muttering through his handkerchief. Dobbs said to me:

'Up on the feet, boy friend.'

I got up and rubbed behind my knee. The nerve of the leg was jumping like an angry monkey.

'Get in the car,' Dobbs said. 'Our car.'

I went over and climbed into the police car.

Dobbs said: 'You drive the other heap, Charlie.'

'I'll tear every god-damn fender off'n it,' Cooney roared.

Dobbs picked the whisky bottle off the ground, threw it over the fence, and slid into the car beside me. He pressed the starter.

'This is going to cost you,' he said. 'You hadn't ought to have socked him.'

I said: 'Just why not?'

'He's a good guy,' Dobbs said. 'A little loud.'

'But not funny,' I said. 'Not at all funny.'

'Don't tell him,' Dobbs said. The police car began to move. 'You'd hurt his feelings.'

Cooney slammed into the Chrysler and started it and clashed the gears as if he was trying to strip them. Dobbs tooled the police car smoothly around and started north again along the brickyard.

'You'll like our new jail,' he said.

'What will the charge be?'

He thought a moment, guiding the car with a gentle hand and watching in the mirror to see that Cooney followed along behind.

'Speeding,' he said. 'Resisting arrest. H.B.D. H.B.D. is police slang for "had been drinking".'

'How about being slammed in the belly, kicked in the shoulder, forced to drink liquor under threat of bodily harm, threatened with a gun and struck with a blackjack while unarmed? Couldn't you make a little something more out of that?'

'Aw, forget it,' he said wearily. 'You think this sort of thing is my idea of a good time?'

'I thought they cleaned this town up,' I said. 'I thought they had it so that a decent man could walk the streets at night without wearing a bullet-proof vest.'

'They cleaned it up some,' he said. 'They wouldn't want it too clean. They might scare away a dirty dollar.'

'Better not talk like that,' I said. 'You'll lose your union card.'

He laughed. 'The hell with them,' he said. 'I'll be in the army in two weeks.'

The incident was over for him. It meant nothing. He took it as a matter of course. He wasn't even bitter about it.

26

The cell block was almost brand-new. The battleship-grey paint on the steel walls and door still had the fresh gloss of newness disfigured in two or three places by squirted tobacco juice. The overhead light was sunk in the ceiling behind a heavy frosted panel. There were two bunks on one side of the cell and a man snored in the top bunk, with a dark-grey blanket wrapped around him. Since he was asleep that early and didn't smell of whisky or gin and had chosen the top berth where he would be out of the way, I judged he was an old lodger.

I sat on the lower bunk. They had tapped me for a gun but they hadn't stripped my pockets. I got out a cigarette and rubbed the hot swelling behind my knee. The pain radiated all the way to the ankle. The whisky I had coughed on my coat front had a rank smell. I held the cloth up and breathed smoke into it. The smoke floated up around the flat square of lighted glass in the ceiling. The jail seemed very quiet. A woman was making a shrill racket somewhere very far off in another part of the jail. My part was as peaceful as a church.

The woman was screaming, wherever she was. The screaming had a thin, sharp, unreal sound, something like the screaming of coyotes in the moonlight, but it didn't have the rising keening note of the coyote. After a while the sound stopped.

I smoked two cigarettes through and dropped the butts into the small toilet in the corner. The man in the upper berth still snored. All I could see of him was damp greasy hair sticking out over the edge of the blanket. He slept on his stomach. He slept well. He was one of the best.

I sat down on the bunk again. It was made of flat steel slats with a thin hard mattress over them. Two dark-grey blankets were folded on it quite neatly. It was a very nice jail. It was on the twelfth floor of the new city hall. It was a very nice city hall. Bay City was a very nice place. People lived there and thought so. If I lived there, I would probably think so. I would see the nice blue bay and the cliffs and the yacht harbour and the quiet streets of houses, old houses brooding under old trees and new houses with sharp green lawns and wire fences and staked saplings set into the parkway in front of them. I knew a girl who lived on Twenty-fifth Street. It was a nice street. She was a nice girl. She liked Bay City.

She wouldn't think about the Mexican and Negro slums stretched out on the dismal flats south of the old interurban tracks. Nor of the waterfront dives along the flat shore south of the cliffs, the sweaty little dance halls on the pike, the marijuana joints, the narrow fox faces watching over the tops of newspapers in far too quiet hotel lobbies, nor the pickpockets and grifters and con men and drunk rollers and pimps and queans on the board walk.

I went over to stand by the door. There was nobody stirring across the way. The lights in the cell block were bleak and silent. Business in the jail was rotten.

I looked at my watch. Nine fifty-four. Time to go home and get your slippers on and play over a game of chess. Time for a tall cool drink and a long quiet pipe. Time to sit with your feet up and think of nothing. Time to start yawning over your magazine. Time to be a human being, a householder, a man with nothing to do but rest and suck in the night air and rebuild the brain for tomorrow.

A man in the blue-grey jail uniform came along between the cells reading numbers. He stopped in front of mine and unlocked the door and gave me the hard stare they think they have to wear on their pans for ever and for ever and for ever. I'm a cop, brother, I'm tough, watch your step, brother, or we'll fix you up so you'll crawl on your hands and knees, brother, snap out of it, brother, let's get a load of the truth, brother, let's go, and let's not forget we're tough guys, we're cops, and we do what we like with punks like you.

'Out,' he said.

I stepped out of the cell and he relocked the door and jerked his thumb and we went along to a wide steel gate and he unlocked that and we went through and he relocked it and the keys tinkled pleasantly on the big steel ring, and after a while we went through a steel door that was painted like wood on the outside and battleship-grey on the inside.

Degarmo was standing there by the counter talking to the desk sergeant.

He turned his metallic blue eyes on me and said: 'How you doing?'

'Fine.'

'Like our jail?'

'I like your jail fine.'

'Captain Webber wants to talk to you.'

'That's fine,' I said.

'Don't you know any words but fine?'

'Not right now,' I said. 'Not in here.'

'You're limping a little,' he said. 'You trip over something?'

'Yeah,' I said. 'I tripped over a blackjack. It jumped up and bit me behind the left knee.'

'That's too bad,' Degarmo said, blank-eyed. 'Get your stuff from the property clerk.'

'I've got it,' I said. 'It wasn't taken away from me.'

'Well, that's fine,' he said.

'It sure is,' I said. 'It's fine.'

The desk sergeant lifted his shaggy head and gave us both a long stare. 'You ought to see Cooney's little Irish nose,' he said. 'If you want to see something fine. It's spread over his face like syrup on a waffle.'

Degarmo said absently: 'What's the matter? He get in a fight?'

'I wouldn't know,' the desk sergeant said. 'Maybe it was the same blackjack that jumped up and bit him.'

'For a desk sergeant you talk too damn much,' Degarmo said.

'A desk sergeant always talks too god-damn much,' the desk sergeant said. 'Maybe that's why he isn't a lieutenant on homicide.'

'You see how we are here,' Degarmo said. 'Just one great big happy family.'

'With beaming smiles on our faces,' the desk sergeant said, 'and our arms spread wide in welcome, and a rock in each hand.'

Degarmo jerked his head at me and we went out.

27

Captain Webber pushed his sharp bent nose across the desk at me and said: 'Sit down.'

I sat down in a round-backed wooden armchair and eased my left leg away from the sharp edge of the seat. It was a large neat corner office. Degarmo sat at the end of the desk and crossed his legs and rubbed his ankle thoughtfully, and looked out of a window.

Webber went on: 'You asked for trouble, and you got it. You were doing fifty-five miles an hour in a residential zone and you attempted to get away from a police car that signalled you to stop with its siren and red spotlight. You were abusive when stopped and you struck an officer in the face.'

I said nothing. Webber picked a match off his desk and broke it in half and threw the pieces over his shoulder.

'Or are they lying – as usual?' he asked.

'I didn't see their report,' I said. 'I was probably doing fifty-five in a residential district, or anyhow within city limits. The police car was parked outside a house I visited. It followed me when I drove away and I didn't at that time know it was a police car. It had no good reason to follow me and I didn't like the look of it. I went a little fast, but all I was trying to do was get to a better-lighted part of town.'

Degarmo moved his eyes to give a bleak meaningless stare. Webber snapped his teeth impatiently.

He said: 'After you knew it was a police car you made a half-turn in the middle of the block and still tried to get away. Is that right?'

I said: 'Yes. It's going to take a little frank talk to explain that.'

'I'm not afraid of a little frank talk,' Webber said. 'I tend to kind of specialize in frank talk.'

I said: 'These cops that picked me up were parked in front of the house where George Talley's wife lives. They were there before I got there. George Talley is the man who used to be a private detective down here. I wanted to see him. Degarmo knows why I wanted to see him.'

Degarmo picked a match out of his pocket and chewed on the soft end of it quietly. He nodded, without expression. Webber didn't look at him.

I said: 'You are a stupid man, Degarmo. Everything you do is stupid, and done in a stupid way. When you went up against me yesterday in front of Almore's house you had to get tough when there was nothing to get tough about. You even had to drop hints which showed me how I could satisfy that curiosity, if it became important. All you had to do to protect your friends was to keep your mouth shut until I made a move. I never would have made one, and you would have saved all this.'

Webber said: 'What the devil has all this got to do with your being arrested in the twelve hundred block on Westmore Street?'

'It has to do with the Almore case,' I said. 'George Talley worked on the Almore case – until he was pinched for drunk-driving.'

'Well, I never worked on the Almore case,' Webber snapped. 'I don't know who stuck the first knife into Julius Caesar either. Stick to the point, can't you?'

'I am sticking to the point. Degarmo knows about the Almore case and he doesn't like it talked about. Even your prowl-car boys know about it. Cooney and Dobbs had no reason to follow me unless it was because I visited the wife of a man who had worked on the Almore case. I wasn't doing fifty-five miles an hour when they started to follow me. I tried to get away from them because I had a good idea I might get beaten up for going there. Degarmo had given me that idea.'

Webber looked quickly at Degarmo. Degarmo's hard blue eyes looked across the room at the wall in front of him.

I said: 'And I didn't bust Cooney in the nose until after he had forced me to drink whisky and then hit me in the stomach when I drank it, so that I would spill it down my coat front and smell of it. This can't be the first time you have heard of that trick, captain.'

Webber broke another match. He leaned back and looked at his small tight knuckles. He looked again at Degarmo and said: 'If you got made chief of police today, you might let me in on it.'

Degarmo said: 'Hell, the shamus just got a couple of playful taps. Kind of kidding. If a guy can't take a joke –'

Webber said: 'You put Cooney and Dobbs over there?'

'Well – yes, I did,' Degarmo said. 'I don't see why we have to put up with these snoopers coming into our town and stirring up a lot of dead leaves just to promote themselves a job and work a couple of old suckers for a big fee. Guys like that need a good sharp lesson.'

'Is that how it looks to you?' Webber asked.

'That's exactly how it looks to me,' Degarmo said.

'I wonder what fellows like you need,' Webber said. 'Right now I think you need a little air. Would you please take it, lieutenant?'

Degarmo opened his mouth slowly. 'You mean you want me to breeze on out?'

Webber leaned forward suddenly and his sharp little chin seemed to cut the air like the forefoot of a cruiser. 'Would you be so kind?'

Degarmo stood up slowly, a dark flush staining his cheekbones. He leaned a hard hand flat on the desk and looked at Webber. There was a little charged silence. He said:

'Okay, captain. But you're playing this wrong.'

Webber didn't answer him. Degarmo walked to the door and out. Webber waited for the door to close before he spoke.

'Is it your line that you can tie this Almore business a year and a half ago to the shooting in Lavery's place today? Or is it just a smoke-screen you're laying down because you know damn well Kingsley's wife shot Lavery?'

I said: 'It was tied to Lavery before he was shot. In a rough sort of way, perhaps only with a granny knot. But enough to make a man think.'

'I've been into this matter a little more thoroughly than you might think,' Webber said coldly. 'Although I never had anything personally to do with the death of Almore's wife and I wasn't chief of detectives at that time. If you didn't even know Almore yesterday morning, you must have heard a lot about him since.'

I told him exactly what I had heard, both from Miss Fromsett and from the Graysons.

'Then it's your theory that Lavery may have blackmailed Dr Almore?' he asked at the end. 'And that that may have something to do with the murder?'

'It's not a theory. It's no more than a possibility. I wouldn't be doing a job if I ignored it. The relations, if any, between Lavery and Almore might have been deep and dangerous or just the merest acquaintance, or not even that. For all I positively know they may never even have spoken to each other. But if there was nothing funny about the Almore case, why get so tough with anybody who shows an interest in it? It could be coincidence that George Talley was hooked for drunk-driving just when he was working on it. It could be coincidence that Almore called a cop because I stared at his house, and that Lavery was shot before I could talk to him a second time. But it's no coincidence that two of your men were watching Talley's home tonight, ready, willing and able to make trouble for me, if I went there.'

'I grant you that,' Webber said. 'And I'm not done with that incident. Do you want to file charges?'

'Life's too short for me to be filing charges of assault against police officers,' I said.

He winced a little. 'Then we'll wash all that out and charge it to experience,' he said. 'And as I understand you were not even booked, you're free to go home any time you want to. And if I were you, I'd leave Captain Webber to deal with the Lavery case and with any remote connexion it might turn out to have with the Almore case.'

I said: 'And with any remote connexion it might have with a woman named Muriel Chess being found drowned in a mountain lake near Puma Point yesterday?'

He raised his little eyebrows. 'You think that?'

'Only you might not know her as Muriel Chess. Supposing that you knew her at all you might have known her as Mildred Haviland, who used to be Dr Almore's office nurse. Who put Mrs Almore to bed the night she was found dead in the garage, and who, if there was any hanky-panky about that, might know who it was, and be bribed or scared into leaving town shortly thereafter.'

Webber picked up two matches and broke them. His small bleak eyes were fixed on my face. He said nothing.

'And at that point,' I said, 'you run into a real basic coincidence, the only one I'm willing to admit in the whole picture. For this Mildred Haviland met a man named Bill Chess in a Riverside beer parlour and for reasons of her own married him and went to live with him at Little Fawn Lake. And Little Fawn Lake was the property of a man whose wife was intimate with Lavery, who had found Mrs Almore's body. That's what I call a real coincidence. It can't be anything else, but it's basic, fundamental. Everything else flows from it.'

Webber got up from his desk and went over to the water-cooler and drank two paper cups of water. He crushed the cups slowly in his hand and twisted them into a ball and dropped the ball into a brown metal basket under the cooler. He walked to the windows and stood looking out over the bay. This was before the dim-out went into effect, and there were many lights in the yacht harbour.

He came slowly back to the desk and sat down. He reached up and pinched his nose. He was making up his mind about something.

He said slowly: 'I can't see what the hell sense there is in trying to mix that up with something that happened a year and a half later.'

'Okay,' I said, 'and thanks for giving me so much of your time.' I got up to go.

'Your leg feel pretty bad?' he asked, as I leaned down to rub it.

'Bad enough, but it's getting better.'

'Police business,' he said almost gently, 'is a hell of a problem. It's a good deal like politics. It asks for the highest type of men, and there's nothing in it to attract the highest type of men. So we have to work with what we get – and we get things like this.'

'I know,' I said. 'I've always known that. I'm not bitter about it. Good night, Captain Webber.'

'Wait a minute,' he said. 'Sit down a minute. If we've got to have the Almore case in this, let's drag it out into the open and look at it.'

'It's about time somebody did that,' I said. I sat down again.

28

Webber said quietly: 'I suppose some people think we're just a bunch of crooks down here. I suppose they think a fellow kills his wife and then calls me up on the phone and says: "Hi, Cap, I got a little murder down here cluttering up the front-room. And I've got five hundred iron men that are not working." And then I say: "Fine. Hold everything and I'll be right down with a blanket."'

'Not quite that bad,' I said.

'What did you want to see Talley about when you went to his house tonight?'

'He had some line on Florence Almore's death. Her parents hired him to follow it up, but he never told them what it was.'

'And you thought he would tell you?' Webber asked sarcastically.

'All I could do was try.'

'Or was it just that Degarmo getting tough with you made you feel like getting tough right back at him?'

'There might be a little of that in it too,' I said.

'Talley was a petty blackmailer,' Webber said contemptuously. 'On more than one occasion. Anyway, to get rid of him was good enough. So I'll tell you what it was he had. He had a slipper he had stolen from Florence Almore's foot.'

'A slipper?'

He smiled faintly. 'Just a slipper. It was later found hidden in his house. It was a green velvet dancing-pump with some little stones set into the heel. It was custom-made, by a man in Hollywood who makes theatrical footwear and such. Now ask me what was important about this slipper.'

'What was important about it, captain?'

'She had two pairs of them, exactly alike, made on the same order. It seems that is not unusual. In case one of them gets scuffed or some drunken ox tries to walk up a lady's leg.' He paused and smiled thinly. 'It seems that one pair had never been worn.'

'I think I'm beginning to get it,' I said.

He leaned back and tapped the arms of his chair. He waited.

'The walk from the side door of the house to the garage is rough concrete,' I said. 'Fairly rough. Suppose she didn't walk it, but was carried. And suppose whoever carried her put her slippers on – and got one that had not been worn.'

'Yes?'

'And suppose Talley noticed this while Lavery was telephoning to the doctor, who was out on his rounds. So he took the unworn slipper, regarding it as evidence that Florence Almore had been murdered.'

Webber nodded his head. 'It was evidence if he left it where it was, for the police to find it. After he took it, it was just evidence that he was a rat.'

'Was a monoxide test made of her blood?'

He put his hands flat on his desk and looked down at them. 'Yes,' he said. 'And there was monoxide all right. Also the investigating officers were satisfied with appearances. There was no sign of violence. They were satisfied that Dr Almore had not murdered his wife. Perhaps they were wrong. I think the investigation was a little superficial.'

'And who was in charge of it?' I asked.

'I think you know the answer to that.'

'When the police came, didn't they notice that a slipper was missing?'

'When the police came there was no slipper missing. You must remember that Dr Almore was back at his home, in response to Lavery's call, before the police were called. All we know about the missing shoe is from Talley himself. He might have taken the unworn shoe from the house. The side door was unlocked. The maids were asleep. The objection to that is that he wouldn't have been likely to know there was an unworn slipper to take. I wouldn't put it past him to think of it. He's a sharp sneaky little devil. But I can't fix the necessary knowledge on him.'

We sat there and looked at each other, thinking about it.

'Unless,' Webber said slowly, 'we can suppose that this nurse of Almore's was involved with Talley in a scheme to put the bite on Almore. It's possible. There are things in favour of it. There are more things against it. What reasons have you for claiming that the girl drowned up in the mountains was this nurse?'

'Two reasons, neither one conclusive separately, but pretty powerful taken together. A tough guy who looked and acted like Degarmo was up there a few weeks ago showing a photograph of Mildred Haviland that looked something like Muriel Chess. Different hair and eyebrows and so on, but a fair resemblance. Nobody helped him much. He called himself De Soto and said he was a Los Angeles cop. There isn't any Los Angeles cop named De Soto. When Muriel Chess heard about it, she looked scared. If it was Degarmo, that's easily established. The other reason is that a golden anklet with a heart on it was hidden in a box of powdered sugar in the Chess cabin. It was found after her death, after her husband had been arrested. On the back of the heart was engraved: "Al to Mildred. June 28th. 1938. With all my love."'

'It could have been some other Al and some other Mildred,' Webber said.

'You don't really believe that, captain.'

He leaned forward and made a hole in the air with his forefinger. 'What do you want to make of all this exactly?'

'I want to make it that Kingsley's wife didn't shoot Lavery. That his death had something to do with the Almore business. And with Mildred Haviland. And possibly with Dr Almore. I want to make it that Kingsley's wife disappeared because something happened that gave her a bad fright, that she may or may not have guilty knowledge, but that she hasn't murdered anybody. There's five hundred dollars in it for me, if I can determine that. It's legitimate to try.'

He nodded. 'Certainly it is. And I'm the man that would help you, if I could see any grounds for it. We haven't found the woman, but the time has been very short. But I can't help you put something on one of my boys.'

I said: 'I heard you call Degarmo Al. But I was thinking of Almore. His name's Albert.'

Webber looked at his thumb. 'But he was never married to the girl,' he said quietly. 'Degarmo was. I can tell you she led him a pretty dance. A lot of what seems bad in him is the result of it.'

I sat very still. After a moment I said: 'I'm beginning to see things I didn't know existed. What kind of a girl was she?'

'Smart, smooth and no good. She had a way with men. She could make them crawl over her shoes. The big boob would tear your head off right now, if you said anything against her. She divorced him, but that didn't end it for him.'

'Does he know she is dead?'

Webber sat quiet for a long moment before he said: 'Not from anything he has said. But how could he help it, if it's the same girl?'

'He never found her in the mountains – so far as we know.' I stood up and leaned down on the desk. 'Look, captain, you're not kidding me, are you?'

'No. Not one damn bit. Some men are like that and some women can make them like it. If you think Degarmo went up there looking for her because he wanted to hurt her, you're as wet as a bar towel.'

'I never quite thought that,' I said. 'It would be possible, provided Degarmo knew the country up there pretty well. Whoever murdered the girl did.'

'This is all between us,' he said. 'I'd like you to keep it that way.'

I nodded, but I didn't promise him. I said good night again and left. He looked after me as I went down the room. He looked hurt and sad.

The Chrysler was in the police lot at the side of the building with the keys in the ignition and none of the fenders smashed. Cooney hadn't made good on his threat. I drove back to Hollywood and went up to my apartment in the Bristol. It was late, almost midnight.

The green and ivory hallway was empty of all sound except that a telephone bell was ringing in one of the apartments. It rang insistently and got louder as I came near to my door. I unlocked the door. It was my telephone.

I walked across the room in darkness to where the phone stood on the ledge of an oak desk against the side wall. It must have rung at least ten times before I got to it.

I lifted it out of the cradle and answered, and it was Derace Kingsley on the line.

His voice sounded tight and brittle and strained. 'Good Lord, where in hell have you been?' he snapped. 'I've been trying to reach you for hours.'

'All right. I'm here now,' I said. 'What is it?'

'I've heard from her.'

I held the telephone very tight and drew my breath in slowly and let it out slowly. 'Go ahead,' I said.

'I'm not far away. I'll be over there in five or six minutes. Be prepared to move.'

He hung up.

I stood there holding the telephone half-way between my ear and the cradle. Then I put it down very slowly and looked at the hand that had held it. It was half-open and clenched stiff, as if it was still holding the instrument.

29

The discreet midnight tapping sounded on the door and I went over and opened it. Kingsley looked as big as a horse in a creamy Shetland sports coat with a green and yellow scarf around the neck inside the loosely turned-up collar. A dark reddish-brown snapbrim hat was pulled low on his forehead and under its brim his eyes looked like the eyes of a sick animal.

Miss Fromsett was with him. She was wearing slacks and sandals and a dark-green coat and no hat and her hair had a wicked lustre. In her ears hung ear-drops made of a pair of tiny artificial gardenia blooms, hanging one above the other, two on each ear. Gillerlain Regal, the Champagne of Perfumes, came in at the door with her.

I shut the door and indicated the furniture and said: 'A drink will probably help.'

Miss Fromsett sat in an armchair and crossed her legs and looked around for cigarettes. She found one and lit it with a long casual flourish and smiled bleakly at a corner of the ceiling.

Kingsley stood in the middle of the floor trying to bite his chin. I went out to the dinette and mixed three drinks and brought them in and handed them. I went over to the chair by the chess table with mine.

Kingsley said: 'What have you been doing and what's the matter with the leg?'

I said: 'A cop kicked me. A present from the Bay City police department. It's a regular service they give down there. As to where I've been – in jail for drunk-driving. And from the expression on your face, I think I may be right back there soon.'

'I don't know what you're talking about,' he said shortly. 'I haven't the foggiest idea. This is no time to kid around.'

'All right, don't,' I said. 'What did you hear and where is she?'

He sat down with his drink and flexed the fingers of his right hand and put it inside his coat. It came out with an envelope, a long one.

'You have to take this to her,' he said. 'Five hundred dollars. She wanted more, but this is all I could raise. I cashed a cheque at a night-club. It wasn't easy. She has to get out of town.'

I said: 'Out of what town?'

'Bay City somewhere. I don't know where. She'll meet you at a place called the Peacock Lounge, on Arguello Boulevard, at Eighth Street, or near it.'

I looked at Miss Fromsett. She was still looking at the corner of the ceiling as if she had just come along for the ride.

Kingsley tossed the envelope across and it fell on the chess table. I looked inside it. It was money all right. That much of his story made sense. I let it lie on the small polished table with its inlaid squares of brown and pale gold.

I said: 'What's the matter with her drawing her own money? Any hotel would clear a cheque for her. Most of them would cash one. Has her bank account got lockjaw or something?'

'That's no way to talk,' Kingsley said heavily. 'She's in trouble. I don't know how she knows she's in trouble. Unless a pick-up order has been broadcast. Has it?'

I said I didn't know. I hadn't had much time to listen to police calls. I had been too busy listening to live policemen. Kingsley said: 'Well, she won't risk cashing a cheque now. It was all right before. But not now.' He lifted his eyes slowly and gave me one of the emptiest stares I had ever seen.

'All right, we can't make sense where there isn't any,' I said. 'So she's in Bay City. Did you talk to her?'

'No. Miss Fromsett talked to her. She called the office. It was just after hours but that cop from the beach, Captain Webber, was with me. Miss Fromsett naturally didn't want her to talk at all then. She told her to call back. She wouldn't give any number we could call.'

I looked at Miss Fromsett. She brought her glance down from the ceiling and pointed it at the top of my head. There was nothing in her eyes at all. They were like drawn curtains.

Kingsley went on: 'I didn't want to talk to her. She didn't want to talk to me. I don't want to see her. I guess there's no doubt she shot Lavery. Webber seemed quite sure of it.'

'That doesn't mean anything,' I said. 'What he says and what he thinks don't even have to be on the same map. I don't like her knowing the cops were after her. It's a long time since anybody listened to the police short-wave for amusement. So she called back later. And then?'

'It was almost half-past six,' Kingsley said. 'We had to sit there in the office and wait for her to call. You tell him.' He turned his head to the girl.

Miss Fromsett said: 'I took the call in Mr Kingsley's office. He was sitting right beside me, but he didn't speak. She said to send the money down to the Peacock place and asked who would bring it.'

'Did she sound scared?'

'Not in the least. Completely calm. I might say, icily calm. She had it all worked out. She realized somebody would have to bring the money she might not know. She seemed to know Derry – Mr Kingsley wouldn't bring it.'

'Call him Derry,' I said. 'I'll be able to guess who you mean.'

She smiled faintly. 'She will go into this Peacock Lounge every hour about fifteen minutes past the hour. I – I guess I assumed you would be the one to go. I described you to her. And you're to wear Derry's scarf. I described that. He keeps some clothes at the office and this was among them. It's distinctive enough.'

It was all of that. It was an affair of fat green kidneys laid down on an egg-yolk background. It would be almost as distinctive as if I went in there wheeling a red, white and blue wheelbarrow.

'For a blimp brain she's doing all right,' I said.

'This is no time to fool around,' Kingsley put in sharply.

'You said that before,' I told him. 'You've got a hell of a crust assuming I'll go down there and take a getaway stake to somebody I know the police are looking for.'

He twisted a hand on his knee and his face twisted into a crooked grin.

'I admit it's a bit thick,' he said. 'Well, how about it?'

'It makes accessories after the fact out of all three of us. That might not be too tough for her husband and his confidential secretary to talk out of, but what they would do to me would be nobody's dream of a vacation.'

'I'm going to make it worth your while,' he said. 'And we wouldn't be accessories if she hasn't done anything.'

'I'm willing to suppose it,' I said. 'Otherwise I wouldn't be talking to you. And in addition to that, if I decide she did do any murder, I'm going to turn her over to the police.'

'She won't talk to you,' he said.

I reached for the envelope and put it in my pocket. 'She will, if she wants this.' I looked at my strap watch. 'If I start right away, I might make the one-fifteen deadline. They must know her by heart in that bar after all these hours. That makes it nice too.'

'She's dyed her hair dark brown,' Miss Fromsett said. 'That ought to help a little.'

I said: 'It doesn't help me to think she is just an innocent wayfarer.' I finished my drink and stood up. Kingsley swallowed his at a gulp and stood up and got the scarf off his neck and handed it to me.

'What did you do to get the police on your neck down there?' he asked.

'I was using some information Miss Fromsett very kindly got for me. And that led to my looking for a man named Talley who worked on the Almore case. And that led to the clink. They had the house staked. Talley was the dick the Graysons hired,' I added, looking at the tall dark girl. 'You'll probably be able to explain to him what it's all about. It doesn't matter anyway. I haven't time to go into it now. You two want to wait here?'

Kingsley shook his head. 'We'll go to my place and wait for a call from you.'

Miss Fromsett stood up and yawned. 'No. I'm tired, Derry. I'm going home and going to bed.'

'You'll come with me,' he said sharply. 'You've got to keep me from going nuts.'

'Where do you live, Miss Fromsett?' I asked.

'Bryson Tower on Sunset Place. Apartment 716. Why?' She gave me a speculative look.

'I might want to reach you some time.'

Kingsley's face looked bleakly irritated, but his eyes still were the eyes of a sick animal. I wound his scarf around my neck and went out to the dinette to switch off the light. When I came back they were both standing by the door. Kingsley had his arm around her shoulders. She looked very tired and rather bored.

333

'Well, I certainly hope –' he started to stay, then took a quick step and put his hand out. 'You're a pretty level guy, Marlowe.'

'Go on, beat it,' I said. 'Go away. Go far away.'

He gave a queer look and they went out.

I waited until I heard the elevator come up and stop, and the doors open and close again, and the elevator start down. Then I went out myself and took the stairs down to the basement garage and got the Chrysler awake again.

30

The Peacock Lounge was a narrow front next to a gift shop in whose window a tray of small crystal animals shimmered in the street light. The Peacock had a glass brick front and soft light glowed out around the stained-glass peacock that was set into the brick. I went in around a Chinese screen and looked along the bar and then sat at the outer edge of a small booth. The light was amber, the leather was Chinese red and the booths had polished plastic tables. In one booth four soldiers were drinking beer moodily, a little glassy in the eyes and obviously bored even with drinking beer. Across from them a party of two girls and two flashy-looking men were making the only noise in the place. I saw nobody that looked like my idea of Crystal Kingsley.

A wizened waiter with evil eyes and a face like a gnawed bone put a napkin with a printed peacock on it down on the table in front of me and gave me a bacardi cocktail. I sipped it and looked at the amber face of the bar clock. It was just past one-fifteen.

One of the men with the two girls got up suddenly and stalked along to the door and went out. The voice of the other man said:

'What did you have to insult the guy for?'

A girl's tinny voice said: 'Insult him? I like that. He propositioned me.'

The man's voice said complainingly: 'Well, you didn't have to insult him, did you?'

One of the soldiers suddenly laughed deep in his chest and then wiped the laugh off his face with a brown hand and drank a little more beer. I rubbed the back of my knee. It was hot and swollen still but the paralysed feeling had gone away.

A tiny, white-faced Mexican boy with enormous black eyes came in with morning papers and scuttled along the booths trying to make a few sales before the barman threw him out. I bought a paper and looked through it to see if there were any interesting murders. There were not.

I folded it and looked up as a slim, brown-haired girl in coal-black slacks and a yellow shirt and a long grey coat came out of somewhere and passed the booth without looking at me. I tried to make up my mind whether her face was familiar or just such a standard type of lean, rather hard, prettiness that I must have seen it ten thousand times. She went out of the street door around the screen. Two minutes later the little Mexican boy came back in, shot a quick look at the barman, and scuttled over to stand in front of me.

'Mister,' he said, his great big eyes shining with mischief. Then he made a beckoning sign and scuttled out again.

I finished my drink and went after him. The girl in the grey coat and yellow shirt and black slacks was standing in front of the gift shop, looking in at the window. Her eyes moved as I went out. I went and stood beside her.

She looked at me again. Her face was white and tired. Her hair looked darker than dark brown. She looked away and spoke to the window.

'Give me the money, please.' A little mist formed on the plate-glass from her breath.

I said: 'I'd have to know who you are.'

'You know who I am,' she said softly. 'How much did you bring?'

'Five hundred.'

'It's not enough,' she said. 'Not nearly enough. Give it to me quickly. I've been waiting half of eternity for somebody to get here.'

'Where can we talk?'

'We don't have to talk. Just give me the money and go the other way.'

'It's not that simple. I'm doing this at quite a risk. I'm at least going to have the satisfaction of knowing what goes on and where I stand.'

335

'Damn you,' she said acidly. 'Why couldn't he come himself? I don't want to talk. I want to get away as soon as I can.'

'You didn't want him to come himself. He understood that you didn't even want to talk to him on the phone.'

'That's right,' she said quickly and tossed her head.

'But you've got to talk to me,' I said. 'I'm not as easy as he is. Either to me or to the law. There's no way out of it. I'm a private detective and I have to have some protection too.'

'Well, isn't he charming,' she said. 'Private detective and all.' Her voice held a low sneer.

'He did the best he knew how. It wasn't easy for him to know what to do.'

'What do you want to talk about?'

'You, and what you've been doing and where you've been and what you expect to do. Things like that. Little things, but important.'

She breathed on the glass of the shop window and waited while the mist of her breath disappeared.

'I think it would be much better,' she said in the same cool empty voice, 'for you to give me the money and let me work things out for myself.'

'No.'

She gave me another sharp sideways glance. She shrugged the shoulders of the grey coat impatiently.

'Very well, if it has to be that way. I'm at the Granada, two blocks north on Eighth. Apartment 618. Give me ten minutes. I'd rather go in alone.'

'I have a car.'

'I'd rather go alone.' She turned quickly and walked away.

She walked back to the corner and crossed the boulevard and disappeared along the block under a line of pepper trees. I went and sat in the Chrysler and gave her the ten minutes before I started it.

The Granada was an ugly grey building on a corner. The plate-glass entrance-door was level with the street. I drove around the corner and saw a milky globe with 'Garage' painted on it. The entrance to the garage was down a ramp into the hard rubber-smelling silence of parked cars in rows. A lanky Negro came out of a glassed-in office and looked the Chrysler over.

'How much to leave this here a short time? I'm going upstairs.'

He gave me a shady leer. 'Kinda late, boss. She needs a good dustin' too. Be a dollar.'

'What goes on here?'

'Be a dollar,' he said woodenly.

I got out. He gave me a ticket. I gave him the dollar. Without my asking him he said the elevator was in back of the office, by the men's room.

I rode up to the sixth floor and looked at numbers on doors and listened to stillness and smelled beach air coming in at the ends of corridors. The place seemed decent enough. There would be a few happy ladies in any apartment house. That would explain the lanky Negro's dollar. A great judge of character, that boy.

I came to the door of Apartment 618 and stood outside it a moment and then knocked softly.

31

She still had the grey coat on. She stood back from the door and I went past her into a square room with twin wall beds and a minimum of uninteresting furniture. A small lamp on a window-table made a dim yellowish light. The window behind it was open.

The girl said: 'Sit down and talk then.'

She closed the door and went to sit in a gloomy Boston rocker across the room. I sat down on a thick davenport. There was a dull-green curtain hanging across an open door space at one end of the davenport. That would lead to dressing-room and bathroom. There was a closed door at the other end. That would be the kitchenette. That would be all there was.

The girl crossed her ankles and leaned her head back against the chair and looked at me under long beaded lashes. Her eyebrows were thin and arched and as brown as her hair. It was a quiet, secret face. It didn't look like the face of a woman who would waste a lot of motion.

'I got a rather different idea of you,' I said, 'from Kingsley.'

Her lips twisted a little. She said nothing.

'From Lavery too,' I said. 'It just goes to show that we talk different languages to different people.'

'I haven't time for this sort of talk,' she said. 'What is it you have to know?'

'He hired me to find you. I've been working on it. I supposed you would know that.'

'Yes. His office sweetie told me that over the phone. She told me you would be a man named Marlowe. She told me about the scarf.'

I took the scarf off my neck and folded it up and slipped it into a pocket. I said:

'So I know a little about your movements. Not very much. I know you left your car at the Prescott Hotel in San Bernardino and that you met Lavery there. I know you sent a wire from El Paso. What did you do then?'

'All I want from you is the money he sent. I don't see that my movements are any of your business.'

'I don't have to argue about that,' I said. 'It's a question of whether you want the money.'

'Well, we went to El Paso,' she said, in a tired voice. 'I thought of marrying him then. So I sent that wire. You saw the wire?'

'Yes.'

'Well, I changed my mind. I asked him to go home and leave me. He made a scene.'

'Did he go home and leave you?'

'Yes. Why not?'

'What did you do then?'

'I went to Santa Barbara and stayed there a few days. Over a week, in fact. Then to Pasadena. Same thing. Then to Hollywood. Then I came down here. That's all.'

'You were alone all this time?'

She hesitated a little and then said: 'Yes.'

'Not with Lavery – any part of it?'

'Not after he went home.'

'What was the idea?'

'Idea of what?' Her voice was a little sharp.

'Idea of going these places and not sending any word. Didn't you know he would be very anxious?'

'Oh, you mean my husband,' she said coolly. 'I don't think I worried much about him. He'd think I was in Mexico, wouldn't he? As for the idea of it all – well, I just had to think things out. My life had got to be a hopeless tangle. I had to be somewhere quite alone and try to straighten myself out.'

'Before that,' I said, 'you spent a month at Little Fawn Lake trying to straighten it out and not getting anywhere. Is that it?'

She looked down at her shoes and then up at me and nodded earnestly. The wavy brown hair surged forward along her cheeks. She put her left hand up and pushed it back and then rubbed her temple with one finger.

'I seemed to need a new place,' she said. 'Not necessarily an interesting place. Just a strange place. Without associations. A place where I would be very much alone. Like an hotel.'

'How are you getting on with it?'

'Not very well. But I'm not going back to Derace Kingsley. Does he want me to?'

'I don't know. Why did you come down here to the town where Lavery was?'

She bit a knuckle and looked at me over her hand.

'I wanted to see him again. He's all mixed up in my mind. I'm in love with him and yet – well, I suppose in a way I am. But I don't think I want to marry him. Does that make sense?'

'That part of it makes sense. But staying away from home in a lot of crummy hotels doesn't. You've lived your own life for years, as I understand it.'

'I had to be alone to – to think things out,' she said a little desperately and bit the knuckle again, hard. 'Won't you please give me the money and go away?'

'Sure. Right away. But wasn't there any other reason for your going away from Little Fawn Lake just then? Anything connected with Muriel Chess, for instance?'

339

She looked surprised. But anyone can look surprised. 'Good heavens, what would there be? That frozen-faced little drip – what is she to me?'

'I thought you might have had a fight with her – about Bill.'

'Bill? Bill Chess?' She seemed even more surprised. Almost too surprised.

'Bill claims you made a pass at him.'

She put her head back and let out a tinny and unreal laugh. 'Good heavens, that muddy-faced boozer?' Her face sobered suddenly. 'What's happened? Why all the mystery?'

'He might be a muddy-faced boozer,' I said. 'The police think he's a murderer too. Of his wife. She's been found drowned in the lake. After a month.'

She moistened her lips and held her head on one side, staring at me fixedly. There was a quiet little silence. The damp breath of the Pacific slid into the room around us.

'I'm not too surprised,' she said slowly. 'So it came to that in the end. They fought terribly at times. Did you think that had something to do with my leaving?'

I nodded. 'There was a chance of it.'

'It didn't have anything to do with it at all,' she said seriously, and shook her head back and forth. 'It was just the way I told you. Nothing else.'

'Muriel's dead,' I said. 'Drowned in the lake. You don't get much of a boot out of that, do you?'

'I hardly knew the girl,' she said. 'Really. She kept to herself. After all –'

'I don't suppose you knew she had once worked in Dr Almore's office?'

She looked completely puzzled now. 'I was never in Dr Almore's office,' she said slowly. 'He made a few house calls a long time ago. I – what are you talking about?'

'Muriel Chess was really a girl called Mildred Haviland, who had been Dr Almore's office nurse.'

'That's a queer coincidence,' she said wonderingly. 'I knew Bill met her in Riverside. I didn't know how or under what circumstances or where she came from. Dr Almore's office, eh? It doesn't have to mean anything, does it?'

I said, 'No. I guess it's a genuine coincidence. They do happen. But you see why I had to talk to you. Muriel being found drowned and you having gone away and Muriel being Mildred Haviland who was connected with Dr Almore at one time – as Lavery was also, in a different way. And, of course, Lavery lives across the street from Dr Almore. Did he, Lavery, seem to know Muriel from somewhere else?'

She thought about it, biting her lower lip gently. 'He saw her up there,' she said finally. 'He didn't act as if he had ever seen her before.'

'And he would have,' I said. 'Being the kind of guy he was.'

'I don't think Chris had anything to do with Dr Almore,' she said. 'He knew Dr Almore's wife. I don't think he knew the doctor at all. So he probably wouldn't know Dr Almore's office nurse.'

'Well, I guess there's nothing in all this to help me,' I said. 'But you can see why I had to talk to you. I guess I can give you the money now.'

I got the envelope out and stood up to drop it on her knee. She let it lie there. I sat down again.

'You do this character very well,' I said. 'This confused innocence with an undertone of hardness and bitterness. People have made a bad mistake about you. They have been thinking of you as a reckless little idiot with no brains and no control. They have been very wrong.'

She stared at me, lifting her eyebrows. She said nothing. Then a small smile lifted the corners of her mouth. She reached for the envelope, tapped it on her knee, and laid it aside on the table. She stared at me all the time.

'You did the Fallbrook character very well too,' I said. 'Looking back on it, I think it was a shade overdone. But at the time it had me going all right. That purple hat that would have been all right on blonde hair but looked like hell on straggly brown, that messed-up make-up that looked as if it had been put on in the dark by somebody with a sprained wrist, the jittery screwball manner. All very good. And when you put the gun in my hand like that – I fell like a brick.'

She snickered and put her hands in the deep pockets of her coat. Her heels tapped on the floor.

'But why did you go back at all?' I asked. 'Why take such a risk in broad daylight, in the middle of the morning?'

'So you think I shot Chris Lavery?' she said quietly.

'I don't think it. I know it.'

'Why did I go back? Is that what you want to know?'

'I don't really care,' I said.

She laughed. A sharp cold laugh. 'He had all my money,' she said. 'He had stripped my purse. He had it all, even silver. That's why I went back. There wasn't any risk at all. I know how he lived. It was really safer to go back. To take in the milk and the newspaper, for instance. People lose their heads in these situations. I don't, I didn't see why I should. It's so very much safer not to.'

'I see,' I said. 'Then, of course, you shot him the night before. I ought to have thought of that, not that it matters. He had been shaving. But guys with dark beards and lady friends sometimes shave the last thing at night, don't they?'

'It has been heard of,' she said almost gaily. 'And just what are you going to do about it?'

'You're a cold-blooded little bitch if ever I saw one,' I said. 'Do about it? Turn you over to the police, naturally. It will be a pleasure.'

'I don't think so.' She threw the words out, almost with a lilt. 'You wondered why I gave you the empty gun. Why not? I had another one in my bag. Like this.'

Her right hand came up from her coat pocket and she pointed it at me.

I grinned. It may not have been the heartiest grin in the world, but it was a grin.

'I've never liked this scene,' I said. 'Detective confronts murderer. Murderer produces gun, points same at detective. Murderer tells detective the whole sad story, with the idea of shooting him at the end of it. Thus wasting a lot of valuable time, even if in the end murderer did shoot detective. Only murderer never does. Something always happens to prevent it. The gods don't like this scene either. They always manage to spoil it.'

'But this time,' she said softly and got up and moved towards me softly across the carpet, 'suppose we make it a little different. Suppose I don't tell you, anything and nothing happens and I do shoot you?'

'I still wouldn't like the scene,' I said.

'You don't seem to be afraid,' she said, and slowly licked her lips, coming towards me very gently without any sound of footfalls on the carpet.

'I'm not afraid,' I lied. 'It's too late at night, too still, and the window is open and the gun would make too much noise. It's too long a journey down to the street and you're not good with guns. You would probably miss me. You missed Lavery three times.'

'Stand up,' she said.

I stood up.

'I'm going to be too close to miss,' she said. She pushed the gun against my chest. 'Like this. I really can't miss now, can I? Now be very still. Hold your hands up by your shoulders and then don't move at all. If you move at all, the gun will go off.'

I put my hands up beside my shoulders. I looked down at the gun. My tongue felt a little thick, but I could still wave it.

Her probing left hand didn't find a gun on me. It dropped and she bit her lip, staring at me. The gun bored into my chest. 'You'll have to turn around now,' she said, polite as a tailor at a fitting.

'There's something a little off key about everything you do,' I said. 'You're definitely not good with guns. You're much too close to me, and I hate to bring this up – but there's that old business of the safety-catch not being off. You've overlooked that too.'

So she started to do two things at once. To take a long step backwards and to feel with her thumb for the safety-catch, without taking her eyes off my face. Two very simple things, needing only a second to do. But she didn't like my telling her. She didn't like my thought riding over hers. The minute confusion of it jarred her.

She let out a small choked sound and I dropped my right hand and yanked her face hard against my chest. My left hand smashed down on her right wrist, the heel of my hand against the base of her thumb. The gun jerked out of her hand to the floor. Her face writhed against my chest and I think she was trying to scream.

Then she tried to kick me and lost what little balance she had left. Her hands came up to claw at me. I caught her wrist and began to twist it behind her back. She was very strong, but I was very much stronger. So she decided to go limp and let her whole weight sag against the hand that was holding her head. I couldn't hold her up with one hand. She started to go down and I had to bend down with her.

There were vague sounds of our scuffling on the floor by the davenport, and hard breathing, and if a floorboard creaked I didn't hear it. I thought a curtain-ring checked sharply on a rod. I wasn't sure and I had no time to consider the question. A figure loomed up suddenly on my left, just behind, and out of range of clear vision. I knew there was a man there and that he was a big man.

That was all I knew. The scene exploded into fire and darkness. I didn't even remember being slugged. Fire and darkness and just before the darkness a sharp flash of nausea.

32

I smelled of gin. Not just casually, as if I had taken four or five drinks of a winter morning to get out of bed on, but as if the Pacific Ocean was pure gin and I had nosedived off the boat deck. The gin was in my hair and eyebrows, on my chin and under my chin. It was on my shirt. I smelled like dead toads.

My coat was off and I was lying flat on my back beside the davenport on somebody's carpet and I was looking at a framed picture. The frame was of cheap soft wood varnished and the picture showed part of an enormously high pale-yellow viaduct across which a shiny black locomotive was dragging a Prussian-blue train. Through one lofty arch of the viaduct a wide yellow beach showed and was dotted with sprawled bathers and striped beach umbrellas. Three girls walked close up, with paper parasols, one girl in cerise, one in pale blue, one in green. Beyond the beach a curving bay was bluer than any bay has any right to be. It was drenched with sunshine and flecked and dotted with aching white sails. Beyond the inland curve of the bay three ranges of hills rose in three precisely opposed colours, gold and terracotta and lavender.

Across the bottom of the picture was printed in large capitals, SEE THE FRENCH RIVIERA BY THE BLUE TRAIN.

It was a fine time to bring that up.

I reached up wearily and felt the back of my head. It felt pulpy. A shoot of pain from the touch went clear to the soles of my feet. I groaned, and made a grunt out of the groan, from professional pride – what was left of it. I rolled over slowly and carefully and looked at the foot of a pulled-down wall-bed; one twin, the other being still up in the wall. The flourish of design on the painted wood was familiar. The picture had hung over the davenport and I hadn't even looked at it.

When I rolled a square gin bottle rolled off my chest and hit the floor. It was water white, and empty. It didn't seem possible there could be so much gin in just one bottle.

I got my knees under me and stayed on all fours for a while, sniffing like a dog who can't finish his dinner, but hates to leave it. I moved my head around on my neck. It hurt. I moved it around some more and it still hurt, so I climbed up on my feet and discovered I didn't have any shoes on.

The shoes were lying against the baseboard, looking as dissipated as shoes ever looked. I put them on wearily. I was an old man now. I was going down the last long hill. I still had a tooth left though. I felt it with my tongue. It didn't seem to taste of gin.

'It will all come back to you,' I said. 'Some day it will all come back to you. And you won't like it.'

There was the lamp on the table by the open window. There was the fat green davenport. There was the doorway with the green curtain across it. Never sit with your back to a green curtain. It always turns out badly. Something always happens. Who had I said that to? A girl with a gun. A girl with a clear, empty face and dark-brown hair that had been blonde.

I looked around for her. She was still there. She was lying on the pulled-down twin bed.

She was wearing a pair of tan stockings and nothing else. Her hair was tumbled. There were dark bruises on her throat. Her mouth was open and a swollen tongue filled it to overflowing. Her eyes bulged and the whites of them were not white.

Across her naked belly four angry scratches leered crimson red against the whiteness of flesh. Deep angry scratches, gouged out by four bitter finger-nails.

On the davenport there were tumbled clothes, mostly hers. My coat was there also. I disentangled it and put it on. Something crackled under my hand in the tumbled clothes. I drew out a long envelope with money still in it. I put it in my pocket. Marlowe, five hundred dollars. I hoped it was all there. There didn't seem much else to hope for.

I stepped on the balls of my feet softly, as if walking on very thin ice. I bent down to rub behind my knee and wondered which hurt most, my knee, or my head when I bent down to rub the knee.

Heavy feet came along the hallway and there was a hard mutter of voices. The feet stopped. A hard fist knocked on the door.

I stood there leering at the door, with my lips drawn back tight against my teeth. I waited for somebody to open the door and walk in. The knob was tried, but nobody walked in. The knocking began again, stopped, the voices muttered again. The steps went away. I wondered how long it would take to get the manager with a passkey. Not very long.

Not nearly long enough for Marlowe to get home from the French Riviera.

I went to the green curtain and brushed it aside and looked down a short dark hallway into a bathroom. I went in there and put the light on. Two wash rugs on the floor, a bath mat folded over the edge of the tub, a pebbled glass window at the corner of the tub. I shut the bathroom door and stood on the edge of the tub and eased the window up. This was the sixth floor. There was no screen. I put my head out and looked into darkness and a narrow glimpse of a street with trees. I looked sideways and saw that the bathroom window of the next apartment was not more than three feet away. A well-nourished mountain goat could make it without any trouble at all.

The question was whether a battered private detective could make it, and if so, what the harvest would be.

Behind me a rather remote and muffled voice seemed to be chanting the policeman's litany: 'Open it up or we'll kick it in.' I sneered back at the voice. They wouldn't kick it in because kicking in a door is hard on the feet. Policemen are kind to their feet. Their feet are about all they are kind to.

I grabbed a towel off the rack and pulled the two halves of the window down and eased out on the sill. I swung half of me over to the next sill, holding on to the frame of the open window. I could just reach to push the next window down, if it was unlocked. It wasn't unlocked. I got my foot over there and kicked the glass over the catch. It made a noise that ought to have been heard in Reno. I wrapped the towel around my left hand and reached in to turn the catch. Down on the street a car went by, but nobody yelled at me.

I pushed the broken window down and climbed across to the other sill. The towel fell out of my hand and fluttered down into the darkness to a strip of grass far below, between the two wings of the building.

I climbed in at the window of the other bathroom.

33

I climbed down into darkness and groped through darkness to a door and opened it and listened. Filtered moonlight coming through north windows showed a bedroom with twin beds, made up and empty. Not wall beds. This was a larger apartment. I moved past the beds to another door and into a living-room. Both rooms were closed up and smelled musty. I felt my way to a lamp and switched it on. I ran a finger along the wood of a table edge. There was a light film of dust, such as accumulates in the cleanest room when it is left shut up.

The room contained a library dining-table, an armchair radio, a book-rack built like a hod, a big bookcase full of novels with their jackets still on them, a dark wood highboy with a siphon and a cut-glass bottle of liquor and four striped glasses upside down on an Indian brass tray. Beside this paired photographs in a double silver frame, a youngish middle-aged man and woman, with round healthy faces and cheerful eyes. They looked out at me as if they didn't mind my being there at all.

I sniffed the liquor, which was Scotch, and used some of it. It made my head feel worse but it made the rest of me feel better. I put a light on in the bedroom and poked into closets. One of them had a man's clothes, tailor-made, plenty of them. The tailor's label inside a coat pocket declared the owner's name to be H. G. Talbot. I went to the bureau and poked around and found a soft blue shirt that looked a little small for me. I carried it into the bathroom and stripped mine off and washed my face and chest and wiped my hair off with a wet towel and put the blue shirt on. I used plenty of Mr Talbot's rather insistent hair tonic on my hair and used his brush and comb to tidy it up. By that time I smelled of gin only remotely, if at all.

The top button of the shirt wouldn't meet its buttonhole, so I poked into the bureau again and found a dark-blue crêpe tie and strung it around my neck. I got my coat back on and looked at myself in the mirror. I looked slightly too neat for that hour of the night, even for as careful a man as Mr Talbot's clothes indicated him to be. Too neat and too sober.

I rumpled my hair a little and pulled the tie loose, and went back to the whisky decanter and did what I could about being too sober. I lit one of Mr Talbot's cigarettes and hoped that Mr and Mrs Talbot, wherever they were, were having a much better time than I was. I hoped I would live long enough to come and visit them.

I went to the living-room door, the one giving on the hallway, and opened it and leaned in the opening smoking. I didn't think it was going to work. But I didn't think waiting there for them to follow my trail through the window was going to work any better.

A man coughed a little way down the hall and I poked my head out farther and he was looking at me. He came towards me briskly, a small sharp man in a neatly pressed police uniform. He had reddish hair and red-gold eyes.

I yawned and said languidly: 'What goes on, officer?'

He stared at me thoughtfully. 'Little trouble next door to you. Hear anything?'

'I thought I heard knocking. I just got home a little while ago.'

'Little late,' he said.

'That's a matter of opinion,' I said. 'Trouble next door, eh?'

'A dame,' he said. 'Know her?'

'I think I've seen her.'

'Yeah,' he said. 'You ought to see her now –' He put his hands to his throat and bulged his eyes out and gurgled unpleasantly. 'Like that,' he said. 'You didn't hear nothing, huh?'

'Nothing I noticed – except the knocking.'

'Yeah. What was the name?'

'Talbot.'

'Just a minute, Mr Talbot. Wait there just a minute.'

He went along the hallway and leaned into an open doorway through which light streamed out. 'Oh, Lieutenant,' he said. 'The man next door is on deck.'

A tall man came out of the doorway and stood looking along the hall straight at me. A tall man with rusty hair and very blue, blue eyes. Degarmo. That made it perfect.

'Here's the guy lives next door,' the small neat cop said helpfully. 'His name's Talbot.'

Degarmo looked straight at me, but nothing in his acid blue eyes showed that he had ever seen me before. He came quietly along the hall and put a hard hand against my chest and pushed me back into the room. When he had me half a dozen feet from the door he said over his shoulder:

'Come in here and shut the door, Shorty.'

The small cop came in and shut the door.

'Quite a gag,' Degarmo said lazily. 'Put a gun on him, Shorty.'

Shorty flicked his black belt holster open and had his .38 in his hand like a flash. He licked his lips.

'Oh boy,' he said softly, whistling a little, 'Oh boy. How'd you know, Lieutenant?'

'Know what?' Degarmo asked, keeping his eyes fixed on mine. 'What were you thinking of doing, pal – going down to get a paper – to find out if she was dead?'

'Oh boy,' Shorty said. 'A sex-killer. He pulled the girl's clothes off and choked her with his hands, Lieutenant. How'd you know?'

Degarmo didn't answer him. He just stood there, rocking a little on his heels, his face empty and granite-hard.

'Yah, he's the killer, sure,' Shorty said suddenly. 'Sniff the air in here, Lieutenant. The place ain't been aired out for days. And look at the dust on those bookshelves. And the clock on the mantel's stopped, Lieutenant. He come in through the – lemme look a minute, can I, Lieutenant?'

He ran out of the room into the bedroom. I heard him fumbling around. Degarmo stood woodenly.

Shorty came back. 'Come in at the bathroom window. There's broken glass in the tub. And something stinks of gin in there something awful. You remember how that apartment smelled of gin when we went in? Here's a shirt, Lieutenant. Smells like it was washed in gin.'

He held the shirt up. It perfumed the air rapidly. Degarmo looked at it vaguely and then stepped forward and yanked my coat open and looked at the shirt I was wearing.

'I know what he done,' Shorty said. 'He stole one of the guy's shirts, that lives here. You see what he done, Lieutenant?'

'Yeah.' Degarmo held his hand against my chest and let it fall slowly. They were talking about me as if I was a piece of wood.

'Frisk him, Shorty.'

Shorty ran around me feeling here and there for a gun. 'Nothing on him,' he said.

'Let's get him out the back way,' Degarmo said. 'It's our pinch, if we make it before Webber gets here. That lug Reed couldn't find a moth in a shoe-box.'

'You ain't even detailed on the case,' Shorty said doubtfully. 'Didn't I hear you was suspended or something?'

'What can I lose,' Degarmo asked, 'if I'm suspended?'

'I can lose this here uniform,' Shorty said.

Degarmo looked at him wearily. The small cop blushed and his bright red-gold eyes were anxious.

'Okay, Shorty. Go and tell Reed.'

The small cop licked his lip. 'You say the word, Lieutenant, and I'm with you. I don't have to know you got suspended.'

'We'll take him down ourselves, just the two of us,' Degarmo said.

'Yeah, sure.'

Degarmo put his finger against my chin. 'A sex-killer,' he said quietly. 'Well, I'll be damned.' He smiled at me thinly, moving only the extreme corners of his wide brutal mouth.

34

We went out of the apartment and along the hall the other way from Apartment 618. Light streamed from the still open door. Two men in plain clothes now stood outside it smoking cigarettes inside their cupped hands, as if a wind was blowing. There was a sound of wrangling voices from the apartment.

We went around the bend of the hall and came to the elevator. Degarmo opened the fire door beyond the elevator shaft and we went down echoing concrete steps, floor after floor. At the lobby floor Degarmo stopped and held his hand on the doorknob and listened. He looked back over his shoulder.

'You got a car?' he asked me.

'In the basement garage.'

'That's an idea.'

We went on down the steps and came out into the shadowy basement. The lanky Negro came out of the little office and I gave him my car check. He looked furtively at the police uniform on Shorty. He said nothing. He pointed to the Chrysler.

Degarmo climbed under the wheel of the Chrysler. I got in beside him and Shorty got into the back seat. We went up the ramp and out into the damp cool night air. A big car with twin red spotlights was charging towards us from a couple of blocks away.

Degarmo spat out of the car window and yanked the Chrysler the other way. 'That will be Webber,' he said. 'Late for the funeral again. We sure skinned his nose on that one, Shorty.'

'I don't like it too well, Lieutenant. I don't, honest.'

'Keep the chin up, kid. You might get back on homicide.'

'I'd rather wear buttons and eat,' Shorty said. The courage was oozing out of him fast.

Degarmo drove the car hard for ten blocks and then slowed a little. Shorty said uneasily:

'I guess you know what you're doing, Lieutenant, but this ain't the way to the Hall.'

'That's right,' Degarmo said. 'It never was, was it?'

He let the car slow down to a crawl and then turned into a residential street of small exact houses squatting behind small exact lawns. He braked the car gently and coasted over to the kerb and stopped about the middle of the block. He threw an arm over the back of the seat and turned his head to look back at Shorty.

'You think this guy killed her, Shorty?'

'I'm listening,' Shorty said in a tight voice.

'Got a flash?'

'No.'

I said: 'There's one in the car pocket on the left side.'

Shorty fumbled around and metal clicked and the white beam of the flashlight came on. Degarmo said:

'Take a look at the back of this guy's head.'

The beam moved and settled. I heard the small man's breathing behind me and felt it on my neck. Something felt for and touched the bump on my head. I grunted. The light went off and the darkness of the street rushed in again.

Shorty said: 'I guess maybe he was sapped, Lieutenant. I don't get it.'

'So was the girl,' Degarmo said. 'It didn't show much but it's there. She was sapped so she could have her clothes pulled off and be clawed up before she was killed. So the scratches would bleed. Then she was throttled. And none of this made any noise. Why would it? And there's no telephone in that apartment. Who reported it, Shorty?'

'How the hell would I know? A guy called up and said a woman had been murdered in 618 Granada Apartments on Eighth. Reed was still looking for a cameraman when you come in. The desk said a guy with a thick voice, likely disguised. Didn't give any name at all.'

'All right then,' Degarmo said. 'If you had murdered the girl, how would you get out of there?'

'I'd walk out,' Shorty said. 'Why not? Hey,' he barked at me suddenly, 'why didn't you?'

I didn't answer him. Degarmo said tonelessly: 'You wouldn't climb out of a bathroom window six floors up and then bust in another bathroom window into a strange apartment where people would likely be sleeping, would you? You wouldn't pretend to be the guy that lived there and you wouldn't throw away a lot of your time by calling the police, would you? Hell, that girl could have laid there for a week. You wouldn't throw away the chance of a start like that, would you, Shorty?'

'I don't guess I would,' Shorty said cautiously. 'I don't guess I would call up at all. But you know these sex fiends do funny things, Lieutenant. They ain't normal like us. And this guy could have had help and the other guy could have knocked him out to put him in the middle.'

'Don't tell me you thought that last bit up all by yourself,' Degarmo grunted. 'So here we sit, and the fellow that knows all the answers is sitting here with us and not saying a word.' He turned his big head and stared at me. 'What were you doing there?'

'I can't remember,' I said. 'The crack on the head seems to have blanked me out.'

'We'll help you to remember,' Degarmo said. 'We'll take you up back in the hills a few miles where you can be quiet and look at the stars and remember. You'll remember all right.'

Shorty said: 'That ain't no way to talk, Lieutenant. Why don't we just go back to the Hall and play this the way it says in the rule book?'

'To hell with the rule book,' Degarmo said. 'I like this guy. I want to have one long sweet talk with him. He just needs a little coaxing, Shorty. He's just bashful.'

'I don't want any part of it,' Shorty said.

'What you want to do, Shorty?'

'I want to go back to the Hall.'

'Nobody's stopping you, kid. You want to walk?'

Shorty was silent for a moment. 'That's right,' he said at last, quietly. 'I want to walk.' He opened the car door and stepped out on to the kerbing. 'And I guess you know I have to report all this, Lieutenant?'

'Right,' Degarmo said. 'Tell Webber I was asking for him. Next time he buys a hamburger, tell him to turn down an empty plate for me.'

'That don't make any sense to me,' the small cop said. He slammed the car door shut. Degarmo let the clutch in and gunned the motor and hit forty in the first block and a half. In the third block he hit fifty. He slowed down at the boulevard and turned east and began to cruise along at a legal speed. A few late cars drifted by both ways, but for the most part the world lay in the cold silence of early morning.

After a little while we passed the city limits and Degarmo spoke. 'Let's hear you talk,' he said quietly. 'Maybe we can work this out.'

The car topped a long rise and dipped down to where the boulevard wound through the park-like grounds of the veterans' hospital. The tall triple electroliers had haloes from the beach fog that had drifted in during the night. I began to talk.

'Kingsley came over to my apartment tonight and said he had heard from his wife over the phone. She wanted some money quick. The idea was I was to take it to her and get her out of whatever trouble she was in. My idea was a little different. She was told how to identify me and I was to be at the Peacock Lounge at Eighth and Arguello at fifteen minutes past the hour. Any hour.'

Degarmo said slowly: 'She had to breeze and that meant she had something to breeze from, such as murder.' He lifted his hands lightly and let them fall on the wheel again.

'I went down there, hours after she had called. I had been told her hair was dyed brown. She passed me going out of the bar, but I didn't know her. I had never seen her in the flesh. All I had seen was what looked like a pretty good snapshot, but could be that and still not a very good likeness. She sent a Mexican kid in to call me out. She wanted the money and no conversation. I wanted her story. Finally she saw she would have to talk a little and told me she was at the Granada. She made me wait ten minutes before I followed her over.'

Degarmo said: 'Time to fix up a plant.'

'There was a plant all right, but I'm not sure she was in on it. She didn't want me to come up there, didn't want to talk. Yet she ought to have known I would insist on some explanation before I gave up the money, so her reluctance could have been just an act, to make me feel that I was controlling the situation. She could act all right. I found that out. Anyhow I went and we talked. Nothing she said made very much sense until we talked about Lavery getting shot. Then she made too much sense too quick. I told her I was going to turn her over to the police.'

Westwood Village, dark except for one all-night service station and a few distant windows in apartment houses, slid away to the north of us.

'So she pulled a gun,' I said. 'I think she meant to use it, but she got too close to me and I got a headlock on her. While we were wrestling around, somebody came out from behind a green curtain and slugged me. When I came out of that the murder was done.'

Degarmo said slowly: 'You get any kind of a look at who slugged you?'

'No. I felt or half-saw he was a man and a big one. And this lying on the davenport, mixed in with clothes.' I reached Kingsley's yellow-and-green scarf out of my pocket and draped it over his knee. 'I saw Kingsley wearing this earlier this evening,' I said.

Degarmo looked down at the scarf. He lifted it under the dashlight. 'You wouldn't forget that too quick,' he said. 'It steps right up and smacks you in the eye. Kingsley, huh? Well, I'm damned. What happened then?'

'Knocking on the door. Me still woozy in the head, not too bright and a bit panicked. I had been flooded with gin and my shoes and coat stripped off and maybe I looked and smelled a little like somebody who would yank a woman's clothes off and strangle her. So I got out through the bathroom window, cleaned myself up as well as I could, and the rest you know.'

Degarmo said: 'Why didn't you lie dormy in the place you climbed into?'

'What was the use? I guess even a Bay City cop would have found the way I had gone in a little while. If I had any chance at all, it was to walk out before that was discovered. If nobody was there who knew me, I had a fair chance of getting out of the building.'

'I don't think so,' Degarmo said. 'But I can see where you didn't lose much trying. What's your idea of the motivation here?'

'Why did Kingsley kill her – if he did? That's not hard. She had been cheating on him, making him a lot of trouble, endangering his job and now she had killed a man. Also, she had money and Kingsley wanted to marry another woman. He might have been afraid that with money to spend she could beat the rap and be left laughing at him. If she didn't beat the rap, and got sent up, her money would be just as thoroughly beyond his reach. He'd have to divorce her to get rid of her. There's plenty of motive for murder in all that. Also he saw a chance to make me the goat. It wouldn't stick, but it would make confusion and delay. If murderers didn't think they could get away with their murders, very few would be committed.'

Degarmo said: 'All the same it could be somebody else, somebody who isn't in the picture at all. Even if he went down there to see her, it could still be somebody else. Somebody else could have killed Lavery too.'

'If you like it that way.'

He turned his head. 'I don't like it any way at all. But if I crack the case, I'll get by with a reprimand from the police board. If I don't crack it, I'll be thumbing a ride out of town. You said I was dumb. Okay, I'm dumb. Where does Kingsley live? One thing I know is how to make people talk.'

'Nine-six-five Carson Drive, Beverly Hills. About five blocks on you turn north to the foothills. It's on the left side, just below Sunset. I've never been there, but I know how the block numbers run.'

He handed me the green-and-yellow scarf. 'Tuck that back into your pocket until we want to spring it on him.'

35

It was a two-storeyed white house with a dark roof. Bright moonlight lay against its wall like a fresh coat of paint. There were wrought-iron grilles against the lower halves of the front windows. A level lawn swept up to the front door which was set diagonally into the angle of a jutting wall. All the visible windows were dark.

Degarmo got out of the car and walked along the parkway and looked back along the drive to the garage. He moved down the driveway and the corner of the house hid him. I heard the sound of a garage door going up, then the thud as it was lowered again. He reappeared at the corner of the house, shook his head at me, and walked across the grass to the front door. He leaned his thumb on the bell and juggled a cigarette out of his pocket with one hand and put it between his lips.

He turned away from the door to light it and the flare of the match cut deep lines into his face. After a while there was light on the fan over the door. The peephole in the door swung back. I saw Degarmo holding up his shield. Slowly and as if unwillingly the door was opened. He went in.

He was gone four or five minutes. Light went on behind various windows, then off again. Then he came out of the house and while he was walking back to the car the light went off in the fan and the whole house was again as dark as we had found it.

He stood beside the car smoking and looking off down the curve of the street.

'One small car in the garage,' he said. 'The cook says it's hers. No sign of Kingsley. They say they haven't seen him since this morning. I looked in all the rooms. I guess they told the truth. Webber and a print man were there late this afternoon and the dusting-powder is still all over the main bedroom. Webber would be getting prints to check against what we found in Lavery's house. He didn't tell me what he got. Where would he be – Kingsley?'

'Anywhere,' I said. 'On the road, in an hotel, in a Turkish bath getting the kinks out of his nerves. But we'll have to try his girl friend first. Her name is Fromsett and she lives at the Bryson Tower on Sunset Place. That's away downtown, near Bullock's Wilshire.'

'She does what?' Degarmo asked, getting in under the wheel.

'She holds the fort in his office and holds his hand out of office hours. She's no office cutie, though. She has brains and style.'

'This situation is going to use all she has,' Degarmo said. He drove down to Wilshire and we turned east again.

Twenty-five minutes brought us to the Bryson Tower, a white stucco palace with fretted lanterns in the forecourt and tall date-palms. The entrance was in an L, up marble steps, through a Moorish archway, and over a lobby that was too big and a carpet that was too blue. Blue Ali Baba oil jars were dotted around, big enough to keep tigers in. There was a desk and a night clerk with one of those moustaches that get stuck under your finger-nail.

Degarmo lunged past the desk towards an open elevator beside which a tired old man sat on a stool waiting for a customer. The clerk snapped at Degarmo's back like a terrier.

'One moment, please. Whom did you wish to see?'

Degarmo spun on his heel and looked at me wonderingly. 'Did he say "whom"?'

'Yeah, but don't hit him,' I said. 'There is such a word.'

Degarmo licked his lips. 'I knew there was,' he said. 'I often wondered where they kept it. Look, buddy,' he said to the clerk, 'we want up seven-sixteen. Any objections?'

'Certainly I have,' the clerk said coldly. 'We don't announce guests at' – he lifted his arm and turned it neatly to look at the narrow oblong watch on the inside of his wrist – 'at twenty-three minutes past four in the morning.'

'That's what I thought,' Degarmo said. 'So I wasn't going to bother you. You get the idea?' He took his shield out of his pocket and held it so that the light glinted on the gold and the blue enamel. 'I'm a police lieutenant.'

The clerk shrugged. 'Very well. I hope there isn't going to be any trouble. I'd better announce you then. What names?'

'Lieutenant Degarmo and Mr Marlowe.'

'Apartment 716. That will be Miss Fromsett. One moment.'

He went behind a glass screen and we heard him talking on the phone after a longish pause. He came back and nodded.

'Miss Fromsett is in. She will receive you.'

'That's certainly a load off my mind,' Degarmo said. 'And don't bother to call your house-peeper and send him up to the scatter. I'm allergic to house-peepers.'

The clerk gave a small cold smile and we got into the elevator.

The seventh floor was cool and quiet. The corridor seemed a mile long. We came at last to a door with 716 on it in gilt numbers in a circle of gilt leaves. There was an ivory button beside the door. Degarmo pushed it and chimes rang inside the door and it was opened.

Miss Fromsett wore a quilted blue robe over her pyjamas. On her feet were small tufted slippers with high heels. Her dark hair was fluffed out engagingly and the cold cream had been wiped from her face and just enough make-up applied.

We went past her into a rather narrow room with several handsome oval mirrors and grey period furniture upholstered in blue damask. It didn't look like apartment-house furniture. She sat down on a slender love seat and leaned back and waited calmly for somebody to say something.

I said: 'This is Lieutenant Degarmo of the Bay City police. We're looking for Kingsley. He's not at his house. We thought you might be able to give us an idea where to find him.'

She spoke to me without looking at me. 'Is it that urgent?'

'Yes. Something has happened.'

'What has happened?'

Degarmo said bluntly: 'We just want to know where Kingsley is, sister. We don't have time to build up a scene.'

The girl looked at him with complete absence of expression. She looked back at me and said:

'I think you had better tell me, Mr Marlowe.'

'I went down there with the money,' I said. 'I met her as arranged. I went to her apartment to talk to her. While there I was slugged by a man who was hidden behind a curtain. I didn't see the man. When I came out of it she had been murdered.'

'Murdered?'

I said: 'Murdered.'

She closed her fine eyes and the corners of her lovely mouth drew in. Then she stood up with a quick shrug and went over to a small, marble-topped table with spindly legs. She took a cigarette out of a small embossed silver box and lit it, staring emptily down at the table. The match in her hand was waved more and more slowly until it stopped, still burning, and she dropped it into a tray. She turned and put her back to the table.

'I suppose I ought to scream or something,' she said. 'I don't seem to have any feeling about it at all.'

Degarmo said: 'We don't feel so interested in your feelings right now. What we want to know is where Kingsley is. You can tell us or not tell us. Either way you can skip the attitudes. Just make your mind up.'

She said to me quietly: 'The lieutenant here is a Bay City officer?'

I nodded. She turned at him slowly, with a lovely contemptuous dignity. 'In that case,' she said, 'he has no more right in my apartment than any other loud-mouthed bum that might try to toss his weight around.'

Degarmo looked at her bleakly. He grinned and walked across the room and stretched his long legs from a deep downy chair. He waved his hand at me.

'Okay, you work on her. I can get all the co-operation I need from the L.A. boys, but by the time I had things explained to them, it would be a week from next Tuesday.'

I said: 'Miss Fromsett, if you know where he is, or where he started to go, please tell us. You can understand that he has to be found.'

She said calmly, 'Why?'

Degarmo put his head back and laughed. 'This babe is good,' he said. 'Maybe she thinks we should keep it a secret from him that his wife has been knocked off.'

'She's better than you think,' I told him. His face sobered and he bit his thumb. He looked her up and down insolently.

She said: 'Is it just because he has to be told?'

I took the yellow-and-green scarf out of my pocket and shook it out loose and held it in front of her.

'This was found in the apartment where she was murdered. I think you have seen it.'

She looked at the scarf and she looked at me, and in neither of the glances was there any meaning. She said: 'You ask for a great deal of confidence, Mr Marlowe. Considering that you haven't been such a very smart detective after all.'

'I ask for it,' I said, 'and I expect to get it. And how smart I've been is something you don't really know anything about.'

'This is cute,' Degarmo put it. 'You two make a nice team. All you need is acrobats to follow you. But right now –'

She cut through his voice as if he didn't exist. 'How was she murdered?'

'She was strangled and stripped naked and scratched up.'

'Derry wouldn't have done anything like that,' she said quietly.

Degarmo made a noise with his lips. 'Nobody ever knows what anybody else will do, sister. A cop knows that much.'

She still didn't look at him. In the same level tone she asked: 'Do you want to know where we went after we left your apartment and whether he brought me home – things like that?'

'Yes.'

'Because if he did, he wouldn't have had time to go down to the beach and kill her? Is that it?'

I said, 'That's a good part of it.'

'He didn't bring me home,' she said slowly. 'I took a taxi on Hollywood Boulevard, not more than five minutes after we left your place. I didn't see him again. I supposed he went home.'

Degarmo said: 'Usually the bim tries to give her boy friend a bit more alibi than that. But it takes all kinds, don't it?'

Miss Fromsett said to me: 'He wanted to bring me home, but it was a long way out of his way and we were both tired. The reason I was telling you this is because I know it doesn't matter in the least. If I thought it did, I wouldn't tell you.'

'So he did have time,' I said.

She shook her head. 'I don't know. I don't know how much time was needed. I don't know how he could have known where to go. Not from me, not from her through me. She didn't tell me.' Her dark eyes were on mine, searching, probing. 'Is this the kind of confidence you ask for?'

I folded the scarf up and put it back in my pocket. 'We want to know where he is now.'

'I can't tell you because I have no idea.' Her eyes had followed the scarf down to my pocket. They stayed there. 'You say you were slugged. You mean knocked unconscious?'

'Yes. By somebody who was hidden out behind a curtain. We still fall for it. She pulled a gun on me and I was busy trying to take it away from her. There's no doubt she shot Lavery.'

Degarmo stood up suddenly: 'You're making yourself a nice smooth scene, fellow,' he growled. 'But you're not getting anywhere. Let's blow.'

I said: 'Wait a minute. I'm not finished. Suppose he had something on his mind, Miss Fromsett, something that was eating pretty deep into him. That was how he looked tonight. Suppose he knew more about all this than we realized – or than I realized – and knew things were coming to a head. He would want to go somewhere quietly and try to figure out what to do. Don't you think he might?'

I stopped and waited, looking sideways at Degarmo's impatience. After a moment the girl said tonelessly: 'He wouldn't run away or hide, because it wasn't anything he could run away and hide from. But he might want a time to himself to think.'

'In a strange place, in an hotel,' I said, thinking of the story that had been told me in the Granada. 'Or in a much quieter place than that.'

I looked around for the telephone.

'It's in my bedroom,' Miss Fromsett said, knowing at once what I was looking for.

I went down the room and through the door at the end. Degarmo was right behind me. The bedroom was ivory and ashes of roses. There was a big bed with no footboard and a pillow with the rounded hollow of a head. Toilet articles glistened on a built-in dresser with panelled mirrors on the wall above it. An open door showed mulberry bathroom tiles. The phone was on a night table by the bed.

I sat down on the edge of the bed and patted the place where Miss Fromsett's head had been and lifted the phone and dialled long distance. When the operator answered I asked for Constable Jim Patton at Puma Point, person to person, very urgent. I put the phone back in the cradle and lit a cigarette. Degarmo glowered down at me, standing with his legs apart, tough and tireless and ready to be nasty. 'What now?' he grunted.

'Wait and see.'

'Who's running this show?'

'Your asking me shows that. I am – unless you want the Los Angeles police to run it.'

He scratched a match on his thumb-nail and watched it burn and tried to blow it out with a long steady breath that just bent the flame over. He got rid of that match and put another between his teeth and chewed on it. The phone rang in a moment.

'Ready with your Puma Point call.'

Patton's sleepy voice came on the line. 'Yes? This is Patton at Puma Point.'

'This is Marlowe in Los Angeles,' I said. 'Remember me?'

'Sure I remember you, son. I ain't only half awake though.'

'Do me a favour,' I said. 'Although I don't know why you should. Go or send over to Little Fawn Lake and see if Kingsley is there. Don't let him see you. You can spot his car outside the cabin or maybe see lights. And see that he stays put. Call me back as soon as you know. I'm coming up. Can you do that?'

Patton said: 'I got no reason to stop him if he wants to leave.'

'I'll have a Bay City police officer with me who wants to question him about a murder. Not your murder, another one.'

There was a drumming silence along the wire. Patton said: 'You ain't just bein' tricky, are you, son?'

'No. Call me back at Tunbridge 2722.'

'Should likely take me half an hour,' he said.

I hung up. Degarmo was grinning now. 'This babe flash you a signal I couldn't read?'

I stood up off the bed. 'No. I'm just trying to read his mind. He's no cold killer. Whatever fire there was is all burned out of him by now. I thought he might go to the quietest and most remote place he knows – just to get a grip of himself. In a few hours he'll probably turn himself in. It would look better for you if you got to him before he did that.'

'Unless he puts a slug in his head,' Degarmo said coldly. 'Guys like him are very apt to do that.'

'You can't stop him until you find him.'

'That's right.'

We went back into the living-room. Miss Fromsett poked her head out of her kitchenette and said she was making coffee, and did we want any. We had some coffee and sat around looking like people seeing friends off at the railroad station.

The call from Patton came through in about twenty-five minutes. There was light in the Kingsley cabin and a car was parked beside it.

36

We ate some breakfast at Alhambra and I had the tank filled. We drove out Highway 70 and started moving past the trucks into the rolling ranch country. I was driving. Degarmo sat moodily in the corner, his hands deep in his pockets.

I watched the fat straight rows of orange trees spin by like the spokes of a wheel. I listened to the whine of the tyres on the pavement and I felt tired and stale from lack of sleep and too much emotion.

We reached the long slope south of San Dimas that goes up to a ridge and drops down into Pomona. This is the ultimate end of the fog belt, and the beginning of that semi-desert region where the sun is as light and dry as old sherry in the morning, as hot as a blast furnace at noon, and drops like an angry brick at nightfall.

- Degarmo stuck a match in the corner of his mouth and said almost sneeringly:

'Webber gave me hell last night. He said he was talking to you and what about.'

I said nothing. He looked at me and looked away again. He waved a hand outwards. 'I wouldn't live in this damn country if they gave it to me. The air's stale before it gets up in the morning.'

'We'll be coming to Ontario in a minute. We'll switch over to Foothill Boulevard and you'll see five miles of the finest grevillea trees in the world.'

'I wouldn't know one from a fireplug,' Degarmo said.

We came to the centre of town and turned north on Euclid, along the splendid parkway. Degarmo sneered at the grevillea trees.

After a while he said: 'That was my girl that drowned in the lake up there. I haven't been right in the head since I heard about it. All I can see is red. If I could get my hands on that guy Chess –'

'You made enough trouble,' I said, 'letting her get away with murdering Almore's wife.'

I stared straight ahead through the windshield. I knew his head moved and his eyes froze on me. I didn't know what his hands were doing. I didn't know what expression was on his face. After a long time his words came. They came through tight teeth and edgeways, and they scraped a little as they came out.

'You a little crazy or something?'

'No,' I said. 'Neither are you. You know as well as anybody could know anything that Florence Almore didn't get up out of bed and walk down to that garage. You know she was carried. You know that was why Talley stole her slipper, the slipper that had never walked on a concrete path. You knew that Almore gave his wife a shot in the arm at Condy's place and that it was just enough and not any too much. He knew his shots in the arm the way you know how to rough up a bum that hasn't any money or any place to sleep. You know that Almore didn't murder his wife with morphine and that if he wanted to murder her, morphine would be the last thing in the world he would use. But you know that somebody else did, and that Almore carried her down to the garage and put here there – technically still alive to breathe in some monoxide, but medically just as dead as though she had stopped breathing. You know all that.'

Degarmo said softly: 'Brother, how did you ever manage to live so long?'

I said: 'By not falling for too many gags and not getting too much afraid of professional hard guys. Only a heel would have done what Almore did, only a heel and a badly scared man who had things on his soul that wouldn't stand daylight. Technically he may even have been guilty of murder. I don't think the point has ever been settled. Certainly he would have a hell of a time proving that she was in such a deep coma that she was beyond any possibility of help. But as a practical matter of who killed her, you know the girl killed her.'

Degarmo laughed. It was a grating unpleasant laugh, not only mirthless, but meaningless.

We reached Foothill Boulevard and turned east again. I thought it was still cool, but Degarmo was sweating. He couldn't take his coat off because of the gun under his arm.

I said: 'The girl, Mildred Haviland, was playing house with Almore and his wife knew it. She had threatened him. I got that from her parents.

365

The girl, Mildred Haviland, knew all about morphine and where to get all of it she needed and how much to use. She was alone in the house with Florence Almore, after she put her to bed. She was in a perfect spot to load a needle with four or five grains and shoot it into an unconscious woman through the same puncture Almore had already made. She would die, perhaps while Almore was still out of the house, and he would come home and find her dead. The problem would be his. He would have to solve it. Nobody would believe anybody else had doped his wife to death. Nobody that didn't know all the circumstances. But you knew. I'd have to think you much more of a damn fool than I think you are to believe you didn't know. You covered the girl up. You were in love with her still. You scared her out of town, out of danger, out of reach, but you covered up for her. You let the murder ride. She had you that way. Why did you go up to the mountains looking for her?'

'And how did I know where to look?' he said harshly. 'It wouldn't bother you to add an explanation of that, would it?'

'Not at all,' I said. 'She got sick of Bill Chess and his boozing and his tempers and his down-at-heels living. But she had to have money to make a break. She thought she was safe now, that she had something on Almore that was safe to use. So she wrote him for money. He sent you up to talk to her. She didn't tell Almore what her present name was or any details or where or how she was living. A letter addressed to Mildred Haviland at Puma Point would reach her. All she had to do was ask for it. But no letter came and nobody connected her with Mildred Haviland. All you had was an old photo and your usual bad manners, and they didn't get you anywhere with those people.'

Degarmo said gratingly: 'Who told you she tried to get money from Almore?'

'Nobody. I had to think of something to fit what happened. If Lavery or Mrs Kingsley had known who Muriel Chess had been, and had tipped it off, you would have known where to find her and what name she was using. You didn't know those things. Therefore the lead had to come from the only person up there who knew who she was, and that was herself. So I assume she wrote to Almore.'

'Okay,' he said at last. 'Let's forget it. It doesn't make any difference any more now. If I'm in a jam, that's my business. I'd do it again, in the same circumstances.'

'That's all right,' I said. 'I'm not planning to put the bite on anybody myself. Not even on you. I'm telling you this mostly so you won't try to hang any murders on Kingsley that don't belong to him. If there is one that does, let it hang.'

'Is that why you're telling me?' he asked.

'Yeah.'

'I thought maybe it was because you hated my guts,' he said.

'I'm all done with hating you,' I said. 'It's all washed out of me. I hate people hard, but I don't hate them very long.'

We were going through the grape country now, the open sandy grape country along the scarred flanks of the foothills. We came in a little while to San Bernardino and I kept on through it without stopping.

37

At Crestline, elevation 5,000 feet, it had not yet started to warm up. We stopped for a beer. When we got back into the car, Degarmo took the gun from his under-arm holster and looked it over. It was .38 Smith and Wesson on a .44 frame, a wicked weapon with a kick like a .45 and a much greater effective range.

'You won't need that,' I said. 'He's big and strong, but he's not that kind of tough.'

He put the gun back under his arm and grunted. We didn't talk any more now. We had no more to talk about. We rolled around the curves and along the sharp sheer edges walled with white guard rails and in some places with walls of field stone and heavy iron chains. We climbed through the tall oaks and on to the altitudes where the oaks are not so tall and the pines are taller and taller. We came at last to the dam at the end of Puma Lake.

I stopped the car and the sentry threw his piece across his body and stepped up to the window.

'Close all the windows of your car before proceeding across the dam, please.'

I reached back to wind up the rear window on my side. Degarmo held his shield up. 'Forget it, buddy. I'm a police officer,' he said with his usual tact.

The sentry gave him a solid expressionless stare. 'Close all windows, please,' he said in the same tone he had used before.

'Nuts to you,' Degarmo said. 'Nuts to you, soldier boy.'

'It's an order,' the sentry said. His jaw muscles bulged very slightly. His dull greyish eyes stared at Degarmo. 'And I didn't write the order, mister. Up with the windows.'

'Suppose I told you to go jump in the lake,' Degarmo sneered.

The sentry said: 'I might do it. I scare easily.' He patted the breech of his rifle with a leathery hand.

Degarmo turned and closed the windows on his side. We drove across the dam. There was a sentry in the middle and one at the far end. The first one must have flashed them some kind of signal. They looked at us with steady watchful eyes, without friendliness.

I drove on through the piled masses of granite and down through the meadows of coarse grass where cows grazed. The same gaudy slacks and short shorts and peasant handkerchiefs as yesterday, the same light breeze and golden sun and clear blue sky, the same smell of pine needles, the same cool softness of a mountain summer. But yesterday was a hundred years ago, something crystallized in time, like a fly in amber.

I turned off on the road to Little Fawn Lake and wound around the huge rocks and past the little gurgling waterfall. The gate into Kingsley's property was open and Patton's car was standing in the road pointing towards the lake, which was invisible from that point. There was nobody in it. The card sign on the windshield still read, *'Keep Jim Patton Constable. He Is Too Old To Go To Work.'*

Close to it and pointed the other way was a small battered coupé. Inside the coupé a lion-hunter's hat. I stopped my car behind Patton's and locked it and got out. Andy got out of the coupé and stood staring at us woodenly.

I said: 'This is Lieutenant Degarmo of the Bay City police.'

Andy said: 'Jim's just over the ridge. He's waiting for you. He ain't had any breakfast.'

We walked up the road to the ridge as Andy got back into his coupé. Beyond it the road dropped to the tiny blue lake. Kingsley's cabin across the water seemed to be without life.

'That's the lake,' I said.

Degarmo looked down at it silently. His shoulders moved in a heavy shrug. 'Let's go get the bastard,' was all he said.

We went on and Patton stood up from behind a rock. He was wearing the same old Stetson and khaki pants and shirt buttoned to his thick neck. The star on his left breast still had a bent point. His jaws moved slowly, munching.

'Nice to see you again,' he said, not looking at me, but at Degarmo.

He put his hand out and shook Degarmo's hard paw. 'Last time I seen you, Lieutenant, you was wearing another name. Kind of undercover, I guess you'd call it. I guess I didn't treat you right neither. I apologize. Guess I know who that photo of yours was all the time.'

Degarmo nodded and said nothing.

'Likely if I'd of been on my toes and played the game right, a lot of trouble would have been saved,' Patton said. 'Maybe a life would have been saved. I feel kind of bad about it, but then again I ain't a fellow that feels too bad about anything very long. Suppose we sit down here and you tell me what it is we're supposed to be doing now.'

Degarmo said: 'Kingsley's wife was murdered in Bay City last night. I have to talk to him about it.'

'You mean you suspect him?' Patton asked.

'And how,' Degarmo grunted.

Patton rubbed his neck and looked across the lake. 'He ain't showed outside the cabin at all. Likely he's still asleep. Early this morning I snuck around the cabin. There was a radio goin' then and I heard sounds like a man would make playing with a bottle and a glass. I stayed away from him. Was that right?'

'We'll go over there now,' Degarmo said.

'You got a gun, Lieutenant?'

Degarmo patted under his left arm. Patton looked at me. I shook my head, no gun.

'Kingsley might have one, too,' Patton said. 'I don't hanker after no fast shooting around here, Lieutenant. It wouldn't do me no good to have a gun-fight. We don't have that kind of community up here. You look to me like a fellow who would jack his gun out kind of fast.'

'I've got plenty of swift, if that's what you mean,' Degarmo said: 'But I want this guy talking.'

Patton looked at Degarmo, looked at me, looked back at Degarmo and spat tobacco juice in a long stream to one side.

'I ain't heard enough to even approach him,' he said stubbornly.

So we sat down on the ground and told him the story. He listened silently, not blinking an eye. At the end he said to me: 'You got a funny way of working for people, seems to me. Personally I think you boys are plumb misinformed. We'll go over and see. I'll go in first – in case you would know what you are talking about and Kingsley would have a gun and would be a little desperate. I got a big belly. Makes a nice target.'

We stood up off the ground and started around the lake the long way. When we came to the little pier I said:

'Did they autopsy her yet, sheriff?'

Patton nodded. 'She drowned all right. They say they're satisfied that's how she died. She wasn't knifed or shot or had her head cracked in or anything. There's marks on the body, but too many to mean anything. And it ain't a very nice body to work with.'

Degarmo looked white and angry.

'I guess I oughtn't to have said that, Lieutenant,' Patton added mildly. 'Kind of tough to take. Seeing you knew the lady pretty well.'

Degarmo said: 'Let's get it over and do what we have to do.'

We went on along the shore of the lake and came to Kingsley's cabin. We went up the heavy steps. Patton went quietly across the porch to the door. He tried the screen. It was not hooked. He opened it and tried the door. That was unlocked also. He held the door shut, with the knob turned in his hand, and Degarmo took hold of the screen and pulled it wide. Patton opened the door and we walked into the room.

Derace Kingsley lay back in a deep chair by the cold fireplace with his eyes closed. There was an empty glass and an almost empty whisky bottle on the table beside him. The room smelled of whisky. A dish near the bottle was choked with cigarette-stubs. Two crushed empty packs lay on top of the stubs.

All the windows in the room were shut. It was already close and hot in there. Kingsley was wearing a sweater and his face was flushed and heavy. He snored and his hands hung lax outside the arms of the chair, the finger-tips touching the floor.

Patton moved to within a few feet of him and stood looking silently down at him for a long moment before he spoke.

'Mr Kingsley,' he said then, in a calm, steady voice, 'we got to talk to you a little.'

38

Kingsley moved with a kind of jerk, and opened his eyes and moved them without moving his head. He looked at Patton, then at Degarmo, lastly at me. His eyes were heavy, but the light sharpened in them. He sat up slowly in the chair and rubbed his hands up and down the sides of his face.

'I was asleep,' he said. 'Fell asleep a couple of hours ago. I was as drunk as a skunk, I guess. Anyway, much drunker than I like to be.' He dropped his hands and let them hang.

Patton said: 'This is Lieutenant Degarmo of the Bay City police. He has to talk to you.'

Kingsley looked briefly at Degarmo and his eyes came around to stare at me. His voice when he spoke again sounded sober and quiet and tired to death.

'So you let them get her?' he said.

I said: 'I would have, but I didn't.'

Kingsley thought about that, looking at Degarmo. Patton had left the front door open. He pulled the brown venetian blinds up at two front windows and pulled the windows up. He sat in a chair near one of them and clasped his hands over his stomach. Degarmo stood glowering down at Kingsley.

'Your wife is dead, Kingsley,' he said brutally. 'If it's any news to you.'

Kingsley stared at him and moistened his lips.

'Takes it easy, don't he?' Degarmo said. 'Show him the scarf.'

I took the green-and-yellow scarf out and dangled it. Degarmo jerked a thumb. 'Yours?'

Kingsley nodded. He moistened his lips again.

'Careless of you to leave it behind you,' Degarmo said. He was breathing a little hard. His nose was pinched and deep lines ran from his nostrils to the corners of his mouth.

Kingsley said very quietly: 'Leave it behind me where?' He had barely glanced at the scarf. He hadn't looked at all at me.

'In the Granada Apartments, on Eighth Street, in Bay City. Apartment 618. Am I telling you something?'

Kingsley now very slowly lifted his eyes to meet mine. 'Is that where she was?' he breathed.

I nodded. 'She didn't want me to go there. I wouldn't give her the money until she talked to me. She admitted she killed Lavery. She pulled a gun and planned to give me the same treatment. Somebody came from behind the curtain and knocked me out without letting me see him. When I came to she was dead.' I told him how she was dead and how she looked. I told him what I had done and what had been done to me.

He listened without moving a muscle of his face. When I had done talking he made a vague gesture towards the scarf. 'What has that got to do with it?'

'The lieutenant regards it as evidence that you were the party hidden out in the apartment.'

Kingsley thought that over. He didn't seem to get the implications of it very quickly. He leaned back in the chair and rested his head against the back. 'Go on,' he said at length. 'I suppose you know what you're talking about. I'm quite sure I don't.'

Degarmo said: 'All right, play dumb. See what it gets you. You could begin by accounting for your time last night after you dropped your biddy at her apartment house.'

Kingsley said evenly: 'If you mean Miss Fromsett, I didn't. She went home in a taxi. I was going home myself, but I didn't. I came up here instead. I thought the trip and the night air and the quiet might help me to get straightened out.'

'Just think of that,' Degarmo jeered. 'Straightened out from what, if I might ask?'

'Straightened out from all the worry I had been having.'

'Hell,' Degarmo said, 'a little thing like strangling your wife and clawing her belly wouldn't worry you that much, would it?'

'Son, you hadn't ought to say things like that,' Patton put in from the background. 'That ain't no way to talk. You ain't produced anything yet that sounds like evidence.'

'No?' Degarmo swung his hard head at him. 'What about this scarf, fatty? Isn't that evidence?'

'You didn't fit it in to anything – not that I heard,' Patton said peacefully. 'And I ain't fat, either, just well covered.'

Degarmo swung away from him disgustedly. He jabbed his finger at Kingsley.

'I suppose you didn't go down to Bay City at all?' he said harshly.

'No. Why should I? Marlowe was taking care of that. And I don't see why you are making a point of the scarf. Marlowe was wearing it.'

Degarmo stood rooted and savage. He turned very slowly and gave me his bleak angry stare.

'I don't get this,' he said. 'Honest, I don't. It wouldn't be that somebody is kidding me, would it? Somebody like you?'

I said: 'All I told about the scarf was that it was in the apartment and that I had seen Kingsley wearing it earlier in the evening. That seemed to be all you wanted. I might have added that I had later worn the scarf myself, so the girl I was to meet could identify me that much easier.'

Degarmo backed away from Kingsley and leaned against the wall at the end of the fireplace. He pulled his lower lip out with thumb and forefinger of his left hand. His right hand hung lax at his side, the fingers slightly curved.

I said: 'I told you all I had ever seen of Mrs Kingsley was a snapshot. One of us had to be sure of being able to identify the other. The scarf seemed obvious enough for identification. As a matter of fact I had seen her once before, although I didn't know it when I went to meet her. But

I didn't recognize her at once.' I turned to Kingsley. 'Mrs Fallbrook,' I said.

'I thought you said Mrs Fallbrook was the owner of the house,' he answered slowly.

'That's what she said at the time. That's what I believed at the time. Why wouldn't I?'

Degarmo made a sound in his throat. His eyes were a little crazy. I told him about Mrs Fallbrook and her purple hat and her fluttery manner and the empty gun she had been holding and how she gave it to me.

When I stopped, he said very carefully: 'I didn't hear you tell Webber any of that.'

'I didn't tell him. I didn't want to admit I had already been in the house three hours before. That I had gone to talk it over with Kingsley before I reported it to the police.'

'That's something we're going to love you for,' Degarmo said with a cold grin. 'Jesus, what a sucker I've been. How much you paying this shamus to cover up your murders for you, Kingsley?'

'His usual rates,' Kingsley told him emptily. 'And a five hundred dollar bonus if he can prove my wife didn't murder Lavery.'

'Too bad he can't earn that,' Degarmo sneered.

'Don't be silly,' I said. 'I've already earned it.'

There was a silence in the room. One of those charged silences which seem about to split apart with a peal of thunder. It didn't. It remained, hung heavy and solid, like a wall. Kingsley moved a little in his chair, and after a long moment, he nodded his head.

'Nobody could possibly know that better than you know it, Degarmo,' I said.

Patton had as much expression on his face as a chunk of wood. He watched Degarmo quietly. He didn't look at Kingsley at all. Degarmo looked at a point between my eyes, but not as if that was anything in the room with him. Rather as if he was looking at something very far away, like a mountain across a valley.

After what seemed a very long time, Degarmo said quietly: 'I don't see why. I don't know anything about Kingsley's wife. To the best of my knowledge I never laid eyes on her – until last night.'

He lowered his eyelids a little and watched me broodingly. He knew perfectly well what I was going to say. I said it anyway.

'And you never saw her last night. Because she had already been dead for over a month. Because she had been drowned in Little Fawn Lake. Because the woman you saw dead in the Granada Apartments was Mildred Haviland, and Mildred Haviland was Muriel Chess. And since Mrs Kingsley was dead long before Lavery was shot, it follows that Mrs Kingsley did not shoot him.'

Kingsley clenched his fists on the arms of his chair, but he made no sound, no sound at all.

39

There was another heavy silence. Patton broke it by saying in his careful slow voice: 'That's kind of a wild statement, ain't it? Don't you kind of think Bill Chess would know his own wife?'

I said: 'After a month in the water? With his wife's clothes on her and some of his wife's trinkets? With water-soaked blonde hair like his wife's hair and almost no recognizable face? Why would he even have a doubt about it? She left a note that might be a suicide note. She was gone away. They had quarrelled. Her clothes and car had gone away. During the month she was gone, he had heard nothing from her. He had no idea where she had gone. And then this corpse comes up out of the water with Muriel's clothes on it. A blonde woman about his wife's size. Of course there would be differences and if any substitution had been suspected, they would have been found and checked. But there was no reason to suspect any such thing. Crystal Kingsley was still alive. She had gone off with Lavery. She had left her car in San Bernardino. She had sent a wire to her husband from El Paso. She was all taken care of, so far as Bill Chess was concerned. He had no thoughts about her at all. She didn't enter the picture anywhere for him. Why should she?'

Patton said: 'I ought to of thought of it myself. But if I had, it would

375

be one of those ideas a fellow would throw away almost as quick as he thought of it. It would look too kind of far-fetched.'

'Superficially, yes,' I said. 'But only superficially. Suppose the body had not come up out of the lake for a year, or not at all, unless the lake was dragged for it. Muriel Chess was gone and nobody was going to spend much time looking for her. We might never have heard of her again. Mrs Kingsley was a different proposition. She had money and connexions and an anxious husband. She would be searched for, as she was, eventually. But not very soon, unless something happened to start suspicion. It might have been a matter of months before anything was found out. The lake might have been dragged, but if a search along her trail seemed to indicate that she had actually left the lake and gone down the hill, even as far as San Bernardino, and the train from there, east, then the lake might never have been dragged. And even if it was and the body was found, there was rather better than an even chance that the body would not be correctly identified. Bill Chess was arrested for his wife's murder. For all I know he might even have been convicted of it; and that would have been that, as far as the body in the lake was concerned. Crystal Kingsley would still be missing, and it would be an unsolved mystery. Eventually it would be assumed that something had happened to her and that she was no longer alive. But nobody would know where or when or how it had happened. If it hadn't been for Lavery, we might not be here talking about it now. Lavery is the key to the whole thing. He was in the Prescott Hotel in San Bernardino the night Crystal Kingsley was supposed to have left here. He saw a woman there who had Crystal Kingsley's car, who was wearing Crystal Kingsley's clothes, and of course he knew who she was. But he didn't have to know there was anything wrong. He didn't have to know they were Crystal Kingsley's clothes or that the woman had put Crystal Kingsley's car in the hotel garage. All he had to know was that he met Muriel Chess. Muriel took care of the rest.'

I stopped and waited for somebody to say anything. Nobody did. Patton sat immovable in his chair, his plump, hairless hands clasped comfortably across his stomach. Kingsley leaned his head back and he had his eyes half-closed and he was not moving. Degarmo leaned against the wall by the fireplace, taut and white-faced and cold, a big, hard, solemn man whose thoughts were deeply hidden.

I went on talking.

'If Muriel Chess impersonated Crystal Kingsley, she murdered her. That's elementary. All right, let's look at it. We know who she was and what kind of woman she was. She had already murdered before she met and married Bill Chess. She had been Dr Almore's office nurse and his little pal and she had murdered Dr Almore's wife in such a neat way that Almore had to cover up for her. And she had been married to a man in the Bay City police who also was sucker enough to cover up for her. She got the men that way, she could make them jump through hoops. I didn't know her long enough to see why, but her record proves it. What she was able to do with Lavery proves it. Very well, she killed people who got in her way, and Kingsley's wife got in her way too. I hadn't meant to talk about this, but it doesn't matter much now. Crystal Kingsley could make the men do a little jumping through hoops too. She made Bill Chess jump and Bill Chess's wife wasn't the girl to take that and smile. Also, she was sick to death of her life up here – she must have been – and she wanted to get away. But she needed money. She had tried to get it from Almore, and that sent Degarmo up here looking for her. That scared her a little. Degarmo is the sort of fellow you are never quite sure of. She was right not to be sure of him, wasn't she, Degarmo?'

Degarmo moved his foot on the ground. 'The sands are running against you, fellow,' he said grimly. 'Speak your little piece while you can.'

'Mildred didn't positively have to have Crystal Kingsley's car and clothes and credentials and what not, but they helped. What money she had must have helped a great deal, and Kingsley says she liked to have a good deal of money with her. Also she must have had jewellery which could eventually be turned into money. All this made killing her a rational as well as an agreeable thing to do. That disposes of motive, and we come to means and opportunity.

'The opportunity was made to order for her. She had quarrelled with Bill and he had gone off to get drunk. She knew her Bill and how drunk he could get and how long he would stay away. She needed time. Time was of the essence. She had to assume that there was time. Otherwise the whole thing flopped. She had to pack her own clothes and take them in her car to Coon Lake and hide them there, because they had to be gone. She had to walk back. She had to murder Crystal Kingsley and dress her in Muriel's clothes and get her down in the lake. All that took time. As to the murder itself, I imagine she got her drunk or knocked her on the head and drowned her in the bathtub in this cabin. That would be logic and simple too. She was a nurse, she knew how to handle things like bodies. She knew how to swim – we have it from Bill that she was a fine swimmer. And a drowned body will sink. All she had to do was guide it down into the deep water where she wanted it. There is nothing in all this beyond the powers of one woman who could swim. She did it, she dressed in Crystal Kingsley's clothes, packed what else of hers she wanted, got into Crystal Kingsley's car and departed. And at San Bernardino she ran into her first snag – Lavery.

'Lavery knew her as Muriel Chess. We have no evidence and no reason whatever to assume that he knew her as anything else. He had seen her up here and he was probably on his way up here again when he met her. She wouldn't want that. All he would find would be a locked-up cabin, but he might get talking to Bill and it was part of her plan that Bill should not know positively that she had ever left Little Fawn Lake. So that when, and if, the body was found, he would identify it. So she put her hooks into Lavery at once, and that wouldn't be too hard. If there is one thing we know for certain about Lavery, it is that he couldn't keep his hands off the women. The more of them, the better. He would be easy for a smart girl like Mildred Haviland. So she played him and took him away with her. She took him to El Paso and there sent a wire he knew nothing about. Finally she played him back to Bay City. She probably couldn't help that. He wanted to go home and she couldn't let him get too far from her. Because Lavery was dangerous to her. Lavery alone could destroy all the indications that Crystal Kingsley had actually left Little Fawn Lake. When the search for Crystal Kingsley eventually began, it had to come to Lavery, and at that moment Lavery's life wasn't worth a plugged nickel. His first denials might not be believed, as they were not, but when he opened up with the whole story, that would be believed, because it could be checked. So the search began and immediately Lavery was shot dead in his bathroom, the very night after I went down to talk to him. That's about all there is to it, except why she went back to the house the next morning. That's just one of those things that murderers seem to do. She said he had taken her money, but I don't believe it. I think more likely she got to thinking he had some of his own hidden away, or that she had better edit the job with a cool head and make sure it was all in order and pointing the right way; or perhaps it was just what she said, and to take in the paper and the milk. Anything is possible. She went back and I found her there and she put on an act that left me with both feet in my mouth.'

Patton said: 'Who killed her, son? I gather you don't like Kingsley for that little job.'

I looked at Kingsley and said: 'You didn't talk to her on the phone, you said. What about Miss Fromsett? Did she think she was talking to your wife?'

Kingsley shook his head. 'I doubt it. It would be pretty hard to fool her that way. All she said was that she seemed very changed and subdued. I had no suspicion then. I didn't have any until I got up here. When I walked into this cabin last night, I felt there was something wrong. It was too clean and neat and orderly. Crystal didn't leave things that way. There would have been clothes all over the bedroom, cigarette-stubs all over the house, bottles and glasses all over the kitchen. There would have been unwashed dishes and ants and flies. I thought Bill's wife might have cleaned up, and then I remembered that Bill's wife wouldn't have, not on that particular day. She had been too busy quarrelling with Bill and being murdered, or committing suicide, whichever it was. I thought about all this in a confused sort of way, but I don't claim I actually made anything of it.'

Patton got up from his chair and went out on the porch. He came back wiping his lips with his tan handkerchief. He sat down again, and eased himself over on his left hip, on account of the hip holster on the other side. He looked thoughtfully at Degarmo. Degarmo stood against the wall, hard and rigid, a stone man. His right hand still hung down at his side, with the fingers curled.

Patton said: 'I still ain't heard who killed Muriel. Is that part of the show or is that something that still has to be worked out?'

I said: 'Somebody who thought she needed killing, somebody who had loved her and hated her, somebody who was too much of a cop to let her get away with any more murders, but not enough of a cop to pull her in and let the whole story come out. Somebody like Degarmo.'

40

Degarmo straightened away from the wall and smiled bleakly. His right hand made a hard clean movement and was holding a gun. He held it with a lax wrist, so that it pointed down at the floor in front of him. He spoke to me without looking at me.

'I don't think you have a gun,' he said. 'Patton has a gun but I don't think he can get it out fast enough to do him any good. Maybe you have a little evidence to go with that last guess. Or wouldn't that be important enough for you to bother with?'

'A little evidence,' I said. 'Not very much. But it will grow. Somebody stood behind that green curtain in the Granada for more than half an hour and stood as silently as only a cop on a stake-out knows how to stand. Somebody who had a blackjack. Somebody who knew I had been hit with one without looking at the back of my head. You told Shorty, remember? Somebody who knew the dead girl had been hit with one, too, although it wouldn't have showed and he wouldn't have been likely at that time to have handled the body enough to find out. Somebody who stripped her and raked her body with scratches in the kind of sadistic hate a man like you might feel for a woman who had made a small private hell for him. Somebody who has blood and cuticle under his finger-nails right now, plenty enough for a chemist to work on. I bet you won't let Patton look at the finger-nails of your right hand, Degarmo.'

Degarmo lifted the gun a little and smiled. A wide white smile.

'And just how did I know where to find her?' he asked.

'Almore saw her – coming out of, or going into, Lavery's house. That's what made him so nervous, that's why he called you when he saw me hanging around. As to how exactly you trailed her to the apartment, I don't know. I don't see anything difficult about it. You could have hid out in Almore's house and followed her, or followed Lavery. All that would be routine work for a copper.'

Degarmo nodded and stood silent for a moment, thinking. His face was grim, but his metallic blue eyes held a light that was almost amusement. The room was hot and heavy with a disaster that could no longer be mended. He seemed to feel it less than any of us.

'I want to get out of here,' he said at last. 'Not very far, maybe, but no hick cop is going to put the arm on me. Any objections?'

Patton said quietly: 'Can't be done, son. You know I got to take you. None of this ain't proved, but I can't just let you walk out.'

'You have a nice fat belly, Patton. I'm a good shot. How do you figure to take me?'

'I been trying to figure,' Patton said and rumpled his hair under his pushed-back hat. 'I ain't got very far with it. I don't want no holes in my belly. But I can't let you make a monkey of me in my own territory either.'

'Let him go,' I said. 'He can't get out of these mountains. That's why I brought him up here.'

Patton said soberly: 'Somebody might get hurt taking him. That wouldn't be right. If it's anybody, it's got to be me.'

Degarmo grinned. 'You're a nice boy, Patton,' he said. 'Look, I'll put the gun back under my arm and we'll start from scratch. I'm good enough for that too.'

He tucked the gun under his arm. He stood with his arms hanging, his chin pushed forward a little, watching. Patton chewed softly, with his pale eyes on Degarmo's vivid eyes.

'I'm sitting down,' he complained. 'I ain't as fast as you anyways. I just don't like to look yellow.' He looked at me sadly. 'Why the hell did you have to bring this up here? It ain't any part of my troubles. Now look at the jam I'm in.' He sounded hurt and confused and rather feeble.

Degarmo put his head back a little and laughed. While he was still laughing, his right hand jumped for his gun again.

I didn't see Patton move at all. The room throbbed with the roar of his frontier Colt.

Degarmo's arm shot straight out to one side and the heavy Smith and Wesson was torn out of his hand and thudded against the knotty pine wall behind him. He shook his numbed right hand and looked down at it with wonder in his eyes.

Patton stood up slowly. He walked slowly across the room and kicked the revolver under a chair. He looked at Degarmo sadly. Degarmo was sucking a little blood off his knuckles.

'You give me a break,' Patton said sadly. 'You hadn't ought ever to give a man like me a break. I been a shooter more years than you been alive, son.'

Degarmo nodded to him and straightened his back and started for the door.

'Don't do that,' Patton told him calmly.

Degarmo kept on going. He reached the door and pushed on the screen. He looked back at Patton and his face was very white now.

'I'm going out of here,' he said. 'There's only one way you can stop me. So long, fatty.'

Patton didn't move a muscle.

Degarmo went out through the door. His feet made heavy sounds on the porch and then on the steps. I went to the front window and looked out. Patton still hadn't moved. Degarmo came down off the steps and started across the top of the little dam.

'He's crossing the dam,' I said. 'Has Andy got a gun?'

'I don't figure he'd use one if he had,' Patton said calmly. 'He don't know any reason why he should.'

'Well, I'll be damned,' I said.

Patton sighed. 'He hadn't ought to have given me a break like that,' he said. 'Had me cold. I got to give it back to him. Kind of puny too. Won't do him a lot of good.'

'He's a killer,' I said.

'He ain't that kind of killer,' Patton said. 'You lock your car?'

I nodded. 'Andy's coming down to the other end of the dam,' I said. 'Degarmo has stopped him. He's speaking to him.'

'He'll take Andy's car maybe,' Patton said sadly.

'Well, I'll be damned,' I said again. I looked back at Kingsley. He had his head in his hands and he was staring at the floor. I turned back to the window. Degarmo was out of sight beyond the rise. Andy was half-way across the dam, coming slowly, looking back over his shoulder now and then. The sound of a starting car came distinctly. Andy looked up at the cabin, then turned back and started to run back along the dam.

The sound of the motor died away. When it was quite gone, Patton said: 'Well, I guess we better go back to the office and do some telephoning.'

Kingsley got up suddenly and went out to the kitchen and came back with a bottle of whisky. He poured himself a stiff drink and drank it standing. He waved a hand at it and walked heavily out of the room. I heard bed-springs creak.

Patton and I went quietly out of the cabin.

41

Patton had just finished putting his calls through to block the highways when a call came through from the sergeant in charge of the guard detail at Puma Lake dam. We went out and got into Patton's car and Andy drove very fast along the lake road through the village and along the lake shore back to the big dam at the end. We were waved across the dam to where the sergeant was waiting in a jeep beside the headquarters hut.

The sergeant waved his arm and started the jeep and we followed him a couple of hundred feet along the highway to where a few soldiers stood on the edge of the canyon looking down. Several cars had stopped there and a cluster of people was grouped near the soldiers. The sergeant got out of the jeep and Patton and Andy and I climbed out of the official car and went over by the sergeant.

'Guy didn't stop for the sentry,' the sergeant said, and there was bitterness in his voice. 'Damn near knocked him off the road. The sentry in the middle of the bridge had to jump fast to get missed. The one at this end had enough. He called the guy to halt. Guy kept going.'

The sergeant chewed his gun and looked down into the canyon.

'Orders are to shoot in a case like that,' he said. 'The sentry shot.' He pointed down to the grooves in the shoulder at the edge of the drop. 'This is where he went off.'

A hundred feet down in the canyon a small coupé was smashed against the side of a huge granite boulder. It was almost upside down, leaning a little. There were three men down there. They had moved the car enough to lift something out.

Something that had been a man.

The Little Sister

1

The pebbled glass door panel is lettered in flaked black paint: 'Philip Marlowe . . . Investigations'. It is a reasonably shabby door at the end of a reasonably shabby corridor in the sort of building that was new about the year the all-tile bathroom became the basis of civilization. The door is locked, but next to it is another door with the same legend which is not locked. Come on in – there's nobody in here but me and a big bluebottle fly. But not if you're from Manhattan, Kansas.

It was one of those clear, bright summer mornings we get in the early spring in California before the high fog sets in. The rains are over. The hills are still green and in the valley across the Hollywood hills you can see snow on the high mountains. The fur stores are advertising their annual sales. The call houses that specialize in sixteen-year-old virgins are doing a land-office business. And in Beverly Hills the jacaranda trees are beginning to bloom.

I had been stalking the bluebottle fly for five minutes, waiting for him to sit down. He didn't want to sit down. He just wanted to do wing-overs and sing the prologue to *Pagliacci*. I had the fly swatter poised in mid-air and I was all set. There was a patch of bright sunlight on the corner of the desk and I knew that sooner or later that was where he was going to alight. But when he did I didn't even see him at first. The buzzing stopped and there he was. And then the phone rang.

I reached for it inch by inch with a slow and patient left hand. I lifted the phone slowly and spoke into it softly: 'Hold the line a moment, please.'

I laid the phone down gently on the brown blotter. He was still there, shining and blue-green and full of sin. I took a deep breath and swung. What was left of him sailed half-way across the room and dropped to the carpet. I went over and picked him up by his good wing and dropped him into the waste-basket.

'Thanks for waiting,' I said into the phone.

'Is this Mr Marlowe, the detective?' It was a small, rather hurried, little-girlish voice. I said it was Mr Marlowe, the detective. 'How much do you charge for your services, Mr Marlowe?'

'What was it you wanted done?'

The voice sharped a little. 'I can't very well tell you over the phone. It's – it's very confidential. Before I'd waste time coming to your office I'd have to have some idea –'

'Forty bucks a day and expenses. Unless it's the kind of job that can be done for a flat fee.'

'That's far too much,' the little voice said. 'Why, it might cost hundreds of dollars and I only get a small salary and –'

'Where are you now?'

'Why, I'm in a drug store. It's right next to the building where your office is.'

'You could have saved a nickel. The elevator's free.'

'I – I beg your pardon?'

I said it all over again. 'Come on up and let's have a look at you,' I added. 'If you're in my kind of trouble, I can give you a pretty good idea –'

'I have to know something about you,' the small voice said very firmly. 'This is a very delicate matter, very personal. I couldn't talk to just anybody.'

'If it's that delicate,' I said, 'maybe you need a lady detective.'

'Goodness, I didn't know there were any.' Pause. 'But I don't think a lady detective would do at all. You see, Orrin was living in a very tough neighbourhood, Mr Marlowe. At least I thought it was tough. The manager of the rooming house is a most unpleasant person. He smelled of liquor. Do you drink, Mr Marlowe?'

'Well, now that you mention it –'

'I don't think I'd care to employ a detective that uses liquor in any form. I don't even approve of tobacco.'

'Would it be all right if I peeled an orange?'

I caught the sharp intake of breath at the far end of the line. 'You might at least talk like a gentleman,' she said.

'Better try the University Club,' I told her. 'I heard they had a couple left over there, but I'm not sure they'll let you handle them.' I hung up.

It was a step in the right direction, but it didn't go far enough. I ought to have locked the door and hid under the desk.

2

Five minutes later the buzzer sounded on the outer door of the half-office I use for a reception room. I heard the door close again. Then I didn't hear anything more. The door between me and there was half open. I listened and decided somebody had just looked in at the wrong office and left without entering. Then there was a small knocking on wood. Then the kind of cough you use for the same purpose. I got my feet off the desk, stood up and looked out. There she was. She didn't have to open her mouth for me to know who she was. And nobody ever looked less like Lady Macbeth. She was a small, neat, rather prissy-looking girl with primly smooth brown hair and rimless glasses. She was wearing a brown tailor-made and from a strap over her shoulder hung one of those awkward-looking square bags that make you think of a Sister of Mercy taking first aid to the wounded. On the smooth brown hair was a hat that had been taken from its mother too young. She had no make-up, no lipstick, and no jewellery. The rimless glasses gave her that librarian's look.

'That's no way to talk to people over the telephone,' she said sharply. 'You ought to be ashamed of yourself.'

'I'm just too proud to show it,' I said. 'Come on in.' I held the door for her. Then I held the chair for her.

She sat down on about two inches of the edge. 'If I talked like that to one of Dr Zugsmith's patients,' she said, 'I'd lose my position. He's most particular how I speak to the patients – even the difficult ones.'

'How is the old boy? I haven't seen him since that time I fell off the garage roof.'

She looked surprised and quite serious. 'Why surely you can't know Dr Zugsmith.' The tip of a rather anaemic tongue came out between her lips and searched furtively for nothing.

'I know a Dr George Zugsmith,' I said, 'in Santa Rosa.'

'Oh no. This is Dr Alfred Zugsmith, in Manhattan. Manhattan, Kansas, you know, not Manhattan, New York.'

'Must be a different Dr Zugsmith,' I said. 'And your name?'

'I'm not sure I'd care to tell you.'

'Just window shopping, huh?'

'I suppose you could call it that. If I have to tell my family affairs to a total stranger, I at least have the right to decide whether he's the kind of person I could trust.'

'Anybody ever tell you you're a cute little trick?'

The eyes behind the rimless cheaters flashed. 'I should hope not.'

I reached for a pipe and started to fill it. 'Hope isn't exactly the word,' I said. 'Get rid of that hat and get yourself a pair of those slinky glasses with coloured rims. You know, the ones that are all cockeyed and oriental –'

'Dr Zugsmith wouldn't permit anything like that,' she said quickly. Then, 'Do you really think so?' she asked, and blushed ever so slightly.

I put a match to the pipe and puffed smoke across the desk. She winced back.

'If you hire me,' I said, 'I'm the guy you hire. Me. Just as I am. If you think you're going to find any lay readers in this business, you're crazy. I hung up on you, but you came up here all the same. So you need help. What's your name and trouble?'

She just stared at me.

'Look,' I said. 'You come from Manhattan, Kansas. The last time I memorized the *World Almanac* that was a little town not far from Topeka. Population around twelve thousand. You work for Dr Alfred Zugsmith and you're looking for somebody named Orrin. Manhattan is a small town. It has to be. Only half a dozen places in Kansas are anything else.

I already have enough information about you to find out your whole family history.'

'But why should you want to?' she asked, troubled.

'Me?' I said. 'I don't want to. I'm fed up with people telling me histories. I'm just sitting here because I don't have any place to go. I don't want to work. I don't want anything.'

'You talk too much.'

'Yes,' I said, 'I talk too much. Lonely men always talk too much. Either that or they don't talk at all. Shall we get down to business? You don't look like the type that goes to see private detectives, and especially private detectives you don't know.'

'I know that,' she said quietly. 'And Orrin would be absolutely livid. Mother would be furious too. I just picked your name out of the phone book –'

'What principle?' I asked. 'And with the eyes closed or open?'

She stared at me for a moment as if I were some kind of freak. 'Seven and thirteen,' she said quietly.

'How?'

'Marlowe has seven letters,' she said, 'and Philip Marlowe has thirteen. Seven together with thirteen –'

'What's *your* name?' I almost snarled.

'Orfamay Quest.' She crinkled her eyes as if she could cry. She spelled the first name out for me, all one word. 'I live with my mother,' she went on, her voice getting rapid now as if my time was costing her. 'My father died four years ago. He was a doctor. My brother Orrin was going to be a surgeon, too, but he changed into engineering after two years of medical. Then a year ago Orrin came out to work for the Cal-Western Aircraft Company in Bay City. He didn't have to. He had a good job in Wichita. I guess he just sort of wanted to come out here to California. Most everybody does.'

'Almost everybody,' I said. 'If you're going to wear those rimless glasses, you might at least try to live up to them.'

She giggled and drew a line along the desk with her fingertip, looking down. 'Did you mean those slanting kind of glasses that make you look kind of oriental?'

'Uh-huh. Now about Orrin. We've got him to California, and we've got him to Bay City. What do we do with him?'

She thought a moment and frowned. Then she studied my face as if making up her mind. Then her words came with a burst: 'It wasn't like Orrin not to write to us regularly. He only wrote twice to mother and three times to me in the last six months. And the last letter was several months ago. Mother and I got worried. So it was my vacation and I came out to see him. He'd never been away from Kansas before.' She stopped. 'Aren't you going to take any notes?' she asked.

I grunted.

'I thought detectives always wrote things down in little note-books.'

'I'll make the gags,' I said. 'You tell the story. You came out on your vacation. Then what?'

'I'd written to Orrin that I was coming but I didn't get any answer. Then I sent a wire to him from Salt Lake City but he didn't answer that either. So all I could do was go down where he lived. It's an awful long way. I went in a bus. It's in Bay City. No. 449 Idaho Street.'

She stopped again, then repeated the address, and I still didn't write it down. I just sat there looking at her glasses and her smooth brown hair and the silly little hat and the finger-nails with no colour and her mouth with no lipstick and the tip of the little tongue that came and went between the pale lips.

'Maybe you don't know Bay City, Mr Marlowe.'

'Ha,' I said. 'All I know about Bay City is that every time I go there I have to buy a new head. You want me to finish your story for you?'

'Wha-a-at?' Her eyes opened so wide that the glasses made them look like something you see in the deep-sea fish tanks.

'He's moved,' I said. 'And you don't know where he's moved to. And you're afraid he's living a life of sin in a penthouse on top of the Regency Towers with something in a long mink coat and an interesting perfume.'

'Well, for goodness' sakes!'

'Or am I being coarse?' I asked.

'Please, Mr Marlowe,' she said at last, 'I don't think anything of the sort about Orrin. And if Orrin heard you say that you'd be sorry. He can be awfully mean. But I know something has happened. It was just a cheap rooming house, and I didn't like the manager at all. A horrid kind of man. He said Orrin had moved away a couple of weeks before and he didn't know where to and he didn't care, and all he wanted was a good slug of gin. I don't know why Orrin would even live in a place like that.'

'Did you say slug of gin?' I asked.

She blushed. 'That's what the manager said. I'm just telling you.'

'All right,' I said. 'Go on.'

'Well, I called the place where he worked. The Cal-Western Company, you know. And they said he'd been laid off like a lot of others and that was all they knew. So then I went to the Post Office and asked if Orrin had put in a change of address to anywhere. And they said they couldn't give me any information. It was against the regulations. So I told them how it was and the man said, well if I was his sister he'd go look. So he went and looked and came back and said no. Orrin hadn't put in any change of address. So then I began to get a little frightened. He might have had an accident or something.'

'Did it occur to you to ask the police about that?'

'I wouldn't dare ask the police. Orrin would never forgive me. He's difficult enough at the best of times. Our family –' She hesitated and there was something behind her eyes she tried not to have there. So she went on breathlessly: 'Our family's not the kind of family –'

'Look,' I said wearily, 'I'm not talking about the guy lifting a wallet. I'm talking about him getting knocked down by a car and losing his memory or being too badly hurt to talk.'

She gave me a level look which was not too admiring. 'If it was anything like that, we'd know,' she said. 'Everybody has things in their pockets to tell who they are.'

'Sometimes all they have left is the pockets.'

'Are you trying to scare me, Mr Marlowe?'

'If I am, I'm certainly getting nowhere fast. Just what do you think might have happened?'

She put her slim forefinger to her lips and touched it very carefully with the tip of that tongue. 'I guess if I knew that I wouldn't have to come and see you. How much would you charge to find him?'

I didn't answer for a long moment, then I said: 'You mean alone, without telling anybody?'

'Yes. I mean alone, without telling anybody.'

'Uh-huh. Well, that depends. I told you what my rates were.'

She clasped her hands on the edge of the desk and squeezed them together hard. She had about the most meaningless set of gestures I had ever laid eyes on. 'I thought you being a detective and all you could find him right away,' she said. 'I couldn't possibly afford more than twenty dollars. I've got to buy my meals here and my hotel and the train going back and you know the hotel is so terribly expensive and the food on the train –'

'Which one are you staying at?'

'I – I'd rather not tell you, if you don't mind.'

'Why?'

'I'd just rather not. I'm terribly afraid of Orrin's temper. And, well, I can always call you up, can't I?'

'Uh-huh. Just what is it you're scared of, besides Orrin's temper, Miss Quest?' I had let my pipe go out. I struck a match and held it to the bowl, watching her over it.

'Isn't pipe smoking a very dirty habit?' she asked.

'Probably,' I said. 'But it would take more than twenty bucks to have me drop it. And don't try to side-step my questions.'

'You can't talk to me like that,' she flared up. 'Pipe smoking *is* a dirty habit. Mother never let father smoke in the house, even the last two years after he had his stroke. He used to sit with that empty pipe in his mouth sometimes. But she didn't like him to do that really. We owed a lot of money too and she said she couldn't afford to give him money for useless things like tobacco. The church needed it much more than he did.'

'I'm beginning to get it,' I said slowly. 'Take a family like yours and somebody in it has to be the dark meat.'

She stood up sharply and clasped the first aid kit to her body. 'I don't like you,' she said. 'I don't think I'm going to employ you. If you're insinuating that Orrin has done something wrong, well, I can assure you that it's not Orrin who's the black sheep of our family.'

I didn't move an eyelash. She swung around and marched to the door and put her hand on the knob and then she swung around again and marched back and suddenly began to cry. I reacted to that just the way a stuffed fish reacts to cut bait. She got out her little handkerchief and tickled the corners of her eyes.

'And now I suppose you'll call the p-police,' she said with a catch in her voice. 'And the Manhattan p-paper will hear all about it and they'll print something n-nasty about us.'

'You don't suppose anything of the sort. Stop chipping at my emotions. Let's see a photo of him.'

She put the handkerchief away in a hurry and dug something else out of her bag. She passed it across the desk. An envelope. Thin, but there could be a couple of snapshots in it. I didn't look inside.

'Describe him the way you see him,' I said.

She concentrated. That gave her a chance to do something with her eyebrows. 'He was twenty-eight years old last March. He has light brown hair, much lighter than mine, and lighter blue eyes, and he brushes his hair straight back. He's very tall, over six feet. But he only weighs about a hundred and forty pounds. He's sort of bony. He used to wear a little blond moustache but mother made him cut it off. She said –'

'Don't tell me. The minister needed it to stuff a cushion.'

'You can't talk like that about my mother,' she yelped, getting pale with rage.

'Oh, stop being silly. There's a lot of things about you I don't know. But you can stop pretending to be an Easter lily right now. Does Orrin have any distinguishing marks on him, like moles or scars, or a tattoo of the Twenty-third Psalm on his chest? And don't bother to blush.'

'Well, you don't have to yell at me. Why don't you look at the photograph?'

'He probably has his clothes on. After all, you're his sister. You ought to know.'

'No, he hasn't,' she said tightly. 'He has a little scar on his left hand where he had a wen removed.'

'What about his habits? What does he do for fun – besides not smoking or drinking or going out with girls?'

'Why – how did you know that?'

'Your mother told me.'

She smiled. I was beginning to wonder if she had one in her. She had very even white teeth and she didn't wave her gums. That was something. 'Aren't you silly,' she said. 'He studies a lot and he has a very expensive camera he likes to snap people with when they don't know. Sometimes it makes them mad. But Orrin says people ought to see themselves as they really are.'

'Let's hope it never happens to him,' I said. 'What kind of camera is it?'

'One of those little cameras with a very fine lens. You can take snaps in almost any kind of light. A Leica.'

I opened the envelope and took out a couple of small prints, very clear. 'These weren't taken with anything like that,' I said.

'Oh no. Philip took those, Philip Anderson. A boy I was going with for a while.' She paused and sighed. 'And I guess that's really why I came here, Mr Marlowe. Just because your name's Philip too.'

I just said: 'Uh-huh,' but I felt touched in some vague sort of way. 'What happened to Philip Anderson?'

'But it's about Orrin – '

'I know,' I interrupted. 'But what happened to Philip Anderson?'

'He's still there in Manhattan.' She looked away. 'Mother doesn't like him very much. I guess you know how it is.'

'Yes,' I said, 'I know how it is. You can cry if you want to. I won't hold it against you. I'm just a big soft slob myself.'

I looked at the two prints. One of them was looking down and was no good to me. The other was a fairly good shot of a tall angular bird with narrow-set eyes and a thin straight mouth and a pointed chin. He had the expression I expected to see. If you forgot to wipe the mud off your shoes, he was the boy who would tell you. I laid the photos aside and looked at Orfamay Quest, trying to find something in her face even remotely like his. I couldn't. Not the slightest trace of family resemblance, which of course means absolutely nothing. It never has.

'All right,' I said. 'I'll go down there and take a look. But you ought to be able to guess what's happened. He's in a strange city. He's making good money for a while. More than he's ever made in his life, perhaps. He's meeting a kind of people he never met before. And it's not the kind of town – believe me it isn't, I know Bay City – that Manhattan, Kansas, is. So he just broke training and he doesn't want his family to know about it. He'll straighten out.'

She just stared at me for a moment in silence, then she shook her head. 'No. Orrin's not the type to do that, Mr Marlowe.'

'Anyone is,' I said. 'Especially a fellow like Orrin. The small-town sanctimonious type of guy who's lived his entire life with his mother on his neck and the minister holding his hand. Out here he's lonely. He's got dough. He'd like to buy a little sweetness and light, and not the kind that comes through the east window of a church. Not that I have anything against that. I mean he already had enough of that, didn't he?'

She nodded her head silently.

'So he starts to play,' I went on, 'and he doesn't know how to play. That takes experience too. He's got himself all jammed up with some floozy and a bottle of hooch and what he's done looks to him as if he'd stolen the bishop's pants. After all, the guy's going on twenty-nine years old and if he wants to roll in the gutter that's his business. He'll find somebody to blame it on after a while.'

'I hate to believe you, Mr Marlowe,' she said slowly. 'I'd hate for mother –'

'Something was said about twenty dollars,' I cut in.

She looked shocked. 'Do I have to pay you now?'

'What would be the custom in Manhattan, Kansas?'

'We don't have any private detectives in Manhattan. Just the regular police. That is, I don't think we do.'

She probed in the inside of her tool kit again and dragged out a red change purse and from that she took a number of bills, all neatly folded and separate. Three fives and five ones. There didn't seem to be much left. She kind of held the purse so I could see how empty it was. Then she straightened the bills out on the desk and put one on top of the other and pushed them across. Very slowly, very sadly, as if she was drowning a favourite kitten.

'I'll give you a receipt,' I said.

'I don't need a receipt, Mr Marlowe.'

'I do. You won't give me your name and address, so I want something with your name on it.'

'What for?'

'To show I'm representing you.' I got the receipt book out and made the receipt and held the book for her to sign the duplicate. She didn't want to. After a moment reluctantly she took the hard pencil and wrote

'Orfamay Quest' in a neat secretary's writing across the face of the duplicate.

'Still no address?' I asked.

'I'd rather not.'

'Call me any time then. My home number is in the phone book, too. Bristol Apartments, Apartment 428.'

'I shan't be very likely to visit you,' she said coldly.

'I haven't asked you yet,' I said. 'Call me around four if you like. I might have something. And then again I might not.'

She stood up. 'I hope mother won't think I've done wrong,' she said, picking at her lip now with the pale finger-nail. 'Coming here, I mean.'

'Just don't tell me any more of the things your mother won't like,' I said. 'Just leave that part out.'

'Well, really!'

'And stop saying "Well, really".'

'I think you are a very offensive person,' she said.

'No, you don't. You think I'm cute. And I think you're a fascinating little liar. You don't think I'm doing this for any twenty bucks, do you?'

She gave me a level, suddenly cool stare. 'Then why?' Then when I didn't answer she added, 'Because spring is in the air?'

I still didn't answer. She blushed a little. Then she giggled.

I didn't have the heart to tell her I was just plain bored with doing nothing. Perhaps it *was* the spring too. And something in her eyes that was much older than Manhattan, Kansas.

'I think you're very nice – really,' she said softly. Then she turned quickly and almost ran out of the office. Her steps along the corridor outside made tiny, sharp, pecky sounds, kind of like mother drumming on the edge of the dinner table when father tried to promote himself a second piece of pie. And him with no money any more. No nothing. Just sitting in a rocker on the front porch back there in Manhattan, Kansas, with his empty pipe in his mouth. Rocking on the front porch, slow and easy, because when you've had a stroke you have to take it slow and easy. And wait for the next one. And the empty pipe in his mouth. No tobacco. Nothing to do but wait.

I put Orfamay Quest's twenty hard-earned dollars in an envelope and wrote her name on it and dropped it in the desk drawer. I didn't like the idea of running around loose with that much currency on me.

3

You could know Bay City a long time without knowing Idaho Street. And you could know a lot of Idaho Street without knowing No. 449. The block in front of it had a broken paving that had almost gone back to dirt. The warped fence of a lumberyard bordered the cracked sidewalk on the opposite side of the street. Half-way up the block the rusted rails of a spur track turned into a pair of high, chained wooden gates that seemed not to have been opened for twenty years. Little boys with chalk had been writing and drawing pictures on the gates and all along the fence.

No. 449 had a shallow, paintless front porch on which five wood and cane rockers loafed dissolutely, held together with wire and the moisture of the beach air. The green shades over the lower windows of the house were two-thirds down and full of cracks. Besides the front door there was a large printed sign 'No Vacancies'. That had been there a long time too. It had got faded and fly-specked. The door opened on a long hall from which stairs went up a third of the way back. To the right there was a narrow shelf with a chained, indelible pencil hanging beside it. There was a push button and a yellow and black sign above which read 'Manager', and was held up by three thumbtacks no two of which matched. There was a pay phone on the opposite wall.

I pushed the bell. It rang somewhere nearby but nothing happened. I rang it again. The same nothing happened. I prowled along to a door with a black and white metal sign on it – 'Manager'. I knocked on that. Then I kicked it. Nobody seemed to mind my kicking it.

I went back out of the house and down around the side where a narrow concrete walk led to the service entrance. It looked as if it was in the right place to belong to the manager's apartment. The rest of the house would be just rooms. There was a dirty garbage pail on the small porch and a wooden box full of liquor bottles. Behind the screen the back door of the house was open. It was gloomy inside. I put my face against the screen and peered in. Through the open inner door beyond the service porch I could see a straight chair with a man's coat hanging over it and in the chair a man in shirt-sleeves with his hat on. He was a small man. I couldn't see what he was doing, but he seemed to be sitting at the end of the built-in breakfast table in the breakfast nook.

I banged on the screen door. The man paid no attention. I banged again, harder. This time he tilted his chair back and showed me a small pale face with a cigarette in it. 'Whatcha want?' he barked.

'Manager.'

'Not in, Bub.'

'Who are you?'

'What's it to you?'

'I want a room.'

'No vacancies, Bub. Can't you read large print?'

'I happen to have different information,' I said.

'Yeah?' He shook ash from his cigarette by flicking it with a nail without removing it from his small said mouth. 'Go fry your head in it.'

He tilted his chair forward again and went on doing whatever it was he was doing.

I made noise getting down off the porch and none whatever coming back up on it. I felt the screen door carefully. It was hooked. With the open blade of a penknife I lifted the hook and eased it out of the eye. It made a small tinkle but louder tinkling sounds were being made beyond, in the kitchen.

I stepped into the house, crossed the service porch, went through the door into the kitchen. The little man was too busy to notice me. The kitchen had a three-burner gas stove, a few shelves of greasy dishes, a chipped icebox and the breakfast nook. The table in the breakfast nook was covered with money. Most of it was paper, but there was silver also, in all sizes up to dollars. The little man was counting and stacking it and making entries in a small book. He wetted his pencil without bothering the cigarette that lived in his face.

There must have been several hundred dollars on that table.

'Rent day?' I asked genially.

The small man turned very suddenly. For a moment he smiled and said nothing. It was the smile of a man whose mind is not smiling. He removed the stub of cigarette from his mouth, dropped it on the floor and stepped on it. He reached a fresh one out of his shirt and put it in the same hole in his face and started fumbling for a match.

'You came in nice,' he said pleasantly.

Finding no match, he turned casually in his chair and reached into a pocket of his coat. Something heavy knocked against the wood of the chair. I got hold of his wrist before the heavy thing came out of the pocket. He threw his weight backwards and the pocket of the coat started to lift towards me. I yanked the chair out from under him.

He sat down hard on the floor and knocked his head against the end of the breakfast table. That didn't keep him from trying to kick me in the groin. I stepped back with his coat and took a .38 out of the pocket he had been playing with.

'Don't sit on the floor just to be chummy,' I said. He got up slowly, pretending to be groggier than he was. His hand fumbled at the back of his collar and light winked on metal as his arm swept towards me. He was a game little rooster. I side-swiped his jaw with his own gun and he sat down on the floor again. I stepped on the hand that held the knife. His face twisted with pain but he didn't make a sound. So I kicked the knife into a corner. It was a long thin knife and it looked very sharp.

'You ought to be ashamed of yourself,' I said. 'Pulling guns and knives on people that are just looking for a place to live. Even for these times that's out of line.'

He held his hurt hand between his knees and squeezed it and began to whistle through his teeth. The slap on the jaw didn't seem to have hurt him. 'Okay,' he said, 'Okay. I ain't supposed to be perfect. Take the dough and beat it. But don't ever think we won't catch up with you.'

I looked at the collection of small bills and medium bills and silver on the table. 'You must meet a lot of sales resistance, the weapons you carry,' I told him. I walked across to the inner door and tried it. It was not locked. I turned back.

'I'll leave your gun in the mailbox,' I said. 'Next time ask to see the buzzer.'

He was still whistling gently between his teeth and holding his hand. He gave me a narrow, thoughtful eye, then shovelled the money into a shabby brief-case and slipped its catch. He took his hat off, straightened it around, put it back jauntily on the back of his head and gave me a quiet efficient smile.

'Never mind about the heater,' he said. 'The town's full of old iron. But you could leave the skiv with Clausen. I've done quite a bit of work on it to get it in shape.'

'And with it?' I said.

'Could be.' He flicked a finger at me airily. 'Maybe we meet again some day soon. When I got a friend with me.'

'Tell him to wear a clean shirt,' I said. 'And lend you one.'

'My, my,' the little man said chidingly. 'How tough we get how quick once we get that badge pinned on.'

He went softly past me and down the wooden steps from the back porch. His footsteps tapped to the street and faded.

They sounded very much like Orfamay's heels clicking along the corridor in my office building. And for some reason I had that empty feeling of having miscounted the trumps. No reason for it at all. Maybe it was the steely quality about the little man. No whimper, no bluster, just the smile, the whistling between the teeth, the light voice and the unforgetting eyes.

I went over and picked up the knife. The blade was long and round and thin, like a rat-tailed file that has been ground smooth. The handle and guard were lightweight plastic and seemed all one piece. I held the knife by the handle and gave it a quick flip at the table. The blade came loose and quivered in the wood.

I took a deep breath and slid the handle down over the end again and worked the blade loose from the table. A curious knife, with design and purpose in it, and neither of them agreeable.

I opened the door beyond the kitchen and went through it with the gun and knife in one hand.

It was a wall-bed living-room, with the wall-bed down and rumpled. There was an overstuffed chair with a hole burnt in the arm. A high oak desk with tilted doors like old-fashioned cellar doors stood against the wall by the front window. Near this there was a studio couch and on the studio couch lay a man. His feet hung over the end of the couch in knobby grey socks. His head had missed the pillow by two feet. It was nothing much to miss from the colour of the slip on it. The upper part of him was contained in a colourless shirt and a thread-bare grey coat-sweater. His mouth was open and his face was shining with sweat and he breathed like an old Ford with a leaky head gasket. On a table beside him was a plate full of cigarette stubs, some of which had a home-made look. On the floor a near-full gin bottle and a cup that seemed to have contained coffee but not at all recently. The room was full mostly of gin and bad air, but there was also a reminiscence of marijuana smoke.

I opened a window and leaned my forehead against the screen to get a little cleaner air into my lungs and looked out into the street. Two kids were wheeling bicycles along the lumberyard fence, stopping from time to time to study the examples of rest-room art on the boarding. Nothing else moved in the neighbourhood. Not even a dog. Down at the corner was dust in the air as though a car had passed that way.

I went over to the desk. Inside it was the house register, so I leafed back until I came to the name 'Orrin P. Quest', written in a sharp meticulous handwriting, and the number 214 added in pencil by another hand that was by no means sharp or meticulous. I followed on through to the end of the register but found no new registration for Room 214. A party named G. W. Hicks had Room 215. I shut the register in the desk and crossed to the couch. The man stopped his snoring and bubbling and threw his right arm across his body as if he thought he was making a speech. I leaned down and gripped his nose tight between my first and second fingers and stuffed a handful of his sweater into his mouth. He stopped snoring and jerked his eyes open. They were glazed and blood-shot. He struggled against my hand. When I was sure he was fully awake I let go of him, picked the bottle full of gin off the floor and poured some into a glass that lay on its side near the bottle. I showed the glass to the man.

His hand came out to it with the beautiful anxiety of a mother welcoming a lost child.

I moved it out of his reach and said: 'You the manager?'

He licked his lips stickily and said: 'Gr-r-r-r'.

He made a grab for the glass. I put it on the table in front of him. He grasped it carefully in both hands and poured the gin into his face. Then he laughed heartily and threw the glass at me. I managed to catch it and up-end it on the table again. The man looked me over with a studied but unsuccessful attempt at sternness.

'What gives?' he croaked in an annoyed tone.

'Manager?'

He nodded and almost fell off the couch. 'Must be I'm drunky,' he said. 'Kind of a bit of a little bit drunky.'

'You're not bad,' I said. 'You're still breathing.'

He put his feet on the ground and pushed himself upright. He cackled with sudden amusement, took three uneven steps, went down on his hands and knees and tried to bite the leg of a chair.

I pulled him up on his feet again, set him down in the over-stuffed chair with the burned arm and poured him another slug of his medicine. He drank it, shuddered violently and all at once his eyes seemed to get sane and cunning. Drunks of his type have a certain balanced moment of reality. You never know when it will come or how long it will last.

'Who the hell are you?' he growled.

'I'm looking for a man named Orrin P. Quest.'

'Huh?'

I said it again. He smeared his face with his hands and said tersely: 'Moved away.'

'Moved away when?'

He waved his hand, almost fell out of his chair and waved it again the other way to restore his balance. 'Gimme a drink,' he said.

I poured another slug of the gin and held it out of his reach.

'Gimme,' the man said urgently. 'I'm not happy.'

'All I want is the present address of Orrin P. Quest.'

'Just think of that,' he said wittily and made a loose pass at the glass I was holding.

I put the glass down on the floor and got one of my business cards out for him. 'This might help you to concentrate,' I told him.

He peered at the card closely, sneered, bent it in half and bent it again.

He held it on the flat of his hand, spat on it, and tossed it over his shoulder.

I handed him the glass of gin. He drank it to my health, nodded solemnly, and threw the glass over his shoulder too. It rolled along the floor and thumped the baseboard. The man stood up with surprising ease, jerked a thumb towards the ceiling, doubled the fingers of his hand under it and made a sharp noise with his tongue and teeth.

'Beat it,' he said. 'I got friends.' He looked at the telephone on the wall and back at me with cunning. 'A couple of boys to take care of you,' he sneered. I said nothing. 'Don't believe me, huh?' he snarled, suddenly angry. I shook my head.

He started for the telephone, clawed the receiver off the hook, and dialled the five digits of a number. I watched him. One-three-five-seven-two.

That took all he had for the time being. He let the receiver fall and bang against the wall and he sat down on the floor beside it. He put it to his ear and growled at the wall: 'Lemme talk to the Doc.' I listened silently. 'Vince! The Doc!' he shouted angrily. He shook the receiver and threw it away from him. He put his hands down on the floor and started to crawl in a circle. When he saw me he looked surprised and annoyed. He got shakily to his feet again and held his hand out. 'Gimme a drink.'

I retrieved the fallen glass and milked the gin bottle into it. He accepted it with the dignity of an intoxicated dowager, drank it down with an airy flourish, walked calmly over to the couch and lay down, putting the glass under his head for a pillow. He went to sleep instantly.

I put the telephone receiver back on its hook, glanced out in the kitchen again, felt the man on the couch over and dug some keys out of his pocket. One of them was a pass-key. The door to the hallway had a spring lock and I fixed it so that I could come in again and started up the stairs. I paused on the way to write 'Doc – Vince, 13572' on an envelope. Maybe it was a clue.

The house was quite silent as I went on up.

4

The manager's much filed pass-key turned the lock of Room 214 without noise. I pushed the door open. The room was not empty. A chunky, strongly-built man was bending over a suitcase on the bed, with his back to the door. Shirts and socks and underwear were laid out on the bed cover, and he was packing them leisurely and carefully, whistling between his teeth in a low monotone.

He stiffened as the door hinge creaked. His hand moved fast for the pillow on the bed.

'I beg your pardon,' I said. 'The manager told me this room was vacant.'

He was as bald as a grapefruit. He wore dark grey flannel slacks and transparent plastic suspenders over a blue shirt. His hands came up from the pillow, went to his head, and down again. He turned and he had hair.

It looked as natural as hair ever looked, smooth, brown, not parted. He glared at me from under it.

'You can always try knocking,' he said.

He had a thick voice and a broad careful face that had been around.

'Why would I? If the manager said the room was empty?'

He nodded, satisfied. The glare went out of his eyes.

I came further into the room without invitation. An open love-pulp magazine lay face down on the bed near the suitcase. A cigar smoked in a green glass ash-tray. The room was careful and orderly, and, for that house, clean.

'He must have thought you had already moved out,' I said, trying to look like a well-meaning party with some talent for the truth.

'Have it in half an hour,' the man said.

'Okay if I look around?'

He smiled mirthlessly. 'Ain't been in town long, have you?'

'Why?'

'New around here, ain't you?'

'Why?'

'Like the house and the neighbourhood?'

'Not much,' I said. 'The room looks all right.'

He grinned, showing a porcelain jacket crown that was too white for his other teeth. 'How long you been looking?'

'Just started,' I said. 'Why all the questions?'

'You make me laugh,' the man said, not laughing. 'You don't look at rooms in this town. You grab them sight unseen. This burg's so jam-packed even now that I could get ten bucks just for telling there's a vacancy here.'

'That's too bad,' I said. 'A man named Orrin P. Quest told me about the room. So there's one sawbuck you don't get to spend.'

'That so?' Not a flicker of an eye. Not a movement of a muscle. I might as well have been talking to a turtle.

'Don't get tough with me,' the man said. 'I'm a bad man to get tough with.'

He picked his cigar out of the green glass ash-tray and blew a little smoke. Through it he gave me the cold grey eye. I got a cigarette out and scratched my chin with it.

'What happens to people that get tough with you?' I asked him. 'You make them hold your toupee?'

'You lay off my toupee,' he said savagely.

'So sorry,' I said.

'There's a "No Vacancy" sign on the house,' the man said. 'So what makes you come here and find one?'

'You didn't catch the name,' I said. 'Orrin P. Quest.' I spelled it for him. Even that didn't make him happy. There was a dead-air pause.

He turned abruptly and put a pile of handkerchiefs into his suitcase. I moved a little closer to him. When he turned back there was what might have been a watchful look on his face. But it had been a watchful face to start with.

'Friend of yours?' he asked casually.

'We grew up together,' I said.

'Quiet sort of guy,' the man said easily. 'I used to pass the time of day with him. Works for Cal-Western, don't he?'

'He did,' I said.

'Oh. He quit?'

'Let out.'

We went on staring at each other. It didn't get either of us anywhere. We both had done too much of it in our lives to expect miracles.

The man put the cigar back in his face and sat down on the side of the bed beside the open suitcase. Glancing into it I saw the square butt of an automatic peeping out from under a pair of badly folded shorts.

'This Quest party's been out of here ten days,' the man said thoughtfully. 'So he still thinks the room is vacant, huh?'

'According to the register it *is* vacant,' I said.

He made a contemptuous noise. 'That rummy downstairs probably ain't looked at the register in a month. Say – wait a minute.' His eyes sharpened and his hand wandered idly over the open suitcase and gave an idle pat to something that was close to the gun. When the hand moved away, the gun was no longer visible.

'I've been kind of dreamy all morning or I'd have wised up,' he said. 'You're a dick.'

'All right. Say I'm a dick.'

'What's the beef?'

'No beef at all. I just wondered why you had the room.'

'I moved from 215 across the hall. This here is a better room. That's all. Simple. Satisfied?'

'Perfectly,' I said, watching the hand that could be near the gun if it wanted to.

'What kind of dick? City? Let's see the buzzer.'

I didn't say anything.

'I don't believe you got no buzzer.'

'If I showed it to you, you're the type of guy who would say it was counterfeit. So you're Hicks.'

He looked surprised.

'George W. Hicks,' I said. 'It's in the register. Room 215. You just got through telling me you moved from 215.' I glanced around the room. 'If you had a blackboard here, I'd write it out for you.'

'Strictly speaking, we don't have to get into no snarling match,' he said. 'Sure I'm Hicks. Pleased to meetcha. What's yours?'

He held his hand out. I shook hands with him, but not as if I had been longing for the moment to arrive.

'My name's Marlowe,' I said. 'Philip Marlowe.'

'You know something,' Hicks said politely, 'you're a goddamn liar.'

I laughed in his face.

'You ain't getting no place with that breezy manner, bub. What's your connexion?'

I got my wallet out and handed him one of my business cards. He read it thoughtfully and tapped the edge against his porcelain crown.

'He coulda went somewhere without telling me,' he mused.

'Your grammar,' I said, 'is almost as loose as your toupee.'

'You lay off my toupee, if you know what's good for you,' he shouted.

'I wasn't going to eat it,' I said. 'I'm not that hungry.'

He took a step towards me, and dropped his right shoulder. A scowl of fury dropped his lip almost as far.

'Don't hit me. I'm insured,' I told him.

'Oh hell. Just another screwball.' He shrugged and put his lip back up on his face. 'What's the lay?'

'I have to find this Orrin P. Quest,' I said.

'Why?'

I didn't answer that.

After a moment he said: 'Okay. I'm a careful guy myself. That's why I'm movin' out.'

'Maybe you don't like the reefer smoke.'

'That,' he said emptily, 'and other things. That's why Quest left. Respectable type. Like me. I think a couple of hard boys threw a scare into him.'

'I see,' I said. 'That would be why he left no forwarding address. And why did they throw a scare into him?'

'You just mentioned reefer smoke, didn't you? Wouldn't he be the type to go to headquarters about that?'

'In Bay City?' I asked. 'Why would he bother? Well, thanks a lot, Mr Hicks. Going far?'

'Not far,' he said. 'No. Not very far. Just far enough.'

'What's your racket?' I asked him.

'Racket?' He looked hurt.

'Sure. What do you shake them for? How do you make your dibs?'

'You got me wrong, brother. I'm a retired optometrist.'

'That why you have the .45 gun in there?' I pointed to the suitcase.

'Nothing to get cute about,' he said sourly. 'It's been in the family for years.' He looked down at the card again. 'Private investigator, huh?' he said thoughtfully. 'What kind of work do you do mostly?'

'Anything that's reasonably honest,' I said.

He nodded. 'Reasonably is a word you could stretch. So is honest.'

I gave him a shady leer. 'You're so right,' I agreed. 'Let's get together some quiet afternoon and stretch them.' I reached out and slipped the card from between his fingers and dropped it into my pocket. 'Thanks for the time,' I said.

I went out and closed the door, then stood against it listening. I don't know what I expected to hear. Whatever it was I didn't hear it. I had a feeling he was standing exactly where I had left him and looking at the spot where I had made my exit. I made noise going along the hall and stood at the head of the stairs.

A car drove away from in front of the house. Somewhere a door closed. I went quietly back to Room 215 and used the pass-key to enter. I closed and locked its door silently, and waited just inside.

5

Not more than two minutes passed before Mr George W. Hicks was on his way. He came out so quietly that I wouldn't have heard him if I hadn't been listening for precisely that kind of movement. I heard the slight metallic sound of the door-knob turning. Then slow steps. Then very gently the door was closed. The steps moved off. The faint distant creak of the stairs. Then nothing. I waited for the sound of the front door. It didn't come. I opened the door of 215 and moved along the hall to the stairhead again. Below there was the careful sound of a door being tried. I looked down to see Hicks going into the manager's apartment. The door closed behind him. I waited for the sound of voices. No voices.

I shrugged and went back to 215.

The room showed signs of occupancy. There was a small radio on a night table, an unmade bed with shoes under it, and an old bathrobe hung over the cracked, pull-down green shade to keep the glare out.

I looked at all this as if it meant something, then stepped back into the hall and relocked the door. Then I made another pilgrimage into Room 214. Its door was now unlocked. I searched the room with care and patience and found nothing that connected it in any way with Orrin P. Quest. I didn't expect to. There was no reason why I should. But you always have to look.

I went downstairs, listened outside the manager's door, heard nothing, went in and crossed to put the keys on the desk. Lester B. Clausen lay on his side on the couch with his face to the wall, dead to the world. I went through the desk, found an old account book that seemed to be concerned with rent taken in and expenses paid out and nothing else. I looked at the register again. It wasn't up to date but the party on the couch seemed enough explanation for that. Orrin P. Quest had moved away. Somebody had taken over his room. Somebody else had the room registered to Hicks. The little man counting money in the kitchen went nicely with the neighbourhood. The fact that he carried a gun and a knife was a social eccentricity that would cause no comment at all on Idaho Street.

I reached the small Bay City telephone book off the hook beside the desk. I didn't think it would be much of a job to sift out the party that went by the name of 'Doc' or 'Vince' and the phone number one-three-five-seven-two. First of all I leafed back through the register. Something which I ought to have done first. The page with Orrin Quest's registration had been torn out. A careful man, Mr George W. Hicks. Very careful.

I closed the register, glanced over at Lester B. Clausen again, wrinkled my nose at the stale air and the sickly sweetish smell of gin and of something else, and started back to the entrance door. As I reached it, something for the first time penetrated my mind. A drunk like Clausen ought to be snoring very loudly. He ought to be snoring his head off with a nice assortment of checks and gurgles and snorts. He wasn't making any sound at all. A brown Army blanket was pulled up around his shoulders and the lower part of his head. He looked very comfortable, very calm. I stood over him and looked down. Something which was not an accidental fold held the Army blanket away from the back of his neck. I moved it. A square yellow wooden handle was attached to the back of Lester B. Clausen's neck. On the side of the yellow handle were printed the words 'Compliments of the Crumsen Hardware Company'. The position of the handle was just below the occipital bulge.

It was the handle of an ice-pick . . .

I did a nice quiet thirty-five getting away from the neighbourhood. On the edge of the city, a frog's jump from the line, I shut myself in an outdoor telephone booth and called the Police Department.

'Bay City Police. Moot talking,' a furry voice said.

I said: 'Number 449 Idaho Street. In the apartment of the manager. His name's Clausen.'

'Yeah?' the voice said. 'What do we do?'

'I don't know,' I said. 'It's a bit of a puzzle to me. But the man's name is Lester B. Clausen. Got that?'

'What makes it important?' the furry voice said without suspicion.

'The coroner will want to know,' I said, and hung up.

6

I drove back to Hollywood and locked myself in the office with the Bay City telephone book. It took me a quarter-hour to find out that the party who went with the telephone number one-three-five-seven-two in Bay City was a Dr Vincent Lagardie, who called himself a neurologist, had his home and offices on Wyoming Street, which according to my map was not quite in the best residential neighbourhood and not quite out of it. I locked the Bay City telephone book up in my desk and went down to the corner drug store for a sandwich and a cup of coffee and used a pay booth to call Dr Vincent Lagardie. A woman answered and I had some trouble getting through to Dr Lagardie himself. When I did his voice was impatient. He was very busy, in the middle of an examination he said. I never knew a doctor who wasn't. Did he know Lester B. Clausen? He never heard of him. What was the purpose of my inquiry?

'Mr Clausen tried to telephone you this morning,' I said. 'He was too drunk to talk properly.'

'But I don't know Mr Clausen,' the doctor's cool voice answered. He didn't seem to be in quite such a hurry now.

'Well, that's all right then,' I said. 'Just wanted to make sure. Somebody stuck an ice-pick into the back of his neck.'

There was a quiet pause. Dr Lagardie's voice was now almost unctuously polite. 'Has this been reported to the police?'

'Naturally,' I said. 'But it shouldn't bother you – unless of course it was your ice-pick.'

He passed that one up. 'And who is this speaking?' he inquired suavely.

'The name is Hicks,' I said. 'George W. Hicks. I just moved out of there. I don't want to get mixed up with that sort of thing. I just figured when Clausen tried to call you – this was before he was dead, you understand – that you might be interested.'

'I'm sorry, Mr Hicks,' Dr Lagardie's voice said. 'But I don't *know* Mr Clausen. I have never *heard* of Mr Clausen or had any contact with him whatsoever. And I have an excellent memory for names.'

'Well, that's fine,' I said. 'And you won't meet him now. But somebody *may* want to know why he tried to telephone you – unless I forget to pass the information along.'

There was a dead pause. Dr Lagardie said: 'I can't think of any comment to make on that.'

I said: 'Neither can I. I may call you again. Don't get me wrong, Dr Lagardie. This isn't any kind of a shake. I'm just a mixed-up little man who needs a friend. I kind of felt that a doctor – like a clergyman –'

'I'm at your entire disposal,' Dr Lagardie said. 'Please feel free to consult me.'

'Thank you, Doctor,' I said fervently. 'Thank you very very much.'

I hung up. If Dr Vincent Lagardie was on the level, he would now telephone the Bay City Police Department and tell them the story. If he didn't telephone the police, he wasn't on the level. Which might or might not be useful to know.

7

The phone on my desk rang at four o'clock sharp.

'Did you find Orrin yet, Mr Marlowe?'

'Not yet. Where are you?'

'Why, I'm in the drug store next to –'

'Come on up and stop acting like Mata Hari,' I said.

'Aren't you ever polite to anybody?' she snapped.

I hung up and fed myself a slug of Old Forester to brace my nerves for the interview. As I was inhaling it I heard her steps tripping along the corridor. I moved across and opened the door.

'Come in this way and miss the crowd,' I said.

She seated herself demurely and waited.

'All I could find out,' I told her, 'is that the dump on Idaho Street is peddling reefers. That's marijuana cigarettes.'

'Why, how disgusting,' she said.

'We have to take the bad with the good in this life,' I said. 'Orrin must have got wise and threatened to report it to the police.'

'You mean,' she said in her little-girl manner, 'that they might hurt him for doing that?'

'Well, most likely they'd just throw a scare into him first.'

'Oh, they couldn't scare Orrin, Mr Marlowe,' she said decisively. 'He just gets mean when people try to run him.'

'Yeah,' I said. 'But we're not talking about the same things. You can scare anybody – with the right technique.'

She set her mouth stubbornly. 'No, Mr Marlowe. They couldn't scare Orrin.'

'Okay,' I said. 'So they didn't scare him. Say they just cut off one of his legs and beat him over the head with it. What would he do then – write to the Better Business Bureau?'

'You're making fun of me,' she said politely. Her voice was as cool as boarding-house soup. 'Is that all you did all day? Just find Orrin had moved and it was a bad neighbourhood? Why, I found that out for myself,

Mr Marlowe. I thought you being a detective and all – ' She trailed off, leaving the rest of it in the air.

'I did a little more than that,' I said. 'I gave the landlord a little gin and went through the register and talked to a man named Hicks. George W. Hicks. He wears a toupee. I guess maybe you didn't meet him. He has, or had, Orrin's room. So I thought maybe – ' It was my turn to do a little trailing in the air.

She fixed me with her pale blue eyes enlarged by the glasses. Her mouth was small and firm and tight, her hands clasped on the desk in front of her over her large square bag, her whole body stiff and erect and formal and disapproving.

'I paid you twenty dollars, Mr Marlowe,' she said coldly. 'I understood that was in payment of a day's work. It doesn't seem to me that you've done a day's work.'

'No,' I said. 'That's true. But the day isn't over yet. And don't bother about the twenty bucks. You can have it back if you like. I didn't even bruise it.'

I opened the desk drawer and got out her money. I pushed it across the desk. She looked at it but didn't touch it. Her eyes came up slowly to meet mine.

'I didn't mean it like that. I know you're doing the best you can, Mr Marlowe.'

'With the facts I have.'

'But I've told you all I know.'

'I don't think so,' I said.

'Well, I'm sure I can't help what you think,' she said tartly. 'After all, if I knew what I wanted to know already, I wouldn't have come here and asked you to find it out, would I?'

'I'm not saying you know all you want to know,' I answered. 'The point is I don't know in order to do a job for you. And what you tell me doesn't add up.'

'What doesn't add up? I've told you the truth. I'm Orrin's sister. I guess I know what kind of person he is.'

'How long did he work for Cal-Western?'

'I've told you that. He came out to California just about a year ago. He got work right away because he practically had the job before he left.'

'He wrote home how often? Before he stopped writing.'

'Every week. Sometimes oftener. He'd take turns writing to mother and me. Of course the letters were for both of us.'

'About what?'

'You mean what did he write about?'

'What did you think I meant?'

'Well, you don't have to snap at me. He wrote about his work and the plant and the people there, and sometimes about a show he'd been to. Or it was about California. He'd write about church too.'

'Nothing about girls?'

'I don't think Orrin cared much for girls.'

'And lived at the same address all this time?'

She nodded, looking puzzled.

'And he stopped writing how long ago?'

That took thought. She pressed her lips and pushed a finger-tip around the middle of the lower one. 'About three or four months,' she said at last.

'What was the date of his last letter?'

'I – I'm afraid I can't tell you exactly the date. But it was like I said, three or four –'

I waved a hand at her. 'Anything out of the ordinary in it? Anything unusual said or anything unusual unsaid?'

'Why no. It seemed just like all the rest.'

'Don't you have any friends or relatives in this part of the country?'

She gave me a funny stare, started to say something, then shook her head sharply. 'No.'

'Okay. Now I'll tell you what's wrong. I'll skip over your not telling me where you're staying, because it might be just that you're afraid I'll show up with a quart of hooch under my arm and make a pass at you.'

'That's not a very nice way to talk,' she said.

'Nothing I say is nice. I'm not nice. By your standards nobody with less than three prayer-books could be nice. But I *am* inquisitive. What's wrong with this picture is that you're not scared. Neither you personally nor your mother. And you ought to be scared as hell.'

She clutched her bag to her bosom with tight little fingers. 'You mean something has happened to him?' Her voice faded off into a sort of sad whisper, like a mortician asking for a down payment.

'I don't know that anything has. But in your position, knowing the kind of guy Orrin was, the way his letters came through and then didn't, I can't see myself waiting for my summer vacation to come around before I start asking questions. I can't see myself bypassing the police who have an organization for finding people. And going to a lone-wolf operator you never heard of, asking him to root around for you in the rubble. And I can't see your dear old mother just sitting there in Manhattan, Kansas, week after week darning the minister's winter underwear. No letter from Orrin. No news. And all she does about it is take a long breath and mend up another pair of pants.'

She came to her feet with a lunge. 'You're a horrid, disgusting person,' she said angrily. 'I think you're vile. Don't you dare say mother and I weren't worried. Just don't you dare.'

I pushed the twenty dollars' worth of currency a little closer to the other side of the desk. 'You were worried twenty dollars' worth, honey,' I said. 'But about what I wouldn't know. I guess I don't really want to know. Just put this hunk of the folding back in your saddle bag and forget you ever met me. You might want to lend it to another detective tomorrow.'

She snapped her bag shut viciously on the money. 'I'm not very likely to forget your rudeness,' she said between her teeth. 'Nobody in the world's ever talked to me the way you have.'

I stood up and wandered around the end of the desk. 'Don't think about it too much. You might get to like it.'

I reached up and twitched her glasses off. She took half a step back, almost stumbled, and I reached an arm around her by pure instinct. Her eyes widened and she put her hands against my chest and pushed. I've been pushed harder by a kitten.

'Without the cheaters those eyes are really something,' I said in an awed voice.

She relaxed and let her head go back and her lips open a little. 'I suppose you do this to all the clients,' she said softly. Her hands now had dropped to her sides. The bag whacked against my leg. She leaned her weight on my arm. If she wanted me to let go of her, she had her signals mixed.

'I just didn't want you to lose your balance,' I said.

'I knew you were the thoughtful type.' She relaxed still more. Her head went back now. Her upper lids drooped, fluttered a bit, and her lips came open a little farther. On them appeared the faint provocative smile that nobody ever has to teach them. 'I suppose you thought I did it on purpose,' she said.

'Did what on purpose?'

'Stumbled, sort of.'

'Wel-l-l-l.'

She reached a quick arm around my neck and started to pull. So I kissed her. It was either that or slug her. She pushed her mouth hard at me for a long moment, then quietly and very comfortably wriggled around in my arms and nestled. She let out a long easy sigh.

'In Manhattan, Kansas, you could be arrested for this,' she said.

'If there was any justice, I could be arrested just for being there,' I said.

She giggled and poked the end of my nose with a finger-tip. 'I suppose you really prefer fast girls,' she said, looking up at me sideways. 'At least you won't have to wipe off any lip rouge. Maybe I'll wear some next time.'

'Maybe we'd better sit down on the floor,' I said. 'My arm's getting tired.'

She giggled again and disengaged herself gracefully. 'I guess you think I've been kissed lots of times,' she said.

'What girl hasn't?'

She nodded, gave me the up-from-under look that made her eyelashes cut across the iris. 'Even at the church socials they play kissing games,' she said.

'Or there wouldn't be any church socials,' I said.

We looked at each other with no particular expression.

'Well-l-l –' she began at last. I handed her back her glasses. She put them on. She opened her bag, looked at herself in a small mirror, rooted around in her bag and came out with her hand clenched.

'I'm sorry I was mean,' she said, and pushed something under the blotter of my desk. She gave me another little frail smile and marched to the door and opened it.

'I'll call you,' she said intimately. And out she went, tap, tap, tap down the hall.

I went over and lifted the blotter and smoothed out the crumpled currency that lay under it. It hadn't been much of a kiss, but it looked like I had another chance at the twenty dollars.

The phone rang before I had quite started to worry about Mr Lester B. Clausen. I reached for it absently. The voice I heard was an abrupt voice, but thick and clogged, as if it was being strained through a curtain or somebody's long white beard.

'You Marlowe?' it said.

'Speaking.'

'You got a safe deposit box, Marlowe?'

I had had enough of being polite for one afternoon. 'Stop asking and start telling,' I said.

'I asked you a question, Marlowe.'

'I didn't answer it,' I said. 'Like this,' I reached over and pressed down the riser on the phone. Held it that way while I fumbled around for a cigarette. I knew he would call right back. They always do when they think they're tough. They haven't used their exit line. When it rang again I started right in.

'If you have a proposition, state it. And I get called "mister" until you give me some money.'

'Don't let that temper ride you so hard, friend. I'm in a jam. I need help. I need something kept in a safe place. For a few days. Not longer. And for that you make a little quick money.'

'How little?' I asked. 'And how quick?'

'A C note. Right here and waiting. I'm warming it for you.'

'I can hear it purr,' I said. 'Right where and waiting?' I was listening to the voice twice, once when I heard it and once when it echoed in my mind.

'Room 332, Van Nuys Hotel. Knock two quick ones and two slow ones. Not too loud. I got to have live action. How fast can you –'

'What is it you want me to keep?'

'That'll wait till you get here. I said I was in a hurry.'

'What's your name?'

'Just Room 332.'

'Thanks for the time,' I said. 'Good-bye.'

'Hey. Wait a minute, dope. It's nothing hot like you think. No ice. No emerald pendants. It just happens to be worth a lot of money to me – and nothing at all to anybody else.'

'The hotel has a safe.'

'Do you want to die poor, Marlowe?'

'Why not? Rockefeller did. Good-bye again.'

The voice changed. The furriness went out of it. It said sharply and swiftly: 'How's every little thing in Bay City?'

I didn't speak. Just waited. There was a dim chuckle over the wire. 'Thought that might interest you, Marlowe. Room 332 it is. Tramp on it, friend. Make speed.'

The phone clicked in my ear. I hung up. For no reason a pencil rolled off the desk and broke its point on the glass doohickey under one of the desk legs. I picked it up and slowly and carefully sharpened it in the Boston sharpener screwed to the edge of the window frame, turning the pencil around to get it nice and even. I laid it down in the tray on the desk and dusted off my hands. I had all the time in the world. I looked out of the window. I didn't see anything. I didn't hear anything.

And then, for even less reason, I saw Orfamay Quest's face without the glasses, and polished and painted and with blonde hair piled up high on the forehead with a braid around the middle of it. And bedroom eyes. They all have to have bedroom eyes. I tried to imagine this face in a vast close-up being gnawed by some virile character from the wide-open spaces of Romanoff's bar.

It took me twenty-nine minutes to get to the Van Nuys Hotel.

8

Once, long ago, it must have had a certain elegance. But no more. The memories of old cigars clung to its lobby like the dirty gilt on its ceiling and the sagging springs of its leather lounging chairs. The marble of the desk had turned a yellowish brown with age. But the floor carpet was new and had a hard look, like the room clerk. I passed him up and strolled over to the cigar counter in the corner and put down a quarter for a package of Camels. The girl behind the counter was a straw blonde with a long neck and tired eyes. She put the cigarettes in front of me, added a packet of matches, dropped my change into a slotted box marked 'The Community Chest Thanks You'.

'You'd want me to do that, wouldn't you?' she said, smiling patiently. 'You'd want to give your change to the poor little underprivileged kids with bent legs and stuff, wouldn't you?'

'Suppose I didn't,' I said.

'I dig up seven cents,' the girl said, 'and it would be very painful.' She had a low lingering voice with a sort of moist caress in it like a damp bath towel. I put a quarter after the seven cents. She gave me her big smile then. It showed more of her tonsils.

'You're nice,' she said. 'I can see you're nice. A lot of fellows would have come in here and made a pass at a girl. Just think. Over seven cents. A pass.'

'Who's the house keeper here now?' I asked her, without taking up the option.

'There's two of them.' She did something slow and elegant to the back of her head, exhibiting what seemed like more than one handful of blood-red fingernails in the process. 'Mr Hady is on nights and Mr Flack is on days. It's day now, so it would be Mr Flack would be on.'

'Where could I find him?'

She leaned over the counter and let me smell her hair, pointing with a half-inch fingernail towards the elevator bank. 'It's down along that corridor there, next to the porter's room. You can't miss the porter's room on account of it has a half-door and says PORTER on the upper part in gold letters. Only that half is folded back like, so I guess maybe you can't see it.'

'I'll see it,' I said. 'Even if I have to get a hinge screwed to my neck. What does this Flack look like?'

'Well,' she said, 'he's a little squatty number, with a bit of a moustache. A sort of chunky type. Thick-set like, only not tall.' Her fingers moved languidly along the counter to where I could have touched them without jumping. 'He's not interesting,' she said. 'Why bother?'

'Business,' I said, and made off before she threw a half-nelson on me.

I looked back at her from the elevators. She was staring after me with an expression she probably would have said was thoughtful.

The porter's room was half-way down the corridor to the Spring Street entrance. The door beyond it was half-open. I looked around its edge, then went in and closed it behind me.

A man was sitting at a small desk which had dust on it, a very large ash-tray and very little else. He was short and thick-set. He had something dark and bristly under his nose about an inch long. I sat down across from him and put a card on the desk.

He reached for the card without excitement, read it, turned it over and read the back with as much care as the front. There was nothing on the back to read. He picked half of a cigar out of his ash-tray and turned his nose lighting it.

'What's the gripe?' he growled at me.

'No gripe. You Flack?'

He didn't bother to answer. He gave me a steady look, which may or may not have concealed his thoughts, depending on whether he had any to conceal.

'Like to get a line on one of the customers,' I said.

'What name?' Flack asked, with no enthusiasm.

'I don't know what name he's using here. He's in Room 332.'

'What name was he using before he came here?' Flack asked.

'I don't know that either.'

'Well, what did he look like?' Flack was suspicious now. He re-read my card but it added nothing to his knowledge.

'I never saw him, so far as I know.'

Flack said: 'I must be overworked. I don't get it.'

'I had a call from him,' I said. 'He wanted to see me.'

'Am I stopping you?'

'Look, Flack. A man in my business makes enemies at times. You ought to know that. This party wants something done. Tells me to come on over, forgets to give his name, and hangs up. I figured I'd do a little checking before I went up there.'

Flack took the cigar out of his mouth and said patiently: 'I'm in terrible shape. I still don't get it. Nothing makes sense to me any more.'

I leaned over the desk and spoke to him slowly and distinctly: 'The whole thing could be a nice way to get me into a hotel room and knock me off and then quietly check out. You wouldn't want anything like that to happen in your hotel, would you, Flack?'

'Supposing I cared,' he said, 'you figure you're that important?'

'Do you smoke that piece of rope because you like it or because you think it makes you look tough?'

'For forty-five bucks a week,' Flack said, 'would I smoke anything better?' He eyed me steadily.

'No expense account yet,' I told him. 'No deal yet.'

He made a sad sound and got up wearily and went out of the room. I lit one of my cigarettes and waited. He came back in a short time and dropped a registration card on the desk. *Dr G. W. Hambleton, El Centro, California* was written on it in a firm round hand in ink. The clerk had written other things on it, including the room number and daily rate. Flack pointed a finger that needed a manicure or, failing that, a nail brush.

'Came in at 2.47 p.m.,' he said. 'Just today, that is. Nothing on his bill. One day's rent. No phone calls. No nothing. That what you want?'

'What does he look like?' I asked.

'I didn't see him. You think I stand out there by the desk and take pictures of them while they register?'

'Thanks,' I said. 'Dr G. W. Hambleton, El Centro. Much obliged.' I handed him back the registration card.

'Anything I ought to know,' Flack said as I went out. 'Don't forget where I live. That is, if you call it living.'

I nodded and went out. There are days like that. Everybody you meet is a dope. You begin to look at yourself in the glass and wonder.

9

Room 332 was at the back of the building near the door to the fire escape. The corridor which led to it had a smell of old carpet and furniture oil and the drab anonymity of a thousand shabby lives. The sand bucket under the racked fire hose was full of cigarette and cigar stubs, an accumulation of several days. A radio pounded brassy music through an open transom. Through another transom people were laughing fit to kill themselves. Down at the end by Room 332 it was quieter.

I knocked the two longs and two shorts as instructed. Nothing happened. I felt jaded and old. I felt as if I had spent my life knocking at doors in cheap hotels that nobody bothered to open. I tried again. Then turned the knob and walked in. A key with a red fibre tab hung in the inside keyhole.

There was a short hall with a bathroom on the right. Beyond the hall the upper half of a bed was in view, and a man lay on it in shirt and pants.

I said: 'Dr Hambleton?'

The man didn't answer. I went past the bathroom door towards him. A whiff of perfume reached me and I started to turn, but not quickly enough. A woman who had been in the bathroom was standing there holding a towel in front of the lower part of her face. Dark glasses showed above the towel. And then the brim of a wide-brimmed straw hat in a sort of dusty delphinium blue. Under that was fluffed-out pale blonde hair. Blue ear-buttons lurked somewhere back in the shadows. The sun-glasses were in white frames with broad flat sidebows. Her dress matched her hat. An embroidered silk or rayon coat was open over the dress. She wore gauntleted gloves and there was an automatic in her right hand. White bone grip. Looked like a .32.

'Turn around and put your hands behind you,' she said through the towel. The voice muffled by the towel meant as little to me as the dark glasses. It was not the voice which had talked to me on the telephone. I didn't move.

'Don't ever think I'm fooling,' she said. 'I'll give you exactly three seconds to do what I say.'

'Couldn't you make it a minute? I like looking at you.'

She made a threatening gesture with the little gun. 'Turn around,' she snapped. 'But fast.'

'I like the sound of your voice too.'

'All right,' she said, in a tight dangerous tone. 'If that's the way you want it, that's the way you want it.'

'Don't forget you're a lady,' I said, and turned around and put my hands up to my shoulders. A gun muzzle poked into the back of my neck. Breath almost tickled my skin. The perfume was an elegant something or other, not strong, not decisive. The gun against my neck went away and a white flame burned for an instant behind my eyes. I grunted and fell forward on my hands and knees and reached back quickly. My hand touched a leg in a nylon stocking, but slipped off, which seemed a pity. It felt like a nice leg. The jar of another blow on the head took the pleasure out of this and I made the hoarse sound of a man in desperate shape. I collapsed on the floor. The door opened. A key rattled. The door closed. The key turned. Silence.

I climbed up to my feet and went into the bathroom. I bathed my head with a towel from the rack soaked with cold water. It felt as if the heel of a shoe had hit me. Certainly it was not a gun butt. There was a little blood, not much. I rinsed the towel out and stood there patting the bruise and wondering why I didn't run after her screaming. But what I was doing was staring into the open medicine cabinet over the basin. The upper part of a can of talcum had been pried off the shoulder. There was talcum all over the shelf. A toothpaste tube had been cut open. Someone had been looking for something.

I went back to the little hallway and tried the room door. Locked from the outside. I bent down and looked through the keyhole. But it was an up-and-down lock, with the outer and inner keyholes on different levels. The girl in the dark glasses with the white rims didn't know much about hotels. I twisted the night latch, which opened the outside lock, opened the door, looked along the empty corridor, and closed the door again.

Then I went towards the man on the bed. He had not moved during all this time, for a somewhat obvious reason.

Beyond the little hallway the room widened towards a pair of windows through which the evening sun slanted in a shaft that reached almost across the bed and came to a stop under the neck of the man that lay there. What it stopped on was blue and white and shining and round. He lay quite comfortably half on his face with his hands down at his sides and his shoes off. The side of his face was on the pillow and he seemed relaxed. He was wearing a toupee. The last time I had talked to him his name had been George W. Hicks. Now it was Dr G. W. Hambleton. Same initials. Not that it mattered any more. I wasn't going to be talking to him again. There was no blood. None at all, which is one of the few nice things about an expert ice-pick job.

I touched his neck. It was still warm. While I was doing it the shaft of sunlight moved away from the knob of the ice-pick towards his left ear. I turned away and looked the room over. The telephone bell box had been opened and left open. The Gideon Bible was thrown in the corner. The desk had been searched. I went to a closet and looked into that. There were clothes in it and a suitcase I had seen before. I found nothing that seemed important. I picked a snap-brim hat off the floor and put it on the desk and went back to the bathroom. The point of interest now was whether the people who had ice-picked Dr Hambleton had found what they came for. They had had very little time.

I searched the bathroom carefully. I moved the top of the toilet and drained it. There was nothing in it. I peered down the overflow pipe. No thread hung there with a small object at the end of it. I searched the bureau. It was empty except for an old envelope. I unhooked the window screens and felt under the sills outside. I picked the Gideon Bible off the floor and leafed through it again. I examined the backs of three pictures and studied the edge of the carpet. It was tacked close to the wall and there were little pockets of dust in the depressions made by the tacks. I got down on the floor and examined the part under the bed. Just the same. I stood on a chair, looked into the bowl of the light fixture. It contained dust and dead moths. I looked the bed over. It had been made up by a professional and not touched since. I felt the pillow under the dead man's head, then got the extra pillow out of the closet and examined its edges. Nothing.

Dr Hambleton's coat hung over a chair back. I went through that, knowing it was the least likely place to find anything. Somebody with a knife had worked on the lining and the shoulder padding. There were matches, a couple of cigars, a pair of dark glasses, a cheap handkerchief not used, a Bay City movie theatre ticket stub, a small comb, an unopened package of cigarettes. I looked at it in the light. It showed no sign of having been disturbed. I disturbed it. I tore off the cover, went through it, found nothing but cigarettes.

That left Dr Hambleton himself. I eased him over and got into his trousers pockets. Loose change, another handkerchief, a small tube of dental floss, more matches, a bunch of keys, a folder of bus schedules. In a pig-skin wallet was a book of stamps, a second comb (here was a man who really took care of his toupee), three flat packages of white powder, seven printed cards reading *Dr G. W. Hambleton, O.D. Tustin Building, El Centro, California, Hours 9–12 and 2–4, and by Appointment. Telephone El Centro 50406.* There was no driver's licence, no social security card, no insurance cards, no real identification at all. There was $164.00 in currency in the wallet. I put the wallet back where I found it.

I lifted Dr Hambleton's hat off the desk and examined the sweat band and the ribbon. The ribbon bow had been picked loose with a knife point, leaving hanging threads. There was nothing hidden inside the bow. No evidence of any previous ripping and restitching.

This was the take. If the killers knew what they were looking for, it was something that could be hidden in a book, a telephone box, a tube of toothpaste, or a hat band. I went back into the bathroom and looked at my head again. It was still oozing a tiny trickle of blood. I gave it more cold water and dried the cut with toilet paper and flushed that down the bowl. I went back and stood a moment looking down on Dr Hambleton, wondering what his mistake had been. He had seemed a fairly wise bird. The sunlight had moved over to the far edge of the room now, off the bed and down into a sad dusty corner.

I grinned suddenly, bent over and quickly and with the grin still on my face, out of place as it was, pulled off Dr Hambleton's toupee and turned it inside out. As simple as all that. To the lining of the toupee a piece of orange-coloured paper was fastened by Scotch tape, protected by a square of cellophane. I pulled it loose, turned it over, and saw that it was a numbered claim check belonging to the Bay City Camera Shop. I put it in my wallet and put the toupee carefully back on the dead egg-bald head.

I left the room unlocked because I had no way to lock it.

Down the hall the radio still blared through the transom and the exaggerated alcoholic laughter accompanied it from across the corridor.

10

Over the telephone the Bay City Camera Shop man said: 'Yes, Mr Hicks. We have them for you. Six enlarged prints on glossy from your negative.'

'What time do you close?' I asked.

'Oh, in about five minutes. We open at nine in the morning.'

'I'll pick them up in the morning. Thanks.'

I hung up, reached mechanically into the slot and found somebody else's nickel. I walked over to the lunch counter and bought myself a cup of coffee with it, and sat there sipping and listening to the auto horns complaining on the street outside. It was time to go home. Whistles blew. Motors raced. Old brake linings squeaked. There was a dull steady mutter of feet on the sidewalk outside. It was just after five-thirty. I finished the coffee, stuffed a pipe, and strolled a half-block back to the Van Nuys Hotel. In the writing-room I folded the orange camera shop cheque into a sheet of hotel stationery and addressed an envelope to myself. I put a special delivery stamp on it and dropped it in the mail chute by the elevator bank. Then I went along to Flack's office again.

Again I closed his door and sat down across from him. Flack didn't seem to have moved an inch. He was chewing morosely on the same cigar butt and his eyes were still full of nothing. I relit my pipe by striking a match on the side of his desk. He frowned.

'Dr Hambleton doesn't answer his door,' I said.

'Huh?' Flack looked at me vacantly.

'Party in 332. Remember? He doesn't answer his door.'

'What should I do – bust my girdle?' Flack asked.

'I knocked several times,' I said. 'No answer. Thought he might be taking a bath or something, although I couldn't hear anything. Went away for a while, then tried again. Same no answer again.'

Flack looked at a turnip watch he got from his vest. 'I'm off at seven,' he said. 'Christ. A whole hour to go, and more. Boy, am I hungry.'

'Working the way you do,' I said, 'you must be. You have to keep your strength up. Do I interest you at all in Room 332?'

'You said he wasn't in,' Flack said irritably. 'So what? He wasn't in.'

'I didn't say he wasn't in. I said he didn't answer his door.'

Flack leaned forward. Very slowly he removed the debris of the cigar from his mouth and put it in the glass tray. 'Go on. Make me like it,' he said, carefully.

'Maybe you'd like to run up and look,' I said. 'Maybe you didn't see a first-class ice-pick job lately.'

Flack put his hands on the arms of his chair and squeezed the wood hard. 'Aw,' he said painfully. 'Aw.' He got to his feet and opened the desk drawer. He took out a large black gun, flicked the gate open, studied the cartridges, squinted down the barrel, snapped the cylinder back into place. He unbuttoned his vest and tucked the gun down inside his waistband. In an emergency he could probably have got to it in less than a minute. He put his hat on firmly and jerked a thumb at the door.

We went up to the third floor in silence. We went down the corridor. Nothing had changed. No sound had increased or diminished. Flack hurried along to 332 and knocked from force of habit. Then tried the door. He looked back at me with a twisted mouth.

'You said the door wasn't locked,' he complained.

'I didn't exactly say that. It *was* unlocked, though.'

'It ain't now,' Flack said, and unshipped a key on a long chain. He unlocked the door and glanced up and down the hall. He twisted the knob slowly without sound and eased the door a couple of inches. He listened. No sound came from within. Flack stepped back, took the black gun out of his waistband. He removed the key from the door, kicked it wide open, and brought the gun up hard and straight, like the wicked foreman of the Lazy Q. 'Let's go,' he said out of the corner of his mouth.

Over his shoulder I could see that Dr Hambleton lay exactly as before, but the ice-pick handle didn't show from the entrance. Flack leaned forward and edged cautiously into the room. He reached the bathroom door and put his eye to the crack, then pushed the door open until it bounced against the tub. He went in and came out, stepped down into the room, a tense and wary man who was taking no chances.

He tried the closet door, levelled his gun and jerked it wide open. No suspects in the closet.

'Look under the bed,' I said.

Flack bent swiftly and looked under the bed.

'Look under the carpet,' I said.

'You kidding me?' Flack added nastily.

'I just like to watch you work.'

He bent over the dead man and studied the ice-pick.

'Somebody locked that door,' he sneered. 'Unless you're lying about its being unlocked.'

I said nothing.

'Well, I guess it's the cops,' he said slowly. 'No chance to cover up on this one.'

'It's not your fault,' I told him. 'It happens even in good hotels.'

11

The red-headed intern filled out a D.O.A. form and clipped his stylus to the outside pocket of his white jacket. He snapped the book shut with a faint grin on his face.

'Punctured spinal cord just below the occipital bulge, I'd say,' he said carelessly. 'A very vulnerable spot. If you know how to find it. And I suppose you do.'

Detective Lieutenant Christy French growled. 'Think it's the first time I've seen one?'

'No, I guess not,' the intern said. He gave a last quick look at the dead man, turned and walked out of the room. 'I'll call the coroner,' he said over his shoulder. The door closed behind him.

'What a stiff means to those birds is what a plate of warmed-up cabbage means to me,' Christy French said sourly to the closed door. His partner, a cop named Fred Beifus, was down on one knee by the telephone box. He had dusted it for finger prints and blown off the loose powder. He was looking at the smudge through a small magnifying glass. He shook, his head, then picked something off the screw with which the box had been fastened shut.

'Grey cotton undertaker's gloves,' he said disgustedly. 'Cost about four cents a pair wholesale. Fat lot of good printing this joint. They were looking for something in the telephone box, huh?'

'Evidently something that could be there,' French said. 'I didn't expect prints. These ice-pick jobs are a speciality. We'll get the experts after a while. This is just a quickover.'

He was stripping the dead man's pockets and laying what had been in them out on the bed beside the quiet and already waxy corpse. Flack was sitting in a chair by the window, looking out morosely. The assistant manager had been up, said nothing with a worried expression, and gone away. I was leaning against the bathroom wall and sorting out my fingers.

Flack said suddenly: 'I figure an ice-pick job's a dame's work. You can buy them anywhere. Ten cents. If you want one fast, you can slip it down inside a garter and let it hang there.'

Christy French gave him a brief glance which had a kind of wonder in it. Beifus said: 'What kind of dames you been running around with, honey? The way stockings cost nowadays a dame would as soon stick a saw down her sock.'

'I never thought of that,' Flack said.

Beifus said: 'Leave us do the thinking, sweetheart. It takes equipment.'

'No need to get tough,' Flack said.

Beifus took his hat off and bowed. 'You mustn't deny us our little pleasures, Mr Flack.'

Christy French said: 'Besides, a woman would keep on jabbing. She wouldn't even know how much was enough. Lots of the punks don't. Whoever did this one was a performer. He got the spinal cord the first try. And another thing – you have to have the guy quiet to do it. That means more than one guy, unless he was doped, or the killer was a friend of his.'

I said: 'I don't see how he could have been doped, if he's the party that called me on the phone.'

French and Beifus both looked at me with the same expression of patient boredom. 'If,' French said, 'and since you don't know the guy – according to you – there's always the faint possibility that you wouldn't know his voice. Or am I being too subtle?'

'I don't know,' I said. 'I haven't read your fan mail.'

French grinned.

'Don't waste it on him,' Beifus told French. 'Save it for when you talk to the Friday Morning Club. Some of them old ladies in the shiny-nose league go big for the nicer angles of murder.'

French rolled himself a cigarette and lit it with a kitchen match he struck on the back of a chair. He sighed.

'They worked the technique out in Brooklyn,' he explained. 'Sunny Moe Stein's boys specialized in it, but they run it into the ground. It got so you couldn't walk across a vacant lot without finding some of their work. Then they came out here, what was left of them. I wonder why did they do that?'

'Maybe we just got more vacant lots,' Beifus said.

'Funny thing, though,' French said, almost dreamily. 'When Weepy Moyer had the chill put on Sunny Moe Stein over on Franklin Avenue last February, the killer used a gun. Moe wouldn't have liked that at all.'

'I betcha that was why his face had that disappointed look, after they washed the blood off,' Beifus remarked.

'Who's Weepy Moyer?' Flack asked.

'He was next to Moe in the organization,' French told him. 'This could easily be his work. Not that he'd have done it personal.'

'Why not?' Flack asked sourly.

'Don't you guys ever read a paper? Moyer's a gentleman now. He knows the nicest people. Even has another name. And as for the Sunny Moe Stein job, it just happened we had him in jail on a gambling rap. We didn't get anywhere. But we did make him a very sweet alibi. Anyhow he's a gentleman like I said, and gentlemen don't go around sticking ice-picks into people. They hire it done.'

'Did you ever have anything on Moyer?' I asked.

French looked at me sharply. 'Why?'

'I just had an idea. But it's very fragile,' I said.

French eyed me slowly. 'Just between us girls in the powder room,' he said, 'we never even proved the guy we had *was* Moyer. But don't broadcast it. Nobody's supposed to know but him and his lawyer and the D.A. and the police beat and the city hall and maybe two or three hundred other people.'

He slapped the dead man's empty wallet against his thigh and sat down on the bed. He leaned casually against the corpse's leg, lit a cigarette and pointed with it.

'That's enough time on the vaudeville circuit. Here's what we got, Fred. First off, the customer here was not too bright. He was going by the name of Dr G. W. Hambleton and had the cards printed with an El Centro address and a phone number. It took just two minutes to find out there ain't any such address or any such phone number. A bright boy doesn't lay open that easy. Next, the guy is definitely not in the chips. He has fourteen smackerooes folding in here and about two bucks loose change. On his key ring he don't have any car key or any safe-deposit key or any house key. All he's got is a suitcase key and seven filed Yale master keys. Filed fairly recently at that. I figure he was planning to sneak the hotel a little. Do you think these keys would work in your dump, Flack?'

Flack went over and stared at the keys. 'Two of them are the right size,' he said. 'I couldn't tell if they'd work by just looking. If I want a master key I have to get it from the office. All I carry is a pass-key. I can only use that if the guest is out.' He took a key out of his pocket, a key on a long chain, and compared it. He shook his head. 'They're no good without more work,' he said. 'Far too much metal on them.'

French flicked ash into the palm of his hand and blew it off as dust. Flack went back to his chair by the window.

'Next point,' Christy French announced. 'He don't have a driver's licence or any identification. None of his outside clothes were bought in El Centro. He had some kind of a grift, but he don't have the looks or personality to bounce cheques.'

'You didn't really see him at his best,' Beifus put in.

'And this hotel is the wrong dump for that anyway,' French went on. 'It's got a crummy reputation.'

'Now wait a minute!' Flack began.

French cut him short with a gesture. 'I know every hotel in the metropolitan district, Flack. It's my business to know. For fifty bucks I could organize a double-strip act with French trimmings inside of an hour in any room in this hotel. Don't kid me. You earn your living and I'll earn mine. Just don't kid me. All right. The customer had something he was afraid to keep around. That means he knew somebody was after him and getting close. So he offers Marlowe a hundred bucks to keep it for him. But he doesn't have that much money on him. So what he must have been planning on was getting Marlowe to gamble with him. It couldn't have been hot jewellery then. It had to be something semi-legitimate. That right, Marlowe?'

'You could leave out the semi,' I said.

French grinned faintly. 'So what he had was something that could be kept flat or rolled up – in a phone box, a hat band, a Bible, a can of talcum. We don't know whether it was found or not. But we do know there was very little time. Not much more than half an hour.'

'If Dr Hambleton did the phoning,' I said. 'You opened that can of beans yourself.'

'It's kind of pointless any other way. The killers wouldn't be in a hurry to have him found. Why should they ask anybody to come over to his room?' He turned to Flack. 'Any chance to check his visitors?'

Flack shook his head gloomily. 'You don't even have to pass the desk to get to the elevators.'

Beifus said: 'Maybe that was one reason he came here. That, and the homey atmosphere.'

'All right,' French said. 'Whoever knocked him off could come and go without any questions asked. All he had to know was his room number. And that's about all we know. Okay, Fred?'

Beifus nodded.

I said: 'Not quite all. It's a nice toupee, but it's still a toupee.'

French and Beifus both swung around quickly. French reached, carefully removed the dead man's hair, and whistled. 'I wondered what that damn intern was grinning at,' he said. 'The bastard didn't even mention it. See what I see, Fred?'

'All I see is a guy without no hair,' Beifus answered.

'Maybe you never knew him at that. Mileaway Marston. Used to be a runner for Ace Devore.'

'Why, sure enough,' Beifus chuckled. He leaned over and patted the dead bald head gently. 'How you been all this time, Mileaway? I didn't see you in so long I forgot. But you know me, pal. Once a softy always a softy.'

The man on the bed looked old and hard and shrunken without his toupee. The yellow mask of death was beginning to set his face into rigid lines.

French said calmly: 'Well, that takes a load off my mind. This punk ain't going to be no twenty-four-hour-a-day job. The hell with him.' He replaced the toupee over one eye and stood up off the bed. 'That's all for you two,' he said to Flack and me.

Flack stood up.

'Thanks for the murder, honey,' Beifus told him. 'You get any more in your nice hotel, don't forget our services. Even when it ain't good, it's quick.'

Flack went down the short hall and yanked the door open. I followed him out. On the way to the elevator we didn't speak. Nor on the way down. I walked with him along to his little office, followed him in and shut the door. He seemed surprised.

He sat down at his desk and reached for his telephone. 'I got to make a report to the Assistant Manager,' he said. 'Something you want?'

I rolled a cigarette around on my fingers, put a match to it and blew smoke softly across the desk. 'One hundred and fifty dollars,' I said.

Flack's small, intent eyes became round holes in a face washed clean of expression. 'Don't get funny in the wrong place,' he said.

'After those two comedians upstairs, you could hardly blame me if I did. But I'm not being funny.' I beat a tattoo on the edge of the desk and waited.

Tiny beads of sweat showed on Flack's lip above his little moustache. 'I got business to attend to,' he said, more throatily this time. 'Beat it and keep going.'

'Such a tough little man,' I said. 'Dr Hambleton had $164.00 currency in his wallet when I searched him. He promised me a hundred as retainer, remember? Now, in the same wallet, he has fourteen dollars. And I *did* leave the door of his room unlocked. And somebody else locked it. You locked it, Flack.'

Flack took hold of the arms of his chair and squeezed. His voice came from the bottom of a well, saying: 'You can't prove a damn thing.'

'Do I have to try?'

He took the gun out of his waistband and laid it on the desk in front of him. He stared down at it. It didn't have any message for him. He looked up at me again. 'Fifty-fifty, huh?' he said brokenly.

There was a moment of silence between us. He got his old shabby wallet out and rooted in it. He came up with a handful of currency and spread bills out on the desk, sorted them into two piles and pushed one pile my way.

I said: 'I want the whole hundred and fifty.'

He hunched down in his chair and stared at a corner of the desk. After a long time, he sighed. He put the two piles together and pushed them over – to my side of the desk.

'It wasn't doing him any good,' Flack said. 'Take the dough and breeze. I'll remember you, buddy. All you guys make me sick to my stomach. How do I know you didn't take half a grand off him?'

'I'd take it all. So would the killer. Why leave fourteen dollars?'

'So why did I leave fourteen dollars?' Flack asked, in a tired voice, making vague movements along the desk edge with his fingers. I picked up the money, counted it and threw it back at him.

'Because you're in the business and could size him up. You knew he'd at least have room rent, and a few dollars for loose change. The cops would expect the same thing. Here, I don't want the money. I want something else.'

He stared at me with his mouth open.

'Put that dough out of sight,' I said.

He reached for it and crammed it back in his wallet. 'What something else?' His eyes were small and thoughtful. His tongue pushed out his lower lip. 'It don't seem to me *you're* in a very hot trading position either.'

'You could be a little wrong about that. If I have to go back up there and tell Christy French and Beifus I was up there before and searched the body, I'd get a tongue lashing all right. But he'd understand that I haven't been holding out just to be smart. He'd know that somewhere in the background I had a client I was trying to protect. I'd get tough talk and bluster. But that's not what *you'd* get.' I stopped and watched the faint glisten of moisture forming on his forehead now. He swallowed hard. His eyes were sick.

'Cut out the wise talk and lay your deal on the desk,' he said. He grinned suddenly, rather wolfishly. 'Got here a little late to protect her, didn't you?' The fat sneer he lived with was coming home again, slowly, but gladly.

I killed my cigarette and got another one out and went through all the slow futile face-saving motions of lighting it, getting rid of the match, blowing smoke off to one side, inhaling deeply as though that scrubby little office was a hilltop overlooking the bouncing ocean – all the tired clichéd mannerisms of my trade.

'All right,' I said. 'I'll admit it was a woman. I'll admit she must have been up there while he was dead, if that makes you happy. I guess it was just shock that made her run away.'

'Oh, sure,' Flack said nastily. The fat sneer was all the way home now. 'Or maybe she hadn't ice-picked a guy in a month. Kind of lost touch.'

'But why would she take his key?' I said, talking to myself. 'And why leave it at the desk? Why not just walk away and leave the whole thing? What if she did think she had to lock the door? Why not drop the key in a sand jar and cover it up? Or take it away with her and lose it? Why do anything with that key that would connect her with that room?' I brought my eyes down and gave Flack a thick leaden stare. 'Unless of course she was seen to leave the room – with the key already in her hand – and followed out of the hotel.'

'What for would anybody do that?' Flack asked.

'Because whoever saw her could have got into that room at once. He had a pass-key.'

Flack's eyes flicked up at me and dropped all in one motion.

'So he must have followed her,' I said. 'He must have seen her dump the key at the desk and stroll out of the hotel and he must have followed her a little farther than that.'

Flack said derisively: 'What makes you so wonderful?'

I leaned down and pulled the telephone towards me. 'I'd better call Christy and get this over with,' I said. 'The more I think about it the scareder I get. Maybe she did kill him. I can't cover up for a murderer.'

I took the receiver off the hook. Flack slammed his moist paw down hard on top of my hand. The phone jumped on the desk. 'Lay off.' His voice was almost a sob. 'I followed her to a car parked down the street. Got the number. Christ sake, pal, give me some kind of a break.' He was fumbling wildly in his pockets. 'Know what I make on this job? Cigarette and cigar money and hardly a dime more. Wait a minute now. I think –' He looked down and played solitaire with some dirty envelopes, finally selected one and tossed it over to me. 'Licence number,' he said wearily, 'and if it's any satisfaction to you, I can't even remember what it was.'

I looked down at the envelope. There was a scrawled licence number on it all right. Ill-written and faint and oblique, the way it would be written hastily on a paper held in a man's hand on the street. 6 N 333. California 1947.

'Satisfied?' This was Flack's voice. Or it came out of his mouth. I tore the number off and tossed the envelope back to him.

'4 P 327,' I said, watching his eyes. Nothing flicked in them. No trace of derision or concealment. 'But how do I know this isn't just some licence number you had already?'

'You just got to take my word for it.'

'Describe the car,' I said.

'Caddy convertible, not new, top up. About 1942 model. Sort of dusty blue colour.'

'Describe the woman.'

'Want a lot for your dough, don't you, peeper?'

'Dr Hambleton's dough.'

He winced. 'All right. Blonde. White coat with some coloured stitching on it. Wide blue straw hat. Dark glasses. Height about five two. Built like a Conover model.'

'Would you know her again – without the glasses?' I asked carefully.

He pretended to think. Then shook his head, no.

'What was that licence number again, Flackie?' I caught him off his guard.

'Which one?' he said.

I leaned across the desk and dropped some cigarette ash on his gun. I did some more staring into his eyes. But I knew he was licked now. He seemed to know too. He reached for his gun, blew off the ash and put it back in the drawer of his desk.

'Go on. Beat it,' he said between his teeth. 'Tell the cops I frisked the stiff. So what? Maybe I lose a job. Maybe I get tossed in the fish-bowl. So what? When I come out I'm solid. Little Flackie don't have to worry about coffee and crullers. Don't think for a minute those dark cheaters fool little Flackie. I've seen too many movies to miss that lovely puss. And if you ask me that babe'll be around for a long time. She's a comer – and who knows –' he leered at me triumphantly '– she'll need a bodyguard one of these days. A guy to have around, watch things, keep her out of jams. Somebody that knows the ropes and ain't unreasonable about dough. . . . What's the matter?'

I had put my head on one side and was leaning forward. I was listening. 'I thought I heard a church bell,' I said.

'There ain't any church around here,' he said contemptuously. 'It's that platinum brain of yours getting cracks in it.'

'Just one bell,' I said. 'Very slow. Tolling is the word, I believe.'

Flack listened with me. 'I don't hear anything,' he said sharply.

'Oh, you wouldn't hear it,' I said. 'You'd be the one guy in the whole world who wouldn't hear it.'

He just sat there and stared at me with his nasty little eyes half closed and his nasty little moustache shining. One of his hands twitched on the desk, an aimless movement.

I left him to his thoughts, which were probably as small, ugly and frightened as the man himself.

12

The apartment house was over on Doheny Drive, just down the hill from the Strip. It was really two buildings, one behind the other, loosely connected by a floored patio with a fountain and a room built over the arch. There were mail boxes and bells in the imitation marble foyer. Three out of the sixteen had no names over them. The names that I read meant nothing to me. The job needed a little more work. I tried the front door, found it unlocked, and the job still needed more work.

Outside stood two Cadillacs, a Lincoln Continental and a Packard Clipper. Neither of the Cadillacs had the right colour or licence. Across the way a guy in riding breeches was sprawled with his legs over the door of a low-cut Lancia. He was smoking and looking up at the pale stars which know enough to keep their distance from Hollywood. I walked up the steep hill to the boulevard and a block east and smothered myself in an outdoor sweat-box phone booth. I dialled a man named Peoria Smith, who was so-called because he stuttered – another little mystery I hadn't had time to work out.

'Mavis Weld,' I said. 'Phone number. This is Marlowe.'

'S-s-s-sure,' he said. 'M-M-Mavis Weld huh? You want h-h-her ph-ph-phone number?'

'How much?'

'Be-b-b-be ten b-b-b-bucks,' he said.

'Just forget I called,' I said.

'W-W-Wait a minute! I ain't supposed to give out with them b-b-babes' phone numbers. An assistant prop man is taking a hell of a chance.'

I waited and breathed back my own breath.

'The address goes with it naturally,' Peoria whined, forgetting to stutter.

'Five bucks,' I said. 'I've got the address already. And don't haggle. If you think you're the only studio grifter in the business of selling unlisted telephone numbers –'

'Hold it,' he said wearily, and went to get his little red book. A left-handed stutterer. He only stuttered when he wasn't excited. He came back and gave it to me. A Crestview number, of course. If you don't have a Crestview number in Hollywood you're a bum.

I opened up the steel-and-glass cell to let in some air while I dialled again. After two rings a drawling sexy voice answered. I pulled the door shut.

'Ye-e-e-s', the voice cooed.

'Miss Weld, please.'

'And who is calling Miss Weld, if you please?'

'I have some stills Whitey wants me to deliver tonight.'

'Whitey? And who is Whitey, amigo?'

'The head still-photographer at the studio,' I said. 'Don't you know that much? I'll come up if you'll tell me which apartment. I'm only a couple of blocks away.'

'Miss Weld is taking a bath.' She laughed. I guess it was a silvery tinkle where she was. It sounded like somebody putting away saucepans where I was. 'But of course bring up the photographs. I am sure she is dying to see them. The apartment number is fourteen.'

'Will you be there too?'

'But of course. But naturally. Why do you ask that?'

I hung up and staggered out into the fresh air. I went down the hill. The guy in the riding breeches was still hanging out of the Lancia but one of the Cadillacs was gone and two Buick convertibles had joined the cars in front. I pushed the bell to number 14, went on through the patio where scarlet Chinese honeysuckle was lit by a peanut spotlight. Another light glowed down on the big ornamental pool full of fat goldfish and silent lily ponds, the lilies folded tight for the night. There were a couple of stone seats and a lawn swing. The place didn't look very expensive except that every place was expensive that year. The apartment was on the second floor, one of two doors facing across a wide landing.

The bell chimed and a tall dark girl in jodhpurs opened the door. Sexy was very faint praise for her. The jodhpurs, like her hair, were coal black. She wore a white silk shirt with a scarlet scarf loose around her throat. It was not as vivid as her mouth. She held a long brown cigarette in a pair of tiny golden tweezers. The fingers holding it were more than adequately jewelled. Her black hair was parted in the middle and a line of scalp as white as snow went over the top of her head and dropped out of sight behind. Two thick braids of her shining black hair lay one on each side of her slim brown neck. Each was tied with a small scarlet bow. But it was a long time since she was a little girl.

She looked sharply down at my empty hands. Studio stills are usually a little too big to put in your pocket.

I said: 'Miss Weld, please.'

'You can give me the stills.' The voice was cool, drawling and insolent, but the eyes were something else. She looked almost as hard to get as a haircut.

'For Miss Weld personally. Sorry.'

'I told you she was taking a bath.'

'I'll wait.'

'Are you quite sure you have the stills, amigo?'

'As sure as I'll ever be. Why?'

'Your name?' Her voice froze on the second word, like a feather taking off in a sudden draught. Then it cooed and hovered and soared and eddied and the silent invitation of a smile picked delicately at the corners of her lips, very slowly like a child trying to pick up a snowflake.

'Your last picture was wonderful, Miss Gonzales.'

The smile flashed like lightning and changed her whole face. The body came erect and vibrant with delight. 'But it was stinking,' she glowed. 'Positively goddamned stinking, you sweet lovely man. You know but positively goddamn well it was stinking.'

'Nothing with you in it stinks for me, Miss Gonzales.'

She stood away from the door and waved me in. 'We will have a drink,' she said. 'The goddamnedest drink we will have. I adore flattery, however dishonest.'

I went in. A gun in the kidney wouldn't have surprised me a bit. She stood so that I had to practically push her mammaries out of the way to get through the door. She smelled the way the Taj Mahal looks by moonlight. She closed the door and danced over to a small portable bar.

'Scotch? Or would you prefer a mixed drink? I mix a perfectly loathsome Martini,' she said.

'Scotch is fine, thanks.'

She made a couple of drinks in a couple of glasses you could almost have stood umbrellas in. I sat down in a chintz chair and looked around.

The place was old-fashioned. It had a false fireplace with gas logs and a marble mantel, cracks in the plaster, a couple of vigorously coloured daubs on the walls that looked lousy enough to have cost money, an old black chipped Steinway and for once no Spanish shawl on it. There were a lot of new-looking books in bright jackets scattered around and a double-barrelled shotgun with a handsomely carved stock stood in the corner with a white satin bow tied around the barrels. Hollywood wit.

The dark lady in the jodhpurs handed me a glass and perched on the arm of my chair. 'You may call me Dolores if you wish,' she said, taking a hearty swig out of her own tumbler.

'Thanks.'

'And what may I call you?'

I grinned.

'Of course,' she said, 'I am most fully aware that you are a goddamn liar and that you have no stills in your pockets. Not that I wish to inquire into your no doubt very private business.'

'Yeah?' I inhaled a couple of inches of my liquor. 'Just what kind of bath is Miss Weld taking? An old-fashioned soap or something with Arabian spices in it?'

She waved the remains of the brown cigarette in the small gold clasp. 'Perhaps you would like to help her. The bathroom is over there – through the arch and to the right. Most probably the door is not locked.'

'Not if it's that easy,' I said.

'Oh,' she gave me the brilliant smile again. 'You like to do the difficult things in life. I must remember to be less approachable, must I not?' She removed herself elegantly from the arm of my chair and ditched her cigarette, bending over so that I could trace the outline of her hips.

'Don't bother, Miss Gonzales. I'm just a guy who came here on business. I don't have any idea of raping anybody.'

'No?' The smile became soft, lazy and, if you can't think of a better word, provocative.

'But I'm sure as hell working up to it,' I said.

'You are an amusing son-of-a-bitch,' she said with a shrug and went off through the arch, carrying her half-quart of Scotch and water with her. I heard a gentle tapping on a door and her voice: 'Darling, there's a man here who says he has some stills from the studio. He says. Muy simpático. Muy guapo también. Con cojones.'

A voice I had heard before said sharply: 'Shut up, you little bitch. I'll be out in a second.'

The Gonzales came back through the archway humming. Her glass was empty. She went to the bar again. 'But you are not drinking,' she cried, looking at my glass.

'I ate dinner. I only have a two-quart stomach anyway. I understand a little Spanish.'

She tossed her head. 'You are shocked?' Her eyes rolled. Her shoulders did a fan dance.

'I'm pretty hard to shock.'

'But you heard what I said? Madre de Dios. I'm so terribly sorry.'

'I'll bet,' I said.

She finished making herself another highball.

'Yes. I am so sorry,' she sighed. 'That is, I think I am. Sometimes I am not sure. Sometimes I do not give a good goddamn. It is so confusing. All my friends tell me I am far too outspoken. I do shock you, don't I?' She was on the arm of my chair again.

'No. But if I wanted to be shocked I'd know right where to come.' She reached her glass behind her indolently and leaned towards me.

'But I do not live here,' she said. 'I live at the Chateau Bercy.'

'Alone?'

She slapped me delicately across the tip of my nose. The next thing I knew I had her in my lap and she was trying to bite a piece off my tongue. 'You are a very sweet son-of-a-bitch,' she said. Her mouth was as hot as ever a mouth was. Her lips burned like dry ice. Her tongue was driving hard against my teeth. Her eyes looked enormous and black and the whites showed under them.

'I am so tired,' she whispered into my mouth. 'I am so worn, so incredibly tired.'

I felt her hand in my breast pocket. I shoved her off hard, but she had my wallet. She danced away with it laughing, flicked it open and went through it with fingers that darted like little snakes.

'So glad you two got acquainted,' a voice off to one side said coolly. Mavis Weld stood in the archway.

Her hair was fluffed out carelessly and she hadn't bothered with make-up. She wore a hostess gown and very little else. Her legs ended in little green and silver slippers. Her eyes were empty, her lips contemptuous. But she was the same girl all right, dark glasses on or off.

The Gonzales gave her a quick darting glance, closed my wallet and tossed it. I caught it and put it away. She strolled to a table and picked up a black bag with a long strap, hooked it over her shoulder and moved towards the door.

Mavis Weld didn't move, didn't look at her. She looked at me. But there was no emotion of any kind in her face. The Gonzales opened the door and glanced outside and almost closed it and turned.

'The name is Philip Marlowe,' she said to Mavis Weld. 'Nice, don't you think?'

'I didn't know you bothered to ask them their names,' Mavis Weld said. 'You so seldom know them long enough.'

'I see,' the Gonzales answered gently. She turned and smiled at me faintly. 'Such a charming way to call a girl a whore, don't you think?'

Mavis Weld said nothing. Her face had no expression.

'At least,' the Gonzales said smoothly as she pulled the door open again, 'I haven't been sleeping with any gunmen lately.'

'Are you sure you can remember?' Mavis Weld asked her in exactly the same tone. 'Open the door, honey. This is the day we put the garbage out.'

The Gonzales looked back at her slowly, levelly, and with a knife in her eyes. Then she made a faint sound with her lips and teeth and yanked the door wide. It closed behind her with a jarring smash. The noise didn't even flicker the steady dark blue glare in Mavis Weld's eyes.

'Now suppose you do the same – but more quietly,' she said.

I got out a handkerchief and scrubbed the lipstick over my face. It looked exactly the colour of blood, fresh blood. 'That could happen to anybody,' I said. 'I wasn't petting her. She was petting me.'

She marched to the door and heaved it open. 'On your way, dreamboat. Make with the feet.'

'I came here on business, Miss Weld.'

'Yes. I can imagine. Out. I don't know you. I don't want to know you. And if I did, this wouldn't be either the day or the hour.'

'Never the time and place and the loved one all together,' I said.

'What's that?' She tried to throw me out with the point of her chin, but even she wasn't that good.

'Browning. The poet, not the automatic. I feel sure you'd prefer the automatic.'

'Look, little man, do I have to call the manager to bounce you downstairs like a basketball?'

I went over and pushed the door shut. She held on to the last moment. She didn't quite kick me, but it cost her an effort not to. I tried to ease her away from the door without appearing to. She didn't ease worth a darn. She stood her ground, one hand still reaching for the door-knob, her eyes full of dark-blue rage.

'If you're going to stand that close to me,' I said, 'maybe you'd better put some clothes on.'

She took her hand back and swung it hard. The slap sounded like Miss Gonzales slamming the door, but it stung. And it reminded me of the sore place on the back of my head.

'Did I hurt you?' she asked softly.

I nodded.

'That's fine.' She hauled off and slapped me again, harder if anything. 'I think you'd better kiss me,' she breathed. Her eyes were clear and limpid and melting. I glanced down casually. Her right hand was balled into a very business-like fist. It wasn't too small to work with, either.

'Believe me,' I said. 'There's only one reason I don't. Even if you had your little black gun with you. Or the brass knuckles you probably keep on your night table.'

She smiled politely.

'I might just happen to be working for you,' I said. 'And I don't go whoring around after every pair of legs I see.' I looked down at hers. I could see them all right and the flag that marked the goal line was no larger than it had to be. She pulled the hostess gown together and turned and walked over to the little bar shaking her head.

'I'm free, white and twenty-one,' she said. 'I've seen all the approaches there are. I think I have. If I can't scare you, lick you, or seduce you, what the hell can I buy you with?'

'Well –'

'Don't tell me,' she interrupted sharply and turned with a glass in her hand. She drank and tossed the loose hair around and smiled a thin little smile. 'Money, of course. How damned stupid of me to overlook that.'

'Money would help,' I said.

Her mouth twisted in wry disgust but the voice was almost affectionate. 'How much money?'

'Oh, a hundred bucks would do to start with.'

'You're cheap. It's a cheap little bastard, isn't it? A hundred bucks it says. Is a hundred bucks money in your circle, darling?'

'Make it two hundred then. I could retire on that.'

'Still cheap. Every week of course. In a nice clean envelope?'

'You could skip the envelope. I'd only get it dirty.'

'And just what would I get for this money, my charming little gumshoe? I'm quite sure of what you are, of course.'

'You'd get a receipt. Who told you I was a gum-shoe?'

She stared out of her own eyes for a brief instant before the act dropped over her again. 'It must have been the smell.' She sipped her drink and stared at me over it with a faint smile of contempt.

'I'm beginning to think you write your own dialogue,' I said. 'I've been wondering just what was the matter with it.'

I ducked. A few drops splattered me. The glass splintered on the wall behind me. The broken pieces fell soundlessly.

'And with that,' she said, completely calm, 'I believe I must have used up my entire stock of girlish charm.'

I went over and picked up my hat. 'I never thought *you* killed him,' I said. 'But it would help to have some sort of reason for not telling you were there. It's a help to have money enough for a retainer just to establish myself. And enough information to justify my accepting the retainer.'

She picked a cigarette out of a box, tossed it in the air, caught it between her lips effortlessly and lit it with a match that came from nowhere.

'My goodness. Am I supposed to have killed somebody?' she asked. I was still holding the hat. It made me feel foolish. I don't know why. I put it on and started for the door.

'I trust you have your car fare home,' the contemptuous voice said behind me.

I didn't answer. I just kept going. When I had the door ready to open she said: 'I also trust Miss Gonzales gave you her address and phone number. You should be able to get almost anything out of her – including, I am told, money.'

I let go of the door-knob and went back across the room fast. She stood her ground and the smile on her lips didn't slip a millimetre.

'Look,' I said. 'You're going to find this hard to believe. But I came over here with the quaint idea that you might be a girl who needed some help – and would find it rather hard to get anyone you could bank on. I figured you went to that hotel room to make some kind of a pay-off. And the fact that you went by yourself and took chances on being recognized – and *were* recognized by a house dick whose standard of ethics would take about as much strain as a very tired old cobweb – all this made me think you might be in one of those Hollywood jams that really mean curtains. But you're not in any jam. You're right up front under the baby spot pulling every tired ham gesture you ever used in the most tired B-picture you ever acted in – if acting is the word –'

'Shut up,' she said, between teeth so tight they grated. 'Shut up, you slimy, blackmailing keyhole peeper.'

'You don't need me,' I said. 'You don't need anybody. You're so goddamn smart you could talk your way out of a safe-deposit box. Okay. Go ahead and talk your way out. I won't stop you. Just don't make me listen to it. I'd burst out crying to think a mere slip of an innocent little girl like you should be so clever. You do things to me, honey. Just like Margaret O'Brien.'

She didn't move or breathe when I reached the door, nor when I opened it. I don't know why. The stuff wasn't *that* good.

I went down the stairs and across the court and out of the front door, almost bumping into a slim dark-eyed man who was standing there lighting a cigarette.

'Excuse me,' he said quietly, 'I'm afraid I'm in your way.'

I started to go around him, then I noticed that his lifted right hand held a key. I reached out and snapped it out of his hand for no reason at all. I looked at the number stamped on it. No. 14. Mavis Weld's apartment. I threw it off behind some bushes.

'You don't need that,' I said. 'The door isn't locked.'

'Of course,' he said. There was a peculiar smile on his face. 'How stupid of me.'

'Yeah,' I said. 'We're both stupid. Anybody's stupid that bothers with that tramp.'

'I wouldn't quite say that,' he answered quietly, his small sad eyes watching me without any particular expression.

'You don't have to,' I said. 'I just said it for you. I beg your pardon. I'll get your key.' I went over behind the bushes, picked it up and handed it to him.

'Thank you very much,' he said. 'And by the way –' He stopped. I stopped. 'I hope I don't interrupt an interesting quarrel,' he said. 'I should hate to do that. No?' He smiled. 'Well, since Miss Weld is a friend in common, may I introduce myself. My name is Steelgrave. Haven't I seen you somewhere?'

'No, you haven't seen me anywhere, Mr Steelgrave,' I said. 'My name's Marlowe, Philip Marlowe. It's extremely unlikely that we've met. And, strange to relate, I never heard of you, Mr Steelgrave. And I wouldn't give a damn, even if your name was Weepy Moyer.' I never knew quite why I said that. There was nothing to make me say it, except that the name had been mentioned. A peculiar stillness came over his face. A peculiar fixed look in his silent black eyes. He took the cigarette out of his mouth, looked at the tip, flicked a little ash off it, although there was no ash to flick off, looking down as he said: 'Weepy Moyer. Peculiar name. I don't think I ever heard that. Is he somebody I should know?'

'Not unless you're unusually fond of ice-picks,' I said, and left him. I went on down the steps, crossed to my car, looked back before I got in. He was standing there looking down at me, the cigarette between his lips. From that distance I couldn't see whether there was any expression on his face. He didn't move or make any kind of gesture when I looked back at him. He didn't turn away. He just stood there. I got in and drove off.

13

I drove east on Sunset but I didn't go home. At La Brea I turned north and swung over to Highland, out over Cahuenga Pass and down on to Ventura Boulevard, past Studio City and Sherman Oaks and Encino. There was nothing lonely about the trip. There never is on that road. Fast boys in stripped-down Fords shot in and out of the traffic streams, missing fenders by a sixteenth of an inch, but somehow always missing them. Tired men in dusty coupés and sedans winced and tightened their grip on the wheel and ploughed on north and west towards home and dinner, an evening with the sports page, the blatting of the radio, the whining of their spoiled children and the gabble of their silly wives. I drove on past the gaudy neons and the false fronts behind them, the sleazy hamburger joints that look like palaces under the colours, the circular drive-ins as gay as circuses with the chipper hard-eyed car-hops, the brilliant counters, and the sweaty greasy kitchens that would have poisoned a toad. Great double trucks rumbled down over Sepulveda from Wilmington and San Pedro and crossed towards the Ridge Route, starting up in low from the traffic lights with a growl of lions in the zoo.

Behind Encino an occasional light winked from the hills through thick trees. The homes of screen stars. Screen stars, phooey. The veterans of a thousand beds. Hold it, Marlowe, you're not human tonight.

The air got cooler. The highway narrowed. The cars were so few now that the headlights hurt. The grade rose against chalk walls and at the top a breeze, unbroken from the ocean, danced casually across the night.

I ate dinner at a place near Thousand Oaks. Bad but quick. Feed 'em and throw 'em out. Lots of business. We can't bother with you sitting over your second cup of coffee, mister. You're using money space. See those people over there behind the rope? They want to eat. Anyway they think they have to. God knows why they want to eat here. They could do better home out of a can. They're just restless. Like you. They have to get the car out and go somewhere. Suckerbait for the racketeers that have taken over the restaurants. Here we go again. You're not human tonight, Marlowe.

I paid off and stopped in a bar to drop a brandy on top of the New York cut. Why New York, I thought. It was Detroit where they made machine tools. I stepped out into the night air that nobody had yet found out how to option. But a lot of people were probably trying. They'd get around to it.

I drove on to the Oxnard cut-off and turned back along the ocean. The big eight-wheelers and sixteen-wheelers were streaming north, all hung over with orange lights. On the right the great fat solid Pacific trudging into shore like a scrub-woman going home. No moon, no fuss, hardly a sound of the surf. No smell. None of the harsh wild smell of the sea. A California ocean. California, the department-store state. The most of everything and the best of nothing. Here we go again. You're not human tonight, Marlowe.

All right. Why should I be? I'm sitting in that office, playing with a dead fly and in pops this dowdy little item from Manhattan, Kansas, and chisels me down to a shop-worn twenty to find her brother. He sounds like a creep but she wants to find him. So with this fortune clasped to my chest, I trundle down to Bay City and the routine I go through is so tired I'm half asleep on my feet. I meet nice people, with and without ice-picks in their necks. I leave, and I leave myself wide-open too. Then she comes in and takes the twenty away from me and gives me a kiss and gives it back to me because I didn't do a full day's work.

So I go see Dr Hambleton, retired (and how) optometrist from El Centro, and meet again the new style in neckwear. And I don't tell the cops. I just frisk the customer's toupee and put on an act. Why? Who am I cutting my throat for this time? A blonde with sexy eyes and too many door keys? A girl from Manhattan, Kansas? I don't know. All I know is that something isn't what it seems and the old tired but always reliable hunch tells me that if the hand is played the way it is dealt the wrong person is going to lose the pot. Is that my business? Well, what is my business? Do I know? Did I ever know? Let's not go into that. You're not human tonight, Marlowe. Maybe I never was nor ever will be. Maybe I'm an ectoplasm with a private licence. Maybe we all get like this in the cold half-lit world where always the wrong thing happens and never the right.

Malibu. More movie stars. More pink and blue bath-tubs. More tufted beds. More Chanel No. 5. More Lincoln Continentals and Cadillacs. More wind-blown hair and sunglasses and attitudes and pseudo-refined voices and waterfront morals. Now, wait a minute. Lots of nice people work in pictures. You've got the wrong attitude, Marlowe. You're not human tonight.

I smelled Los Angeles before I got to it. It smelled stale and old like a living-room that had been closed too long. But the coloured lights fooled you. The lights were wonderful. There ought to be a monument to the man who invented neon lights. Fifteen stories high, solid marble. There's a boy who really made something out of nothing.

So I went to a picture show and it had to have Mavis Weld in it. One of those glass-and-chromium deals where everybody smiled too much and talked too much and knew it. The women were always going up a long curving staircase to change their clothes. The men were always taking monogrammed cigarettes out of expensive cases and snapping expensive lighters at each other. And the help was round-shouldered from carrying trays with drinks across the terrace to a swimming pool about the size of Lake Huron but a lot neater.

The leading man was an amiable ham with a lot of charm, some of it turning a little yellow at the edges. The star was a bad-tempered brunette with contemptuous eyes and a couple of bad close-ups that showed her pushing forty-five backwards almost hard enough to break a wrist. Mavis Weld played second lead and she played it with wraps on. She was good, but she could have been ten times better. But if she had been ten times better half her scenes would have been yanked out to protect the star. It was as neat a bit of tight-rope walking as I ever saw. Well, it wouldn't be a tightrope she'd be walking from now on. It would be a piano wire. It would be very high. And there wouldn't be any net under it.

14

I had a reason for going back to the office. A special delivery letter with an orange claim check ought to have arrived there by now. Most of the windows were dark in the building, but not all. People work nights in other businesses than mine. The elevator man said 'Howdy' from the depths of his throat and trundled me up. The corridor had lighted open doors where the scrub-women were still cleaning up the debris of the wasted hours. I turned a corner past the slobbery hum of a vacuum cleaner, let myself into my dark office and opened the windows. I sat there at the desk doing nothing, not even thinking. No special delivery letter. All the noise of the building, except the vacuum cleaner, seemed to have flowed out into the street and lost itself among the turning wheels of innumerable cars. Then, somewhere along the hall outside, a man started whistling 'Lili Marlene' with elegance and virtuosity. I knew who that was. The night man checking office doors. I switched the desk lamp on and he passed without trying mine. His steps went away, then came back with a different sound, more of a shuffle. The buzzer sounded in the other office which was still unlocked. That would be special delivery. I went out to get it, only it wasn't.

A fat man in sky-blue pants was closing the door with that beautiful leisure only fat men ever achieve. He wasn't alone, but I looked at him first. He was a large man and wide. Not young nor handsome, but he looked durable. Above the sky-blue gabardine slacks he wore a two-tone leisure jacket which would have been revolting on a zebra. The neck of his canary-yellow shirt was open wide, which it had to be if his neck was going to get out. He was hatless and his large head was decorated with a reasonable amount of pale salmon-coloured hair. His nose had been broken but well set, and it hadn't been a collector's item in the first place.

The creature with him was a weedy number with red eyes and sniffles. Age about twenty, five feet nine, thin as a broom straw. His nose twitched and his mouth twitched and his hands twitched and he looked very unhappy.

453

The big man smiled genially. 'Mr Marlowe, no doubt?'

I said: 'Who else?'

'It's a little late for a business call,' the big man said and hid half the office by spreading out his hands. 'I hope you don't mind. Or do you already have all the business you can handle?'

'Don't kid me. My nerves are frayed,' I said. 'Who's the junky?'

'Come along, Alfred,' the big man said to his companion. 'And stop acting girlish.'

'In a pig's valise,' Alfred told him.

The big man turned to me placidly. 'Why do all these punks keep saying that? It isn't funny. It isn't witty. It doesn't mean anything. Quite a problem, this Alfred. I got him off the stuff, you know, temporarily at least. Say "How do you do" to Mr Marlowe, Alfred.'

'Screw him,' Alfred said.

The big man sighed. 'My name's Toad,' he said. 'Joseph P. Toad.'

I didn't say anything.

'Go ahead and laugh,' the big man said. 'I'm used to it. Had the name all my life.' He came towards me with his hand out. I took it. The big man smiled pleasantly into my eyes. 'Okay, Alfred,' he said without looking back.

Alfred made what seemed to be a very slight and unimportant movement at the end of which a heavy automatic was pointing at me.

'Careful, Alfred,' the big man said, holding my hand with a grip that would have bent a girder. 'Not yet.'

'In a pig's valise,' Alfred said. The gun pointed at my chest. His fingers tightened around the trigger. I watched it tighten. I knew at precisely what moment that tightening would release the hammer. It didn't seem to make any difference. This was happening somewhere else in a cheesy programme picture. It wasn't happening to me.

The hammer of the automatic clicked dryly on nothing. Alfred lowered the gun with a grunt of annoyance and it disappeared whence it had come. He started to twitch again. There was nothing nervous about his movements with the gun. I wondered just what junk he was off of.

The big man let go of my hand, the genial smile still over his large healthy face.

He patted a pocket. 'I got the magazine,' he said. 'Alfred ain't reliable lately. The little bastard might have shot you.'

Alfred sat down in a chair and tilted it against the wall and breathed through his mouth.

I let my heels down on the floor again.

'I bet he scared you,' Joseph P. Toad said.

I tasted salt on my tongue.

'You ain't so tough,' Toad said, poking me in the stomach with a fat finger.

I stepped away from the finger and watched his eyes.

'What does it cost?' he asked almost gently.

'Let's go into my parlour,' I said.

I turned my back on him and walked through the door into the other office. It was hard work but I made it. I sweated all the way. I went around behind the desk and stood there waiting. Mr Toad followed me in placidly. The junky came twitching in behind him.

'You don't have a comic book around, do you?' Toad asked. 'Keeps him quiet.'

'Sit down,' I said. 'I'll look.'

He reached for the chair arms, I jerked a drawer open and got my hand around the butt of a Luger. I brought it up slowly, looking at Alfred. Alfred didn't even look at me. He was studying the corner of the ceiling and trying to keep his mouth out of his eye.

'This is as comic as I get,' I said.

'You won't need that,' the big man said, genially.

'That's fine,' I said, like somebody else talking, far away behind a wall. I could just barely hear the words. 'But if I do, here it is. And this one's loaded. Want me to prove it to you?'

The big man looked as near worried as he would ever look. 'I'm sorry you take it like that,' he said. 'I'm so used to Alfred I hardly notice him. Maybe you're right. Maybe I ought to do something about him.'

'Yeah,' I said. 'Do it this afternoon before you come up here. It's too late now.'

'Now wait a minute, Mr Marlowe.' He put his hand out. I slashed at it with the Luger. He was fast, but not fast enough. I cut the back of his hand open with the sight on the gun. He grabbed at it and sucked at the cut. 'Hey, please! Alfred's my nephew. My sister's kid. I kind of look after him. He wouldn't hurt a fly, really.'

'Next time you come up I'll have one for him not to hurt,' I said.

'Now don't be like that, mister. Please don't be like that. I've got quite a nice little proposition –'

'Shut up,' I said. I sat down very slowly. My face burned. I had difficulty speaking clearly at all. I felt a little drunk. I said, slowly and thickly: 'A friend of mine told me about a fellow that had something like this pulled on him. He was at a desk the way I am. He had a gun, just the way I have. There were two men on the other side of the desk, like you and Alfred. The man on my side began to get mad. He couldn't help himself. He began to shake. He couldn't speak a word. He just had this gun in his hand. So without a word he shot twice under the desk, right where your belly is.'

The big man turned a sallow green colour and started to get up. But he changed his mind. He got a violent-looking handkerchief out of his pocket and mopped his face. 'You seen that in a picture,' he said.

'That's right,' I said. 'But the man who made the picture told me where he got the idea. *That* wasn't in any picture.' I put the Luger down on the desk in front of me and said in a more natural voice: 'You've got to be careful about firearms, Mr Toad. You never know but what it may upset a man to have an Army .45 snapped in his face – especially when he doesn't know it's not loaded. It made me kind of nervous for a minute. I haven't had a shot of morphine since lunch-time.'

Toad studied me carefully with narrow eyes. The junky got up and went to another chair and kicked it around and sat down and tilted his greasy head against the wall. But his nose and hands kept on twitching.

'I heard you were kind of hard-boiled,' Toad said slowly, his eyes cool and watchful.

'You heard wrong. I'm a very sensitive guy. I go all to pieces over nothing.'

'Yeah. I understand.' He stared at me a long time without speaking. 'Maybe we played this wrong. Mind if I put my hand in my pocket? I don't wear a gun.'

'Go ahead,' I said. 'It would give me the greatest possible pleasure to see you try to pull a gun.'

He frowned, then very slowly got out a flat pigskin wallet and drew out a crisp new one-hundred-dollar bill. He laid it on the edge of the glass top, drew out another just like it, then, one by one, three more. He laid them carefully in a row along the desk, end to end. Alfred let his chair settle to the floor and stared at the money with his mouth quivering.

'Five C's,' the big man said. He folded his wallet and put it away. I watched every movement he made. 'For nothing at all but keeping the nose clean. Check?'

I just looked at him.

'You ain't looking for nobody,' the big man said. 'You couldn't find nobody. You don't have time to work for nobody. You didn't hear a thing or see a thing. You're clean. Five C's clean. Okay?'

There was no sound in the office but Alfred's sniffling. The big man half turned his head. 'Quiet, Alfred. I'll give you a shot when we leave,' the big man told him. 'Try to act nice.' He sucked again at the cut on the back of his hand.

'With you for a model that ought to be easy,' I said.

'Screw you,' Alfred said.

'Limited vocabulary,' the big man told me. 'Very limited. Get the idea, chum?' He indicated the money. I fingered the butt of the Luger. He leaned forward a little. 'Relax, can't you. It's simple. This is a retainer. You don't do a thing for it. Nothing is what you do. If you keep on doing nothing for a reasonable length of time you get the same amount later on. That's simple, isn't it?'

'And who am I doing this nothing for?' I asked.

'Me. Joseph P. Toad.'

'What's your racket?'

'Business representative, you might call me.'

'What else could I call you? Besides what I could think up myself?'

'You could call me a guy that wants to help out a guy that don't want to make trouble for a guy.'

'And what could I call that lovable character?' I asked.

Joseph P. Toad gathered the five hundred-dollar bills together, lined up the edges neatly and pushed the packet across the desk. 'You can call him a guy that would rather spill money than blood,' he said. 'But he don't mind spilling blood if it looks like that's what he's got to do.'

'How is he with an ice-pick?' I asked. 'I can see how lousy he is with a
.45.'

The big man chewed his lower lip, then pulled it out with a blunt
forefinger and thumb and nibbled on the inside of it softly, like a milch
cow chewing her cud. 'We're not talking about ice-picks,' he said at
length. 'All we're talking about is how you might get off on the wrong
foot and do yourself a lot of harm. Whereas if you don't get off on no foot
at all, you're sitting pretty and money coming in.'

'Who is the blonde?' I asked.

He thought about that and nodded. 'Maybe you're into this too far
already,' he sighed. 'Maybe it's too late to do business.'

After a moment he leaned forward and said gently: 'Okay. I'll check
back with my principal and see how far out he wants to come. Maybe
we can still do business. Everything stands as it is until you hear from
me. Check?'

I let him have that one. He put his hands on the desk and very slowly
stood up, watching the gun I was pushing around on the blotter.

'You can keep the dough,' he said. 'Come on, Alfred.' He turned and
walked solidly out of the office.

Alfred's eyes crawled sideways watching him, then jerked to the money
on the desk. The big automatic appeared with the same magic in his right
hand. Dartingly as an eel he moved over to the desk. He kept the gun on
me and reached for the money with his left hand. It disappeared into his
pocket. He gave me a smooth cool empty grin, nodded and moved away,
apparently not realizing for a moment that I was holding a gun too.

'Come on, Alfred,' the big man called sharply from outside the door.
Alfred slipped through the door and was gone.

The outer door opened and closed. Steps went along the hall. Then
silence. I sat there thinking back over it, trying to make up my mind
whether it was pure idiocy or just a new way to toss a scare.

Five minutes later the telephone rang.

A thick pleasant voice said: 'Oh, by the way, Mr Marlowe, I guess you
know Sherry Ballou, don't you?'

'Nope.'

'Sheridan Ballou, Incorporated. The big agent? You ought to look him
up sometime.'

I held the phone silently for a moment. Then I said: 'Is he her agent?'

'He might be,' Joseph P. Toad said, and paused a moment. 'I suppose you realize we're just a couple of bit players, Mr Marlowe. That's all. Just a couple of bit players. Somebody wanted to find out a little something about you. It seemed the simplest way to do it. Now, I'm not so sure.'

I didn't answer. He hung up. Almost at once the phone rang again.

A seductive voice said: 'You do not like me so well, do you, amigo?'

'Sure I do. Just don't keep biting me.'

'I am at home at the Chateau Bercy. I am lonely.'

'Call an escort bureau.'

'But please. That is no way to talk. This is business of a great importance.'

'I bet. But not the business I'm in.'

'That slut – What does she say about me?' she hissed.

'Nothing. Oh, she might have called you a Tijuana hooker in riding pants. Would you mind?'

That amused her. The silvery giggle went on for a little while. 'Always the wisecrack with you. Is it not so? But you see I did not then know you were a detective. That makes a very big difference.'

I could have told her how wrong she was. I just said: 'Miss Gonzales, you said something about business. What kind of business, if you're not kidding me?'

'Would you like to make a great deal of money? A very great deal of money?'

'You mean without getting shot?' I asked.

Her incaught breath came over the wire. '*Si*,' she said thoughtfully. 'There is also that to consider. But you are so brave, so big, so – '

'I'll be at my office at nine in the morning, Miss Gonzales. I'll be a lot braver then. Now if you'll excuse me – '

'You have a date? Is she beautiful? More beautiful than I am?'

'For Christ's sake,' I said. 'Don't you ever think of anything but one thing?'

'The hell with you, darling,' she said, and hung up in my face.

I turned out the lights and left. Half-way down the hall I met a man looking at numbers. He had a special delivery in his hand. So I had to

459

go back to the office and put it in the safe. And the phone rang again while I was doing this.

I let it ring. I had had enough for one day. I just didn't care. It could have been the Queen of Sheba with her cellophane pyjamas on – or off – I was too tired to bother. My brain felt like a bucket of wet sand.

It was still ringing as I reached the door. No use. I had to go back. Instinct was stronger than weariness. I lifted the receiver.

Orfamay Quest's twittery little voice said: 'Oh, Mr Marlowe, I've been trying to get you for just the longest time. I'm so upset. I'm –'

'In the morning.' I said. 'The office is closed.'

'Please, Mr Marlowe – Just because I lost my temper for a moment –'

'In the morning.'

'But I tell you I have to see you.' The voice didn't quite rise to a yell. 'It's terribly important.'

'Uh-huh.'

She sniffled. 'You – you kissed me.'

'I've kissed better since,' I said. To hell with her. To hell with all women.

'I've heard from Orrin,' she said.

That stopped me for a moment, then I laughed. 'You're a nice little liar,' I said. 'Good-bye.'

'But really I have. He called me. On the telephone. Right here where I'm staying.'

'Fine,' I said. 'Then you don't need a detective at all. And if you did, you've got a better one than I am right in the family, I couldn't even find out where you were staying.'

There was a little pause. She still had me talking to her anyway. She'd kept me from hanging up. I had to give her that much.

'I wrote to him where I'd be staying,' she said at last.

'Uh-huh. Only he didn't get the letter because he had moved and he didn't leave any forwarding address. Remember? Try again some time when I'm not so tired. Good night, Miss Quest. And you don't have to tell me where you are staying now. I'm not working for you.'

'Very well, Mr Marlowe. I'm ready to call the police now. But I don't think you'll like it. I don't think you'll like it at all.'

'Why?'

'Because there's murder in it, Mr Marlowe, and murder is a very nasty word – don't you think?'

'Come on up,' I said. 'I'll wait.'

I hung up. I got the bottle of Old Forester out. There was nothing slow about the way I poured myself a drink and dropped it down my throat.

15

She came in briskly enough this time. Her motions were small and quick and determined. There was one of those thin little, bright little smiles on her face. She put her bag down firmly, settled herself in the customer's chair and went on smiling.

'It's nice of you to wait for me,' she said. 'I bet you haven't had your dinner yet, either.'

'Wrong,' I said. 'I have had my dinner. I am now drinking whisky. You don't approve of whisky drinking, do you?'

'I certainly do not.'

'That's just dandy,' I said. 'I hoped you hadn't changed your mind.' I put the bottle up on the desk and poured myself another slug. I drank a little of it and gave her a leer above the glass.

'If you keep on with that you won't be in any condition to listen to what I have to say,' she snapped.

'About this murder,' I said. 'Anybody I know? I can see you're not murdered – yet.'

'Please don't be unnecessarily horrid. It's not my fault. You doubted me over the telephone so I had to convince you. Orrin did call me up. But he wouldn't tell me where he was or what he was doing. I don't know why.'

'He wanted you to find out for yourself,' I said. 'He's building your character.'

'That's not funny. It's not even smart.'

'But you've got to admit it's nasty,' I said. 'Who was murdered? Or is that a secret too?'

She fiddled a little with her bag, not enough to overcome her embarrassment, because she wasn't embarrassed. But enough to needle me into taking another drink.

'That horrid man in the rooming house was murdered. Mr – Mr – I forget his name.'

'Let's both forget it,' I said. 'Let's do something together for once.' I dropped the whisky bottle into the desk drawer and stood up. 'Look, Orfamay, I'm not asking you how you know all this. Or rather how Orrin knows it all. Or if he *does* know it. You've found him. That's what you wanted me to do. Or he's found you, which comes to much the same thing.'

'It's not the same thing,' she cried. 'I haven't really found him. He wouldn't tell me where he was living.'

'Well, if it is anything like the last place, I don't blame him.'

She set her lips in a firm line of distaste. 'He wouldn't tell me anything really.'

'Just about murders,' I said. 'Trifles like that.'

She laughed bubblingly. 'I just said that to scare you. I don't really mean anybody was murdered, Mr Marlowe. You sounded so cold and distant. I thought you wouldn't help me any more. And – well, I just made it up.'

I took a couple of deep breaths and looked down at my hands. I straightened out the fingers slowly. Then I stood up. I didn't say anything.

'Are you mad at me?' she asked timidly, making a little circle on the desk with the point of a finger.

'I ought to slap your face off,' I said. 'And quit acting innocent. Or it mightn't be your face I'd slap.'

Her breath caught with a jerk. 'Why, how dare you!'

'You used that line,' I said. 'You used it too often. Shut up and get to hell out of here. Do you think I enjoy being scared to death? Oh – there's this.' I yanked a drawer open, got out her twenty dollars and threw them down in front of her. 'Take this money away. Endow a hospital or a research laboratory with it. It makes me nervous having it around.'

Her hand reached automatically for the money. Her eyes behind the cheaters were round and wondering. 'Goodness,' she said, assembling her handbag with a nice dignity. 'I'm sure I didn't know you scared that easy. I thought you were tough.'

'That's just an act,' I growled, moving around the desk. She leaned back in her chair away from me. 'I'm only tough with little girls like you that don't let their fingernails grow too long. I'm all mush inside.' I took hold of her arm and yanked her to her feet. Her head went back. Her lips parted. I was hell with the women that day.

'But you will find Orrin for me, won't you?' she whispered. 'It was all a lie. Everything I've told you was a lie. He didn't call me up. I – I don't know anything.'

'Perfume,' I said, sniffing. 'Why, you little darling. You put perfume behind your ears – and all for me!'

She nodded her little chin half an inch. Her eyes were melting. 'Take my glasses off,' she whispered. 'Philip. I don't mind if you take a little whisky once in a while. Really I don't.'

Our faces were about six inches apart. I was afraid to take her glasses off. I might have socked her on the nose.

'Yes,' I said in a voice that sounded like Orson Welles with his mouth full of crackers. 'I'll find him for you, honey, if he's still alive. And for free. Not a dime of expenses involved. I only ask one thing.'

'What, Philip?' she asked softly and opened her lips a little wider.

'Who was the black sheep in your family?'

She jerked away from me like a startled fawn might, if I had a startled fawn and it jerked away from me. She stared at me stony-faced.

'You said Orrin wasn't the black sheep in your family. Remember? With a very peculiar emphasis. And when you mentioned your sister Leila, you sort of passed on quickly as if the subject was distasteful.'

'I – I don't remember saying anything like that,' she said very slowly.

'So I was wondering,' I said. 'What name does your sister Leila use in pictures?'

'Pictures?' she sounded vague.'Oh, you mean motion pictures? Why, I never said she was in pictures. I never said anything about her like that.'

I gave her my big homely lop-sided grin. She suddenly flew into a rage.

'Mind your own business about my sister Leila,' she spat at me. 'You leave my sister Leila out of your dirty remarks.'

'What dirty remarks?' I asked. 'Or should I try to guess?'

'All you think about is liquor and women,' she screamed. 'I hate you!' She rushed to the door and yanked it open and went out. She practically ran down the hall.

I went back around my desk and slumped into the chair. A very strange little girl. Very strange indeed. After a while the phone started ringing again, as it would. On the fourth ring I leaned my head on my hand and groped for it, fumbled it to my face.

'Utter McKinley Funeral Parlours,' I said.

A female voice said: 'Wha-a-t?' and went off into a shriek of laughter. That one was a riot at the police smoker in 1921. What a wit. Like a humming-bird's beak. I put the lights out and went home.

16

Eight-forty-five the next morning found me parked a couple of doors from the Bay City Camera Shop, breakfasted and peaceful and reading the local paper through a pair of sunglasses. I had already chewed my way through the Los Angeles paper, which contained no item about ice-picks in the Van Nuys or any other hotel. Not even MYSTERIOUS DEATH IN DOWNTOWN HOTEL, with no names or weapon specified. The Bay City News wasn't too busy to write up a murder. They put it on the first page, right next to the price of meat.

LOCAL MAN FOUND STABBED IN
IDAHO STREET ROOMING HOUSE

'An anonymous telephone call late yesterday sent police speeding to an address on Idaho Street opposite the Seamans and Jansing Company's lumber yard. Entering the unlocked door of his apartment, officers found Lester B. Clausen, 45, manager of the rooming house, dead on the couch in his apartment. Clausen had been stabbed in the neck with an ice-pick which was still in his body. After a preliminary examination, Coroner Frank L. Crowdy announced that Clausen had been drinking heavily and may have been unconscious at the time of his death. No signs of a struggle were observed by the police.

'Detective Lieutenant Moses Maglashan immediately took charge and questioned tenants of the rooming house on their return from work, but no light has so far been thrown on the circumstances of the crime. Interviewed by this reporter, Coroner Crowdy stated that Clausen's death might have been suicide but that the position of the wound made this unlikely. Examination of the rooming house register disclosed that a page had recently been torn out. Lieutenant Maglashan, after questioning the tenants at length, stated that a thick-set middle-aged man with brown hair and heavy features had been noticed in the hallway of the rooming house on several occasions, but that none of the tenants knew his name or occupation. After carefully checking all rooms, Maglashan further gave it as his opinion that one of the roomers had left recently and in some haste. The mutilation of the register, however, the character of the neighbourhood, the lack of an accurate description of the missing man, made the job of tracing him extremely difficult.

' "I have no idea at present why Clausen was murdered," Maglashan announced at a late hour last night. "But I have had my eye on this man for some time. Many of his associates are known to me. It's a tough case, but we'll crack it." '

It was a nice piece and only mentioned Maglashan's name twelve times in the text and twice more in picture captions. There was a photo of him on page three holding an ice-pick and looking at it with profound thought wrinkling his brows. There was a photo of 449 Idaho Street which did it more than justice, and a photo of something with a sheet over it on a couch and Lieutenant Maglashan pointing at it sternly. There was also a close-up of the mayor looking as executive as hell behind his official desk and an interview with him on the subject of post-war crime. He said just what you would expect a mayor to say – a watered-down shot of J. Edgar Hoover with some extra bad grammar thrown in.

At three minutes to nine the door of the Bay City Camera Shop opened and an elderly Negro began to sweep dirt across the sidewalk into the gutter. At nine a.m. a neat-appearing young guy in glasses fixed the lock on the door and I went in there with the black-and-orange check Dr G. W. Hambleton had pasted to the inside of his toupee.

The neat-appearing young man gave me a searching glance as I exchanged the check and some money for an envelope containing a tiny negative and half a dozen shiny prints blown up to eight times the size of the negative. He didn't say anything, but the way he looked at me gave me the impression that he remembered I was not the man who had left the negative.

I went out and sat in my car and looked over the catch. The prints showed a man and a blonde girl sitting in a crowded booth in a restaurant with food in front of them. They were looking up as though their attention had suddenly been attracted and they had only just had time to react before the camera had clicked. It was clear from the lighting that no flashbulb had been used.

The girl was Mavis Weld. The man was rather small, rather dark, rather expressionless. I didn't recognize him. There was no reason why I should. The padded leather seat was covered with tiny figures of dancing couples. That made the restaurant The Dancers. This added to the confusion. Any amateur camera hound that tried to flash a lens in there without getting an okay from the management would have been thrown out so hard that he would have bounced all the way down to Hollywood and Vine. I figured it must have been the hidden camera trick, the way they took Ruth Snyder in the electric chair. He would have the little camera up hanging by a strap under his coat collar, the lens just peeping out from his open jacket, and he would have rigged a bulb release that he could hold in his pocket. It wasn't too hard for me to guess who had taken the picture. Mr Orrin P. Quest must have moved fast and smooth to get out of there with his face still in front of his head.

I put the pictures in my vest pocket and my fingers touched a crumpled piece of paper. I got it out and read: 'Doctor Vincent Lagardie, 965 Wyoming Street, Bay City.' That was the Vince I had talked to on the phone, the one Lester B. Clausen might have been trying to call.

An elderly flat-foot was strolling down the line of parked cars, marking tyres with yellow chalk. He told me where Wyoming Street was. I drove out there. It was a cross-town street well out beyond the business district, parallel with two numbered streets. Number 965, a grey-white frame house, was on a corner. On its door a brass plate said *Vincent Lagardie, M.D., Hours* 10.00 *to* 12.00 *and* 2.30 *to* 4.00.

The house looked quiet and decent. A woman with an unwilling small boy was going up the steps. She read the plate, looked at a watch pinned to her lapel and chewed irresolutely on her lip. The small boy looked around carefully, then kicked her on the ankle. She winced but her voice was patient. 'Now, Johnny, you mustn't do that to Aunty Fern,' she said mildly.

She opened the door and dragged the little ape in with her. Diagonally across the intersection was a big white colonial mansion with a portico which was roofed and much too small for the house. Floodlight reflectors were set into the front lawn. The walk was bordered by tree roses in bloom. A large black and silver sign over the portico said: *'The Garland Home of Peace.'* I wondered how Dr Lagardie liked looking out of his front windows at a funeral parlour. Maybe it made him careful.

I turned around at the intersection and drove back to Los Angeles, and went up to the office to look at my mail and lock my catch from the Bay City Camera Shop up in the battered green safe – all but one print. I sat down at the desk and studied this through a magnifying glass. Even with that and the camera shop blow-up the detail was still clear. There was an evening paper, a *News-Chronicle*, lying on the table in front of the dark thin expressionless man who sat beside Mavis Weld. I could just read the headline. LIGHTHEAVYWEIGHT CONTENDER SUCCUMBS TO RING INJURIES. Only a noon or late sports edition would use a headline like that. I pulled the phone towards me. It rang just as I got my hand on it.

'Marlowe? This is Christy French downtown. Any ideas this morning?'

'Not if your teletype's working. I've seen a Bay City paper.'

'Yeah, we got that,' he said casually. 'Sounds like the same guy, don't it? Same initials, same description, same method of murder, and the time element seems to check. I hope to Christ this doesn't mean Sunny Moe Stein's mob have started in business again.'

'If they have, they've changed their technique,' I said. 'I was reading up on it last night. The Stein mob used to jab their victims full of holes. One of them had over a hundred stab wounds in him.'

'They could learn better,' French said a little evasively, as if he didn't want to talk about it. 'What I called you about was Flack. Seen anything of him since yesterday afternoon?'

'No.'

'He skipped out. Didn't come to work. Hotel called his landlady. Packed up and left last night. Destination unknown.'

'I haven't seen him or heard from him,' I said.

'Didn't it strike you as kind of funny our stiff only had fourteen bucks in his kick?'

'It did a little. You answered that yourself.'

'I was just talking. I don't buy that any more. Flack's either scared out or come into money. Either he saw something he didn't tell and got paid to breeze, or else he lifted the customer's case dough, leaving the fourteen bucks to make it look better.'

I said: 'I'll buy either one. Or both at the same time. Whoever searched that room so thoroughly wasn't looking for money.'

'Why not?'

'Because when this Dr Hambleton called me up I suggested the hotel safe to him. He wasn't interested.'

'A type like that wouldn't have hired you to hold his dough anyway,' French said. 'He wouldn't have hired you to keep anything for him. He wanted protection or he wanted a sidekick – or maybe just a messenger.'

'Sorry,' I said. 'He told me just what I told you.'

'And seeing he was dead when you got over there,' French said with a too casual drawl, 'you couldn't hardly have given him one of your business cards.'

I held the phone too tight and thought back rapidly over my talk with Hicks in the Idaho Street rooming house. I saw him holding my card between his fingers, looking down at it. And then I saw myself taking it out of his hand quickly, before he froze to it. I took a deep breath and let it out slowly.

'Hardly,' I said. 'And stop trying to scare me to death.'

'He had one, chum. Folded twice across in his pants watch pocket. We missed it the first time.'

'I gave Flack a card,' I said, stiff-lipped.

There was a silence. I could hear voices in the background and the clack of a typewriter. Finally French said drily: 'Fair enough. See you later.' He hung up abruptly.

I put the phone down very slowly in its cradle and flexed my cramped fingers. I stared down at the photo lying on the desk in front of me. All it told me was that two people, one of whom I knew, were having lunch at The Dancers. The paper on the table told me the date, or would.

I dialled the *News-Chronicle* and asked for the sports section. Four minutes later I wrote on a pad: 'Ritchy Belleau, popular young light heavyweight contender, died in the Sisters Hospital just before midnight February 19th as a result of ring injuries sustained the previous evening in the main event at the Hollywood Legion Stadium. The *News-Chronicle* Noon Sports Edition for February 20th carried the headline.'

I dialled the same number again and asked for Kenny Haste in the City Room. He was an ex-crime reporter I had known for years. We chatted around for a minute and then I said:

'Who covered the Sunny Moe Stein killing for you?'

'Tod Barrow. He's on the *Post-Despatch* now. Why?'

'I'd like the details, if any.'

He said he would send to the morgue for the file and call me, which he did ten minutes later. 'He was shot twice in the head, in his car, about two blocks from the Chateau Bercy on Franklin. Time, about 11.15 p.m.'

'Date, February 20th,' I said, 'or was it?'

'Check, it was. No witnesses, no arrests except the usual police stock company of book-handlers, out-of-work fight managers and other professional suspects. What's in it?'

'Wasn't a pal of his supposed to be in town about that time?'

'Nothing here says so. What name?'

'Weepy Moyer. A cop friend of mine said something about a Hollywood money man being held on suspicion and then released for lack of evidence.'

Kenny said: 'Wait a minute. Something's coming back to me – yeah. Fellow named Steelgrave, owns The Dancers, supposed to be a gambler and so on. Nice guy, I've met him. That was a bust.'

'How do you mean, a bust?'

'Some smart monkey tipped the cops he was Weepy Moyer and they held him for ten days on an open charge for Cleveland. Cleveland brushed it off. That didn't have anything to do with the Stein killing. Steelgrave was under glass all that week. No connexion at all. Your cop friend has been reading pulp magazines.'

'They all do,' I said. 'That's why they talk so tough. Thanks, Kenny.'

We said good-bye and hung up and I sat leaning in my chair and looking at my photograph. After a while I took scissors and cut out the piece that contained the folded newspaper with the headline. I put the two pieces in separate envelopes and put them in my pocket with the sheet from the pad.

I dialled Miss Mavis Weld's Crestview number. A woman's voice answered after several rings. It was a remote and formal voice that I might or might not have heard before. All it said was, 'Hello?'

'This is Philip Marlowe. Is Miss Weld in?'

'Miss Weld will not be in until late this evening. Do you care to leave a message?'

'Very important. Where could I reach her?'

'I'm sorry. I have no information.'

'Would her agents know?'

'Possibly.'

'You're quite sure *you're* not Miss Weld?'

'Miss Weld is not in.' She hung up.

I sat there and listened to the voice. At first I thought yes, then I thought no. The longer I thought the less I knew. I went down to the parking lot and got my car out.

17

On the terrace at The Dancers a few early birds were getting ready to drink their lunch. The glass-fronted upstairs room had the awning let down in front of it. I drove on past the curve that goes down into the Strip and stopped across the street from a square building of two stories of rose-red brick with small white leaded bay windows and a Greek porch over the front door and what looked, from across the street, like an antique pewter door-knob. Over the door was a fanlight and the name Sheridan Ballou, Inc. in black wooden letters severely stylized. I locked my car and crossed to the front door. It was white and tall and wide and had a keyhole big enough for a mouse to crawl through. Inside this keyhole was the real lock. I went for the knocker, but they had thought of that too. It was all in one piece and didn't knock.

So I patted one of the slim fluted white pillars and opened the door and walked directly into the reception room which filled the entire front of the building. It was furnished in dark antique-looking furniture and many chairs and settees of quilted chintz-like material. There were lace curtains at the windows and chintz boxes around them that matched the chintz of the furniture. There was a flowered carpet and a lot of people waiting to see Mr Sheridan Ballou.

Some of them were bright and cheerful and full of hope. Some looked as if they had been there for days. One small dark girl was sniffling into her handkerchief in the corner. Nobody paid any attention to her. I got a couple of profiles at nice angles before the company decided I wasn't buying anything and didn't work there.

A dangerous-looking redhead sat languidly at an Adam desk talking into a pure-white telephone. I went over there and she put a couple of cold blue pellets into me with her eyes and then stared at the cornice that ran around the room.

'No,' she said into the phone. 'No. So sorry. I'm afraid it's no use. Far, far too busy.' She hung up and ticked off something on a list and gave me some more of her steely glance.

'Good morning. I'd like to see Mr Ballou,' I said. I put my plain card on her desk. She lifted it by one corner, smiled at it amusedly.

'Today?' she inquired amiably. 'This week?'

'How long does it usually take?'

'It *has* taken six months,' she said cheerfully. 'Can't somebody else help you?'

'No.'

'So sorry. Not a chance. Drop in again, won't you? Somewhere about Thanksgiving.' She was wearing a white wool skirt, a burgundy silk blouse and a black velvet over-jacket with short sleeves. Her hair was a hot sunset. She wore a golden topaz bracelet and topaz ear-rings and a topaz dinner ring in the shape of a shield. Her fingernails matched her blouse exactly. She looked as if it would take a couple of weeks to get her dressed.

'I've got to see him,' I said.

She read my card again. She smiled beautifully. 'Everyone has,' she said. 'Why – er – Mr Marlowe. Look at all these lovely people. Every one of them has been here since the office opened two hours ago.'

'This is important.'

'No doubt. In what way if I may ask?'

'I want to peddle a little dirt.'

She picked a cigarette out of a crystal box and lit it with a crystal lighter. 'Peddle? You mean for money – in Hollywood?'

'Could be.'

'What kind of dirt? Don't be afraid to shock me.'

'It's a bit obscene, Miss – Miss –' I screwed my head around to read the plaque on her desk.

'Helen Grady,' she said. 'Well, a little well-bred obscenity never did any harm, did it?'

'I didn't say it was well-bred.'

She leaned back carefully and puffed smoke in my face.

'Blackmail, in short.' She sighed. 'Why the hell don't you lam out of here, bud? Before I throw a handful of fat coppers in your lap?'

I sat on the corner of her desk, grabbed a double handful of her cigarette smoke and blew it into her hair. She dodged angrily. 'Beat it, lug,' she said in a voice that could have been used for paint remover.

'Oh, oh. What happened to the Bryn Mawr accent?'

Without turning her head she said sharply: 'Miss Vane.'

A tall slim elegant dark girl with supercilious eyebrows looked up. She had just come through an inner door camouflaged as a stained-glass window. The dark girl came over. Miss Grady handed her my card: 'Spink.'

Miss Vane went back through the stained-glass window with the card.

'Sit down and rest your ankles, big stuff,' Miss Grady informed me. 'You may be here all week.'

I sat down in a chintz winged chair, the back of which came eight inches above my head. It made me feel shrunken, Miss Grady gave me her smile again, the one with the hand-honed edge, and bent to the telephone once more.

I looked around. The little girl in the corner had stopped crying and was making up her face with calm unconcern. A very tall distinguished-looking party swung up a graceful arm to stare at his elegant wrist watch and oozed gently to his feet. He set a pearl-grey homburg at a rakish angle on the side of his head, checked his yellow chamois gloves and his silver-knobbed cane, and strolled languidly over to the red-headed receptionist.

'I have been waiting two hours to see Mr Ballou,' he said icily in a rich sweet voice that had been modulated by a lot of training. 'I'm not accustomed to waiting two hours to see anybody.'

'So sorry, Mr Fortescue. Mr Ballou is just too busy for words this a.m.'

'I'm sorry I cannot leave him a cheque,' the elegant tall party remarked with a weary contempt. 'Probably the only thing that would interest him. But in default of that –'

'Just a minute, kid.' The redhead picked up a phone and said into it: 'Yes? . . . Who says so besides Goldwyn? Can't you reach somebody that's not crazy? . . . Well, try again.' She slammed the telephone down. The tall party had not moved.

'In default of that,' he resumed as if he had never stopped speaking, 'I should like to leave a short personal message.'

'Please do,' Miss Grady told him. 'I'll get it to him somehow.'

'Tell him with my love that he is a dirty polecat.'

'Make it skunk, darling,' she said. 'He doesn't know any English words.'

'Make it skunk and double skunk,' Fortescue told her. 'With a slight added nuance of sulphuretted hydrogen and a very cheap grade of whore-house perfume.' He adjusted his hat and gave his profile the once over in a mirror. 'I now bid you good morning and to hell with Sheridan Ballou, Incorporated.'

The tall actor stalked out elegantly, using his cane to open the door.

'What's the matter with him?' I asked.

She looked at me pityingly. 'Billy Fortescue? Nothing's the matter with him. He isn't getting any parts so he comes in every day and goes through that routine. He figures somebody might see him and like it.'

I shut my mouth slowly. You can live a long time in Hollywood and never see the part they use in pictures.

Miss Vane appeared through the inner door and made a chin-jerk at me. I went in past her. 'This way. Second on the right.' She watched me while I went down the corridor to the second door which was open. I went in and closed the door.

A plump white-haired Jew sat at the desk smiling at me tenderly. 'Greetings,' he said. 'I'm Moss Spink. What's on the thinker, pal? Park the body. Cigarette?' He opened a thing that looked like a trunk and presented me with a cigarette which was not more than a foot long. It was in an individual glass tube.

'No thanks,' I said. 'I smoke tobacco.'

He sighed. 'All right. Give. Let's see. Your name's Marlowe. Huh? Marlowe. Marlowe. Have I ever heard of anybody named Marlowe?'

'Probably not,' I said. 'I never heard of anybody named Spink. I asked to see a man named Ballou. Does that sound like Spink? I'm not looking for anybody named Spink. And just between you and me, the hell with people named Spink.'

'Anti-Semitic, huh?' Spink said. He waved a generous hand on which a canary-yellow diamond looked like an amber traffic light. 'Don't be like that,' he said. 'Sit down and dust off the brains. You don't know me. You don't want to know me. O.K. I ain't offended. In a business like this you got to have somebody around that don't get offended.'

'Ballou,' I said.

'Now be reasonable, pal. Sherry Ballou's a very busy guy. He works twenty hours a day and even then he's way behind schedule. Sit down and talk it out with little Spinky.'

'You're what around here?' I asked him.

'I'm his protection, pal. I gotta protect him. A guy like Sherry can't see everybody. I see people for him. I'm the same as him – up to a point you understand.'

'Could be I'm past the point you're up to,' I said.

'Could be,' Spink agreed pleasantly. He peeled a thick tape off an aluminium individual cigar container, reached the cigar out tenderly and looked it over for birthmarks. 'I don't say not. Why not demonstrate a little? Then we'll know. Up to now all you're doing is throwing a line. We get so much of that in here it don't mean a thing to us.'

I watched him clip and light the expensive-looking cigar. 'How do I know you wouldn't double-cross him?' I asked cunningly.

Spink's small tight eyes blinked and I wasn't sure but that there were tears in them. 'Me cross Sherry Ballou?' he asked brokenly in a hushed voice, like a six-hundred-dollar funeral. 'Me? I'd sooner double-cross my own mother.'

'That doesn't mean anything to me either,' I said. 'I never met your mother.'

Spink laid his cigar aside in an ash-tray the size of a bird bath. He waved both his arms. Sorrow was eating into him. 'Oh, pal. What a way to talk,' he wailed. 'I love Sherry Ballou like he was my own father. Better. My father – well, skip it. Come on, pal. Be human. Give with a little of the old trust and friendliness. Spill the dirt to little Spinky, huh?'

I drew an envelope from my pocket and tossed it across the desk to him. He pulled the single photograph from it and stared at it solemnly. He laid it down on the desk. He looked up at me, down at the photo, up at me. 'Well,' he said woodenly, in a voice suddenly empty of the old trust and friendliness he had been talking about. 'What's it got that's so wonderful?'

'Do I have to tell you who the girl is?'

'Who's the guy?' Spink snapped.

I said nothing.

'I said who's the guy?' Spink almost yelled at me. 'Cough up, mug. Cough up.'

I still didn't say anything. Spink reached slowly for his telephone, keeping his hard bright eyes on my face.

'Go on. Call them,' I said. 'Call downtown and ask for Lieutenant Christy French in the homicide bureau. There's another boy that's hard to convince.'

Spink took his hand off the phone. He got up slowly and went out with the photograph. I waited. Outside on Sunset Boulevard traffic went by distantly, monotonously. The minutes dropped silently down a well. The smoke of Spink's fresh-lit cigar played in the air for a moment, then was sucked through the vent of the air-conditioning apparatus. I looked at the innumerable inscribed photos on the walls, all inscribed to Sherry Ballou with somebody's eternal love. I figured they were back numbers if they were in Spink's office.

18

After a while Spink came back and gestured to me. I followed him along the corridor through double doors into an ante-room with two secretaries. Past them towards more double doors of heavy black glass with silver peacocks etched into the panels. As we neared the doors they opened of themselves.

We went down three carpeted steps into an office that had everything in it but a swimming pool. It was two stories high, surrounded by a balcony loaded with bookshelves. There was a concert grand Steinway in the corner and a lot of glass and bleached wood furniture and a desk about the size of a badminton court and chairs and couches and tables and a man lying on one of the couches with his coat off and his shirt open over a Charvet scarf you could have found in the dark by listening to it purr. A white cloth was over his eyes and forehead, and a lissom blonde girl was wringing out another in a silver bowl of ice water at a table beside him.

The man was a big shapely guy with wavy dark hair and a strong brown face below the white cloth. An arm dropped to the carpet and a cigarette hung between fingers, wisping a tiny thread of smoke.

The blonde girl changed the cloth deftly. The man on the couch groaned. Spink said: 'This is the boy, Sherry. Name of Marlowe.'

The man on the couch groaned. 'What does he want?'

Spink said: 'Won't spill.'

The man on the couch said: 'What did you bring him in for then? I'm tired.'

Spink said: 'Well, you know how it is, Sherry. Sometimes you kind of got to.'

The man on the couch said: 'What did you say his beautiful name was?'

Spink turned to me. 'You can tell us what you want now. And make it snappy, Marlowe.'

I said nothing.

After a moment the man on the couch slowly raised the arm with the cigarette at the end of it. He got the cigarette wearily into his mouth and drew on it with the infinite languor of a decadent aristocrat mouldering in a ruined château.

'I'm talking to you, pal,' Spink said harshly. The blonde changed the cloth again, looking at nobody. The silence hung in the room as acrid as the smoke of the cigarette. 'Come on, mug. Snap it up.'

I got one of my Camels out and lit it and picked out a chair and sat down. I stretched my hand out and looked at it. The thumb twitched up and down slowly every few seconds.

Spink's voice cut into this furiously: 'Sherry don't have all day, you.'

'What would he do with the rest of the day?' I heard myself asking. 'Sit on a white satin couch and have his toenails gilded?'

The blonde turned suddenly and stared at me. Spink's mouth fell open. He blinked. The man on the couch lifted a slow hand to the corner of the towel over his eyes. He removed enough so that one seal-brown eye looked at me. The towel fell softly back into place.

'You can't talk like that in here,' Spink said in a tough voice.

I stood up. I said: 'I forgot to bring my prayer-book. This is the first time I knew God worked on commission.'

Nobody said anything for a minute. The blonde changed the towel again.

From under it the man on the couch said calmly: 'Get the hell out of here, darlings. All but the new chum.'

Spink gave me a narrow glare of hate. The blonde left silently.

Spink said: 'Why don't I just toss him out on his can?'

The tired voice under the towel said: 'I've been wondering about that so long I've lost interest in the problem. Beat it.'

'Okay, boss,' Spink said. He withdrew reluctantly. He paused at the door, gave me one more silent snarl and disappeared.

The man on the couch listened to the door close and then said: 'How much?'

'You don't want to buy anything.'

He pushed the towel off his head, tossed it to one side and sat up slowly. He put his bench-made pebble grain brogues on the carpet and passed a hand across his forehead. He looked tired but not dissipated. He fumbled another cigarette from somewhere, lit it and stared morosely through the smoke at the floor.

'Go on,' he said.

'I don't know why you wasted all the build-up on me,' I said. 'But I credit you with enough brains to know you couldn't buy anything, and know it would stay bought.'

Ballou picked up the photo that Spink had put down near him on a long low table. He reached out a languid hand. 'The piece that's cut out would be the punch line, no doubt,' he said.

I got the envelope out of my pocket and gave him the cut-out corner, watched him fit the two pieces together.

'With a glass you can read the headline,' I said.

'There's one on my desk. Please.'

I went over and got the magnifying glass off his desk. 'You're used to a lot of service, aren't you, Mr Ballou?'

'I pay for it.' He studied the photograph through the glass and sighed. 'Seems to me I saw that fight. They ought to take more care of these boys.'

'Like you do of your clients,' I said.

He laid down the magnifying glass and leaned back to stare at me with cool untroubled eyes.

'That's the chap that owns The Dancers. Name's Steelgrave. The girl is a client of mine, of course.' He made a vague gesture towards a chair. I sat down on it. 'What were you thinking of asking, Mr Marlowe?'

'For what?'

'All the prints and the negative. The works.'

'Ten grand,' I said, and watched his mouth. The mouth smiled, rather pleasantly.

'It needs a little more explanation, doesn't it? All I see is two people having lunch in a public place. Hardly disastrous to the reputation of my client. I assume that was what you had in mind.'

I grinned. 'You can't buy anything, Mr Ballou. I could have had a positive made from the negative and another negative from the positive. If that snap is evidence of something, you could never know you had suppressed it.'

'Not much of a sales talk for a blackmailer,' he said, still smiling.

'I always wonder why people pay blackmailers. They can't buy anything. Yet they do pay them, sometimes over and over and over again. And in the end are just where they started.'

'The fear of today,' he said, 'always overrides the fear of tomorrow. It's a basic fact of the dramatic emotions that the part is greater than the whole. If you see a glamour star on the screen in a position of great danger, you fear for her with one part of your mind, the emotional part. Notwithstanding that, your reasoning mind knows that she is the star of the picture and nothing very bad is going to happen to her. If suspense and menace didn't defeat reason, there would be very little drama.'

I said: 'Very true, I guess,' and puffed some of my Camel smoke around.

His eyes narrowed a little. 'As to really being able to buy anything, if I paid you a substantial price and didn't get what I bought, I'd have you taken care of. Beaten to a pulp. And when you got out of the hospital, if you felt aggressive enough, you could try to get me arrested.'

'It's happened to me,' I said. 'I'm a private eye. I know what you mean. Why are you talking to me?'

He laughed. He had a deep pleasant effortless laugh. 'I'm an agent, sonny. I always tend to think traders have a little something in reserve. But we won't talk about any ten grand. She hasn't got it. She only makes a grand a week so far. I admit she's very close to the big money, though.'

'That would stop her cold,' I said, pointing to the photo. 'No big money, no swimming pool with underwater lights, no platinum mink, no name in neons, no nothing. All blown away like dust.'

He laughed contemptuously.

'Okay if I show this to the johns down town, then?' I said.

He stopped laughing. His eyes narrowed. Very quietly he asked:

'Why would they be interested?'

I stood up. 'I don't think we're going to do any business, Mr Ballou. And you're a busy man. I'll take myself off.'

He got up off the couch and stretched, all six feet two of him. He was a very fine hunk of man. He came over and stood close to me. His seal-brown eyes had little gold flecks in them. 'Let's see who are you, sonny.'

He put his hand out. I dropped my open wallet into it. He read the photostat of my licence, poked a few more things out of the wallet and glanced at them. He handed it back.

'What would happen, if you did show your little picture to the cops?'

'I'd first of all have to connect it up with something they're working on – something that happened in the Van Nuys Hotel yesterday afternoon. I'd connect it up through the girl – who won't talk to me – that's why I'm talking to you.'

'She told me about it last night,' he sighed.

'Told you how much?' I asked.

'That a private detective named Marlowe had tried to force her to hire him, on the ground that she was seen in a downtown hotel inconveniently close to where a murder was committed.'

'How close?' I asked.

'She didn't say.'

'Nuts she didn't.'

He walked away from me to a tall cylindrical jar in the corner. From this he took one of a number of short thin malacca canes. He began to walk up and down the carpet, swinging the cane deftly past his right shoe.

I sat down again and killed my cigarette and took a deep breath. 'It could only happen in Hollywood,' I grunted.

He made a neat about turn and glanced at me. 'I beg your pardon.'

'That an apparently sane man could walk up and down inside the house with a Piccadilly stroll and a monkey stick in his hand.'

He nodded. 'I caught the disease from a producer at M.G.M. Charming fellow. Or so I've been told.' He stopped and pointed the cane at me. 'You amuse the hell out of me, Marlowe. Really you do. You're so transparent. You're trying to use me for a shovel to dig yourself out of a jam.'

'There's some truth in that. But the jam I'm in is nothing to the jam your client would be in if I hadn't done the thing that put me in the jam.'

He stood quite still for a moment. Then the threw the cane away from him and walked over to a liquor cabinet and swung the two halves of it open. He poured something into a couple of pot-bellied glasses. He carried one of them over to me. Then he went back and got his own. He sat down with it on the couch.

'Armagnac,' he said. 'If you knew me, you'd appreciate the compliment. This stuff is pretty scarce. The Krauts cleaned most of it out. Our brass got the rest. Here's to you.'

He lifted the glass, sniffed and sipped a tiny sip. I put mine down in a lump. It tasted like good French brandy.

Ballou looked shocked. 'My God, you sip that stuff, you don't swallow it whole.'

'I swallow it whole,' I said. 'Sorry. She also told you that if somebody didn't shut my mouth, she would be in a lot of trouble.'

He nodded.

'Did she suggest how to go about shutting my mouth?'

'I got the impression she was in favour of doing it with some kind of heavy blunt instrument. So I tried out a mixture of threat and bribery. We have an outfit down the street that specializes in protecting picture people. Apparently they didn't scare you and the bribe wasn't big enough.'

'They scared me plenty,' I said. 'I damn near fanned a Luger at them. That junky with the .45 puts on a terrific act. And as for the money not being big enough, it's all a question of how it's offered to me.'

He sipped a little more of his Armagnac. He pointed at the photograph lying in front of him with the two pieces fitted together.

'We got to where you were taking that to the cops. What then?'

'I don't think we got that far. We got to why she took this up with you instead of with her boy friend. He arrived just as I left. He has his own key.'

'Apparently she just didn't.' He frowned and looked down into his Armagnac.

'I like that fine,' I said. 'I'd like it still better if the guy didn't have her door-key.'

He looked up rather sadly. 'So would I. So would we all. But show business has always been like that – any kind of show business. If these people didn't live intense and rather disordered lives, if their emotions didn't ride them too hard – well, they wouldn't be able to catch those emotions in flight and imprint them on a few feet of celluloid or project them across the footlights.'

'I'm not talking about her love life,' I said. 'She doesn't have to shack up with a red-hot.'

'There's no proof of that, Marlowe.'

I pointed to the photograph. 'The man that took that is missing and can't be found. He's probably dead. Two other men who lived at the same address are dead. One of them was trying to peddle those pictures just before he got dead. She went to his hotel in person to take delivery. So did whoever killed him. She didn't get delivery and neither did the killer. They didn't know where to look.'

'And you did?'

'I was lucky. I'd seen him without his toupee. None of this is what I call proof, maybe. You could build an argument against it. Why bother? Two men have been killed, perhaps three. She took an awful chance. Why? She wanted that picture. Getting it was worth an awful chance. Why, again? It's just two people having lunch on a certain day. The day Moe Stein was shot to death on Franklin Avenue. The day a character named Steelgrave was in jail because the cops got a tip he was a Cleveland red-hot named Weepy Moyer. That's what the record shows. But the photo says he was out of jail. And by saying that about him on that particular day it says who he is. And she knows it. And he still has her door-key.'

I paused and we eyed each other solidly for a while. I said:

'You don't really want the cops to have that picture, do you? Win, lose or draw, they'd crucify her. And when it was all over it wouldn't make a damn bit of difference whether Steelgrave was Moyer or whether Moyer killed Stein or had him killed or just happened to be out on a jail pass the day he was killed. If he got away with it, there'd always be enough people to think it was a fix. She wouldn't get away with anything. She's a gangster's girl in the public mind. And as far as your business is concerned, she's definitely and completely through.'

Ballou was silent for a moment, staring at me without expression. 'And where are you all this time?' he asked softly.

'That depends a good deal on you, Mr Ballou.'

'What do you really want?' His voice was thin and bitter now.

'What I wanted from her and couldn't get. Something that gives me a colourable right to act in her interests up to the point where I decide I can't go any farther.'

'By suppressing evidence?' he asked tightly.

'If it *is* evidence. The cops couldn't find out without smearing Miss Weld. Maybe I can. They wouldn't be bothered to try; they don't care enough. I do.'

'Why?'

'Let's say it's the way I earn my living. I might have other motives, but that one's enough.'

'What's your price?'

'You sent it to me last night. I wouldn't take it then. I'll take it now. With a signed letter employing my services to investigate an attempt to blackmail one of your clients.'

I got up with my empty glass and went over and put it down on the desk. As I bent down I heard a soft whirring noise. I went around behind the desk and yanked open a drawer. A wire recorder slid out on a hinged shelf. The motor was running and the fine steel wire was moving steadily from one spool to the other. I looked across at Ballou.

'You can shut it off and take the record with you,' he said. 'You can't blame me for using it.'

I moved the switch over to rewind and the wire reversed direction and picked up speed until the wire was winding so fast I couldn't see it. It made a sort of high keening noise, like a couple of pansies fighting for a piece of silk. The wire came loose and the machine stopped. I took the spool off and dropped it into my pocket.

'You might have another one,' I said. 'I'll have to chance that.'

'Pretty sure of yourself, aren't you, Marlowe?'

'I only wish I was.'

'Press that button on the end of the desk, will you?'

I pressed it. The black glass doors opened and a dark girl came in with a stenographer's note-book.

Without looking at her, Ballou began to dictate. 'Letter to Mr Philip Marlowe, with his address. Dear Mr Marlowe: This agency herewith employs you to investigate an attempt to blackmail one of its clients, particulars of which have been given to you verbally. Your fee is to be one hundred dollars a day with a retainer of five hundred dollars, receipt of which you can acknowledge on the copy of this letter. Blah, blah, blah. That's all, Eileen. Right away, please.'

I gave the girl my address and she went out.

I took the wire spool out of my pocket and put it back in the drawer.

Ballou crossed his knees and danced the shiny tip of his shoe up and down, staring at it. He ran his hand through crisp dark hair.

'One of these days,' he said, 'I'm going to make the mistake which a man in my business dreads above all other mistakes. I'm going to find myself doing business with a man I can trust and I'm going to be just too goddamn smart to trust him. Here, you'd better keep this.' He held out the two pieces of the photograph.

Five minutes later I left. The glass doors opened when I was three feet from them. I went past the two secretaries and down the corridor past the open door of Spink's office. There was no sound in there, but I could smell his cigar smoke. In the reception room exactly the same people seemed to be sitting around in the chintzy chairs. Miss Helen Grady gave me her Saturday night smile. Miss Vane beamed at me.

I had been forty minutes with the boss. That made me as gaudy as a chiropractor's chart.

19

The studio cop at the semi-circular glassed-in desk put down his telephone and scribbled on a pad. He tore off the sheet and pushed it through the narrow slit not more than three-quarters of an inch wide where the glass did not quite meet the top of his desk. His voice coming through the speaking device set into the glass panel had a metallic ring.

'Straight through to the end of the corridor,' he said, 'you'll find a drinking fountain in the middle of the patio. George Wilson will pick up there.'

I said: 'Thanks. Is this bullet-proof glass?'

'Sure. Why?'

'I just wondered,' I said. 'I never heard of anybody shooting his way into the picture business.'

Behind me somebody snickered. I turned to look at a girl in slacks with a red carnation behind her ear. She was grinning.

'Oh, brother, if a gun was all it took.'

I went over to an olive-green door that didn't have any handle. It made a buzzing sound and let me push it open. Beyond was an olive green corridor with bare walls and a door at the far end. A rat trap. If you got into that and something was wrong, they could still stop you. The far door made the same buzz and click. I wondered how the cop knew I was at it. So I looked up and found his eyes staring at me in a tilted mirror. As I touched the door the mirror went blank. They thought of everything.

Outside in the hot midday sun, flowers rioted in a small patio with tiled walks and a pool in the middle and a marble seat. The drinking fountain was beside the marble seat. An elderly and beautifully dressed man was lounging on the marble seat watching three tan-coloured boxer dogs root up some tea rose begonias. There was an expression of intense but quiet satisfaction on his face. He didn't glance at me as I came up. One of the boxers, the biggest one, came over and made a wet on the marble seat beside his pants leg. He leaned down and patted the dog's hard short-haired head.

'You Mr Wilson?' I asked.

He looked up at me vaguely. The middle-sized boxer trotted up and sniffed and wet after the first one.

'Wilson?' He had a lazy voice with a touch of drawl to it. 'Oh no. My name's not Wilson. Should it be?'

'Sorry.' I went over to the drinking fountain and hit myself in the face with a stream of water. While I was wiping it off with a handkerchief the smallest boxer did his duty on the marble bench.

The man whose name was not Wilson said lovingly: 'Always do it in the exact same order. Fascinates me.'

'Do what?' I asked.

'Pee,' he said. 'Question of seniority it seems. Very orderly. First Maisie. She's the mother. Then Mac. Year older than Jock, the baby. Always the same. Even in my office.'

'In your office?' I said, and nobody ever looked stupider saying anything.

He lifted his whitish eyebrows at me, took a plain brown cigar out of his mouth, bit the end off and spat it into the pool.

'That won't do the fish any good,' I said.

He gave me an up-from-under look. 'I raise boxers. The hell with fish.'

I figured it was just Hollywood. I lit a cigarette and sat down on the bench. 'In your office,' I said. 'Well, every day has its new idea, hasn't it.'

'Up against the corner of the desk. Do it all the time. Drives my secretaries crazy. Gets into the carpet, they say. What's the matter with women nowadays? Never bothers me. Rather like it. You get fond of dogs, you even like to watch them pee.'

One of the dogs heaved a full-blown begonia plant into the middle of the tiled walk at his feet. He picked it up and threw it into the pool.

'Bothers the gardeners, I suppose,' he remarked as he sat down again. 'Oh well, if they're not satisfied, they can always –' he stopped dead and watched a slim mail girl in yellow slacks deliberately detour in order to pass through the patio. She gave him a quick side glance and went off making music with her hips.

'You know what's the matter with this business?' he asked me.

'Nobody does,' I said.

'Too much sex,' he said. 'All right in its proper time and place. But we get it in carload lots. Wade through it. Stand up to our necks in it. Gets to be like fly paper.' He stood up. 'We have too many flies too. Nice to have met you. Mister –'

'Marlowe,' I said. 'I'm afraid you don't know me.'

'Don't know anybody,' he said. 'Memory's going. Meet too many people. Name's Oppenheimer.'

'Jules Oppenheimer?'

He nodded. 'Right. Have a cigar.' He held one out to me. I showed my cigarette. He threw the cigar into the pool, then frowned. 'Memory's going,' he said sadly. 'Wasted fifty cents. Oughtn't to do that.'

'You run this studio,' I said.

He nodded absently. 'Ought to have saved that cigar. Save fifty cents and what have you got?'

'Fifty cents,' I said, wondering what the hell he was talking about.

'Not in this business. Save fifty cents in this business and all you have is five dollars' worth of book-keeping.' He paused and made a motion to the three boxers. They stopped whatever they were rooting at and watched him. 'Just run the financial end,' he said. 'That's easy. Come on, children, back to the brothel.' He sighed. 'Fifteen hundred theatres,' he added.

I must have been wearing my stupid expression again. He waved a hand around the patio. 'Fifteen hundred theatres is all you need. A damn sight easier than raising pure-bred boxers. The motion picture business is the only business in the world in which you can make all the mistakes there are and still make money.'

'Must be the only business in the world where you can have three dogs pee up against your office desk,' I said.

'You have to have the fifteen hundred theatres.'

'That makes it a little harder to get a start,' I said.

He looked pleased. 'Yes. That *is* the hard part.' He looked across the green clipped lawn at a four-storey building which made one side of the open square. 'All offices over there,' he said. 'I never go there. Always redecorating. Makes me sick to look at the stuff some of these people put in their suites. Most expensive talent in the world. Give them anything they like, all the money they want. Why? No reason at all. Just habit. Doesn't matter a damn what they do or how they do it. Just give me fifteen hundred theatres.'

'You wouldn't want to be quoted on that, Mr Oppenheimer?'

'You a newspaper man?'

'No.'

'Too bad. Just for the hell of it I'd like to see somebody try to get that simple elementary fact of life into the papers.' He paused and snorted. 'Nobody'd print it. Afraid to. Come on, children!'

The big one, Maisie, came over and stood beside him. The middle-sized one paused to ruin another begonia and then trotted up beside Maisie. The little one, Jock, lined up in order, then, with a sudden inspiration, lifted a hind leg at the cuff of Oppenheimer's pants. Maisie blocked him off casually.

'See that?' Oppenheimer beamed. 'Jock tried to get out of turn. Maisie wouldn't stand for it.' He leaned down and patted Maisie's head. She looked up at him adoringly.

'The eyes of your dog,' Oppenheimer mused. 'The most unforgettable thing in the world.'

He strolled off down the tiled path towards the executive building, the three boxers trotting sedately beside him.

'Mr Marlowe?'

I turned to find that a tall sandy-haired man with a nose like a straphanger's elbow had sneaked up on me.

'I'm George Wilson. Glad to know you. I see you know Mr Oppenheimer.'

'Been talking to him. He told me how to run the picture business. Seems all it takes is fifteen hundred theatres.'

'I've been working here five years. I've never even spoken to him.'

'You just don't get pee'd on by the right dogs.'

'You could be right. Just what can I do for you, Mr Marlowe?'

'I want to see Mavis Weld.'

'She's on the set. She's in a picture that's shooting.'

'Could I see her on the set for a minute?'

He looked doubtful. 'What kind of pass did they give you?'

'Just a pass, I guess.' I held it out to him. He looked it over.

'Ballou sent you. He's her agent. I guess we can manage Stage 12. Want to go over there now?'

'If you have time.'

'I'm the unit publicity man. That's what my time is for.'

We walked along the tiled path towards the corners of two buildings. A concrete roadway went between them towards the back lot and the stages.

'You in Ballou's office?' Wilson asked.

'Just came from there.'

'Quite an organization, I hear. I've thought of trying that business myself. There's nothing in this but a lot of grief.'

We passed a couple of uniformed cops, then turned into a narrow

alley between two stages. A red wig-wag was swinging in the middle of
the alley, a red light was on over a door marked 12, and a bell was ringing
steadily above the red light. Wilson stopped beside the door. Another
cop in a tilted back chair nodded to him, and looked me over with that
dead grey expression that grows on them like scum on a watertank.

The bell and the wig-wag stopped and the red light went off. Wilson
pulled a heavy door open and I went in past him. Inside was another
door. Inside that what seemed after the sunlight to be pitch darkness.
Then I saw a concentration of lights in the far corner. The rest of the
enormous sound stage seemed to be empty.

We went towards the lights. As we drew near the floor seemed to be
covered with thick black cables. There were rows of folding chairs, a
cluster of portable dressing-rooms with names on the doors. We were
wrong way on to the set and all I could see was the wooden backing and
on either side a big screen. A couple of back-projection machines sizzled
off to the side.

A voice shouted: 'Roll 'em.' A bell rang loudly. The two screens
came alive with tossing waves. Another calmer voice said: 'Watch your
positions, please, we may have to end up matching this little vignette.
All right, action.'

Wilson stopped dead and touched my arm. The voices of the actors
came out of nowhere, neither loud nor distinct, an unimportant murmur
with no meaning.

One of the screens suddenly went blank. The smooth voice, without
change of tone, said: 'Cut.'

The bell rang again and there was a general sound of movement.
Wilson and I went on. He whispered in my ear: 'If Ned Gammon doesn't
get this take before lunch, he'll bust Torrance on the nose.'

'Oh. Torrance in this?' Dick Torrance at the time was a ranking star
of the second grade, a not uncommon type of Hollywood actor that
nobody really wants but a lot of people in the end have to take for lack
of better.

'Care to run over the scene again, Dick?' the calm voice asked, as we
came around the corner of the set and saw what it was – the deck of a
pleasure yacht near the stern. There were two girls and three men in the
scene. One of them was middle-aged, in sports clothes, lounging in a

deck chair. One wore whites and had red hair and looked like the yacht's captain. The third was the amateur yachtsman, with the handsome cap, the blue jacket with gold buttons, the white shoes and slacks and the supercilious charm. This was Torrance. One of the girls was a dark beauty who had been younger; Susan Crawley. The other was Mavis Weld. She wore a wet white sharkskin swim suit, and had evidently just come aboard. A make-up man was spraying water on her face and arms and the edges of her blonde hair.

Torrance hadn't answered. He turned suddenly and stared at the camera. 'You think I don't know my lines?'

A grey-haired man in grey clothes came forward into the light from the shadowy background. He had hot black eyes, but there was no heat in his voice.

'Unless you changed them intentionally,' he said, his eyes steady on Torrance.

'It's just possible that I'm not used to playing in front of a back projection screen that has a habit of running out of film only in the middle of a take.'

'That's a fair complaint,' Ned Gammon said. 'Trouble is he only has two hundred and twelve feet of film, and that's my fault. If you could take the scene just a little faster –'

'Huh.' Torrance snorted. 'If *I* could take it a little faster. Perhaps Miss Weld could be prevailed upon to climb aboard this yacht in rather less time than it would take to build the damn boat.'

Mavis Weld gave him a quick, contemptuous look.

'Weld's timing is just right,' Gammon said. 'Her performance is just right too.'

Susan Crawley shrugged elegantly. 'I had the impression she could speed it up a trifle, Ned. It's good, but it *could* be better.'

'If it was any better, darling,' Mavis Weld told her smoothly, 'somebody might call it acting. You wouldn't want anything like that to happen in *your* picture, would you?'

Torrance laughed. Susan Crawley turned and glared at him. 'What's funny, Mister Thirteen?'

Torrance's face settled into an icy mask. 'The name again?' He almost hissed.

'Good heavens, you mean you didn't know,' Susan Crawley said wonderingly. 'They call you Mister Thirteen because any time you play a part it means twelve other guys have turned it down.'

'I see,' Torrance said coolly, then burst out laughing again. He turned to Ned Gammon. 'Okay, Ned. Now everybody's got the rat poison out of their system, maybe we can give it to you the way you want it.'

Ned Gammon nodded. 'Nothing like a little hamming to clear the air. All right, here we go.'

He went back beside the camera. The assistant shouted 'roll 'em' and the scene went through without a hitch.

'Cut,' Gammon said. 'Print that one. Break for lunch everybody.'

The actors came down a flight of rough wooden steps and nodded to Wilson. Mavis Weld came last, having stopped to put on a terrycloth robe and a pair of beach sandals. She stopped dead when she saw me. Wilson stepped forward.

'Hello, George,' Mavis Weld said, staring at me. 'Want something from me?'

'Mr Marlowe would like a few words with you. Okay?'

'Mr Marlowe?'

Wilson gave me a quick sharp look. 'From Ballou's office. I supposed you knew him.'

'I may have seen him.' She was still staring at me. 'What is it?'

I didn't speak.

After a moment she said: 'Thanks, George. Better come along to my dressing-room, Mr Marlowe.'

She turned and walked off around the far side of the set. A green and white dressing-room stood against the wall. The name on the door was Miss Weld. At the door she turned and looked around carefully. Then she fixed her lovely blue eyes on my face.

'And now, Mr Marlowe?'

'You *do* remember me?'

'I believe so.'

'Do we take up where we left off – or have a new deal with a clean deck?'

'Somebody let you in here. Who? Why? That takes explaining.'

'I'm working for you. I've been paid a retainer and Ballou has the receipt.'

'How very thoughtful. And suppose I don't want you to work for me? Whatever your work is.'

'All right, be fancy,' I said. I took the Dancers photo out of my pocket and held it out. She looked at me a long and steady moment before she dropped her eyes. Then she looked at the snapshot of herself and Steelgrave in the booth. She looked at it gravely without movement. Then very slowly she reached up and touched the tendrils of damp hair at the side of her face. Ever so slightly she shivered. Her hand came out and she took the photograph. She stared at it. Her eyes came up again slowly, slowly.

'Well?' she asked.

'I have the negative and some other prints. You would have had them, if you had had more time and known where to look. Or if he had stayed alive to sell them to you.'

'I'm a little chilly,' she said. 'And I have to eat some lunch.' She held the photo out to me.

'You're a little chilly and you have to eat some lunch,' I said.

I thought a pulse beat in her throat. But the light was not too good. She smiled faintly. The bored aristocrat touch.

'The significance of all this escapes me,' she said.

'You're spending too much time on yachts. What you mean is I know you and I know Steelgrave, so what has this photo got that makes anybody give me a diamond dog collar?'

'All right,' she said. 'What?'

'I don't know,' I said. 'But if finding out is what it takes to shake you out of this duchess routine, I'll find out. And in the meantime you're still chilly and you still have to eat some lunch.'

'And you've waited too long,' she said quietly. 'You haven't anything to sell. Except perhaps your life.'

'I'd sell that cheap. For love of a pair of dark glasses and a delphinium blue hat and a crack on the head from a high-heeled slipper.'

Her mouth twitched as if she was going to laugh. But there was no laughter in her eyes.

'Not to mention three slaps in the face,' she said. 'Good-bye, Mr Marlowe. You came too late. Much, much too late.'

'For me – or for you?' She reached back and opened the door of the dressing-room.

'I think for both of us.' She went in quickly, leaving the door open.

'Come in and shut the door,' her voice said from the dressing-room.

I went in and shut the door. It was no fancy custom-built star's dressing-room. Strictly utility only. There was a shabby couch, one easy chair, a small dressing-table with mirror and two lights, a straight chair in front of it, a tray that had held coffee.

Mavis Weld reached down and plugged in a round electric heater. Then she grabbed up a towel and rubbed the damp edges of her hair. I sat down on the couch and waited.

'Give me a cigarette.' She tossed the towel to one side. Her eyes came close to my face as I lit the cigarette for her. 'How did you like that little scene we adlibbed on the yacht?'

'Bitchy.'

'We're all bitches. Some smile more than others, that's all. Show business. There's something cheap about it. There always has been. There was a time when actors went in at the back door. Most of them still should. Great strain, great urgency, great hatred, and it comes out in nasty little scenes. They don't mean a thing.'

'Cat talk,' I said.

She reached up and pulled a fingertip down the side of my cheek. It burned like a hot iron. 'How much money do you make, Marlowe?'

'Forty bucks a day and expenses. That's the asking price. I take twenty-five. I've taken less.' I thought about Orfamay's worn twenty.

She did that with her finger again and I just didn't grab hold of her. She moved away from me and sat in the chair, drawing the robe close. The electric heater was making the little room warm.

'Twenty-five dollars a day,' she said wonderingly.

'Little lonely dollars.'

'Are they very lonely?'

'Lonely as lighthouses.'

She crossed her legs and the pale glow of her skin in the light seemed to fill the room.

'So ask me the questions,' she said, making no attempt to cover her thighs.

'Who's Steelgrave?'

'A man I've known for years. And liked. He owns things. A restaurant or two. Where he comes from – that I don't know.'

'But you know him very well.'

'Why don't you ask me if I sleep with him?'

'I don't ask that kind of questions.'

She laughed and snapped ash from her cigarette. 'Miss Gonzales would be glad to tell you.'

'The hell with Miss Gonzales.'

'She's dark and lovely and passionate. And very, very kind.'

'And exclusive as a mailbox,' I said. 'The hell with her. About Steelgrave – has he ever been in trouble?'

'Who hasn't?'

'With the police.'

Her eyes widened a little too innocently. Her laugh was a little too silvery. 'Don't be ridiculous. The man is worth a couple of million dollars.'

'How did he get it?'

'How would I know?'

'All right. You wouldn't. That cigarette's going to burn your fingers.' I leaned across and took the stub out of her hand. Her hand lay open on her bare leg. I touched the palm with a fingertip. She drew away from me and tightened the hand into a fist.

'Don't do that,' she said sharply.

'Why? I used to do that to girls when I was a kid.'

'I know.' She was breathing a little fast. 'It makes me feel very young and innocent and kind of naughty. And I'm far from being young and innocent any more.'

'Then you don't really know anything about Steelgrave.'

'I wish you'd make up your mind whether you are giving me a third degree or making love to me.'

'My mind has nothing to do with it,' I said.

After a silence she said: 'I really do have to eat something, Marlowe.

I'm working this afternoon. You wouldn't want me to collapse on the set, would you?'

'Only stars do that.' I stood up. 'Okay, I'll leave. Don't forget I'm working for you. I wouldn't be if I thought you'd killed anybody. But you were there. You took a big chance. There was something you wanted very badly.'

She reached the photo out from somewhere and stared at it, biting her lip. Her eyes came up without her head moving.

'It could hardly have been this.'

'That was the one thing he had so well hidden that it was not found. But what good is it? You and a man called Steelgrave in a booth at The Dancers. Nothing in that.'

'Nothing at all,' she said.

'So it has to be something about Steelgrave – or something about the date.'

Her eyes snapped down to the picture again. 'There's nothing to tell the date,' she said quickly. 'Even if it meant something. Unless the cut-out piece –'

'Here.' I gave her the cut-out piece. 'But you'll need a magnifier. Show it to Steelgrave. Ask *him* if it means anything. Or ask Ballou.'

I started towards the exit of the dressing-room. 'Don't kid yourself the date can't be fixed,' I said over my shoulder. 'Steelgrave won't.'

'You're just building a sand castle, Marlowe.'

'Really?' I looked back at her, not grinning. 'You really think that? Oh no you don't. You went there. The man was murdered. You had a gun. He was a known crook. And I found something the police would love to have me hide from them. Because it must be as full of motive as the ocean is full of salt. As long as the cops don't find it I have a licence. And as long as somebody else doesn't find it I don't have an ice-pick in the back of my neck. Would you say I was in an overpaid profession?'

She just sat there and looked at me, one hand on her kneecap, squeezing it. The other moving restlessly, finger by finger, on the arm of the chair.

All I had to do was turn the knob and go on out. I don't know why it had to be so hard to do.

495

20

There was the usual coming and going in the corridor outside my office, and when I opened the door and walked into the musty silence of the little waiting-room there was the usual feeling of having been dropped down a well dried up twenty years ago to which no one would come back ever. The smell of old dust hung in the air as flat and stale as a football interview.

I opened the inner door and inside there it was the same dead air, the same dust along the veneer, the same broken promise of a life of ease. I opened the windows and turned on the radio. It came up too loud and when I had it tuned down to normal the phone sounded as if it had been ringing for some time. I took my hat off it and lifted the receiver.

It was high time I heard from her again. Her cool compact voice said: 'This time I really mean it.'

'Go on.'

'I lied before. I'm not lying now. I really have heard from Orrin.'

'Go on.'

'You're not believing me. I can tell by your voice.'

'You can't tell anything by my voice. I'm a detective. Heard from him how?'

'By phone from Bay City.'

'Wait a minute.' I put the receiver down on the stained brown blotter and lit my pipe. No hurry. Lies are always patient. I took it up again.

'We've been through that routine,' I said. 'You're pretty forgetful for your age. I don't think Dr Zugsmith would like it.'

'Please don't tease me. This is very serious. He got my letter. He went to the post office and asked for his mail. He knew where I'd be staying. And about when I'd be here. So he called up. He's staying with a doctor he got to know down there. Doing some kind of work for him. I told you he had two years medical.'

'Doctor have a name?'

'Yes. A funny name. Dr Vincent Lagardie.'

'Just a minute. There's somebody at the door.'

I laid the phone down very carefully. It might be brittle. It might be made of spun glass. I got a handkerchief out and wiped the palm of my hand, the one that had been holding it. I got up and went to the built-in wardrobe and looked at my face in the flawed mirror. It was me all right. I had a strained look. I'd been living too fast.

Dr Vincent Lagardie, 965 Wyoming Street. Catty-corners from The Garland Home of Peace. Frame house on the corner. Quiet. Nice neighbourhood. Friend of the extinct Clausen. Maybe. Not according to him. But still maybe.

I went back to the telephone and squeezed the jerks out of my voice. 'How would you spell that?' I asked.

She spelled it – with ease and precision. 'Nothing to do then, is there?' I said. 'All jake to the angels – or whatever they say in Manhattan, Kansas.'

'Stop sneering at me, Orrin's in a lot of trouble. Some –' her voice quivered a little and her breath came quickly. 'Some gangsters are after him.'

'Don't be silly, Orfamay. They don't have gangsters in Bay City. They're all working in pictures. What's Dr Lagardie's phone number?'

She gave it to me. It was right. I won't say the pieces were beginning to fall into place, but at least they were getting to look like parts of the same puzzle. Which is all I ever get or ask.

'Please go down there and see him and help him. He's afraid to leave the house. After all, I did pay you.'

'I gave it back.'

'Well. I offered it to you again.'

'You more or less offered me other things that are more than I'd care to take.'

There was silence.

'All right,' I said. 'All right. If I can stay free that long. I'm in a lot of trouble myself.'

'Why?'

'Telling lies and not telling the truth. It always catches up with me. I'm not as lucky as some people.'

'But I'm not lying, Philip. I'm not lying. I'm frantic.'

'Take a deep breath and get frantic so I can hear it.'

'They might kill him,' she said quietly.

'And what is Dr Vincent Lagardie doing all this time?'

'He doesn't know, of course. Please, please go at once. I have the address here. Just a moment.'

And the little bell rang, the one that rings far back at the end of the corridor, and is not loud, but you'd better hear it. No matter what other noises there are you'd better hear it.

'He'll be in the phone book,' I said. 'And by an odd coincidence I have a Bay City phone book. Call me around four. Or five. Better make it five.'

I hung up quickly. I stood up and turned the radio off, not having heard a thing it said. I closed the windows again. I opened the drawer of my desk and took out the Luger and strapped it on. I fitted my hat on my head. On the way out I had another look at the face in the mirror.

I looked as if I had made up my mind to drive off a cliff.

21

They were just finishing a funeral service at The Garland Home of Peace. A big grey hearse was waiting at the side entrance. Cars were clotted along both sides of the street, three black sedans in a row at the side of Dr Vincent Lagardie's establishment. People were coming sedately down the walk from the funeral chapel to the corner and getting into their cars. I stopped a third of a block away and waited. The cars didn't move. Then three people came out with a woman heavily veiled and all in black. They half carried her down to a big limousine. The boss mortician fluttered around making elegant little gestures and body movements as graceful as a Chopin ending. His composed grey face was long enough to wrap twice around his neck.

The amateur pallbearers carried the coffin out the side door and professionals eased the weight from them and slid it into the back of the hearse as smoothly as if it had no more weight than a pan of butter rolls.

Flowers began to grow into a mound over it. The glass doors were closed and motors started all over the block.

A few moments later nothing was left but one sedan across the way and the boss mortician sniffing a tree-rose on his way back to count the take. With a beaming smile he faded into his neat colonial doorway and the world was still and empty again. The sedan that was left hadn't moved. I drove along and made a U-turn and came up behind it. The driver wore blue serge and a soft cap with a shiny peak. He was doing a crossword puzzle from the morning paper. I stuck a pair of those diaphanous mirror sunglasses on my nose and strolled past him towards Dr Lagardie's place. He didn't look up. When I was a few yards ahead I took the glasses off and pretended to polish them on my handkerchief. I caught him in one of the mirror lenses. He still didn't look up. He was just a guy doing a crossword puzzle. I put the mirror glasses back on my nose, and went around to Dr Lagardie's front door.

The sign over the door said: Ring and Enter. I rang, but the door wouldn't let me enter. I waited. I rang again. I waited again. There was silence inside. Then the door opened a crack very slowly, and a thin expressionless face over a white uniform looked out at me.

'I'm sorry. Doctor is not seeing any patients today.' She blinked at the mirror glasses. She didn't like them. Her tongue moved restlessly inside her lips.

'I'm looking for a Mr Quest. Orrin P. Quest.'

'Who?' There was a dim reflection of shock behind her eyes.

'Quest. Q as in quintessential, U as in uninhibited, E as in Extrasensory, S as in Subliminal, T as in Toots. Put them all together and they spell Brother.'

She looked at me as if I had just come up from the floor of the ocean with a drowned mermaid under my arm.

'I beg your pardon. Dr Lagardie is not –'

She was pushed out of the way by invisible hands and a thin dark haunted man stood in the half-open doorway.

'I am Dr Lagardie. What is it, please?'

I gave him a card. He read it. He looked at me. He had the white pinched look of a man who is waiting for a disaster to happen.

'We talked over the phone,' I said. 'About a man named Clausen.'

499

'Please come in,' he said quickly. 'I don't remember, but come in.'

I went in. The room was dark, the blinds drawn, the windows closed. It was dark, and it was cold.

The nurse backed away and sat down behind a small desk. It was an ordinary living-room with light painted woodwork which had once been dark, judging by the probable age of the house. A square arch divided the living-room from the dining-room. There were easy-chairs and a centre table with magazines. It looked like what it was – the reception room of a doctor practising in what had been a private home.

The telephone rang on the desk in front of the nurse. She started and her hand went out and then stopped. She stared at the telephone. After a while it stopped ringing.

'What was the name you mentioned?' Dr Lagardie asked me softly.

'Orrin Quest. His sister told me he was doing some kind of work for you, Doctor. I've been looking for him for days. Last night he called her up. From here, she said.'

'There is no one of that name here,' Dr Lagardie said politely. 'There hasn't been.'

'You don't know him at all?'

'I have never heard of him.'

'I can't figure why he would say that to his sister.'

The nurse dabbed at her eyes furtively. The telephone on her desk burred and made her jump again. 'Don't answer it,' Dr Lagardie said without turning his head.

We waited while it rang. Everybody waits while a telephone rings. After a while it stopped.

'Why don't you go home, Miss Watson? There's nothing for you to do here.'

'Thank you. Doctor.' She sat without moving, looking down at the desk. She squeezed her eyes shut and blinked them open. She shook her head hopelessly.

Dr Lagardie turned back to me. 'Shall we go into my office?'

We went across through another door leading to a hallway. I walked on eggs. The atmosphere of the house was charged with foreboding. He opened a door and ushered me into what must have once been a bedroom, but nothing suggested a bedroom. It was a small compact doctor's office. An open door showed a part of an examination room. A sterilizer was working in the corner. There were a lot of needles cooking in it.

'That's a lot of needles,' I said, always quick with an idea.

'Sit down, Mr Marlowe.'

He went behind the desk and sat down and picked up a long thin letter-opening knife.

He looked at me levelly from his sorrowful eyes. 'No, I don't know anyone named Orrin Quest, Mr Marlowe. I can't imagine any reason in the world why a person of that name should say he was in my house.'

'Hiding out,' I said.

His eyebrows went up. 'From what?'

'From some guys that might want to stick an ice-pick in the back of his neck. On account of he is a little too quick with his little Leica. Taking people's photographs when they want to be private. Or it could be something else, like peddling reefers and he got wise. Am I talking in riddles?'

'It was you who sent the police here,' he said coldly.

I didn't say anything.

'It was you who called up and reported Clausen's death.'

I said the same as before.

'It was you who called me up and asked me if I knew Clausen. I said I did not.'

'But it wasn't true.'

'I was under no obligation to give you information, Mr Marlowe.'

I nodded and got a cigarette out and lit it. Dr Lagardie glanced at his watch. He turned in his chair and switched off the sterilizer. I looked at the needles. A lot of needles. Once before I had had trouble in Bay City with a guy who cooked a lot of needles.

'What makes it?' I asked him. 'The yacht harbour?'

He picked up the wicked-looking paper knife with a silver handle in the shape of a nude woman. He pricked the ball of his thumb. A pearl of dark blood showed on it. He put it to his mouth and licked it. 'I like the taste of blood,' he said softly.

There was a distant sound as of the front door opening and closing.

We both listened to it carefully. We listened to retreating steps on the front steps of the house. We listened hard.

'Miss Watson has gone home,' Dr Lagardie said. 'We are all alone in the house.' He mulled that over and licked his thumb again. He laid the knife down carefully on the desk blotter. 'Ah, the question of the yacht harbour,' he added. 'The proximity of Mexico you are thinking of, no doubt. The ease with which marijuana –'

'I wasn't thinking so much of marijuana any more.' I stared again at the needles. He followed my stare. He shrugged.

I said: 'Why so many of them?'

'Is it any of your business?'

'Nothing's any of my business.'

'But you seem to expect your questions to be answered.'

'I'm just talking,' I said. 'Waiting for something to happen. Something's going to happen in this house. It's leering at me from corners.'

Dr Lagardie licked another pearl of blood off his thumb.

I looked hard at him. It didn't buy me a way into his soul. He was quiet, dark and shattered and all the misery of life was in his eyes. But he was still gentle.

'Let me tell you about the needles,' I said.

'By all means.' He picked the long thin knife up again.

'Don't do that,' I said sharply. 'It gives me the creeps. Like petting snakes.'

He put the knife down again gently and smiled. 'We do seem to talk in circles,' he suggested.

'We'll get there. About the needles. A couple of years back I had a case that brought me down here and mixed me up with a doctor named Almore. Lived over on Altair Street. He had a funny practice. Went out nights with a big case of hypodermic needles – all ready to go. Loaded with the stuff. He had a peculiar practice. Drunks, rich junkies, of whom there are far more than people think, over-stimulated people who had driven themselves beyond the possibility of relaxing. Insomniacs – all the neurotic types that can't take it cold. Have to have their little pills and little shots in the arm. Have to help them over the humps. It gets to be all humps after a while. Good business for the doctor. Almore was the doctor for them. It's all right to say it now. He died a year or so back. Of his own medicine.'

'And you think I may have inherited his practice?'

'Somebody would. As long as there are the patients, there will be the doctor.'

He looked even more exhausted than before. 'I think you are an ass, my friend. I did not know Dr Almore. And I do not have the sort of practice you attribute to him. As for the needles – just to get that trifle out of the way – they are in somewhat constant use in the medical profession today, often for such innocent medicaments as vitamin injections. And needles get dull. And when they are dull they are painful. Therefore in the course of the day one may use a dozen or more. Without narcotics in a single one.'

He raised his head slowly and stared at me with a fixed contempt.

'I can be wrong,' I said. 'Smelling that reefer smoke over at Clausen's place yesterday, and having him call your number on the telephone – and call you by your first name – all this probably made me jump to wrong conclusions.'

'I have dealt with addicts,' he said. 'What doctor has not? It is a complete waste of time.'

'They get cured sometimes.'

'They can be deprived of their drug. Eventually after great suffering they can do without it. That is not curing them, my friend. That is not removing the nervous or emotional flaw which made them become addicts. It is making them dull negative people who sit in the sun and twirl their thumbs and die of sheer boredom and inanition.'

'That's a pretty raw theory, Doctor.'

'You raised the subject. I have disposed of it. I will raise another subject. You may have noticed a certain atmosphere and strain about this house. Even with those silly mirror glasses on. Which you may now remove. They don't make you look in the least like Cary Grant.'

I took them off. 'I'd forgotten all about them.'

'The police have been here, Mr Marlowe. A certain Lieutenant Maglashan, who is investigating Clausen's death. He would be pleased to meet you. Shall I call him? I'm sure he would come back.'

'Go ahead, call him,' I said. 'I just stopped off here on my way to commit suicide.'

His hand went towards the telephone but was pulled to one side by the magnetism of the paper knife. He picked it up again. Couldn't leave it alone, it seemed.

'You could kill a man with that,' I said.

'Very easily,' and he smiled a little.

'An inch and a half in the back of the neck, square in the centre, just under the occipital bulge.'

'An ice-pick would be better,' he said. 'Especially a short one, filed down very sharp. It would not bend. If you miss the spinal cord, you do no great damage.'

'Takes a bit of medical knowledge then?' I got out a poor old package of Camels and untangled one from the cellophane.

He just kept on smiling. Very faintly, rather sadly. It was not the smile of a man in fear. 'That would help,' he said softly. 'But any reasonably dexterous person could acquire the technique in ten minutes.'

'Orrin Quest had a couple of years' medical,' I said.

'I told you I did not know anybody of that name.'

'Yeah, I know you did. I didn't quite believe you.'

He shrugged his shoulders. But his eyes as always went to the knife in the end.

'We're a couple of sweethearts,' I said. 'We just sit here making with the old over-the-desk dialogue. As though we hadn't a care in the world. Because both of us are going to be in the clink by nightfall.'

He raised his eyebrows again. I went on:

'You, because Clausen knew you by your first name. And you may have been the last man he talked to. Me, because I've been doing all the things a P.I. never gets away with. Hiding evidence, hiding information, finding bodies and not coming in with my hat in my hand to these lovely incorruptible Bay City cops. Oh, I'm through. Very much through. But there's a wild perfume in the air this afternoon. I don't seem to care. Or I'm in love. I just don't seem to care.'

'You have been drinking,' he said slowly.

'Only Chanel No. 5, and kisses, and the pale glow of lovely legs, and the mocking invitation in deep blue eyes. Innocent things like that.'

He just looked sadder than ever. 'Women can weaken a man terribly, can they not?' he said.

'Clausen.'

'A hopeless alcoholic. You probably know how they are. They drink and drink and don't eat. And little by little the vitamin deficiency brings on the symptoms of delirium. There is only one thing to do for them.' He turned and looked at the sterilizer. 'Needles, and more needles. It makes me feel dirty. I am a graduate of the Sorbonne. But I practise among dirty little people in a dirty little town.'

'Why?'

'Because of something that happened years ago – in another city. Don't ask me too much, Mr Marlowe.'

'He used your first name.'

'It is a habit with people of a certain class. One-time actors especially. And one-time crooks.'

'Oh,' I said. 'That all there is to it?'

'All.'

'Then the cops coming here doesn't bother you on account of Clausen. You're just afraid of this other thing that happened somewhere else long gone. Or it could even be love.'

'Love?' He dropped the word slowly off the end of his tongue, tasting it to the last. A bitter little smile stayed after the word, like powder smell in the air after a gun is fired. He shrugged and pushed a desk cigarette box from behind a filing tray and over to my side of the desk.

'Not love then,' I said. 'I'm trying to read your mind. Here you are, a guy with a Sorbonne degree and a cheap little practice in a cheap and nasty little town. I know it well. So what are you doing here? What are you doing with people like Clausen? What was the rap, Doctor? Narcotics, abortions, or were you by any chance a medic for the gang boys in some hot Eastern city?'

'As for instance?' he smiled thinly.

'As for instance Cleveland.'

'A very wild suggestion, my friend.' His voice was like ice now.

'Wild as all hell,' I said. 'But a fellow like me with very limited brains tends to try to fit the things he knows into a pattern. It's often wrong, but it's an occupational disease with me. It goes like this, if you want to listen.'

'I am listening.' He picked the knife up again and pricked lightly at the blotter on his desk.

'You knew Clausen. Clausen was killed very skilfully with an ice-pick, killed while I was in the house, upstairs talking to a grifter named Hicks. Hicks moved out fast, taking a page of the register with him, the page that had Orrin Quest's name on it. Later that afternoon Hicks was killed with an ice-pick in L.A. His room had been searched. There was a woman there who had come to buy something from him. She didn't get it. I had more time to search. I did get it. Presumption A. Clausen and Hicks killed by same man, not necessarily for same reason. Hicks killed because he muscled in on another guy's racket and muscled the other guy out. Clausen killed because he was a babbling drunk and might know who would be likely to kill Hicks. Any good so far?'

'Not the slightest interest to me,' Dr Lagardie said.

'But you *are* listening. Sheer good manners, I suppose. Okay. Now what did I find? A photo of a movie queen and an ex-Cleveland gangster, maybe, now a Hollywood restaurant owner, etc. having lunch on a particular day. Day when this ex-Cleveland gangster was supposed to be in hock at the County Jail, also day when ex-Cleveland gangster's one-time sidekick was shot dead on Franklin Avenue in Los Angeles. Why was he in hock? Tipoff that he was who he was, and say what you like against the L.A. cops, they do try to run back-East hot shots out of town. Who gave them the tip? The guy they pinched gave it to them himself, because his ex-partner was being troublesome and had to be rubbed out, and being in jail was a first-class alibi when it happened.'

'All fantastic,' Dr Lagardie smiled wearily. 'Utterly fantastic.'

'Sure. It gets worse. Cops couldn't prove anything on ex-gangster. Cleveland police not interested. The L.A. cops turn him loose. But they wouldn't have turned him loose if they'd seen that photo. Photo therefore strong blackmail material, first against ex-Cleveland character, if he really is the guy; secondly against movie queen for being seen around with him in public. A good man could make a fortune out of that photo. Hicks not good enough. Paragraph. Presumption B: Orrin Quest, the boy I'm trying to find, took that photo. Taken with Contax or Leica, without flashbulb, without subjects knowing they were being photographed. Quest had a Leica and liked to do things like that. In this case of course he had a more commercial motive. Question, how did he get a chance to take photo? Answer, the movie queen was his sister. She would let him come up and speak to her. He was out of work, needed money. Likely enough she gave him some and made it a condition he stay away from her. She wants no part of her family. Is it still utterly fantastic, Doctor?'

He stared at me moodily. 'I don't know,' he said slowly. 'It begins to have possibilities. But why are you telling this rather dangerous story to me?'

He reached a cigarette out of the box and tossed me one casually. I caught it and looked it over. Egyptian, oval and fat, a little rich for my blood. I didn't light it, just sat holding it between my fingers, watching his dark unhappy eyes. He lit his own cigarette and puffed nervously.

'I'll tie you in on it now,' I said. 'You knew Clausen. Professionally, you said. I showed him I was a dick. He tried at once to call you up. He was too drunk to talk to you. I caught the number and later told you he was dead. Why? If you were on the level, you would call the cops. You didn't. Why? You knew Clausen, you could have known some of his roomers. No proof either way. Paragraph. Presumption C: you knew Hicks or Orrin Quest or both. The L.A. cops couldn't or didn't establish identity of ex-Cleveland character – let's give him his new name, call him Steelgrave. But *somebody* had to be able to – if that photo was worth killing people over. Did you ever practise medicine in Cleveland, Doctor?'

'Certainly not.' His voice seemed to come from far off. His eyes were remote too. His lips opened barely enough to admit his cigarette. He was very still.

I said: 'They have a whole roomful of directories over at the telephone office. From all over the country. I checked you up.'

'A suite in a downtown office building,' I said. 'And now this – an almost furtive practice in a little beach town. You'd have liked to change your name – but you couldn't and keep your licence. Somebody had to master-mind this deal, Doctor. Clausen was a bum, Hicks a stupid lout, Orrin Quest a nasty-minded creep. But they could be used. You couldn't go up against Steelgrave directly. You wouldn't have stayed alive long enough to brush your teeth. You had to work through pawns – expendable pawns. Well – are we getting anywhere?'

He smiled faintly and leaned back in his chair with a sigh. 'Presumption D, Mr Marlowe,' he almost whispered. 'You are an unmitigated idiot.'

I grinned and reached for a match to light his fat Egyptian cigarette.

'Added to all the rest,' I said, 'Orrin's sister calls me up and tells me he is in your house. There are a lot of weak arguments taken one at a time, I admit. But they do seem to sort of focus on you.' I puffed peacefully on the cigarette.

He watched me. His face seemed to fluctuate and become vague, to move far off and come back. I felt a tightness in my chest. My mind had slowed to a turtle's gallop.

'What's going on here?' I heard myself mumble.

I put my hands on the arms of the chair and pushed myself up. 'Been dumb, haven't I?' I said, with the cigarette still in my mouth and me still smoking it. Dumb was hardly the word. Have to coin a new word.

I was out of the chair and my feet were stuck in two barrels of cement. When I spoke my voice seemed to come through cottonwool.

I let go of the arms of the chair and reached for the cigarette. I missed it clean a couple of times, then got my hand around it. It didn't feel like a cigarette. It felt like the hind leg of an elephant. With sharp toenails. They stuck into my hand. I shook my hand and the elephant took his leg away.

A vague but enormously tall figure swung around in front of me and a mule kicked me in the chest. I sat down on the floor.

'A little potassium hydrocyanide,' a voice said, over the transatlantic telephone. 'Not fatal, not even dangerous. Merely relaxing. . . .'

I started to get up off the floor. You ought to try it sometime. But have somebody nail the floor down first. This one looped the loop. After a while it steadied a little. I settled for an angle of forty-five degrees. I took hold of myself and started to go somewhere. There was a thing that might have been Napoleon's tomb on the horizon. That was a good enough objective. I started that way. My heart beat fast and thick and I was having trouble opening my lungs. Like after being winded at football. You think your breath will never come back. Never, never, never.

Then it wasn't Napoleon's tomb any more. It was a raft on a swell. There was a man on it. I'd seen him somewhere. Nice fellow, we'd got on fine. I started towards him and hit a wall with my shoulder. That spun me around. I started clawing for something to hold on to. There was nothing but the carpet. How did I get down there? No use asking. It's a secret. Every time you ask a question they just push the floor in your face. Okay, I started to crawl along the carpet. I was on what formerly had been my hands and knees. No sensation proved it. I crawled towards a dark wooden wall. Or it could have been black marble. Napoleon's tomb again. What did I ever do to Napoleon? What for should he keep shoving his tomb at me?

'Need a drink of water,' I said.

I listened for the echo. No echo. Nobody said anything. Maybe I didn't say it. Maybe it was just an idea I thought better of. Potassium cyanide. That's a couple of long words to be worrying about when you're crawling through tunnels. Nothing fatal, he said. Okay, this is just fun. What you might call semi-fatal. Philip Marlowe, 38, a private licence operator of shady reputation, was apprehended by police last night while crawling through the Ballona Storm Drain with a grand piano on his back. Questioned at the University Heights Police Station, Marlowe declared he was taking the piano to the Maharajah of Coot-Berar. Asked why he was wearing spurs, Marlowe declared that a client's confidence was sacred. Marlowe is being held for investigation. Chief Hornside said police were not yet ready to say more. Asked if the piano was in tune, Chief Hornside declared that he had played the Minute Waltz on it in thirty-five seconds and so far as he could tell there were no strings in the piano. He intimated that something else was. A complete statement to the press will be made within twelve hours, Chief Hornside said abruptly. Speculation is rife that Marlowe was attempting to dispose of a body.

A face swam towards me out of the darkness. I changed direction and started for the face. But it was too late in the afternoon. The sun was setting. It was getting dark rapidly. There was no face. There was no wall, no desk. Then there was no floor. There was nothing at all.

I wasn't even there.

22

A big black gorilla with a big black paw had his big black paw over my face and was trying to push it through the back of my neck. I pushed back. Taking the weak side of an argument is my speciality. Then I realized that he was trying to keep me from opening my eyes.

I decided to open my eyes just the same. Others have done it, why not me? I gathered my strength and very slowly, keeping the back straight, flexing the thighs and knees, using the arms as ropes, I lifted the enormous weight of my eyelids.

I was looking at the ceiling, lying on my back on the floor, a position in which my calling has occasionally placed me. I rolled my head. My lungs felt stiff and my mouth felt dry. The room was just Dr Lagardie's consulting room. Same chair, same desk, same walls and window. There was a shuttered silence hanging around.

I got up on my haunches and braced myself on the floor and shook my head. It went into a flat spin. It spun down about five thousand feet and then I dragged it out and levelled off. I blinked. Same floor, same desk, same walls. But no Dr Lagardie.

I wet my lips and made some kind of a vague noise to which nobody paid any attention. I got up on my feet. I was as dizzy as a dervish, as weak as a worn-out washer, as low as a badger's belly, as timid as a titmouse, and as unlikely to succeed as a ballet dancer with a wooden leg.

I groped my way over behind the desk and slumped into Lagardie's chair and began to paw fitfully through his equipment for a likely looking bottle of liquid fertilizer. Nothing doing. I got up again. I was as hard to lift as a dead elephant. I staggered around looking into cabinets of shining white enamel which contained everything somebody else was in a hurry for. Finally, after what seemed like four years on the road gang, my little hand closed around six ounces of ethyl alcohol. Just what the label said. All I needed now was a glass and some water. A good man ought to be able to get that far. I started through the door to the examination room.

The air still had the aromatic perfume of overripe peaches. I hit both sides of the doorway going through and paused to take a fresh sighting.

At that moment I was aware that steps were coming down the hall. I leaned against the wall wearily and listened.

Slow, dragging steps, with a long pause between each. At first they seemed furtive. Then they just seemed very, very tired. An old man trying to make it to his last armchair. That made two of us. And then I thought, for no reason at all, of Orfamay's father back there on the porch in Manhattan, Kansas, moving quietly along to his rocking chair with his cold pipe in his hand, to sit down and look out over the front lawn and have himself a nice economical smoke that required no matches and no tobacco and didn't mess up the living-room carpet. I arranged his chair for him. In the shade at the end of the porch where the bougainvillaea was thick I helped him sit down. He looked up and thanked me with the good side of his face. His fingernails scratched on the arms of the chair as he leaned back.

The fingernails scratched, but it wasn't on the arm of any chair. It was a real sound. It was close by, on the outside of a closed door that led from the examination room to the hallway. A thin, feeble scratch, possibly a young kitten wanting to be let in. Okay, Marlowe, you're an old animal lover. Go over and let the kitten in. I started. I made it with the help of the nice examination couch with the rings on the end and the nice clean towels. The scratching had stopped. Poor little kitten, outside and wanting to come in. A tear formed itself in my eye and trickled down my furrowed cheek. I let go of the examination table and made a smooth four yards to the door. The heart was bumping inside me. And the lungs still had that feeling of having been in storage for a couple of years. I took a deep breath and got hold of the door-knob and opened it. Just at the last moment it occurred to me to reach for a gun. It occurred to me but that's as far as I got. I'm a fellow that likes to take an idea over by the light and have a good look at it. I'd have had to let go of the door-knob. It seemed like too big an operation. I just twisted the knob and opened the door instead.

He was braced to the door-frame by four hooked fingers made of white wax. He had eyes an eighth of an inch deep, pale grey-blue, wide open. They looked at me but they didn't see me. Our faces were inches apart.

Our breathing met in mid-air. Mine was quick and harsh, his was the far-off whisper which has not yet begun to rattle. Blood bubbled from his mouth and ran down his chin. Something made me look down. Blood drained slowly down the inside of his trouser leg and out on his shoe and from his shoe it flowed without haste to the floor. It was already a small pool.

I couldn't see where he had been shot. His teeth clicked and I thought he was going to speak, or try to speak. But that was the only sound from him. He had stopped breathing. His jaw fell slack. Then the rattle started. It isn't a rattle at all, of course. It isn't anything like a rattle.

Rubber heels squeaked on the linoleum between the rug and the door sill. The white fingers slid away from the door frame. The man's body started to wind up on the legs. The legs refused to hold it. They scissored. His torso turned in mid-air, like a swimmer in a wave, and jumped at me.

In the same moment his other arm, the one that had been out of sight, came up and over in a galvanic sweep that seemed not to have any possible living impetus behind it. It fell across my left shoulder as I reached for him. A bee stung me between the shoulder blades. Something besides the bottle of alcohol I had been holding thumped to the floor and rattled against the bottom of the wall.

I clamped my teeth hard and spread my feet and caught him under the arms. He weighed like five men. I took a step back and tried to hold him up. It was like trying to lift one end of a fallen tree. I went down with him. His head bumped the floor. I couldn't help it. There wasn't enough of me working to stop it. I straightened him out a bit and got away from him. I climbed up on my knees, and bent down and listened. The rattle stopped. There was a long silence. Then there was a muted sigh, very quiet and indolent and without urgency. Another silence. Another still slower sigh, languid and peaceful as a summer breeze drifting past the nodding roses.

Something happened to his face and behind his face, the indefinable thing that happens in that always baffling and inscrutable moment, the smoothing out, the going back over the years to the age of innocence. The face now had a vague inner amusement, an almost roguish lift at the corners of the mouth. All of which was very silly, because I knew damn well, if I ever knew anything at all, that Orrin P. Quest had not been that kind of boy.

In the distance a siren wailed. I stayed kneeling and listened. It wailed and went away. I got to my feet and went over and looked out of the side window. In front of The Garland Home of Peace another funeral was forming up. The street was thick with cars again. People walked slowly up the path past the tree roses. Very slowly, the men with their hats in their hands long before they reached the little colonial porch.

I dropped the curtain and went over and picked up the bottle of ethyl alcohol and wiped it off with my handkerchief and laid it aside. I was no longer interested in alcohol. I bent down again and the bee-sting between my shoulder blades reminded me that there was something else to pick up. A thing with a round white wooden handle that lay against the baseboard. An ice-pick with a filed down blade not more than three inches long. I held it against the light and looked at the needle sharp tip. There might or might not have been a faint stain of my blood on it. I pulled a finger gently beside the point. No blood. The point was very sharp.

I did some more work with my handkerchief and then bent down and put the ice-pick on the palm of his right hand, white and waxy against the dull nap of the carpet. It looked too arranged. I shook his arm enough to make it roll off his hand to the floor. I thought about going through his pockets, but a more ruthless hand than mine would have done that already.

In a flash of sudden panic I went through mine instead. Nothing had been taken. Even the Luger under my arm had been left. I dragged it out and sniffed at it. It had not been fired, something I should have known without looking. You don't walk around much after being shot with a Luger.

I stepped over the dark red pool in the doorway and looked along the hall. The house was still silent and waiting. The blood trail led me back and across to a room furnished like a den. There was a studio couch and a desk, some books and medical journals, an ashtray with five fat oval stubs in it. A metallic glitter near the leg of the studio couch turned out to be a used shell from an automatic .32 calibre. I found another under the desk. I put them in my pocket.

I went back out and up the stairs. There were two bedrooms both in use, one pretty thoroughly stripped of clothes. In an ash-tray more of Dr Lagardie's oval stubs. The other contained Orrin Quest's meagre wardrobe, his spare suit and overcoat neatly hung in the closet, his shirts and socks and underwear equally neat in the drawers of a chest. Under the shirts at the back I found a Leica and an F.2 lens.

I left all these things as they were and went back downstairs into the room where the dead man lay indifferent to these trifles. I wiped off a few more door-knobs out of sheer perverseness, hesitated over the phone in the front room, and left without touching it. The fact that I was still walking around was a pretty good indication that the good Dr Lagardie hadn't killed anybody.

People were still crawling up the walk to the oddly undersized colonial porch of the funeral parlours across the street. An organ was moaning inside.

I went around the corner of the house and got into my car and left. I drove slowly and breathed deeply from the bottom of my lungs, but I still couldn't seem to get enough oxygen.

Bay City ends about four miles from the ocean. I stopped in front of the last drug store. It was time for me to make one more of my anonymous phone calls. Come and pick up the body, fellows. Who am I? Just a lucky boy who keeps finding them for you. Modest too. Don't even want my name mentioned.

I looked at the drug store and in through the plate-glass front. A girl with slanted cheaters was reading a magazine. She looked something like Orfamay Quest. Something tightened up my throat.

I let the clutch in and drove on. She had a right to know first, law or no law. And I was far outside the law already.

23

I stopped at the office door with the key in my hand. Then I went noiselessly along to the other door, the one that was always unlocked, and stood there and listened. She might be in there already, waiting, with her eyes shining behind the slanted cheaters and the small moist mouth willing to be kissed. I would have to tell her a harder thing than she dreamed of, and then after a while she would go and I would never see her again.

I didn't hear anything. I went back and unlocked the other door and picked the mail up and carried it over and dumped it on the desk. Nothing in it made me feel any taller. I left it and crossed to turn the latch in the other door and after a long slow moment I opened it and looked out. Silence and emptiness. A folded piece of paper lay at my feet. It had been pushed under the door. I picked it up and unfolded it.

'Please call me at the apartment house. Most urgent. I must see you.' It was signed D.

I dialled the number of the Chateau Bercy and asked for Miss Gonzales. Who was calling, please? One moment please, Mr Marlowe. Buzz, buzz. Buzz, buzz.

' 'Allo?'

'The accent's a bit thick this afternoon.'

'Ah, it is you, amigo. I waited so long in your funny little office. Can you come over here and talk to me?'

'Impossible. I'm waiting for a call.'

'Well, may I come there?'

'What's it all about?'

'Nothing I could discuss on the telephone, amigo.'

'Come ahead.'

I sat there and waited for the telephone to ring. It didn't ring. I looked out of the window. The crowd was seething on the boulevard, the kitchen of the coffee shop next door was pouring the smell of Blue Plate Specials out of its ventilator shaft. Time passed and I sat there hunched over the desk, my chin in a hand, staring at the mustard yellow plaster of the end wall, seeing on it the vague figure of a dying man with a short ice-pick in his hand, and feeling the sting of its point between my shoulder-blades. Wonderful what Hollywood will do to a nobody. It will make a radiant glamour queen out of a drab little wench who ought to be ironing a truck driver's shirts, a he-man hero with shining eyes and brilliant smile reeking of sexual charm out of some overgrown kid who was meant to go to work with a lunch-box. Out of a Texas car hop with the literacy of a character in a comic strip it will make an international courtesan, married six times to six millionaires and so blasé and decadent at the end of it that her idea of a thrill is to seduce a furniture-mover in a sweaty undershirt.

And by remote control it might even take a small town prig like Orrin Quest and make an ice-pick murderer out of him in a matter of months, elevating his simple meanness into the classic sadism of the multiple killer.

It took her a little over ten minutes to get there. I heard the door open and close and I went through to the waiting-room and there she was, the All-American Gardenia. She hit me right between the eyes. Her own were deep and dark and unsmiling.

She was all in black, like the night before, but a tailor-made outfit this time, a wide black straw hat set at a rakish angle, the collar of a white silk shirt folded out over the collar of her jacket, and her throat brown and supple and her mouth as red as a new fire engine.

'I waited a long time,' she said. 'I have not had any lunch.'

'I had mine,' I said. 'Cyanide. Very satisfying. I've only just stopped looking blue.'

'I am not in an amusing mood this morning, amigo.'

'You don't have to amuse me,' I said. 'I amuse myself. I do a brother act that has me rolling in the aisle. Let's go inside.'

We went into my private thinking parlour and sat down.

'You always wear black?' I asked.

'But yes. It is more exciting when I take my clothes off.'

'Do you have to talk like a whore?'

'You do not know much about whores, amigo. They are always most respectable. Except, of course, the very cheap ones.'

'Yeah,' I said. 'Thanks for telling me. What is the urgent matter we have to talk about? Going to bed with you is not urgent. It can be done any day.'

'You are in a nasty mood.'

'Okay, I'm in a nasty mood.'

She got one of her long brown cigarettes out of her bag and fitted it carefully into the golden tweezers. She waited for me to light it for her. I didn't, so she lit it herself with a golden lighter.

She held this doohickey in a black gauntleted glove and stared at me out of depthless black eyes that had no laughter in them now.

'Would you like to go to bed with me?'

'Most anyone would. But let's leave sex out of it for now.'

'I do not draw a very sharp line between business and sex,' she said evenly. 'And you cannot humiliate me. Sex is a net with which I catch fools. Some of these fools are useful and generous. Occasionally one is dangerous.'

She paused thoughtfully.

I said: 'If you're waiting for me to say something that lets on I know who a certain party is – Okay, I know who he is.'

'Can you prove it?'

'Probably not. The cops couldn't.'

'The cops,' she said contemptuously, 'do not always tell all they know. They do not always prove everything they could prove. I suppose you know he was in jail for ten days last February.'

'Yes.'

'Did it not occur to you as strange that he did not get bail?'

'I don't know what charge they had him on. If it was as a material witness –'

'Do you not think he could get the charge changed to something bailable – if he really wanted to?'

'I haven't thought much about it,' I lied. 'I don't know the man.'

'You have never spoken to him?' she asked idly, a little too idly.

I didn't answer.

She laughed shortly. 'Last night, amigo. Outside Mavis Weld's apartment. I was sitting in a car across the street.'

'I may have bumped into him accidentally. Was that the guy?'

'You do not fool me at all.'

'Okay. Miss Weld was pretty rough with me. I went away sore. Then I met this ginzo with her door-key in his hand. I yank it out of his hand and toss it behind some bushes. Then I apologize and go get it for him. He seemed like a nice little guy too.'

'Ver-ry nice,' she drawled. 'He was *my* boy friend also.'

I grunted.

'Strange as it may seem I'm not a hell of a lot interested in your love life, Miss Gonzales. I assume it covers a wild field – all the way from Stein to Steelgrave.'

'Stein?' she asked softly. 'Who is Stein?'

'A Cleveland hot shot that got himself gunned in front of your apartment house last February. He had an apartment there. I thought perhaps you might have met him.'

She let out a silvery little laugh. 'Amigo, there are men I do not know. Even at the Chateau Bercy.'

'Reports say he was gunned two blocks away,' I said. 'I like it better that it happened right in front. And you were looking out of the window and saw it happen. And saw the killer run away and just under a street light he turned back and the light caught his face and darned if it wasn't old man Steelgrave. You recognized him by his rubber nose and the fact that he was wearing his tall hat with the pigeons on it.'

She didn't laugh.

'You like it better that way,' she purred.

'We could make more money that way.'

'But Steelgrave was in jail,' she smiled. 'And even if he was not in jail – even if, for example, I happened to be friendly with a certain Dr Chalmers who was county jail physician at the time and he told me, in an intimate moment, that he had given Steelgrave a pass to go to the dentist – with a guard, of course, but the guard was a reasonable man – on the very day Stein was shot – even if this happened to be true, would it not be a very poor way to use the information by blackmailing Steelgrave?'

'I hate to talk big,' I said, 'but I'm not afraid of Steelgrave – or a dozen like him in one package.'

'But I am, amigo. A witness to a gang murder is not in a very safe position in this country. No, we will not blackmail Steelgrave. And we will not say anything about Mr Stein, whom I may or may not have known. It is enough that Mavis Weld is a close friend of a known gangster and is seen in public with him.'

'We'd have to prove he was a known gangster,' I said.

'Can we not do that?'

'How?'

She made a disappointed mouth. 'But I felt sure that was what you had been doing these last couple of days.'

'Why?'

'I have private reasons.'

'They mean nothing to me while you keep them private.'

She got rid of the brown cigarette stub in my ashtray. I leaned over and squashed it out with the stub of a pencil. She touched my hand lightly with a gauntleted finger. Her smile was the reverse of anaesthetic. She leaned back and crossed her legs. The little lights began to dance in her eyes. It was a long time between passes – for her.

'Love is such a dull word,' she mused. 'It amazed me that the English language, so rich in the poetry of love, can accept such a feeble word for it. It has no life, no resonance. It suggests to me little girls in ruffled summer dresses, with little pink smiles, and little shy voices, and probably the most unbecoming underwear.'

I said nothing. With an effortless change of pace she became business-like again.

'Mavis will get seventy-five thousand dollars a picture from now on, and eventually one hundred and fifty thousand dollars. She has started to climb and nothing will stop her. Except possibly a bad scandal.'

'Then somebody ought to tell her who Steelgrave is,' I said. 'Why don't you? And incidentally, suppose we did have all this proof, what's Steelgrave doing all the time we're putting the bite on Weld?'

'Does he have to know? I hardly think she would tell him. In fact, I hardly think she would go on having anything to do with him. But that would matter to us – if we had our proof. And if she knew we had it.'

Her black gauntleted hand moved towards her black bag, stopped, drummed lightly on the edge of the desk, and so got back to where she could drop it in her lap. She hadn't looked at the bag. I hadn't either.

I stood up. 'I might happen to be under some obligation to Miss Weld. Ever think of that?'

She just smiled.

'And if that was so,' I said, 'don't you think it's about time you got the hell out of my office?'

She put her hands on the arms of her chair and started to get up, still smiling. I scooped the bag before she could change direction. Her eyes filled with glare. She made a spitting sound.

I opened the bag and went through and found a white envelope that looked a little familiar. Out of it I shook the photo at The Dancers, the two pieces fitted together and pasted on another piece of paper.

I closed the bag and tossed it to her.

She was on her feet now, her lips drawn back over her teeth. She was very silent.

'Interesting,' I said, and snapped a digit at the glazed surface of the print. 'If it's not a fake. Is that Steelgrave?'

The silvery laugh bubbled up again. 'You are a ridiculous character, amigo. You really are. I did not know they made such people any more.'

'Pre-war stock,' I said. 'We're getting scarcer every day. Where did you get this?'

'From Mavis Weld's purse in Mavis Weld's dressing-room. While she was on the set.'

'She know?'

'She does not know.'

'I wonder where she got it.'

'From you.'

'Nonsense.' I raised my eyebrows a few inches. 'Where would I get it?'

She reached the gauntleted hand across the desk. Her voice was cold. 'Give it back to me, please.'

'I'll give it back to Mavis Weld. And I hate to tell you this, Miss Gonzales, but I'd never get anywhere as a blackmailer. I just don't have the engaging personality.'

'Give it back to me!' she said sharply. 'If you do not –'

She cut herself off. I waited for her to finish. A look of contempt showed on her smooth features.

'Very well,' she said. 'It is my mistake. I thought you were smart. I can see that you are just another dumb private eye. This shabby little office,' she waved a black gloved hand at it, 'and the shabby little life that goes on here – they ought to tell me what sort of idiot you are.'

'They do,' I said.

She turned slowly and walked to the door. I got around the desk and she let me open it for her.

She went out slowly. The way she did it hadn't been learned at business college.

She went on down the hall without looking back. She had a beautiful walk.

The door bumped against the pneumatic door-closer and very softly clicked shut. It seemed to take a long time to do that. I stood there watching it as if I had never seen it happen before. Then I turned and started back towards my desk and the phone rang.

I picked it up and answered it. It was Christy French. 'Marlowe? We'd like to see you down at headquarters.'

'Right away?'

'If not sooner,' he said and hung up.

I slipped the pasted-together print from under the blotter and went over to put it in the safe with the others. I put my hat on and closed the window. There was nothing to wait for. I looked at the green tip on the sweep hand of my watch. It was a long time until five o'clock. The sweep hand went around and around the dial like a door to door salesman. The hands stood at four-ten. You'd think she'd have called up by now. I peeled my coat off and unstrapped the shoulder harness and locked it with the Luger in the desk drawer. The cops don't like you to be wearing a gun in their territory. Even if you have the right to wear one. They like you to come in properly humble, with your hat in your hand, and your voice low and polite, and your eyes full of nothing.

I looked at the watch again. I listened. The building seemed quiet this afternoon. After a while it would be silent and then the madonna of the dark grey mop would come shuffling along the hall, trying door-knobs.

I put my coat back on and locked the communicating door and switched off the buzzer and let myself out into the hallway. And then the phone rang. I nearly took the door off its hinges getting back to it. It was her voice all right, but it had a tone I had never heard before. A cool,

521

balanced tone, not flat or empty or dead, or even childish. Just the voice of a girl I didn't know and yet did know. What was in that voice I knew before she said more than three words.

'I called you up because you told me to,' she said. 'But you don't have to tell me anything. I went down there.'

I was holding the phone with both hands.

'You went down there,' I said. 'Yes. I heard that. So?'

'I – borrowed a car,' she said. 'I parked across the street. There were so many cars you would never have noticed me. There's a funeral home there. I wasn't following you. I tried to go after you when you came out but I don't know the streets down there at all. I lost you. So I went back.'

'What did you go back for?'

'I don't really know. I thought you looked kind of funny when you came out of the house. Or maybe I just had a feeling. He being my brother and all. So I went back and rang the bell. And nobody answered the door. I thought that was funny too. Maybe I'm psychic or something. All of a sudden I seemed to have to get into that house. And I didn't know how to do it, but I had to.'

'That's happened to me,' I said, and it was my voice, but somebody had been using my tongue for sandpaper.

'I called the police and told them I had heard shots,' she said. 'They came and one of them got into the house through a window. And then he let the other one in. And after a while they let me in. And they wouldn't let me go. I had to tell them all about it, who he was, and that I had lied about the shots, but I was afraid something had happened to Orrin. And I had to tell them about you too.'

'That's all right,' I said. 'I'd have told them myself as soon as I could get a chance to tell *you*.'

'It's kind of awkward for you, isn't it?'

'Yes.'

'Will they arrest you or something?'

'They could.'

'You left him lying there on the floor. Dead. You had to, I guess.'

'I had my reasons,' I said. 'They won't sound too good, but I had them. It made no difference to him.'

'Oh, you'd have your reasons all right,' she said. 'You're very smart.

You'd always have reasons for things. Well, I guess you'll have to tell the police your reasons too.'

'Not necessarily.'

'Oh yes, you will,' the voice said, and there was a ring of pleasure in it I couldn't account for. 'You certainly will. They'll make you.'

'We won't argue about that,' I said. 'In my business a fellow does what he can to protect a client. Sometimes he goes a little too far. That's what I did. I've put myself where they can hurt me. But not entirely for you.'

'You left him lying on the floor, dead,' she said. 'And I don't care what they do to you. If they put you in prison, I think I would like that. I bet you'll be awfully brave about it.'

'Sure,' I said. 'Always a gay smile. Do you see what he had in his hand?'

'He didn't have anything in his hand.'

'Well, lying near his hand.'

'There wasn't anything. There wasn't anything at all. What sort of thing?'

'That's fine,' I said. 'I'm glad of that. Well, good-bye. I'm going down to headquarters now. They want to see me. Good luck, if I don't see you again.'

'You'd better keep your good luck,' she said. 'You might need it. And I wouldn't want it.'

'I did my best for you,' I said. 'Perhaps if you'd given me a little more information in the beginning –'

She hung up while I was saying it.

I put the phone down in its cradle as gently as if it was a baby. I got out a handkerchief and wiped the palms of my hands. I went over to the wash-basin and washed my hands and face. I sloshed cold water on my face and dried it off hard with the towel and looked at it in the mirror.

'You drove off a cliff all right,' I said to the face.

24

In the centre of the room was a long yellow oak table. Its edges were unevenly grooved with cigarette burns. Behind it was a window with wire over the stippled glass. Also behind it with a mess of papers spread out untidily in front of him was Detective-Lieutenant Fred Beifus. At the end of the table leaning back on two legs of an armchair was a big burly man whose face had for me the vague familiarity of a face previously seen in a halftone on newsprint. He had a jaw like a park bench. He had the butt end of a carpenter's pencil between his teeth. He seemed to be awake and breathing, but apart from that he just sat.

There were two roll-top desks at the other side of the table and there was another window. One of the roll-top desks was backed to the window. A woman with orange-coloured hair was typing out a report on a typewriter stand beside the desk. At the other desk, which was endways to the window, Christy French sat in a tilted back swivel chair with his feet on the corner of the desk. He was looking out of the window, which was open and afforded a magnificent view of the police parking lot and the back of a billboard.

'Sit down there,' Beifus said, pointing.

I sat down across from him in a straight oak chair without arms. It was far from new and when new had not been beautiful.

'This is Lieutenant Moses Maglashan of the Bay City police,' Beifus said. 'He don't like you any better than we do.'

Lieutenant Moses Maglashan took the carpenter's pencil out of his mouth and looked at the teeth marks in the fat octagonal pencil butt. Then he looked at me. His eyes went over me slowly exploring me, noting me, cataloguing me. He said nothing. He put the pencil back in his mouth.

Beifus said: 'Maybe I'm a queer, but for me you don't have no more sex appeal than a turtle.' He half turned to the typing woman in the corner. 'Millie.'

She swung around from the typewriter to a shorthand notebook.

'Name's Philip Marlowe,' Beifus said. 'With an "e" on the end, if you're fussy. Licence number?'

He looked back at me. I told him. The orange queen wrote without looking up. To say she had a face that would have stopped a clock would have been to insult her. It would have stopped a runaway horse.

'Now if you're in the mood,' Beifus told me, 'you could start in at the beginning and give us all the stuff you left out yesterday. Don't try to sort it out. Just let it flow natural. We got enough stuff to check you as you go along.'

'You want me to make a statement?'

'A very full statement,' Beifus said. 'Fun, huh?'

'This statement is to be voluntary and without coercion?'

'Yeah. They all are.' Beifus grinned.

Maglashan looked at me steadily for a moment. The orange queen turned back to her typing. Nothing for her yet. Thirty years of it had perfected her timing.

Maglashan took a heavy worn pigskin glove out of his pocket and put it on his right hand and flexed his fingers.

'What's that for?' Beifus asked him.

'I bite my nails times,' Maglashan said. 'Funny. Only bite 'em on my right hand.' He raised his slow eyes to stare at me. 'Some guys are more voluntary than others,' he said idly. 'Something to do with the kidneys, they tell me. I've known guys of the not so voluntary type that had to go to the can every fifteen minutes for weeks after they got voluntary. Couldn't seem to hold water.'

'Just think of that,' Beifus said wonderingly.

'Then there's the guys can't talk above a husky whisper,' Maglashan went on. 'Like punch-drunk fighters that have stopped too many with their necks.'

Maglashan looked at me. It seemed to be my turn.

'Then there's the type that won't go to the can at all,' I said. 'They try too hard. Sit in a chair like this for thirty hours straight. Then they fall down and rupture a spleen or burst a bladder. They over-co-operate. And after sunrise court, when the tank is empty, you find them dead in a dark corner. Maybe they ought to have seen a doctor, but you can't figure everything, can you, Lieutenant?'

'We figure pretty close down in Bay City,' he said. 'When we got anything to figure with.'

There were hard lumps of muscle at the corners of his jaws. His eyes had a reddish glare behind them.

'I could do lovely business with you,' he said, staring at me. 'Just lovely.'

'I'm sure you could, Lieutenant. I've always had a swell time in Bay City – while I stayed conscious.'

'I'd keep you conscious a long long time, baby. I'd make a point of it. I'd give it my personal attention.'

Christy French turned his head slowly and yawned. 'What makes you Bay City cops so tough?' he asked. 'You pickle your nuts in salt-water or something?'

Beifus put his tongue out so that the tip showed and ran it along his lips.

'We've always been tough,' Maglashan said, not looking at him. 'We like to be tough. Jokers like this character here keep us tuned up.' He turned back to me. 'So you're the sweetheart that phoned in about Clausen. You're right handy with a pay phone, ain't you, sweetheart?'

I didn't say nothing.

'I'm talking to you, sweetheart,' Maglashan said. 'I asked you a question, sweetheart. When I ask a question I get answered. Get that, sweetheart?'

'Keep on talking and you'll answer yourself,' Christy French said. 'And maybe you won't like the answer, and maybe you'll be so damn tough you'll have to knock yourself out with that glove. Just to prove it.'

Maglashan straightened up. Red spots the size of half-dollars glowed dully on his cheeks.

'I come up here to get co-operation,' he told French slowly. 'The big razzoo I can get to home. From my wife. Here I don't expect the wise numbers to work out on me.'

'You'll get co-operation,' French said. 'Just don't try to steal the picture with that nineteen-thirty dialogue.' He swung his chair around and looked at me. 'Let's take out a clean sheet of paper and play like we're just starting this investigation. I know all your arguments. I'm no judge of them. The point is, do you want to talk or get booked as a material witness?'

'Ask the questions,' I said. 'If you don't like the answers, you can book me. If you book me, I get to make a phone call.'

'Correct,' French said, '*if* we book you. But we don't have to. We can ride the circuit with you. It might take days.'

'And canned cornbeef hash to eat,' Beifus put in cheerfully.

'Strictly speaking, it wouldn't be legal,' French said. 'But we do it all the time. Like you do a few things which you hadn't ought to do maybe. Would you say you were legal in this picture?'

'No.'

Maglashan let out a deep-throated 'Ha!'

I looked across at the orange queen who was back to her notebook, silent and indifferent.

'You got a client to protect,' French said.

'Maybe.'

'You mean you did have a client. She ratted on you.'

I said nothing.

'Name's Orfamay Quest,' French said, watching me.

'Ask your questions,' I said.

'What happened down there on Idaho Street?'

'I went there looking for her brother. He'd moved away, she said, and she'd come out here to see him. She was worried. The manager, Clausen, was too drunk to talk sense. I looked at the register and saw another man had moved into Quest's room. I talked to this man. He told me nothing that helped.'

French reached around and picked a pencil off the desk and tapped it against his teeth. 'Ever see this man again?'

'Yes. I told him who I was. When I went back downstairs Clausen was dead. And somebody had torn a page out of the register. The page with Quest's name on it. I called the police.'

'But you didn't stick around?'

'I had no information about Clausen's death.'

'But you didn't stick around,' French repeated. Maglashan made a savage noise in his throat and threw the carpenter's pencil clear across the room. I watched it bounce against the wall and floor and come to a stop.

'That's correct,' I said.

'In Bay City,' Maglashan said, 'we could murder you for that.'

'In Bay City you could murder me for wearing a blue tie,' I said.

He started to get up. Beifus looked sideways at him and said: 'Leave Christy handle it. There's always a second show.'

'We could break you for that,' French said to me without inflection.

'Consider me broke,' I said. 'I never liked the business anyway.'

'So you came back to your office. What then?'

'I reported to the client. Then a guy called me up and asked me over to the Van Nuys Hotel. He was the same guy I had talked to down on Idaho Street, but with a different name.'

'You could have told us that, couldn't you?'

'If I had, I'd have had to tell you everything. That would have violated the conditions of my employment.'

French nodded and tapped his pencil. He said slowly: 'A murder wipes out agreements like that. Two murders ought to do it double. And two murders by the same method, treble. You don't look good, Marlowe. You don't look good at all.'

'I don't even look good to the client,' I said, 'after today.'

'What happened today?'

'She told me her brother had called her up from this doctor's house. Dr Lagardie. The brother was in danger. I was to hurry on down and take care of him. I hurried on down. Dr Lagardie and his nurse had the office closed. They acted scared. The police had been there.' I looked at Maglashan.

'Another of his phone calls,' Maglashan snarled.

'Not me this time,' I said.

'All right. Go on,' French said, after a pause.

'Lagardie denied knowing anything about Orrin Quest. He sent his nurse home. Then he slipped me a doped cigarette and I went away from there for a while. When I came to I was alone in the house. Then I wasn't. Orrin Quest, or what was left of him, was scratching at the door. He fell through it and died as I opened it. With his last ounce of strength he tried to stick me with an ice-pick.' I moved my shoulders. The place between them was a little stiff and sore, nothing more.

French looked hard at Maglashan. Maglashan shook his head, but French kept on looking at him. Beifus began to whistle under his breath.

I couldn't make out the tune at first, and then I could. It was Old Man Mose is Dead.

French turned his head and said slowly: 'No ice-pick was found by the body.'

'I left it where it fell,' I said.

Maglashan said: 'Looks like I ought to be putting on my glove again.' He stretched it between his fingers. 'Somebody's a goddam liar and it ain't me.'

'All right,' French said. 'All right. Let's not be theatrical. Suppose the kid did have an ice-pick in his hand, that doesn't prove he was born holding one.'

'Filed down,' I said. 'Short. Three inches from the handle to the tip of the point. That's not the way they come from the hardware store.'

'Why would he want to stick you?' Beifus asked with his derisive grin. 'You were his pal. You were down there to keep him safe for his sister.'

'I was just something between him and the light,' I said. 'Something that moved and could have been a man and could have been the man that hurt him. He was dying on his feet. I'd never seen him before. If he ever saw me, I didn't know it.'

'It could have been a beautiful friendship,' Beifus said with a sigh. 'Except for the ice-pick, of course.'

'And the fact that he had it in his hand and tried to stick me with it could mean something.'

'For instance what?'

'A man in his condition acts from instinct. He doesn't invent new techniques. He got me between the shoulder-blades, a sting, the feeble last effort of a dying man. Maybe it would have been a different place and a much deeper penetration if he had had his health.'

Maglashan said: 'How much longer we have to barber round with this monkey? You talk to him like he was human. Leave me talk to him my way.'

'The captain doesn't like it,' French said casually.

'Hell with the captain.'

'The captain doesn't like small town cops saying the hell with him,' French said.

Maglashan clamped his teeth tight and the line of his jaw showed white. His eyes narrowed and glistened. He took a deep breath through his nose.

'Thanks for the co-operation,' he said, and stood up. 'I'll be on my way.' He rounded the corner of the table and stopped beside me. He put his left hand out and tilted my chin up again.

'See you again, sweetheart. In *my* town.'

He lashed me across the face twice with the wrist end of the glove. The buttons stung sharply. I put my hand up and rubbed my lower lip.

French said: 'For Chrissake, Maglashan, sit down and let the guy speak his piece. And keep your hands off him.'

Maglashan looked back at him and said: 'Think you can make me?'

French just shrugged. After a moment Maglashan rubbed his big hand across his mouth and strolled back to his chair. French said:

'Let's have your ideas about all this, Marlowe.'

'Among other things Clausen was probably pushing reefers,' I said. 'I sniffed marijuana smoke in his apartment. A tough little guy was counting money in the kitchen when I got there. He had a gun and a sharpened rat-tail file, both of which he tried to use on me. I took them away from him and he left. He would be the runner. But Clausen was liquored to a point where you wouldn't want to trust him any more. They don't go for that in the organizations. The runner thought I was a dick. Those people wouldn't want Clausen picked up. He would be too easy to milk. The minute they smelled dick around the house Clausen would be missing.'

French looked at Maglashan. 'That make any sense to you?'

'It could happen,' Maglashan said grudgingly.

French said: 'Suppose it was so, what's it got to do with this Orrin Quest?'

'Anybody can smoke reefers,' I said. 'If you're dull and lonely and depressed and out of a job, they might be very attractive. But when you smoke them you get warped and calloused emotions. And marijuana affects different people different ways. Some it makes very tough and some it just makes never-no-mind. Suppose Quest tried to put the bite on somebody and threatened to go to the police. Quite possibly all three murders are connected with the reefer gang.'

'That don't jibe with Quest having a filed down ice-pick,' Beifus said.

I said: 'According to the lieutenant here he didn't have one. So I must have imagined that. Anyhow, he might just have picked it up. They might be standard equipment around Dr Lagardie's house. Get anything on him?'

He shook his head. 'Not so far.'

'He didn't kill me, probably he didn't kill anybody,' I said. 'Quest told his sister – according to her – that he was working for Dr Lagardie, but that some gangsters were after him.'

'This Lagardie,' French said, prodding at his blotter with a pen point, 'what do you make of him?'

'He used to practise in Cleveland. Downtown in a large way. He must have had his reasons for hiding out in Bay City.'

'Cleveland, huh?' French drawled and looked at a corner of the ceiling. Beifus looked down at his papers. Maglashan said:

'Probably an abortionist. I've had my eye on him for some time.'

'Which eye?' Beifus asked him mildly.

Maglashan flushed.

French said: 'Probably the one he didn't have on Idaho Street.'

Maglashan stood up violently. 'You boys think you're so goddam smart it might interest you to know that we're just a small town police force. We got to double in brass once in a while. Just the same, I like that reefer angle. It might cut down my work considerable. I'm looking into it right now.'

He marched solidly to the door and left. French looked after him. Beifus did the same. When the door closed they looked at each other.

'I betcha they pull that raid again tonight,' Beifus said.

French nodded.

Beifus said: 'In a flat over a laundry. They'll go down on the beach and pull in three or four vagrants and stash them in the flat and then they'll line them up for the camera boys after they pull the raid.'

French said: 'You're talking too much, Fred.'

Beifus grinned and was silent. French said to me: 'If you were guessing, what would you guess they were looking for in that room at the Van Nuys?'

'A claimcheck for a suitcase full of weed.'

'Not bad,' French said. 'And still guessing where would it have been?'

'I thought about that. When I talked to Hicks down at Bay City he wasn't wearing his muff. A man doesn't around the house. But he was wearing it on the bed at the Van Nuys. Maybe he didn't put it on himself.'

French said: 'So?'

I said: 'Wouldn't be a bad place to stash a claimcheck.'

French said: 'You could pin it down with a piece of scotch tape. Quite an idea.'

There was a silence. The orange queen went back to her typing. I looked at my nails. They weren't as clean as they might be. After the pause French said slowly:

'Don't think for a minute you're in the clear, Marlowe. Still guessing, how come Dr Lagardie to mention Cleveland to you?'

'I took the trouble to look him up. A doctor can't change his name if he wants to go on practising. The ice-pick made you think of Weepy Moyer. Weepy Moyer operated in Cleveland. Sunny Moe Stein operated in Cleveland. It's true the ice-pick technique was different, but it was an ice-pick. You said yourself the boys might have learned. And always with these gangs there's a doctor somewhere in the background.'

'Pretty wild,' French said. 'Pretty loose connexion.'

'Would I do myself any good if I tightened it up?'

'Can you?'

'I can try.'

French sighed. 'The little Quest girl is okay,' he said. 'I talked to her mother back in Kansas. She really did come out here to look for her brother. And she really did hire you to do it. She gives you a good write-up. Up to a point. She really did suspect her brother was mixed up in something wrong. You make any money on the deal?'

'Not much,' I said. 'I gave her back the fee. She didn't have much.'

'That way you don't have to pay income tax on it,' Beifus said.

French said: 'Let's break this off. The next move is up to the D.A. And if I know Endicott, it will be a week from Tuesday before he decides how to play it.' He made a gesture towards the door.

I stood up. 'Will it be all right if I don't leave town?' I asked.

They didn't bother to answer that one.

I just stood there and looked at them. The ice-pick wound between my shoulders had a dry sting, and the flesh around the place was stiff.

The side of my face and mouth smarted where Maglashan had sideswiped me with his well-used pigskin glove. I was in the deep water. It was dark and unclear and the taste of the salt was in my mouth.

They just sat there and looked back at me. The orange queen was clacking her typewriter. Cop talk was no more treat to her than legs to a dance director. They had the calm weathered faces of healthy men in hard condition. They had the eyes they always have, cloudy and grey like freezing water. The firm set mouth, the hard little wrinkles at the corners of the eyes, the hard hollow meaningless stare, not quite cruel and a thousand miles from kind. The dull ready-made clothes, worn without style, with a sort of contempt; the look of men who are poor and yet proud of their power, watching always for ways to make it felt, to shove it into you and twist it and grin and watch you squirm, ruthless without malice, cruel and yet not always unkind. What would you expect them to be? Civilization had no meaning for them. All they saw of it was the failures, the dirt, the dregs, the aberrations and the disgust.

'What you standing there for?' Beifus asked sharply. 'You want us to give you a great big spitty kiss? No snappy comeback, huh? Too bad.' His voice fell away into a dull drone. He frowned and reached a pencil off the desk. With a quick motion of his fingers he snapped it in half and held the two halves out on his palm.

'We're giving you that much break,' he said thinly, the smile all gone. 'Go on out and square things up. What the hell you think we're turning you loose for? Maglashan bought you a rain check. Use it.'

I put my hand up and rubbed my lip. My mouth had too many teeth in it.

Beifus lowered his eyes to the table, picked up a paper and began to read it. Christy French swung around in his chair and put his feet on the desk and stared out of the open window at the parking lot. The orange queen stopped typing. The room was suddenly full of heavy silence, like a fallen cake.

I went on out, parting the silence as if I was pushing my way through water.

25

The office was empty again. No leggy brunettes, no little girls with slanted glasses, no neat dark men with gangster's eyes.

I sat down at the desk and watched the light fade. The going home sounds had died away. Outside the neon signs began to glare at one another across the boulevard. There was something to be done, but I didn't know what. Whatever it was it would be useless. I tidied up my desk, listening to the scrape of a bucket on the tiling of the corridor. I put my papers away in the drawer, straightened the pen stand, got out a duster and wiped off the glass and then the telephone. It was dark and sleek in the fading light. It wouldn't ring tonight. Nobody would call me again. Not now, not this time. Perhaps not ever.

I put the duster away folded with the dust in it, leaned back and just sat, not smoking, not even thinking. I was a blank man. I had no face, no meaning, no personality, hardly a name. I didn't want to eat. I didn't even want a drink. I was the page from yesterday's calendar crumpled at the bottom of the waste basket.

So I pulled the phone towards me and dialled Mavis Weld's number. It rang and rang and rang. Nine times. That's a lot of ringing, Marlowe. I guess there's nobody home. Nobody home to you. I hung up. Who would you like to call now? You got a friend somewhere that might like to hear your voice? No. Nobody.

Let the telephone ring, please. Let there be somebody to call up and plug me into the human race again. Even a cop. Even a Maglashan. Nobody has to like me. I just want to get off this frozen star.

The telephone rang.

'Amigo,' her voice said. 'There is trouble. Bad trouble. She wants to see you. She likes you. She thinks you are an honest man.'

'Where?' I asked. It wasn't really a question, just a sound I made. I sucked on a cold pipe and leaned my head on my hand, brooding at the telephone. It was a voice to talk to anyway.

'You will come?'

'I'd sit with a sick parrot tonight. Where do I go?'

'I will come for you. I will be before your building in fifteen minutes. It is not easy to get where we go.'

'How is it coming back,' I asked, 'or don't we care?'

But she had already hung up.

Down at the drug-store lunch counter I had time to inhale two cups of coffee and a melted cheese sandwich with two slivers of ersatz bacon embedded in it, like dead fish in the silt at the bottom of a drained pool.

I was crazy. I liked it.

26

It was a black Mercury convertible with a light top. The top was up. When I leaned in at the door Dolores Gonzales slid over towards me along the leather seat.

'You drive please, amigo. I do not really ever like to drive.'

The light from the drug-store caught her face. She had changed her clothes again, but it was still all black, save for a flame-coloured shirt. Slacks and kind of loose coat like a man's leisure jacket.

I leaned on the door of the car. 'Why didn't she call me ?'

'She couldn't. She did not have the number and she had very little time.'

'Why?'

'It seemed to be while someone was out of the room for just a moment.'

'And where is this place she called from?'

'I do not know the name of the street. But I can find the house. That is why I come. Please get into the car and let us hurry.'

'Maybe,' I said. 'And again maybe I am not getting into the car. Old age and arthritis have made me cautious.'

'Always the wisecrack,' she said. 'It is a very strange man.'

'Always the wisecrack where possible,' I said, 'and it is a very ordinary guy with only one head – which has been rather harshly used at times. The times usually started out like this.'

'Will you make love to me tonight?' she asked softly.

'That is an open question. Probably not.'

'You would not waste your time. I am not one of those synthetic blondes with a skin you could strike matches on. These ex-laundresses with large bony hands and sharp knees and unsuccessful breasts.'

'Just for half an hour,' I said, 'let's leave the sex to one side. It's great stuff, like chocolate sundaes. But there comes a time you would rather cut your throat. I guess maybe I'd better cut mine.'

I went around the car and slid under the wheel and started the motor.

'We go west,' she said, 'through the Beverly Hills and then farther on.'

I let the clutch in and drifted around the corner to go south to Sunset. Dolores got one of her long brown cigarettes out.

'Did you bring a gun?' she asked.

'No. What would I want a gun for ?' The inside of my left arm pressed against the Luger in the shoulder harness.

'It is better not perhaps.' She fitted the cigarette into the little golden tweezer thing and lit it with the golden lighter. The light flaring in her face seemed to be swallowed up by her depthless black eyes.

I turned west on Sunset and swallowed myself up in three lanes of race track drivers who were pushing their mounts hard to get nowhere and do nothing.

'What kind of trouble is Miss Weld in?'

'I do not know. She just said that it was trouble and she was much afraid and she needed you.'

'You ought to be able to think up a better story than that.'

She didn't answer. I stopped for a traffic signal and turned to look at her. She was crying softly in the dark.

'I would not hurt a hair of Mavis Weld's head,' she said. 'I do not quite expect that you would believe me.'

'On the other hand,' I said, 'maybe the fact that you don't have a story helps.'

She started to slide along the seat towards me.

'Keep to your own side of the car,' I said. 'I've got to drive this heap.'

'You do not want my head on your shoulder?'

'Not in this traffic.'

I stopped at Fairfax with the green light to let a man make a left turn. Horns blew violently behind. When I started again the car that had been right behind swung out and pulled level and a fat guy in a sweatshirt yelled:

'Aw go get yourself a hammock!'

He went on, cutting in so hard that I had to brake.

'I used to like this town,' I said, just to be saying something and not be thinking too hard. 'A long time ago. There were trees along Wilshire Boulevard. Beverly Hills was a country town. Westwood was bare hills and lots offering at eleven hundred dollars and no takers. Hollywood was a bunch of frame houses on the inter-urban line. Los Angeles was just a big dry sunny place with ugly homes and no style, but good hearted and peaceful. It had the climate they just yap about now. People used to sleep out on porches. Little groups who thought they were intellectual used to call it the Athens of America. It wasn't that, but it wasn't a neon-lighted slum either.'

We crossed La Cienega and went into the curve of the Strip. The Dancers was a blaze of light. The terrace was packed. The parking lot was like ants on a piece of over-ripe fruit.

'Now we get characters like this Steelgrave owning restaurants. We get guys like that fat boy that balled me out back there. We've got the big money, the sharp shooters, the percentage workers, the fast dollar boys, the hoodlums out of New York and Chicago and Detroit – and Cleveland. We've got the flash restaurants and night clubs they run, and the hotels and apartment houses they own, and the grifters and con men and female bandits that live in them. The luxury trades, the pansy decorators, the Lesbian dress designers, the riff-raff of a big hard-boiled city with no more personality than a paper cup. Out in the fancy suburbs dear old Dad is reading the sports page in front of a picture window, with his shoes off, thinking he is high class because he has a three-car garage. Mom is in front of her princess dresser trying to paint the suitcases out from under her eyes. And Junior is clamped on to the telephone calling up a succession of high school girls that talk pidgin English and carry contraceptives in their make-up kit.'

'It is the same in all big cities, amigo.'

'Real cities have something else, some individual bony structure under the muck. Los Angeles has Hollywood – and hates it. It ought to consider itself damn lucky. Without Hollywood it would be a mail order city. Everything in the catalogue you could get better somewhere else.'

'You are bitter, tonight, amigo.'

'I've got a few troubles. The only reason I'm driving this car with you beside me is that I've got so much trouble a little more will seem like icing.'

'You have done something wrong?' she asked, and came close to me along the seat.

'Well, just collecting a few bodies,' I said. 'Depends on the point of view. The cops don't like the work done by us amateurs. They have their own service.'

'What will they do to you?'

'They might run me out of town and I couldn't care less. Don't push me so hard. I need this arm to shift gears with.'

She pulled away in a huff. 'I think you are very nasty to get along with,' she said. 'Turn right at the Lost Canyon Road.'

After a while we passed the University. All the lights of the city were on now, a vast carpet of them stretching down the slope to the south and on into the almost infinite distance. A plane droned overhead, losing altitude, its two signal lights winking on and off alternately. At Lost Canyon I swung right, skirting the big gates that led into Bel-Air. The road began to twist and climb. There were too many cars; the headlights glared angrily down the twisting white concrete. A little breeze blew down over the pass. There was the odour of wild sage, the acrid tang of eucalyptus, and the quiet smell of dust. Windows glowed on the hill-side. We passed a big white two-storied Monterey house that must have cost $70,000 and had a cut-out illuminated sign in front: 'Cairn Terriers.'

'The next to the right,' Dolores said.

I made the turn. The road got steeper and narrower. There were houses behind walls and masses of shrubbery but you couldn't see anything. Then we came to the fork and there was a police car with a red spotlight parked at it and across the right side of the fork two cars parked at right angles. A torch waved up and down. I slowed the car and stopped level with the police car. Two cops sat in it smoking. They didn't move.

'What goes on?'

'Amigo, I have no idea at all.' Her voice had a hushed withdrawn sound. She might have been a little scared. I didn't know what of.

A tall man, the one with the torch, came around the side of the car and poked the flash at me, then lowered it.

'We're not using this road tonight,' he said. 'Going anywhere in particular?'

I set the brake, reached for a flash which Dolores got out of the glove compartment. I snapped the light on to the tall man. He wore expensive-looking slacks, a sports shirt with initials on the pocket and a polka dot scarf knotted around his neck. He had horn-rimmed glasses and glossy wavy black hair. He looked as Hollywood as all hell.

I said: 'Any explanation – or are you just making law?'

'The law is over there, if you want to talk to them.' His voice held a tone of contempt. 'We are merely private citizens. We live around here. This is a residential neighbourhood. We mean to keep it that way.'

A man with a sporting gun came out of the shadows and stood beside the tall man. He held the gun in the crook of his left arm, pointed muzzle down. But he didn't look as if he just had it for ballast.

'That's jake with me,' I said. 'I didn't have any other plans. We just want to go to a place.'

'What place?' the tall man asked coolly.

I turned to Dolores. 'What place?'

'It is a white house on the hill, high up,' she said.

'And what did you plan to do up there?' the tall man asked.

'The man who lives there is my friend,' she said tartly.

He shone the flash in her face for a moment. 'You look swell,' he said. 'But we don't like your friend. We don't like characters that try to run gambling joints in this kind of neighbourhood.'

'I know nothing about a gambling joint,' Dolores told him sharply.

'Neither do the cops,' the tall man said. 'They don't even want to find out. What's your friend's name, darling?'

'That is not of your business,' Dolores spat at him.

'Go on home and knit socks, darling,' the tall man said. He turned to me.

'The road's not in use tonight,' he said. 'Now you know why.'

'Think you can make it stick?' I asked him.

'It will take more than you to change our plans. You ought to see our tax assessments. And those monkeys in the prowl car – and a lot more like them down at the City Hall – just sit on their hands when we ask for the law to be enforced.'

I unlatched the car door and swung it open. He stepped back and let me get out. I walked over to the prowl car. The two cops in it were leaning back lazily. Their loudspeaker was turned low, just audibly muttering. One of them was chewing gum rhythmically.

'How's to break up this road block and let the citizens through?' I asked him.

'No orders, buddy. We're just here to keep the peace. Anybody starts anything, we finish it.'

'They say there's a gambling house up the line.'

'They say,' the cop said.

'You don't believe them?'

'I don't even try, buddy,' he said, and spat past my shoulder.

'Suppose I have urgent business up there.'

He looked at me without expression and yawned.

'Thanks a lot, buddy,' I said.

I went back to the Mercury, got my wallet out and handed the tall man a card. He put his flash on it, and said: 'Well?'

He snapped the flash off and stood silent. His face began to take form palely in the darkness.

'I'm on business. To me it's important business. Let me through and perhaps you won't need this block tomorrow.'

'You talk large, friend.'

'Would I have the kind of money it takes to patronize a private gambling club?'

'She might,' he flicked an eye at Dolores. 'She might have brought you along for protection.'

He turned to the shotgun man. 'What do you think?'

'Chance it. Just two of them and both sober.'

The tall one snapped his flash on again and made a side-sweep with it back and forth. A car motor started. One of the block cars backed around on to the shoulder. I got in and started the Mercury, went on through the gap and watched the block car in the mirror as it took up position again, then cut its high beam lights.

'Is this the only way in and out of here?'

'They think it is, amigo. There is another way, but it is a private road through an estate. We would have had to go around by the valley side.'

'We nearly didn't get through,' I told her. 'This can't be very bad trouble anybody is in.'

'I knew you would find a way, amigo.'

'Something stinks,' I said nastily. 'And it isn't wild lilac.'

'Such a suspicious man. Do you not even want to kiss me?'

'You ought to have used a little of that back at the road block. That tall guy looked lonely. You could have taken him off in the bushes.'

She hit me across the mouth with the back of her hand. 'You son of a bitch,' she said casually. 'The next driveway on the left, if you please.'

We topped a rise and the road ended suddenly in a wide black circle edged with whitewashed stones. Directly ahead was a wire fence with a wide gate in it, and a sign on the gate: 'Private Road. No Trespassing.' The gate was open and a padlock hung from one end of a loose chain on the posts. I turned the car around a white oleander bush and was in the motor yard of a long low white house with a tile roof and a four-car garage in the corner, under a walled balcony. Both the wide garage doors were closed. There was no light in the house. A high moon made a bluish radiance on the white stucco walls. Some of the lower windows were shuttered. Four packing cases full of trash stood in a row at the foot of the steps. There was a big garbage can upended and empty. There were two steel drums with papers in them.

There was no sound from the house, no sign of life. I stopped the Mercury, cut the lights and the motor, and just sat. Dolores moved in the corner. The seat seemed to be shaking. I reached across and touched her. She was shivering.

'What's the matter?'

'Get – get out, please,' she said as if her teeth chattered.

'How about you?'

She opened the door on her side and jumped out. I got out my side and left the door hanging open, the keys in the lock. She came around the back of the car and as she got close to me I could almost feel her shaking before she touched me. Then she leaned up against me hard, thigh to thigh and breast to breast. Her arms went around my neck.

'I am being very foolish,' she said softly. 'He will kill me for this – just as he killed Stein. Kiss me.'

I kissed her. Her lips were hot and dry. 'Is he in there?'

'Yes.'

'Who else?'

'Nobody else – except Mavis. He will kill her too.'

'Listen –'

'Kiss me again. I have not very long to live, amigo. When you are the finger for a man like that – you die young.'

I pushed her away from me, but gently.

She stepped back and lifted her right hand quickly. There was a gun in it now.

I looked at the gun. There was a dull shine on it from the high moon. She held it level and her hand wasn't shaking now.

'What a friend I would make if I pulled this trigger,' she said.

'They'd hear the shot down the road.'

She shook her head. 'No, there is a little hill between. I do not think they would hear, amigo.'

I thought the gun would jump when she pulled the trigger. If I dropped just at the right moment –

I wasn't that good. I didn't say nothing. My tongue felt large in my mouth.

She went on slowly, in a soft, tired voice: 'With Stein it did not matter. I would have killed him myself, gladly. That filth. To die is not much, to kill is not much. But to entice people to their deaths –' She broke off with what might have been a sob. 'Amigo, I liked you for some strange reason. I should be far beyond such nonsense. Mavis took him away from me, but I did not want him to kill her. The world is full of men who have enough money.'

'He seems like a nice little guy,' I said, still watching the hand that held the gun. Not a quiver in it now.

She laughed contemptuously. 'Of course he does. That is why he is what he is. You think you are tough, amigo. You are a very soft peach compared with Steelgrave.' She lowered the gun and now it was my time to jump. I still wasn't good enough.

'He has killed a dozen men,' she said. 'With a smile for each one. I have known him for a long time. I knew him in Cleveland.'

'With ice-picks?' I asked.

'If I give you the gun, will you kill him for me?'

'Would you believe me if I promised?'

'Yes.' Somewhere down the hill there was the sound of a car. But it seemed as remote as Mars, as meaningless as the chattering of monkeys in the Brazilian jungle. It had nothing to do with me.

'I'd kill him if I had to,' I said, licking along my lips.

I was leaning a little, knees bent, all set for a jump again.

'Good night, amigo. I wear black because I am beautiful and wicked – and lost.'

She held the gun out to me. I took it. I just stood there holding it. For another silent moment neither of us moved. Then she smiled and tossed her head and jumped into the car. She started the motor and slammed the door shut. She idled the motor down and sat looking out at me. There was a smile on her face now.

'I was pretty good in there, no?' she said softly.

Then the car backed violently with a harsh tearing of the tyres on the asphalt paving. The lights jumped on. The car curved away and was gone past the oleander bush. The lights turned left, into the private road. The lights drifted off among trees and the sound faded into the long-drawn whee of tree frogs. Then that stopped and for a moment there was no sound at all. And no light except the tired old moon.

I broke the magazine from the gun. It had seven shells in it. There was another in the breach. Two less than a full load. I sniffed at the muzzle. It had been fired since it was cleaned. Fired twice, perhaps.

I pushed the magazine into place again and held the gun on the flat of my hand. It had a white bone grip. .32 calibre.

Orrin Quest had been shot twice. The two exploded shells I picked up on the floor of the room were .32 calibre.

And yesterday afternoon, in Room 332 of the Hotel Van Nuys, a blonde girl with a towel in front of her face had pointed a .32 calibre automatic with a white bone grip at me.

You can get too fancy about these things. You can also not get fancy enough.

27

I walked on rubber heels across to the garage and tried to open one of the two wide doors. There were no handles, so it must have been operated by a switch. I played a tiny pencil flash on the frame, but no switch looked at me.

I left that and prowled over to the trash barrels. Wooden steps went up to a service entrance. I didn't think the door would be unlocked for my convenience. Under the porch was another door. This was unlocked and gave on darkness and the smell of corded eucalyptus wood. I closed the door behind me and put the little flash on again. In the corner there was another staircase, with a thing like a dumb waiter beside it. It wasn't dumb enough to let me work it. I started up the steps.

Somewhere remotely something buzzed. I stopped. The buzzing stopped. I started again. The buzzing didn't. I went on up to a door with no knob, set flush. Another gadget.

But I found the switch to this one. It was an oblong movable plate set into the door frame. Too many dusty hands had touched it. I pressed it and the door clicked and fell back off the latch. I pushed it open, with the tenderness of a young intern delivering his first baby.

Inside was a hallway. Through shuttered windows moonlight caught the white corner of a stove and the chromed griddle on top of it. The kitchen was big enough for a dancing class. An open arch led to a butler's pantry tiled to the ceiling. A sink, a huge ice-box set into the wall, a lot of electrical stuff for making drinks without trying. You pick your poison, press a button, and four days later you wake up on the rubbing table in a reconditioning parlour.

Beyond the butler's pantry a swing door. Beyond the swing door a dark dining-room with an open end to a glassed-in lounge into which the moonlight poured like water through the flood-gates of a dam.

A carpeted hall led off somewhere. From another flat arch a flying buttress of a staircase went up into more darkness, but shimmered as it went in what might have been glass brick and stainless steel.

At last I came to what should be the living-room. It was curtained and quite dark, but it had the feel of great size. The darkness was heavy in it and my nose twitched at a lingering odour that said somebody had been there not too long ago. I stopped breathing and listened. Tigers could be in the darkness watching me. Or guys with large guns, standing flat-footed, breathing softly with their mouths open. Or nothing and nobody and too much imagination in the wrong place.

I edged back to the wall and felt around for a light switch. There's always a light switch. Everybody has light switches. Usually on the right side as you go in. You go into a dark room and you want light. Okay, you have a light switch in a natural place at a natural height. This room hadn't. This was a different kind of house. They had odd ways of handling doors and lights. The gadget this time might be something fancy like having to sing A above High C, or stepping on a flat button under the carpet, or maybe you just spoke and said: 'Let there be light,' and a mike picked it up and turned the voice vibration into a low-power electrical impulse and a transformer built that up to enough voltage to throw a silent mercury switch.

I was psychic that night. I was a fellow who wanted company in a dark place and was willing to pay a high price for it. The Luger under my arm and the .32 in my hand made me tough. Two-gun Marlowe, the kid from Cyanide Gulch.

I took the wrinkles out of my lip and said aloud:

'Hello again. Anybody here needing a detective?'

Nothing answered me, not even a stand-in for an echo. The sound of my voice fell on silence like a tired head on a swansdown pillow.

And then amber light began to grow high up behind the cornice that circumnavigated the huge room. It brightened very slowly, as if controlled by the rheostat panel in a theatre. Heavy apricot coloured curtains covered the windows.

The walls were apricot too. At the far end was a bar off to one side, a little catty-corner, reaching back into the space by the butler's pantry. There was an alcove with small tables and padded seats. There were floor lamps and soft chairs and love seats and the usual paraphernalia of a living-room, and there were long shrouded tables in the middle of the floor space.

The boys back at the road block had something after all. But the joint was dead. The room was empty of life. It was almost empty. Not quite empty.

A blonde in a pale cocoa fur coat stood leaning against the side of a grandfather's chair. Her hands were in the pockets of the chair. Her hair was fluffed out carelessly and her face was not chalk white because the light was not white.

'Hello again yourself,' she said in a dead voice. 'I still think you came too late.'

'Too late for what?'

I walked towards her, a movement which was always a pleasure. Even then, even in that too silent house.

'You're kind of cute,' she said. 'I didn't think you were cute. You found a way in. You –' her voice clicked off and strangled itself in her throat.

'I need a drink,' she said after a thick pause. 'Or maybe I'll fall down.'

'That's a lovely coat,' I said. I was up to her now. I reached out and touched it. She didn't move. Her mouth moved in and out, trembling.

'Stone marten,' she whispered. 'Forty thousand dollars. Rented. For the picture.'

'Is this part of the picture?' I gestured around the room.

'This is the picture to end all pictures – for me. I – I do need that drink. If I try to walk –' the clear voice whispered away into nothing. Her eyelids fluttered up and down.

'Go ahead and faint,' I said. 'I'll catch you on the first bounce.'

A smile struggled to arrange her face for smiling. She pressed her lips together, fighting hard to stay on her feet.

'Why did I come too late?' I asked. 'Too late for what?

'Too late to be shot.'

'Shucks. I've been looking forward to it all evening. Miss Gonzales brought me.'

'I know.'

I reached out and touched the fur again. Forty thousand dollars is nice to touch, even rented.

'Dolores will be disappointed as hell,' she said, her mouth edged with white.

'No.'

'She put you on the spot – just as she did Stein.'

'She may have started out to. But she changed her mind.'

She laughed. It was a silly pooped out little laugh like a child trying to be supercilious at a playroom tea party.

'What a way you have with the girls,' she whispered. 'How the hell do you do it, wonderful? With doped cigarettes? It can't be your clothes or your money or your personality. You don't have any. You're not too young, nor too beautiful. You've seen your best days and –'

Her voice had been coming faster and faster, like a motor with a broken governor. At the end she was chattering. When she stopped a spent sigh drifted along the silence and she caved at the knees and fell straight forward into my arms.

If it was an act it worked perfectly. I might have had guns in all nine pockets and they would have been as much use to me as nine little pink candles on a birthday cake.

But nothing happened. No hard characters peeked at me with automatics in their hands. No Steelgrave smiled at me with the faint dry remote killer's smile. No stealthy footstep crept up behind me.

She hung in my arms as limp as a wet tea towel and not as heavy as Orrin Quest, being less dead, but heavy enough to make the tendons in my knee joints ache. Her eyes were closed when I pushed her head away from my chest. Her breath was inaudible and she had that bluish look on the parted lips.

I got my right hand under her knees and carried her over to a gold couch and spread her out on it. I straightened up and went along to the bar. There was a telephone on the corner of it but I couldn't find the way through to the bottles. So I had to swing over the top. I got a likely looking bottle with a blue and silver label and five stars on it. The cork had been loosened. I poured dark and pungent brandy into the wrong kind of glass and went back over the bar top, taking the bottle with me.

547

She was lying as I had left her, but her eyes were open.

'Can you hold a glass?'

She could, with a little help. She drank the brandy and pressed the edge of the glass hard against her lips as if she wanted to hold them still. I watched her breathe into the glass and cloud it. A slow smile formed itself on her mouth.

'It's cold tonight,' she said.

She swung her legs over the edge of the couch and put her feet on the floor.

'More,' she said, holding the glass out. I poured into it. 'Where's yours?'

'Not drinking. My emotions are being worked on enough without that.'

The second drink made her shudder. But the blue look had gone away from her mouth and her lips didn't glare like stop lights and the little etched lines at the corners of her eyes were not in relief any more.

'Who's working on your emotions?'

'Oh, a lot of women that keep throwing their arms around my neck and fainting on me and getting kissed and so forth. Quite a full couple of days for a beat-up gumshoe with no yacht.'

'No yacht,' she said. 'I'd hate that. I was brought up rich.'

'Yeah,' I said. 'You were born with a Cadillac in your mouth. And I could guess where.'

Her eyes narrowed. 'Could you?'

'Didn't think it was a very tight secret, did you?'

'I – I –' she broke off and made a helpless gesture. 'I can't think of any lines tonight.'

'It's the technicolor dialogue,' I said. 'It freezes up on you.'

'Aren't we talking like a couple of nuts?'

'We could get sensible. Where's Steelgrave?'

She just looked at me. She held the empty glass out and I took it, and put it somewhere or other without taking my eyes off her. Nor she hers off me. It seemed as if a long minute went by.

'He was here,' she said at last, as slowly as if she had to invent the words one at a time. 'May I have a cigarette?'

'The old cigarette stall,' I said. I got a couple out and put them in my mouth and lit them. I leaned across and tucked one between her ruby lips.

'Nothing's cornier than that,' she said. 'Except maybe butterfly kisses.'

'Sex is a wonderful thing,' I said. 'When you don't want to answer questions.'

She puffed loosely and blinked, then put her hand up to adjust the cigarette. After all these years I can never put a cigarette in a girl's mouth where she wants it.

She gave her head a toss and swung the soft loose hair around her cheeks and watched me to see how hard that hit me. All the whiteness had gone now. Her cheeks were a little flushed. But behind her eyes things watched and waited.

'You're rather nice,' she said, when I didn't do anything sensational. 'For the kind of guy you are.'

I stood that well too.

'But I don't really know what kind of guy you are, do I?' She laughed suddenly and a tear came from nowhere and slid down her cheek. 'For all I know you might be nice for any kind of guy.' She snatched the cigarette loose and put her hand to her mouth and bit on it. 'What's the matter with me? Am I drunk?'

'You're stalling for time,' I said. 'But I can't make up my mind whether it's to give someone time to get here – or to give somebody time to get far away from here. And again it could just be brandy on top of shock. You're a little girl and you want to cry into your mother's apron.'

'Not my mother,' she said. 'I could get as far crying into a rain barrel.'

'Dealt and passed. So where is Steelgrave?'

'You ought to be glad wherever he is. He had to kill you. Or thought he had.'

'You wanted me here, didn't you? Were you that fond of him?'

She blew cigarette ash off the back of her hand. A flake of it went into my eye and made me blink.

'I must have been,' she said, 'once.' She put a hand down on her knee and spread the fingers out, studying the nails. She brought her eyes up slowly without moving her head. 'It seems like about a thousand years ago I met a nice quiet little guy who knew how to behave in public and didn't shoot his charm around every bistro in town. Yes, I liked him. I liked him a lot.'

She put her hand up to her mouth and bit a knuckle. Then she put the same hand into the pocket of the fur coat and brought out a white-handled automatic, the brother of the one I had myself.

'And in the end I liked him with this,' she said.

I went over and took it out of her hand. I sniffed the muzzle. Yes. That made two of them fired around.

'Aren't you going to wrap it up in a handkerchief, the way they do in the movies?'

I just dropped it into my other pocket, where it could pick up a few interesting crumbs of tobacco and some seeds that grow only on the south-east slope of the Beverly Hills City Hall. It might amuse a police chemist for a while.

28

I watched her for a minute, biting at the end of my lip. She watched me. I saw no change of expression. Then I started prowling the room with my eyes. I lifted up the dust cover on one of the long tables. Under it was a roulette layout but no wheel. Under the table was nothing.

'Try that chair with the magnolias on it,' she said.

She didn't look towards it so I had to find it myself. Surprising how long it took me. It was a high-backed wing chair, covered in flowered chintz, the kind of chair that a long time ago was intended to keep the draught off while you sat crouched over a fire of cannel coal.

It was turned away from me. I went over there, walking softly, in low gear. It almost faced the wall. Even at that it seemed ridiculous that I hadn't spotted him on my way back from the bar. He leaned in the corner of the chair with his head tilted back. His carnation was red and white and looked as fresh as though the flower girl had just pinned it into his lapel. His eyes were half open as such eyes usually are. They stared at a point in the corner of the ceiling. The bullet had gone through the outside pocket of his double-breasted jacket. It had been fired by someone who knew where the heart was.

I touched his cheek and it was still warm. I lifted his hand and let it fall. It was quite limp. It felt like the back of somebody's hand. I reached for the big artery in his neck. No blood moved in him and very little had stained his jacket. I wiped my hands off on my handkerchief and stood for a little longer looking down at his quiet little face. Everything I had done or not done, everything wrong and everything right – all wasted.

I went back and sat down near her and squeezed my kneecaps.

'What did you expect me to do?' she asked. 'He killed my brother.'

'Your brother was no angel.'

'He didn't have to kill him.'

'Somebody had to – and quick.'

Her eyes widened suddenly.

I said: 'Didn't you ever wonder why Steelgrave never went after me and why he let you go to the Van Nuys yesterday instead of going himself? Didn't you ever wonder why a fellow with his resources and experience never tried to get hold of those photographs, no matter what he had to do to get them?'

She didn't answer.

'How long have you known the photographs existed?' I asked.

'Weeks, nearly two months. I got one in the mail a couple of days after – after that time we had lunch together.'

'After Stein was killed.'

'Yes, of course.'

'Did you think Steelgrave had killed Stein?'

'No. Why should I? Until tonight, that is.'

'What happened after you got the photo?'

'My brother Orrin called me up and said he had lost his job and was broke. He wanted money. He didn't say anything about the photo. He didn't have to. There was only one time it could have been taken.'

'How did he get your number?'

'Telephone? How did you?'

'Bought it.'

'Well –' she made a vague movement with her hand. 'Why not call the police and get it over with.'

'Wait a minute. Then what? More prints of the photo?'

'One every week. I showed them to *him*.' She gestured towards the chintzy chair. 'He didn't like it. I didn't tell him about Orrin.'

'He must have known. His kind find things out.'

'I suppose so.'

'But not where Orrin was hiding out,' I said. 'Or he wouldn't have waited this long. *When* did you tell Steelgrave?'

She looked away from me. Her fingers kneaded her arm. 'Today,' she said in a distant voice.

'Why today?'

Her breath caught in her throat. 'Please,' she said. 'Don't ask me a lot of useless questions. Don't torment me. There's nothing you can do. I thought there was – when I called Dolores. There isn't now.'

I said: 'All right. There's something you don't seem to understand. Steelgrave knew that whoever was behind that photograph wanted money – a lot of money. He knew that sooner or later the blackmailer would have to show himself. That was what Steelgrave was waiting for. He didn't care anything about the photo itself, except for your sake.'

'He certainly proved that,' she said wearily.

'In his own way,' I said.

Her voice came to me with glacial calm. 'He killed my brother. He told me so himself. The gangster showed through then all right. Funny people you meet in Hollywood, don't you – including me.'

'You were fond of him once,' I said brutally.

Red spots flared in her cheeks.

'I'm not fond of anybody,' she said. 'I'm all through being fond of people.' She glanced briefly towards the high-backed chair. 'I stopped being fond of him last night. He asked me about you, who you were and so on. I told him. I told him that I would have to admit that I was at the Van Nuys Hotel when that man was lying there dead.'

'You were going to tell the police that?'

'I was going to tell Julius Oppenheimer. He would know how to handle it.'

'If he didn't one of his dogs would,' I said.

She didn't smile. I didn't either.

'If Oppenheimer couldn't handle it, I'd be through in pictures,' she added without interest. 'Now I'm through everywhere else as well.'

I got a cigarette out and lit it. I offered her one. She didn't want one. I wasn't in any hurry. Time seemed to have lost its grip on me. And almost everything else. I was flat out.

'You're going too fast for me,' I said, after a moment. 'You didn't know when you went to the Van Nuys that Steelgrave was Weepy Moyer.'

'No.'

'Then what did you go there for?'

'To buy back those photographs.'

'That doesn't check. The photographs didn't mean anything to you then. They were just you and him having lunch.'

She stared at me and winked her eyes tight, then opened them wide. 'I'm not going to cry,' she said. 'I said I didn't *know*. But when he was in jail that time, I had to know there was something about him that he didn't care to have known. I knew he had been in some kind of racket, I guess. But not killing people.'

I said: 'Uh-huh.' I got up and walked around the high-backed chair again. Her eyes travelled slowly to watch me. I leaned over the dead Steelgrave and felt under his arm on the left side. There was a gun there in the holster. I didn't touch it. I went back and sat down opposite her again.

'It's going to cost a lot of money to fix this,' I said.

For the first time she smiled. It was a very small smile, but it was a smile. 'I don't have a lot of money,' she said. 'So that's out.'

'Oppenheimer has. You're worth millions to him by now.'

'He wouldn't chance it. Too many people have their knives into the picture business these days. He'll take his loss and forget it in six months.'

'You said you'd go to him.'

'I said if I got into a jam and hadn't really done anything, I'd go to him. But I have done something now.'

'How about Ballou? You're worth a lot to him too.'

'I'm not worth a plugged nickel to anybody. Forget it, Marlowe. You mean well, but I know these people.'

'That puts it up to me,' I said. 'That would be why you sent for me.'

'Wonderful,' she said. 'You fix it, darling. For free.' Her voice was brittle and shallow again.

I went and sat beside her on the davenport. I took hold of her arm and pulled her hand out of the fur pocket and took hold of that. It was almost ice cold, in spite of the fur.

She turned her head and looked at me squarely. She shook her head a little. 'Believe me, darling, I'm not worth it – even to sleep with.'

I turned the hand over and opened the fingers out. They were stiff and resisted. I opened them out one by one. I smoothed the palm of her hand.

'Tell me why you had the gun with you.'

'The gun?'

'Don't take time to think. Just tell me. Did you mean to kill him?'

'Why not, darling? I thought I meant something to him, I guess I'm a little vain. He fooled me. Nobody means anything to the Steelgraves of this world. And nobody means anything to the Mavis Welds of this world any more.'

She pulled away from me and smiled thinly. 'I oughtn't to have given you that gun. If I killed you I might get clear yet.'

I took it out and held it towards her. She took it and stood up quickly. The gun pointed at me. The small tired smile moved her lips again. Her finger was very firm on the trigger.

'Shoot high,' I said. 'I'm wearing my bullet-proof underwear.'

She dropped the gun to her side and for a moment she just stood staring at me. Then she tossed the gun down on the davenport.

'I guess I don't like the script,' she said. 'I don't like the lines. It just isn't me, if you know what I mean.'

She laughed and looked down at the floor. The point of her shoe moved back and forth on the carpeting. 'We've had a nice chat, darling. The phone's over there at the end of the bar.'

'Thanks, do you remember Dolores' number?'

'Why Dolores?'

When I didn't answer she told me. I went along the room to the corner of the bar and dialled. The same routine as before. Good evening, the Chateau Bercy, who is calling Miss Gonzales please. One moment, please, buzz, buzz, and then a sultry voice saying: 'Hello?'

'This is Marlowe. Did you really mean to put me on a spot?'

I could almost hear her breath catch. Not quite. You can't really hear it over the phone. Sometimes you think you can.

'Amigo, but I am glad to hear your voice,' she said. 'I am so very glad.'

'Did you or didn't you?'

'I – I don't know. I am very sad to think that I might have. I like you very much.'

'I'm in a little trouble here.'

'Is he –' long pause. Apartment house phone. Careful. 'Is he there?'

'Well – in a way. He is and yet he isn't.'

I really did hear her breath this time. A long indrawn sigh that was almost a whistle.

'Who else is there?'

'Nobody. Just me and my homework. I want to ask you something. It is deadly important. Tell me the truth. Where did you get that thing you gave me tonight?'

'Why, from him. He gave it to me.'

'When?'

'Early this evening. Why?'

'How early?'

'About six o'clock, I think.'

'*Why* did he give it to you?'

'He asked me to keep it. He always carried one.'

'Asked you to keep it, why?'

'He did not say, amigo. He was a man that did things like that. He did not often explain himself.'

'Notice anything unusual about it? About what he gave you?'

'Why – no, I did not.'

'Yes, you did. You noticed that it had been fired and that it smelled of burned powder.'

'But I did not –'

'Yes, you did. Just like that. You wondered about it. You didn't like to keep it. You didn't keep it. You gave it back to him. You don't like them around anyhow.'

There was a long silence. She said a last: 'But of course. But why did he want me to have it? I mean, if that was what happened.'

'He didn't tell you why. He just tried to ditch a gun on you and you weren't having any. Remember?'

'That is something I have to tell?'

'*Si.*'

'Will it be safe for me to do that?'

'When did you ever try to be safe?'

She laughed softly. 'Amigo, you understand me very well.'

'Good night,' I said.

'One moment, you have not told me what happened.'

'I haven't even telephoned you.'

I hung up and turned.

Mavis Weld was standing in the middle of the floor watching me.

'You have your car here?' I asked.

'Yes.'

'Get going.'

'And do what?'

'Just go home. That's all.'

'You can't get away with it,' she said softly.

'You're my client.'

'I can't let you. I killed him. Why should you be dragged into it?'

'Don't stall. And when you leave go the back way. Not the way Dolores brought me.'

She stared me straight in the eyes and repeated in a tense voice: 'But I killed him.'

'I can't hear a word you say.'

Her teeth took hold of her lower lip and held it cruelly. She seemed hardly to breathe. She stood rigid. I went over close to her and touched her cheek with a fingertip. I pressed it hard and watched the white spot turn red.

'If you want to know my motive,' I said, 'it has nothing to do with you. I owe it to the johns. I haven't played clean cards in this game. They know. I know. I'm just giving them a chance to use the loud pedal.'

'As if anyone ever had to give them that,' she said, and turned abruptly and walked away. I watched her to the arch and waited for her to look back. She went on through without turning. After a long time I heard a whirring noise. Then the bump of something heavy – the garage door going up. A car started a long way off. It idled down and after another pause the whirring noise again.

When that stopped, the motor faded off into the distance. I heard nothing now. The silence of the house hung around me in thick loose folds like that fur coat around the shoulders of Mavis Weld.

I carried the glass and bottle of brandy over to the bar and climbed over it. I rinsed the glass in a little sink and set the bottle back on the shelf. I found the trick catch this time and swung the door open at the end opposite the telephone. I went back to Steelgrave.

I took the gun Dolores had given me out and wiped it off and put his small limp hand around the butt, held it there and let go. The gun thudded to the carpet. The position looked natural. I wasn't thinking about finger-prints. He would have learned long ago not to leave them on any gun.

That left me with three guns. The weapon in his holster I took out and went and put it on the bar shelf under the counter, wrapped in a towel. The Luger I didn't touch. The other white-handled automatic was left. I tried to decide about how far away from him it had been fired. Beyond scorching distance, but probably very close beyond. I stood about three feet from him and fired two shots past him. They nicked peacefully into the wall. I dragged the chair around until it faced into the room. I laid the small automatic down on the dust cover of one of the roulette tables. I touched the big muscle in the side of his neck, usually the first to harden. I couldn't tell whether it had begun to set or not. But his skin was colder than it had been.

There was not a hell of a lot of time to play around with.

I went to the telephone and dialled the number of the Los Angeles Police Department. I asked the police operator for Christy French. A voice from homicide came on, said he had gone home and what was it. I said it was a personal call he was expecting. They gave me his phone number at home, reluctantly, not because they cared, but because they hate to give anybody anything any time.

I dialled and a woman answered and screamed his name. He sounded rested and calm.

'This is Marlowe. What were you doing?'

'Reading the funnies to my kid. He ought to be in bed. What's doing?'

'Remember over at the Van Nuys yesterday you said a man could make a friend if he got you something on Weepy Moyer?'

'Yeah.'

'I need a friend.'

He didn't sound very interested. 'What you got on him?'

'I'm assuming it's the same guy. Steelgrave.'

'Too much assuming, kid. We had him in the fish-bowl because we thought the same. It didn't pan any gold.'

'You got a tip. He set that tip up himself. So the night Stein was squibbed off he would be where you knew.'

'You just making this up – or got evidence?' He sounded a little less relaxed.

'If a man got out of jail on a pass from the jail doctor, could you prove that?'

There was a silence. I heard a child's voice complaining and a woman's voice speaking to the child.

'It's happened,' French said heavily. 'I dunno. That's a tough order to fill. They'd send him under guard. Did he get to the guard?'

'That's my theory.'

'Better sleep on it. Anything else?'

'I'm out at Stillwood Heights. In a big house where they were setting up for gambling and the local residents didn't like it.'

'Read about it. Steelgrave there?'

'He's here. I'm here alone with him.'

Another silence. The kid yelled and I thought I heard a slap. The kid yelled louder. French yelled at somebody.

'Put him on the phone,' French said at last.

'You're not bright tonight, Christy. Why would I call *you?*'

'Yeah,' he said. 'Stupid of me. What's the address there?'

'I don't know. But it's up at the end of Tower Road in Stillwood Heights, and the phone number is Halldale 9–5033. I'll be waiting for you.'

He repeated the number and said slowly: 'This time you wait, huh?'

'It had to come sometime.'

The phone clicked and I hung up.

I went back through the house putting on lights as I found them, and came out at the back door at the top of the stairs. There was a flood light for the motor yard. I put that on. I went down the steps and walked along to the oleander bush. The private gate stood open as before. I swung it shut, hooked up the chain and clicked the padlock. I went back, walking slowly, looking up at the moon, sniffing the night air, listening to the tree-frogs and the crickets. I went into the house and found the front door and put the light on over that. There was a big parking space in front and a circular lawn with roses. But you had to slide back around the house to the rear to get away.

The place was a dead end except for the driveway through the neighbouring grounds. I wondered who lived there. A long way off through trees I could see the lights of a big house. Some Hollywood big shot, probably, some wizard of the slobbery kiss, and the pornographic dissolve.

I went back in and felt the gun I had just fired. It was cold enough. And Mr Steelgrave was beginning to look as if he meant to stay dead.

No siren. But the sound of a car coming up the hill at last. I went out to meet it, me and my beautiful dream.

29

They came in as they should, big, tough and quiet, their eyes flickering with watchfulness and cautious with disbelief.

'Nice place,' French said. 'Where's the customer?'

'In there,' Beifus said, without waiting for me to answer.

They went along the room without haste and stood in front of him looking down solemnly.

'Dead, wouldn't you say?' Beifus remarked, opening up the act.

French leaned down and took the gun that lay on the floor with thumb and finger on the trigger guard. His eyes flicked sideways and he jerked his chin. Beifus took the other white-handled gun by sliding a pencil into the end of the barrel.

'Finger prints all in the right places, I hope,' Beifus said. He sniffed. 'Oh yeah, this baby's been working. How's yours, Christy?'

'Fired,' French said. He sniffed again. 'But not recently.' He took a clip flash from his pocket and shone it into the barrel of the black gun. 'Hours ago.'

'Down at Bay City, in a house on Wyoming Street,' I said.

Their heads swung around to me in unison.

'Guessing?' French asked slowly.

'Yes.'

He walked over to the covered table and laid the gun down some distance from the other. 'Better tag them right away, Fred. They're twins. We'll both sign the tags.'

Beifus nodded and rooted around in his pockets. He came up with a couple of tie-on tags. The things cops carry around with them.

French moved back to me. 'Let's stop guessing and get to the part you know.'

'A girl I know called me this evening and said a client of mine was in danger up here – from him.' I pointed with my chin at the dead man in the chair. 'This girl rode me up here. We passed the road block. A number of people saw us both. She left me in back of the house and went home.'

'Somebody with a name?' French asked.

'Dolores Gonzales, Chateau Bercy Apartments. On Franklin. She's in pictures.'

'Oh ho,' Beifus said and rolled his eyes.

'Who's your client? Same one?' French asked.

'No. This is another party altogether.'

'She have a name?'

'Not yet.'

They stared at me with hard bright faces. French's jaw moved almost with a jerk. Knots of muscles showed at the sides of his jaw bone.

'New rules, huh?' he said softly.

I said: 'There has to be some agreement about publicity. The D.A. ought to be willing.'

Beifus said: 'You don't know the D.A. good, Marlowe. He eats publicity like I eat tender young garden peas.'

French said: 'We don't give you any undertaking whatsoever.'

'She hasn't any name,' I said.

'There's a dozen ways we can find out, kid,' Beifus said. 'Why go into this routine that makes it tough for all of us?'

'No publicity,' I said, 'unless charges are actually filed.'

'You can't get away with it, Marlowe.'

'Goddamn it,' I said, 'this man killed Orrin Quest. You take that gun down town and check it against the bullets in Quest. Give me that much at least, before you force me into an impossible position.'

'I wouldn't give you the dirty end of a burnt match,' French said.

I didn't say anything. He stared at me with cold hate in his eyes. His lips moved slowly and his voice was thick saying: 'You here when he got it?'

'No.'

'Who was?'

'He was,' I said, looking across at the dead Steelgrave.

'Who else?'

'I won't lie to you,' I said. 'And I won't tell you anything I don't want to tell – except on the terms I stated. I don't know who was here when he got it.'

'Who was here when you got here?'

I didn't answer. He turned his head slowly and said to Beifus: 'Put the cuffs on him. Behind.'

Beifus hesitated. Then he took a pair of steel handcuffs out of his left hip pocket and came over to me. 'Put your hands behind you,' he said in an uncomfortable voice.

I did. He clicked the cuffs on. French walked over slowly and stood in front of me. His eyes were half-closed. The skin around them was greyish with fatigue.

'I'm going to make a little speech,' he said. 'You're not going to like it.'

I didn't say anything.

French said: 'It's like this with us, baby. We're coppers and everybody hates our guts. And as if we didn't have enough trouble, we have to have you. As if we didn't get pushed around enough by the guys in the corner offices, the City Hall gang, the day chief, the night chief, the chamber of commerce, His Honour the Mayor in his panelled office four times as big as the three lousy rooms the whole homicide staff has to work out of. As if we didn't have to handle one hundred and fourteen homicides last year out of three rooms that don't have enough chairs for the whole duty squad to sit down in at once. We spend our lives turning over dirty underwear and sniffing rotten teeth. We go up dark stairways to get a gun punk with a skinful of hop and sometimes we don't get all the way up, and our wives wait dinner that night and all the other nights. We don't come home any more. And nights we do come home, we come home so goddam tired we can't eat or sleep or even read the lies the papers print about us. So we lie awake in the dark in a cheap house on a cheap street and listen to the drunks down the block having fun. And just about the time we drop off the phone rings and we get up and start all over again. Nothing we do is right, not ever. Not once. If we get a confession, we beat it out of the guy, they say, and some shyster calls us Gestapo in courts and sneers at us when we muddle our grammar. If we make a mistake they put us back in uniform on Skid Row and we spend the nice cool summer evenings picking drunks out of the gutter and being yelled at by whores and taking knives away from grease-balls in zoot suits. But all that ain't enough to make us entirely happy. We got to have you.'

He stopped and drew in his breath. His face glistened a little as if with sweat. He leaned forward from his hips.

'We got to have you,' he reported. 'We got to have sharpers with private licences hiding information and dodging around corners and stirring up dust for us to breathe in. We got to have you suppressing evidence and framing set-ups that wouldn't fool a sick baby. You wouldn't mind me calling you a goddam cheap double-crossing keyhole peeper, would you, baby?'

'You want me to mind?' I asked him.

He straightened up. 'I'd love it,' he said. 'In spades redoubled.'

'Some of what you say is true,' I said. 'Not all. Any private eye wants to play ball with the police. Sometimes it's a little hard to find out who's making the rules of the ball game. Sometimes he doesn't trust the police, and with cause. Sometimes he just gets in a jam without meaning to and has to play his hand out the way it's dealt. He'd usually rather have a new deal. He'd like to keep on earning a living.'

'Your licence is dead,' French said. 'As of now. That problem won't bother you any more.'

'It's dead when the commission that gave it to me says so. Not before.'

Beifus said quietly: 'Let's get on with it, Christy. This could wait.'

'I'm getting on with it,' French said. 'My way. This bird hasn't cracked wise yet. I'm waiting for him to crack wise. The bright repartee. Don't tell me you're all out of the quick stuff, Marlowe.'

'Just what is it you want me to say?' I asked him.

'Guess,' he said.

'You're a man eater tonight,' I said. 'You want to break me in half. But you want an excuse. And you want me to give it to you?'

'That might help,' he said between his teeth.

'What would you have done in my place?' I asked him.

'I couldn't imagine myself getting that low.'

He licked at the point of his upper lip. His right hand was hanging loose at his side. He was clenching and unclenching the fingers without knowing it.

'Take it easy, Christy,' Beifus said. 'Lay off.'

French didn't move. Beifus came over and stepped between us. French said: 'Get out of there, Fred.'

'No.'

French doubled his fist and slugged him hard on the point of the jaw. Beifus stumbled back and knocked me out of the way. His knees wobbled. He bent forward and coughed. He shook his head slowly in a bent-over position. After a while he straightened up with a grunt. He turned and looked at me. He grinned.

'It's a new kind of third degree,' he said. 'The cops beat hell out of each other and the suspect cracks up from the agony of watching.'

His hand went up and felt the angle of his jaw. It already showed swelling. His mouth grinned but his eyes were still a little vague. French stood rooted and silent.

Beifus got out a pack of cigarettes and shook one loose and held the pack out to French. French looked at the cigarette, looked at Beifus.

'Seventeen years of it,' he said. 'Even my wife hates me.'

He lifted his open hand and slapped Beifus across the cheek with it lightly. Beifus kept on grinning.

French said: 'Was it you I hit, Fred?'

Beifus said: 'Nobody hit me, Christy. Nobody that I can remember.'

French said: 'Take the cuffs off him and take him out to the car. He's under arrest. Cuff him to the rail if you think it's necessary.'

'Okay.' Beifus went around behind me. The cuffs came loose. 'Come along, baby,' Beifus said.

I stared hard at French. He looked at me as if I was the wallpaper. His eyes didn't seem to see me at all.

I went out under the archway and out of the house.

30

I never knew his name, but he was rather short and thin for a cop, which was what he must have been, partly because he was there, and partly because when he leaned across the table to reach a card I could see the leather under-arm holster and the butt end of a police .38.

He didn't speak much, but when he did he had a nice voice, a soft-water voice. And he had a smile that warmed the whole room.

'Wonderful casting,' I said, looking at him across the cards.

We were playing double Canfield. Or he was. I was just there, watching him, watching his small and very neat and very clean hands go out across the table and touch a card and lift it delicately and put it somewhere else. When he did this he pursed his lips a little and whistled without tune, a low soft whistle, like a very young engine that is not yet sure of itself.

He smiled and put a red nine on a black ten.

'What do you do in your spare time?' I asked him.

'I play the piano a good deal,' he said. 'I have a seven-foot Steinway. Mozart and Bach mostly. I'm a bit old-fashioned. Most people find it dull stuff. I don't.'

'Perfect casting,' I said, and put a card somewhere.

'You'd be surprised how difficult some of that Mozart is,' he said. 'It sounds so simple when you hear it played well.'

'Who can play it well?' I asked.

'Schnabel.'

'Rubinstein?'

He shook his head. 'Too heavy. Too emotional. Mozart is just music. No comment needed from the performer.'

'I bet you get a lot of them in the confession mood,' I said. 'Like the job?'

He moved another card and flexed his fingers lightly. His nails were bright but short. You could see he was a man who loved to move his hands, to make little neat inconspicuous motions with them, motions without any special meaning, but smooth and flowing and light as swansdown. They gave him a feel of delicate things delicately done, but not weak. Mozart, all right. I could see that.

It was about five-thirty, and the sky behind the screened window was getting light. The roll-top desk in the corner was rolled shut. The room was the same room I had been in the afternoon before. Down at the end of the table the square carpenter's pencil was lying where somebody had picked it up and put it back after Lieutenant Maglashan of Bay City threw it against the wall. The flat desk at which Christy French had sat was littered with ash. An old cigar butt clung to the extreme edge of a glass ash-tray. A moth circled around the overhead light on a drop cord that had one of those green and white glass shades they still have in country hotels.

'Tired?' he asked.

'Pooped.'

'You oughtn't to get yourself involved in these elaborate messes. No point in it that I can see.'

'No point in shooting a man?'

He smiled the warm smile. 'You never shot anybody.'

'What makes you say that?'

'Common sense – and a lot of experience sitting here with people.'

'I guess you do like the job,' I said.

'It's night work. Gives me the days to practise. I've had it for twelve years now. Seen a lot of funny ones come and go.'

He got another ace out, just in time. We were almost blocked.

'Get many confessions?'

'I don't take confessions,' he said. 'I just establish a mood.'

'Why give it all away?'

He leaned back and tapped lightly with the edge of a card on the edge of the table. The smile came again. 'I'm not giving anything away. We got you figured long ago.'

'Then what are they holding me for?'

He wouldn't answer that. He looked around at the clock on the wall. 'I think we could get some food now.' He got up and went to the door. He half opened it and spoke softly to someone outside. Then he came back and sat down again and looked at what we had in the way of cards.

'No use,' he said. 'Three more up and we're blocked. Okay with you to start over?'

'Okay with me if we never started at all. I don't play cards. Chess.'

He looked up at me quickly. 'Why didn't you say so? I'd rather have played chess too.'

'I'd rather drink some hot black coffee as bitter as sin.'

'Any minute now. But I won't promise the coffee's what you're used to.'

'Hell, I eat anywhere . . . Well, if I didn't shoot him, who did?'

'Guess that's what is annoying them.'

'They ought to be glad to have him shot.'

'They probably are,' he said. 'But they don't like the way it was done.'

'Personally I thought it was as neat a job as you could find.'

He looked at me in silence. He had the cards between his hands, all in a lump. He smoothed them out and flicked them over on their faces and dealt them rapidly into the two decks. The cards seemed to pour from his hands in a stream, in a blur.

'If you were that fast with a gun,' I began.

The stream of cards stopped. Without apparent motion a gun took their place. He held it lightly in his right hand pointed at a distant corner of the room. It went away and the cards started flowing again.

'You're wasted in here,' I said. 'You ought to be in Las Vegas.'

He picked up one of the packs and shuffled it slightly and quickly, cut it, and dealt me a king high flush in spades.

'I'm safer with a Steinway,' he said.

The door opened and a uniformed man came in with a tray.

We ate canned cornbeef hash and drank hot but weak coffee. By that time it was full morning.

At eight-fifteen Christy French came in and stood with his hat on the back of his head and dark smudges under his eyes.

I looked from him to the little man across the table. But he wasn't there any more. The cards weren't there either. Nothing was there but a chair pushed in neatly to the table and the dishes we had eaten off gathered on a tray. For a moment I had that creepy feeling.

Then Christy French walked around the table and jerked the chair out and sat down and leaned his chin on his hand. He took his hat off and rumpled his hair. He stared at me with hard morose eyes. I was back in cop-town again.

31

'The D.A. wants to see you at nine o'clock,' he said. 'After that I guess you can go on home. That is, if he doesn't hang a pinch on you. I'm sorry you had it sit up in that chair all night.'

'It's all right,' I said. 'I needed the exercise.'

'Yeah, back in the groove again,' he said. He stared moodily at the dishes on the tray.

'Got Lagardie?' I asked him.

'No. He's a doctor all right, though.' His eyes moved to mine. 'He practised in Cleveland.'

I said: 'I hate it to be that tidy.'

'How do you mean?'

'Young Quest wants to put the bite on Steelgrave. So he just by pure accident runs into the one guy in Bay City that could prove who Steelgrave was. *That's* too tidy.'

'Aren't you forgetting something?'

'I'm tired enough to forget my name. What?'

'Me too,' French said. '*Somebody* had to tell him who Steelgrave was. When that photo was taken Moe Stein hadn't been squibbed off. So what good was the photo unless somebody knew who Steelgrave was?'

'I guess Miss Weld knew,' I said. 'And Quest was her brother.'

'You're not making much sense, chum.' He grinned a tired grin. 'Would she help her brother put the bite on her boy friend and on her too?'

'I give up. Maybe the photo was just a fluke. His other sister – my client that was – said he liked to take candid camera shots. The candider the better. If he'd lived long enough you'd have had him up for mopery.'

'For murder,' French said indifferently.

'Oh?'

'Maglashan found that ice-pick all right. He just wouldn't give out to you.'

'There'd have to be more than that.'

'There is, but it's a dead issue. Clausen and Mileaway Marston both had records. The kid's dead. His family's respectable. He had an off streak in him and he got in with the wrong people. No point in smearing his family just to prove the police can solve a case.'

'That's white of you. How about Steelgrave?'

'That's out of my hands.' He started to get up. 'When a gangster gets his, how long does the investigation last?'

'Just as long as it's front page stuff,' I said. 'But there's a question of identity involved here.'

'No.'

I stared at him. 'How do you mean, no?'

'Just no. We're sure.' He was on his feet now. He combed his hair with his fingers and rearranged his tie and hat. Out of the corner of his mouth he said in a low voice: 'Off the record – we were always sure. We just didn't have a thing on him.'

'Thanks,' I said, 'I'll keep it to myself. How about the guns?'

He stopped and stared down at the table. His eyes came up to mine rather slowly. 'They both belonged to Steelgrave. What's more, he had a permit to carry a gun. From the sheriff's office in another county. Don't ask me why. One of them' – he paused and looked up at the wall over my head – 'one of them killed Quest . . . The same gun killed Stein.'

'Which one?'

He smiled faintly. 'It would be hell if the ballistics man got them mixed up and we didn't know,' he said.

He waited for me to say something. I didn't have anything to say. He made a gesture with his hand.

'Well, so long. Nothing personal you know, but I hope the D.A. takes your hide off – in long, thin strips.'

He turned and went out.

I could have done the same, but I just sat there and stared across the table at the wall, as if I had forgotten how to get up. After a while the door opened and the orange queen came in. She unlocked her roll-top desk and took her hat off her impossible hair and hung her jacket on a bare hook in the bare wall. She opened the window near her and uncovered her typewriter and put paper in it. Then she looked across at me.

'Waiting for somebody?'

'I room here,' I said. 'Been here all night.'

She looked at me steadily for a moment. 'You were here yesterday afternoon. I remember.'

She turned to her typewriter and her fingers began to fly. From the open window behind her came the growl of cars filling up the parking lot. The sky had a white glare and there was not much smog. It was going to be a hot day.

The telephone rang on the orange queen's desk. She talked into it inaudibly, and hung up. She looked across at me again.

'Mr Endicott's in his office,' she said. 'Know the way?'

'I worked there once. Not for him, though. I got fired.'

She looked at me with that City Hall look they have. A voice that seemed to come from anywhere but her mouth said:

'Hit him in the face with a wet glove.'

I went over near her and stood looking down at the orange hair. There was plenty of grey at the roots.

'Who said that?'

'It's the wall,' she said. 'It talks. The voices of the dead men who have passed through on the way to hell.'

I went out of the room walking softly and shut the door against the closer so that it wouldn't make any noise.

32

You go in through double swing doors. Inside the double doors there is a combination PBX and Information desk at which sits one of those ageless women you see around municipal offices everywhere in the world. They were never young and will never be old. They have no beauty, no charm, no style. They don't have to please anybody. They are safe. They are civil without ever quite being polite and intelligent and knowledgeable without any real interest in anything. They are what human beings turn into when they trade life for existence and ambition for security.

Beyond this desk there is a row of glassed-in cubicles stretching along one side of a very long room. On the other side is the waiting-room, a row of hard chairs all facing one way, towards the cubicles.

About half the chairs were filled with people waiting and the look of long waiting on their faces and the expectation of still longer waiting to come. Most of them were shabby. One was from the jail, in denim, with a guard. A white-faced kid built like a tackle, with sick, empty eyes.

At the back of the line of cubicles a door was lettered SEWELL ENDICOTT DISTRICT ATTORNEY. I knocked and went on into a big airy corner room. A nice enough room, old fashioned with padded black leather chairs and pictures of former D.A.s and Governors on the walls. Breeze fluttered the net curtain at four windows. A fan on a high shelf purred and swung slowly in a languid arc.

Sewell Endicott sat behind a flat dark desk and watched me come. He pointed to a chair across from him. I sat down. He was tall, thin and dark with loose black hair and long delicate fingers.

'You're Marlowe?' he said in a voice that had a touch of the soft South.

I didn't think he really needed an answer to that. I just waited.

'You're in a bad spot, Marlowe. You don't look good at all. You've been caught suppressing evidence helpful to the solution of a murder. That is obstructing justice. You could go up for it.'

'Suppressing what evidence?' I asked.

He picked a photo off his desk and frowned at it. I looked across at the other two people in the room. They sat in chairs side by side. One of them was Mavis Weld. She wore the dark glasses with the wide white bows. I couldn't see her eyes, but I thought she was looking at me. She didn't smile. She sat very still.

By her side sat a man in an angelic pale grey flannel suit with a carnation the size of a dahlia in his lapel. He was smoking a mono-grammed cigarette and flicking the ashes on the floor, ignoring the smoking stand at his elbow. I knew him by pictures I had seen in the papers. Lee Farrell, one of the hottest trouble-shooting lawyers in the country. His hair was white but his eyes were bright and young. He had a deep outdoor tan. He looked as if it would cost a thousand dollars to shake hands with him.

Endicott leaned back and tapped the arm of his chair with his long fingers. He turned with polite deference to Mavis Weld.

'And how well did you know Steelgrave, Miss Weld?'

'Intimately. He was very charming in some ways. I can hardly believe –' she broke off and shrugged.

'And you are prepared to take the stand and swear as to the time and place when this photograph was taken?' He turned the photograph over and showed it to her.

Farrell said indifferently: 'Just a moment. Is that the evidence Mr Marlowe is supposed to have suppressed?'

'I ask the questions,' Endicott said sharply.

Farrell smiled. 'Well, in case the answer is yes, that photo isn't evidence of anything.'

Endicott said softly: 'Will you answer my question, Miss Weld?'

She said quietly and easily: 'No, Mr Endicott, I couldn't swear when that picture was taken or where. I didn't know it was being taken.'

'All you have to do is look at it,' Endicott suggested.

'And all I know is what I get from looking at it,' she told him.

I grinned. Farrell looked at me with a twinkle. Endicott caught the grin out of the corner of his eye. 'Something you find amusing?' he snapped at me.

'I've been up all night. My face keeps slipping,' I said.

He gave me a stern look and turned to Mavis Weld again.

'Will you amplify that, Miss Weld?'

'I've had a lot of photos taken of me, Mr Endicott. In a lot of different places and with a lot of different people. I have had lunch and dinner at The Dancers with Mr Steelgrave and with various other men. I don't know what you want me to say.'

Farrell put in smoothly: 'If I understand your point, you would like Miss Weld to be your witness to connect this photo up. In what kind of proceeding?'

'That's my business,' Endicott said shortly. 'Somebody shot Steelgrave to death last night. It could have been a woman. It could even have been Miss Weld. I'm sorry to say that, but it seems to be in the cards.'

Mavis Weld looked down at her hands. She twisted a white glove between her fingers.

'Well, let's assume a proceeding,' Farrell said. 'One in which that photo is part of your evidence – if you can get it in. But you can't get it in. Miss Weld won't get it in for you. All she knows about the photo is what she sees by looking at it. What anybody can see. You'd have to connect it up with a witness who could swear as to when, how and where it was taken. Otherwise I'd object – if I happened to be on the other side. I could even introduce experts to swear the photo was faked.'

'I'm sure you could,' Endicott said dryly.

'The only man who could connect it up for you is the man who took it,' Farrell went on without haste or heat. 'I understand he's dead. I suspect that was why he was killed.'

Endicott said: 'This photo is clear evidence of itself that at a certain time and place Steelgrave was not in jail and therefore had no alibi for the killing of Stein.'

Farrell said: 'It's evidence when and if you get it introduced in evidence, Endicott. For Pete's sake, I'm not trying to tell you the law. You know it. Forget that picture. It proves nothing whatsoever. No paper would dare print it. No judge would admit it in evidence, because no competent witness can connect it up. And if that's the evidence Marlowe suppressed, then he didn't in a legal sense suppress evidence at all.'

'I wasn't thinking of trying Steelgrave for murder,' Endicott said, dryly. 'But I *am* a little interested in who killed him. The police department, fantastically enough, also has an interest in that. I hope our interest doesn't offend you.'

Farrell said: 'Nothing offends me. That's why I'm where I am. Are you sure Steelgrave was murdered?'

Endicott just stared at him. Farrell said easily: 'I understand two guns were found, both the property of Steelgrave.'

'Who told you?' Endicott asked sharply. He leaned forward, frowning.

Farrell dropped his cigarette into the smoking stand and shrugged. 'Hell, these things come out. One of these guns had killed Quest and also Stein. The other had killed Steelgrave. Fired at close quarters too. I admit those boys don't as a rule take that way out. But it could happen.'

Endicott said gravely: 'No doubt. Thanks for the suggestion. It happens to be wrong.'

Farrell smiled a little and was silent. Endicott turned slowly to Mavis Weld.

'Miss Weld, this office – or the present incumbent of it at least – doesn't believe in seeking publicity at the expense of people to whom a certain kind of publicity might be fatal. It is my duty to determine whether anyone should be brought to trial for any of these murders, and to prosecute them, if the evidence warrants it. It is not my duty to ruin your career by exploiting the fact that you had the bad luck or bad judgement to be the friend of a man who, although never convicted or even indicted for any crime, was undoubtedly a member of a criminal mob at one time. I don't think you have been quite candid with me about this photograph, but I won't press the matter now. There is not much point in my asking you whether you shot Steelgrave. But I do ask you whether you have any knowledge that would point to who may have or might have killed him.'

Farrell said quickly: 'Knowledge, Miss Weld – not mere suspicion.'

She faced Endicott squarely. 'No.'

He stood up and bowed. 'That will be all for now then. Thanks for coming in.'

Farrell and Mavis Weld stood up. I didn't move. Farrell said: 'Are you calling a press conference?'

'I think I'll leave that to you, Mr Farrell. You have always been very skilful in handling the press.'

Farrell nodded and went to open the door. They went out. She didn't seem to look at me when she went out, but something touched the back of my neck lightly. Probably accidental. Her sleeve.

Endicott watched the door close. He looked across the desk at me. 'Is Farrell representing you? I forgot to ask him.'

'I can't afford him. So I'm vulnerable.'

He smiled thinly. 'I let them take all the tricks and then salve my dignity by working out on you, eh?'

'I couldn't stop you.'

'You're not exactly proud of the way you have handled things, are you, Marlowe?'

'I got off on the wrong foot. After that I just had to take my lumps.'

'Don't you think you owe a certain obligation to the law?'

'I would – if the law was like you.'

He ran his long pale fingers through his tousled black hair.

'I could make a lot of answers to that,' he said. 'They'd all sound about the same. The citizen is the law. In this country we haven't got around to understanding that. We think of the law as an enemy. We're a nation of cop-haters.'

'It'll take a lot to change that,' I said. 'On both sides.'

He leaned forward and pressed a buzzer. 'Yes,' he said quietly. 'It will. But somebody has to make a beginning. Thanks for coming in.'

As I went out a secretary came in at another door with a fat file in her hand.

33

A shave and a second breakfast made me feel a little less like the box of shavings the cat had had kittens in. I went up to the office and unlocked the door and sniffed in the twice-breathed air and the smell of dust. I opened a window and inhaled the fry cook smell from the coffee shop next door. I sat down at my desk and felt the grit on it with my fingertips. I filled a pipe and lit it and leaned back and looked around.

'Hello,' I said.

I was just talking to the office equipment, the three green filing cases, the threadbare piece of carpet, the customers' chair across from me, and the light fixture in the ceiling with three dead moths in it that had been there for at least six months. I was talking to the pebbled glass panel and the grimy woodwork and the pen set on the desk and the tired, tired telephone. I was talking to the scales on an alligator, the name of the alligator being Marlowe, a private detective in our thriving little community. Not the brainiest guy in the world, but cheap. He started out cheap and he ended cheaper still.

I reached down and put the bottle of Old Forester up on the desk. It was about a third full. Old Forester. Now who gave you that, pal? That's green label stuff. Out of your class entirely. Must have been a client. I had a client once.

And that got me thinking about her, and maybe I have stronger thoughts than I know. The telephone rang, and the funny little precise voice sounded just as it had the first time she called me up.

'I'm in that telephone booth,' she said. 'If you're alone, I'm coming up.'

'Uh-huh.'

'I suppose you're mad at me,' she said.

'I'm not mad at anybody. Just tired.'

'Oh yes you are,' her tight little voice said. 'But I'm coming up anyway. I don't care if you *are* mad at me.'

She hung up. I took the cork out of the bottle of Old Forester and gave a sniff at it. I shuddered. That settled it. Any time I couldn't smell whisky without shuddering I was through.

I put the bottle away and got up to unlock the communicating door. Then I heard her tripping along the hall. I'd know those tight little footsteps anywhere. I opened the door and she came up to me and looked at me shyly.

It was all gone. The slanted cheaters, and the new hair-do and the smart little hat and the perfume and the prettied-up touch. The costume jewellery, the rouge, the everything. All gone. She was right back where she started that first morning. Same brown tailor-made, same square bag, same rimless glasses, same prim little narrow-minded smile.

'It's me,' she said. 'I'm going home.'

She followed me into my private thinking parlour and sat down primly, and I sat down just any old way and stared at her.

'Back to Manhattan,' I said. 'I'm surprised they let you.'

'I may have to come back.'

'Can you afford it?'

She gave a quick little half-embarrassed laugh. 'It won't cost me anything,' she said. She reached up and touched the rimless glasses. 'These feel all wrong now,' she said. 'I liked the others. But Dr Zugsmith wouldn't like them at all.' She put her bag on the desk and drew a line along the desk with her fingertip. That was just like the first time too.

'I can't remember whether I gave you back your twenty dollars or not,' I said. 'We kept passing it back and forth until I lost count.'

'Oh, you gave it to me,' she said. 'Thank you.'

'Sure?'

'I never make mistakes about money. Are you all right? Did they hurt you?'

'The police? No. And it was as tough a job as they ever didn't do.'

She looked innocently surprised. Then her eyes glowed. 'You must be awfully brave,' she said.

'Just luck,' I said. I picked up a pencil and felt the point. It was a good sharp point, if anybody wanted to write anything. I didn't. I reached across and slipped the pencil through the strap of her bag and pulled it towards me.

'Don't touch my bag,' she said quickly and reached for it.

I grinned and drew it out of her reach. 'All right. But it's such a cute little bag. It's so like you.'

She leaned back. There was a vague worry behind her eyes, but she smiled. 'You think I'm cute – Philip? I'm so ordinary.'

'I wouldn't say so.'

'You wouldn't?'

'Hell no, I think you're one of the most unusual girls I ever met.' I swung the bag by its strap and set it down on the corner of the desk. Her eyes fastened on it quickly, but she licked her lip and kept on smiling at me.

'And I bet you've known an awful lot of girls,' she said. 'Why' – she looked down and did that with her fingertip on the desk again – 'why didn't you ever get married?'

I thought of all the ways you answer that. I thought of all the women I had liked that much. No, not all. But some of them.

'I suppose I know the answer,' I said. 'But it would just sound corny. The ones I'd maybe like to marry – well, I haven't what they need. The others you don't have to marry. You just seduce them – if they don't beat you to it.'

She flushed to the roots of her mousey hair.

'You're horrid when you talk like that.'

'That goes for some of the nice ones too,' I said. 'Not what you said. What I said. You wouldn't have been so hard to take yourself.'

'Don't talk like that, please!'

'Well, would you?'

She looked down at the desk. 'I wish you'd tell me,' she said slowly, 'what happened to Orrin. I'm all confused.'

'I told you he probably went off the rails. The first time you came in. Remember?'

She nodded slowly, still blushing.

'Abnormal sort of home life,' I said. 'Very inhibited sort of guy with a very highly developed sense of his own importance. It looked at you out of the picture you gave me. I don't want to go psychological on you, but I figure he was just the type to go very completely haywire, if he went haywire at all. Then there's that awful money hunger that runs in your family – all except one.'

She smiled at me now. If she thought I meant her, that was jake with me.

'There's one question I want to ask you,' I said. 'Was your father married before?'

She nodded, yes.

'That helps. Leila had another mother. That suits me fine. Tell me some more. After all, I did a lot of work for you, for a very low fee of no dollars net.'

'You got paid,' she said sharply. 'Well paid. By Leila. And don't expect me to call her Mavis Weld. I won't do it.'

'You didn't know I was going to get paid.'

'Well' – there was a long pause, during which her eyes went to her bag again – 'you did get paid.'

'Okay, pass that. Why wouldn't you tell me who she was?'

'I was ashamed. Mother and I were both ashamed.'

'Orrin wasn't. He loved it.'

'Orrin?' There was a tidy little silence while she looked at her bag again. I was beginning to get curious about that bag. 'But he had been out here and I suppose he'd got used to it.'

'Being in pictures isn't that bad, surely.'

'It wasn't just that,' she said swiftly, and her tooth came down on the outer edge of her lower lip and something flared in her eyes and very slowly died away. I just put another match to my pipe. I was too tired to show emotions, even if I felt any.

'I know. Or anyway I kind of guessed. How did Orrin find out something about Steelgrave that the cops didn't know?'

'I – I don't know,' she said slowly, picking her way among her words like a cat on a fence. 'Could it have been that doctor?'

'Oh sure,' I said, with a big warm smile. 'He and Orrin got to be friends somehow. A common interest in sharp tools maybe.'

She leaned back in her chair. Her little face was thin and angular now. Her eyes had a watchful look.

'Now you're just being nasty,' she said. 'Every so often you have to be that way.'

'Such a pity,' I said. 'I'd be a lovable character if I'd let myself alone. Nice bag.' I reached for it and pulled it in front of me and snapped it open.

She came up out of her chair and lunged.

'You let my bag alone!'

I looked her straight in the rimless glasses. 'You want to go home to Manhattan, Kansas, don't you? Today? You got your ticket and everything?'

She worked her lips and slowly sat down again.

'Okay,' I said. 'I'm not stopping you. I just wondered how much dough you squeezed out of the deal.'

She began to cry. I opened the bag and went through it. Nothing until I came to the zipper pocket at the back. I unzipped and reached in. There was a flat packet of new bills in there. I took them out and riffled them. Ten centuries. All new. All nice. An even thousand dollars. Nice travelling money.

I leaned back and tapped the edge of the packet on my desk. She sat silent now, staring at me with wet eyes. I got a handkerchief out of her bag and tossed it across to her. She dabbed at her eyes. She watched me around the handkerchief. Once in a while she made a nice little appealing sob in her throat.

'Leila gave the money to me,' she said softly.

'What size chisel did you use?'

She just opened her mouth and a tear ran down her cheek into it.

'Skip it,' I said. I dropped the pack of money back into the bag, snapped the bag shut and pushed it across the desk to her. 'I guess you and Orrin belong to that class of people that can convince themselves that everything they do is right. He can blackmail his sister and then when a couple of small time crooks get wise to his racket and take it away from him, he can sneak up on them and knock them off with an ice-pick in the back of the neck. Probably didn't even keep him awake that night. You can do much the same. Leila didn't give you that money. Steelgrave gave it to you. For what?'

'You're filthy,' she said. 'You're vile. How dare you say such things to me?'

'Who tipped off the law that Dr Lagardie knew Clausen? Lagardie thought I did. I didn't. So you did. Why? To smoke out your brother who was not cutting you in – because right then he had lost his deck of cards and was hiding out. I'd like to see some of those letters he wrote home.

I bet they're meaty. I can see him working at it, watching his sister, trying to get her lined up for his Leica, with the good Dr Lagardie waiting quietly in the background for his share of the take. What did you hire me for?'

'I didn't know,' she said evenly. She wiped her eyes again and put the handkerchief away in the bag and got herself all collected and ready to leave. 'Orrin never mentioned any names. I didn't even know Orrin had lost his pictures. But I knew he had taken them and that they were very valuable. I came out to make sure.'

'Sure of what?'

'That Orrin treated me right. He could be awfully mean sometimes. He might have kept all the money himself.'

'Why did he call you up night before last?'

'He was scared. Dr Lagardie wasn't pleased with him any more. He didn't have the pictures. Somebody else had them. Orrin didn't know who. But he was scared.'

'I had them. I still have,' I said. 'They're in that safe.'

She turned her head very slowly to look at the safe. She ran a fingertip questioningly along her lip. She turned back.

'I don't believe you,' she said, and her eyes watched me like a cat watching a mousehole.

'How's to split that grand with me. You get the pictures.'

She thought about it. 'I could hardly give you all that money for something that doesn't belong to you,' she said, and smiled. 'Please give them to me. Please, Philip. Leila ought to have them back.'

'For how much dough?'

She frowned and looked hurt.

'She's my client now,' I said. 'But double-crossing her wouldn't be bad business – at the right price.'

'I don't believe you have them.'

'Okay.' I got up and went to the safe. In a moment I was back with the envelope. I poured the prints and the negative out on the desk – my side of the desk. She looked down at them and started to reach.

I picked them up and shuffled them together and held one so that she could look at it. When she reached for it I moved it back.

'But I can't see it so far away,' she complained.

'It costs money to get closer.'

'I never thought you were a crook,' she said with dignity.

I didn't say anything. I relit my pipe.

'I could make you give them to the police,' she said.

'You could try.'

Suddenly she spoke rapidly. 'I couldn't give you this money I have, really I couldn't. We – well, mother and I owe money still on account of father and the house isn't clear and –'

'What did you sell Steelgrave for the grand?'

Her mouth fell open and she looked ugly. She closed her lips and pressed them together. It was a tight hard little face that I was looking at.

'You had one thing to sell,' I said. 'You knew where Orrin was. To Steelgrave that information was worth a grand. Easy. It's a question of connecting up evidence. You wouldn't understand. Steelgrave went down there and killed him. He paid you the money for the address.'

'Leila told him,' she said in a far-away voice.

'Leila told me she told him,' I said. 'If necessary Leila would tell the world she told him. Just as she would tell the world she killed Steelgrave – if that was the only way out. Leila is a sort of free and easy Hollywood babe that doesn't have very good morals. But when it comes to bedrock guts – she has what it takes. She's not the ice-pick type. And she's not the blood money type.'

The colour flowed away from her face and left her as pale as ice. Her mouth quivered, then tightened up hard into a little knot. She pushed her chair back and leaned forward to get up.

'Blood money,' I said quietly. 'Your own brother. And you set him up so they could kill him. A thousand dollars blood money. I hope you'll be happy with it.'

She stood away from the chair and took a couple of steps backward. Then suddenly she giggled.

'Who could prove it?' she half squealed. 'Who's alive to prove it? You? Who are you? A cheap shyster, a nobody.' She went off into a shrill peal of laughter. 'Why, even twenty dollars buys you.'

I was still holding the packet of photos. I struck a match and dropped the negative into the ash-tray and watched it flare up.

She stopped dead, frozen in a kind of horror. I started to tear the pictures up into strips. I grinned at her.

'A cheap shyster,' I said. 'Well, what would you expect. I don't have any brothers or sisters to sell out. So I sell out my clients.'

She stood rigid and glaring. I finished my tearing-up job and lit the scraps of paper in the tray.

'One thing I regret,' I said. 'Not seeing your meeting back in Manhattan, Kansas, with dear old Mom. Not seeing the fight over how to split that grand. I bet that would be something to watch.'

I poked at the paper with a pencil to keep it burning. She came slowly, step by step, to the desk, and her eyes were fixed on the little smouldering heap of torn prints.

'I could tell the police,' she whispered. 'I could tell them a lot of things. They'd believe me.'

'I could tell them who shot Steelgrave,' I said. 'Because I know who didn't. They might believe *me*.'

The small head jerked up. The light glinted on the glasses. There were no eyes behind them.

'Don't worry,' I said. 'I'm not going to. It wouldn't cost me enough. And it would cost somebody else too much.'

The telephone rang and she jumped a foot. I turned and reached for it and put my face against it and said: 'Hello.'

'Amigo, are you all right?'

There was a sound in the background. I swung around and saw the door click shut. I was alone in the room.

'Are you all right, amigo?'

'I'm tired. I've been up all night. Apart from –'

'Has the little one called you up?'

'The little sister? She was just in here. She's on her way back to Manhattan with the swag.'

'The swag?'

'The pocket money she got from Steelgrave for fingering her brother.'

There was a silence, then she said gravely: 'You cannot know that, amigo.'

'Like I know I'm sitting leaning on this desk holding on to this telephone. Like I know I hear your voice. And not quite so certainly, but certainly enough like I know who shot Steelgrave.'

'You are somewhat foolish to say that to me, amigo. I am not above reproach. You should not trust me too much.'

'I make mistakes, but this won't be one. I've burned all the photographs. I tried to sell them to Orfamay. She wouldn't bid high enough.'

'Surely you are making fun, amigo.'

'Am I? Who of?'

She tinkled her laugh over the wire. 'Would you like to take me to lunch?'

'I might. Are you home?'

'*Si.*'

'I'll come over in a little while.'

'But I shall be delighted.'

I hung up.

The play was over. I was sitting in the empty theatre. The curtain was down and projected on it dimly I could see the action. But already some of the actors were getting vague and unreal. The little sister above all. In a couple of days I would forget what she looked like. Because in a way she *was* so unreal. I thought of her tripping back to Manhattan, Kansas, and dear old Mom, with that fat little new little thousand dollars in her purse. A few people had been killed so she could get it, but I didn't think that would bother her for long. I thought of her getting down to the office in the morning – what was the man's name? Oh yes. Dr Zugsmith – and dusting off his desk before he arrived and arranging the magazines in the waiting-room. She'd have her rimless cheaters on and a plain dress and her face would be without make-up and her manners to the patients would be most correct.

'Dr Zugsmith will see you now, Mrs Whoosis.'

She would hold the door open with a little smile and Mrs Whoosis would go in past her and Dr Zugsmith would be sitting behind his desk as professional as hell with a white coat on and his stethoscope hanging around his neck. A case file would be in front of him and his note pad and prescription pad would be neatly squared off. Nothing that Dr Zugsmith didn't know. You couldn't fool him. He had it all at his fingertips. When he looked at a patient he knew the answers to all his questions he was going to ask just as a matter of form.

When he looked at his receptionist, Miss Orfamay Quest, he saw a nice quiet young lady, properly dressed for a doctor's office, no red nails, no loud make-up, nothing to offend the old-fashioned type of customer. An ideal receptionist, Miss Quest.

Dr Zugsmith, when he thought about her at all, thought of her with self-satisfaction. He had made her what she was. She was just what the doctor ordered.

Most probably he hadn't made a pass at her yet. Maybe they don't in those small towns. Ha, ha! I grew up in one.

I changed position and looked at my watch and got that bottle of Old Forester up out of the drawer after all. I sniffed it. It smelled good. I poured myself a good stiff jolt and held it up against the light.

'Well, Dr Zugsmith,' I said out loud, just as if he was sitting there on the other side of the desk with a drink in his hand, 'I don't know you very well and you don't know me at all. Ordinarily I don't believe in giving advice to strangers, but I've had a short intensive course of Miss Orfamay Quest and I'm breaking my rule. If ever that little girl wants anything from you, give it to her quick. Don't stall around or gobble about your income tax and your overhead. Just wrap yourself in a smile and shell out. Don't you get involved in any discussions about what belongs to who. Keep the little girl happy, that's the main thing. Good luck to you, Doctor, and don't leave any harpoons lying around the office.'

I drank off half of my drink and waited for it to warm me up. When it did that I drank the rest and put the bottle away.

I knocked the cold ashes out of my pipe and refilled it from the leather humidor an admirer had given me for Christmas, the admirer by an odd coincidence having the same name as mine.

When I had the pipe filled I lit it carefully, without haste, and went on out and down the hall, as breezy as a Britisher coming in from a tiger hunt.

34

The Chateau Bercy was old but made over. It had the sort of lobby that asks for plush and india rubber plants, but gets glass brick, cornice lighting, three-cornered glass tables, and a general air of having been re-decorated by a parolee from a nut hatch. Its colour scheme was bile green, linseed poultice brown, sidewalk grey and monkey-bottom blue. It was as restful as a split lip.

The small desk was empty but the mirror behind it could be diaphanous, so I didn't try to sneak up the stairs. I rang a bell and a large soft man oozed out from behind a wall and smiled at me with moist soft lips and bluish-white teeth and unnaturally bright eyes.

'Miss Gonzales,' I said. 'Name's Marlowe. She's expecting me.'

'Why, yes, of course,' he said, fluttering his hands. 'Yes, of course. I'll telephone up at once.' He had a voice that fluttered too.

He picked up the telephone and gurgled into it and put it down.

'Yes, Mr Marlowe. Miss Gonzales says to come right up. Apartment 412.' He giggled. 'But I suppose you know.'

'I know now,' I said. 'By the way, were you here last February?'

'Last February? Last February? Oh yes, I was here last February.' He pronounced it exactly as spelled.

'Remember the night Stein got chilled out front?'

The smile went away from the fat face in a hurry. 'Are you a police officer?' His voice was now thin and reedy.

'No. But your pants are unzipped, if you care.'

He looked down with horror and zipped them up with hands that almost trembled.

'Why, thank you,' he said. 'Thank you.' He leaned across the low desk. 'It was not exactly out front,' he said. 'That is not exactly. It was almost to the next corner.'

'Living here, wasn't he?'

'I'd really rather not talk about it. Really I'd rather not talk about it.' He paused and ran his pinkie along his lower lip. 'Why do you ask?'

585

'Just to keep you talking. You want to be more careful, bud. I can smell it on your breath.'

The pink flowed all over him right down to his neck. 'If you suggest I have been drinking –'

'Only tea,' I said. 'And not from a cup.'

I turned away. He was silent. As I reached the elevator I looked back. He stood with his hands flat on the desk and his head strained around to watch me. Even from a distance he seemed to be trembling.

The elevator was self-service. The fourth floor was cool grey, the carpet thick. There was a small bell-push beside Apartment 412. It chimed softly inside. The door was swung open instantly. The beautiful deep dark eyes looked at me and the red red mouth smiled at me. Black slacks and the flame-coloured shirt, just like last night.

'Amigo,' she said softly. She put her arms out. I took hold of her wrists and brought them together and made her palms touch. I played patacake with her for a moment. The expression in her eyes was languorous and fiery at the same time.

I let go of her wrists, closed the door with my elbow and slid past her. It was like the first time.

'You ought to carry insurance on those,' I said, touching one. It was real enough. The nipple was as hard as a ruby.

She went into her joyous laugh. I went on in and looked the place over. It was French grey and dusty blue. Not her colours, but very nice. There was a false fireplace with gas logs, and enough chairs and tables and lamps, but not too many. There was a neat little cellarette in the corner.

'You like my little apartment, amigo?'

'Don't say little apartment. That sounds like a whore too.'

I didn't look at her. I didn't want to look at her. I sat down on a davenport and rubbed a hand across my forehead.

'Four hours' sleep and a couple of drinks,' I said. 'And I'd be able to talk nonsense to you again. Right now I've barely strength to talk sense. But I've got to.'

She came to sit close to me. I shook my head. 'Over there. I really do have to talk sense.'

She sat down opposite and looked at me with grave dark eye. 'But yes, amigo, whatever you wish. I am your girl – at least I would gladly be your girl.'

'Where did you live in Cleveland?'

'In Cleveland?' Her voice was very soft, almost cooing. 'Did I say I had lived in Cleveland?'

'You said you knew him there.'

She thought back and then nodded. 'I was married then, amigo. What is the matter?'

'You did live in Cleveland then?'

'Yes,' she said softly.

'You got to know Steelgrave how?'

'It was just that in those days it was fun to know a gangster. A form of inverted snobbery, I suppose. One went to the places where they were said to go, and if one was lucky, perhaps some evening –'

'You let him pick you up.'

She nodded brightly. 'Let us say *I* picked *him* up. He was a very nice little man. Really, he was.'

'What about the husband? *Your* husband. Or don't you remember?'

She smiled. 'The streets of the world are paved with discarded husbands,' she said.

'Isn't it the truth? You find them everywhere. Even in Bay City.'

That bought me nothing. She shrugged politely. 'I would not doubt it.'

'Might even be a graduate of the Sorbonne. Might even be mooning away in a measly small town practice. Waiting and hoping. That's one coincidence I'd like to eat. It has a touch of poetry.'

The polite smile stayed in place on her lovely face.

'We've slipped far apart,' I said. 'Ever so far. And we got to be pretty clubby there for a while.'

I looked down at my fingers. My head ached. I wasn't even forty per cent of what I ought to be. She reached me a crystal cigarette box and I took one. She fitted one for herself into the golden tweezers. She took it from a different box.

'I'd like to try one of yours,' I said.

'But Mexican tobacco is so harsh to most people.'

'As long as it's tobacco,' I said, watching her. I made up my mind. 'No, you're right. I wouldn't like it.'

'What,' she asked carefully, 'is the meaning of this by-play?'

'Desk clerk's a muggle-smoker.'

She nodded slowly. 'I have warned him,' she said. 'Several times.'

'Amigo,' I said.

'What?'

'You don't use much Spanish, do you? Perhaps you don't know much Spanish. Amigo gets worn to shreds.'

'We are not going to be like yesterday afternoon, I hope,' she said slowly.

'We're not. The only thing Mexican about you is a few words and a careful way of talking that's supposed to give the impression of a person speaking a language they had to learn. Like saying "do not" instead of "don't". That sort of thing.'

She didn't answer. She puffed gently on her cigarette and smiled.

'I'm in bad trouble downtown,' I went on. 'Apparently Miss Weld had the good sense to tell it to her boss – Julius Oppenheimer – and he came through. Got Lee Farrell for her. I don't think they think she shot Steelgrave. But they think I know who did, and they don't love me any more.'

'And do you know, amigo?'

'Told you over the phone I did.'

She looked at me steadily for a longish moment. 'I was there.' Her voice had a dry serious sound for once.

'It was very curious, really. The little girl wanted to see the gambling house. She had never seen anything like that and there had been in the papers –'

'She was staying here – with you?'

'Not in my apartment, amigo. In a room I got for her here.'

'No wonder she wouldn't tell me,' I said. 'But I guess you didn't have time to teach her the business.'

She frowned very slightly and made a motion in the air with the brown cigarette. I watched its smoke write something unreadable in the still air.

'Please. As I was saying, she wanted to go to that house. So I called him up and he said to come along. When we got there he was drunk. I have never seen him drunk before. He laughed and put his arm around little Orfamay and told her she had earned her money well. He said he had something for her, then he took from his pocket a bill-fold wrapped in a cloth of some kind and gave it to her. When she unwrapped it there was a hole in the middle of it and the hole was stained with blood.'

'That wasn't nice,' I said. 'I wouldn't even call it characteristic.'

'You did not know him very well.'

'True. Go on.'

'Little Orfamay took the bill-fold and stared at it and then stared at him, and her white little face was very still. Then she thanked him and opened her bag to put the bill-fold in it, as I thought – it was all very curious –'

'A scream,' I said. 'It would have had me gasping on the floor.'

' – but instead she took a gun out of her bag. It was a gun he had given Mavis, I think. It was like the one –'

'I know exactly what it was like,' I said. 'I played with it some.'

'She turned around and shot him dead with one shot. It was very dramatic.'

She put the brown cigarette back in her mouth and smiled at me. A curious, rather distant smile, as if she was thinking of something far away.

'You made her confess to Mavis Weld,' I said.

She nodded.

'Mavis wouldn't have believed *you*, I guess.'

'I did not care to risk it.'

'It wasn't you gave Orfamay the thousand bucks, was it, darling? To make her tell? She's a little girl who would go a long way for a thousand bucks.'

'I do not care to answer that,' she said with dignity.

'No. So last night when you rushed me out there, you already knew Steelgrave was dead and there wasn't anything to be afraid of and all that act with the gun was just an act.'

'I do not like to play God,' she said softly. 'There was a situation and I knew that somehow or other you would get Mavis out of it. There was no one else who would. Mavis was determined to take the blame.'

'I'd better have a drink,' I said. 'I'm sunk.'

She jumped up and went to the little cellarette. She came back with a couple of huge glasses of Scotch and water. She handed me one and watched me over her glass as I tried it out. It was wonderful. I drank some more. She sank down into her chair again, and reached for the golden tweezers.

'I chased her out,' I said, finally. 'Mavis, I'm talking about. She told me she had shot him. She had the gun. The twin of the one you gave me. You didn't probably notice that yours had been fired.'

'I know very little about guns,' she said softly.

'Sure. I counted the shells in it, and assuming it had been full to start with, two had been fired. Quest was killed with two shots from a .32 automatic. Same calibre. I picked up the empty shells in the den down there.'

'Down where, amigo?'

It was beginning to grate. Too much amigo, far too much.

'Of course I couldn't know it was the same gun, but it seemed worth trying out. Only confuse things up a little anyhow, and give Mavis that much break. So I switched guns on him, and put his behind the bar. His was a black .38. More like what he would carry, if he carried one at all. Even with a checked grip you can leave prints, but with an ivory grip you're apt to leave a fair set of finger marks on the left side. Steelgrave wouldn't carry that kind of gun.'

Her eyes were round and empty and puzzled. 'I am afraid I am not following you too well.'

'And if he killed a man he would kill him dead, and be sure of it. This guy got up and walked a bit.'

A flash of something showed in her eyes and was gone.

'I'd like to say he talked a bit,' I went on. 'But he didn't. His lungs were full of blood. He died at my feet. Down there.'

'But down where? You have not told me where it was that this —'

'Do I have to?'

She sipped from her glass. She smiled. She put the glass down. I said:

'You were present when little Orfamay told him where to go.'

'Oh yes, of course.' Nice recovery. Fast and clean. But her smile looked a little more tired.

'Only he didn't go,' I said.

Her cigarette stopped in mid-air. That was all. Nothing else. It went on slowly to her lips. She puffed elegantly.

'That's what's been the matter all long,' I said. 'I just wouldn't buy what was staring me in the face. Steelgrave is Weepy Moyer. That's solid, isn't it?'

'Most certainly. And it can be proved.'

'Steelgrave is a reformed character and doing fine. Then this Stein comes out bothering him, wanting to cut in. I'm guessing, but that's about how it would happen. Okay, Stein has to go. Steelgrave doesn't want to kill anybody – and he has never been accused of killing anybody. The Cleveland cops wouldn't come out and get him. No charges pending. No mystery – except that he had been connected with a mob in some capacity. But he has to get rid of Stein. So he gets himself pinched. And then he gets out of jail by bribing the jail doctor, and he kills Stein and goes back into jail at once. When the killing shows up, whoever let him out of jail is going to run like hell and destroy any records there might be of his going out. Because the cops will come over and ask questions.'

'Very naturally, amigo.'

I looked her over for cracks, but there weren't any yet.

'So far so good. But we've got to give this lad credit for a few brains. Why did he let them hold him in jail for ten days? Answer One, to make himself an alibi. Answer Two, because he knew that sooner or later this question of him being Moyer was going to get aired, so why not give them the time and get it over with? That way any time a racket boy gets blown down around here they're not going to keep pulling Steelgrave in and trying to hang the rap on him.'

'You like that idea, amigo?'

'Yes. Look at it this way. Why would he have lunch in a public place the very day he was out of the cooler to knock Stein off? And if he did, why would young Quest happen around to snap that picture? Stein hadn't been killed, so the picture wasn't evidence of anything. I like people to be lucky, but that's *too* lucky. Again, even if Steelgrave didn't know his picture had been taken, he knew who Quest was. Must have. Quest had been tapping his sister for eating money since he lost his job, maybe before. Steelgrave had a key to her apartment. He must have known something about this brother of hers. Which simply adds up to the result, that *that* night of all nights Steelgrave would *not* have shot Stein – even if he had planned to.'

'It is now for me to ask you who did,' she said politely.

'Somebody who knew Stein and could get close to him. Somebody who already knew that photo had been taken, knew who Stein was, knew that Mavis Weld was on the edge of becoming a big star, knew that her association with Steelgrave was dangerous, but would be a thousand times more dangerous if Steelgrave could be framed for the murder of Stein. Knew Quest, because he had been to Mavis Weld's apartment, and had met him there and given him the works, and he was a boy that could be knocked clean out of his mind by that sort of treatment. Knew that those bone-handled .32s were registered to Steelgrave, although he had only bought them to give to a couple of girls, and if he carried a gun himself, it would be one that was not registered and could not be traced to him. Knew –'

'Stop!' Her voice was a sharp stab of sound, but neither frightened nor even angry. 'You will stop at once, please! I will not tolerate this another minute. You will now go!'

I stood up. She leaned back and a pulse beat in her throat. She was exquisite, she was dark, she was deadly. And nothing would ever touch her, not even the law . . .

'Why did you kill Quest?' I asked her.

She stood up and came close to me, smiling again. 'For two reasons, amigo. He was more than a little crazy and in the end he would have killed me. And the other reason is that none of this – absolutely none of it – was for money. It was for love.'

I started to laugh in her face. She didn't. She was dead serious. It was out of this world.

'No matter how many lovers a woman may have,' she said softly, 'there is always one she cannot bear to lose to another woman. He was the one.'

I just stared into her lovely dark eyes. 'I believe you,' I said at last.

'Kiss me, amigo.'

'Good God!'

'I must have men, amigo. But the man I loved is dead. I killed him. That man I would not share.'

'You waited a long time.'

'I can be patient – as long as there is hope.'

'Oh, nuts.'

She smiled a free, beautiful, and perfectly natural smile. 'And you cannot do a damn thing about all this, darling, unless you destroy Mavis Weld utterly and finally.'

'Last night she proved she was willing to destroy herself.'

'If she was not acting.' She looked at me sharply and laughed. 'That hurt, did it not? You are in love with her.'

I said slowly: 'That would be kind of silly. I could sit in the dark with her and hold hands, but for how long? In a little while she will drift off into a haze of glamour and expensive clothes and froth and unreality and muted sex. She won't be a real person any more. Just a voice from a sound track, a face on a screen. I'd want more than that.'

I moved towards the door without putting my back to her. I didn't really expect a slug. I thought she liked better having me the way I was – and not being able to do a damn thing about any of it.

I looked back as I opened the door. Slim, dark and lovely and smiling. Reeking with sex. Utterly beyond the moral laws of this or any world I could imagine.

She was one for the book all right. I went out quietly. Very softly her voice came to me as I closed the door.

'Querido – I have liked you very much. It is too bad.'

I shut the door.

As the elevator opened at the lobby a man stood there waiting for it. He was tall and thin and his hat was pulled low over his eyes. It was a warm day but he wore a thin topcoat with the collar up. He kept his chin low.

'Dr Lagardie,' I said softly.

He glanced at me with no trace of recognition. He moved into the elevator. It started up.

I went across to the desk and banged the bell. The large fat soft man came out and stood with a pained smile on his loose mouth. His eyes were not quite so bright.

'Give me the phone.'

He reached down and put it on the desk. I dialled Madison 7911. The voice said: 'Police.' This was the Emergency Board.

'Chateau Bercy Apartments, Franklin and Girard in Hollywood. A man named Dr Vincent Lagardie wanted for questioning by homicide

Lieutenants French and Beifus, has just gone up to Apartment 412. This is Philip Marlowe, a private detective.'

'Franklin and Girard. Wait there please. Are you armed?'

'Yes.'

'Hold him if he tries to leave.'

I hung up and wiped my mouth off. The fat softy was leaning against the counter, white around the eyes.

They came fast – but not fast enough. Perhaps I ought to have stopped him. Perhaps I had a hunch what he would do, and deliberately let him do it. Sometimes when I'm low I try to reason it out. But it gets too complicated. The whole damn case was that way. There was never a point where I could do the natural obvious thing without stopping to rack my head dizzy with figuring how it would affect somebody I owed something to.

When they cracked the door he was sitting on the couch holding her pressed against his heart. His eyes were blind and there was bloody foam on his lips. He had bitten through his tongue.

Under her left breast and tight against the flame-coloured shirt lay the silver handle of a knife I had seen before. The handle was in the shape of a naked woman. The eyes of Miss Dolores Gonzales were half-open and on her lips there was the dim ghost of a provocative smile.

'The Hippocrates smile,' the ambulance intern said, and sighed. 'On her it looks good.'

He glanced across at Dr Lagardie who saw nothing and heard nothing, if you could judge by his face.

'I guess somebody lost a dream,' the intern said. He bent over and closed her eyes.

PENGUIN CLASSICS

www.penguinclassics.com

- Details about every Penguin Classic

- Advanced information about forthcoming titles

- Hundreds of author biographies

- FREE resources including critical essays on the books and their historical background, reader's and teacher's guides.

- Links to other web resources for the Classics

- Discussion area

- Online review copy ordering for academics

- Competitions with prizes, and challenging Classics trivia quizzes

PENGUIN CLASSICS ONLINE

READ MORE IN PENGUIN

In every corner of the world, on every subject under the sun, Penguin represents quality and variety – the very best in publishing today.

For complete information about books available from Penguin – including Puffins, Penguin Classics and Arkana – and how to order them, write to us at the appropriate address below. Please note that for copyright reasons the selection of books varies from country to country.

In the United Kingdom: Please write to *Dept. EP, Penguin Books Ltd, Bath Road, Harmondsworth, West Drayton, Middlesex UB7 ODA*

In the United States: Please write to *Consumer Sales, Penguin Putnam Inc., P.O. Box 12289 Dept. B, Newark, New Jersey 07101-5289.* VISA and MasterCard holders call 1-800-788-6262 to order Penguin titles

In Canada: Please write to *Penguin Books Canada Ltd, 10 Alcorn Avenue, Suite 300, Toronto, Ontario M4V 3B2*

In Australia: Please write to *Penguin Books Australia Ltd, P.O. Box 257, Ringwood, Victoria 3134*

In New Zealand: Please write to *Penguin Books (NZ) Ltd, Private Bag 102902, North Shore Mail Centre, Auckland 10*

In India: Please write to *Penguin Books India Pvt Ltd, 11 Community Centre, Panchsheel Park, New Delhi 110017*

In the Netherlands: Please write to *Penguin Books Netherlands bv, Postbus 3507, NL-1001 AH Amsterdam*

In Germany: Please write to *Penguin Books Deutschland GmbH, Metzlerstrasse 26, 60594 Frankfurt am Main*

In Spain: Please write to *Penguin Books S. A., Bravo Murillo 19, 1° B, 28015 Madrid*

In Italy: Please write to *Penguin Italia s.r.l., Via Benedetto Croce 2, 20094 Corsico, Milano*

In France: Please write to *Penguin France, Le Carré Wilson, 62 rue Benjamin Baillaud, 31500 Toulouse*

In Japan: Please write to *Penguin Books Japan Ltd, Kaneko Building, 2-3-25 Koraku, Bunkyo-Ku, Tokyo 112*

In South Africa: Please write to *Penguin Books South Africa (Pty) Ltd, Private Bag X14, Parkview, 2122 Johannesburg*

READ MORE IN PENGUIN

Published or forthcoming:

A Clockwork Orange Anthony Burgess

Fifteen-year-old Alex enjoys rape, drugs and Beethoven's Ninth. He and his gang rampage through a dystopian future, hunting for terrible thrills, until he finds himself at the mercy of the state and the ministrations of Dr Brodsky, the government psychologist. *A Clockwork Orange* is both a virtuoso performance from an electrifying prose stylist and a serious exploration of the morality of free will.

On the Road Jack Kerouac

On the Road swings to the rhythms of 1950s underground America, with Sal Paradise and his hero Dean Moriarty, traveller and mystic, the living epitome of Beat. Now recognized as a modern classic, its American Dream is nearer that of Walt Whitman than F. Scott Fitzgerald, and it goes racing towards the sunset with unforgettable exuberance, poignancy and autobiographical passion.

Zazie in the Metro Raymond Queneau

Impish, foul-mouthed Zazie arrives in Paris from the country to stay with her female-impersonator Uncle Gabriel. All she really wants to do is ride the metro, but finding it shut because of a strike, Zazie looks for other means of amusement and is soon caught up in a comic adventure that becomes wilder and more manic by the minute. Queneau's cult classic is stylish, witty and packed full of wordplay and phonetic games.

Lolita Vladimir Nabokov

Poet and pervert Humbert Humbert becomes obsessed by twelve-year-old Lolita and seeks to possess her, first carnally and then artistically. This seduction is one of many dimensions in Nabokov's dizzying masterpiece, which is suffused with a savage humour and rich verbal textures. 'You read Lolita sprawling limply in your chair, ravished, overcome, nodding scandalized assent' Martin Amis

READ MORE IN PENGUIN

Published or forthcoming:

Swann's Way Marcel Proust

This first book of Proust's supreme masterpiece, *A la recherche du temps perdu*, recalls the early youth of Charles Swann in the small, provincial backwater of Combray through the eyes of the adult narrator. The story then moves forward to Swann's life as a man of fashion in the glittering world of *belle-époque* Paris. A scathing, often comic dissection of French society, *Swann's Way* is also a story of past moments tantalizingly lost and, finally, triumphantly rediscovered.

Metamorphosis and Other Stories Franz Kafka

A companion volume to *The Great Wall of China and Other Short Works*, these translations bring together the small proportion of Kafka's works that he thought worthy of publication. This volume contains his most famous story, 'Metamorphosis'. All the stories reveal the breadth of Kafka's literary vision and the extraordinary imaginative depth of his thought.

Cancer Ward Aleksandr Solzhenitsyn

One of the great allegorical masterpieces of world literature, *Cancer Ward* is both a deeply compassionate study of people facing terminal illness and a brilliant dissection of the 'cancerous' Soviet police state. Withdrawn from publication in Russia in 1964, it became a work that awoke the conscience of the world. 'Without doubt the greatest Russian novelist of this century' *Sunday Times*

Peter Camenzind Hermann Hesse

In a moment of 'emotion recollected in tranquility' Peter Camenzind recounts the days of his youth: his childhood in a remote mountain village, his abiding love of nature, and the discovery of literature which inspires him to leave the village and become a writer. 'One of the most penetrating accounts of a young man trying to discover the nature of his creative talent' *The Times Literary Supplement*

READ MORE IN PENGUIN

Published or forthcoming:

A Confederacy of Dunces John Kennedy Toole

A monument to sloth, rant and contempt, a behemoth of fat, flatulence and furious suspicion of anything modern – this is Ignatius J. Reilly of New Orleans. In magnificent revolt against the twentieth century, he propels his monstrous bulk among the flesh-pots of a fallen city, a noble crusader against a world of dunces. 'A masterwork of comedy' *The New York Times*

Giovanni's Room James Baldwin

Set in the bohemian world of 1950s Paris, *Giovanni's Room* is a landmark in gay writing. David is casually introduced to a barman named Giovanni and stays overnight with him. One night lengthens to more than three months of covert passion in his room. As he waits for his fiancée to arrive from Spain, David idealizes his planned marriage while tragically failing to see Giovanni's real love.

Breakfast at Tiffany's Truman Capote

It's New York in the 1940s, where the Martinis flow from cocktail-hour to breakfast at Tiffany's. And nice girls don't, except, of course, Holly Golightly. Pursued by Mafia gangsters and playboy millionaires, Holly is a fragile eyeful of tawny hair and turned-up nose. She is irrepressibly 'top banana in the shock department', and one of the shining flowers of American fiction.

Delta of Venus Anaïs Nin

In *Delta of Venus* Anaïs Nin conjures up a glittering cascade of sexual encounters. Creating her own 'language of the senses', she explores an area that was previously the domain of male writers and brings to it her own unique perceptions. Her vibrant and impassioned prose evokes the essence of female sexuality in a world where only love has meaning.